THE HOUSE BY THE CHURCHYARD

by

Joseph Sheridan Le Fanu

with an introduction by
Paul M. Chapman

WORDSWORTH EDITIONS

1

Readers who are interested in other titles from
Wordsworth Editions are invited to visit our website at
www.wordsworth-editions.com

For our latest list and a full mail-order service contact
Bibliophile Books, 5 Thomas Road, London E14 7BN
Tel: +44 0207 515 9222 Fax: +44 0207 538 4115
e-mail: orders@bibliophilebooks.com

This edition published 2007 by
Wordsworth Editions Limited
8B East Street, Ware, Hertfordshire SG12 9HJ

ISBN 978 1 84022 574 7

© Wordsworth Editions Limited 2007

Wordsworth® is a registered trademark of
Wordsworth Editions Limited

Typeset in Great Britain by Chrissie Madden
Printed by Clays Ltd, St Ives plc

CONTENTS

INTRODUCTION

It would be an exaggeration to claim that Sheridan Le Fanu is a forgotten writer of the Victorian period, but he has been somewhat overlooked by posterity – certainly when compared with such of his contemporaries as Charles Dickens, Wilkie Collins and Edgar Allan Poe, with all of whom he shared literary affinities. Le Fanu was a unique voice, perhaps as a result of both French and Irish ancestry. Yet despite this, and his versatility – in addition to writing fiction he was an active journalist – he found himself classed as a sensationalist, an imputation which rather irked him, as he made clear in a preface to his most famous novel, *Uncle Silas* (1864):

> May he [the writer] be permitted a few words also of remonstrance against the promiscuous application of the term 'sensation' to that large school of fiction which transgresses no one of those canons of construction and morality which in producing the unapproachable *Waverley Novels*, their great author imposed upon himself? No-one, it is assumed, would describe Sir Walter Scott's romances as 'sensation novels'; yet in that marvellous series there is not a single tale in which death, crime, and, in some form, mystery, have not a place.

Yet if, in his lifetime, Le Fanu was regarded primarily as an exponent of sensational mystery stories, he is best known today as a master of the ghost story; so much so that many who associate him with supernatural fiction are disappointed to discover that there is little ghostly activity in most of his best-known novels, such as *Uncle Silas*, *The House by the Churchyard* (1863), *Wylder's Hand* (1864) and *The Wyvern Mystery* (1869).

Much of Le Fanu's posthumous rehabilitation, such as it is, can be attributed to the proselytising zeal of Montague Rhodes James, one of the greatest of all ghost-story writers, who wrote of him:

> He stands absolutely in the first rank as a writer of ghost stories. That is my deliberate verdict, after reading all the supernatural tales

I have been able to get hold of. Nobody sets the scene better than he, nobody touches in the effective detail more deftly.

James wrote this in the introduction to his anthology of rare Le Fanu short stories, *Madam Crowl's Ghost and Other Tales of Mystery* (1923), and they have been influential words, which – ironically, for it was not James's intention – once more helped to place Le Fanu in a box. This labelling is probably best expressed via an aside from Henry James's short story 'The Liar' (which, in typically Jamesian fashion, can be read as both compliment and condescension): 'There was the customary novel of Mr Le Fanu for the bed-side; the ideal reading in a country house for the hours after midnight.'

However, the current growth of interest in Victorian literary studies could once more see Le Fanu's reputation change, as specialists in social and political history and gender studies begin to analyse his work, whilst literary scholars digest his influence upon a range of writers as diverse as M. R. James, Bram Stoker, Elizabeth Bowen and James Joyce.

Joseph Thomas Sheridan Le Fanu was born on 28 August 1814, at 45 Lower Dominick Street, Dublin. His father, Thomas, was a curate of Dr William Dobbin, rector of Finglas, whose daughter, Emma, he married in July 1811. *His* father, Joseph, was of Huguenot descent. There was also a literary touch, for his paternal grandmother was the sister of the dramatist Richard Brinsley Sheridan, writer of *The Rivals* and *School for Scandal*.

In 1815 Thomas Le Fanu was appointed as chaplain to the Royal Hibernian Military School and moved his family to the Phoenix Park in the west of Dublin. Joseph thus spent his early childhood amid a picturesque, if changing, landscape, and surrounded by military glamour. The environs of the Phoenix Park, and particularly the village of Chapelizod, would later influence some of his fiction, including the novels *The Cock and Anchor* (1845) and, more significantly, *The House by the Churchyard*.

The Le Fanus moved again in 1826, this time to Abington in County Limerick, where Thomas had been appointed rector, in addition to holding the deanship of Emly. It was during his years here that young Joseph first really encountered the conditions of life in rural Ireland and the disparity between the Protestant ruling élite, of which he was an example, by birth if not entirely by inclination, and the bulk of the Catholic population. This was thrown into sharp relief by the agrarian disturbances of the time, which affected his family personally. Despite his father's empathy with the sufferings of the rural population Joseph's brother William, and sister Catherine, were stoned by local Catholics. Yet throughout his life, and in almost wilful contrast to the High Tory views he espoused in his journalism, Joseph could understand the Catholic and nationalist perspective. He even produced a number of popular ballads, among them 'Shamus O'Brien' and 'Phaudhrig Crohoore', as if to prove the point.

After a childhood in which self-education had played a part Joseph Sheridan Le Fanu entered Trinity College, Dublin in 1832 to read classics and train for the law. He was called to the Irish Bar in 1839, but soon abandoned law for journalism, and embarked upon a joint career of writing and newspaper proprietorship, during which he would own, or have part shares in, *The Warder*, *The Protestant Guardian*, *The Statesman*, *The Dublin Evening Packet* and *Evening Mail*.

Le Fanu's first published short story was 'The Ghost and the Bone-Setter', which appeared in the January 1838 issue of *The Dublin University Magazine* (henceforward *DUM*) – a periodical with no official connection to the university, which would publish many of his stories and novels, and which he actually owned between 1861 and 1869. His first novel, *The Cock and Anchor*, an historical romance, was published in 1845. His second, *The Fortunes of Colonel Torlogh O'Brien*, another historical adventure, appeared in 1847, and it has been commented that had he continued in this vein he might have become an Irish version of his literary hero Sir Walter Scott.

But rather than producing further novels Le Fanu concentrated once more upon short stories until the publication of 'An Account of Some Strange Disturbances in Aungier Street' in the *DUM* for December 1853, which would mark an eight-year hiatus in his production of fiction, due largely to a number of domestic and personal crises.

He had married Susanna Bennett, daughter of George Bennett, Q.C., in 1843, a union which produced four children and appeared on the surface to be very successful. In 1850 the couple took over residence of 18 Merrion Square, Dublin, a prestigious address, when it was vacated by Susanna's father, but the 1850s were marked by a number of upheavals including debts, Susanna's ill-health, William Le Fanu's religious conversion and a number of family deaths. Finally, in 1858, Susanna herself died, an event which devastated her husband and from which he never entirely recovered: 'The greatest misfortune of my life has overtaken me. My darling wife is gone. The most affectionate the truest I think . . . I adored her.'

In the years following her death he became more reclusive and returned to writing fiction, which he used both as a distraction and a means of channelling his feelings, as is shown by the degree of modified self-portraiture in the character of Austin Ruthyn in *Uncle Silas*:

> Rather late in life he married and his beautiful young wife died, leaving me, their only child, to his care. This bereavement, I have been told, changed him – made him more odd and taciturn than ever . . . My father had left the Church of England for some odd sect, I forget its name, and ultimately became, I was told, a Swedenborgian.

One of the greatest early products of this new round of fiction was the sprawling novel *The House by the Churchyard*, which first appeared pseudonymously (Le Fanu published it under an ancestral name, Charles de Cresseron) in the *DUM* between 1861 and 1862.

The novel had been prefigured ten years earlier by the short piece 'Ghost Stories of Chapelizod', which comprised 'The Village Bully', 'The Sexton's Adventure' and 'The Spectre Lovers', and had appeared in the DUM in January 1851. After the second of these stories Le Fanu almost apologetically wrote:

> I don't mean to say that I cannot tell a great many more stories, equally authentic and marvellous, touching this old town; but as I may possibly have to perform a like office for other localities . . . I consider it, on the whole, safe to despatch the traditions of Chapelizod with one tale more.

However, so strong were the nostalgic associations of Chapelizod, taking the author back to a less troubled period of his life, that his imagination was unable to leave it be, and he was inspired to write this diffuse, at points almost shapeless, but rather enjoyable, novel.

It opens in characteristic Le Fanu fashion with the accidental disinterment of an old skull in Chapelizod churchyard whilst a new grave is being dug. The skull shows marked signs of violence, inviting speculation as to its history. But this supplies only one of the enigmas of the novel, linking directly into the book's primary mystery, the curtain of which is raised by a strange late-night funeral which takes place as:

. . . an awfully dark night came down on Chapelizod and all the country round.

I believe there was no moon, and the stars had been quite put out under the wet 'blanket of the night', which impenetrable muffler overspread the sky with a funereal darkness.

There was a little of that sheet-lightning early in the evening, which betokens sultry weather. The clouds, column after column, came up sullenly over the Dublin mountains, rolling themselves from one horizon to the other into one black dome of vapour, their slow but steady motion contrasting with the awful stillness of the air. There was a weight in the atmosphere, and a sort of undefined menace brooding over the little town, as if unseen crime or danger – some mystery of iniquity – was stealing into the heart of it, and the disapproving heavens scowled a melancholy warning.

This is the Le Fanu touch which M. R. James so admired: the ability to build a menacing and expectant atmosphere without the need to resort to Gothic histrionics.

The mood is further heightened by the appearance of the chief mourner, Mr Mervyn, ' . . . a tall, very pale, and peculiar-looking young man, with very large, melancholy eyes, and a certain cast of evil pride in his handsome face', who does conform to the romantic type and, unfortunately, remains rather undeveloped throughout the novel.

As if to confirm his dark and mysterious persona, Mervyn takes up residence at Chapelizod's haunted locale, the Tiled House, which is supposedly troubled by the apparition of a disembodied hand. The history of this spectral visitation, 'Some odd facts about the Tiled House – being an authentic narrative of the ghost of a hand', is one of the book's most well-known passages, having been anthologised separately, its familiarity perhaps over-emphasising the importance of this unconnected anecdote.

However, even in this single chapter Le Fanu demonstrates that deftness of touch which separates his supernatural writing from that of his predecessors. Le Fanu had grown up with such works as Ann Radcliffe's *The Mysteries of Udolpho* and Jane Webb's *The Mummy* and was fully conversant with their failings. He was also genuinely interested in the world of the occult and supernatural, and wanted his readers to suspend their disbelief and question, if only for a time, the material reality around them. An additional thrill of unease was all for the good.

Given the familiarity of the 'narrative of the ghost of a hand' and the novel's very title – *The House by the Churchyard* (which is actually the spiritually untroubled home of the military surgeon Dr Sturk, and bears no relation to the unquiet Tiled House), it is unsurprising that it is often assumed to be part of Le Fanu's ghostly *oeuvre*, whereas it is really a curious mixture of social comedy and the veiled mystery surrounding two interconnected murders, one historical and one committed during the story itself.

The mystery aspect constitutes the main plot, but it is often lost beneath passages of social interaction, as if the author were more interested in following the personal dramas of secondary characters (of whom there are rather too many) and the general ebb and flow of life amongst Chapelizod's military and professional residents in the late 1760s. Much of this digression is light-hearted and humorous but, as this is a work tinged with nostalgia written by a still-suffering widower, there are moments of wistfulness and melancholy, as when the Byronic Captain Devereux reflects upon his misspent, but enjoyable, youth, which seems inexorably to be passing into memory:

> They were his young days – beautiful and wicked – days of clear rich tints, and sanguine throbbings, and *gloria mundi* – when we fancy the spirit perfect, and the body needs no redemption – when, fresh from the fountains of life, death is but a dream, and we walk the earth like heathen gods and goddesses, in celestial egotism and beauty. Oh fair youth! – gone for ever . . . But to the last those young days will be remembered and worth remembering; for be we what else we may, young mortals we shall never be again.

Throughout the second half of the novel this melancholic tone hardens into something darker, as murder and discord threaten the former social equilibrium and the community realises that it has been unwittingly sheltering a notorious criminal who is described in the sort of florid Gothic terms which doubtless helped to characterise Le Fanu as a writer of sensational fiction:

> They had been bringing into their homes and families an undivulged and terrible monster. The wehr-wolf had walked the homely streets of their village. The ghoul, unrecognised, had prowled among the graves of their churchyard. One of their fairest princesses, the lady of Belmont, had been on the point of being sacrificed to a vampire.

Despite its undeniable faults – a profusion of characters, a constantly disappearing storyline, an occasional reliance upon coincidence and cliché – *The House by the Churchyard* remains a powerful and engaging work. As a mystery story its lack of a driving plot is a serious disadvantage, but (unlike so many mystery stories) it is a book which repays repeated reading. It is a pleasure to revisit the well-delineated, if slightly unreal, world of late-eighteenth century Chapelizod. M. R. James obviously felt that way, as it was his favourite amongst Le Fanu's novels and he claimed to have lost count of the number of times he had read it, whilst S. M. Ellis, author of the well-regarded study *Wilkie Collins, Le Fanu and Others*, referred to it as 'that fine – his finest – romance'.

Following serial publication Le Fanu issued the book himself, having 1000 copies printed, of which he sold 500 to the London publisher William Tinsley, who had them rebound, but remembered that 'the book sold very well indeed'.

Towards the end of his life Le Fanu developed curious nocturnal working habits and reportedly suffered from a recurring nightmare about being caught beneath a collapsing house. Upon viewing the author's body his doctor is supposed to have remarked: 'I feared this – that house fell at last.' The house may have fallen, but Le Fanu's reputation appears to be rising and is built on strong enough foundations to resist any sudden collapse. The only mystery is that it has taken so long.

PAUL M. CHAPMAN

THE HOUSE BY THE CHURCHYARD

A Prologue – being a dish of village chat

We are going to talk, if you please, in the ensuing chapters, of what was going on in Chapelizod about a hundred years ago. A hundred years, to be sure, is a good while; but though fashions have changed, some old phrases dropped out, and new ones come in; and snuff and hair-powder, and sacques and solitaires quite passed away – yet men and women were men and women all the same – as elderly fellows, like your humble servant, who have seen and talked with rearward stragglers of that generation – now all and long marched off – can testify, if they will.

In those days Chapelizod was about the gayest and prettiest of the outpost villages in which old Dublin took a complacent pride. The poplars which stood, in military rows, here and there, just showed a glimpse of formality among the orchards and old timber that lined the banks of the river and the valley of the Liffey, with a lively sort of richness. The broad old street looked hospitable and merry, with steep roofs and many coloured hall-doors. The jolly old inn, just beyond the turnpike at the sweep of the road, leading over the buttressed bridge by the mill, was first to welcome the excursionist from Dublin, under the sign of the Phoenix. There, in the grand wainscoted back-parlour, with 'the great and good King William', in his robe, garter, periwig, and sceptre presiding in the panel over the chimneypiece, and confronting the large projecting window, through which the river, and the daffodils, and the summer foliage looked so bright and quiet, the Aldermen of Skinner's Alley – a club of the 'true blue' dye, as old as the Jacobite wars of the previous century – the corporation of shoemakers, or of tailors, or the free-masons, or the musical clubs, loved to dine at the stately hour of five, and deliver their jokes, sentiments, songs, and wisdom, on a pleasant summer's evening. Alas! the inn is as clean gone as the guests – a dream of the shadow of smoke.

Lately, too, came down the old 'Salmon House' – so called from the blazonry of that noble fish upon its painted sign-board – at the other end of the town, that, with a couple more, wheeled out at right angles from the line of the broad street, and directly confronting the passenger from Dublin, gave to it something of the character of a square, and just left room for the high road and Martin's Row to slip between its flank and the orchard that overtopped the river wall. Well! it is gone. I blame nobody. I suppose it was quite rotten, and that the rats would soon have thrown up their lease of it; and that it was taken down, in short, chiefly, as one of the players said of 'Old Drury', to prevent the inconvenience of its coming down of itself. Still a peevish but harmless old fellow – who hates change, and would wish things to stay as they were just a little, till his own great change comes; who haunts the places where his childhood was passed, and reverences the homeliest relics of bygone generations – may be permitted to grumble a little at the impertinences of improving proprietors with a taste for accurate parallelograms and pale new brick.

Then there was the village church, with its tower dark and rustling from base to summit, with thick piled, bowering ivy. The royal arms cut in bold relief in the broad stone over the porch – where, pray, is that stone now, the memento of its old viceregal dignity? Where is the elevated pew, where many a lord lieutenant, in point and gold lace, and thunder-cloud periwig, sate in awful isolation, and listened to orthodox and loyal sermons, and took French rappee; whence too, he stepped forth between the files of the guard of honour of the Royal Irish Artillery from the barrack over the way, in their courtly uniform, white, scarlet and blue, cocked hats, and cues, and ruffles, presenting arms – into his emblazoned coach and six, with hanging footmen, as wonderful as Cinderella's, and outriders out-blazing the liveries of the troops, and rolling grandly away in sunshine and dust.

The 'Ecclesiastical Commissioners' have done their office here. The tower, indeed, remains, with half its antique growth of ivy gone; but the body of the church is new, and I, and perhaps an elderly fellow or two more, miss the old-fashioned square pews, distributed by a traditional tenure among the families and dignitaries of the town and vicinage (who are they now?), and sigh for the queer, old, clumsy reading-desk and pulpit, grown dearer from the long and hopeless separation; and wonder where the tables of the Ten Commandments, in long gold letters of Queen Anne's date, upon a vivid blue ground, arched above, and flanking the communion-table, with its tall thin rails, and fifty other things that appeared to me in my nonage as stable as the earth, and as sacred as the heavens, are gone to.

As for the barrack of the Royal Irish Artillery, the great gate leading into the parade ground, by the river side, and all that, I believe the earth, or rather that grim giant factory, which is now the grand feature and centre of Chapelizod, throbbing all over with steam, and whizzing with wheels, and vomiting pitchy smoke, has swallowed them up.

A line of houses fronting this – old familiar faces – still look blank and regretfully forth, through their glassy eyes, upon the changed scene. How different the company they kept some ninety or a hundred years ago!

Where is the mill, too, standing fast by the bridge, the manorial appendage of the town, which I loved in my boyhood for its gaunt and crazy aspect and dim interior, whence the clapper kept time mysteriously to the drone of the mill-sluice? I think it is gone. Surely *that* confounded thing can't be my venerable old friend in masquerade!

But I can't expect you, my reader – polite and patient as you manifestly are – to potter about with me, all the summer day, through this melancholy and mangled old town, with a canopy of factory soot between your head and the pleasant sky. One glance, however, before you go, you will vouchsafe at the village tree – that stalworth elm. It has not grown an inch these hundred years. It does not look a day older than it did fifty years ago, *I* can tell you. There he stands the same; and yet a stranger in the place of his birth, in a new order of things, joyless, busy, transformed Chapelizod, listening, as it seems to me, always to the unchanged song and prattle of the river, with his reveries and affections far away among bygone times and a buried race. Thou hast a story, too, to tell, thou slighted and solitary sage, if only the winds would steal it musically forth, like the secret of Mildas from the moaning reeds.

The palmy days of Chapelizod were just about a hundred years ago, and those days – though I am jealous of their pleasant and kindly fame, and specially for the preservation of the few memorials they have left behind, were yet, I may say, in your ear, with all their colour and adventure – perhaps, on the whole, more pleasant to read about and dream of, than they were to live in. Still their violence, follies and hospitalities, softened by distance, and illuminated with a sort of barbaric splendour, have long presented to my fancy the glowing and ever-shifting combinations upon which, as on the red embers, in a winter's gloaming, I love to gaze, propping my white head upon my hand, in a lazy luxury of reverie, from my own armchair, while they drop, ever and anon, into new shapes, and silently tell their 'winter's tales'.

When your humble servant, Charles de Cresseron, the compiler of this narrative, was a boy some fourteen years old – how long ago precisely that was, is nothing to the purpose, 'tis enough to say he remembers what he then saw and heard a good deal better than what happened a week ago – it came to pass that he was spending a pleasant week of his holidays with his benign uncle and godfather, the curate of Chapelizod. On the second day of his, or rather *my* sojourn (I take leave to return to the first person), there was a notable funeral of an old lady. Her name was Darby, and her journey to her last home was very considerable, being made in a hearse, by easy stages, from her house of Lisnabane, in the county of Sligo, to the churchyard of Chapelizod. There was a great flat stone over that small parcel of the rector's freehold, which the family held by a tenure, not of lives, but of deaths, renewable for ever. So that my uncle, who was a man of an anxious temperament, had little trouble in satisfying himself of the meerings and identity of this narrow tenement, to which Lemuel Mattocks, the sexton, led him as straight and confidently as he could have done to the communion-table.

My uncle, therefore, fiated the sexton's presentment, and the work commenced forthwith. I don't know whether all boys have the same liking for horrors which I am conscious of having possessed – I only know that I liked the churchyard, and deciphering tombstones, and watching the labours of the sexton, and hearing the old world village talk that often got up over the relics.

When this particular grave was pretty nearly finished – it lay from east to west – a lot of earth fell out at the northern side, where an old coffin had lain, and good store of brown dust and grimy bones, and the yellow skull itself came tumbling about the sexton's feet. These fossils, after his wont, he lifted decently with the point of his shovel, and pitched into a little nook beside the great mound of mould at top.

'Be the powers o' war! Here's a battered head-piece for yez,' said young Tim Moran, who had picked up the cranium, and was eyeing it curiously, turning it round the while.

'Show it here, Tim;' 'let *me* look,' cried two or three neighbours, getting round as quickly as they could.

'Oh! murdher,' said one.

'Oh! be the powers o' Moll Kelly!' cried another.

'Oh! bloody wars!' exclaimed a third.

'That poor fellow got no chance for his life at all, at all!' said Tim.

'That was a bullet,' said one of them, putting his finger into a clean circular aperture as large as a half-penny.

'An' look at them two cracks. Och, murther!'

'There's only one. Oh, I see you're right, *two*, begorra!'

'Aich o' them a wipe iv a poker.'

Mattocks had climbed nimbly to the upper level, and taking the skull in his fist, turned it about this way and that, curiously. But though he was no chicken, his memory did not go far enough back to throw any light upon the matter.

'Could it be the Mattross that was shot in the year '90, as I often heerd, for sthrikin' his captain?' suggested a by-stander.

'Oh! that poor fellow's buried round by the north side of the church,' said Mattocks, still eyeing the skull. 'It could not be Counsellor Gallagher, that was kilt in the jewel with Colonel Ruck – he was hot in the head – bud it could not be – augh! not at all.'

'Why not, Misther Mattocks?'

'No, nor the Mattross neither. This, ye see, is a dhry bit o' the yard here; there's ould Darby's coffin, at the bottom, down there, sound enough to stand on, as you see, wid a plank; an' he was buried in the year '93. Why, look at the coffin this skull belongs to, 'tid go into powdher between your fingers; 'tis nothin' but tindher.'

'I believe you're right, Mr Mattocks.'

'Phiat! To be sure, 'tis longer undher ground by thirty years, good, or more maybe.'

Just then the slim figure of my tall mild uncle the curate appeared, and his long thin legs, in black worsted stockings and knee-breeches, stepped reverently and lightly among the graves. The men raised their hats, and Mattocks jumped lightly into the grave again, while my uncle returned their salute with the sad sort of smile, a regretful kindness, which he never exceeded, in these solemn precincts.

It was his custom to care very tenderly for the bones turned up by the sexton, and to wait with an awful solicitude until, after the reading of the funeral service, he saw them gently replaced, as nearly as might be, in their old bed; and discouraging all idle curiosity or levity respecting them, with a solemn rebuke, which all respected. Therefore it was, that so soon as he appeared the skull was, in Hibernian phrase, 'dropt like a hot potato', and the grave-digger betook himself to his spade so nimbly.

'Oh! Uncle Charles,' I said, taking his hand, and leading him towards the foot of the grave; 'such a wonderful skull has come up! It is shot through with a bullet, and cracked with a poker besides.'

''Tis thrue for him, your raverence; he was murthered twiste over, whoever he was – rest his sowl;' and the sexton, who had nearly completed his work, got out of the grave again, with a demure activity, and raising the brown relic with great reverence, out of regard for my good uncle, he turned it about slowly before the eyes of the curate, who scrutinised it, from a little distance, with a sort of melancholy horror.

'Yes, Lemuel,' said my uncle, still holding my hand, ''twas undoubtedly a murder; ay, indeed! He sustained two heavy blows, beside that gunshot through the head.'

''Twasn't gunshot, Sir; why the hole 'id take in a grape-shot,' said an old fellow, just from behind my uncle, in a pensioner's cocked hat, leggings, and long old-world red frock-coat, speaking with a harsh reedy voice, and a grim sort of reserved smile.

I moved a little aside, with a sort of thrill, to give him freer access to my uncle, in the hope that he might, perhaps, throw a light upon the history of this remarkable memorial. The old fellow had a rat-like grey eye – the other was hid under a black patch – and there was a deep red scar across his forehead, slanting from the patch that covered the extinguished orb. His face was purplish, the tinge deepening towards the lumpish top of his nose, on the side of which stood a big wart, and he carried a great walking-cane over his shoulder, and bore, as it seemed to me, an intimidating but caricatured resemblance to an old portrait of Oliver Cromwell in my Whig grandfather's parlour.

'You don't think it a bullet wound, Sir?' said my uncle, mildly, and touching his hat – for coming of a military stock himself, he always treated an old soldier with uncommon respect.

'Why, please your raverence,' replied the man, reciprocating his courtesy; 'I *know* it's not.'

'And what *is* it, then, my good man?' interrogated the sexton, as one in authority, and standing on his own dunghill.

'The trepan,' said the fogey, in the tone in which he'd have cried 'attention' to a raw recruit, without turning his head, and with a scornful momentary skew-glance from his grey eye.

'And do you know whose skull that was, Sir?' asked the curate.

'Ay do I, Sir, *well*,' with the same queer smile, he answered. 'Come, now, you're a grave-digger, my fine fellow,' he continued, accosting the sexton cynically; 'how long do you suppose that skull's been under ground?'

'Long enough; but not so long, *my* fine fellow, as yours has been above ground.'

'Well, you're right there, for *I* seen him buried,' and he took the skull from the sexton's hands; 'and I'll tell you more, there was some dry eyes, too, at his funeral – ha, ha, ha!'

'You were a resident in the town, then?' said my uncle, who did not like the turn his recollections were taking.

'Ay, Sir, that I was,' he replied; 'see that broken tooth, there – I forgot 'twas there – and the minute I seen it, I remembered it like this morning – I could swear to it – when he laughed; ay, and that sharp corner to it – hang him,' and he twirled the loose tooth, the last but two of all its fellows, from its socket, and chucked it into the grave.

'And were you – you weren't in the army, *then*?' enquired the curate, who could not understand the sort of scoffing dislike he seemed to bear it.

'Be my faith I was *so*, Sir – the Royal Irish Artillery,' replied he, promptly.

'And in what capacity?' pursued his reverence.

'Drummer,' answered the mulberry-faced veteran.

'Ho! – Drummer? That's a good time ago, I dare say,' said my uncle, looking on him reflectively.

'Well, so it is, not far off fifty years,' answered he. 'He was a hard-headed codger, he was; but you see the sprig of shillelagh was too hard for him – ha, ha, ha!' and he gave the skull a smart knock with his walking-cane, as he grinned at it and wagged his head.

'Gently, gently, my good man,' said the curate, placing his hand hastily upon his arm, for the knock was harder than was needed for the purpose of demonstration.

'You see, Sir, at that time, our Colonel-in-Chief was my Lord Blackwater,' continued the old soldier, 'not that we often seen him, for he lived in France mostly; the Colonel-en-Second was General Chattesworth, and Colonel Stafford was Lieutenant-Colonel, and under him Major O'Neill; Captains, four – Cluffe, Devereux, Barton, and Burgh: First Lieutenants – Puddock, Delany, Sackville, and Armstrong; Second Lieutenants – Salt; Barber, Lillyman, and Pringle; Lieutenant Fireworkers – O'Flaherty – '

'I beg your pardon,' interposed my uncle, '*Fireworkers*, did you say?'

'Yes, Sir.'

'And what, pray, does a Lieutenant *Fireworker* mean?'

'Why, law bless you, Sir! A Fireworker! 'Twas his business to see that the men loaded, sarved, laid, and fired the gun all right. But that doesn't signify; you see this old skull, Sir: well, 'twas a nine days' wonder, and the queerest business you ever heerd tell of. Why, Sir, the women was frightened out of their senses, an' the men puzzled out o' their wits – they wor – ha, ha, ha! An' I can tell you all about it – a mighty black and bloody business it was – '

'I – I beg your pardon, Sir: but I think – yes – the funeral has arrived; and for the present, I must bid you good-morning.'

And so my uncle hurried to the church, where he assumed his gown, and the solemn rite proceeded.

When all was over, my uncle, after his wont, waited until he had seen the disturbed remains re-deposited decently in their place; and then, having disrobed, I saw him look with some interest about the churchyard, and I knew 'twas in quest of the old soldier.

'I saw him go away during the funeral,' I said.

'Ay, the old pensioner,' said my uncle, peering about in quest of him.

And we walked through the town, and over the bridge, and we saw nothing of his cocked hat and red single-breasted frock, and returned rather disappointed to tea.

I ran into the back room which commanded the churchyard in the hope of seeing the old fellow once more, with his cane shouldered, grinning among the tombstones in the evening sun. But there was no sign of him, or indeed of anyone else there. So I returned, just as my uncle, having made the tea, shut down the lid of his silver tea-pot with a little smack; and with a kind but absent smile upon me, he took his book, sat down and crossed one of his thin legs over the other, and waited pleasantly until the delightful infusion should be ready for our lips, reading his old volume, and with his disengaged hand gently stroking his long shin-bone.

In the meantime, I, who thirsted more for that tale of terror which the old soldier had all but begun, of which in that strangely battered skull I had only an hour ago seen face to face so grisly a memento, and of which in all human probability I never was to hear more, looked out dejectedly from the window, when, whom should I behold marching up the street, at slow time, towards the Salmon House, but the identical old soldier, cocked hat, copper nose, great red single-breasted coat with its prodigious wide button-holes, leggings, cane and all, just under the village tree.

'Here he is, oh! Uncle Charles, here he comes,' I cried.

'Eh, the soldier, is he?' said my uncle, tripping in the carpet in his eagerness, and all but breaking the window. 'So it is, indeed; run down, my boy, and beg him to come up.'

But by the time I had reached the street, which you may be sure was not very long, I found my uncle had got the window up and was himself inviting the old boy, who having brought his left shoulder forward, thanked the curate, saluting soldier-fashion, with his hand to his hat, palm foremost. I've observed, indeed, than those grim old campaigners who have seen the world, make it a principle to accept anything in the shape of a treat. If it's bad, why, it costs them nothing; and if good, so much the better.

So up he marched, and into the room with soldierly self-possession, and being offered tea, preferred punch, and the ingredients were soon on the little round table by the fire, which, the evening being sharp, was pleasant; and the old fellow being seated, he brewed his nectar, to his heart's content; and as we sipped our tea in pleased attention he, after his own fashion, commenced the story, to which I listened with an interest which I confess has never subsided.

Many years after, as will sometimes happen, a flood of light was unexpectedly poured over the details of his narrative; on my coming into possession of the diary, curiously minute, and the voluminous correspondence of Rebecca, sister to General Chattesworth, with whose family I had the honour to be connected. And this journal, to me, with my queer cat-like affection for this old village, a perfect treasure – and the interminable *bundles* of letters, sorted and arranged so neatly, with little abstracts of their contents in red ink, in her own firm thin hand upon the covers, from all and to all manner of persons – for the industrious lady made fair copies of all the letters she wrote – formed for many years my occasional, and always pleasant, winter night's reading.

I wish I could infuse their spirit into what I am going to tell, and above all that I could inspire my readers with ever so little of the peculiar interest with which the old town has always been tinted and saddened to my eye. My boyish imagination, perhaps, kindled all the more at the story, by reason of it being a good deal connected with the identical old house in which we three – my dear uncle, my idle self, and the queer old soldier – were then sitting. But wishes are as vain as regrets; so I'll just do my best, bespeaking your attention, and submissively abiding your judgment.

Chapter One

The rector's night-walk to his church

A. D. 1767, in the beginning of the month of May – I mention it
because, as I said, I write from memoranda – an awfully dark night
came down on Chapelizod and all the country round.

I believe there was no moon, and the stars had been quite put out
under the wet 'blanket of the night', which impenetrable muffler
overspread the sky with a funereal darkness.

There was a little of that sheet-lightning early in the evening,
which betokens sultry weather. The clouds, column after column,
came up sullenly over the Dublin mountains, rolling themselves
from one horizon to the other into one black dome of vapour, their
slow but steady motion contrasting with the awful stillness of the air.
There was a weight in the atmosphere, and a sort of undefined
menace brooding over the little town, as if unseen crime or danger –
some mystery of iniquity – was stealing into the heart of it, and the
disapproving heavens scowled a melancholy warning.

That morning old Sally, the rector's housekeeper, was disquieted.
She had dreamed of making the great four-post, state bed, with the
dark green damask curtains – a dream that betokened some coming
trouble – it might, to be sure, be ever so small – (it had once come
with no worse result than Dr Walsingham's dropping his purse,
containing something under a guinea in silver, over the side of the
ferry boat) – but again it might be tremendous. The omen hung over
them doubtful.

A large square letter, with a great round seal, as big as a crown piece,
addressed to the Rev. Hugh Walsingham, Doctor of Divinity, at his
house, by the bridge, in Chapelizod, had reached him in the morning, and plainly troubled him. He kept the messenger a good hour
awaiting his answer; and, just at two o'clock, the same messenger
returned with a second letter – but this time a note sufficed for reply.
' 'Twill seem ungracious,' said the doctor, knitting his brows over his
closed folio in the study; 'but I cannot choose but walk clear in my

calling before the Lord. How can I honestly pronounce hope, when in my mind there is nothing but *fear* – let another do it if he see his way – I do enough in being present, as 'tis right I should.'

It was, indeed, a remarkably dark night – a rush and downpour of rain! The doctor stood just under the porch of the stout brick house – of King William's date, which was then the residence of the worthy rector of Chapelizod – with his great surtout and cape on – his leggings buttoned up – and his capacious leather 'overalls' pulled up and strapped over these – and his broad-leafed hat tied down over his wig and ears with a mighty silk kerchief. I dare say he looked absurd enough – but it was the women's doing – who always, upon emergencies, took the doctor's wardrobe in hand. Old Sally, with her kind, mild, grave face, and grey locks, stood modestly behind in the hall; and pretty Lilias, his only child, gave him her parting kiss, and her last grand charge about his shoes and other exterior toggery, in the porch; and he patted her cheek with a little fond laugh, taking old John Tracy's, the butler's, arm. John carried a handsome horn-lantern, which flashed now on a roadside bush – now on the discoloured battlements of the bridge – and now on a streaming window. They stepped out – there were no umbrellas in those days – splashing among the wide and widening pools; while Sally and Lilias stood in the porch, holding candles for full five minutes after the doctor and his 'Jack-o'-the-lantern', as he called honest John, whose arm and candle always befriended him in his night excursions, had got round the corner.

Through the back bow-window of the Phoenix, there pealed forth – faint in the distance and rain – a solemn royal ditty, piped by the tuneful Aldermen of Skinner's Alley, and neither unmusical nor somehow uncongenial with the darkness and the melancholy object of the doctor's walk, the chant being rather monastic, wild, and dirge-like. It was a quarter past ten, and no other sound of life or human neighbourhood was stirring. If secrecy were an object, it was well secured by the sable sky, and the steady torrent which rolled down with electric weight and perpendicularity, making all nature resound with one long hush – sh – sh – sh – sh – deluging the broad street, and turning the channels and gutters into mimic mill-streams which snorted and hurtled headlong through their uneven beds, and round the corners towards the turbid Liffey, which, battered all over with rain, muddy and sullen, reeled its way towards the sea, rolling up to the heavens an aspect black as their own.

As they passed by the Phoenix (a little rivulet, by-the-bye, was spouting down from the corner of the sign; and indeed the night was such as might well have caused that suicidal fowl to abandon all thoughts of self-incremation, and submit to an unprecedented death by drowning), there was no idle officer, or lounging waiter upon the threshold. Military and civilians were all snug in their quarters that night; and the inn, except for the 'Aldermen' in the back parlour, was doing no business. The door was nearly closed, and only let out a tall, narrow slice of candle-light upon the lake of mud, over every inch of which the rain was drumming.

The doctor's lantern glided by – and then across the street – and so leisurely along the foot-way, by the range of lightless hall doors towards the Salmon House, also dark; and so, sharp round the corner, and up to the churchyard gate, which stood a little open, as also the church door beyond, as was evidenced by the feeble glow of a lantern from within.

I dare say old Bob Martin, the sexton, and grave Mr Irons, the clerk, were reassured when they heard the cheery voice of the rector hailing them by name. There were now three candles in church; but the edifice looked unpleasantly dim, and went off at the far end into total darkness. Zekiel Irons was a lean, reserved fellow, with a black wig and blue chin, and something shy and sinister in his phiz. I don't think he had entertained honest Bob with much conversation from those thin lips of his during their grisly *tête-à-tête* among the black windows and the mural tablets that overhung the aisle.

But the rector had lots to say – though deliberately and gravely, still the voice was genial and inspiring – and exorcised the shadows that had been gathering stealthily around the lesser Church functionaries. Mrs Irons's tooth, he learned, was still bad; but she was no longer troubled with 'that sour humour in her stomach'. There were sour humours, alas! still remaining – enough, and to spare, as the clerk knew to his cost. Bob Martin thanked his reverence; the cold rheumatism in his hip was better. Irons, the clerk, replied, 'he had brought two prayer-books'. Bob averred 'he could not be mistaken; the old lady was buried in the near-vault; though it was forty years before, he remembered it like last night. They changed her into her lead coffin in the vault – he and the undertaker together – her own servants would not put a hand to her. She was buried in white satin, and with her rings on her fingers. It was her fancy, and so ordered in her will. They said she was mad. He'd know her face again if he saw her. She had a long hooked nose; and her eyes were open. For, as he was told, she died in her sleep, and was quite cold and stiff when they found her in the morning. He went down and saw the coffin today, half an hour after meeting his reverence.'

The rector consulted his great warming-pan of a watch. It was drawing near eleven. He fell into a reverie, and rambled slowly up and down the aisle, with his hands behind his back, and his dripping hat in them, swinging nearly to the flags – now lost in the darkness – now emerging again, dim, nebulous, in the foggy light of the lanterns. When this clerical portrait came near, he was looking down, with gathered brows, upon the flags, moving his lips and nodding, as if counting them, as was his way. The doctor was thinking all the time upon the one text: why should this livid memorial of two great crimes be now disturbed, after an obscurity of twenty-one years, as if to jog the memory of scandal, and set the great throat of the monster baying once more at the old midnight horror?

And as for that old house at Ballyfermot, why anyone could have looked after it as well as he. 'Still he must live somewhere, and certainly this little town is quieter than the city, and the people, on the whole, very kindly, and by no means curious.' This latter was a mistake of the doctor's, who, like other simple persons, was fond of regarding others as harmless repetitions of himself. 'And his sojourn will be,' he says, 'but a matter of weeks; and the doctor's mind wandered back again to the dead, and forward to the remoter consequences of his guilt, so he heaved a heavy, honest sigh, and lifted up his head and slackened his pace for a little prayer, and with that there came the rumble of wheels to the church door.

Chapter Two

The nameless coffin

Three vehicles with flambeaux, and the clang and snorting of horses came close to the church porch, and there appeared suddenly, standing within the disc of candle-light at the church door, before one would have thought there was time, a tall, very pale, and peculiar-looking young man, with very large, melancholy eyes, and a certain cast of evil pride in his handsome face.

John Tracy lighted the wax candles which he had brought, and Bob Martin stuck them in the sockets at either side of the cushion, on the ledge of the pew, beside the aisle, where the prayer-book lay open at 'the burial of the dead', and the rest of the party drew about the door, while the doctor was shaking hands very ceremoniously with that tall young man, who had now stepped into the circle of light, with a short, black mantle on, and his black curls uncovered, and a certain air of high breeding in his movements. 'He reminded me painfully of him who is gone, whom we name not,' said the doctor to pretty Lilias, when he got home; 'he has his pale, delicately-formed features, with a shadow of his evil passions too, and his mother's large, sad eyes.'

And an elderly clergyman, in surplice, band, and white wig, with a hard, yellow, furrowed face, hovered in, like a white bird of night, from the darkness behind, and was introduced to Dr Walsingham, and whispered for a while to Mr Irons, and then to Bob Martin, who had two short forms placed transversely in the aisle to receive what was coming, and a shovel full of earth – all ready. So, while the angular clergyman ruffled into the front of the pew, with Irons on one side, a little in the rear, both books open; the plump little undertaker, diffusing a steam from his moist garments, making a prismatic halo round the candles and lanterns as he moved successively by them, whispered a word or two to the young gentleman [Mr Mervyn, the doctor called him], and Mr Mervyn disappeared. Dr Walsingham and John Tracy got into contiguous seats, and Bob Martin went out to lend a hand. Then came the shuffling of feet, and the sound of hard-tugging respiration, and the suppressed energetic mutual directions of the undertaker's men, who supported the ponderous coffin. How much heavier, it always seems to me, that sort of load than any other of the same size!

A great oak shell: the lid was outside in the porch, Mr Tressels was unwilling to screw it down, having heard that the entrance to the vault was so narrow, and apprehending it might be necessary to take the coffin out. So it lay its length with a dull weight on the two forms. The lead coffin inside, with its dusty black velvet, was plainly much older. There was a plate on it with two bold capitals, and a full stop after each, thus –

R. D.
obiit May 11th
A.D. 1746
aetat 38

And above this plain, oval plate was a little bit of an ornament no bigger than a sixpence. John Tracy took it for a star, Bob Martin said he knew it to be a Freemason's order, and Mr Tressels, who almost overlooked it, thought it was nothing better than a fourpenny cherub. But Mr Irons, the clerk, knew that it was a coronet; and when he heard the other theories thrown out, being a man of few words he let them have it their own way, and with his thin lips closed, with their changeless and unpleasant character of an imperfect smile, he coldly kept this little bit of knowledge to himself.

Earth to earth (rumble), dust to dust (tumble), ashes to ashes (rattle).

And now the coffin must go out again, and down to its final abode. The flag that closed the entrance of the vault had been removed. But the descent of Avernus was not facile, the steps being steep and broken, and the roof so low. Young Mervyn had gone down the steps to see it duly placed; a murky, fiery light came up, against which the descending figures looked black and cyclopean.

Dr Walsingham offered his brother-clergyman his hospitalities; but somehow that cleric preferred returning to town for his supper and his bed. Mervyn also excused himself. It was late, and he meant to stay that night at the Phoenix, and tomorrow designed to make his compliments in person to Dr Walsingham. So the bilious clergyman from town climbed into the vehicle in which he had come, and the undertaker and his troop got into the hearse and the mourning coach and drove off demurely through the town; but once a hundred yards or so beyond the turnpike, at such a pace that they overtook the rollicking *cortège* of the Alderman of Skinner's Alley upon the Dublin road, all singing and hallooing, and crowing and shouting scraps of banter at one another, in which recreations these professional mourners forthwith joined them; and they cracked screaming jokes, and drove wild chariot races the whole way into town, to the terror of the divine, whose presence they forgot, and whom, though he shrieked from the window, they never heard until getting out, when the coach came to a standstill, he gave Mr Tressels a piece of his mind, and that in so alarming a sort, that the jolly undertaker, expressing a funereal concern at the accident, was obliged to explain that all the noise came from the scandalous party they had so unfortunately overtaken, and that 'the drunken blackguards had lashed and frightened his horses to a runaway pace, singing and hallooing in the filthy way he heard, it being a standing joke among such roisterers to put quiet tradesmen of his melancholy profession into a false and ridiculous position.' He did not convince, but only half-puzzled the ecclesiastic, who muttering '*credat Judaeus*', turned his back upon Mr Tressels with an angry whisk, without bidding him good-night.

Dr Walsingham, with the aid of his guide, in the meantime, had reached the little garden in front of the old house, and the gay tinkle of a harpsichord and the notes of a sweet contralto suddenly ceased as he did so; and he said – smiling in the dark, in a pleasant soliloquy, for he did not mind John Tracy – old John was not in the way – 'She always hears my step – always – little Lily, no matter how she's employed,' and the hall-door opened, and a voice that was gentle, and yet somehow very spirited and sweet, cried a loving and playful welcome to the old man.

Chapter Three

Mr Mervyn in his inn

The morning was fine – the sun shone out with a yellow splendour – all nature was refreshed – a pleasant smell rose up from tree and flower and earth. The now dry pavement and all the row of village windows were glittering merrily – the sparrows twittered their lively morning gossip among the thick ivy of the old church tower – here and there the village cock challenged his neighbour with high and vaunting crow, and the bugle notes soared sweetly into the air from the artillery ground beside the river.

Moore, the barber, was already busy making his morning circuit, servant men and maids were dropping in and out at the baker's, and old Poll Delany, in her weather-stained red hood, and neat little Kitty Lane, with her bright young careful face and white basket, were calling at the doors of their customers with new-laid eggs. Through half-opened hall doors you might see the powdered servant, or the sprightly maid in her mob-cap in hot haste steaming away with the red japanned 'tea kitchen' into the parlour. The town of Chapelizod, in short, was just sitting down to its breakfast.

Mervyn, in the meantime, had had his solitary meal in the famous back parlour of the Phoenix, where the newspapers lay, and all comers were welcome. He was by no means a bad hero to look at, if such a thing were needed. His face was pale, melancholy, statuesque – and his large enthusiastic eyes suggested a story and a secret – perhaps a horror. Most men, had they known all, would have wondered with good Doctor Walsingham, why, of all places in the world, he should have chosen the little town where he now stood for even a temporary residence. It was not a perversity, but rather a fascination. His whole life had been a flight and a pursuit – a vain endeavour to escape from the evil spirit that pursued him – and a chase of a chimera.

He was standing at the window, not indeed enjoying, as another man might, the quiet verdure of the scene, and the fragrant air, and all the mellowed sounds of village life, but lost in a sad and dreadful reverie, when in bounced little red-faced bustling Dr Toole – the joke and the chuckle with which he had just requited the fat old barmaid still ringing in the passage – 'Stay there, sweetheart,' addressed to a dog squeezing by him, and which screeched out as he kicked it neatly round the door-post.

'Hey, your most obedient, Sir,' cried the doctor, with a short but grand bow, affecting surprise, though his chief object in visiting the back parlour at that moment was precisely to make a personal inspection of the stranger. 'Pray, don't mind me, Sir – your – ho! breakfast ended, eh? Coffee not so bad, Sir; rather good coffee, I hold it, at the Phoenix. Cream very choice, Sir? – I don't tell 'em so though;' [a wink] 'it might not improve it, you know. I hope they gave you – eh? – eh?' [he peeped into the cream-ewer, which he turned towards the light, with a whisk] 'And no disputing the eggs – forty-eight hens in the poultry yard, and ninety ducks in Tresham's little garden, next door to Sturk's. They make a precious noise, I can tell you, when it showers. Sturk threatens to shoot 'em. He's the artillery surgeon here; and Tom Larkin said, last night, it's because they only dabble and quack – and two of a trade, you know – ha! ha! ha! And what a night we had – dark as Erebus – pouring like pumps, by Jove. I'll remember it, I warrant you. Out on business – a medical man, you know, can't always choose – and near meeting a bad accident too. Anything in the paper, eh? Ho! I see, Sir, haven't read it. Well, and what do you think – a queer night for the purpose, eh? you'll say – we had a funeral in the town last night, Sir – someone from Dublin. It was Tressel's men came out. The turnpike rogue – just round the corner there – one of the talkingest gossips in the town – and a confounded prying, tattling place it is, I can tell you – knows the driver; and Bob Martin, the sexton, you know – tells me there were two parsons, no less – hey! cauliflowers in season, by Jove. Old Dr Walsingham, our rector, a pious man, Sir, and does a world of good – that is to say, relieves half the blackguards in the parish – ha! ha! when we're on the point of getting rid of them – but means well, only he's a little bit lazy, and queer, you know; and that rancid, raw-boned parson, Gillespie – how the plague did they pick him up? – one of the mutes told Bob 'twas he. He's from Donegal; I know all about him; the sourest dog I ever broke bread with – and mason, if you please, by Jove – a prince pelican! He supped at the Grand Lodge after labour, one night – *you're* not a mason, I see; tipt you the sign – and his face was so pinched, and so yellow, by Jupiter, I was near squeezing it into the punch-bowl for a lemon – ha! ha! Hey?'

Mervyn's large eyes expressed a well-bred surprise. Dr Toole paused for nearly a minute, as if expecting something in return; but it did not come.

So the doctor started afresh, never caring for Mervyn's somewhat dangerous looks.

'Mighty pretty prospects about here, Sir. The painters come out by dozens in the summer, with their books and pencils, and scratch away like so many Scotchmen. Ha! ha! ha! If you draw, Sir, there's one prospect up the river, by the mills – upon my conscience – but you don't draw?'

No answer.

'A little, Sir, maybe? Just for a maggot, I'll wager – like *my* good lady, Mrs Toole.' A nearer glance at his dress had satisfied Toole that he was too much of a macaroni for an artist, and he was thinking of placing him upon the lord lieutenant's staff. 'We've capital horses here, if you want to go on to Leixlip,' (where – this between ourselves and the reader – during the summer months His Excellency and Lady Townshend resided, and where, the old newspapers tell us, they 'kept a public day every Monday,' and he 'had a *levée*, as usual, every Thursday.') But this had no better success.

'If you design to stay over the day, and care for shooting, we'll have some ball practice on Palmerstown fair-green today. Seven baronies to shoot for ten and five guineas. One o'clock, hey?'

At this moment entered Major O'Neill, of the Royal Irish Artillery, a small man, very neatly got up, and with a decidedly Milesian cast of countenance, who said little, but smiled agreeably – 'Gentlemen, your most obedient. Ha, doctor; how goes it? – Anything new – anything on the *Freeman*?'

Toole had scanned that paper, and hummed out, as he rumpled it over – 'nothing – very – particular. Here's Lady Moira's ball: fancy dresses – all Irish; no masks; a numerous appearance of the nobility and gentry – upwards of five hundred persons. A good many of your corps there, major?'

'Ay, Lord Blackwater, of course, and the general, and Devereux, and little Puddock, and – '

'*Sturk* wasn't,' with a grin interrupted Toole, who bore that practitioner no good-will. 'A gentleman robbed, by two footpads, on Chapelizod-road, on Wednesday night, of his watch and money, together with his hat, wig and cane, and lies now in a dangerous state, having been much abused; one of them dressed in an old light-coloured coat, wore a wig. By Jupiter, major, if I was in General Chattesworth's place, with two hundred strapping fellows at my orders, I'd get a commission from Government to clear that road. It's too bad, Sir, we can't go in and out of town, unless in a body, after nightfall, but at the risk of our lives.' [The convivial doctor felt this public scandal acutely.] 'The bloody-minded miscreants, I'd catch every living soul of them, and burn them alive in tar-barrels. By Jove! here's old Joe Napper, of Dirty-lane's dead. Plenty of dry eyes after *him*. And stay, here's another row.' And so he read on.

In the meantime, stout, tightly-braced Captain Cluffe of the same corps, and little dark, hard-faced, and solemn Mr Nutter, of the Mills, Lord Castlemallard's agents, came in, and half a dozen more, chiefly members of the club, which met by night in the front parlour on the left, opposite the bar, where they entertained themselves with agreeable conversation, cards, backgammon, draughts, and an occasional song by Dr Toole, who was a florid tenor, and used to give them 'While gentlefolks strut in silver and satins' or 'A maiden of late had a merry design', or some other such ditty, with a recitation by plump little stage-stricken Ensign Puddock, who, in 'thpite of hith lithp', gave rather spirited imitations of some of the players – Mossop, Sheridan, Macklin, Barry and the rest. So Mervyn, the stranger, by no means affecting this agreeable society, took his cane and cocked hat, and went out – the dark and handsome apparition – followed by curious glances from two or three pairs of eyes, and a whispered commentary and criticism from Toole.

So, taking a meditative ramble in 'His Majesty's Park, the Phoenix'; and passing out at Castleknock gate, he walked up the river, between the wooded slopes, which make the valley of the Liffey so pleasant and picturesque, until he reached the ferry, which crossing, he at the other side found himself not very far from Palmerstown, through which village his return route to Chapelizod lay.

Chapter Four
The fair-green of Palmerstown

There were half-a-dozen carriages, and a score of led horses, outside the fair-green, a precious lot of ragamuffins, and a good resort to the public-house opposite; and the gate being open, the artillery band, rousing all the echoes round with harmonious and exhilarating thunder within – an occasional crack of a 'Brown Bess', with a puff of white smoke over the hedge, being heard, and the cheers of the spectators, and sometimes a jolly chorus of many-toned laughter, all mixed together, and carried on with a pleasant running hum of voices – Mervyn, the stranger, reckoning on being unobserved in the crowd, and weary of the very solitude he courted, turned to his right, and so found himself upon the renowned fair-green of Palmerstown.

It was really a gay rural sight. The circular target stood, with its bright concentric rings, in conspicuous isolation, about a hundred yards away, against the green slope of the hill. The competitors in their best Sunday suits, some armed with muskets and some with fowling pieces – for they were not particular – and with bunches of ribbons fluttering in their three-cornered hats, and sprigs of gay flowers in their breasts, stood in the foreground, in an irregular cluster, while the spectators, in pleasant disorder, formed two broad, and many-coloured parterres, broken into little groups, and separated by a wide, clear sweep of greensward, running up from the marksmen to the target.

In the luminous atmosphere the men of those days showed bright and gay. Such fine scarlet and gold waistcoats – such sky-blue and silver – such pea-green lutestrings – and pink silk linings – and flashing buckles – and courtly wigs – or becoming powder – went pleasantly with the brilliant costume of the stately dames and smiling lasses. There was a pretty sprinkling of uniforms, too – the whole picture in gentle motion, and the bugles and drums of the Royal Irish Artillery filling the air with inspiring music.

All the neighbours were there – merry little Dr Toole in his grandest wig and gold-headed cane, with three dogs at his heels – he seldom appeared without this sort of train – sometimes three, sometimes five – sometimes as many as seven – and his hearty voice was heard bawling at them by name, as he sauntered through the town of a morning, and theirs occasionally in short screeches, responsive to the touch of his cane. Now it was, 'Fairy, you savage, let that pig alone!' a yell and a scuffle – 'Juno, drop it, you slut' – or 'Cæsar, you blackguard, where are you going?'

'Look at Sturk there, with his lordship,' said Toole, to the fair Magnolia, with a wink and a nod, and a sneering grin. 'Good natured dog that – ha! ha! You'll find he'll oust Nutter at last, and get the agency; that's what he's driving at – always undermining somebody.' Doctor Sturk and Lord Castlemallard were talking apart on the high ground, and the artillery surgeon was pointing with his cane at distant objects. 'I'll lay you fifty he's picking holes in Nutter's management this moment.'

I'm afraid there was some truth in the theory, and Toole – though he did not remember to mention it – had an instinctive notion that Sturk had an eye upon the civil practice of the neighbourhood, and was meditating a retirement from the army, and a serious invasion of his domain.

Sturk and Toole, behind backs, did not spare one another. Toole called Sturk a 'horse doctor', and 'the smuggler' – in reference to some affair about French brandy, never made quite clear to me, but in which, I believe, Sturk was really not to blame; and Sturk called him 'that drunken little apothecary' – for Toole had a boy who compounded, under the rose, his draughts, pills, and powders in the back parlour – and sometimes, 'that smutty little ballad singer', or 'that whiskeyfied dog-fancier, Toole'. There was no actual quarrel, however; they met freely – told one another the news – their mutual disagreeabilities were administered guardedly – and, on the whole, they hated one another in a neighbourly way.

Fat, short, radiant, General Chattesworth – in full artillery uniform – was there, smiling and making little speeches to the ladies, and bowing stiffly from his hips upward – his great cue playing all the time up and down his back, and sometimes so near the ground when he stood erect and threw back his head, that Toole, seeing Juno eyeing the appendage rather viciously, thought it prudent to cut her speculations short with a smart kick.

His sister Rebecca – tall, erect, with grand lace, in a splendid stiff brocade, and with a fine fan – was certainly five-and-fifty, but still wonderfully fresh, and sometimes had quite a pretty little pink colour – perfectly genuine – in her cheeks; command sat in her eye and energy on her lip – but though it was imperious and restless, there was something provokingly likeable and even pleasant in her face. Her niece, Gertrude, the general's daughter, was also tall, graceful – and, I am told, perfectly handsome.

'Be the powers, she's mighty handsome!' observed 'Lieutenant Fireworker' O'Flaherty, who, being a little stupid, did not remember that such a remark was not likely to pleasure the charming Magnolia Macnamara, to whom he had transferred the adoration of a passionate, but somewhat battered heart.

'They must not see with my eyes that think so,' said Mag, with a disdainful toss of her head.

'They say she's not twenty, but I'll wager a pipe of claret she's something to the back of it,' said O'Flaherty, mending his hand.

'Why, bless your innocence, she'll never see five-and-twenty, and a bit to spare,' sneered Miss Mag, who might more truly have told that tale of herself. 'Who's that pretty young man my Lord Castlemallard is introducing to her and old Chattesworth?' The commendation was a shot at poor O'Flaherty.

'Hey – so, my Lord knows him!' says Toole, very much interested. 'Why that's Mr Mervyn, that's stopping at the Phoenix. A. Mervyn – I saw it on his dressing case. See how she smiles.'

'Ay, she simpers like a firmity kettle,' said scornful Miss Mag.

'They're very grand today, the Chattesworths, with them two livery footmen behind them,' threw in O'Flaherty, accommodating his remarks to the spirit of his lady-love.

'That young buck's a man of consequence,' Toole rattled on; 'Miss does not smile on everybody.'

'Ay, she looks as if butter would not melt in her mouth, but I warrant cheese won't choke her,' Magnolia laughed out with angry eyes.

Magnolia's fat and highly painted parent – poor bragging, good-natured, cunning, foolish Mrs Macnamara, the widow – joined, with a venomous wheeze in the laugh.

Those who suppose that all this rancour was produced by mere feminine emulations and jealousy do these ladies of the ancient sept Macnamara foul wrong. Mrs Mack, on the contrary, had a fat and genial soul of her own, and Magnolia was by no means a particularly ungenerous rival in the lists of love. But Aunt Rebecca was hoitytoity upon the Macnamaras, whom she would never consent to more than half-know, seeing them with difficulty, often failing to see them altogether – though Magnolia's stature and activity did not always render that easy. Today, for instance, when the firing was brisk, and some of the ladies uttered pretty little timid squalls, Miss Magnolia not only stood fire like brick, but with her own fair hands cracked off a firelock, and was more complimented and applauded than all the marksmen beside, although she shot most dangerously wide, and was much nearer hitting old Arthur Slowe than that respectable gentleman, who waved his hat and smirked gallantly, was at all aware. Aunt Rebecca, notwithstanding all this, and although she looked straight at her from a distance of only ten steps, yet she could not see that large and highly-coloured heroine; and Magnolia was so incensed at her serene impertinence that when Gertrude afterwards smiled and courtesied twice, she only held her head the higher and flung a flashing defiance from her fine eyes right at that unoffending virgin.

Everybody knew that Miss Rebecca Chattesworth ruled supreme at Belmont. With a docile old general and a niece so young, she had less resistance to encounter than, perhaps, her ardent soul would have relished. Fortunately for the general it was only now and then that Aunt Becky took a whim to command the Royal Irish Artillery. She had other hobbies just as odd, though not quite so scandalous. It had struck her active mind that such of the ancient women of Chapelizod as were destitute of letters – mendicants and the like – should learn to read. Twice a week her 'old women's school', under that energetic lady's presidency, brought together its muster-roll of rheumatism, paralysis, dim eyes, bothered ears, and invincible stupidity. Over the fireplace in large black letters was the legend, 'BETTER LATE THAN NEVER!' and out came the horn-books and spectacles, and to it they went with their A-B ab, etc., and plenty of wheezing and coughing. Aunt Becky kept good fires, and served out a mess of bread and broth, along with some pungent ethics, to each of her hopeful old girls. In winter she further encouraged them with a flannel petticoat apiece, and there was besides a monthly dole. So that although after a year there was, perhaps, on the whole, no progress in learning, the affair wore a tolerably encouraging aspect; for the academy had increased in numbers, and two old fellows, liking the notion of the broth and the 6d. a month – one a barber, Will Potts, ruined by a shake in his right hand, the other a drunken pensioner, Phil Doolan, with a wooden leg – petitioned to be en-rolled, and were, accordingly, admitted. Then Aunt Becky visited the gaols, and had a knack of picking up the worst characters there, and had generally two or three discharged felons on her hands. Some people said she was a bit of a Voltarian, but unjustly; for though she now and then came out with a bouncing social para-dox, she was a good bitter Church-woman. So she was liberal and troublesome – off-handed and dictatorial – not without good nature, but administering her benevolences somewhat tyrannically, and, for the most part, doing more or less of positive mischief in the process.

And now the general ('old Chattesworth', as the scornful Mag-nolia called him) drew near, with his benevolent smirk, and his stiff bows, and all his good-natured formalities – for the general had no notion of ignoring his good friend and officer, Major O'Neill, or his sister or niece – and so he made up to Mrs Macnamara, who arrested a narrative in which she was demonstrating to O'Flah-erty the general's lineal descent from old Chattesworth – an army tailor in Queen Anne's time – and his cousinship to a live butter dealer in Cork – and spicing her little history with not a very nice epigram on his uncle, 'the counsellor', by Dr Swift, which she delivered with a vicious chuckle in the 'Fireworker's' ear, who also laughed, though he did not quite see the joke, and said, 'Oh-ho-ho, murdher!'

The good Mrs Mack received the general haughtily and slightly, and Miss Magnolia with a short courtesy and a little toss of her head, and up went her fan, and she giggled something in Toole's ear, who grinned, and glanced uneasily out of the corner of his shrewd little eye at the unsuspicious general and on to Aunt Rebecca; for it was very important to Dr Toole to stand well at Belmont. So, seeing that Miss Mag was disposed to be vicious, and not caring to be compromised by her tricks, he whistled and bawled to his dogs, and with a jolly smirk and flourish of his cocked hat, off he went to seek other adventures.

Thus was there feud and malice between two houses, and Aunt Rebecca's wrong-headed freak of cutting the Macnamaras (for it was not 'snobbery', and she would talk for hours on band-days publicly and familiarly with scrubby little Mrs Toole), involved her innocent relations in scorn and ill-will; for this sort of offence, like Chinese treason, is not visited on the arch-offender only, but according to a scale of consanguinity, upon his kith and kin. The criminal is minced – his sons lashed – his nephews reduced to cutlets – his cousins to joints – and so on – none of the family quite escapes; and seeing the bitter reprisals provoked by this kind of uncharity, fiercer and more enduring by much than any begotten of more tangible wrongs, Christian people who pray, 'lead us not into temptation', and repeat 'blessed are the peacemakers', will, on the whole, do wisely to forbear practising it.

As handsome, slender Captain Devereux, with his dark face, and great, strange, earnest eyes, and that look of intelligence so racy and peculiar, that gave him a sort of enigmatical interest, stepped into the fair-green, the dark blue glance of poor Nan Glynn, of Palmerstown, from under her red Sunday riding-hood, followed the tall, dashing, graceful apparition with a stolen glance of wild loyalty and admiration. Poor Nan! With thy fun and thy rascalities, thy strong affections and thy fatal gift of beauty, where does thy head rest now?

Handsome Captain Devereux! – Gypsy Devereux, as they called him for his clear dark complexion – was talking a few minutes later to Lilias Walsingham. Oh, pretty Lilias – oh, true lady – I never saw the pleasant crayon sketch that my mother used to speak of, but the tradition of thee has come to me – so bright and tender, with its rose and violet tints, and merry, melancholy dimples, that I see thee now, as then, with the dew of thy youth still on thee, and sigh as I look, as if on a lost, early love of mine.

'I'm out of conceit with myself,' he said; 'I'm so idle and useless; I wish that were all – I wish myself better, but I'm such a weak coxcomb – a father-confessor might keep me nearer to my duty – someone to scold and exhort me. Perhaps if some charitable lady would take me in hand, something might be made of me still.'

There was a vein of seriousness in this reverie which amused the young lady; for she had never heard anything worse of him – very young ladies seldom do hear the worst – than that he had played once or twice rather high.

'Shall I ask Gertrude Chattesworth to speak to her Aunt Rebecca?' said Lilias slyly. 'Suppose you attend her school in Martin's Row, with "better late than never" over her chimneypiece: there are two pupils of your own sex, you know, and you might sit on the bench with poor Potts and good old Doolan.'

'Thank you, Miss Lilias,' he answered, with a bow and a little laugh, as it seemed just the least bit in the world piqued; 'I know she would do it zealously; but neither so well nor so wisely as others might; I wish I dare ask *you* to lecture me.'

'I!' said that young lady. 'Oh, yes, I forgot,' she went on merrily, 'five years ago, when I was a little girl, you once called me Dr Walsingham's curate, I was so grave – do you remember?'

She did not know how much obliged Devereux was to her for remembering that poor little joke, and how much the handsome lieutenant would have given, at that instant, to kiss the hand of the grave little girl of five years ago.

'I was a more impudent fellow then,' he said, 'than I am now; won't you forget my old impertinences, and allow me to make atonement, and be your – your *very* humble servant now?'

She laughed. 'Not my servant – but you know I can't help you being my parishioner.'

'And as such surely I may plead an humble right to your counsels and reproof. Yes, you *shall* lecture me – I'll bear it from none but *you*, and the more you do it, the happier, at least, you make me,' he said.

'Alas, if my censure is pleasant to you, 'tis a certain sign it can do you no good.'

'It *shall* do me good, and be it never so bitter and so true, it will be pleasant to me too,' he answered, with an honest and very peculiar light in his dark, strange eyes; and after a little pause, 'I'll tell you why, just because I had rather you remembered my faults, than that you did not remember me at all.'

'But,'tis not my business to make people angry.'

'More likely you should make me sad, or perhaps happy, that is to say, better. I think you'd like to see your parish improve.'

'So I would – but by means of my example, not my preaching. No; I leave that to wiser heads – to the rector, for instance' – and she drew closer to the dear old man, with a quick fond glance of such proud affection, for she thought the sun never shone upon his like, as made Devereux sigh a little unconscious sigh. The old man did not hear her – he was too absorbed in his talk – he only felt the pressure of his darling's little hand, and returned it, after his wont, with a gentle squeeze of his cassocked arm, while he continued the learned essay he was addressing to young, queer, erudite, simple Dan Loftus, on the descent of the Decie branch of the Desmonds. There was, by-the-bye, a rumour – I know not how true – that these two sages were concocting between them, beside their folios on the Castle of Chapelizod, an interminable history of Ireland.

Devereux was secretly chafed at the sort of invisible, but insuperable resistance which pretty Lilias Walsingham, as it seemed, unconsciously opposed to his approaches to a nearer and tenderer sort of trifling. 'The little Siren! There are air-drawn circles round her which I cannot pass – and why should I? How is it that she interests me, and yet repels me so easily? And – and when I came here first,' he continued aloud, 'you were, oh dear! How mere a child, hardly eleven years old. How long I've known you, Miss Lilias, and yet how formal you are with me.' There was reproach almost fierce in his eye, though his tones were low and gentle. 'Well!' he said, with an odd changed little laugh, 'you *did* commit yourself at first – you spoke against card-playing, and I tell you frankly I mean to play a great deal more, and a great deal higher than I've ever done before, and so adieu.'

He did not choose to see the little motion which indicated that she was going to shake hands with him, and only bowed the lower, and answered her grave smile, which seemed to say, 'Now, you are vexed,' with another little laugh, and turned gaily away, and so was gone.

'She thinks she has wounded me, and she thinks, I suppose, that I can't be happy away from her. I'll let her see I can; I shan't speak to her, no, nor look at her, for a month!'

The Chattesworths by this time, as well as others, were moving away – and that young Mr Mervyn, more remarked upon than he suspected, walked with them to the gate of the fair-green. As he passed he bowed low to good Parson Walsingham, who returned his salute, not unkindly – that never was – but very gravely, and with his gentle and thoughtful blue eyes followed the party sadly on their way.

'Ay – there he goes – Mervyn! Well! – so – so – pray Heaven, sorrow and a blight follow him not into this place,' the rector murmured to himself, and sighed, still following him with his glance.

Little Lilias, with her hand within his arm, wondered, as she glanced upward into that beloved face, what could have darkened it with a look so sad and anxious; and then her eyes also followed the retreating figure of that pale young man, with a sort of interest not quite unmixed with uneasiness.

Chapter Five

How the Royal Irish Artillery entertained some of the
neighbours at dinner

If I stuck at a fib as little as some historians, I might easily tell you
who won the prizes at this shooting on Palmerstown Green. But the
truth is, I don't know; my grand-uncle could have told me, for he had
a marvellous memory, but he died, a pleasant old gentleman of four-
score and upwards, when I was a small urchin. I remember his lively
old face, his powdered bald head and pigtail, his slight erect figure,
and how merrily he used to play the fiddle for his juvenile posterity
to dance to. But I was not of an age to comprehend the value of this
thin, living volume of old lore, or to question the oracle. Well, it
can't be helped now, and the papers I've got are silent upon the
point. But there were jollifications to no end both in Palmerstown
and Chapelizod that night, and declamatory conversations rising up
in the street at very late hours, and singing, and '*hurooing*' along the
moonlit roads.

There was a large and pleasant dinner-party, too, in the mess-
room of the Royal Irish Artillery. Lord Castlemallard was there in
the place of honour, next to jolly old General Chattesworth, and the
worthy rector, Doctor Walsingham, and Father Roach, the dapper,
florid little priest of the parish, with his silk waistcoat and well-
placed paunch, and his keen relish for funny stories, side-dishes, and
convivial glass; and Dan Loftus, that simple, meek, semi-barbarous
young scholar, his head in a state of chronic dishevelment, his harmless little round light-blue eyes, pinkish from late night reading,
generally betraying the absence of his vagrant thoughts, and I know
not what of goodness, as well as queerness, in his homely features.

Good Dr Walsingham, indeed, in his simple benevolence, had
helped the strange, kindly creature through college, and had a high
opinion of him, and a great delight in his company. They were both
much given to books, and according to their lights zealous archae-
ologists. They had got hold of Chapelizod Castle, a good tough

enigma. It was a theme they never tired of. Loftus had already two folios of extracts copied from all the records to which Dr Walsing-ham could procure him access. They could not have worked harder, indeed, if they were getting up evidence to prove their joint title to Lord Castlemallard's estates. This pursuit was a bond of close sym-pathy between the rector and the student, and they spent more time than appeared to his parishioners quite consistent with sanity in the paddock by the river, pacing up and down, and across, poking sticks into the earth and grubbing for old walls underground.

Loftus, moreover, was a good Irish scholar, and from Celtic MSS. had elicited some cross-lights upon his subject – not very bright or steady, I allow – but enough to delight the rector, and inspire him with a tender reverence for the indefatigable and versatile youth, who was devoting to the successful equitation of their hobby so many of his hours, and so much of his languages, labour, and brains.

Lord Castlemallard was accustomed to be listened to, and was not aware how confoundedly dull his talk sometimes was. It was measured, and dreamy, and every way slow. He was entertaining the courteous old general at the head of the table, with an oration in praise of Paul Dangerfield – a wonderful man – immensely wealthy – the cleverest man of his age – he might have been anything he pleased. His lordship really believed his English property would drop to pieces if Dangerfield retired from its management, and he was vastly obliged to him inwardly, for retaining the agency even for a little time longer. He was coming over to visit the Irish estates – perhaps to give Nutter a wrinkle or two. He was a bachelor, and his lordship averred would be a prodigious great match for some of our Irish ladies. Chapelizod would be his headquarters while in Ireland. No, he was not sure – he rather thought he was *not* of the Thorley family; and so on for a mighty long time. But though he tired them prodigiously, he contrived to evoke before their minds' eyes a very gigantic, though somewhat hazy figure, and a good deal stimulated the interest with which a new arrival was commonly looked for in that pleasant suburban village. There is no know-ing how long Lord Castlemallard might have prosed upon this theme, had he not been accidentally cut short, and himself laid fast asleep in his chair, without his or anybody else's intending it. For overhearing, during a short pause, in which he sipped some claret, Surgeon Sturk applying some very strong, and indeed, fright-ful language to a little pamphlet upon magnetism, a subject then making a stir – as from a much earlier date it has periodically done down to the present day – he languidly asked Dr Walsingham his opinion upon the subject.

Now, Dr Walsingham was a great reader of out-of-the-way lore, and retained it with a sometimes painful accuracy; and he forthwith began – 'There is, my Lord Castlemallard, a curious old tract of the learned Van Helmont, in which he says, as near as I can remember his words, that magnetism is a magical faculty, which lieth dormant in us by the opiate of primitive sin, and, therefore, stands in need of an excitator, which excitator may be either good or evil; but is more frequently Satan himself, by reason of some previous oppignoration or compact with witches. The power, indeed, is in the witch, and not conferred by him; but this versipellous or Protean impostor – these are his words – will not suffer her to know that it is of her own natural endowment, though for the present charmed into somnolent inactivity by the narcotic of primitive sin.'

I verily believe that a fair description – none of your poetical balderdash, but an honest plodding description of a perfectly comfortable bed, and of the process of going to sleep, would, judiciously administered soon after dinner, overpower the vivacity of any tranquil gentleman who loves a nap after that meal – gently draw the curtains of his senses, and extinguish the bedroom candle of his consciousness. In the doctor's address and quotation there was so much about somnolency and narcotics, and lying dormant, and opiates, that my Lord Castlemallard's senses forsook him, and he lost, as you, my kind reader, must, all the latter portion of the doctor's lullaby.

'I'd give half I'm pothethed of, Thir, and all my prothpecth in life,' lisped vehemently plump little Lieutenant Puddock, in one of those stage frenzies to which he was prone, 'to be the firtht Alecthander on the boardth.'

Between ourselves, Puddock was short and fat, very sentimental, and a little bit of a *gourmet*; his desk stuffed with amorous sonnets and receipts for side-dishes; he, always in love, and often in the kitchen, where, under the rose, he loved to direct the cooking of critical little *plats*, very good-natured, rather literal, very courteous, a *chevalier*, indeed, *sans reproche*. He had a profound faith in his genius for tragedy, but those who liked him best could not help thinking that his plump cheeks, round, little light eyes, his lisp, and a certain lackadaisical, though solemn expression of surprise, which Nature, in one of her jocular moods, seemed to have fixed upon his countenance, were against his shining in that walk of the drama. He was blessed, too, with a pleasant belief in his acceptance with the fair sex, but had a real one with his comrades, who knew his absurdities and his virtues, and laughed at and loved him.

'But hang it, there'th no uthe in doing things by halves. Melpomene's the most jealous of the Muses. I tell you if you stand well in her gratheth, by Jove, Thir, you mutht give yourthelf up to her body and thoul. How the deuthe can a fellow that's out at drill at hicth in the morning, and all day with his head filled with tacticth and gunnery, and – and – '

'And "farced pigeons" and lovely women,' said Devereux.

'And such dry professional matterth,' continued he, without noticing, perhaps hearing, the interpolation, 'How can he pothibly have a chance againth geniuses, no doubt – vathly thuperior by nature' – (Puddock, the rogue, believed no such thing) – 'but who devote themthelveth to the thtudy of the art incethantly, exclusively, and – and – '

'Impossible,' said O'Flaherty. 'There now, was Tommy Shycock, of Ballybaisly, that larned himself to balance a fiddle-stick on his chin; and the young leedies, and especially Miss Kitty Mahony, used to be all around him in the ball-room at Thralee, lookin', wondhrin', and laughin'; and I that had twiste his brains, could not come round it, though I got up every morning for a month at four o'clock, and was obleeged to give over be rason of a soart iv a squint I was gettin' be looking continually at the fiddle-stick. I began with a double bass, the way he did – it's it that was the powerful fateaguin' exercise, I can tell you. Two blessed hours a day, regular practice, besides an odd half-hour, now and agin, for three mortial years, it took him to larn it, and dhrilled a dimple in his chin you could put a marrow-fat pay in.'

'Practice,' resumed Puddock, I need not spell his lisp, 'study – time to devote – industry in great things as in small – there's the secret. *Nature*, to be sure – '

'Ay, Nature, to be sure – we must sustain Nature, dear Puddock, so pass the bottle,' said Devereux, who liked his glass.

'Be the powers, Mr Puddock, if I had half your janius for play-acting,' persisted O'Flaherty, 'nothing i'd keep me from the boards iv Smock-alley play-house – incog., I mean, of course. There's that wonderful little Mr Garrick – why he's the talk of the three kingdoms as long as I can remember – an' making his thousand pounds a week – coining, be gannies – an' he can't be much taller than you, for he's contimptably small.'

'I'm the taller man of the two,' said little Puddock, haughtily, who had made enquiries, and claimed half an inch over Rocius, honestly, let us hope. 'But this is building castles in the air; joking apart, however, I do confess I should dearly love – just for a maggot – to play two parts – Richard the Third and Tamerlane.'

'Was not that the part you spoke that sympathetic speech out of for me before dinner?'

'No, that was Justice Greedy,' said Devereux.

'Ay, so it was – was it? – that smothered his wife.'

'With a pudding clout,' persisted Devereux.

'No. With a – pooh! – a – you know – and stabbed himself,' continued O'Flaherty.

'With a larding-pin – 'tis written in good Italian.'

'Augh, not at all – it isn't Italian, but English, I'm thinking of – a pilla, Puddock, you know – the *black* rascal.'

'Well, English or Italian – tragedy or comedy,' said Devereux, who liked Puddock, and would not annoy him, and saw he was hurt by Othello's borrowing his properties from the kitchen; 'I venture to say you were well entertained: and for my part, Sir, there are some characters' – (in farce Puddock was really highly diverting) – 'in which I prefer Puddock to any player I every saw.'

'Oh – ho-ho!' laughed poor little Puddock, with a most gratified derisiveness, for he cherished in secret a great admiration for Devereux.

And so they talked stage-talk. Puddock lithping away, grand and garrulous; O'Flaherty, the illiterate, blundering in with sincere applause; and Devereux sipping his claret and dropping a quiet saucy word now and again.

'I shall never forget Mrs Cibber's countenance in that last scene – you know – in the "Orphan" – Monimia *you* know, Devereux.' And the table being by this time in high chat, and the chairs a little irregular, Puddock slipped off his, and addressing himself to Devereux and O'Flaherty – just to give them a notion of Mrs Cibber – began, with a countenance the most woebegone, and in a piping falsetto –

When I am laid low, i' the grave, and quite forgotten.

Monimia dies at the end of the speech – as the reader may not be aware; but when Puddock came to the line –

When I am dead, as presently I shall be,

all Mrs Cibber's best points being still to come, the little lieutenant's heel caught in the edge of the carpet, as he sailed with an imaginary hoop on grandly backward, and in spite of a surprising flick-flack cut in the attempt to recover his equipoise, down came the 'orphan', together with a table-load of spoons and plates, with a crash that stopt all conversation.

Lord Castlemallard waked up, with a snort and a 'hollo, gentlemen!'

'It's only poor dear Monimia, general,' said Devereux with a melancholy bow, in reply to a fiery and startled stare darted to the point by that gallant officer.

'Hey – eh?' said his lordship, brightening up, and gazing glassily round with a wan smile; and I fancy he thought a lady had somehow introduced herself during his nap, and was pleased, for he admired the sex.

'If there's any recitation going on, I think it had better be for the benefit of the company,' said the general, a little surly, and looking full upon the plump Monimia, who was arranging his frill and hair, and getting a little awkwardly into his place.

'And I think 'twould be no harm, Lieutenant Puddock, my dear,' says Father Roach, testily, for he had been himself frightened by the crash, 'if you'd die a little aisier the next time.'

Puddock began to apologise.

'Never mind,' said the general, recovering, 'let's fill our glasses – my Lord Castlemallard, they tell me this claret is a pretty wine.'

'A very pretty wine,' said my lord.

'And suppose, my lord, we ask these gentlemen to give us a song? I say, gentlemen, there are fine voices among you. Will some gentleman oblige the company with a song?'

'Mr Loftus sings a very fine song, I'm told,' said Captain Cluffe, with a wink at Father Roach.

'Ay,' cried Roach, backing up the joke (a good old one, and not yet quite off the hooks), 'Mr Loftus sings, I'll take my davy – I've heard him!'

Loftus was shy, simple, and grotesque, and looked like a man who could not sing a note. So when he opened his eyes, looked round, and blushed, there was a general knocking of glasses, and a very flattering clamour for Mr Loftus's song.

But when silence came, to the surprise of the company he submitted, though with manifest trepidation, and told them that he would sing as the company desired. It was a song from a good old writer upon fasting in Lent, and was, in fact, a reproof to all hypocrisy. Hereupon there was a great ringing of glasses and a jolly round of laughter rose up in the cheer that welcomed the announcement. Father Roach looked queer and disconcerted, and shot a look of suspicion at Devereux, for poor Dan Loftus had, in truth, hit that divine strait in a very tender spot.

The fact is, Father Roach was, as Irish priests were sometimes then, a bit of a sportsman. He and Toole used occasionally to make mysterious excursions to the Dublin mountains. He had a couple of mighty good dogs, which he lent freely, being a good-natured fellow. He liked good living and jolly young fellows, and was popular among the officers, who used to pop in freely enough at his reverence's green hall-door whenever they wanted a loan of his dogs, or to take counsel of the ghostly father (whose opinion was valued more highly even than Toole's) upon the case of a sick dog or a lame nag.

Well, one morning – only a few weeks before – Devereux and Toole together had looked in on some such business upon his reverence – a little suddenly – and found him eating a hare! – by all the gods, it *was* – hare-pie in the middle of Lent!

It was at breakfast. His dinner was the meal of an anchorite, and who would have guessed that these confounded sparks would have bounced into his little refectory at that hour of the morning? There was no room for equivocation; he had been caught in the very act of criminal conversation with the hare-pie. He rose with a spring, like a Jack-in-a-box, as they entered, and knife and fork in hand, and with shining chops, stared at them with an angry, bothered, and alarmed countenance, which increased their laughter. It was a good while before he obtained a hearing, such was the hilarity, so sustained the fire of ironical compliments, enquiries, and pleasantries, and the general uproar.

When he did, with hand uplifted, after the manner of a prisoner arraigned for murder, he pleaded 'a dispensation'. I suppose it was true, for he backed the allegation with several most religious oaths and imprecations, and explained how men were not always quite so strong as they looked; that he might, if he liked it, by permission of his bishop, eat meat at every meal in the day, and every day in the week; that his not doing so was a voluntary abstinence – not conscientious, only expedient – to prevent the 'unreasonable remarks' of his parishioners (a roar of laughter); that he was, perhaps, rightly served for not having publicly availed himself of his bishop's dispensation (renewed peals of merriment). By this foolish delicacy (more of that detestable horse-laughter), he had got himself into a false position; and so on, till the *ad misericordiam* peroration addressed to 'Captain Devereux, dear', and 'Toole, my honey'. Well, they quizzed him unmercifully; they sat down and eat all that was left of the hare-pie, under his wistful ogle. They made him narrate minutely every circumstance connected with the smuggling of the game, and the illicit distillation for the mess. They never passed so pleasant a morning. Of course he bound them over to eternal secrecy, and of course, as in all similar cases, the vow was religiously observed; nothing was ever heard of it at mess – oh, no – and Toole never gave a dramatic representation of the occurrence, heightened and embellished with all the little doctor's genius for farce.

There certainly was a monologue to which he frequently after-wards treated the Aldermen of Skinner's Alley, and other convivial bodies, at supper; the doctor's gestures were made with knife and fork in hand, and it was spoken in a rich brogue and tones sometimes of thrilling pathos, anon of sharp and vehement indignation, and again of childlike endearment, amidst pounding and jingling of glasses, and screams of laughter from the company. Indeed the lord mayor, a fat slob of a fellow, though not much given to undue merriment, laughed his ribs into such a state of breathless torture, that he implored of Toole, with a wave of his hand – he could not speak – to give him breathing time, which that voluble performer disregarding, his lordship had to rise twice, and get to the window, or, as he afterwards said, he should have lost his life; and when the performance was ended, his fat cheeks were covered with tears, his mouth hung down, his head wagged slowly from side to side, and with short gasping 'oohs', and 'aahs', his hands pressed to his pudgy ribs, he looked so pale and breathless, that although they said nothing, several of his comrades stared hard at him, and thought him in rather a queer state.

Shortly after this little surprise, I suppose by way of ratifying the secret treaty of silence, Father Roach gave the officers and Toole a grand Lent dinner of fish, with no less than nineteen different *plats*, baked, boiled, stewed, in fact, a very splendid feast; and Puddock talked of some of those dishes more than twenty years afterwards.

Chapter Six
In which the minstrelsy proceeds

No wonder, then, if Father Roach, when Loftus, in the innocence of his heart, announced his song and its theme, was thoroughly uneasy, and would have given a good deal that he had not helped that simple youth into his difficulty. But things must now take their course. So amid a decorous silence, Dan Loftus lifted up his voice, and sang. That voice was a high small pipe, with a very nervous quaver in it. He leaned back in his chair, and little more than the whites of his upturned eyes were visible; and beating time upon the table with one hand, claw-wise, and with two or three queer, little trills and roulades, which re-appeared with great precision in each verse, he delivered himself thus, in what I suspect was an old psalm tune –

> Now Lent is come, let us refrain
> From carnal creatures, quick or slain;
> Let's fast and macerate the flesh,
> Impound and keep it in distress.

Here there came a wonderful, unspellable choking sound, partly through the mouth, partly through the nose, from several of the officers; and old General Chattesworth, who was frowning hard upon his dessert-plate, cried, 'Order, gentlemen,' in a stern, but very tremulous undertone. Lord Castlemallard, leaning upon his elbow, was staring with a grave and dreamy curiosity at the songster, and neither he nor his lordship heard the interruption, and on went the pleasant ditty; and as the musician regularly repeated the last two lines like a clerk in a piece of psalmody, the young wags, to save themselves from bursting outright, joined in the chorus, while verse after verse waxed more uproarious and hilarious, and gave a singular relief to Loftus's thin, high, quavering solo –

[*Loftus, solo*]
>   But to forbear from flesh, fowl, fish,
>   And eat potatoes in a dish,
>   Done o'er with amber, or a mess
>   Of ringos in a Spanish dress.

[*Chorus of officers*]
>   Done o'er with amber, or a mess
>   Of ringos in a Spanish dress.

''Tis a good song,' murmured Doctor Walsingham in Lord Castle-mallard's ear – 'I know the verses well – the ingenious and pious Howel penned them in the reign of King James the First.'

'Ha! Thank you, Sir,' said his lordship.

[*Loftus, solo*]
>   Or to refrain from all high dishes,
>   But feed our thoughts with wanton wishes,
>   Making the soul, like a light wench,
>   Wear patches of concupiscence.

[*Chorus of officers*]
>   Making the soul, like a light wench,
>   Wear patches of concupiscence.

[*Loftus, solo*]
>   This is not to keep Lent aright,
>   But play the juggling hypocrite;
>   For we must starve the inward man,
>   And feed the outward too on bran.

[*Chorus of officers*]
>   For we must starve the inward man,
>   And feed the outward too on bran.

I believe no song was ever received with heartier bursts of laughter and applause. Puddock indeed was grave, being a good deal interested in the dishes sung by the poet. So, for the sake of its moral point, was Dr Walsingham, who, with brows gathered together judicially, kept time with head and hand, murmuring 'true, true – *good*, Sir, good,' from time to time, as the sentiment liked him.

But honest Father Roach was confoundedly put out by the performance. He sat with his blue double chin buried in his breast, his mouth pursed up tightly, a red scowl all over his face, his quick, little, angry, suspicious eyes peeping cornerwise, now this way, now that, not knowing how to take what seemed to him like a deliberate conspiracy to roast him for the entertainment of the company, who followed the concluding verse with a universal roaring chorus, which went off into a storm of laughter, in which Father Roach made an absurd attempt to join. But it was only a gunpowder glare, swallowed in an instant in darkness, and down came the black portcullis of his scowl with a chop, while clearing his voice, and directing his red face and vicious little eyes straight on simple Dan Loftus he said, rising very erect and square from an unusually ceremonious bow – 'I don't know, Mr Loftus, exactly what you mean by a "ring-goat in a Spanish dress" ' (the priest had just smuggled over a wonderful bit of ecclesiastical toggery from Salamanca): 'and – a – person wearing patches, you said of – of – patches of concupiscence, I think.' (Father Roach's housekeeper unfortunately wore patches, though, it is right to add, she was altogether virtuous, and by no means young); 'but I'm bound to suppose, by the amusement our friends seem to derive from it, Sir, that a ring-goat, whatever it means, is a good joke, as well as a good-natured one.'

'But, by your leave, Sir,' emphatically interposed Puddock, on whose ear the ecclesiastic's blunder grated like a discord, 'Mr Loftus sang nothing about a goat, though kid is not a bad thing: he said, "ringos", meaning, I conclude, eringoeous, a delicious preserve or confection. Have you never eaten them, either preserved or candied – a – why I – a – I happen to have a receipt – a – and if you permit me, Sir – a capital receipt. When I was a boy, I made some once at home, Sir; and, by Jupiter, my brother, Sam, eat of them till he was quite sick – I remember, *so* sick, by Jupiter, my poor mother and old Dorcas had to sit up all night with him – a – and – I was going to say, if you will allow me, Sir, I shall be very happy to send the receipt to your housekeeper.'

'You'll not like it, Sir,' said Devereux, mischievously: 'but there really is a capital one – quite of another kind – a lenten dish – fish, you know, Puddock – the one you described yesterday; but Mr Loftus has, I think, a still better way.'

'Have you, Sir?' asked Puddock, who had a keen appetite for knowledge.

'I don't know, Captain Puddock,' murmured Loftus, bewildered.

'What is it?' remarked his reverence, shortly.

'A roast roach,' answered Puddock, looking quite innocently in that theologian's fiery face.

'*Thank* you,' said Father Roach, with an expression of countenance which polite little Puddock did not in the least understand.

'And how do *you* roast him – we know Loftus's receipt,' persisted Devereux, with remarkable cruelty.

'Just like a lump,' said Puddock, briskly.

'And how is that?' enquired Devereux.

'Flay the lump – splat him – divide him,' answered Puddock, with great volubility; 'and cut each side into two pieces; season with salt, pepper, and nutmeg, and baste with clarified butter; dish him with slices of oranges, barberries, grapes, gooseberries, and butter; and you will find that he eats deliriously either with farced pain or gammon pain.'

This rhapsody, delivered with the rapidity and emphasis of Puddock's earnest lisp, was accompanied with very general tokens of merriment from the company, and the priest, who half suspected him of having invented it, was on the point of falling foul of him, when Lord Castlemallard rose to take leave, and the general forthwith vacated the chair, and so the party broke up, fell into groups, and the greater part sauntered off to the Phoenix, where, in the clubroom, they, with less restraint, and some new recruits, carried on the pleasures of the evening, which pleasures, as will sometimes happen, ended in something rather serious.

Chapter Seven

*Showing how two gentlemen may misundrstand one another, without
enabling the company to understand their quarrel*

Loftus had by this time climbed to the savage lair of his garret,
overstrewn with tattered papers and books; and Father Roach, in the
sanctuary of his little parlour, was growling over the bones of a
devilled-turkey, and about to soothe his fretted soul in a generous
libation of hot whiskey punch. Indeed, he was of an appeasable
nature, and on the whole a very good fellow.

Dr Toole, whom the young fellows found along with Nutter over
the draught-board in the club-room, forsook his game to devour the
story of Loftus's Lenten Hymn, and poor Father Roach's penance,
rubbed his hands, and slapped his thigh, and crowed and shouted
with ecstasy. O'Flaherty, who called for punch, and was unfortunately prone to grow melancholy and pugnacious over his liquor, was
now in a saturnine vein of sentiment, discoursing of the charms of
his peerless mistress, the Lady Magnolia Macnamara – for he was
not one of those maudlin shepherds who pipe their loves in lonely
glens and other sequestered places, but rather loved to exhibit his
bare scars, and roar his tender torments for the edification of the
market-place.

While he was descanting on the attributes of that bewitching
'crature', Puddock, not two yards off, was describing, with scarcely
less unction, the perfections of 'pig roast with the hair on': and the
two made a medley like 'The Roast Beef of Old England', and 'The
Last Rose of Summer', arranged in alternate stanzas. O'Flaherty
suddenly stopped short, and said a little sternly to Lieutenant Puddock – 'Does it very much signify, Sir (or as O'Flaherty pronounced it,
"Sorr") whether the animal has hair upon it or not?'

'*Every*thing, Thir, in thith particular retheipt,' answered Puddock,
a little loftily.

'But,' said Nutter, who, though no great talker, would make an
effort to prevent a quarrel, and at the same time winking to Puddock

in token that O'Flaherty was just a little 'hearty', and so to let him alone; 'what signifies pigs' hair, compared with human tresses?'

'Compared with *human* tresses?' interrupted O'Flaherty, with stern deliberation, and fixing his eyes steadily and rather unpleasantly upon Nutter (I think he saw that wink and perhaps did not understand its import.)

'Ay, Sir, and Mrs Magnolia Macnamara has as rich a head of hair as you could wish to see,' says Nutter, thinking he was drawing him off very cleverly.

'As *I* could wish to see?' repeated O'Flaherty grimly.

'As *you* could desire to see, Sir,' reiterated Nutter, firmly, for he was not easily put down; and they looked for several seconds in silence a little menacingly, though puzzled, at one another.

But O'Flaherty, after a short pause, seemed to forget Nutter, and returned to his celestial theme.

'Be the powers, Sir, that young leedy has the most beautiful dimple in her chin I ever set eyes on!'

'Have you ever put a marrow fat pea in it, Sir?' enquired Devereux, simply, with all the beautiful rashness of youth.

'No, Sorr,' replied O'Flaherty, in a deep tone, and with a very dangerous glare; 'and I'd like to see the man who, in my presence, id preshum to teeke that libertee.'

'What a glorious name Magnolia is!' interposed little Toole in great haste; for it was a practice among these worthies to avert quarrels – very serious affairs in these jolly days – by making timely little diversions, and it is wonderful, at a critical moment, what may be done by suddenly presenting a trifle; a pin's point, sometimes – at least, a marvellously small one – will draw off innocuously the accumulating electricity of a pair of bloated scowling thunderclouds.

'It was her noble godmother, when the family resided at Castlemara, in the county of Roscommon, the Lady Carrick-o'-Gunniol, who conferred it,' said O'Flaherty, grandly, 'upon her god-daughter, as who had a better right – I say, *who* had a better right?' and he smote his hand upon the table, and looked round inviting contradiction. 'My godmothers, in my baptism – that's catechism – and all the town of Chapelizod won't put that down – the Holy Church Catechism – while Hyacinth O'Flaherty, of Coolnaquirk, Lieutenant Fireworker, wears a sword.'

'Nobly said, lieutenant!' exclaimed Toole, with a sly wink over his shoulder.

'And what about that leedy's neeme, Sir?' demanded the enamoured fireworker.

'By Jove, Sir, it is quite true, Lady Carrick-o'-Gunniol *was* her godmother:' and Toole ran off into the story of how that relationship was brought about; narrating it, however, with great caution and mildness, extracting all the satire, and giving it quite a dignified and creditable character, for the Lieutenant Fireworker smelt so confoundedly of powder that the little doctor, though he never flinched when occasion demanded, did not care to give him an open. Those who had heard the same story from the mischievous merry little doctor before, were I dare say, amused at the grand and complimentary turn he gave it now.

The fact was, that poor Magnolia's name came to her in no very gracious way. Young Lady Carrick-o'-Gunniol was a bit of a wag, and was planting a magnolia – one of the first of those botanical rarities seen in Ireland – when good-natured, vapouring, vulgar Mrs Macnamara's note, who wished to secure a peeress for her daughter's spiritual guardian, arrived. Her ladyship pencilled on the back of the note, 'Pray call the dear babe Magnolia', and forthwith forgot all about it. But Madam Macnamara was charmed, and the autograph remained afterwards for two generations among the archives of the family; and, with great smiles and much complacency, she told Lord Carrick-o'-Gunniol all about it, just outside the grand jury-room, where she met him during the assize week; and, being a man of a weak and considerate nature, rather kind, and very courteous – although his smile was very near exploding into a laugh, as he gave the good lady snuff out of his own box – he was yet very much concerned and vexed, and asked his lady, when he went home, how she could have induced old Mrs Macnamara to give that absurd name to her poor infant; whereat her ladyship, who had not thought of it since, was highly diverted; and being assured that the babe was actually christened, and past recovery Magnolia Macnamara, laughed very merrily, kissed her lord, who was shaking his head gravely, and then popped her hood on, kissed him again, and, laughing still, ran out to look at her magnolia, which, by way of reprisal, he henceforth, notwithstanding her entreaties, always called her 'Macnamara'; until, to her infinite delight, he came out with it, as it sometimes happens, at a wrong time, and asked old Mac – a large, mild man, then extant – Madame herself, nurse, infant Magnolia, and all, who had arrived at the castle, to walk out and see Lady Carrick-o'-Gunniol's 'Macnamara', and perceived not the slip, such is the force of habit, though the family stared, and Lady C. laughed in an uncalled-for-way, at a sudden recollection of a tumble she once had, when a child, over a flower-bed; and broke out repeatedly, to my lord's chagrin and bewilderment, as they walked towards the exotic.

When Toole ended his little family anecdote, which, you may be sure, he took care to render as palatable to Magnolia's knight as possible, by not very scrupulous excisions and interpolations, he wound all up, without allowing an instant for criticism or question, by saying briskly, though incoherently.

'And so, what do you say, lieutenant, to a Welsh rabbit for supper?' The lieutenant nodded a stolid assent.

'Will *you* have one, Nutter?' cried Toole.

'No,' said Nutter.

'And why not?' says Toole.

'Why, I believe Tom Rooke's song in praise of oysters,' answered Nutter, 'especially the verse –

> The youth will ne'er live to scratch a grey head,
> On a supper who goes of Welsh rabbit to bed.'

How came it to pass that Nutter hardly opened his lips this evening – on which, as the men who knew him longest all remarked, he was unprecedentedly talkative – without instantaneously becoming the mark at which O'Flaherty directed his fiercest and most suspicious scowls? And now that I know the allusion which the pugnacious lieutenant apprehended, I cannot but admire the fatality with which, without the smallest design, a very serious misunderstanding was brought about.

'As to *youths* living to scratch grey heads or not, Sir,' said the young officer, in most menacing tones; 'I don't see what concern persons of your age can have in that. But I'll take leave to tell you, Sir, that a gentleman, whether he be a "youth" as you *say*, or aged, as you *are*, who endayvours to make himself diverting at the expense of others, runs a murdhering good risk, Sir, of getting himself scratched where he'll like it least.'

Little Nutter, though grave and generally taciturn, had a spirit of his own, and no notion whatever of knocking under to a bully. It is true, he had not the faintest notion why he was singled out for the young gentleman's impertinence; but neither did he mean to enquire. His mahogany features darkened for a moment to logwood, and his eyes showed their whites fiercely.

'We are not accustomed, Sir, in this part of the world, to your Connaught notions of politeness; we meet here for social – a – a – sociality, Sir; and the long and the short of it is, young gentleman, if you don't change your key, you'll find two can play at that game – and – and, I tell you, Sir, there will be wigs on the green, Sir.'

Here several voices interposed.

'Silence, gentlemen, and let me speak, or I'll assault him,' bellowed O'Flaherty, who, to do him justice, at this moment looked capable of anything. 'I believe, Sir,' he continued, addressing Nutter, who confronted him like a little gamecock, 'it is not usual for one gentleman who renders himself offensive to another to oblige him to proceed to the length of manually malthrating his person.'

'Hey! Eh?' said Nutter, drawing his mouth tight on one side with an ugly expression, and clenching his hands in his breeches pockets.

'Manually malthrating his person, Sir,' repeated O'Flaherty, 'by striking, kicking, or whipping any part or mimber of his body; or offering a milder assault, such as a pull by the chin, or a finger-tap upon the nose. It is usual, Sir, for the purpose of avoiding ungentle-manlike noise, inconvenience, and confusion, that one gentleman should request of another to suppose himself affronted in the manner, whatever it may be, most intolerable to his feelings, which request I now, Sir, teeke the libertee of preferring to you; and when you have engaged the services of a friend, I trust that Lieutenant Puddock, who lodges in the same house with me, will, in consideration of my being an officer of the same honourable corps, a sthranger in this part of the counthry, and, above all, a gentleman who can show paydagree like himself' [here a low bow to Puddock, who returned it] 'that Lieu-tenant Puddock will be so feelin' and so kind as to receive him on my behalf, and acting as *my* friend to manage all the particulars for settling, as easily as may be, this most unprovoked affair.'

With which words he made another bow, and a pause of enquiry directed to Puddock, who lisped with dignity – 'Sir, the duty is, for many reasons, painful; but I – I can't refuse, Sir, and I accept the trust.'

So O'Flaherty shook his hand, with another bow; bowed silently and loftily round the room, and disappeared, and a general buzz and a clack of tongues arose.

'Mr Nutter – a – I hope things may be settled pleasantly,' said Puddock, looking as tall and weighty as he could; 'at present I – a – that is, at the moment, I – a – don't quite see – ' [the fact is, he had not a notion what the deuce it was all about] ' – but your friend will find me – your friend – a – at my lodgings up to one o'clock tonight, if necessary.'

And so Puddock's bow. For the moment an affair of this sort presented itself, all concerned therein became reserved and official, and the representatives merely of a ceremonious etiquette and a minutely-regulated ordeal of battle. So, as I said, Puddock bowed grandly and sublimely to Nutter, and then magnificently to the company, and made his exit.

There was a sort of a stun and a lull for several seconds. Something very decisive and serious had occurred. One or two countenances wore that stern and mysterious smile, which implies no hilarity, but a kind of reaction in presence of the astounding and the slightly horrible. There was a silence; the gentlemen kept their attitudes too, for some moments, and all eyes were directed toward the door. Then some turned to Charles Nutter, and then the momentary spell dissolved itself.

Chapter Eight

*Relating how Doctor Toole and Captain Devereux went
on a moonlight errand*

Nearly a dozen gentlemen broke out at once into voluble speech.
Nutter was in a confounded passion; but being a man of few words,
showed his wrath chiefly in his countenance, and stood with his legs
apart and his arms stuffed straight into his coat pockets, his back to
the fireplace, with his chest thrown daringly out, sniffing the air in a
state of high tension, and as like as a respectable little fellow of five
feet six could be to that giant who smelt the blood of the Irishman,
and swore, with a 'Fee! Faw!! Fum!!!' he'd 'eat him for his supper
that night'.

'None of the corps can represent you, Nutter, you know,'
said Captain Cluffe. 'It may go hard enough with Puddock and
O'Flaherty, as the matter stands; but, by Jove! if any of us appear on
the other side, the general would make it a very serious affair,
indeed.'

'Toole, can't you?' asked Devereux.

'Out of the question,' answered he, shutting his eyes, with a frown,
and shaking his head. 'There's no man I'd do it sooner for, Nutter
knows; but I can't – I've refused too often; besides, you'll want me
professionally, you know; for Sturk must attend that Royal Hospital
enquiry tomorrow all day – but hang it, where's the difficulty? Isn't
there? – pooh! – why there must be lots of fellows at hand. Just – a –
just think for a minute.'

'I don't care who,' said Nutter, with dry ferocity, 'so he can load
a pistol.'

'Tom Forsythe would have done capitally, if he was at home,'
said one.

'But he's *not*,' remarked Cluffe.

'Well,' said Toole, getting close up to Devereux, in a coaxing
undertone, 'suppose we try Loftus.'

'Dan Loftus!' ejaculated Devereux.

'Dan Loftus,' repeated the little doctor, testily; 'remember, it's just eleven o'clock. He's no great things, to be sure; but what better can we get.'

'*Allons, donc!*' said Devereux, donning his cocked hat with a shrug, and the least little bit of a satirical smile, and out bustled the doctor beside him.

'Where the deuce did that broganeer, O'Flaherty, come from?' said Cluffe, confidentially, to old Major O'Neill.

'A Connaughtman,' answered the major, with a grim smile, for he was himself of that province and was, perhaps, a little bit proud of his countryman.

'Toole says he's well connected,' pursued Cluffe; 'but, by Jupiter! I never saw so mere a Teague; and the most cross-grained devil of a cat-a-mountain.'

'I could not quite understand why he fastened on Mr Nutter,' observed the major, with a mild smile.

'I'll rid the town of him,' rapped out Nutter, with an oath, leering at his own shoebuckle, and tapping the sole with asperity on the floor.

'If you are thinking of any unpleasant measures, gentlemen, I'd rather, if you please, know nothing of them,' said the sly, quiet major; 'for the general, you are aware, has expressed a strong opinion about such affairs; and as 'tis past my bed-hour, I'll wish you, gentlemen, a good-night,' and off went the major.

'Upon my life, if this Connaught rapparee is permitted to carry on his business of indiscriminate cut-throat here, he'll make the service very pleasant,' resumed Cluffe, who, though a brisk young fellow of eight-and-forty, had no special fancy for being shot. 'I say the general ought to take the matter into his own hands.'

'Not till I'm done with it,' growled Nutter.

'And send the young gentleman home to Connaught,' pursued Cluffe.

'I'll send him first to the other place,' said Nutter, in allusion to the Lord Protector's well-known alternative.

In the open street, under the sly old moon, red little Dr Toole, in his great wig, and Gypsy Devereux, in quest of a squire for the good knight who stood panting for battle in the front parlour of the Phoenix, saw a red glimmer in Loftus's dormant window.

'He's alive and stirring still,' said Devereux, approaching the hall door with a military nonchalance.

'Whisht!' said Toole, plucking him back by the sash: 'we must not make a noise – the house is asleep. I'll manage it – leave it to me.'

And he took up a handful of gravel, but not having got the range, he shied it all against old Tom Drought's bedroom window.

'Deuce take that old sneak,' whispered Toole vehemently, 'he's always in the way; the last man in the town I'd have – but no matter:' and up went a pebble, better directed, for this time it went right through Loftus's window, and a pleasant little shower of broken glass jingled down into the street.

'Confound you, Toole,' said Devereux, 'you'll rouse the town.'

'Plague take the fellow's glass – it's as thin as paper,' sputtered Toole.

'Loftus, we want you,' said Toole, in a hard whispered shout, and making a speaking trumpet of his hands, as the wild head of the student, like nothing in life but a hen's nest, appeared above.

'Cock-Loftus, come down, d'ye hear?' urged Devereux.

'Dr Toole and Lieutenant Devereux – I – I – dear me! Yes. Gentlemen, your most obedient,' murmured Loftus vacantly, and knocking his head smartly on the top of the window frame, in recovering from a little bow. 'I'll be wi' ye, gentlemen, in a moment.' And the hen's nest vanished.

Toole and Devereux drew back a little into the shadow of the opposite buildings, for while they were waiting, a dusky apparition, supposed to be old Drought in his night-shirt, appeared at that gentleman's windows, saluting the ambassadors with mop and moe, in a very threatening and energetic way. Just as this demonstration subsided, the hall door opened wide – and indeed was left so – while our friend Loftus, in a wonderful tattered old silk coat, that looked quite indescribable by moonlight, the torn linings hanging down in loops inside the skirts, pale and discoloured, like the shreds of banners in a cathedral; his shirt loose at the neck, his breeches unbuttoned at the knees, and a gigantic, misshapen, and mouldy pair of slippers clinging and clattering about his feet, came down the steps, his light, round little eyes and queer, quiet face peering at them into the shade, and a smokified volume of divinity tucked under his arm, with his finger between the leaves to keep the place.

When Devereux saw him approaching, the whole thing – mission, service, man, and all – struck him in so absurd a point of view, that he burst out into an explosion of laughter, which only grew more vehement and uproarious the more earnestly and imploringly Toole tried to quiet him, pointing up with both hands, and all his fingers extended, to the windows of the sleeping townsfolk, and making horrible grimaces, shrugs, and ogles. But the young gentleman was not in the habit of denying himself innocent indulgences, and shaking himself loose of Toole, he walked down the dark side of the street in peals of laughter, making, ever and anon, little breathless remarks to himself, which his colleague could not hear, but which seemed to have the effect of setting him off again into new hemi-demi-semiquavers and roars of laughter, and left the doctor to himself, to conduct the negotiation with Loftus.

'Well?' said Devereux, by this time recovering breath, as the little doctor, looking very red and glum, strutted up to him along the shady pavement.

'Well? *Well*? – oh, ay, *very* well, to be sure. I'd like to know what the plague we're to do now,' grumbled Toole.

'Your precious armour-bearer refuses to act then?' asked Devereux.

'To be sure he does. He sees *you* walking down the street, ready to die o' laughing – at *nothing*, by Jove!' swore Toole, in deep disgust; 'and – and – och! hang it! it's all a confounded pack o' nonsense. Sir, if you could not keep grave for five minutes, you ought not to have come at all. But what need *I* care? It's Nutter's affair, not mine.'

'And well for him we failed. Did you ever see such a fish? He'd have shot himself or Nutter, to a certainty. But there's a chance yet: we forgot the Nightingale Club; they're still in the Phoenix.'

'Pooh, Sir! they're all tailors and greengrocers,' said Toole, in high dudgeon.

'There are two or three good names among them, however,' answered Devereux; and by this time they were on the threshold of the Phoenix.

'Larry,' he cried to the waiter, 'the Nightingale Club is *there*, is it not?' glancing at the great back parlour door.

'Be the powers! Captain, you may say that,' said Larry, with a wink, and a grin of exquisite glee.

'See, Larry,' said Toole, with importance, 'we're a little serious now; so just say if there's any of the gentlemen there; you – you understand, now; quite steady? D'ye see me?'

Larry winked – this time a grave wink – looked down at the floor, and up to the cornice, and 'Well,' said he, 'to be candid with you, jest at this minute – half-an-hour ago, you see, it was different – the only gentleman I'd take on myself to recommend to you as perfectly sober is Mr Macan, of Petticoat-lane.'

'Is he in business?' asked Toole.

'Does he keep a shop?' said Devereux.

'A shop! *Two* shops; – a great man in the chandlery line,' responded Larry.

'H'm! Not precisely the thing we want, though,' says Toole.

'There are some of them, surely, that *don't* keep shops,' said Devereux, a little impatiently.

'Millions!' said Larry.

'Come, say their names.'

'Only one of them came this evening, Mr Doolan, of Stonny-batther – he's a retired merchant.'

'That will do,' said Toole, under his breath, to Devereux. Devereux nodded.

'Just, I say, tap him on the shoulder, and tell him that Dr Toole, you know, of this town, with many compliments and excuses, begs one word with him,' said the doctor.

'Hoo! Docthur dear, he was the first of them down, and was carried out to his coach insensible jist when Mr Crozier of Christ Church began "Come Roger and listen"; he's in his bed in Stonny-batther a good hour and a half ago.'

'A retired merchant,' says Devereux; 'well, Toole, what do you advise now?'

'By Jove, I think one of us must go into town. 'Twill never do to leave poor Nutter in the lurch; and between ourselves, that O'Flaherty's a – a bloodthirsty idiot, by Jove – and ought to be put down.'

'Let's see Nutter – you or I must go – we'll take one of these songster's "noddies".'

A 'noddy', give me leave to remark, was the one-horse hack vehicle of Dublin and the country round, which has since given place to the jaunting car, which is, in its turn, half superseded by the cab.

And Devereux, followed by Toole, entered the front parlour again. But without their help, the matter was arranging itself, and a second of whom they knew nothing, was about to emerge.

Chapter Nine

How a squire was found for the knight of the rueful countenance

When Dr Toole grumbled at his disappointment, he was not at all aware how nearly his interview with Loftus had knocked the entire affair on the head. He had no idea how much that worthy person was horrified by his proposition; and Toole walked off in a huff, without bidding him good-night, and making a remark in which the words 'old woman' occurred pretty audibly. But Loftus remained under the glimpses of the moon in perturbation and sore perplexity. It was so late he scarcely dared disturb Dr Walsingham or General Chattesworth. But there came the half-stifled cadence of a song – not bacchanalian, but sentimental – something about Daphne and a swain – struggling through the window-shutters next the green hall-door close by, and Dan instantly bethought himself of Father Roach. So knocking stoutly at the window, he caused the melody to subside and the shutter to open. When the priest, looking out, saw Dan Loftus in his déshabillé, I believe he thought for a moment it was something from the neighbouring churchyard.

However, his reverence came out and stood on the steps, enveloped in a hospital aroma of broiled bones, lemons, and alcohol, and shaking his visitor affectionately by the hand – for he bore no malice, and the Lenten ditty he quite forgave as being no worse in modern parlance than an unhappy 'fluke' – was about to pull him into the parlour, where there was ensconced, he told him, 'a noble friend of his'. This was 'Pat Mahony, from beyond Killarney, just arrived – a man of parts and conversation, and a lovely singer'.

But Dan resisted, and told his tale in an earnest whisper in the hall. The priest made his mouth into a round queer little O, through which he sucked a long breath, elevating his brows, and rolling his eyes slowly about.

'A jewel! And Nutter, of all the men on the face of the airth – though I often heerd he was a fine shot, and a sweet little fencer in his youth, an' game, too – oh, be the powers! You can see that still – game to the backbone – and – whisht a bit now – who's the other?'

'Lieutenant O'Flaherty.'

[A low whistle from his reverence.] 'That's a boy that comes from a fighting county – Galway. I wish you saw them at an election time. Why, there's no end of diversion – the diversion of *stopping* them, of course, I mean (observing a sudden alteration in Loftus's countenance). An' *you*, av coorse, want to stop it? And so, av coorse, do I, my dear. Well, then, wait a bit, now – we must have our eyes open. Don't be in a hurry – let us be harrumless as sarpints, but *wise* as doves. Now, 'tis a fine thing, no doubt, to put an end to a jewel by active intherfarence, though I have known cases, my dear child, where suppressing a simple jewel has been the cause of half a dozen breaking out afterwards in the same neighbourhood, and on the very same quarrel, d'ye mind – though, of coorse, that's no reason here or there, my dear boy! But take it that a jewel is breaking down and coming to the ground of itself (here a hugely cunning wink), in an aisy, natural, accommodating way, the only effect of intherfarence is to bolster it up, d'ye see, so just considher how things are, my dear. Lave it all to me, and mind my words, it *can't* take place without a second. The officers have refused, so has Toole, *you* won't undertake it, and it's too late to go into town. I defy it to come to anything. Jest be said be me, Dan Loftus, and let sleeping dogs lie. Here I am, an old experienced observer, that's up to their tricks, with my eye upon them. Go you to bed – lave them to me – and they're checkmated without so much as seeing how we bring it to pass.'

Dan hesitated.

'Arrah! Go to your bed, Dan Loftus, dear. It's past eleven o'clock – they're nonplussed already; and lave *me* – me that understands it – to manage the rest.'

'Well, Sir, I do confide it altogether to you. I know I might, through ignorance, do a mischief.'

And so they bid a mutual good-night, and Loftus scaled his garret stair and snuffed his candle, and plunged again into the business of two thousand years ago.

'Here's a purty business,' says the priest, extending both his palms, with a face of warlike importance, and shutting the door behind him with what he called 'a cow's kick'; 'a jewel, my dear Pat, no less; bloody work I'm afeared.'

Mr Mahony, who had lighted a pipe during his entertainer's absence, withdrew the fragrant tube from his lips, and opened his capacious mouth with a look of pleasant expectation, for he, like other gentlemen of his day – and, must we confess, not a few jolly clerics of my creed, as well as of honest Father Roach's – regarded the ordeal of battle, and all its belongings, simply as the highest branch of sporting. Not that the worthy father avowed any such sentiment; on the contrary, his voice and his eyes, if not his hands, were always raised against the sanguinary practice; and scarce a duel occurred within a reasonable distance unattended by his reverence, in the capacity, as he said, of 'an unauthorised, but airnest, though he feared unavailing, peacemaker.' There he used to spout little maxims of reconciliation, and Christian brotherhood and forbearance; exhorting to forget and forgive; wringing his hands at each successive discharge; and it must be said, too, in fairness, playing the part of a good Samaritan towards the wounded, to whom his green hall-door was ever open, and for whom the oil of his consolation and the wine of his best bin never refused to flow.

'Pat, my child,' said his reverence, 'that Nutter's a divil of a fellow – at least he *was*, by all accounts; he'll be bad enough, I'm afeared, and hard enough to manage, if everything goes smooth; but if he's kept waiting there, fuming and boiling over, do ye mind, without a natural vent for his feelings, or a *friend*, do ye see, at his side to – to *resthrain* him, and bring about, if possible, a friendly mutual understanding – why, my dear child, he'll get into that state of exasperation an' violence, he'll have half a dozen jewels on his hands before morning.'

'Augh! 'tid be a murther to baulk them for want of a friend,' answered Mr Mahony, standing up like a warrior, and laying the pipe of peace upon the chimney. 'Will I go down, Father Denis, and offer my sarvices?'

'With a view to a *reconciliation*, mind,' said his reverence, raising his finger, closing his eyes, and shaking his florid face impressively.

'Och, bother! Don't I know – of coorse, reconciliation;' and he was buttoning his garments where, being a little 'in flesh', as well as tall, he had loosed them. '*Where* are the gentlemen now, and who will I ask for?'

'I'll show you the light from the steps. Ask for Dr Toole; and he's *certainly* there; and if he's not, for Mr Nutter; and just say you came from my house, where you – a – pooh! accidentally heard, through Mr Loftus, do ye mind, there was a difficulty in finding a friend to – a – strive to make up matters between thim.'

By this time they stood upon the door-steps; and Mr Mahony had clapt on his hat with a pugnacious cock o' one side; and following, with a sporting and mischievous leer, the direction of the priest's hand, that indicated the open door of the Phoenix, through which a hospitable light was issuing.

'There's where you'll find the gentlemen, in the front parlour,' says the priest. 'You remember Dr Toole, and *he'll* remember *you*. An' *mind*, dear, it's to make it up you're goin'.' Mr Mahony was already under weigh, at a brisk stride, and with a keen relish for the business. 'And the blessing of the peacemaker go with you, my child!' added his reverence, lifting his hands and his eyes towards the heavens, 'An' upon my fainy!' looking shrewdly at the stars, and talking to himself, 'they'll have a fine morning for the business, *if*, unfortunately' – and here he re-ascended his door-steps with a melancholy shrug – 'if *unfortunately*, Pat Mahony should fail.'

When Mr Pat Mahony saw occasion for playing the gentleman, he certainly did come out remarkably strong in the part. It was done in a noble, florid, glowing style, according to his private ideal of the complete fine gentleman. Such bows, such pointing of the toes, such graceful flourishes of the three-cocked hat – such immensely engaging smiles and wonderful by-play, such an apparition, in short, of perfect elegance, valour, and courtesy, were never seen before in the front parlour of the Phoenix.

'Mr Mahony, by jingo!' ejaculated Toole, in an accent of thankfulness amounting nearly to rapture. Nutter seemed relieved, too, and advanced to be presented to the man who, instinct told him, was to be his friend. Cluffe, a man of fashion of the military school, eyed the elegant stranger with undisguised disgust and wonder, and Devereux with that sub-acid smile with which men will sometimes quietly relish absurdity.

Mr Mahony, 'discoursin' a country neighbour outside the half-way-house at Muckafubble, or enjoying an easy *tête-à-tête* with Father Roach, was a very inferior person, indeed, to Patrick Mahony, Esq., the full-blown diplomatist and pink of gentility astonishing the front parlour of the Phoenix.

There, Mr Mahony's periods were fluent and florid, and the words chosen occasionally rather for their grandeur and melody than for their exact connection with the context or bearing upon his meaning. The consequence was a certain gorgeous haziness and bewilderment, which made the task of translating his harangues rather troublesome and conjectural.

Having effected the introduction, and made known the object of his visit, Nutter and he withdrew to a small chamber behind the bar, where Nutter, returning some of his bows, and having listened without deriving any very clear ideas to two consecutive addresses from his companion, took the matter in hand himself, and, said he, 'I beg, Sir, to relieve you at once from the trouble of trying to arrange this affair amicably. I have been grossly insulted, he's not going to apologise, and nothing but a meeting will satisfy me. He's a mere murderer. I have not the faintest notion why he wants to kill me; but being reduced to this situation, I hold myself obliged, if I can, to rid the town of him finally.'

'Shake hands, Sir,' cried Mahony, forgetting his rhetoric in his enthusiasm; 'be the hole in the wall, Sir, I honour you.'

Chapter Ten

The dead secret, showing how the fireworker proved to Puddock that Nutter had spied out the nakedness of the land

When Puddock, having taken a short turn or two in the air, by way of tranquillising his mind, mounted his lodging stairs, he found Lieutenant O'Flaherty, not at all more sober than he had last seen him, in the front drawing-room, which apartment was richly perfumed with powerful exhalations of rum punch.

'Dhrink this, Puddock – dhrink it,' said O'Flaherty, filling a large glass in equal quantities with rum and water; 'dhrink it, my sinsare friend; it will studdy you, it will, upon my honour, Puddock!'

'But – a – thank you, Sir, I am anxious to understand exactly' – said Puddock. Here he was interrupted by a frightful grin and a '*ha!*' from O'Flaherty, who darted to the door, and seizing his little withered French servant, who was entering, swung him about the room by his coat collar.

'So, Sorr, you've been prating again, have you, you desateful, idle old dhrunken miscreant; you did it on purpose, you blundherin' old hyena; it's the third jewel you got your masther into; and if I lose my life, divil a penny iv your wages ye'll ever get – that's one comfort. Yes, Sorr! This is the third time you have caused me to brew my hands in human blood; I dono' if it's malice, or only blundherin'. Oh!' he cried, with a still fiercer shake, 'it's I that wishes I could be sure 'twas malice, I'd skiver you, heels and elbows, on my sword, and roast you alive on that fire. Is not it a hard thing, my darlin' Puddock, I can't find out.' He was still holding the little valet by the collar, and stretching out his right hand to Puddock. 'But I am always the sport of misfortunes – small and great. If there was an ould woman to be handed in to supper – or a man to be murthered by mistake – or an ugly girl to be danced with, whose turn was it, ever and always to do the business, but poor Hyacinth O'Flaherty's – ' [tears]. 'I could tell you, Puddock,' he continued, forgetting his wrath, and letting his prisoner go, in his eager pathos – the Frenchman made his escape in a twinkling – 'I was the only man in our regiment that tuck the mazles in Cork, when it was goin' among the children, bad luck to them – I that was near dyin' of it when I was an infant; and I was the only officer in the regiment, when we were at Athlone, that was prevented going to the race ball – and I would not for a hundred pounds. I was to dance the first minuet, and the first country dance, with that beautiful creature, Miss Rose Cox. I was makin' a glass of brandy punch – not feelin' quite myself – and I dhressed and all, in our room, when Ensign Higgins, a most thoughtless young man, said something disrespectful about a beautiful mole she had on her chin; bedad, Sir, he called it a wart, if you plase! And feelin' it sthrongly, I let the jug of scaldin' wather drop on my knees; I wish you felt it, my darlin' Puddock. I was scalded in half a crack from a fut above my knees down to the last joint of my two big toes; and I raly thought my sinses were leving me. I lost the ball by it. Oh, ho, wirresthrue! Poor Hyacinth O'Flaherty!' and thereupon he wept.

'You thee, Lieutenant O'Flaherty,' lisped Puddock, growing impatient, 'we can't say how soon Mr Nutter's friend may apply for an interview, and – a – I must confeth I don't yet quite understand the point of difference between you and him, and therefore – '

'A where the devil's that blackguard little French wazel gone to?' exclaimed O'Flaherty, for the first time perceiving that his captive had escaped. '*Kokang Modate*! Do you hear me, *Kokang Modate*!' he shouted.

'But really, Sir, you must be so good as to place before me, before me, Sir, clearly, the – the cause of this unhappy dispute, the exact offenth, Thir, for otherwithe – '

'Cause, to be sure! And plenty iv cause. I never fought a jewel yet, Puddock, my friend – and this will be the ninth – without cause. They said, I'm tould, in Cork, I was quarrelsome; they lied; I'm not quarrelsome; I only want pace, and quiet, and justice; I hate a quarrelsome man. I tell you, Puddock, if I only knew where to find a quarrelsome man, be the powers I'd go fifty miles out of my way to pull him be the nose. They lied, Puddock, my dear boy, an' I'd give twenty pounds this minute I had them on this flure, to tell them how *damnably* they lied!'

'No doubt, Thir,' said Puddock, 'but if you pleathe I really mutht have a dithtinct answer to my – '

'Get out o' that, Sorr,' thundered O'Flaherty, with an awful stamp on the floor, as the '*coquin maudit*', O'Flaherty's only bit of French, such as it was, in obedience to that form of invocation, appeared nervously at the threshold, 'or I'll fling the contints of the r-r-oo-oo-oom at your head,' [exit Monsieur, again] 'Be gannies! If I thought it was he that done it, I'd jirk his old bones through the top of the window. Will I call him back and give him his desarts, will I, Puddock! Oh, ho, hone! My darlin' Puddock, everything turns agin me; what'll I do, Puddock, jewel, or what's to become o' me?' and he shed some more tears, and drank off the greater part of the beverage which he had prepared for Puddock.

'I believe, Sir, that this is the sixth time I've ventured to ask a distinct statement from your lips, of the cauthe of your dithagreement with Mr Nutter, which I plainly tell you, Thir, I don't at prethent underthtand, said Puddock, loftily and firmly enough.

'To be sure, my darlin' Puddock,' replied O'Flaherty, 'it was that cursed little French whippersnapper, with his monkeyfied intherruptions; be the powers, Puddock, if you knew half the mischief that same little baste has got me into, you would not wondher if I murthered him. It was he was the cause of my jewel with my cousin, Art Considine, and I wanting to be the very pink of politeness to him. I wrote him a note when he came to Athlone, afther two years in France, and jist out o' compliment to him, I unluckily put in a word of French: come an' dine, says I, and we'll have a dish of chat. I knew u-n p-l-a-t (spelling it), was a dish, an' says I to Jerome, that pigimy (so he pronounced it) you seen here at the door, that's his damnable name, what's *chat* in French – c-h-a-t – spelling it to him; "sha," says he; "sha?" says I, "spell it, if you plase," says I; "c-h-a-t," says he, the stupid old viper. Well, I took the trouble to write it out, *"un plat de chat"*; "is that right?" says I, showing it to him. "It is, my lord," says he, looking at me as if I had two heads. I never knew the manin' of it for more than a month afther I shot poor Art through the two calves. An' he that fought two jewels before, all about cats, one of them with a Scotch gentleman that he gave the lie to, for saying that French cooks had a way of stewing cats you could not tell them from hares; and the other immadiately afther, with Lieutenant Rugge, of the Royal Navy, that got one stewed for fun, and afther my Cousin Art dined off it, like a man, showed him the tail and the claws. It's well he did not die of it, and no wondher he resented my invitation, though upon my honour, as a soldier and a gentleman, may I be stewed alive myself in a pot, Puddock my dear, if I had the laste notion of offering him the smallest affront!'

'I begin to despair, Sir,' exclaimed Puddock, 'of receiving the information without which 'tis vain for me to try to be useful to you;

once more, may I entreat to know what *is* the affront of which you complain?'

'You don't know; raly and truly now, you don't know?' said O'Flaherty, fixing a solemn tipsy leer on him.

'I tell you *no*, Thir,' rejoined Puddock.

'And do you mean to tell me you did not hear that vulgar dog Nutter's unmanly jokes?'

'Jokes!' repeated Puddock, in large perplexity, 'why I've been here in this town for more than five years, and I never heard in all that time that Nutter once made a joke – and upon my life, I don't think he could make a joke, Sir, if he tried – I don't, indeed, Lieutenant O'Flaherty, upon my honour!'

'And rat it, Sir, how can I help it?' cried O'Flaherty, relapsing into pathos.

'Help what?' demanded Puddock.

O'Flaherty took him by the hand, and gazing on his face with a maudlin, lacklustre tenderness, said: 'Absalom was caught by the hair of his head – he was, Puddock – long hair or short hair, or (a hiccough) no hair at all, isn't it nature's doing, I ask you my darlin' Puddock, *isn't* it?' He was shedding tears again very fast. 'There was Cicero and Julius Cæsar, wor both as bald as that,' and he thrust a shining sugar basin, bottom upward, into Puddock's face. '*I'm* not bald; I tell you I'm *not* – no, my darlin' Puddock, I'm not – poor Hyacinth O'Flaherty is *not bald*,' shaking Puddock by both hands.

'That's very plain, Sir, but I don't see your drift,' he replied.

'I want to tell you, Puddock dear, if you'll only have a minute's patience. The door can't fasten, divil bother it; come into the next room;' and toppling a little in his walk, he led him solemnly into his bedroom – the door of which he locked – somewhat to Puddock's disquietude, who began to think him insane. Here having informed Puddock that Nutter was driving at the one point the whole evening, as anyone that knew the secret would have seen; and having solemnly imposed the seal of secrecy upon his second, and essayed a wild and broken discourse upon the difference between total baldness and partial loss of hair, he disclosed to him the grand mystery of his existence, by lifting from the summit of his head a circular piece of wig, which in those days they called I believe, a 'topping', leaving a bare shining disc exposed, about the size of a large pat of butter.

'Upon my life, Thir, it'th a very fine piethe of work,' says Puddock, who viewed the wiglet with the eye of a stage-property man, and held it by a top lock near the candle. 'The very finetht piethe of work of the kind I ever thaw. 'Tith thertainly French. Oh, yeth – we can't do such thingth here. By Jove, Thir, what a wig that man would make for Cato!'

'An' he must be a mane crature – I say, a mane crature,' pursued O'Flaherty, 'for there was not a soul in the town but Jerome, the – the treacherous ape, that knew it. It's he that dhresses my head every morning behind the bed-curtain there, with the door locked. And Nutter could never have found it out – *who* was to tell him, unless that ojus French damon, that's never done talkin' about it;' and O'Flaherty strode heavily up and down the room with his hands in his breeches' pockets, muttering savage invectives, pitching his head from side to side, and whisking round at the turns in a way to show how strongly he was wrought upon.

'Come in, Sorr!' thundered O'Flaherty, unlocking the door, in reply to a knock, and expecting to see his 'ojus French damon'. But it was a tall fattish stranger, rather flashily dressed, but a little soiled, with a black wig, and a rollicking red face, showing a good deal of chin and jaw.

O'Flaherty made his grandest bow, quite forgetting the exposure at the top of his head; and Puddock stood rather shocked, with the candle in one hand and O'Flaherty's scalp in the other.

'You come, Sir, I presume, from Mr Nutter,' said O'Flaherty, with lofty courtesy. This, Sir, is my friend, Lieutenant Puddock of the Royal Irish Artillery, who does me the honour to support me with his advice and – '

As he moved his hand towards Puddock, he saw his scalp dangling between that gentleman's finger and thumb, and became suddenly mute. He clapped his hand upon his bare skull, and made an agitated pluck at that article, but missed, and disappeared, with an imprecation in Irish, behind the bed curtains.

'If you will be so obliging, Sir, as to precede me into that room,' lisped Puddock, with grave dignity, and waving O'Flaherty's scalp slightly towards the door – for Puddock never stooped to hide anything, and being a gentleman, pure and simple, was not ashamed or afraid to avow his deeds, words, and situations; 'I shall do myself the honour to follow.'

'Gi' me *that*,' was heard in a vehement whisper from behind the curtains. Puddock understood it, and restored the treasure.

The secret conference in the drawing-room was not tedious, nor indeed very secret, for anyone acquainted with the diplomatic slang in which such affairs were conducted might have learned in the lobby, or indeed in the hall, so mighty was the voice of the stranger, that there was no chance of any settlement without a meeting which was fixed to take place at twelve o'clock next day on the Fifteen Acres.

Chapter Eleven

Some talk about the haunted house – being, as I suppose,
only old woman's tales

Old Sally always attended her young mistress while she prepared for bed – not that Lilias required help, for she had the spirit of neatness and a joyous, gentle alacrity, and only troubled the good old creature enough to prevent her thinking herself grown old and useless.

Sally, in her quiet way, was garrulous, and she had all sorts of old-world tales of wonder and adventure, to which Lilias often went pleasantly to sleep; for there was no danger while old Sally sat knitting there by the fire, and the sound of the rector's mounting upon his chairs, as was his wont, and taking down and putting up his books in the study beneath, though muffled and faint, gave evidence that that good and loving influence was awake and busy.

Old Sally was telling her young mistress, who sometimes listened with a smile, and sometimes lost a good five minutes together of her gentle prattle, how the young gentleman, Mr Mervyn, had taken that awful old haunted habitation, the Tiled House 'beyant at Bally-fermot', and was going to stay there, and wondered no-one had told him of the mysterious dangers of that desolate mansion.

It stood by a lonely bend of the narrow road. Lilias had often looked upon the short, straight, grass-grown avenue with an awful curiosity at the old house which she had learned in childhood to fear as the abode of shadowy tenants and unearthly dangers.

'There are people, Sally, nowadays, who call themselves free-thinkers, and don't believe in anything – even in ghosts,' said Lilias.

'A-then the place he's stopping in now, Miss Lily, 'ill soon cure him of free-thinking, if the half they say about it's true,' answered Sally.

'But I don't say, mind, he's a freethinker, for I don't know anything of Mr Mervyn; but if he be not, he must be very brave, or very good, indeed. I know, Sally, I should be horribly afraid, indeed, to sleep in it myself,' answered Lilias, with a cosy little shudder, as the aërial image of the old house for a moment stood before her, with its peculiar malign, sacred, and skulking aspect, as if it had drawn back in shame and guilt under the melancholy old elms among the tall hemlock and nettles.

'And now, Sally, I'm safe in bed. Stir the fire, my old darling.' For although it was the first week in May, the night was frosty. 'And tell me all about the Tiled House again, and frighten me out of my wits.'

So good old Sally, whose faith in such matters was a religion, went off over the well-known ground in a gentle little amble – sometimes subsiding into a walk as she approached some special horror, and pulling up altogether – that is to say, suspending her knitting, and looking with a mysterious nod at her young mistress in the four-poster, or lowering her voice to a sort of whisper when the crisis came.

So she told her how when the neighbours hired the orchard that ran up to the windows at the back of the house, the dogs they kept there used to howl so wildly and wolfishly all night among the trees, and prowl under the walls of the house so dejectedly, that they were fain to open the door and let them in at last; and, indeed, small need was there for dogs; for no-one, young or old, dared go near the orchard after nightfall. No, the burnished golden pippins that peeped through the leaves in the western rays of evening, and made the mouths of the Ballyfermot schoolboys water, glowed undisturbed in the morning sunbeams, and secure in the mysterious tutelage of the night smiled coyly on their predatory longings. And this was no fanciful reserve and avoidance. Mick Daly, when he had the orchard, used to sleep in the loft over the kitchen; and he swore that within five or six weeks, while he lodged there, he twice saw the same thing, and that was a lady in a hood and a loose dress, her head drooping, and her finger on her lip, walking in silence among the crooked stems, with a little child by the hand, who ran smiling and skipping beside her. And the Widow Cresswell once met them at nightfall, on the path through the orchard to the back-door, and she did not know what it was until she saw the men looking at one another as she told it.

'It's often she told it to me,' said old Sally; 'and how she came on them all of a sudden at the turn of the path, just by the thick clump of alder trees; and how she stopped, thinking it was some lady that had a right to be there; and how they went by as swift as the shadow of a cloud, though she only seemed to be walking slow enough, and the little child pulling by her arm, this way and that way, and took no notice of her, nor even raised her head, though she stopped and courtesied. And old Dalton, don't you remember old Dalton, Miss Lily?'

'I think I do, the old man who limped, and wore the old black wig?'

'Yes, indeed, acushla, so he did. See how well she remembers! That was by a kick of one of the earl's horses – he was groom there,' resumed Sally. 'He used to be troubled with hearing the very sounds his master used to make to bring him and old Oliver to the door, when he came back late. It was only on very dark nights when there was no moon. They used to hear all on a sudden, the whimpering and scraping of dogs at the hall door, and the sound of the whistle, and the light stroke across the window with the lash of the whip, just like as if the earl himself – may his poor soul find rest – was there. First the wind 'id stop, like you'd be holding your breath, then came these sounds they knew so well, and when they made no sign of stirring or opening the door, the wind 'id begin again with such a hoo-hoo-o-o-high, you'd think it was laughing, and crying, and hooting all at once.'

Here old Sally's tale and her knitting ceased for a moment, as if she were listening to the wind outside the haunted precincts of the Tiled House; and she took up her parable again.

'The very night he met his death in England, old Oliver, the butler, was listening to Dalton – for Dalton was a scholar – reading the letter that came to him through the post that day, telling him to get things ready, for his troubles wor nearly over and he expected to be with them again in a few days, and maybe almost as soon as the letter; and sure enough, while he was reading, there comes a frightful rattle at the window, like someone all in a tremble, trying to shake it open, and the earl's voice, as they both conceited, cries from outside, "Let me in, let me in, let me in!" "It's him," says the butler. "'tis so, bedad," says Dalton, and they both looked at the windy, and at one another – and then back again – overjoyed, in a soart of a way, and frightened all at onst. Old Oliver was bad with the rheumatiz. So away goes Dalton to the hall-door, and he calls "who's there?" and no answer. "Maybe," says Dalton, to himself, " 'tis what he's rid round to the back-door;" so to the back-door with him, and there he shouts again – and no answer, and not a sound outside – and he began to feel quare, and to the hall door with him back again. "Who's there? Do you hear? Who's there?" he shouts, and receives no answer still. "I'll open the door at any rate," says he, "maybe it's what he's made his escape," for they knew all about his troubles, "and wants to get in without noise," so praying all the time – for his mind misgave him it might not be all right – he shifts the bars and unlocks the door; but neither man, woman, nor child, nor horse, nor any living shape was standing there, only something or another slipt into the house close by his leg; it might be a dog, or something that way, he could not tell, for he only seen it for a moment with the corner of his eye, and it went in just like as if it belonged to the place. He could not see which way it went, up or down, but the house was never a happy one, or a quiet house after; and Dalton bangs the hall-door, and he took a sort of a turn and a trembling, and back with him to Oliver, the butler, looking as white as the blank leaf of his master's letter, that was between his finger and thumb. "What is it? *What* is it?" says the butler, catching his crutch like a waypon, fastening his eyes on Dalton's white face, and growing almost as pale himself. "The master's dead," says Dalton – and so he was, signs on it.

'After the turn she got by what she seen in the orchard, when she came to know the truth of what it was, Jinny Cresswell, you may be sure, did not stay there an hour longer than she could help: and she began to take notice of things she did not mind before – such as when she went into the big bedroom over the hall, that the lord used to sleep in, whenever she went in at one door the other door used to be pulled to very quick, as if someone avoiding her was getting out in haste; but the thing that frightened her most was just this – that sometimes she used to find a long straight mark from the head to the foot of her bed, as if 'twas made by something heavy lying there, and the place where it was used to feel warm – as if – whoever it was – they only left it as she came into the room.

'But the worst of all was poor Kitty Haplin, the young woman that died of what she seen. Her mother said it was how she was kept awake all the night with the walking about of someone in the next room, tumbling about boxes, and pulling over drawers, and talking and sighing to himself, and she, poor thing, wishing to go asleep, and wondering who it could be, when in he comes, a fine man, in a sort of loose silk morning-dress, an' no wig, but a velvet cap on, and to the windy with him quiet and aisy, and she makes a turn in the bed to let him know there was someone there, thinking he'd go away, but instead of that, over he comes to the side of the bed, looking very bad, and says something to her – but his speech was thick and choakin' like a dummy's that id be trying to spake – and she grew very frightened, and says she, "I ask your honour's pardon, Sir, but I can't hear you right," and with that he stretches up his neck nigh out of his cravat, turning his face up towards the ceiling, and – grace between us and harm! – his throat was cut across, and wide open; she seen no more, but dropped in a dead faint in the bed, and back to her mother with her in the morning, and she never swallied bit or sup more, only she just sat by the fire holding her mother's hand, crying and trembling, and peepin' over her shoulder, and starting with every sound, till she took the fever and died, poor thing, not five weeks after.'

And so on, and on, and on flowed the stream of old Sally's narrative, while Lilias dropped into dreamless sleep, and then the storyteller stole away to her own tidy bedroom and innocent slumbers.

Chapter Twelve

*Some odd facts about the Tiled House – being an authentic
narrative of the ghost of a hand*

I'm sure she believed every word she related, for old Sally was
veracious. But all this was worth just so much as such talk commonly is – marvels, fabulae, what our ancestors called winter's tales –
which gathered details from every narrator, and dilated in the act of
narration. Still it was not quite for nothing that the house was held
to be haunted. Under all this smoke there smouldered just a little
spark of truth – an authenticated mystery, for the solution of which
some of my readers may possibly suggest a theory, though I confess
I can't.

Miss Rebecca Chattesworth, in a letter dated late in the autumn of
1753, gives a minute and curious relation of occurrences in the Tiled
House, which, it is plain, although at starting she protests against
all such fooleries, she has heard with a peculiar sort of interest, and
relates it certainly with an awful sort of particularity.

I was for printing the entire letter, which is really very singular as
well as characteristic. But my publisher meets me with his *veto*; and I
believe he is right. The worthy old lady's letter *is*, perhaps, too long;
and I must rest content with a few hungry notes of its tenor.

That year, and somewhere about the 24th October, there broke
out a strange dispute between Mr Alderman Harper, of High Street,
Dublin, and my Lord Castlemallard, who, in virtue of his cousinship
to the young heir's mother, had undertaken for him the management
of the tiny estate on which the Tiled or Tyled House – for I find it
spelt both ways – stood.

This Alderman Harper had agreed for a lease of the house for his
daughter, who was married to a gentleman named Prosser. He furnished it, and put up hangings, and otherwise went to considerable
expense. Mr and Mrs Prosser came there some time in June, and
after having parted with a good many servants in the interval, she
made up her mind that she could not live in the house, and her father

waited on Lord Castlemallard, and told him plainly that he would not take out the lease because the house was subjected to annoyances which he could not explain. In plain terms, he said it was haunted, and that no servants would live there more than a few weeks, and that after what his son-in-law's family had suffered there, not only should he be excused from taking a lease of it, but that the house itself ought to be pulled down as a nuisance and the habitual haunt of something worse than human malefactors.

Lord Castlemallard filed a bill in the Equity side of the Exchequer to compel Mr Alderman Harper to perform his contract, by taking out the lease. But the Alderman drew an answer, supported by no less than seven long affidavits, copies of all which were furnished to his lordship, and with the desired effect; for rather than compel him to place them upon the file of the court, his lordship struck, and consented to release him.

I am sorry the cause did not proceed at least far enough to place upon the files of the court the very authentic and unaccountable story which Miss Rebecca relates.

The annoyances described did not begin till the end of August, when, one evening, Mrs Prosser, quite alone, was sitting in the twilight at the back parlour window, which was open, looking out into the orchard, and plainly saw a hand stealthily placed upon the stone window-sill outside, as if by someone beneath the window, at her right side, intending to climb up. There was nothing but the hand, which was rather short but handsomely formed, and white and plump, laid on the edge of the window-sill; and it was not a very young hand, but one aged, somewhere about forty, as she conjectured. It was only a few weeks before that the horrible robbery at Clondalkin had taken place, and the lady fancied that the hand was that of one of the miscreants who was now about to scale the windows of the Tiled House. She uttered a loud scream and an ejaculation of terror, and at the same moment the hand was quietly withdrawn.

Search was made in the orchard, but no indications of any person's having been under the window, beneath which, ranged along the wall, stood a great column of flower-pots, which it seemed must have prevented any one's coming within reach of it.

The same night there came a hasty tapping, every now and then, at the window of the kitchen. The women grew frightened, and the servant-man, taking firearms with him, opened the back-door, but discovered nothing. As he shut it, however, he said, 'a thump came on it', and a pressure as of somebody striving to force his way in, which frightened *him*; and though the tapping went on upon the kitchen window panes, he made no further explorations.

About six o'clock on the Saturday evening following, the cook, 'an honest, sober woman, now aged nigh sixty years', being alone in the kitchen, saw, on looking up, it is supposed, the same fat but aristocratic-looking hand, laid with its palm against the glass, near the side of the window, and this time moving slowly up and down, pressed all the while against the glass, as if feeling carefully for some inequality in its surface. She cried out, and said something like a prayer on seeing it. But it was not withdrawn for several seconds after.

After this, for a great many nights, there came at first a low, and afterwards an angry rapping, as it seemed with a set of clenched knuckles, at the back-door. And the servant-man would not open it, but called to know who was there; and there came no answer, only a sound as if the palm of the hand was placed against it, and drawn slowly from side to side with a sort of soft, groping motion.

All this time, sitting in the back parlour, which, for the time, they used as a drawing-room, Mr and Mrs Prosser were disturbed by rappings at the window, sometimes very low and furtive, like a clandestine signal, and at others sudden, and so loud as to threaten the breaking of the pane.

This was all at the back of the house, which looked upon the orchard as you know. But on a Tuesday night, at about half-past nine, there came precisely the same rapping at the hall-door, and went on, to the great annoyance of the master and terror of his wife, at intervals, for nearly two hours.

After this, for several days and nights, they had no annoyance whatsoever, and began to think that nuisance had expended itself. But on the night of the 13th September, Jane Easterbrook, an English maid, having gone into the pantry for the small silver bowl in which her mistress's posset was served, happening to look up at the little window of only four panes, observed through an auger-hole which was drilled through the window frame, for the admission of a bolt to secure the shutter, a white pudgy finger – first the tip, and then the two first joints introduced, and turned about this way and that, crooked against the inside, as if in search of a fastening which its owner designed to push aside. When the maid got back into the kitchen we are told 'she fell into "a swounde", and was all the next day very weak.'

Mr Prosser being, I've heard, a hard-headed and conceited sort of fellow, scouted the ghost, and sneered at the fears of his family. He was privately of opinion that the whole affair was a practical joke or a fraud, and waited an opportunity of catching the rogue *flagrante delicto*. He did not long keep this theory to himself, but let it out by degrees with no stint of oaths and threats, believing that some domestic traitor held the thread of the conspiracy.

Indeed it was time something were done; for not only his servants, but good Mrs Prosser herself, had grown to look unhappy and anxious. They kept at home from the hour of sunset, and would not venture about the house after nightfall, except in couples.

The knocking had ceased for about a week, when one night, Mrs Prosser being in the nursery, her husband, who was in the parlour, heard it begin very softly at the hall-door. The air was quite still, which favoured his hearing distinctly. This was the first time there had been any disturbance at that side of the house, and the character of the summons was changed.

Mr Prosser, leaving the parlour-door open, it seems, went quietly into the hall. The sound was that of beating on the outside of the stout door, softly and regularly, 'with the flat of the hand'. He was going to open it suddenly, but changed his mind; and went back very quietly, and on to the head of the kitchen stair, where was a 'strong closet' over the pantry, in which he kept his firearms, swords, and canes.

Here he called his manservant, whom he believed to be honest, and, with a pair of loaded pistols in his own coat-pockets, and giving another pair to him, he went as lightly as he could, followed by the man, and with a stout walking-cane in his hand, forward to the door.

Everything went as Mr Prosser wished. The besieger of his house, so far from taking fright at their approach, grew more impatient; and the sort of patting which had aroused his attention at first assumed the rhythm and emphasis of a series of double-knocks.

Mr Prosser, angry, opened the door with his right arm across, cane in hand. Looking, he saw nothing; but his arm was jerked up oddly, as it might be with the hollow of a hand, and something passed under it, with a kind of gentle squeeze. The servant neither saw nor felt anything, and did not know why his master looked back so hastily, cutting with his cane, and shutting the door with so sudden a slam.

From that time Mr Prosser discontinued his angry talk and swearing about it, and seemed nearly as averse from the subject as the rest of his family. He grew, in fact, very uncomfortable, feeling an inward persuasion that when, in answer to the summons, he had opened the hall-door, he had actually given admission to the besieger.

He said nothing to Mrs Prosser, but went up earlier to his bed-room, 'where he read a while in his Bible, and said his prayers'. I hope the particular relation of this circumstance does not indicate its singularity. He lay awake a good while, it appears; and, as he supposed, about a quarter past twelve he heard the soft palm of a hand patting on the outside of the bedroom door, and then brushed slowly along it.

Up bounced Mr Prosser, very much frightened, and locked the door, crying, 'Who's there?' but receiving no answer but the same brushing sound of a soft hand drawn over the panels, which he knew only too well.

In the morning the housemaid was terrified by the impression of a hand in the dust of the 'little parlour' table, where they had been unpacking delft and other things the day before. The print of the naked foot in the sea-sand did not frighten Robinson Crusoe half so much. They were by this time all nervous, and some of them half-crazed, about the hand.

Mr Prosser went to examine the mark, and made light of it, but as he swore afterwards, rather to quiet his servants than from any comfortable feeling about it in his own mind; however, he had them all, one by one, into the room, and made each place his or her hand, palm downward, on the same table, thus taking a similar impression from every person in the house, including himself and his wife; and his 'affidavit' deposed that the formation of the hand so impressed differed altogether from those of the living inhabitants of the house, and corresponded with that of the hand seen by Mrs Prosser and by the cook.

Whoever or whatever the owner of that hand might be, they all felt this subtle demonstration to mean that it was declared he was no longer out of doors, but had established himself in the house.

And now Mrs Prosser began to be troubled with strange and horrible dreams, some of which as set out in detail, in Aunt Rebecca's long letter, are really very appalling nightmares. But one night, as Mr Prosser closed his bedchamber-door, he was struck somewhat by the utter silence of the room, there being no sound of breathing, which seemed unaccountable to him, as he knew his wife was in bed, and his ears were particularly sharp.

There was a candle burning on a small table at the foot of the bed, beside the one he held in one hand, a heavy ledger, connected with his father-in-law's business being under his arm. He drew the curtain at the side of the bed, and saw Mrs Prosser lying, as for a few seconds he mortally feared, dead, her face being motionless, white, and covered with a cold dew; and on the pillow, close beside her head, and just within the curtains, was, as he first thought, a toad – but really the same fattish hand, the wrist resting on the pillow, and the fingers extended towards her temple.

Mr Prosser, with a horrified jerk, pitched the ledger right at the curtains, behind which the owner of the hand might be supposed to stand. The hand was instantaneously and smoothly snatched away, the curtains made a great wave, and Mr Prosser got round the bed in time to see the closet-door, which was at the other side, pulled to by the same white, puffy hand, as he believed.

He drew the door open with a fling, and stared in: but the closet was empty, except for the clothes hanging from the pegs on the wall, and the dressing-table and looking-glass facing the windows. He shut it sharply, and locked it, and felt for a minute, he says, 'as if he were like to lose his wits'; then, ringing at the bell, he brought the servants, and with much ado they recovered Mrs Prosser from a sort of 'trance', in which, he says, from her looks, she seemed to have suffered 'the pains of death': and Aunt Rebecca adds, 'from what she told me of her visions, with her own lips, he might have added, "and of hell also".'

But the occurrence which seems to have determined the crisis was the strange sickness of their eldest child, a little boy aged between two and three years. He lay awake, seemingly in paroxysms of terror, and the doctors who were called in, set down the symptoms to incipient water on the brain. Mrs Prosser used to sit up with the nurse by the nursery fire, much troubled in mind about the condition of her child.

His bed was placed sideways along the wall, with its head against the door of a press or cupboard, which, however, did not shut quite close. There was a little valance, about a foot deep, round the top of the child's bed, and this descended within some ten or twelve inches of the pillow on which it lay.

They observed that the little creature was quieter whenever they took it up and held it on their laps. They had just replaced him, as he seemed to have grown quite sleepy and tranquil, but he was not five minutes in his bed when he began to scream in one of his frenzies of terror; at the same moment the nurse, for the first time, detected, and Mrs Prosser equally plainly saw, following the direction of *her* eyes, the real cause of the child's sufferings.

Protruding through the aperture of the press, and shrouded in the shade of the valance, they plainly saw the white fat hand, palm downwards, presented towards the head of the child. The mother uttered a scream, and snatched the child from its little bed, and she and the nurse ran down to the lady's sleeping-room, where Mr Prosser was in bed, shutting the door as they entered; and they had hardly done so, when a gentle tap came to it from the outside.

There is a great deal more, but this will suffice. The singularity of the narrative seems to me to be this, that it describes the ghost of a hand, and no more. The person to whom that hand belonged never once appeared: nor was it a hand separated from a body, but only a hand so manifested and introduced that its owner was always, by some crafty accident, hidden from view.

In the year 1819, at a college breakfast, I met a Mr Prosser – a thin, grave, but rather chatty old gentleman, with very white hair drawn back into a pigtail – and he told us all, with a concise particularity, a story of his cousin, James Prosser, who, when an infant, had slept for some time in what his mother said was a haunted nursery in an old house near Chapelizod, and who, whenever he was ill, over-fatigued, or in any wise feverish, suffered all through his life as he had done from a time he could scarce remember, from a vision of a certain gentleman, fat and pale, every curl of whose wig, every button and fold of whose laced clothes, and every feature and line of whose sensual, benignant, and unwholesome face, was as minutely engraven upon his memory as the dress and lineaments of his own grandfather's portrait, which hung before him every day at breakfast, dinner, and supper.

Mr Prosser mentioned this as an instance of a curiously monotonous, individualised, and persistent nightmare, and hinted the extreme horror and anxiety with which his cousin, of whom he spoke in the past tense as 'poor Jemmie', was at any time induced to mention it.

I hope the reader will pardon me for loitering so long in the Tiled House, but this sort of lore has always had a charm for me; and people, you know, especially old people, will talk of what most interests themselves, too often forgetting that others may have had more than enough of it.

Chapter Thirteen

In which the rector visits the Tiled House, and Dr Toole
looks after the brass castle

Next morning Toole, sauntering along the low road towards the mills, as usual bawling at his dogs, who scampered and nuzzled hither and thither, round and about him, saw two hackney coaches and a 'noddy' arrive at the Brass Castle, a tall old house by the river, with a little bit of a flower-garden, half-a-dozen poplars, and a few old privet hedges about it; and being aware that it had been taken the day before for Mr Dangerfield, for three months, he slackened his pace, in the hope of seeing that personage, of whom he had heard great things, take seisin of his tabernacle. He was disappointed, however; the great man had not arrived, only a sour-faced, fussy old lady, Mrs Jukes, his housekeeper and a servant-wench and a great lot of boxes and trunks; and so leaving the coachman grumbling and swearing at the lady, who, bitter, shrill and voluble, was manifestly well able to fight her own battles, he strolled back to the Phoenix, where a new evidence of the impending arrival met his view in an English groom with three horses, which the hostler and he were leading into the inn-yard.

There were others, too, agreeably fidgeted about this arrival. The fair Miss Magnolia, for instance, and her enterprising parent, the agreeable Mrs Macnamara: who both as they gaped and peeped from the windows, bouncing up from the breakfast-table every minute, to the silent distress of quiet little Major O'Neill, painted all sorts of handsome portraits, and agreeable landscapes, and cloud-clapped castles, each for her private contemplation, on the spreading canvas of her hopes.

Dr Walsingham rode down to the Tiled House, where workmen were already preparing to make things a little more comfortable. The towering hall-door stood half open; and down the broad stairs – his tall, slim figure showing black against the light of the discoloured lobby-window – his raven hair reaching to his shoulders – Mervyn, the pale, large-eyed genius of that haunted place, came to meet him. He led him into the cedar parlour, the stained and dusty windows of which opened upon that moss-grown orchard, among whose great trunks and arches those strange shapes were said sometimes to have walked at night, like penitents and mourners through cathedral pillars.

It was a reception as stately, but as sombre and as beggarly withal as that of the Master of Ravenswood, for there were but two chairs in the cedar-parlour – one with but three legs, the other without a bottom; so they were fain to stand. But Mervyn could smile without bitterness and his desolation had not the sting of actual poverty, as he begged the rector to excuse his dreary welcome, and hoped that he would find things better the next time.

Their little colloquy got on very easily, for Mervyn liked the rector, and felt a confidence in him which was comfortable and almost exhilarating. The doctor had a cheery, kindly, robust voice, and a good, honest emphasis in his talk; a guileless blue eye; a face furrowed, thoughtful, and benevolent; well formed too. He must have been a handsome curate in his day. Not uncourtly, but honest; the politeness of a gentle and tender heart; *very* courteous and popular among ladies, although he sometimes forgot that they knew no Latin.

So Mervyn drew nigh to him in spirit, and liked him and talked to him rather more freely (though even that was enigmatically enough) than he had done to anybody else for a long time. It would seem that the young man had formed no very distinct plan of life. He appeared to have some thought of volunteering to serve in America, and some of entering into a foreign service; but his plans were, I suppose, *in nubibus*. All that was plain was that he was restless and eager for some change – any.

It was not a very long visit, you may suppose; and just as Dr Walsingham rode out of the avenue, Lord Castlemallard was riding leisurely by towards Chapelizod, followed by his groom.

His lordship, though he had a drowsy way with him, was esteemed rather an active man of business, being really, I'm afraid, only what is termed a fidget: and the fact is, his business would have been better done if he had looked after it himself a good deal less.

He was just going down to the town to see whether Dangerfield had arrived, and slackened his pace to allow the doctor to join him, for he could ride with him more comfortably than with parsons generally, the doctor being well descended, and having married, besides, into a good family. He stared, as he passed, at the old house listlessly and peevishly. He had heard of Mervyn's doings there, and did not like them.

'Yes, Sir, he's a very pretty young, man, and very well dressed,' said his lordship, with manifest dissatisfaction: 'but I don't like meeting him, you know. 'Tis not his fault; but one can't help thinking of – of things! And I'd be glad his friends would advise him not to dress in velvets, you know – particularly black velvets you can understand. I could not help thinking, at the time, of a pall, somehow. I'm not – no – not pleasant near him. No – I – I can't – his face is so pale – you don't often see so pale a face – no – it looks like a reflection from one that's still paler – you understand – and in short, even in his perfumes there's a taint of – of – you know – a taint of blood, Sir. Then there was a pause, during which he kept slapping his boot peevishly with his little riding-whip. 'One can't, of course, but be kind,' he recommenced. 'I can't do much – I can't make him acceptable, you know – but I pity him, Dr Walsingham, and I've tried to be kind to him, *you* know that; for ten years I had all the trouble, Sir, of a guardian without the authority of one. Yes, of course we're kind; but body o' me! Sir, he'd be better anywhere else than here, and without occupation, you know, quite idle, and so conspicuous. I promise you there are more than I who think it. And he has commenced fitting up that vile old house – that vile house, Sir. It is ready to tumble down – upon my life they say so; Nutter says so, and Sturk – Dr Sturk, of the Artillery here – an uncommon sensible man, you know, says so too. 'Tis a vile house, and ready to tumble down, and you know the trouble I was put to by that corporation fellow – a – what's his name – about it; and he can't let it – people's servants won't stay in it, you know, the people tell such stories about it, I'm told; and what business has he here, you know? It is all very fine for a week or so, but they'll find him out, they will, Sir. He may call himself Mervyn, or Fitzgerald, or Thompson, Sir, or any other name, but it won't do, Sir. No, Dr Walsingham, it won't do. The people down in this little village here, Sir, are plaguy sharp – they're cunning; upon my life, I believe they are too hard for Nutter.'

In fact, Sturk had been urging on his lordship the purchase of this little property, which, for many reasons ought to be had a bargain, and adjoined Lord Castlemallard's, and had talked him into viewing it quite as an object. No wonder, then, he should look on Mervyn's restorations and residence in the light of an impertinence and an intrusion.

Chapter Fourteen

*Relating how Puddock purged O'Flaherty's head – a chapter which,
it is hoped, no genteel person will read*

Rum disagreed with O'Flaherty confoundedly, but, being sanguine,
and also of an obstinate courage not easily to be put down, and liking
that fluid, and being young withal, he drank it defiantly and liberally
whenever it came in his way. So this morning he announced to his
friend Puddock that he was suffering under a headache 'that 'id burst
a pot'. The gallant fellow's stomach, too, was qualmish and disturbed.
He heard of breakfast with loathing. Puddock rather imperiously
insisted on his drinking some tea, which he abhorred, and of which,
in very imperfect clothing and with deep groans and occasional
imprecations on 'that bastely clar't' – to which he chose to ascribe his
indisposition – he drearily partook.

'I tell you what, Thir,' said Puddock, finding his patient nothing
better, and not relishing the notion of presenting his man in that
seedy condition upon the field: 'I've got a remedy, a very thimple
one; it used to do wonderth for my poor Uncle Neagle, who loved
rum shrub, though it gave him the headache *always*, and sometimes
the gout.'

And Puddock had up Mrs Hogg, his landlady, and ordered a pair
of little muslin bags about the size of a pistol-cartridge each, which
she promised to prepare in five minutes, and he himself tumbled
over the leaves of his private manuscript quarto, a desultory and
miscellaneous album, stuffed with sonnets on Celia's eye – a lock of
hair, or a pansy here or there pressed between the pages – birthday
verses addressed to Sacharissa, receipts for 'puptons', 'farces', &c.;
and several for toilet luxuries, 'Angelica water', 'The Queen of
Hungary's' ditto, 'surfeit waters', and finally, that he was in search
of, to wit, 'My great Aunt Bell's recipe for purging the head' (good
against melancholy or the headache). You are not to suppose that
the volume was slovenly or in anywise unworthy of a gentleman
and officer of those days. It was bound in red and gold, had two

handsome silver-gilt clasps and red edges, the writing being exquisitely straight and legible, and without a single blot.

'I have them all except – two – *three*,' murmured the thoughtful Puddock when he had read over the list of ingredients. These, however, he got from Toole, close at hand, and with a little silver grater and a pretty little agate pocket pestle and mortar – an heirloom derived from poor Aunt Bell – he made a wonderful powder; 'nutmeg and ginger, cinnamon and cloves', as the song says, and every other stinging product of nature and chemistry which the author of this famous family 'purge for the head' could bring to remembrance; and certainly it *was* potent. With this the cartridges were loaded, the ends tied up, and O'Flaherty, placed behind a table on which stood a basin, commenced the serious operation, under Puddock's directions, by introducing a bag at each side of his mouth, which as a man of honour, he was bound to retain there until Puddock had had his morning's *tête-à-tête* with the barber.

Those who please to consult old domestic receipt-books of the last century, will find the whole process very exactly described therein.

'Be the powers, Sorr, that was the stuff!' said O'Flaherty, discussing the composition afterwards, with an awful shake of his head; 'my chops wor blazing before you could count twenty.'

It was martyrdom; but anything was better than the incapacity which threatened, and certainly, by the end of five minutes, his head was something better. In this satisfactory condition – Jerome being in the back garden brushing his regimentals, and preparing his other properties – he suddenly heard voices close to the door, and gracious powers! One was certainly Magnolia's.

'That born devil, Juddy Carrol,' blazed forth. O'Flaherty, afterwards, 'pushed open the door; it served me right for not being in my bedroom, and the door locked – though who'd a thought there was such a cruel eediot on airth – bad luck to her – as to show a leedy in to a gentleman, with scarcely the half of his clothes on, and undhergoin' a soart iv an operation, I may say.'

Happily the table behind which he stood was one of those old-fashioned toilet affairs, with the back part, which was turned toward the door, sheeted over with wood, so that his ungartered stockings and rascally old slippers were invisible. Even so, it was bad enough: he was arrayed in a shabby old silk roquelaire, and there was a towel upon his breast, pinned behind his neck. He had just a second to pop the basin under the table, and to whisk the towel violently from under his chin, drying that feature with merciless violence, when the officious Judy Carrol, Grand Chamberlain in Jerome's absence, with the facetious grin of a good-natured lady about to make two people happy, introduced the bewitching Magnolia, and her meek little uncle, Major O'Neill.

In they came, rejoicing, to ask the gallant fireworker (it was a different element just now), to make one of a party of pleasure to Leixlip. O'Flaherty could not so much as hand the young lady a chair; to emerge from behind the table, or even to attempt a retreat, was of course not to be thought of in the existing state of affairs. The action of Puddock's recipe was such as to make his share in the little complimentary conversation that ensued very indistinct, and to oblige him, to his disgrace and despair, when the poor fellow tried a smile, actually to apply his towel hastily to his mouth.

He saw that his visitors observed those symptoms with some perplexity: the major was looking steadfastly at O'Flaherty's lips, and unconsciously making corresponding movements with his own, and the fair Magnolia was evidently full of pleasant surprise and curiosity. I really think, if O'Flaherty had had a pistol within reach, he would have been tempted to deliver himself summarily from that agonising situation.

'I'm afraid, lieutenant, you've got the toothache,' said Miss Mag, with her usual agreeable simplicity.

In his alacrity to assure her there was no such thing, he actually swallowed one of the bags. 'Twas no easy matter, and he grew very red, and stared frightfully, and swallowed a draught of water precipitately. His misery was indeed so great that at the conclusion of a polite little farewell speech of the major's, he uttered an involuntary groan, and lively Miss Mag, with an odious titter, exclaimed: 'The little creature's teething, uncle, as sure as you're not; either that, or he's got a hot potato in his poor little mouzey-wouzey;' and poor O'Flaherty smiled a great silent moist smile at the well-bred pleasantry. The major, who did not choose to hear Mag's banter, made a formal, but rather smiling salute. The lieutenant returned it, and down came the unlucky mortar and a china plate, on which Puddock had mingled the ingredients, with a shocking crash and jingle on the bare boards; a plate and mortar never made such a noise before, O'Flaherty thought, with a mental imprecation.

'Nothing – hash – 'appened – Shur,' said O'Flaherty, whose articulation was affected a good deal, in terror lest the major should arrest his departure.

So the major and tall Miss Magnolia, with all her roses and lilies, and bold broad talk, and her wicked eyes, went down the stairs; and O'Flaherty, looking with lively emotion in the glass, at the unbecoming *coup-d'oeil*, heard that agreeable young lady laughing most riotously under the windows as she and the major marched away.

It was well for Judy, that, being of the gentler sex, the wrath of the fireworker could not wreak itself upon her. The oftener he viewed himself in the pier-glass, trying in vain to think he did not look so very badly after all, the more bitter were his feelings. Oh, that villainous old silk morning gown! And his eyes so confoundedly red, and his hair all dishevelled – bad luck to that clar't! The wig was all right, that was his only comfort;, and his mouth, 'och, look at it; twiste its natural size,' though that was no trifle.

'Another week I'll not stop in her lodgings,' cried poor O'Flaherty, grinning at himself in the glass, 'if she keeps that savage, Judy Carrol, here a day longer.'

Then he stumbled to the stair-head to call her up for judgment; but changed his mind, and returned to the looking-glass, blowing the cooling air in short whistles through his peppered lips – and I'm sorry to say, blowing out also many an ejaculation and invective, as that sorry sight met his gaze in the oval mirror, which would have been much better not uttered.

Chapter Fifteen

Aesculapius to the rescue

It was not until Puddock had returned, that the gallant fireworker recollected all on a sudden that he had swallowed one of the bags.

'Thwallowed? – Thwallowed it!' said Puddock, looking very blank and uncomfortable; 'why, Thir, I told you you were to be *very* careful.'

'Why, why curse it, it's *not*, 'tisn't – '

'There was a long pause, and O'Flaherty stared a very frightened and hideous stare at the proprietor of the red quarto.

'Not *what*, Thir?' demanded Puddock, briskly, but plainly disconcerted.

'Not anything – anything *bad* – or, or – there's no use in purtendin', Puddock,' he resumed, turning quite yellow. 'I see, Sir, I see by your looks, it's what you think, I'm poisoned!'

'I – I – do *not*, Thir, think you're poisoned,' he replied indignantly, but with some flurry; 'that is, there's a great deal in it that could not pothibly do you harm – there's only one ingredient, yes – or, or, yes, perhapth three, but thertainly no more, that I don't quite know about, depend upon it, 'tis nothing – a – nothing – a – seriouthly – a – But why, my dear Thir, why on earth did you violate the thimple directions – why did you thwallow a particle of it?'

'Och, why did I let it into my mouth at all – the divil go with it!' retorted poor O'Flaherty; 'an' wasn't I the born eediot to put them devil's dumplins inside my mouth? But I did not know what I was doin' – no more I didn't.'

'I hope your head'th better,' said Puddock, vindicating by that dignified enquiry the character of his recipe.

'Auch! My head be smathered, what the puck do I care about it?' O'Flaherty broke out. 'Ah, why the devil, Puddock, do you keep them ould women's charrums and devilments about you? – You'll be the death of someone yet, so you will.'

'It's a recipe, Sir,' replied Puddock, with the same dignity 'from which my great-uncle, General Neagle, derived frequent benefit.'

'And here I am,' says O'Flaherty, vehemently; 'and you don't know whether I'm poisoned or no!'

At this moment he saw Dr Sturk passing by, and drummed violently at the window. The doctor was impressed by the summons; for however queer the apparition, it was plain he was desperately in earnest.

'Let's see the recipe,' said Sturk, drily; 'you think you're poisoned – I know you do;' poor O'Flaherty had shrunk from disclosing the extent of his apprehensions, and only beat about the bush; 'and if you be, I lay you fifty, I can't save you, nor all the doctors in Dublin – show me the recipe.'

Puddock put it before him, and Sturk looked at the back of the volume with a leisurely disdain, but finding no title there, returned to the recipe. They both stared on his face, without breathing, while he conned it over. When he came about half-way, he whistled; and when he arrived at the end, he frowned hard; and squeezed his lips together till the red disappeared altogether, and he looked again at the back of the book, and then turned it round, once more reading the last line over with a severe expression.

'And so you actually swallowed this – this devil's dose, Sir, did you?' demanded Sturk.

'I – I believe he did, some of it; but I warned him, I did, upon my honour! Now, tell him, did I not warn you, my dear lieutenant, not to thwallow,' interposed little Puddock, who began to grow confoundedly agitated; but Sturk, who rather liked shocking and frightening people, and had a knack of making bad worse, and an alacrity in waxing savage without adequate cause, silenced him with 'I p-pity you, Sir,' and 'pity' shot like a pellet from his lips. 'Why the deuce will you dabble in medicine, Sir? Do you think it's a thing to be learnt in an afternoon out of the bottom of an old cookery-book?'

'Cookery-book! Excuse me, Dr Sturk,' replied Puddock offended. 'I'm given to underthtand, Sir, it's to be found in Culpepper.'

'Culpepper!' said Sturk, viciously. 'Cull-*poison* – you have peppered him to a purpose, I promise you! How much of it, pray, Sir,' (to O'Flaherty) 'have you got in your stomach?'

'Tell him, Puddock,' said O'Flaherty, helplessly.

'Only a trifle I assure you,' extenuated Puddock (I need not spell his lisp), 'in a little muslin bag, about the size of the top joint of a lady's little finger.'

'Top joint o' the devil!' roared O'Flaherty, bitterly, rousing himself; 'I tell you, Dr Sturk, it was as big as my thumb, and a miracle it did not choke me.'

'It may do that job for you yet, Sir,' sneered the doctor with a stern disgust. 'I dare say you feel pretty hot here?' jerking his finger into his stomach.

'And – and – and – *what* is it? – is it – do you think it's anything – anyways – *dangerous*?' faltered poor O'Flaherty.

'Dangerous!' responded Sturk, with an angry chuckle – indeed, he was specially vindictive against lay intruders upon the mystery of his craft; 'why, yes – ha, ha! – just maybe a little. It's only *poison*, Sir, deadly, barefaced poison!' he began sardonically, with a grin, and ended with a black glare and a knock on the table, like an auctioneer's 'gone!'

'There are no less than two – three – *five* mortal poisons in it,' said the doctor with emphatic acerbity. 'You and Mr Puddock will allow *that's* rather strong.'

O'Flaherty sat down and looked at Sturk, and wiping his damp face and forehead, he got up without appearing to know where he was going. Puddock stood with his hands in his breeches pockets, staring with his little round eyes on the doctor, I must confess, with a very foolish and rather guilty vacuity all over his plump face, rigid and speechless, for three or four seconds; then he put his hand, which did actually tremble, upon the doctor's arm, and he said, very thickly – 'I feel, Sir, you're right; it is my fault, Sir, I've poisoned him – merthiful goodneth! – I – I – '

Puddock's address acted for a moment on O'Flaherty. He came up to him pale and queer, like a somnambulist, and shook his fingers very cordially with a very cold grasp.

'If it was the last word I ever spoke, Puddock, you're a good-natured – he's a gentleman, Sir – and it was *all* my own fault; he warned me, he did, again' swallyin' a dhrop of it – remember what I'm saying, doctor – 'twas *I* that done it; I was *always* a botch, Puddock, an' a fool; and – and – gentlemen – goodbye.'

And the flowered dressing-gown and ungartered stockings disappeared through the door into the bedroom, from whence they heard a great souse on the bed, and the bedstead gave a dismal groan.

'Is there – *is* there nothing, doctor – for mercy's sake, think – doctor, do – I conjure you – pray think – there must be something – ' urged Puddock, imploringly.

'Ay, that's the way, Sir, fellows quacking themselves and one another; when they get frightened, and with good reason, come to us and expect miracles; but as in this case, the quantity was not very much, 'tis not, you see, overpowering, and he *may* do if he takes what I'll send him.'

Puddock was already at his bedside, shaking his hand hysterically, and tumbling his words out one over the other: 'You're thafe, my dear Thir – *dum thpiro thpero* – he thayth – Dr Thturk – he can thave you, my dear Thir – my dear lieutenant – my dear O'Flaherty – he can thave you, Thir – thafe and thound, Thir.'

O'Flaherty, who had turned his face to the wall in the bitterness of his situation – for like some other men, he had the intensest horror of death when he came peaceably to his bedside, though ready enough to meet him with a 'hurrah!' and a wave of his rapier, if he arrived at a moment's notice, with due dash and éclat – sat up like a shot, and gaping upon Puddock for a few seconds, relieved himself with a long sigh, a devotional upward roll of the eyes, and some muttered words, of which the little ensign heard only 'blessing', very fervently, and 'catch me again', and 'divil bellows it'; and forthwith out came one of the fireworker's long shanks, and O'Flaherty insisted on dressing, shaving, and otherwise preparing as a gentleman and an officer, with great gaiety of heart, to meet his fate on the Fifteen Acres.

In due time arrived the antidote. It was enclosed in a gallipot, and was what I believe they called an electuary. I don't know whether it is an obsolete abomination now, but it looked like brick-dust and treacle, and what it was made of even Puddock could not divine. O'Flaherty, that great Hibernian athlete, unconsciously winced and shuddered like a child at sight of it. Puddock stirred it with the tip of a tea-spoon, and looked into it with inquisitive disgust, and seemed to smell it from a distance, lost for a minute in inward conjecture, and then with a slight bow, pushed it ceremoniously toward his brother in arms.

'There is not much the matter with me now – I feel well enough,' said O'Flaherty, mildly, and eyeing the mixture askance; and after a little while he looked at Puddock. That disciplinarian understood the look, and said, peremptorily, shaking up his little powdered head, and lisping vehemently: 'Lieutenant O'Flaherty, Sir! I insist on your instantly taking that physic. How you may feel, Sir, has nothing to do with it. If you hesitate, I withdraw my sanction to your going to the field, Sir. There's no – there *can* be – no earthly excuse but a – a miserable objection to a – swallowing a – recipe, Sir – that isn't – that is may be – not intended to please the palate, but to save your *life*, Sir, – remember. Sir, you've swallowed a – you – you *require*, Sir – you don't think I fear to say it, Sir! – you have swallowed that you ought not to have swallowed, and don't, Sir – don't – for *both* our sakes – for Heaven's sake – I implore – and insist – don't trifle, Sir.'

O'Flaherty felt himself passing under the chill and dismal shadow of death once more, such was the eloquence of Puddock, and so impressible his own nature, as he followed the appeal of his second. 'Life is sweet', and, though the compound was nauseous, and a necessity upon him of swallowing it in horrid instalments, spoonful after spoonful, yet, though not without many interruptions, and many a shocking apostrophe, and even some sudden paroxysms of horror, which alarmed Puddock, he did contrive to get through it pretty well, except a little residuum in the bottom, which Puddock wisely connived at.

The clink of a horse-shoe drew Puddock to the window. Sturk riding into town, reined in his generous beast, and called up to the little lieutenant.

'Well, he's taken it, eh?'

Puddock smiled a pleasant smile and nodded.

'Walk him about, then, for an hour or so, and he'll do.'

'Thank you, Sir,' said little Puddock, gaily.

'Don't thank *me*, Sir, *either* of you, but remember the lesson you've got,' said the doctor, tartly, and away he plunged into a sharp trot, with a cling-clang and a cloud of dust. And Puddock followed that ungracious leech, with a stare of gratitude and admiration, almost with a benediction. And his anxiety relieved, he and his principal prepared forthwith to provide real work for the surgeons.

Chapter Sixteen
The ordeal by battle

The chronicles of the small-sword and pistol are pregnant with horrid and absurd illustrations of certain great moral facts. Let them pass. A duel, we all know, spirit of 'Punch and Judy' – a farce of murder. Sterne's gallant father expired, or near it, with the point of a small-sword sticking out two feet between his shoulders, all about a goose-pie. I often wondered what the precise quarrel was. But these tragedies smell all over of goose-pie. Why – oh, why – brave Captain Sterne, as with saucy, flashing knife and fork you sported with the outworks of that fated structure, was there no augur at thine elbow, with a shake of his wintry beard, to warn thee that the birds of fate – *thy* fate – sat vigilant under that festive mask of crust? Beware, it is Pandora's pie! Madman! Hold thy hand! The knife's point that seems to thee about to glide through that pasty is palpably levelled at thine own windpipe! But this time Mephistopheles leaves the revellers to use their own cutlery; and now the pie is opened; and now the birds begin to sing! Come along, then to the Fifteen Acres, and let us see what will come of it all.

That flanking demi-bastion of the Magazine, crenelled for musketry, commands, with the aid of a couple of good field-glasses, an excellent and secret view of the arena on which the redoubted O'Flaherty and the grim Nutter were about to put their metal to the proof. General Chattesworth, who happened to have an appointment, as he told his sister at breakfast, in town about that hour, forgot it just as he reached the Magazine, gave his bridle to the groom, and stumped into the fortress, where he had a biscuit and a glass of sherry in the commandant's little parlour, and forth the two cronies sallied mysteriously side by side; the commandant, Colonel Bligh, being remarkably tall, slim, and straight, with an austere, mulberry-coloured face, the general stout and stumpy, and smiling plentifully, short of breath, and double-chinned, they got into the sanctum I have just mentioned.

I don't apologise to my readers, English-born and bred, for ass-uming them to be acquainted with the chief features of the Phoenix Park, near Dublin. Irish scenery is now as accessible as Welsh. Let them study the old problem, not in blue books, but in the green and brown ones of our fields and heaths, and mountains. If Ireland be no more than a great capability and a beautiful land-scape, faintly visible in the blue haze, even from your own head-lands, and separated by hardly four hours of water, and a ten-shilling fare, from your jetties, it is your own shame, not ours, if a nation of bold speculators and indefatigable tourists leave it unexplored.

So I say, from this coign of vantage, looking westward over the broad green level toward the thin smoke that rose from Chapelizod chimneys, lying so snugly in the lap of the hollow by the river, the famous Fifteen Acres, where so many heroes have measured swords, and so many bullies have bit the dust, was distinctly displayed in the near foreground. You all know the artillery butt. Well, that was the centre of a circular enclosure containing just fifteen acres, with broad entrances eastward and westward.

The old fellows knew very well where to look.

Father Roach was quite accidentally there, reading his breviary, when the hostile parties came upon the ground – for except when an accident of this sort occurred, or the troops were being drilled, it was a sequestered spot enough – and he forthwith joined them, as usual, to reconcile the dread debate.

Somehow, I think his arguments were not altogether judicious.

'I don't ask particulars, my dear – I abominate all that concerns a quarrel; but Lieutenant O'Flaherty, jewel, supposin' the very worst – supposin', just for argument, that he has horse-whipped you – '

'An' who dar' suppose it?' glared O'Flaherty.

'Or, we'll take it that he spit in your face, honey. Well,' continued his reverence, not choosing to hear the shocking ejaculations which this hypothesis wrung from the lieutenant; 'what of that, my darlin'? Think of the indignities, insults, and disgraces that the blessed Saint Martellus suffered, without allowing anything worse to cross his lips than an Ave Mary or a smile in resignation.'

'Ordher the priest off the ground, Sorr,' said O'Flaherty, lividly, to little Puddock, who was too busy with Mr Mahony to hear him; and Roach had already transferred his pious offices to Nutter, who speedily flushed up and became, to all appearances, in his own way just as angry as O'Flaherty.

'Lieutenant O'Flaherty, a word in your ear,' once more droned the mellow voice of Father Roach; 'you're a young man, my dear, and here's Lieutenant Puddock by your side, a young man too; I'm as ould, my honeys, as the two of you put together, an' I advise you, for your good – don't shed human blood – don't even draw your swords – don't, my darlins; don't be led or said by them army-gentlemen, that's always standin' up for fightin' because the leedies admire fightin' men. They'll call you cowards, polthroons, curs, sneaks, turn-tails – let them!'

'There's no standin' this any longer, Puddock,' said O'Flaherty, incensed indescribably by the odious names which his reverence was hypothetically accumulating; 'if you want to see the fightin', Father Roach –'

'*Apage, Sathanas!*' murmured his reverence, pettishly, raising his plump, blue chin, and dropping his eyelids with a shake of the head, and waving the back of his fat, red hand gently towards the speaker.

'In that case, stay here, an' look your full, an' welcome, only don't make a noise; behave like a Christian, an' hould your tongue; but if you really hate fightin', as you say –'

Having reached this point in his address, but intending a good deal more, O'Flaherty suddenly stopped short, drew himself into a stooping posture, with a flush and a strange distortion, and his eyes fastened upon Father Roach with an unearthly glare for nearly two minutes; and seized Puddock upon the upper part of his arm with so awful a grip, in his great bony hand, that the gallant little gentleman piped out in a flurry of anguish: 'O – O – O'Flaherty, Thir – *let* go my arm, Thir.'

O'Flaherty drew a long breath, uttered a short, deep groan, and wiping the moisture from his red forehead, and resuming a perpendicular position, was evidently trying to recover the lost thread of his discourse.

'There'th dethidedly thomething the matter with you, Thir,' said Puddock, anxiously, *sotto voce*, while he worked his injured arm a little at the shoulder.

'You may say that,' said O'Flaherty, very dismally, and, perhaps, a little bitterly.

'And – and – and – you don't mean to thay – why – eh?' asked Puddock, uneasily.

'I tell you what, Puddock – there's no use in purtendin' – the poison's working – *that's* what's the matter,' returned poor O'Flaherty, in what romance writers call 'a hissing whisper'.

'Good – merthiful – graciouth – Thir!' ejaculated poor little Puddock, in a panic, and gazing up into the brawny fireworker's face with a pallid fascination; indeed they both looked unpleasantly unlike the popular conception of heroes on the eve of battle.

'But – but it can't be – you forget Dr Sturk and – oh, dear! – the antidote. It – I thay – it can't *be*, Thir,' said Puddock, rapidly.

'It's no use, now; but I shirked two or three spoonfuls, and I left some more in the bottom,' said the gigantic O'Flaherty, with a gloomy sheepishness.

Puddock made an ejaculation – the only violent one recorded of him – and turning his back briskly upon his principal, actually walked several steps away, as if he intended to cut the whole concern. But such a measure was really not to be thought of.

'O'Flaherty – Lieutenant – I won't reproach you,' began Puddock.

'*Reproach* me! An' who *poisoned* me, my tight little fellow?' retorted the fireworker, savagely.

Puddock could only look at him, and then said, quite meekly, 'Well, and my dear Thir, what on earth had we better do?'

'Do,' said O'Flaherty, 'why, isn't it completely Hobson's choice with us? What can we do but go through with it?'

The fact is, I may as well mention, lest the sensitive reader should be concerned for the gallant O'Flaherty, that the poison had very little to do with it, and the antidote a great deal. In fact, it was a reckless compound conceived in a cynical and angry spirit by Sturk, and as the fireworker afterwards declared, while expressing in excited language his wonder how Puddock (for he never suspected Sturk's elixir) had contrived to compound such a poison – 'The torture was such, my dear Madam, as fairly thranslated me into the purlieus of the other world.'

Nutter had already put off his coat and waistcoat, and appeared in a neat little black lutestring vest, with sleeves to it, which the elder officers of the R.I.A. remembered well in by-gone fencing matches.

''Tis a most *miserable* situation,' said Puddock, in extreme distress.

'Never mind,' groaned O'Flaherty, grimly taking off his coat; 'you'll have *two* corpses to carry home with you; don't you show the laste taste iv unaisiness, an' I'll not disgrace you, *if* I'm spared to see it out.'

And now preliminaries were quite adjusted; and Nutter, light and wiry, a good swordsman, though not young, stepped out with his vicious weapon in hand, and his eyes looking white and stony out of his dark face. A word or two to his armour-bearer, and a rapid gesture, right and left, and that magnificent squire spoke low to two or three of the surrounding officers, who forthwith bestirred themselves to keep back the crowd, and as it were to keep the ring unbroken. O'Flaherty took his sword, got his hand well into the hilt, poised the blade, shook himself up as it were, and made a feint or two and a parry in the air, and so began to advance, like Goliath, towards little Nutter.

'Now, Puddock, back him up – encourage your man,' said Devereux, who took a perverse pleasure in joking; 'tell him to flay the lump, splat him, divide him, and cut him in two pieces – '

It was a custom of the corps to quiz Puddock about his cookery; but Puddock, I suppose, did not hear his last night's 'receipt' quoted, and he kept his eye upon his man, who had now got nearly within fencing distance of his adversary. But at this critical moment, O'Flaherty, much to Puddock's disgust, suddenly stopped, and got into the old stooping posture, making an appalling grimace in what looked like an endeavour to swallow, not only his under lip, but his chin also. Uttering a quivering, groan, he continued to stoop nearer to the earth, on which he finally actually sat down and hugged his knees close to his chest, holding his breath all the time till he was perfectly purple, and rocking himself this way and that.

The whole procedure was a mystery to everybody except the guilty Puddock, who changed colour, and in manifest perturbation, skipped to his side.

'Bleth me – bleth me – my dear O'Flaherty, he'th very ill – where ith the pain?'

'Is it "farced pain", Puddock, or "gammon pain"?' asked Devereux, with much concern.

Puddock's plump panic-stricken little face, and staring eyeballs, were approached close to the writhing features of his redoubted principal – as I think I have seen honest Sancho Panza's, in one of Tony Johannot's sketches, to that of the prostrate Knight of the Rueful Countenance.

'I wish to Heaven I had thwallowed it myself – it'th dreadful – what ith to be – are you eathier – I *think* you're eathier.'

I don't think O'Flaherty heard him. He only hugged his knees tighter, and slowly turned up his face, wrung into ten thousand horrid puckers, to the sky, till his chin stood as high as his forehead, with his teeth and eyes shut, and he uttered a sound like a half-stifled screech; and, indeed, looked very black and horrible.

Some of the spectators, rear-rank men, having but an imperfect view of the transaction, thought that O'Flaherty had been hideously run through the body by his solemn opponent, and swelled the general chorus of counsel and ejaculation, by all together advising cobwebs, brown-paper plugs, clergymen, brandy, and the like; but as none of these comforts were at hand, and nobody stirred, O'Flaherty was left to the resources of Nature.

Puddock threw his cocked hat upon the ground and stamped in a momentary frenzy.

'He'th *dying* – Devereux – Cluffe – he'th – I *tell* you, he'th dying;' and he was on the point of declaring himself O'Flaherty's murderer, and surrendering himself as such into the hands of anybody who would accept the custody of his person, when the recollection of his official position as poor O'Flaherty's second flashed upon him, and collecting with a grand effort, his wits and his graces, 'It'th totally impothible, gentlemen,' he said, with his most ceremonious bow; 'conthidering the awful condition of my printhipal – I – I have reathon to fear – in fact I know – Dr Thturk has theen him – that he'th under the action of *poithon* – and it'th quite impractithable, gentlemen, that thith affair of honour can protheed at prethent;' and Puddock drew himself up peremptorily, and replaced his hat, which somebody had slipped into his hand, upon his round powdered head.

Mr Mahony, though a magnificent gentleman, was, perhaps, a little stupid, and he mistook Puddock's agitation, and thought he was in a passion, and disposed to be offensive. He, therefore, with a marked and stern sort of elegance, replied: '*Pison*, Sir, is a remarkably strong alpathet; it's language, Sir, which, if a gentleman uses at all, he's bound in justice, in shivalry, and in dacency to a generous adversary, to define with precision. Mr Nutter is too well known to the best o'society, moving in a circle as he does, to require the panegyric of humble me. They drank together last night, they differed in opinion, that's true, but fourteen clear hours has expired, and pison being mentioned – '

'Why, body o' me! Sir,' lisped Puddock, in fierce horror; 'can you imagine for one moment, Sir, that I or any man living could suppose for an instant, that my respected friend, Mr Nutter, to whom (a low bow to Nutter, returned by that gentleman) I have now the misfortune to be opposed, is capable – capable, Sir, of poisoning any living being – man, woman, or child; and to put an end, Sir, at once to all misapprehension upon this point, it was I – *I*, Sir – myself – who poisoned him, altogether accidentally, of course, by a valuable, but mismanaged receipt, this morning, Sir – you – you *see*, Mr Nutter!'

Nutter, balked of his gentlemanlike satisfaction, stared with a horrified but somewhat foolish countenance from Puddock to O'Flaherty.

'And now, Thir,' pursued Puddock, addressing himself to Mr Mahony, 'if Mr Nutter desires to postpone the combat, I consent; if not, I offer mythelf to maintain it inthead of my printhipal.'

And so he made another low bow, and stood bareheaded, hat in hand, with his right hand on his sword hilt.

'Upon my honour, Captain Puddock, it's precisely what I was going to propose myself, Sir,' said Mahony, with great alacrity; 'as the only way left us of getting honourably out of the great embarrassment in which we are placed by the premature *death*-struggles of your friend; for nothing, Mr Puddock, but being *bona fide in articulo mortis*, can palliate his conduct.'

'My dear Puddock,' whispered Devereux, in his ear, 'surely you would not kill Nutter to oblige two such brutes as these?' indicating by a glance Nutter's splendid second and the magnanimous O'Flaherty, who was still sitting speechless upon the ground.

'Captain Puddock,' pursued that mirror of courtesy, Mr Patrick Mahony, of Muckafubble, who, by-the-bye, persisted in giving him his captaincy, may I enquire who's *your* friend upon this unexpected turn of affairs?'

'There's no need, Sir,' said Nutter, dryly and stoutly, 'I would not hurt a hair of your head, Lieutenant Puddock.'

'Do you hear him?' panted O'Flaherty, for the first time articulate, and stung by the unfortunate phrase – it seemed fated that Nutter should not open his lips without making some allusion to human hair: 'do you *hear* him, Puddock? Mr Nutter – (he spoke with great difficulty, and in jerks) – Sir – Mr Nutter – you shall – ugh – you shall render a strict accow-ow-oh-im-m-m!'

The sound was smothered under his compressed lips, his face wrung itself again crimson with a hideous squeeze, and Puddock thought the moment of his dissolution was come, and almost wished it over.

'Don't try to speak – pray, Sir, don't – there – there, now,' urged Puddock, distractedly; but the injunction was unnecessary.

'Mr Nutter,' said his second sulkily, 'I don't see anything to satisfy your outraged honour in the curious spectacle of that gentleman sitting on the ground making faces; we came here not to trifle, but, as I conceive, to dispatch business, Sir.'

'To dispatch that unfortunate gentleman, you mean, and that seems pretty well done to your hand,' said little Dr Toole, bustling up from the coach where his instruments, lint, and plasters were deposited. 'What's it all, eh? – oh, Dr *Sturk's* been with him, eh? Oh, ho, ho, ho!' and he laughed sarcastically, in an undertone, and shrugged, as he stooped down and took O'Flaherty's pulse in his fingers and thumb.

'I tell you what, Mr a – a – a – Sir,' said Nutter, with a very dangerous look; 'I have had the honour of knowing Lieutenant Puddock since August 1756; I won't hurt him, for I like and respect him; but, if fight I must, I'll fight *you*, Sir!'

'Since August 1756?' repeated Mr Mahony, with prompt surprise. 'Pooh! Why didn't you mention that before? Why, Sir, he's an old friend, and you *could* not pleasantly ask him to volunteer to bare his waypon against the boosom of his friend. No, Sir, shivalry is the handmaid of Christian charity, and honour walks hand in hand with the human heart!'

With this noble sentiment he bowed and shook Nutter's cold, hard hand, and then Puddock's plump little white paw.

You are not to suppose that Pat Mahoney, of Muckafubble, was a poltroon; on the contrary, he had fought several shocking duels, and displayed a remarkable amount of savagery and coolness; but having made a character, he was satisfied therewith. They may talk of fighting for the fun of it, liking it, delighting in it; don't believe a word of it. We all hate it, and the hero is only he who hates it least.

'Ugh, I can't stand it any longer; take me out of this, some of you,' said O'Flaherty, wiping the damp from his red face. 'I don't think there's ten minutes' life in me.'

'*De profundis conclamavi*,' murmured fat father Roach; 'lean upon me, Sir.'

'And me,' said little Toole.

'For the benefit of your poor soul, my honey, just say you forgive Mr Nutter before you leave the field,' said the priest quite sincerely.

'Anything at all, Father Roach,' replied the sufferer; 'only don't bother me.'

'You forgive him then, aroon?' said the priest.

'Och, bother! Forgive him, to be sure I do. *That's* supposin', mind, I don't recover; but if I *do* – '

'Och, pacible, pacible, my son,' said Father Roach, patting his arm, and soothing him with his voice. It was the phrase he used to address to his nag, Brian O'Lynn, when Brian had too much oats, and was disagreeably playful. 'Nansinse, now, can't you be pacible – pacible my son – there now, pacible, pacible.'

Upon his two supporters, and followed by his little second, this towering sufferer was helped, and tumbled into the coach, into which Puddock, Toole, and the priest, who was curious to see O'Flaherty's last moments, all followed; and they drove at a wild canter – for the coachman was 'hearty' – over the green grass, and toward Chapelizod, though Toole broke the check-string without producing any effect, down the hill, quite frightfully, and were all within an ace of being capsized. But ultimately they reached, in various states of mind, but safely enough, O'Flaherty's lodgings.

Here the gigantic invalid, who had suffered another paroxysm on the way, was slowly assisted to the ground by his awestruck and curious friends, and entered the house with a groan, and roared for Judy Carrol with a curse, and invoked Jerome, the *cokang modate*, with horrible vociferation. And as among the hushed exhortations of the good priest, Toole and Puddock, he mounted the stairs, he took occasion over the banister, in stentorian tones, to proclaim to the household his own awful situation, and the imminent approach of the moment of his dissolution.

Chapter Seventeen

Lieutenant Puddock receives an invitation and a rap over the knuckles

The old gentlemen, from their peepholes in the Magazine, watched the progress of this remarkable affair of honour, as well as they could, with the aid of their field-glasses, and through an interposing crowd.

'By Jupiter, Sir, he's through him!' said Colonel Bligh, when he saw O'Flaherty go down.

'So he is, by George!' replied General Chattesworth; 'but, eh, which is he?'

'The *long* fellow,' said Bligh.

'O'Flaherty? – hey! – no, by George! – though so it is – there's work in Frank Nutter yet, by Jove,' said the general, poking his glass and his fat face an inch or two nearer.

'Quick work, general!' said Bligh.

'Devilish,' replied the general.

The two worthies never moved their glasses; as each, on his inquisitive face, wore the grim, wickedish half-smile, with which an old-stager recalls, in the prowess of his juniors, the pleasant devilment of his own youth.

'The cool, old hand, Sir, too much for your new fireworker,' remarked Bligh, cynically.

'Tut, Sir, this O'Flaherty has not been three weeks among us,' spluttered out the general, who was woundily jealous of the honour of his corps. 'There are lads among our fireworkers who would whip Nutter through the liver while you'd count ten!'

'They're removing the – the – (a long pause) the *body*, eh?' said Bligh. 'Hey! No, see, by George, he's walking but he's *hurt*.'

'I'm mighty well pleased it's no worse, Sir,' said the general, honestly glad.

'They're helping him into the coach – long legs the fellow's got,' remarked Bligh.

'These – things – Sir – are – are – very – un – pleasant,' said the general, adjusting the focus of the glass, and speaking slowly – though no Spanish dandy ever relished a bull-fight more than he an affair of the kind. He and old Bligh had witnessed no less than five – not counting this – in which officers of the R.I.A. were principal performers, from the same snug post of observation. The general, indeed, was conventionally supposed to know nothing of them, and to reprobate the practice itself with his whole soul. But somehow, when an affair of the sort came off on the Fifteen Acres, he always happened to drop in, at the proper moment, upon his old crony, the colonel, and they sauntered into the demi-bastion together, and quietly saw what was to be seen. It was Miss Becky Chattesworth who involved the poor general in this hypocrisy. It was not exactly her money; it was her force of will and unflinching audacity that established her control over an easy, harmless, plastic old gentleman.

'They are unpleasant – devilish unpleasant – somewhere in the body, I think, hey? They're stooping again, stooping again – eh? – *plaguey* unpleasant, Sir,' [the general was thinking how Miss Becky's tongue would wag, and what she might not even *do*, if O'Flaherty died]. 'Ha! On they go again, and a – Puddock – getting in – and that's Toole. He's not so much hurt – eh? He helped himself a good deal, you saw; but' [taking heart of grace] 'when a quarrel does occur, Sir, I believe, after all, 'tis better off the stomach at once – a few passes – you know – or the crack of a pistol – who's that got in – the priest – hey? By George!'

'Awkward if he dies a Papist,' said cynical old Bligh – the R.I.A. were Protestant by constitution.

'That never happens in our corps, Sir,' said the general, haughtily; 'but, as I say, when a quarrel – does – occur – Sir – there, they're off at last; when it does occur – I say – heyday! what a thundering pace! A gallop, by George! That don't look well,' [a pause] ' – and – and – a – about what you were saying – you know he *couldn't* die a Papist in our corps – no-one does – no-one ever *did* – it would be, you know – it would be a *trick*, Sir, and O'Flaherty's a gentleman; it *could* not be – [he was thinking of Miss Becky again – she was so fierce on the Gunpowder Plot, the rising of 1642, and Jesuits in general, and he went on a little flustered] 'but then, Sir, as I was saying, though the thing has its uses – '

'I'd like to know where society'd be without it,' interposed Bligh, with a sneer.

'Though it may have its uses, Sir; it's not a thing one can sit down and say is *right* – we *can't*!'

'I've heard your sister, Miss Becky, speak strongly on that point, too,'said Bligh.

'Ah! I dare say,' said the general, quite innocently, and coughing a little. This was a sore point with the hen-pecked warrior, and the grim scarecrow by his side knew it, and grinned through his telescope; 'and you see – I say – eh! I think they're breaking up, a – and – I say – I – it seems all over – eh – and so, dear colonel, I must take my leave, and – '

And after a lingering look, he shut up his glass, and walking thoughtfully back with his friend, said suddenly: 'And, now I think of it – it could not be *that* – Puddock, you know, would not suffer the priest to sit in the same coach with such a design – Puddock's a good officer, eh! And knows his duty.'

A few hours afterwards, General Chattesworth, having just dismounted outside the Artillery barracks, to his surprise met Puddock and O'Flaherty walking leisurely in the street of Chapelizod. O'Flaherty looked pale and shaky, and rather wild; and the general returned his salute, looking deuced hard at him, and wondering all the time in what part of his body (in his phrase) 'he had got it'; and how the plague the doctors had put him so soon on his legs again.

'Ha, Lieutenant Puddock,' with a smile, which Puddock thought significant – 'give you good-evening, Sir. Dr Toole anywhere about, or have you seen Sturk?'

'No, he had not.'

The general wanted to hear by accident, or in confidence, all about it; and having engaged Puddock in talk, that officer followed by his side.

'I should be glad of the honour of your company, Lieutenant Puddock, to dinner this evening – Sturk comes, and Captain Cluffe, and this wonderful Mr Dangerfield too, of whom we all heard so much at mess; at five o'clock, if the invitation's not too late.'

The lieutenant acknowledged and accepted, with a blush and a very low bow, his commanding officer's hospitality; in fact, there was a *tendre* in the direction of Belmont, and little Puddock had inscribed in his private book many charming stanzas of various lengths and structures, in which the name of 'Gertrude' was of frequent recurrence.

'And – a – I say, Puddock – Lieutenant O'Flaherty, I thought – I – I thought, d'ye see, just now, eh? (he looked inquisitively, but there was no answer); I thought, I say, he looked devilish out of sorts, is he – a – *ill*?'

'He *was very* ill, indeed, this afternoon, general; a sudden attack – '

The general looked quickly at Puddock's plump, consequential face; but there was no further light in it. 'He *was* hurt then, I knew it' – he thought – 'who's attending him – and why is he out – and was it a flesh-wound – or where was it?' all these questions silently, but vehemently, solicited an answer – and he repeated the last aloud, in a careless sort of way.

'And – a – Lieutenant Puddock, you were saying – a – tell me – now – *where* was it?'

'In the park, general,' said Puddock, in perfect good faith.

'Eh? Ah! In the park, was it? But I want to know, you know, what part of the body – d'ye see – the shoulder – or – ?'

'The duodenum, Dr Toole called it – just here, general,' and he pressed his fingers to what is vulgarly known as the 'pit' of his stomach.

'What, Sir, do you mean to say the pit of his stomach?' said the general, with more horror and indignation than he often showed.

'Yes, just about that point, general, and the pain was very violent indeed,' answered Puddock, looking with a puzzled stare at the general's stern and horrified countenance – an officer might have a pain in his stomach, he thought, without exciting all that emotion. Had he heard of the poison, and did he know more of the working of such things than, perhaps, the doctors did?

'And what in the name of Bedlam, Sir, does he mean by walking about the town with a hole through his – his what's his name? I'm hanged but I'll place him under arrest this moment,' the general thundered, and his little eyes swept the perspective this way and that, as if they would leap from their sockets, in search of the reckless O'Flaherty. 'Where's the adjutant, Sir?' he bellowed with a crimson scowl and a stamp, to the unoffending sentry.

'That's the way to make him lie quiet, and keep his bed till he heals, Sir.'

Puddock explained, and the storm subsided, rumbling off in half a dozen testy assertions on the general's part that he, Puddock, had distinctly used the word '*wounded*', and now and then renewing faintly, in a muttered explosion, on the troubles and worries of his command, and a great many 'pshaws!' and several fits of coughing, for the general continued out of breath for some time. He had showed his cards, however, and so, in a dignified disconcerted sort of way, he told Puddock that he had heard something about O'Flaherty's having got most improperly into a foolish quarrel, and having met Nutter that afternoon, and for a moment feared he might have been hurt; and then came enquiries about Nutter, and there appeared to have been no-one hurt, and yet the parties on the ground – and no fighting – and yet no reconciliation – and, in fact, the general was so puzzled with this conundrum, and so curious, that he was very near calling after Puddock, when they parted at the bridge, and making him entertain him, at some cost of consistency, with the whole story.

So Puddock – his head full of delicious visions – marched homeward – to powder and perfume, and otherwise equip for that banquet of the gods, of which he was to partake at five o'clock, and just as he turned the corner at the Phoenix, who should he behold, sailing down the Dublin road from the King's House, with a grand powdered footman bearing his cane of office, and a great bouquet behind her, and Gertrude Chattesworth by her side, but the splendid and formidable Aunt Becky, who had just been paying her compliments to old Mrs Colonel Stafford, from whom she had heard all about the duel. So as Puddock's fat cheeks grew pink at sight of Miss Gertrude, all Aunt Becky's colour flushed into her face, as her keen eye pierced the unconscious lieutenant from afar off, and chin and nose high in air, her mouth just a little tucked in, as it were, at one corner – a certain sign of coming storm – an angry hectic in each cheek, a fierce flirt of her fan, and two or three short sniffs that betokened mischief – she quickened her pace, leaving her niece a good way in the rear, in her haste to engage the enemy. Before she came up she commenced the action at a long range, and very abruptly – for an effective rhetorician of Aunt Becky's sort jumps at once, like a good epic poet, *in medias res*; and as Nutter, who, like all her friends in turn, experienced once or twice 'a taste of her quality', observed to his wife, 'by Jove, that woman says things for which she ought to be put in the watch-house,' so now and here she maintained her reputation: 'You ought to be flogged, Sir; yes,' she insisted, answering Puddock's bewildered stare, 'tied up to the halberts and flogged.'

Aunt Rebecca was accompanied by at least half a dozen lapdogs, and those intelligent brutes, aware of his disgrace, beset poor Puddock's legs with a furious vociferation.

'Madam,' said he, his ears tingling, and making a prodigious low bow; 'commissioned officers are never flogged.'

'So much the worse for the service, Sir; and the sooner they abolish that anomalous distinction the better. I'd have them begin, Sir, with you, and your accomplice in murder, Lieutenant O'Flaherty.'

'Madam! Your most obedient humble servant,' said Puddock, with another bow, still more ceremonious, flushing up intensely to the very roots of his powdered hair, and feeling in his swelling heart that all the generals of all the armies of Europe dare not have held such language to him.

'Good-evening, Sir,' said Aunt Becky, with an energetic toss of her head, having discharged her shot; and with an averted countenance, and in high disdain, she swept grandly on, quite forgetting her niece, who said a pleasant word or two to Puddock as she passed, and smiled so kindly, and seemed so entirely unconscious of his mortification, that he was quite consoled, and on the whole was made happy and elated by the rencontre, and went home to his wash-balls and perfumes in a hopeful and radiant, though somewhat excited state.

Indeed, the little lieutenant knew that kind-hearted termagant, Aunt Becky, too well to be long cast down or even flurried by her onset. When the same little Puddock, about a year ago, had that ugly attack of pleurisy, and was so low and so long about recovering, and so puny and fastidious in appetite, she treated him as kindly as if he were her own son, in the matter of jellies, strong soups, and curious light wines, and had afterwards lent him some good books which the little lieutenant had read through, like a man of honour as he was. And, indeed, what specially piqued Aunt Becky's resentment just now was, that having had, about that time, a good deal of talk with Puddock upon the particular subject of duelling, he had, as she thought, taken very kindly to her way of thinking; and she had a dozen times in the last month, cited Puddock to the general; and so his public defection was highly mortifying and intolerable.

So Puddock, in a not unpleasant fuss and excitement, sat down in his dressing-gown before the glass; and while Moore the barber, with tongs, powder, and pomade, repaired the dilapidations of the day, he contemplated his own plump face, not altogether unapprovingly, and thought with a charming anticipation of the adventures of the approaching evening.

Chapter Eighteen

*Relating how the gentlemen sat over their claret, and how
Dr Sturk saw a face*

Puddock drove up the avenue of gentlemanlike old poplars, and over
the little bridge, and under the high-arched bowers of elms, walled up
at either side with evergreens, and so into the courtyard of Belmont.
Three sides of a parellelogram, the white old house being the largest,
and offices white and in keeping, but overgrown with ivy, and opening
to yards of their own on the other sides, facing one another at the
flanks, and in front a straight Dutch-like moat, with a stone balustrade
running all along from the garden to the bridge, with great stone
flower-pots set at intervals, the shrubs and flowers of which associated
themselves in his thoughts with beautiful Gertrude Chattesworth, and
so were wonderfully bright and fragrant. And there were two swans
upon the water, and several peacocks marching dandily in the courtyard, and a grand old Irish dog, with a great collar and a Celtic in-
scription, dreaming on the steps in the evening sun.

It was always pleasant to dine at Belmont. Old General Chattesworth was so genuinely hospitable and so really glad to see you, and
so hilarious himself, and so enjoying. A sage or a scholar, perhaps,
might not have found a great deal in him. Most of his stories had
been heard before. Some of them, I am led to believe, had even been
printed. But they were not very long, and he had a good-natured
word and a cordial smile for everybody; and he had a good cook, and
explained his dishes to those beside him, and used sometimes to
toddle out himself to the cellar in search of a curious bon-bouche;
and of nearly every bin in it he had a little anecdote or a pedigree to
relate. And his laugh was frequent and hearty, and somehow the
room and all in it felt the influence of his presence like the glow, and
cheer, and crackle of a bright Christmas fire.

Miss Becky Chattesworth, very stately in a fine brocade, and a
great deal of point lace, received Puddock very loftily, and only
touched his hand with the tips of her fingers. It was plain he was

not yet taken into favour. When he entered the drawing-room, that handsome stranger, with the large eyes, so wonderfully elegant and easy in the puce-coloured cut velvet – Mr Mervyn – was leaning upon the high back of a chair, and talking agreeably, as it seemed, to Miss Gertrude. He had a shake of the hand and a fashionable greeting from stout, dandified Captain Cluffe, who was by no means so young as he would be supposed, and made up industriously and braced what he called his waist, with great fortitude, and indeed sometimes looked half-stifled, in spite of his smile and his swagger. Sturk, leaning at the window with his shoulders to the wall, beckoned Puddock gruffly, and cross-examined him in an undertone as to the issue of O'Flaherty's case. Of course he knew all about the duel, but the corps also knew that Sturk would not attend on the ground in any affair where the Royal Irish Artillery were concerned, and therefore they could bring what doctor they pleased to the field without an affront.

'And see, my buck,' said Sturk, winding up rather savagely with a sneer; 'you've got out of that scrape, you and your *patient*, by a piece of good luck that's not like to happen twice over; so take my advice, and cut that leaf out of your – your – grandmother's cookery book, and light your pipe with it.'

This slight way of treating both his book and his ancestors nettled little Puddock – who never himself took a liberty, and expected similar treatment – but he knew Sturk, the nature of the beast, and he only bowed grandly, and went to pay his respects to cowed, kindly, querulous little Mrs Sturk, at the other end of the room. An elderly gentleman, with a rather white face, a high forehead and grim look, was chatting briskly with her; and Puddock, the moment his eye lighted on the stranger, felt that there was something remarkable about him. Taken in detail, indeed, he was insignificant. He was dressed as quietly as the style of that day would allow, yet in his toilet there was entire ease and even a latent air of fashion. He wore his own hair; and though there was a little powder upon it and upon his coat collar, it was perfectly white, frizzed out a little at the sides, and gathered into a bag behind. The stranger rose and bowed as Puddock approached the lady, and the lieutenant had a nearer view of his great white forehead – his only good feature – and the pair of silver spectacles that glimmered under it, and his small hooked nose and stern mouth.

' 'Tis a mean countenance,' said the general, talking him over when the company had dispersed.

'No countenance,' said Miss Becky decisively, '*could* be mean with such a forehead.'

The fact is – if they had cared to analyse – the features, taken separately, with that one exception, were insignificant; but the face was singular, with its strange pallor, its intellectual mastery, and sarcastic decision.

The general, who had accidentally omitted the ceremony – in those days essential – now strutted up to introduce them.

'Mr Dangerfield, will you permit me to present my good friend and officer Lieutenant Puddock. Lieutenant Puddock, Mr Dangerfield – Mr Dangerfield, Lieutenant Puddock.'

And there was a great deal of pretty bowing, and each was the other's 'most obedient', and declared himself honoured; and the conventional parenthesis ended, things returned to their former course.

Puddock only perceived that Mrs Sturk was giving Dangerfield a rambling sort of account of the people of Chapelizod. Dangerfield, to do him justice, listened attentively. In fact, he had led her upon that particular theme, and as easily and cleverly kept her close to the subject. For he was not a general to manoeuvre without knowing first how the ground lay, and had an active, enquiring mind, in which he made all sorts of little notes.

So Mrs Sturk prattled on, to her own and Mr Dangerfield's content, for she was garrulous when not under the eye of her lord, and always gentle, though given to lamentation, having commonly many small hardships to mention. So, quite without malice or retention, she poured out the gossip of the town, but not its scandal. Indeed, she was a very harmless and rather sweet, though dolorous, little body, and was very fond of children, especially her own, who would have been ruined were it not that they quailed as much as she did before Sturk, on whom she looked as by far the cleverest and most awful mortal then extant, and never doubted that the world thought so too. For the rest, she preserved her dresses, which were not amiss, for an interminable time, her sheets were always well aired, her maids often saucy, and she often in tears, but Sturk's lace and fine-linen were always forthcoming in exemplary order; she rehearsed the catechism with the children, and loved Dr Walsingham heartily, and made more raspberry jam than any other woman of her means in Chapelizod, except, perhaps, Mrs Nutter, between whom and herself there were points of resemblance, but something as nearly a feud as could subsist between their harmless natures. Each believed the other matched with a bold bad man, who was always scheming something – they never quite understood what – against her own peerless lord; each on seeing the other, hoping that Heaven would defend the right and change the hearts of her enemies, or at all events confound their politics; and each, with a sort of awful second-sight, when they viewed one another across the street, beholding her neighbour draped in a dark film of thunder-cloud, and with a sheaf of pale lightning, instead of a fan flickering in her hand.

When they came down to dinner, the gallant Captain Cluffe contrived to seat himself beside Aunt Becky, to whom the rogue commended himself by making a corner on his chair, next hers, for that odious greedy little brute 'Fancy', and by a hundred other adroit and amiable attentions. And having a perfect acquaintance with all her weak points – as everybody had who lived long in Chapelizod – he had no difficulty in finding topics to interest her, and in conversing acceptably thereupon. And, indeed, whenever he was mentioned for some time after, she used to remark, that Captain Cluffe was a very conversable and worthy young [!] man.

In truth, that dinner went swiftly and pleasantly over for many of the guests. Gertrude Chattesworth was placed between the enamoured Puddock and the large-eyed, handsome, mysterious Mervyn. Of course, the hour flew with light and roseate wings for him. Little Puddock was in great force, and chatted with energy, and his theatrical lore, and his oddities, made him not unamusing. So she smiled on him more than usual, to make amends for the frowns of the higher powers, and he was as happy as a prince and as proud as a peacock, and quite tipsy with his success.

It is not always easy to know what young ladies like best or least, or quite what they are driving at; and Cluffe, from the other side of the table, thought, though Puddock *was* an agreeable fellow, and exerting himself uncommonly (for Cluffe, like other men not deep in the *literae humaniores*, had a sort of veneration for 'book learning', under which category he placed Puddock's endless odds and ends of play lore, and viewed the little lieutenant himself accordingly with some awe as a man of parts and a scholar, and prodigiously admired his verses, which he only half understood); he fancied, I say, although Puddock was unusually entertaining, that Miss Gertrude would have been well content to exchange him for the wooden lay-figure on which she hung her draperies when she sketched, which might have worn his uniform and filled his chair, and spared her his agreeable conversation, and which had eyes and saw not, and ears and heard not.

In short, the cunning fellow fancied he saw, by many small signs, a very decided preference on her part for the handsome and melancholy, but evidently eloquent stranger. Like other cunning fellows, however, Cluffe was not always right; and right or wrong in his own illusions, if such they were, little Puddock was, for the time, substantially blessed.

The plump and happy lieutenant, when the ladies had flown away to the drawing-room and their small tea-cups, waxed silent and sentimental, but being a generous rival, and feeling that he could afford it, made a little effort, and engaged Mervyn in talk, and found him pleasantly versed in many things of which he knew little, and especially in the Continental stage and drama, upon which Puddock heard him greedily; and the general's bustling talk helped to keep the company merry, and he treated them to a bottle of the identical sack of which his own father's wedding posset had been compounded! Dangerfield, in a rather harsh voice, but agreeably and intelligently withal, told some rather pleasant stories about old wines and curious wine fanciers; and Cluffe and Puddock, who often sang together, being called on by the general, chanted a duet rather prettily, though neither, separately, had much of a voice. And the incorrigible Puddock, apropos of a piece of a whale once eaten by Dangerfield, after his wont, related a wonderful receipt – 'a weaver surprised'. The weaver turned out to be a fish, and the 'surprising' was the popping him out of ice into boiling water, with after details, which made the old general shake and laugh till tears bedewed his honest cheeks. And Mervyn and Dangerfield, as much surprised as the weaver, both looked, each in his own way, a little curiously at the young warrior who possessed this remarkable knowledge.

And the claret, like the general's other wines, was very good, and Dangerfield said a stern word or two in its praise, and guessed its vintage, to his host's great elation, who, with Lord Castlemallard, began to think Dangerfield a very wonderful man.

Dr Sturk alone sipped his claret silently, looking thoughtfully a good deal at Dangerfield over the way; and when spoken to, seemed to waken up, but dropped out of the conversation again; though this was odd, for he had intended giving Dangerfield a bit of his mind as to what might be made of the Castlemallard estates, and by implication letting in some light upon Nutter's mismanagement.

When Dr Sturk had come into the drawing-room before dinner, Dangerfield was turning over a portfolio in the shade beyond the window, and the evening sun was shining strongly in his own face;

so that during the ceremony of introduction he had seen next to nothing of him, and then sauntered away to the bow window at the other end, where the ladies were assembled, to make his obeisance.

But at the dinner-table, he was placed directly opposite, with the advantage of a very distinct view; and the face, relieved against the dark stamped leather hangings on the wall, stood out like a sharply-painted portrait, and produced an odd and unpleasant effect upon Sturk, who could not help puzzling himself then, and for a long time after, with unavailing speculations about him.

The grim white man opposite did not appear to trouble his head about Sturk. He eat his dinner energetically, chatted laconically but rather pleasantly. Sturk thought he might be eight-and-forty, or perhaps six or seven-and-fifty – it was a face without a date. He went over all his points, insignificant features, high forehead, stern countenance, abruptly silent, abruptly speaking, spectacles, harsh voice, harsher laugh, something sinister perhaps, and used for the most part when the joking or the story had a flavour of the sarcastic and the devilish. The image, as a whole, seemed to Sturk to fill in the outlines of a recollection, which yet was *not* a recollection. He could not seize it; it was a decidedly unpleasant impression of having seen him before, but where he could not bring to mind. 'He got me into some confounded trouble some time or other,' thought Sturk, in his uneasy dream; 'the sight of him is like a thump in my stomach. Was he the sheriff's deputy at Chester, when that rascally Jew-tailor followed me? Dangerfield – Dangerfield – Dangerfield – no; or could it be that row at Taunton? Or the custom-house officer – let me see – 1751; no, he was a taller man – yes, I remember him; it is *not* he. Or was he at Dick Luscome's duel?' and he lay awake half the night thinking of him; for he was not only a puzzle, but there was a sort of suspicion of danger and he knew not what, throbbing in his soul whenever his reverie conjured up that impenetrable, white scoffing face.

Chapter Nineteen

In which the gentlemen follow the ladies

Having had as much claret as they cared for, the gentlemen fluttered gaily into the drawing-room, and Puddock, who made up to Miss Gertrude, and had just started afresh, and in a rather more sentimental vein, was a good deal scandalised and put out by the general's reciting with jolly emphasis, and calling thereto his daughter's special attention, his receipt for 'surprising a weaver', which he embellished with two or three burlesque improvements of his own, which Puddock, amidst his blushes and confusion, allowed to pass without a protest. Aunt Rebecca was the only person present who pointedly refused to laugh; and with a slight shudder and momentary elevation of her eyes, said, 'wicked and unnatural cruelty!' at which sentiment Puddock used his pocket-handkerchief in rather an agitated manner.

' 'Tis a thing I've never done myself – that is, I've never seen it done,' said Little Puddock, suffused with blushes, as he pleaded his cause at the bar of humanity – for those were the days of Howard, and the fair sex had taken up the philanthropist. 'The – the – receipt – 'tis, you see, a thing I happened to meet – and – and just read it in the – in a book – and the – I – a – '

Aunt Becky, with her shoulders raised in a shudder, and an agonised and peremptory 'there, there, *there*', moved out of hearing in dignified disgust, to the general's high entertainment, who enjoyed her assaults upon innocent Puddock, and indeed took her attacks upon himself, when executed with moderation, hilariously enough – a misplaced good-humour which never failed to fire Aunt Becky's just resentment.

Indeed, the general was so tickled with this joke that he kept it going for the rest of the evening, by sly allusions and mischievous puns. As for instance, at supper, when Aunt Rebecca was deploring the miserable depression of the silk manufacture, and the distress of the poor Protestant artisans of the Liberty, the general, with a solemn wink at Puddock, and to that officer's terror, came out with:

'Yet, who knows, Lieutenant Puddock, but the weavers, poor fellows, may be surprised, you know, by a sudden order from the Court, as happened last year.'

But Aunt Rebecca only raised her eyebrows, and, with a slight toss of her head, looked sternly at a cold fowl on the other side. But, from some cause or other – perhaps it was Miss Gertrude's rebellion in treating the outlawed Puddock with special civility that evening, Miss Becky's asperity seemed to acquire edge and venom as time proceeded. But Puddock rallied quickly. He was on the whole very happy, and did not grudge Mervyn his share of the talk, though he heard him ask leave to send Miss Gertrude Chattesworth a portfolio of his drawings made in Venice, to look over, which she with a smile accepted – and at supper, Puddock, at the general's instigation, gave them a solo, which went off pretty well, and, as they stood about the fire after it, on a similar pressure, an imitation of Barry in *Othello*; and upon this, Miss Becky, who was a furious partisan of Smock-alley Theatre and Mossop against Barry, Woodward, and the Crow-street playhouse, went off again. Indeed, this was a feud which just then divided the ladies of all Dublin, and the greater part of the country, with uncommon acrimony.

'Crow-street was set up,' she harangued, 'to ruin the old house in the spirit of covetousness, *you* say,' (Puddock had not said a word on the subject) 'well, covetousness, we have good authority for saying, is idolatry – nothing less – *idolatry*, Sir – you need not stare.' (Puddock certainly did stare.) 'I suppose you *once* read your Bible, Sir, but every sensible man, woman, child, and infant, Sir, in the kingdom, knows it was malice; and malice, Holy Writ says, is *murder* – but I forgot, that's perhaps no very great objection with Lieutenant Puddock.'

And little Puddock flushed up, and his round eyes grew rounder and rounder, as she proceeded, every moment; and he did not know what to say – for it had not struck him before that Messrs. Barry's and Woodward's theatrical venture might be viewed in the light of idolatry or murder. So dumbfounded as he was, he took half of Lord Chesterfield's advice in such cases, that is, he forgot the smile, but he made a very low bow, and, with this submission, the combat (*si rixa est*) subsided.

Dangerfield had gone away some time – so had Mervyn – Sturk and his wife went next, and Cluffe and Puddock, who lingered as long as was decent, at last took leave. The plump lieutenant went away very happy, notwithstanding the two or three little rubs he had met with, and a good deal more in love than ever. And he and his companion were both thoughtful, and the walk home was quite silent, though very pleasant.

Cluffe was giving shape mentally to his designs upon Miss Rebecca's £20,000 and savings. He knew she had had high offers in her young days and refused; but those were past and gone – and grey hairs bring wisdom – and women grow more practicable as the time for action dwindles – and she was just the woman to take a fancy – and 'once the maggot bit', to go any honest length to make it fact. And Cluffe knew that he had the field to himself, and that he was a well-made, handsome, agreeable officer – not so young as to make the thing absurd, yet young enough to inspire the right sort of feeling. To be sure, there were a few things to be weighed. She was, perhaps – well, she *was* eccentric. She had troublesome pets and pastimes – he knew them all – was well stricken in years, and had a will of her own – that was all. But, then, on the other side was the money – a great and agreeable arithmetical fact not to be shaken – and she could be well-bred when she liked, and a self-possessed, dignified lady, who could sail about a room, and courtesy, and manage her fan, and lead the conversation, and do the honours as Mrs Cluffe, with a certain air of *haut ton*, and in an imposing way, to Cluffe's entire content, who liked the idea of overawing his peers.

And the two warriors, side by side, marched over the bridge in the starlight, and both by common consent, halted silently, and wheeled up to the battlement; and Puddock puffed a complacent little sigh up the river toward Belmont; and Cluffe was a good deal interested in the subject of his contemplation, and in fact, the more he thought of it, the better he liked it.

And they stood, each in his reverie, looking over the battlement toward Belmont, and hearing the hushed roll of the river, and seeing nothing but the deep blue, and the stars, and the black outline of the trees that overhung the bridge, until the enamoured Cluffe, who liked his comforts and knew what gout was, felt the chill air, and remembered suddenly that they had stopped, and ought to be in motion toward their beds, and so he shook up Puddock, and they started anew, and parted just at the Phoenix, shaking hands heartily, like two men who had just done a good stroke of business together.

Chapter Twenty

In which Mr Dangerfield visits the church of Chapelizod,
and Zekiel Irons goes fishing

Early next morning Lord Castlemallard, Dangerfield, and Nutter, rode into Chapelizod, plaguy dusty, having already made the circuit of that portion of his property which lay west of the town. They had poked into the new mills and the old mills, and contemplated the quarries and lime-kilns, and talked with Doyle about his holding, and walked over the two vacant farms, and I know not all besides. And away trotted his lordship to his breakfast in town. And Dangerfield seeing the church door open, dismounted and walked in, and Nutter did likewise.

Bob Martin was up in the gallery, I suppose, doing some good, and making a considerable knocking here and there in the pews, and walking slowly with creaking shoes. Zekiel Irons, the clerk, was down below about his business, at the communion table at the far end, lean, blue-chinned, thin-lipped, stooping over his quarto prayer books, and gliding about without noise, reverent and sinister. When they came in, Nutter led the way to Lord Castlemallard's pew, which brought them up pretty near to the spot where grave Mr Irons was prowling serenely. The pew would soon want new flooring, Mr Dangerfield thought, and the Castlemallard arms and supporters, a rather dingy piece of vainglory, overhanging the main seat on the wall, would be nothing the worse of a little fresh gilding and paint.

'There was a claim – eh – to one foot nine inches off the eastern end of the pew, on the part of – of the family – at Inchicore, I think they call it,' said Dangerfield, laying his riding-whip like a rule along the top to help his imagination – 'Hey – that would spoil the pew.'

'The claim's settled, and Mr Langley goes to the other side of the aisle,' said Nutter, nodding to Irons, who came up, and laid his long clay-coloured fingers on the top of the pew door, and one long, thin foot on the first step, and with half-closed eyes, and a half bow, he awaited their pleasure.

'The Langley family had *this* pew,' said Dangerfield, with a side nod to that next his lordship's.

'Yes, Sir,' said Irons, with the same immutable semblance of a smile, and raising neither his head nor his eyes.

'And who's got it now?'

'His reverence, Dr Walsingham.'

And so it came out, that having purchased Salmonfalls, the rector had compromised the territorial war that was on the point of breaking out among his parishioners, by exchanging with that old coxcomb Langley, the great square pew over the way, that belonged to that house, for the queer little crib in which the tenant of Inchicore had hitherto sat in state; and so there was peace, if not goodwill, in the church.

'Hey – let's see it,' said Dangerfield, crossing the aisle, with Irons at his heels, for he was a man that saw everything for himself, that ever so remotely concerned him or his business.

'We buried Lord — ' (and the title he spoke very low) 'in the vault here, just under where you stand, on Monday last, by night,' said Irons, very gently and grimly, as he stood behind Dangerfield.

A faint galvanic thrill shot up through the flagging and his firmly planted foot to his brain, as though something said, 'Ay, here I am!'

'Oh! Indeed?' said Dangerfield, dryly, making a little nod, and raising his eyebrows, and just moving a little to one side – ''Twas a nasty affair.'

He looked up, with his hands in his breeches' pockets, and read a mural tablet, whistling scarce audibly the while. It was not reverent, but he was a gentleman; and the clerk standing behind him, retained his quiet posture, and that smile that yet was not a smile, but a sort of reflected light – was it patience, or was it secret ridicule? – you could not tell: and it never changed, and somehow it was provoking.

'And some persons, I believe, had an unpleasant duty to do there,' said Dangerfield, abruptly, in the middle of his tune, and turning his spectacles fully and sternly on Mr Irons.

The clerk's head bent lower, and he shook it; and his eyes, but for a little glitter through the eyelashes, seemed to close.

''Tis a pretty church, this – a pretty town, and some good families in the neighbourhood,' said Dangerfield, briskly; 'and I dare say some trout in the river – hey? – the stream looks lively.'

'Middling, only – poor grey troutlings, Sir – not a soul cares to fish it but myself,' he answered.

'You're the clerk – eh?'

'At your service, Sir.'

'*Dublin* man? – or – '

'Born and bred in Dublin, your honour.'

'Ay – well! Irons – you've heard of Mr Dangerfield – Lord Castle-mallard's agent – I am he. Good-morning, Irons;' and he gave him half-a-crown, and he took another look round; and then he and Nutter went out of the church, and took a hasty leave of one another, and away went Nutter on his nag, to the mills. And Dangerfield, just before mounting, popped into Cleary's shop, and in his grim, laconic way, asked the proprietor, among his meal-bags and bacon, about fifty questions in less than five minutes. 'That was one of Lord Castlemallard's houses – eh – with the bad roof, and manure-heap round the corner?' – and 'Where's the pot-house they call the Salmon House? – Doing a good business – eh?' and at last – 'I'm told there's some trout in the stream. Is there anyone in the town who knows the river, and could show me the fishing? – Oh, the clerk! And what sort of fish is *he* – hey? – Oh! an honest, worthy man, is he? Very good, Sir. Then, perhaps, Mr a – perhaps, Sir, you'll do me the favour to let one of your people run down to his house, and say Mr Dangerfield, Lord Castlemallard's agent, who is staying, you know, at the Brass Castle, would be much obliged if he would bring his rod and tackle, and take a walk with him up the river, for a little angling, at ten o'clock!'

Jolly Phil Cleary was deferential, and almost nervous in his presence. The silver-haired, grim man, with his mysterious reputation for money, and that short decisive way of his, and sudden cynical chuckle, inspired a sort of awe, which made his wishes, where expressed with that intent, very generally obeyed; and, sure enough, Irons appeared, with his rod, at the appointed hour, and the interesting anglers – Piscator and his 'honest scholar', as Isaac Walton hath it – set out side by side on their ramble, in the true fraternity of the gentle craft.

The clerk had, I'm afraid, a shrew of a wife – shrill, vehement, and fluent. 'Rogue', 'old miser', 'old sneak', and a great many worse names, she called him. Good Mrs Irons was old, fat, and ugly, and she knew it; and that knowledge made her natural jealousy the fiercer. He had learned, by long experience, the best tactique under fire: he became actually taciturn; or, if he spoke, his speech was laconic and enigmatical, sometimes throwing out a proverb, and sometimes a text; and sometimes when provoked past endurance, spouting mildly a little bit of meek and venomous irony.

He loved his trout-rod and the devious banks of the Liffey, where, saturnine and alone, he filled his basket. It was his helpmate's rule, whenever she did not know to a certainty precisely what Irons was doing, to take it for granted that he was about some mischief. Her lodger, Captain Devereux, was her great resource on these occasions, and few things pleased him better than a stormy visit from his hostess in this temper. The young scapegrace would close his novel, and set down his glass of sherry and water (it sometimes smelt very like brandy, I'm afraid). To hear her rant, one would have supposed, who had not seen him, that her lank-haired, grimly partner, was the prettiest youth in the county of Dublin, and that all the comely lasses in Chapelizod and the country round were sighing and setting caps at him; and Devereux, who had a vein of satire, and loved even farce, enjoyed the heroics of the fat old slut.

'Oh! what am I to do, captain, jewel?' she bounced into the room, with flaming face and eyes swelled, and the end of her apron, with which she had been swobbing them, in her hand, while she gesticulated, with her right; 'there, he's off again to Island Bridge – the owdacious sneak! It's all that dirty hussy's doing. I'm not such a fool, but I know how to put this and that together, though he thinks I don't know of his doings; but I'll be even with you, Meg Partlet, yet – you trollop;' and all this was delivered in renewed floods of tears, and stentorian hysterics, while she shook her fat red fist in the air, at the presumed level of Meg's beautiful features.

'Nay, Madam,' said the gay captain; 'I prithee, weep not; the like discoveries, as you have read, have been made in Rome, Salamanca, Ballyporeen, Babylon, Venice, and fifty other famous cities.' He always felt in these interviews, as if she and he were extemporising a burlesque – she the Queen of Crim Tartary, and he an Archbishop in her court – and would have spoken blank verse, only he feared she might perceive it, and break up the conference.

'And what's that to the purpose? – Don't I know they're the same all over the world – nothing but brutes and barbarians.'

'But suppose, Madam, he has only gone up the river, and just taken his rod – '

'Oh! rod, indeed. I know where he wants a rod, the rascal!'

'I tell you, Madam,' urged the captain, 'you're quite in the wrong. You've discovered after twenty years' wedlock that your husband's – a man! And you're vexed: would you have him anything else?'

'You're all in a story,' she blubbered maniacally; 'there's no justice, nor feeling, nor succour for a poor abused woman; but I'll do it – I will. I'll go to his reverence – don't try to persuade me – the Rev. Hugh Walsingham, Doctor of Divinity and Rector of Chapelizod,' [she used to give him at full length whenever she threatened Zekiel with a visitation from that quarter, by way of adding ponderosity to the menace] ' – I'll go to him straight – don't think to stop me – and we'll see what he'll say;' and so she addressed herself to go.

'And when you see him, Madam, ask the learned doctor – don't ask me – believe the rector of the parish – he'll tell you, that it hath prevailed from the period at which Madam Sarah quarrelled with saucy Miss Hagar; that it hath prevailed among all the principal nations of antiquity, according to Pliny, Strabo, and the chief writers of antiquity; that Juno, Dido, Eleanor Queen of England, and Mrs Partridge, whom I read of here,' [and he pointed to the open volume of *Tom Jones*] 'each made, or thought she made, a like discovery.' And the captain delivered this slowly, with knitted brow and thoughtful face, after the manner of the erudite and simple doctor.

'Pretty Partridges, indeed! And nice game for a parish clerk!' cried the lady, returning. 'I wonder, so I do, when I look at him, and think of his goings on, how he can have the assurance to sit under the minister, and look the congregation in the face, and tune his throat, and sing the blessed psalms.'

'You are not to wonder, Madam; believe the sage, who says, *omnibus hoc vitium est cantoribus.*'

Devereux knew of old that the effect of Latin on Mrs Irons was to heighten the inflammation, and so the matron burst into whole chapters of crimination, enlivened with a sprinkling of strong words, as the sages of the law love to pepper their indictments and informations with hot adverbs and well-spiced parentheses, 'falsely', 'scandalously', 'maliciously', and *suadente diabolo*, to make them sit warm on the stomachs of a loyal judge and jury, and digest easily.

The neighbours were so accustomed to Mrs Irons's griefs, that when her voice was audible, as upon such occasions it was, upon the high road and in the back gardens, it produced next to no sensation; everybody had heard from that loud oracle every sort of story touching Irons which could well be imagined, and it was all so thoroughly published by the good lady, that curiosity on the subject was pretty well dead and gone, and her distant declamation rattled over their heads and boomed in their ears, like the distant guns and trumpets on a review day, signifying nothing.

And all this only shows what every man who has ruralised a little in his lifetime knows, more than in theory, that the golden age lingers in no corner of the earth, but is really quite gone and over every-where, and that peace and *prisca fides* have not fled to the nooks and shadows of deep valleys and bowery brooks, but flown once, and away to heaven again, and left the round world to its general curse. So it is even in pretty old villages, embowered in orchards, with hollyhocks and jessamine in front of the houses, and primeval cocks and hens pecking and scraping in the street, and the modest river dimpling and simpering among osiers and apple trees, and old ivied walls close by – you sometimes hear other things than lowing herds, and small birds singing, and purling streams; and shrill accents and voluble rhetoric will now and then trouble the fragrant air, and wake up the dim old river-god from his nap.

As to Irons, if he was all that his wife gave out, he must have been a mighty sly dog indeed; for on the whole, he presented a tolerably decent exterior to society. It is said, indeed, that he liked a grave tumbler of punch, and was sardonic and silent in his liquor; that his gait was occasionally a little queer and uncertain, as his lank figure glided home by moonlight, from the Salmon House; and that his fingers fumbled longer than need be with the latch, and his tongue, though it tried but a short and grim 'bar th' door, Marjry', or 'gi' me can'le, wench', sometimes lacked its cunning, and slipped and kept not time. There were, too, other scandals, such as the prying and profane love to shoot privily at church celebrities. Perhaps it was his reserve and sanctity that provoked them. Perhaps he was, in truth, though cautious, sometimes indiscreet. Perhaps it was fanciful Mrs Irons's jealous hullabaloos and hysterics that did it – I don't know – but people have been observed, *a propos* of him, to wink at one another, and grin, and shake their heads, and say: 'the nearer the church, you know' – and 'he so ancient, too! But 'tis an old rat that won't eat cheese,' and so forth.

Just as Mrs Irons whisked round for the seventh time to start upon her long threatened march to Dr Walsingham's study to lay her pitiful case before him, Captain Devereux, who was looking toward the Phoenix, saw the truant clerk and Mr Dangerfield turn the corner together on their return.

'Stay, Madam, here comes the traitor,' said he; 'and, on my honour, 'tis worse than we thought; for he has led my Lord Castlemallard's old agent into mischief too – and Meg Partlet has had two swains at her feet this morning; and, see, the hypocrites have got some trout in their basket, and their rods on their shoulders – and look, for all the world, as if they had only been fishing – sly rogues!'

'Well, it's all one,' said Mrs Irons, gaping from the other window, and sobering rapidly; 'if 'tisn't today, 'twill be tomorrow, I suppose; and at any rate 'tis a sin and shame to leave any poor crature in this miserable taking, not knowing but he might be drownded – or worse – dear knows it would not be much trouble to tell his wife when the gentleman wanted him – and sure for any honest matter I'd never say against it.'

Her thoughts were running upon Dangerfield, and what 'compliment' he had probably made her husband at parting; and a minute or two after this, Devereux saw her, with her riding-hood on, trudging up to the Salmon House to make inquisition after the same.

Chapter Twenty-one

Relating among other things how Dr Toole walked up to the Tiled House; and of his pleasant discourse with Mr Mervyn

Dr Sturk's spirits and temper had not become more pleasant lately. In fact he brooded more, and was more savage at home than was at all agreeable. He used to go into town oftener, and to stay there later; and his language about Toole and Nutter, when there was none but submissive little Mrs Sturk by, was more fierce and coarse than ever. To hear him, then, one would have supposed that they were actually plotting to make away with him, and that in self-defence he must smite them hip and thigh. Then, beside their moral offensiveness, they were such 'idiots', and 'noodles', and botching and blundering right and left, so palpably to the danger and ruin of their employers, that no man of conscience could sit easy and see it going on; and all this simply because he had fixed his affections upon the practice of the one, and the agency of the other. For Sturk had, in his own belief, a genius for business of every sort. Everybody on whom his insolent glance fell, who had any sort of business to do, did it wrong, and was a 'precious disciple', or a 'goose', or a 'born jackass', and excited his scoffing chuckle. And little Mrs Sturk, frightened and admiring, used to say, while he grinned and muttered, and tittered into the fire, with his great shoulders buried in his balloon-backed chair, his heels over the fender and his hands in his breeches' pockets – 'But, Barney, you know, you're so clever – there's no-one like you!' And he was fond of just nibbling at speculations in a small safe way, and used to pull out a roll of bank-notes, when he was lucky, and show his winnings to his wife, and chuckle and swear over them, and boast and rail, and tell her, if it was not for the cursed way his time was cut up with hospital, and field days, and such trumpery regimental duties, he could make a fortune while other men were thinking of it; and he very nearly believed it. And he was, doubtless, clear-headed, though wrong-headed, too, at times, and very energetic; but his genius was for pushing men out of their places to make way for himself.

But with all that he had the good brute instincts too, and catered diligently for his brood, and their 'dam' – and took a gruff unacknowledged pride in seeing his wife well-dressed – and had a strong liking for her – and thanked her in his soul for looking after things so well; and thought often about his boys, and looked sharply after their education; and was an efficient and decisive head of a household; and had no vices nor expensive indulgences; and was a hard but tolerably just man to deal with.

All this time his uneasiness and puzzle about Dangerfield continued, and, along with other things, kept him awake often to unseasonable hours at night. He did not tell Mrs Sturk. In fact, he was a man who, though on most occasions he gave the wife of his bosom what he called 'his mind' freely enough, yet did not see fit to give her a great deal of his confidence.

Dangerfield had his plans too. Who has not? Nothing could be more compact and modest than his household. He had just a housekeeper and two maids, who looked nearly as old, and a valet, and a groom, who slept at the Phoenix, and two very pretty horses at livery in the same place. All his appointments were natty and complete, and his servants, everyone, stood in awe of him; for no lip or eye-service would go down with that severe, prompt, and lynx-eyed gentleman. And his groom, among the coachmen and other experts of the Salmon House, used to brag of his hunters in England; and his man, of his riches, and his influence with Lord Castlemallard.

In England, Dangerfield, indeed, spent little more money than he did in Chapelizod, except in his stable; and Lord Castlemallard, who admired his stinginess, as he did everything else about him, used to say: 'He's a wonder of the world! How he retains his influence over all the people he knows without ever giving one among them so much as a mutton-chop or a glass of sherry in his house, I can't conceive. *I* couldn't do it, I know.' But he had ultimate plans, if not of splendour, at least of luxury. His tastes, and perhaps some deeper feelings, pointed to the continent, and he had purchased a little paradise on the Lake of Geneva, where was an Eden of fruits and flowers, and wealth of marbles and coloured canvas, and wonderful wines maturing in his cellars, and aquaria for his fish, and ice-houses and baths, and I know not what refinements of old Roman villa-luxury beside – among which he meant to pass the honoured evening of his days; with just a few more thousands, and, as he sometimes thought, perhaps a wife. He had not quite made up his mind; but he had come to the time when a man must forthwith accept matrimony frankly, or, if he be wise, shake hands with bleak celibacy, and content himself for his earthly future with monastic jollity and solitude.

It is a maxim with charitable persons – and no more than a recognition of a great constitutional axiom – to assume, in the absence of proof to the contrary, that every British subject is an honest man. Now, if we had gone to Lord Castlemallard for his character – and who more competent to give him one – we know very well what we should have heard about Dangerfield; and, on the other hand, we have never found him out – have we, kind reader? – in a shabby action or unworthy thought; and, therefore, it leaves upon our mind an unpleasant impression about that Mr Mervyn, who arrived in the dark, attending upon a coffin as mysterious as himself, and now lives solitarily in the haunted house near Ballyfermot, that the omniscient Dangerfield should follow him, when they pass upon the road, with that peculiar stern glance of surprise which seemed to say – 'Was ever such audacity conceived? Is the man mad?'

But Dangerfield did not choose to talk about him – if indeed he had anything to disclose – though the gentlemen at the club pressed him often with questions, which however, he quietly parried, to the signal vexation of active little Dr Toole, who took up and dropped, in turn, all sorts of curious theories about the young stranger. Lord Castlemallard knew all about him, too, but his lordship was high and huffy, and hardly ever in Chapelizod, except on horseback, and two or three times in the year at a grand dinner at the Artillery mess. And when Mervyn was mentioned he always talked of something else, rather imperiously, as though he said, 'You'll please to observe that upon that subject I don't choose to speak.' And as for Dr Walsingham, when he thought it right to hold his tongue upon a given matter, thumbscrews could not squeeze it from him.

In short, our friend Toole grew so feverish under his disappointment that he made an excuse of old Tim Molloy's toothache to go up in person to the Tiled House, in the hope of meeting the young gentleman, and hearing something from him (the servants, he already knew, were as much in the dark as he) to alleviate his distress. And, sure enough, his luck stood him in stead; for, as he was going away, having pulled out old Molloy's grinder to give a colour to his visit, who should he find upon the steps of the hall-door but the pale, handsome young gentleman himself.

Dr Toole bowed low, and grinned with real satisfaction, reminded him of their interview at the Phoenix, and made by way of apology for his appearance at the Tiled House, a light and kind allusion to poor old Tim, of whose toothache he spoke affectionately, and with water in his eyes – for he half believed for the moment what he was saying – declared how he remembered him when he did not come up to Tim's knee-buckle, and would walk that far any day, and a bit further too, he hoped, to relieve the poor old boy in a less matter. And finding that Mr Mervyn was going toward Chapelizod, he begged him not to delay on his account, and accompanied him down the Ballyfermot road, entertaining him by the way with an inexhaustible affluence of Chapelizod anecdote and scandal, at which the young man stared a good deal, and sometimes even appeared impatient: but the doctor did not perceive it, and rattled on; and told him moreover, everything about himself and his belongings with a minute and voluble frankness, intended to shame the suspicious reserve of the stranger. But nothing came; and being by this time grown bolder, he began a more direct assault, and told him, with a proper scorn of the village curiosity, all the theories which the Chapelizod gossips had spun about him.

'And they say, among other things, that you're not – a – in fact – there's a mystery – a something – about your birth, you know,' said Toole, in a tone implying pity and contempt for his idle townsfolk.

'They lie, then!' cried the young man, stopping short, more fiercely than was pleasant, and fixing his great lurid eyes upon the cunning face of the doctor; and, after a pause, 'Why can't they let me and my concerns alone, Sir?'

'But there's no use in saying so, I can tell you,' exclaimed little Toole, recovering his feet in an instant. 'Why, I suppose there isn't so tattling, prying, lying, scandalous a little colony of Christians on earth: eyes, ears, and mouths all open, Sir; heads busy, tongues wagging; lots of old maids, by Jove; ladies' women, and gentlemen's gentlemen, and drawers and footmen; club talk, Sir, and mess-table talk, and talk on band days, talk over cards, talk at home, Sir – talk in the streets – talk – talk; by Jupiter Tonans! 'tis enough to bother one's ears, and make a man envy Robinson Crusoe!'

'So I do, Sir, if we were rid of his parrot,' answered Mervyn: and with a dry 'I wish you a good-morning, doctor – doctor – a – *Sir*' – turned sharply from him up the Palmerstown-road.

'Going to Belmont,' murmured little Toole, with his face a little redder than usual, and stopping in an undignified way for a moment at the corner to look after him. 'He's close – plaguy close; and Miss Rebecca Chattesworth knows nothing about him neither – I wonder does she though – and doesn't seem to care even. He's not there for nothing though. *Someone* makes him welcome, depend on't,' and he winked to himself. 'A plaguy high stomach, too, by Jove. I bet you fifty, if he stays here three months, he'll be at swords or pistols with some of our hot bloods. And whatever his secret is – and I dare say 'tisn't worth knowing – the people here will ferret it out at last, I warrant you. There's small good in making all the fuss he does about it; if he but knew all, there's no such thing as a secret here – hang the one have *I*, I know, just because there's no use in trying. The whole town knows when I've tripe for dinner, and where I have a patch or a darn. And when I got the fourteen pigeons at Darkey's-bridge, the birds were not ten minutes on my kitchen table when old Widow Foote sends her maid and her compliments, as she knew my pie-dish only held a dozen, to beg the two odd birds. Secret, indeed!' and he whistled a bar or two contemptuously, which subsided into dejected silence, and he muttered, 'I wish I knew it', and walked over the bridge gloomily; and he roared more fiercely on smaller occasions than usual at his dogs on the way home, and they squalled oftener and louder.

Now, for some reason or other, Dangerfield had watched the growing intimacy between Mervyn and Miss Gertrude Chattesworth with an evil eye. He certainly did know something about this Mr Mervyn, with his beautiful sketches, and his talk about Italy, and his fine music. And his own spectacles had carefully surveyed Miss Chattesworth, and she had passed the ordeal satisfactorily. And Dangerfield thought, 'These people can't possibly suspect the actual state of the case, and who and what this gentleman is *to my certain knowledge*; and 'tis a pity so fine a young lady should be sacrificed for want of a word spoken in season.' And when he had decided upon a point, it was not easy to make him stop or swerve.

Chapter Twenty-two

Telling how Mr Mervyn fared at Belmont, and of a pleasant little déjeuner by the margin of the Liffey

Now it happened that on the very same day, the fashion of Dr Walsingham's and of Aunt Rebecca's countenances were one and both changed towards Mr Mervyn, much to his chagrin and puzzle. The doctor, who met him near his own house on the bridge, was something distant in manner, and looked him in the face with very grave eyes, and seemed sad, and as if he had something on his mind, and laid his hand upon the young man's arm, and addressed himself to speak; but glancing round his shoulder, and seeing people astir, and that they were under observation, he reserved himself.

That both the ladies of Belmont looked as if they had heard some strange story, each in her own way. Aunt Rebecca received the young man without a smile, and was unaccountably upon her high horse, and said some dry and sharp things, and looked as if she could say more, and coloured menacingly, and, in short, was odd, and very nearly impertinent. And Gertrude, though very gentle and kind, seemed also much graver, and looked pale, and her eyes larger and more excited, and altogether like a brave young lady who had fought a battle without crying. And Mervyn saw all this and pondered on it, and went away soon; the iron entered into his soul.

Aunt Rebecca was so occupied with her dogs, squirrels, parrots, old women, and convicts, that her eyes being off the cards, she saw little of the game; and when a friendly whisper turned her thoughts that way, and it flashed upon her that tricks and honours were pretty far gone, she never remembered that she had herself to blame for the matter, but turned upon her poor niece with 'Sly creature!' and so forth. And while owing to this inattention, Gertrude had lost the benefit of her sage Aunt Rebecca's counsels altogether, her venerable but frisky old grandmother – Madam Nature – it was to be feared, might have profited by the occasion to giggle and whistle her own advice in her ear, and been indifferently well obeyed. I really don't pretend to say –

maybe there was nothing, or next to nothing in it; or if there was, Miss Gertrude herself might not quite know. And if she did suspect she liked him, ever so little, she had no-one but Lilias Walsingham to tell; and I don't know that young ladies are always quite candid upon these points. Some, at least, I believe, don't make confidences until their secrets become insupportable. However, Aunt Rebecca was now wide awake, and had trumpeted a pretty shrill *reveiller*. And Gertrude had started up, her elbow on the pillow, and her large eyes open; and the dream, I suppose, was shivered and flown, and something rather ghastly at her side.

Coming out of church, Dr Walsingham asked Mervyn to take a turn with him in the park – and so they did – and the doctor talked with him seriously and kindly on that broad plateau. The young man walked darkly beside him, and they often stopped outright. When, on their return, they came near the Chapelizod gate, and Parson's lodge, and the duck-pond, the doctor was telling him that marriage is an affair of the heart – also a spiritual union – and, moreover, a mercantile partnership – and he insisted much upon this latter view – and told him what and how strict was the practice of the ancient Jews, the people of God, upon this particular point. Dr Walsingham had made a love-match, was the most imprudent and open-handed of men, and always preaching to others against his own besetting sin. To hear him talk, indeed, you would have supposed he was a usurer. Then Mr Mervyn, who looked a little pale and excited, turned the doctor about, and they made another little circuit, while he entered somewhat into his affairs and prospects, and told him something about an appointment in connection with the Embassy at Paris, and said he would ask him to read some letters about it; and the doctor seemed a little shaken; and so they parted in a very friendly but grave way.

When Mervyn had turned his back upon Belmont, on the occasion of the unpleasant little visit I mentioned just now, the ladies had some words in the drawing-room.

'I have *not* coquetted, Madam,' said Miss Gertrude, haughtily.

'Then I'm to presume you've been serious; and I take the liberty to ask how far this affair has proceeded?' said Aunt Rebecca, firmly, and laying her gloved hand and folded fan calmly on the table.

'I really forget,' said the young lady, coldly.

'Has he made a declaration of love?' demanded the aunt, the two red spots on her cheeks coming out steadily, and helping the flash of her eyes.

'Certainly not,' answered the young lady, with a stare of haughty surprise that was quite unaffected.

At the pleasant luncheon and dance on the grass that the officers gave, in that pretty field by the river, half-a-dozen of the young people had got beside the little brook that runs simpering and romping into the river just there. Women are often good-natured in love matters where rivalry does not mix, and Miss Gertrude, all on a sudden, found herself alone with Mervyn. Aunt Becky, from under the ash trees at the other end of the field, with great distinctness, for she was not a bit near-sighted, and considerable uneasiness, saw their *tête-à-tête*. It was out of the question getting up in time to prevent the young people speaking their minds if so disposed, and she thought she perceived that in the young man's bearing, which looked like a pleading and eagerness, and 'Gertrude's put out a good deal – I see by her plucking at those flowers – but my head to a China orange – the girl won't think of him. She's not a young woman to rush into a horrible folly, hand-over-head,' thought Aunt Becky; and then she began to think they were talking very much at length indeed, and to regret that she had not started at once from her post for the place of meeting; and one, and two, and three minutes passed, and perhaps some more, and Aunt Becky began to grow wroth, and was on the point of marching upon them, when they began slowly to walk towards the group who were plucking bunches of woodbine from the hedge across the little stream, at the risk of tumbling in, and distributing the flowers among the ladies, amidst a great deal of laughing and gabble. Then Miss Gertrude made Mr Mervyn rather a haughty and slight salutation, her aunt thought, and so dismissed him; he, too, made a bow, but a very low one, and walked straight off to the first lady he saw.

This happened to be mild little Mrs Sturk, and he talked a good deal to her, but restlessly, and, as it seemed, with a wandering mind; and afterwards he conversed, with an affectation of interest – it was only that – Aunt Becky, who observed him with some curiosity, thought – for a few minutes with Lilias Walsingham; and afterwards he talked with an effort, and so much animation and such good acceptance [though it was plain, Aunt Becky said, that he did not listen to one word she said] to the fair Magnolia, that O'Flaherty had serious thoughts of horse-whipping him when the festivities were over – for, as he purposed informing him, his 'ungentlemanlike intherfarence'.

'He has got his quietus,' thought Aunt Becky, with triumph; 'this brisk, laughing carriage, and heightened colour, a woman of experience can see through at a glance.'

Yes, all this frisking and skipping is but the hypocrisy of bleeding vanity – *haeret lateri* – they are just the flush, wriggle, and hysterics of suppressed torture.

Then came her niece, cold and stately, with steady eye and a slight flush, and altogether the air of the conscientious young matron who has returned from the nursery, having there administered the discipline; and so she sat down beside her aunt, serene and silent, and, the little glow passed away, pale and still.

'Well, he *has* spoken?' said her aunt to her, in a sharp aside.

'Yes,' answered the young lady, icily.

'And has had his answer?'

'Yes – and I beg, Aunt Rebecca, the subject may be allowed to drop.' The young lady's eyes encountered her aunt's so directly and were so fully charged with the genuine Chattesworth lightning, that Miss Rebecca, unused to such demonstrations, averted hers, and with a slight sarcastic inclination, and, 'Oh! your servant, young lady,' beckoning with her fan grandly to little Puddock, who was hovering with other designs in the vicinity, and taking his arm, though he was not forgiven, but only employed – a distinction often made by good Queen Elizabeth – marched to the marquee, where, it was soon evident, the plump lieutenant was busy in commending, according to their merits, the best bits of the best *plats* on the table.

'So dear Aunt Becky has forgiven Puddock,' said Devereux, who was sauntering up to the tent between O'Flaherty and Cluffe, and little suspecting that he was descanting upon the intended Mrs Cluffe – 'and they are celebrating the reconciliation over a jelly and a pupton. I love Aunt Rebecca, I tell you – I don't know what we should do without her. She's impertinent, and often nearly insupportable; but isn't she the most placable creature on earth? I venture to say I might kill you, Lieutenant O'Flaherty – of course, with your permission, Sir – and she'd forgive me tomorrow morning! And she really does princely things – doesn't she? She set up that ugly widow – what's her name? – twice in a shop in Dame Street, and gave two hundred pounds to poor Scamper's orphan, and actually pensions that old miscreant, Wagget, who ought to be hanged – and never looks for thanks or compliments, or upbraids her ingrates with past kindnesses. She's noble – Aunt Becky's every inch a gentleman!'

By this time they had reached the tent, and the hearty voice of the general challenged them from the shade, as he filliped a little chime merrily on his empty glass.

Chapter Twenty-three

Which concerns the grand dinner at the King's House, and who were there, and something of their talk, reveries, disputes, and general jollity

It was about this time that the dinner-party at the King's House came off. Old Colonel and Mrs Stafford were hospitable, if not very entertaining, and liked to bring their neighbours together, without ceremony, round a saddle of mutton and a gooseberry pie, and other such solid comforts; and then, hey for a round game! – for the young people, Pope Joan, or what you please, in the drawing-room, with lots of flirting and favouritism, and a jolly little supper of broiled bones and whipt cream, and toasts and sentiments, with plenty of sly allusions and honest laughter all round the table. But twice or thrice in the year the worthy couple made a more imposing gathering at the King's House, and killed the fatted calf, and made a solemn feast to the bigwigs and the notables of Chapelizod, with just such a sprinkling of youngsters as sufficed to keep alive the young people whom they brought in their train. There was eating of venison and farced turkeys, and other stately fare; and they praised the colonel's claret, and gave the servants their 'veils' in the hall, and drove away in their carriages, with flambeaux and footmen, followed by the hearty good-night of the host from the hall-door steps, and amazing the quiet little town with their rattle and glare.

Dinner was a five o'clock affair in those days, and the state parlour was well-filled. There was old Bligh from the Magazine – I take the guests in order of arrival – and the Chattesworths, and the Walsinghams; and old Dowager Lady Glenvarlogh – Colonel Stratford's cousin – who flashed out in the evening sun from Dublin in thunder and dust and her carriage-and-four, bringing her mild little country niece, who watched her fat painted aunt all the time of dinner, with the corners of her frightened little eyes, across the table; and spoke sparingly, and eat with diffidence; and Captain Devereux was there; and the next beau who appeared was – of all men in the world – Mr Mervyn! And Aunt Becky watched, and saw with satisfaction, that he and Gertrude met as formally and coldly as she could have desired. And then there was an elaborate macaroni, one of the Lord Lieutenant's household – Mr Beauchamp; and last, Lord Castlemallard, who liked very well to be the chief man in the room, and dozed after dinner serenely in that consciousness, and loved to lean back upon his sofa in the drawing-room, and gaze in a dozing, smiling, Turkish reverie, after Gertrude Chattesworth and pretty Lilias, whom he admired; and when either came near enough, he would take her hand and say – 'Well, child, how do you do? – and why don't you speak to your old friend? You charming rogue, you know I remember you no bigger than your fan. And what mischief have you been about – eh? What mischief have you been about, I say, young gentlewoman? Turning all the pretty fellows' heads, I warrant you – eh! – turning their heads?' And he used to talk this sort of talk very slowly, and to hold their hands all the while, and even after this talk was exhausted, and grin sleepily, and wag his head, looking with a glittering, unpleasant gaze in their faces all the time. But at present we are all at dinner, in the midst of the row which even the best-bred people, assembled in sufficient numbers, will make over that meal.

Devereux could not help seeing pretty Lilias over the way, who was listening to handsome Mervyn, as it seemed, with interest, and talking also her pleasant little share. He was no dunce, that Mervyn, nor much of a coxcomb, and certainly no clown, Devereux thought, but as fine a gentleman, to speak honestly, and as handsome, as well dressed, and as pleasant to listen to, with that sweet low voice and piquant smile, as any. Besides he could draw, and had more yards of French and English verses by rote than Aunt Becky owned of Venetian lace and satin ribbons, and was more of a scholar than he. He? *He*! – Why 'he'? What the deuce had Devereux to do with it – was he vexed? – A fiddle-stick! He began to flag with Miss Ward, the dowager's niece, and was glad when the refined Beauchamp, at her other side, took her up, and entertained her with Lady Carrickmore's ball and the masquerade, and the last levee, and the withdrawing-room. There are said to have been persons who could attend to half-a-dozen different conversations going on together, and take a rational part in them all, and indulge, all the time, in a distinct consecutive train of thought beside. I dare say, Mr Morphy the chess-player, would find no difficulty in it. But Devereux was not by any means competent to the feat, though there was one conversation, perhaps, the thread of which he would gladly have caught up and disentangled. So the talk at top and bottom and both sides of the table, with its cross-readings, and muddle, and uproar, changed hands, and whisked and rioted, like a dance of Walpurgis, in his lonely brain.

What he heard, on the whole, was very like this – 'hubble-bubble-rubble-dubble – the great match of shuttlecock played between the gentlemen of the north and those of hubble-bubble – the Methodist persuasion; but – ha-ha-ha! – a squeeze of a lemon – rubble-dubble – ha-ha-ha! – wicked man – hubble-bubble – force-meat balls and yolks of eggs – rubble-dubble – musket balls from a steel cross-bow – upon my – hubble-bubble – throwing a sheep's eye – ha-ha-ha – rubble-dubble – at the two remaining heads on Temple Bar – hubble-bubble – and the duke left by his will – rubble-dubble – a quid of tobacco in a brass snuff-box – hubble-bubble – and my Lady Rostrevor's very sweet upon – rubble-dubble – old Alderman Wallop of John's-lane – hubble-bubble – ha-ha-ha – from Jericho to Bethany, where David, Joab, and – rubble-dubble – the whole party upset in the mud in a chaise marine – and – hubble-bubble – shake a little white pepper over them – and – rubble-dubble – his name is Solomon – hubble-bubble – ha-ha-ha – the poor old thing dying of cold, and not a stitch of clothes to cover her nakedness – rubble-dubble – play or pay, on Finchley Common – hubble-bubble – most melancholy truly – ha-ha-ha! – rubble-dubble – and old Lady Ruth is ready to swear she never – hubble-bubble – served High Sheriff for the county of Down in the reign of Queen Anne – rubble-dubble – and Dr and Mrs Sturk – hubble-bubble – Secretaries of State in the room of the Duke of Grafton and General Conway – rubble-dubble – venerable prelate – ha-ha-ha! Hubble-bubble – filthy creature – hubble-bubble-rubble-dubble.'

And this did not make him much wiser or merrier. Love has its fevers, its recoveries, and its relapses. The patient – nay even his nurse and his doctor, if he has taken to himself such officers in his distress – may believe the malady quite cured – the passion burnt out – the flame extinct – even the smoke quite over, when a little chance puff of rivalry blows the white ashes off, and, lo! the old liking is still smouldering. But this was not Devereux's case. He remembered when his fever – not a love one – and his leave of absence at Scarborough, and that long continental tour of hers with Aunt Rebecca and Gertrude Chattesworth, had carried the grave, large-eyed little girl away, and hid her from his sight for more than a year, very nearly *two* years, the strange sort of thrill and surprise with which he saw her again – tall and slight, and very beautiful – no, not *beautiful*, perhaps, if you go to rule and compass, and Greek trigono-metrical theories; but there was an indescribable prettiness in all her features, and movements, and looks, higher and finer and sweeter than all the canons of statuary will give you.

How prettily she stands! How prettily she walks! What a sensitive, spirited, clear-tinted face it is! This was pretty much the interpret-ation of his reverie, as Colonel Stafford's large and respectable party obligingly vanished for a while into air. Is it sad? I think it *is* sad – I don't know – and how sweetly and how drolly it lighted up; at that moment he saw her smile – the pleasant mischief in it – the dark violet glance – the wonderful soft dimple in chin and cheek – the little crimson mouth, and its laughing coronet of pearls – and then all earnest again, and still so animated! What feminine intelligence and character there is in that face! – 'tis pleasanter to me than convers-ation – 'tis a fairy tale, or – or a dream, it's so interesting – I never know, you see, what's coming – is not it wonderful? What is she talking about now? – what does it signify? – she's so strangely beauti-ful – she's like those Irish melodies, I can't reach all their meaning; I only know their changes keep me silent, and are playing with my heartstrings.

Devereux's contemplation of the animated *tête-à-tête*, for such, in effect, it seemed to him at the other side of the table, was, however, by no means altogether pleasurable. He began to think Mervyn conceited; there was a 'provoking probability of succeeding' about him, and altogether something that was beginning to grow offensive and odious.

'She knows well enough I like her,' so his liking said in confidence to his vanity, and even *he* hardly overheard them talk; 'better a great deal than I knew it myself, till old Strafford got together this con-founded stupid dinner-party (he caught Miss Chattesworth glancing at him with a peculiar look of enquiry). Why the plague did he ask *me* here? It was Puddock's turn, and he likes venison and compots, and – and – but 'tis like them – the women fall in love with the man who's in love with himself, like Narcissus yonder – and they can't help it – not they – and what care I? – Hang it! I say, what is't to me? – and yet – if she were to leave it – what a queer unmeaning place Chapelizod would be!'

'And what do you say to that, Captain Devereux?' cried the hearty voice of old General Chattesworth, and, with a little shock, the captain dropped from the clouds into his chair, and a clear view of the larded fowl before him, and his own responsibilities and situation: 'Some turkey!' he said, awaking, and touching the carving-knife and fork, with a smile and a bow; and he mingled once more in the business and bustle of life.

And soon there came in the general talk and business one of those sudden lulls which catch speakers unawares, and Mr Beauchamp was found saying, 'I saw her play on Thursday, and, upon my honour, the Bellamy is a mockery, a skeleton and a spectacle.'

'That's no reason,' said Aunt Becky, who, as usual, had got up a skirmish, and was firing away in the cause of Mossop and Smock-alley play-house; 'why, she would be fraudulently arrested in her own chair, on her way to the play-house, by the contrivance of the rogue Barry, and that wicked mountebank, Woodward.'

'You're rather hard upon them, Madam,' said Mrs Colonel Stafford, who stood up for Crow-street, with a slight elevation of her chin.

'Very true, indeed, Mistress Chattesworth,' cried the dowager, overlooking Madam Stafford's parenthesis, and tapping an applause with her fan, and, at the same time, rewarding the champion of Smock-alley, for she was one of the faction, with one of her large, painted smiles, followed by a grave and somewhat supercilious glance at the gentleman of the household; 'and I don't believe *they*, at least, can think her a spectacle, and – a – the like, or they'd hardly have conspired to lock her in a sponging-house, while she should have been in the play-house. What say you, Mistress Chattesworth?'

'Ha, ha! No, truly, my lady; but you know she's unfortunate, and a stranger, and the good people in this part of the world improve so safe an opportunity of libelling a friendless gentlewoman.'

This little jet of vitriol was intended for the eye of the Castle beau; but he, quite innocent of the injection, went on serenely, 'So they do, upon my honour, Madam, tell prodigious naughty tales about her: yet upon my life I do pity her from my soul: how that fellow Calcraft, by Jove – she says, you know, she's married to him, but we know better – he has half broken her heart, and treated her with most refined meanness, as I live; in the green-room, where she looks an infinity worse than on the stage, she told me – '

'I dare say,' said Aunt Becky, rather stiffly, pulling him up; for though she had fought a round for poor George Anne Bellamy for Mossop's sake, she nevertheless had formed a pretty just estimate of that faded, good-natured, and insolvent demirep, and rather recoiled from any anecdotes of her telling.

'And Calcraft gave her his likeness in miniature,' related the macaroni, never minding; 'set round with diamonds, and, will you believe it? when she came to examine it, they were not brilliants, but rose-diamonds – despicable fellow!'

Here the talk began to spring up again in different places, and the conversation speedily turned into what we have heard it before, and the roar and confusion became universal, and swallowed up what remained of poor George Anne's persecutions.

Chapter Twenty-four

In which two young persons understand one another better, perhaps,
than ever they did before, without saying so

And now the ladies, with their gay plumage, have flown away like
foreign birds of passage, and the jolly old priests of Bacchus, in
the parlour, make their libations of claret; and the young fellows,
after a while, seeing a gathering of painted fans, and rustling hoops,
and fluttering laces, upon the lawn, and a large immigration of
hilarious neighbours besides, and two serious fiddlers, and a black
fellow with a tambourine preparing for action, and the warm glitter
of the western sun among the green foliage about the window,
could stand it no longer, but stole away, notwithstanding a hospitable remonstrance and a protest from old Strafford, to join the
merry muster.

'The young bucks will leave their claret,' said Lord Castlemallard;
'and truly 'tis a rare fine wine, colonel, a mighty choice claret truly,'
[and the colonel bowed low, and smiled a rugged purple smile in
spite of himself, for his claret *was* choice] 'all won't do when Venus
beckons – when she beckons – ha, ha – all won't do, Sir – at the first
flutter of a petticoat, and the invitation of a pair of fine eyes – fine
eyes, colonel – by Jupiter, they're off – you can't keep 'em – I say
your wine won't keep 'em – they'll be off, Sir – peeping under the
hoods, the dogs will – and whispering their wicked nonsense, Dr
Walsingham – ha, ha – and your wine, I say – your claret, colonel,
won't hold 'em – 'twas once so with us – eh, general? – ha! ha! And
we must forgive 'em now.'

And he shoved round his chair lazily, with a left-backward wheel,
so as to command the window, for he liked to see the girls dance, the
little rogues! – with his claret and his French rappee at his elbow;
and he did not hear General Chattesworth, who was talking of the
new comedy called *The Clandestine Marriage*, and how 'the prologue
touches genteelly on the loss of three late geniuses – Hogarth, Quin,
and Cibber – and the epilogue is the picture of a polite company;' for

the tambourine and the fiddles were going merrily, and the lasses and lads in motion.

Aunt Becky and Lilias were chatting just under those pollard osiers by the river. She was always gentle with Lily, and somehow unlike the pugnacious Aunt Becky, whose attack was so spirited and whose thrust so fierce; and when Lily told a diverting little story – and she was often very diverting – Aunt Becky used to watch her pleasant face, with such a droll, good-natured smile; and she used to pat her on the cheek, and look so glad to see her when they met, and often as if she would say – 'I admire you a great deal more, and I am a great deal fonder of you than you think; but you know brave stoical Aunt Becky can't say all that – it would not be in character, you know.' And the old lady knew how good she was to the poor, and she liked her spirit, and candour, and honour – it was so uncommon, and somehow angelic, she thought. 'Little Lily's so true!' she used to say; and perhaps there was there a noble chord of sympathy between the young girl, who had no taste for battle, and the daring Aunt Becky.

I think Devereux liked her for liking Lily – he thought it was for her own sake. Of course, he was often unexpectedly set upon and tomahawked by the impetuous lady; but the gay captain put on his scalp again, and gathered his limbs together, and got up in high good humour, and shook himself and smiled, after his dismemberment, like one of the old soldiers of the Walhalla – and they were never the worse friends.

So, turning his back upon the fiddles and tambourine, Gypsy Devereux sauntered down to the river-bank, and to the osiers, where the ladies are looking down the river, and a bluebell, not half so blue as her own deep eyes, in Lilias' fingers; and the sound of their gay talk came mixed with the twitter and clear evening songs of the small birds. By those same osiers, that see so many things, and tell no tales, there will yet be a parting. But its own sorrow suffices to the day. And now it is a summer sunset, and all around dappled gold and azure, and sweet, dreamy sounds; and Lilias turns her pretty head, and sees him – and oh! was it fancy, or did he see just a little flushing of the colour on her cheek – and her lashes seemed to drop a little, and out came her frank little hand. And Devereux leaned on the paling there, and chatted his best sense and nonsense, I dare say; and they laughed and talked about all sorts of things; and he sang for them a queer little snatch of a ballad, of an enamoured captain, the course of whose true love ran not smooth –

The river ran between them,
And she looked upon the stream,
And the soldier looked upon her
As a dreamer on a dream.
'Believe me – oh! believe,'
He sighed, 'you peerless maid;
My honour is pure,
And my true love sure,
Like the white plume in my hat,
And my shining blade.'

The river ran between them,
And she smiled upon the stream,
Like one that smiles at folly –
A dreamer on a dream.
'I do not trust your promise,
I will not be betrayed;
For your faith is light,
And your cold wit bright,
Like the white plume in your hat,
And your shining blade.'

The river ran between them,
And he rode beside the stream,
And he turned away and parted,
As a dreamer from his dream.
And his comrade brought his message,
From the field where he was laid –
Just his name to repeat,
And to lay at her feet
The white plume from his hat
And his shining blade.*

And he sang it in a tuneful and plaintive tenor, that had power to make rude and ridiculous things pathetic; and Aunt Rebecca thought he was altogether very agreeable. But it was time she should see what Miss Gertrude was about; and Devereux and Lily were such very old friends that she left them to their devices.

'I like the river,' says he; 'it has a soul, Miss Lily, and a character. There are no river *gods*, but nymphs. Look at that river, Miss Lilias;

* These little verses have been several times set to music, and last and very sweetly, by Miss Elizabeth Philp.

what a girlish spirit. I wish she would reveal herself; I could lose my heart to her, I believe – if, indeed, I could be in love with anything, you know. Look at the river – is not it feminine? It's sad and it's merry, musical and sparkling – and oh, so deep! Always changing, yet still the same. 'Twill show you the trees, or the clouds, or yourself, or the stars; and it's so clear and so dark, and so sunny, and – so cold. It tells everything, and yet nothing. It's so pure, and so playful, and so tuneful, and so coy, yet so mysterious and *fatal*. I sometimes think, Miss Lilias, I've seen this river spirit; and she's like – very like you!'

And so he went on; and she was more silent and more a listener than usual. I don't know all that was passing in pretty Lilias's fancy – in her heart – near the hum of the waters and the spell of that musical voice. Love speaks in allegories and a language of signs; looks and tones tell his tale most truly. So Devereux's talk held her for a while in a sort of trance, melancholy and delightful. There must be, of course, the affinity – the rapport – the what you please to call it – to begin with – it matters not how faint and slender; and then the spell steals on and grows. See how the poor little woodbine, or the jessamine, or the vine, will lean towards the rugged elm, appointed by Virgil, in his epic of husbandry (I mean no pun) for their natural support – the elm, you know it hath been said, is the gentleman of the forest – see all the little tendrils turn his way silently, and cling, and long years after, maybe, clothe the broken and blighted tree with a fragrance and beauty not its own. Those feeble feminine plants, are, it sometimes seems to me, the strength and perfection of creation – strength perfected in weakness; the ivy, green among the snows of winter, and clasping together in its true embrace the loveless ruin; and the vine that maketh glad the heart of man amidst the miseries of life. I must not be mistaken, though, for Devereux's talk was only a tender sort of trifling, and Lilias had said nothing to encourage him to risk more; but she now felt sure that Devereux liked her – that, indeed, he took a deep interest in her – and somehow she was happy.

And little Lily drew towards the dancers, and Devereux by her side – not to join in the frolic; it was much pleasanter talking. But the merry thrum and jingle of the tambourine, and vivacious squeak of the fiddles, and the incessant laughter and prattle of the gay company were a sort of protection. And perhaps she fancied that within that pleasant and bustling circle, the discourse, which was to her so charming, might be longer maintained. It was music heard in a dream – strange and sweet – and might never come again.

Chapter Twenty-five

In which the sun sets, and the merrymaking is kept up by candle-light in the King's House, and Lily receives a warning which she does not comprehend

Dr Toole, without whom no jollification of any sort could occur satisfactorily in Chapelizod or the country round, was this evening at the King's House, of course, as usual, with his eyes about him and his tongue busy; and at this moment he was setting Cluffe right about Devereux's relation to the title and estates of Athenry. His uncle Roland Lord Athenry was, as everybody knew, a lunatic – Toole used to call him Orlando Furioso: and Lewis, his first cousin by his father's elder brother – the heir presumptive – was very little better, and reported every winter to be dying. He spends all his time – his spine being made, it is popularly believed, of gristle – stretched on his back upon a deal board, cutting out paper figures with a pair of scissors. Toole used to tell them at the club, when alarming letters arrived about the health of the noble uncle and his hopeful nephew – the heir apparent – 'That's the gentleman whose backbone's made of jelly – eh, Puddock? Two letters come, by Jove, announcing that Dick Devereux's benefit is actually fixed for the Christmas holidays, when his cousin undertakes to die for positively the last time, and his uncle will play in the most natural manner conceivable, the last act of *King Lear*.' In fact, this family calamity was rather a cheerful subject among Devereux's friends; and certainly Devereux had no reason to love that vicious, selfish old lunatic, Lord Athenry, who in his prodigal and heartless reign, before straw and darkness swallowed him, never gave the boy a kind word or gentle look, and owed him a mortal grudge because he stood near the kingdom, and wrote most damaging reports of him at the end of the holidays, and despatched those letters of Bellerophon by the boy's own hand to the schoolmaster, with the natural results.

When Aunt Rebecca rustled into the ring that was gathered round about the fiddles and tambourine, she passed Miss Magnolia very near, with a high countenance, and looking straight before her, and with no more recognition than the tragedy queen bestows upon the painted statue on the wing by which she enters. And Miss Mag followed her with a titter and an angry flash of her eyes. So Aunt Rebecca made up to the little hillock – little bigger than a good tea-cake – on which the dowager was perched in a high-backed chair, smiling over the dancers with a splendid benignity, and beating time with her fat short foot. And Aunt Becky told Mrs Colonel Stafford, standing by, she had extemporised a living Watteau, and indeed it *was* a very pretty picture, or Aunt Becky would not have said so; and 'craning' from this eminence she saw her niece coming leisurely round, not in company of Mervyn.

That interesting stranger, on the contrary, had by this time joined Lilias and Devereux, who had returned toward the dancers, and was talking again with Miss Walsingham. Gertrude's beau was little Puddock, who was all radiant and supremely blest. But encountering rather a black look from Aunt Becky as they drew near, he deferentially surrendered the young lady to the care of her natural guardian, who forthwith presented her to the dowager; and Puddock, warned off by another glance, backed away, and fell, unawares, helplessly into the possession of Miss Magnolia, a lady whom he never quite understood, and whom he regarded with a very kind and polite sort of horror.

So the athletic Magnolia instantly impounded the little lieutenant, and began to rally him, in the sort of slang she delighted in, with plenty of merriment and malice upon his *tendre* for Miss Chattesworth, and made the gallant young gentleman blush and occasionally smile, and bow a great deal, and take some snuff.

'And here comes the Duchess of Belmont again,' said the saucy Miss Magnolia, seeing the stately approach of Aunt Becky, as it seemed to Puddock, through the back of her head. I think the exertion and frolic of the dance had got her high blood up into a sparkling state, and her scorn and hate of Aunt Rebecca was more demonstrative than usual. 'Now you'll see how she'll run against poor little simple me, just because I'm small. And *this* is the way they dance it,' cried she, in a louder tone; and capering backward with a bounce, and an air, and a grace, she came with a sort of a courtesy, and a smart bump, and a shock against the stately Miss Rebecca; and whisking round with a little scream and a look of terrified innocence, and with her fingers to her heart, to suppress an imaginary palpitation, dropped a low courtesy, crying 'I'm blest but I thought 'twas tall Burke, the gunner.'

'You might look behind before you spring backward, young gentlewoman,' said Aunt Becky, with a very bright colour.

'And you might look before you before you spring forward, old gentlewoman,' replied Miss Mag, just as angry.

'Young ladies used to have a respect to decorum,' Aunt Becky went on.

'So they prayed me to tell you, Madam,' replied the young lady, with a very meek courtesy, and a very crimson face.

'Yes, Miss Mac – Mag – Madam – it used to be so,' rejoined Aunt Rebecca, ''twas part of my education, at least, to conduct myself in a polite company like a civilised person.'

'"I wish I could see it," says blind Hugh,' Magnolia retorted; 'but 'twas a good while ago, Madam, and you've had time to forget.'

'I shall acquaint your mother, Mrs – Mug – Mac – Macnamara, with your pretty behaviour tomorrow,' said Miss Rebecca.

'Tomorrow's a new day, and mother may be well enough then to hear your genteel lamentation; but I suppose you mean tomorrow come never,' answered Magnolia, with another of her provoking meek courtesies.

'Oh, this is Lieutenant Puddock,' said Aunt Becky, drawing off in high disdain, 'the bully of the town. Your present company, Sir, will find very pretty work, I warrant, for your sword and pistols; Sir Launcelot and his belle!'

'Do you like a belle or beldame best, Sir Launcelot?' enquired Miss Mag, with a mild little duck to Puddock.

'You'll have your hands pretty full, Sir, ha, ha, ha!' and with scarlet cheeks, and a choking laugh, away sailed Aunt Rebecca.

'Choke, chicken, there's more a-hatching,' said Miss Mag, in a sort of aside, and cutting a flic-flac with a merry devilish laugh, and a wink to Puddock. That officer, being a gentleman, was a good deal disconcerted, and scandalised – too literal to see, and too honest to enjoy, the absurd side of the combat.

'Twas an affair of a few seconds, like two frigates crossing in a gale, with only opportunity for a broadside or two; and when the Rebecca Chattesworth sheered off, it can't be denied, her tackling was a good deal more cut up, and her hull considerably more pierced, than those of the saucy Magnolia, who sent that whistling shot and provoking cheer in her majestic wake.

'I see you want to go, Lieutenant Puddock – Lieutenant O'Flaherty,

I promised to dance this country dance with you; don't let me keep *you*, Ensign Puddock,' said Miss Mag in a huff, observing little Puddock's wandering eye and thoughts.

'I – a – you see, Miss Macnamara, truly you were so hard upon poor Miss Rebecca Chattesworth, that I fear I shall get into trouble, unless I go and make my peace with her,' lisped the little lieutenant, speaking the truth, as was his wont, with a bow and a polite smile, and a gentle indication of beginning to move away.

'Oh, is that all? I was afraid you were sick of the mulligrubs, with eating chopt hay; you had better go back to her at once if she wants you, for if you don't with a good grace, she'll very likely come and take you back by the collar,' and Miss Mag and O'Flaherty joined in a derisive hee-haw, to Puddock's considerable confusion, who bowed and smiled again, and tried to laugh, till the charming couple relieved him by taking their places in the dance.

When I read this speech about the 'mulligrubs', in the old yellow letter which contains a lively account of the skirmish, my breath was fairly taken away, and I could see nothing else for more than a minute; and so soon as I was quite myself again, I struck my revising pen across the monstrous sentence, with uncompromising decision, referring it to a clerical blunder, or some unlucky transposition, and I wondered how any polite person could have made so gross a slip. But see how authentication waits upon truth! Three years afterwards, I picked up in the parlour of the Cat and Fiddle, on the Macclesfield Road, in Derbyshire, a scrubby old duodecimo, which turned out to be an old volume of Dean Swift's works: well, I opened in the middle of 'Polite Conversation', and there, upon my honour, the second sentence I read was '*Lady Smart*', (mark *that* – 'LADY!') 'What, you are sick of the mulligrubs, with eating chopt hay?' So my good old yellow letter-writer ('I' or 'T'. Tresham, I can't decide what he signs himself) – *you* were, no doubt, exact here as in other matters, and *I* was determining the probable and the impossible, unphilosophically, by the *rule* of my own time. And my poor Magnolia, though you spoke some years – thirty or so – later than my Lady Smart, a countess for aught I know, you are not so much to blame. Thirty years! What of that? Don't we, to this hour, more especially in rural districts, encounter among the old folk, every now and then, one of honest Simon Wagstaff's pleasantries, which had served merry ladies and gentlemen so long before that charming compiler, with his *Large Table Book*, took the matter in hands. And I feel, I confess, a queer sort of a thrill, not at all contemptuous – neither altogether sad, nor altogether joyous – but something pleasantly regretful, whenever one of those quaint and faded old servants of the mirth of so many dead and buried generations, turns up in my company.

And now the sun went down behind the tufted trees, and the blue shades of evening began to deepen, and the merry company flocked into the King's House, to dance again and drink tea, and make more love, and play round games, and joke, and sing songs, and eat supper under old Colonel Stafford's snug and kindly roof-tree.

Dangerfield, who arrived rather late, was now in high chat with Aunt Becky. She rather liked him and had very graciously accepted a grey parrot and a monkey, which he had deferentially presented, a step which called forth, to General Chattesworth's consternation, a cockatoo from Cluffe, who felt the necessity of maintaining his ground against the stranger, and wrote off by the next packet to London, in a confounded passion, for he hated wasting money, about a pelican he had got wind of. Dangerfield also entered with much apparent interest into a favourite scheme of Aunt Becky's, for establishing, between Chapelizod and Knockmaroon, a sort of retreat for discharged gaol-birds of her selection, a colony, happily for the character and the silver spoons of the neighbourhood, never eventually established.

It was plain he was playing the frank, good fellow, and aiming at popularity. He had become one of the club. He played at whist, and only smiled, after his sort, when his partner revoked, and he lost like a gentleman. His talk was brisk, and hard, and caustic – that of a Philistine who had seen the world and knew it. He had the Peerage by rote, and knew something out-of-the-way, amusing or damnable about every person of note you could name; and his shrewd gossip had a bouquet its own, and a fine cynical flavour, which secretly awed and delighted the young fellows. He smiled a good deal. He was not aware that a smile did not quite become him. The fact is, he had lost a good many side teeth, and it was a hollow and sinister disclosure. He would laugh, too, occasionally; but his laugh was not rich and joyous, like General Chattesworth's, or even Tom Toole's cosy chuckle, or old Doctor Walsingham's hilarious ha-ha-ha! He did not know it; but there was a cold hard ring in it, like the crash and jingle of broken glass. Then his spectacles, shining like ice in the light, never removed for a moment – never even pushed up to his forehead – he eat in them, drank in them, fished in them, joked in them – he prayed in them, and, no doubt, slept in them, and would, it was believed, be buried in them – heightened that sense of mystery and mask which seemed to challenge curiosity and defy scrutiny with a scornful chuckle.

In the meantime, the mirth, and frolic, and flirtation were drawing to a close. The dowager, in high good humour, was conveyed downstairs to her carriage, by Colonel Stafford and Lord Castlemallard, and rolled away, with blazing flambeaux, like a meteor, into town. There was a breaking-up and leave-taking, and parting jokes on the door-steps; and as the ladies, old and young, were popping on their mantles in the little room off the hall, and Aunt Becky and Mrs Colonel Strafford were exchanging a little bit of eager farewell gossip beside the cabinet, Gertrude Chattesworth – by some chance she and Lilias had not had an opportunity of speaking that evening – drew close to her, and she took her hand and said 'Good-night, dear Lily', and glanced over her shoulder, still holding Lily's hand; and she looked very pale and earnest, and said quickly, in a whisper: 'Lily, darling, if you knew what I could tell you, if I dare, about Mr Mervyn, you would cut your hand off rather than allow him to talk to you, as, I confess, he *has* talked to me, as an admirer, and knowing what I know, and with my eye upon him – Lily – *Lily* – I've been amazed by him tonight. I can only *warn* you now, darling, to beware of a great danger.'

''Tis no danger, however, to me, Gertrude dear,' said Lily, with a pleasant little smile. 'And though he's handsome, there's something, is there not, *funeste* in his deep eyes and black hair; and the dear old man knows something strange about him, too; I suppose 'tis all the same story.'

'And he has not told you,' said Gertrude, looking down with a gloomy face at her fan.

'No; but I'm so curious, I know he will, though he does not like to speak of it; but you know, Gertie, I love a horror, and I know the story's fearful, and I feel uncertain whether he's a man or a ghost; but see, Aunt Rebecca and Mistress Strafford are kissing.'

'Good night, dear Lily, and remember!' said pale Gertrude without a smile, looking at her, for a moment, with a steadfast gaze, and then kissing her with a hasty and earnest pressure. And Lily kissed her again, and so they parted.

Chapter Twenty-six

Relating how the band of the Royal Irish Artillery played, and, while the music was going on, how variously different people were moved

Twice a week the band of the Royal Irish Artillery regaled all comers with their music on the parade-ground by the river; and, as it was reputed the best in Ireland, and Chapelizod was a fashionable resort, and a very pretty village, embowered in orchards, people liked to drive out of town on a fine autumn day like this, by way of listening, and all the neighbours showed there, and there was quite a little fair for an hour or two.

Mervyn, among the rest, was there, but for scarce ten minutes, and, as usual, received little more than a distant salutation, coldly and gravely returned, from Gertrude Chattesworth, to whom Mr Beauchamp, whom she remembered at the Stafford's dinner, addicted himself a good deal. That demigod appeared in a white surtout, with a crimson cape, a French waistcoat, his hair *en papillote*, a feather in his hat, a *couteau de chasse* by his side, with a small cane hanging to his button, and a pair of Italian greyhounds at his heels; and he must have impressed Tresham prodigiously; for I observe no other instance in which he has noted down costume so carefully. Little Puddock, too, was hovering near, and his wooing made uncomfortable by Aunt Becky's renewed severity, as well as by the splendour of 'Mr Redheels', who was expending his small talk and *fleuerets* upon Gertrude. Cluffe, moreover, who was pretty well in favour with Aunt Rebecca, and had been happy and prosperous, had his little jealousies too to plague him, for Dangerfield, with his fishing-rod and basket, no sooner looked in, with his stern front and his remarkable smile, than Aunt Becky, seeming instantaneously to forget Captain Cluffe, and all his winning ways, and the pleasant story, to the point of which he was just arriving, in his best manner, left him abruptly, and walked up to the grim *pescator del onda*, with an outstretched hand and a smile of encouragement, and immediately fell into confidential talk with him.

'The minds of anglers,' says the gentle Colonel Robert Venables, 'be usually more calm and composed than many others; when he hath the worst success he loseth but a hook or line, or perhaps what he never possessed, a fish; and suppose he should take nothing, yet he enjoyeth a delightful walk by pleasant rivers, in sweet pastures, amongst odoriferous flowers, which gratify his senses and delight his mind; and if example, which is the best proof, may sway anything, I know no sort of men less subject to melancholy than anglers.' It was only natural, then, that Dangerfield should be serene and sunny.

Aunt Becky led him a little walk twice or thrice up and down. She seemed grave, earnest, and lofty, and he grinned and chatted after his wont energetically, to stout Captain Cluffe's considerable uneasiness and mortification. He had seen Dangerfield the day before, through his field-glass, from the high wooded grounds in the park, across the river, walk slowly for a good while under the poplars in the meadow at Belmont, beside Aunt Becky, in high chat; and there was something particular and earnest in their manner, which made him uncomfortable then. And fat Captain Cluffe's gall rose and nearly choked him, and he cursed Dangerfield in the bottom of his corpulent, greedy soul, and wondered what fiend had sent that scheming old land-agent three hundred miles out of his way, on purpose to interfere with his little interests, as if there were not plenty of – of – well! – rich old women – in London. And he bethought him of the price of the cockatoo and the probable cost of the pelican, rejoinders to Dangerfield's contributions to Aunt Rebecca's menagerie, for those birds were not to be had for nothing; and Cluffe, who loved money as well, at least, as any man in his Majesty's service, would have seen the two tribes as extinct as the dodo, before he would have expended sixpence upon such tom-foolery, had it not been for Dangerfield's investments in animated nature. 'The hound! As if two could not play at that game.' But he had an uneasy and bitter presentiment that they were birds of paradise, and fifty other cursed birds beside, and that in this costly competition Dangerfield could take a flight beyond and above him; and he thought of the flagitious waste of money, and cursed him for a fool again. Aunt Becky had said, he thought, something in which 'tomorrow' occurred, on taking leave of Dangerfield. 'Tomorrow!' 'What tomorrow? She spoke low and confidentially, and seemed excited and a little flushed, and very distrait when she came back. Altogether, he felt as if Aunt Rebecca was slipping through his fingers, and would have liked to take that selfish old puppy, Dangerfield, by the neck and drown him out of hand in the river. But, notwithstanding the state of his temper, he knew it might be his only chance to shine pre-eminently at that moment in amiability, wit, grace, and gallantry, and, though it was up-hill work, he did labour uncommonly.

When Mr Dangerfield's spectacles gleamed through the crowd upon Dr Sturk, who was thinking of other things beside the music, the angler walked round forthwith, and accosted that universal genius. Mrs Sturk felt the doctor's arm, on which she leaned, vibrate for a second with a slight thrill – an evidence in that hard, fibrous limb of what she used to call 'a start' – and she heard Dangerfield's voice over his shoulder. And the surgeon and the grand vizier were soon deep in talk, and Sturk brightened up, and looked eager and sagacious, and important, and became very voluble and impressive, and, leaving his lady to her own devices, with her maid and children, he got to the other side of the street, where Nutter, with taciturn and black observation, saw them busy pointing with cane and finger, and talking briskly as they surveyed together Dick Fisher's and Tom Tresham's tenements, and the Salmon House; and then beheld them ascend the steps of Tresham's door, and overlook the wall on the other side toward the river, and point this way and that along the near bank, as it seemed to Nutter discussing detailed schemes of alteration and improvement. Sturk actually pulled out his pocket-book and pencil, and then Dangerfield took the pencil, and made notes of what he read to him, on the back of a letter; and Sturk looked eager and elated, and Dangerfield frowned and looked impressed, and nodded again and again. *Diruit aedificat, mutat quadrata rotundis*, under his very nose – he unconsulted! It was such an impertinence as Nutter could ill digest. It was a studied slight, something like a public deposition, and Nutter's jealous soul seethed secretly in a hellbroth of rage and suspicion.

I mentioned that Mistress Sturk felt in that physician's arm the telegraphic thrill with which the brain will occasionally send an invisible message of alarm from the seat of government to the extremities; and as this smallest of all small bits of domestic gossip did innocently escape me, the idle and good-natured reader will, I hope, let me say out my little say upon the matter, in the next chapter.

Chapter Twenty-seven

*Concerning the troubles and the shapes that began to gather
about Dr Sturk*

It was just about that time that our friend, Dr Sturk, had two or three
odd dreams that secretly acted disagreeably upon his spirits. His liver
he thought was a little wrong, and there was certainly a little light
gout sporting about him. His favourite 'pupton', at mess, disagreed
with him; so did his claret, and hot suppers as often as he tried them,
and that was, more or less, nearly every night in the week. So he
was, perhaps, right in ascribing these his visions to the humours, the
spleen, the liver, and the juices. Still they sat uncomfortably upon his
memory, and helped his spirits down, and made him silent and testy,
and more than usually formidable to poor, little, quiet, hard-worked
Mrs Sturk.

Dreams! What talk can be idler? And yet haven't we seen grave
people and gay listening very contentedly at times to that wild and
awful sort of frivolity; and I think there is in most men's minds, sages
or zanies, a secret misgiving that dreams may have an office and a
meaning, and are perhaps more than a fortuitous concourse of symbols, in fact, the language which good or evil spirits whisper over the
sleeping brain.

There was an ugly and ominous consistency in these dreams
which might have made a less dyspeptic man a little nervous. Tom
Dunstan, a sergeant whom Sturk had prosecuted and degraded
before a court-martial, who owed the doctor no good-will, and was
dead and buried in the churchyard close by, six years ago, and whom
Sturk had never thought about in the interval – made a kind of
resurrection now, and was with him every night, figuring in these
dreary visions and somehow in league with a sort of conspirator-in-
chief, who never showed distinctly, but talked in scoffing menaces
from outside the door, or clutched him by the throat from behind his
chair, and yelled some hideous secret into his ear, which his scared
and scattered wits, when he started into consciousness, could never

collect again. And this fellow, with whose sneering cavernous talk – with whose very knock at the door or thump at the partition-wall he was as familiar as with his own wife's voice, and the touch of whose cold convulsive hand he had felt so often on his cheek or throat, and the very suspicion of whose approach made him faint with horror, his dreams would not present to his sight. There was always something interposed, or he stole behind him, or just as he was entering and the door swinging open, Sturk would awake – and he never saw him, at least in a human shape.

But one night he thought he saw, as it were, his sign or symbol. As Sturk lay his length under the bed-clothes, with his back turned upon his slumbering helpmate, he was, in the spirit, sitting perpendicularly in his great balloon-backed chair at his writing-table, in the window of the back one-pair-of-stairs chamber which he called his library, where he sometimes wrote prescriptions, and pondering over his pennyweights, his Roman numerals, his *guttae* and *pillulae*, his 3s, his 5s, his 9s, and the other arabesque and astrological symbols of his mystery, he looked over his pen into the churchyard, which inspiring prospect he thence commanded.

Thus, as out of the body sat our recumbent doctor in the room underneath the bed in which his snoring idolon lay, Tom Dunstan stood beside the table, with the short white threads sticking out on his blue sleeve, where the stitching of the stripes had been cut through on that twilight parade morning when the doctor triumphed, and Tom's rank, fortune, and castles in the air, all tumbled together in the dust of the barrack pavement; and so, with his thin features and evil eye turned sideways to Sturk, says he, with a stiff salute – 'A gentleman, Sir, that means to dine with you', and there was the muffled knock at the door which he knew so well, and a rustling behind him. So the doctor turned him about quickly with a sort of chill between his shoulders, and perched on the back of his chair sat a portentous old quizzical carrion-crow, the antediluvian progenitor of the whole race of carrion-crows, monstrous, with great shining eyes, and head white as snow, and a queer human look, and the crooked beak of an owl, that opened with a loud grating 'caw' close in his ears; and with a 'bo-o-oh!' and a bounce that shook the bed and made poor Mrs Sturk jump out of it, and spin round in the curtain, Sturk's spirit popped back again into his body, which sat up wide awake that moment.

It is not pretended that at this particular time the doctor was a specially good sleeper. The contrary stands admitted; and I don't ask you, sagacious reader, to lay any sort of stress upon his dreams; only as there came a time when people talked of them a good deal over the fireside in Chapelizod, and made winter's tales about them, I thought myself obliged to tell you that such things were.

He did not choose to narrate them to his brother-officers, and to be quizzed about them at mess. But he opened his budget to old Dr Walsingham, of course, only as a matter to be smiled at by a pair of philosophers like them. But Dr Walsingham, who was an absent man, and floated upon the ocean of his learning serenely and lazily, drawn finely and whimsically, now hither, now thither, by the finest hair of association, glided complacently off into the dim region of visionary prognostics and warnings, and reminded him how Joseph dreamed, and Pharaoh, and Benvenuto Cellini's father, and St Dominick's mother, and Edward II of England, and dodged back and forward among patriarchs and pagans, and modern Christians, men and women, not at all suspecting that he was making poor Sturk, who had looked for a cheerful, sceptical sort of essay, confoundedly dismal and uncomfortable.

And, indeed, confoundedly distressed he must have been, for he took his brother-chip, Tom Toole, whom he loved not, to counsel upon his case – of course, strictly as a question of dandelion, or gentian, or camomile flowers; and Tom, who, as we all know, loved him reciprocally, frightened him as well as he could, offered to take charge of his case, and said, looking hard at him out of the corner of his cunning, resolute little eye, as they sauntered in the park: 'But I need not tell *you*, my good Sir, that physic is of small avail, if there is any sort of – a – a – vexation, or – or – in short – a – a – *vexation*, you know, on your mind.'

'A – ha, ha, ha! – what? Murdered my father, and married my grandmother?' snarled Sturk, sneeringly, amused or affecting to be so, and striving to laugh at the daisies before his toes, as he trudged along, with his hands in his breeches' pockets. 'I have not a secret on earth, Sir. 'Tis not a button to me, Sir, who talks about me; and I don't owe a guinea, Sir, that is, that I could not pay tomorrow, if I liked it; and there's nothing to trouble me – nothing, Sir, except this dirty, little, gouty dyspepsy, scarce worth talking about.

Then came a considerable silence; and Toole's active little mind, having just made a note of this, tripped off smartly to half-a-dozen totally different topics, and he was mentally tippling his honest share of a dozen of claret, with a pleasant little masonic party at the Salmon-leap, on Sunday next, and was just going to charm them with his best song, and a new verse of his own compounding, when Sturk, in a moment, dispersed the masons, and brought him back by the ear at a jump from the Salmon-leap, with a savage – 'And I'd like to know, Sir, who the deuce, or, rather, what the — ' [*plague* we'll say] 'could put into your head, Sir, to suppose any such matter?'

But this was only one of Sturk's explosions, and he and little Toole parted no better and no worse friends than usual, in ten minutes more, at the latter's door-step.

So Toole said to Mrs T. that evening – 'Sturk owes money, mark my words, sweetheart. Remember *I* say it – he'll cool his heels in a prison, if he's no wiser than of late, before a twel'month. Since the beginning of February he has lost – just wait a minute, and let me see – ay, that, £150 by the levanting of old Tom Farthingale; and, I had it today from little O'Leary, who had it from Jim Kelly, old Craddock's conducting clerk, he's bit to the tune of three hundred more by the failure of Larkin, Brothers, and Hoolaghan. You see a little bit of usury under the rose is all very well for a vulgar dog like Sturk, if he knows the town, and how to go about it; but hang, it, he knows nothing. Why, the turnpike-man, over the way, would not have taken old Jos. Farthingale's bill for fippence – no, nor his bond neither; and he's stupid beside – but he can't help that, the hound! – and he'll owe a whole year's rent only six weeks hence, and he has not a shilling to bless himself with. Unfortunate devil – I've no reason to like him – but, truly, I do pity him.'

Saying which Tom Toole, with his back to the fire, and a look of concern thrown into his comic little mug, and his eyebrows raised, experienced a very pleasurable glow of commiseration.

Sturk, on the contrary, was more than commonly silent and savage that evening, and sat in his drawing-room, with his fists in his breeches' pockets, and his heels stretched out, lurid and threatening, in a gloomy and highly electric state. Mrs S. did not venture her usual 'would my Barney like a dish of tea?' but plied her worsted and knitting-needles with mild concentration, sometimes peeping under her lashes at Sturk, and sometimes telegraphing faintly to the children if they whispered too loud – all cautious pantomime – *nutu signisque loquuntur*.

Sturk was incensed by the suspicion that Tom Toole knew something of his losses, 'the dirty, little, unscrupulous spy and tattler'. He was confident, however, that he could not know their extent. It was certainly a hard thing, and enough to exasperate a better man than Sturk, that the savings of a shrewd and, in many ways, a self-denying life should have been swept away, and something along with them, by a few unlucky casts in little more than twelve months. And he such a clever dog, too! The best player, all to nothing, driven to the wall, by a cursed obstinate run of infernal luck. And he used to scowl, and grind his teeth, and nearly break the keys and shillings in his gripe in his breeches' pocket, as imprecations, hot and unspoken, coursed one another through his brain. Then up he would get, and walk sulkily to the brandy-flask and have a dram, and feel better, and begin to count up his chances, and what he might yet save out of the fire; and resolve to press vigorously for the agency, which he thought Dangerfield, if he wanted a useful man, could not fail to give him; and he had hinted the matter to Lord Castlemallard, who, he thought, understood and favoured his wishes. Yes; that agency would give him credit and opportunity, and be the foundation of his new fortunes, and the saving of him. A precious, pleasant companion, you may suppose, he was to poor little Mrs Sturk, who knew nothing of his affairs, and could not tell what to make of her Barney's eccentricities.

And so it was, somehow, when Dangerfield spoke his greeting at Sturk's ear, and the doctor turned short round, and saw his white frizzed hair, great glass eyes, and crooked, short beak, quizzical and sinister, close by, it seemed for a second as if the 'caw' and the carrion-crow of his dream was at his shoulder; and, I suppose, he showed his discomfiture a little, for he smiled a good deal more than Sturk usually did at a recognition.

Chapter Twenty-eight

*In which Mr Irons recounts some old recollections about the
Pied Horse and the Flower de Luce*

It was so well known in Chapelizod that Sturk was poking after Lord
Castlemallard's agency that Nutter felt the scene going on before his
eyes between him and Dangerfield like a public affront. His ire was
that of a phlegmatic man, dangerous when stirred, and there was no
mistaking, in his rigid, swarthy countenance, the state of his temper.

Dangerfield took an opportunity, and touched Nutter on the
shoulder, and told him frankly, in effect, though *he* wished things
to go on as heretofore, Sturk had wormed himself into a sort of
confidence with Lord Castlemallard.

'Not confidence, Sir – *talk*, if you please,' said Nutter grimly.

'Well, into talk,' acquiesced Dangerfield; 'and by Jove, I've a hard
card to play, you see. His lordship will have me listen to Doctor
Sturk's talk, such as it is.'

'He has no talk in him, Sir, you mayn't get from any other
impudent dunderhead in the town,' answered Nutter.

'My dear Sir, understand me. I'm your friend,' and he placed his
hand amicably upon Nutter's arm; 'but Lord Castlemallard has, now
and then, a will of his own, I need not tell you; and somebody's been
doing you an ill turn with his lordship; and you're a gentleman, Mr
Nutter, and I like you, and I'll be frank with you, knowing 'twill go
no further. Sturk wants the agency. You have *my* good-will. *I* don't
see why he should take it from you; but – but – you see his lordship
takes odd likings, and he won't always listen to reason.'

Nutter was so shocked and exasperated, that for a moment he felt
stunned, and put his hand toward his head.

'I think, Sir,' said Nutter, with a stern, deliberate oath, 'I'll write
to Lord Castlemallard this evening, and throw up his agency; and
challenge Sturk, and fight him in the morning.'

'You must not resign the agency, Sir; his lordship is whimsical, but
you have a friend at court. I've spoken in full confidence in your

secrecy; and should any words pass between you and Dr Sturk, you'll not mention my name; I rely, Sir, on your honour, as you may on my good-will;' and Dangerfield shook hands with Nutter significantly, and called to Irons, who was waiting to accompany him, and the two anglers walked away together up the river.

Nutter was still possessed with his furious resolution to fling down his office at Lord Castlemallard's feet, and to call Sturk into the lists of mortal combat. One turn by himself as far as the turnpike, however, and he gave up the first, and retained only the second resolve. Half-an-hour more, and he had settled in his mind that there was no need to punish the meddler that way: and so he resolved to bide his time – a short one.

In the meanwhile Dangerfield had reached one of those sweet pastures by the river's bank which, as we have read, delight the simple mind of the angler, and his float was already out, and bobbing up and down on the ripples of the stream; and the verdant valley, in which he and his taciturn companion stood side by side, resounded, from time to time, with Dangerfield's strange harsh laughter; the cause of which Irons did not, of course, presume to ask.

There is a churchyard cough – I don't see why there may not be a churchyard laugh. In Dangerfield's certainly there was an omen – a glee that had nothing to do with mirth; and more dismaying, perhaps, than his sternest rebuke. If a man is not a laugher by nature, he had better let it alone. The bipeds that love mousing and carrion have a chant of their own, and nobody quarrels with it. We respect an owl or a raven, though we mayn't love him, while he sticks to his croak or to-whoo. 'Tisn't pleasant, but quite natural and unaffected, and we acquiesce. All we ask of these gentlemanlike birds is, that they mistake not their talent – affect not music; or if they do, that they treat not us to their queer warblings.

Irons, with that never-failing phantom of a smile on his thin lips, stood a little apart, with a gaff and landing-net, and a second rod, and a little bag of worms, and his other gear, silent, except when spoken to, or sometimes to suggest a change of bait, or fly, or a cast over a particular spot; for Dangerfield was of good Colonel Venables' mind, that 'tis well in the lover of the gentle craft to associate himself with some honest, expert angler, who will freely and candidly communicate his skill unto him.'

Dangerfield was looking straight at his float, but thinking of something else. Whenever Sturk met him at dinner, or the club, the doctor's arrogance and loud lungs failed him, and he fell for a while into a sort of gloom and dreaming; and when he came slowly to himself, he could not talk to anyone but the man with the spectacles; and in the midst of his talk he would grow wandering and thoughtful, as if over some half-remembered dream; and when he took his leave of Dangerfield it was with a lingering look and a stern withdrawal, as if he had still a last word to say, and he went away in a dismal reverie. It was natural, that with his views about the agency, Sturk should regard him with particular interest. But there was something more here, and it did not escape Dangerfield, as, indeed, very little that in any wise concerned him ever did.

'Clever fellow, Doctor Sturk,' said the silver spectacles, looking grimly at the float. 'I like him. You remember him, you say, Irons?'

'Ay, Sir,' said Blue-chin: 'I never forget a face.'

'*Par nobile*,' sneered the angler quietly. 'In the year '45, eh – go on.'

'Ay, Sir; he slept in the Pied Horse, at Newmarket, and was in all the fun. Next day he broke his arm badly, and slept there in the closet off Mr Beauclerc's room that night under laudanum, and remained ten days longer in the house. Mr Beauclerc's chamber was the Flower de Luce. Barnabus Sturk, Esq. When I saw him here, half the length of the street away, I knew him and his name on the instant. I never forget things.'

'But he don't remember you?'

'No,' smiled Blue-chin, looking at the float also.

'Two-and-twenty-years. How came it he was not summoned?'

'He was under laudanum, and could tell nothing.'

'Ay,' said the spectacles, 'ay,' and he let out some more line. 'That's deep.'

'Yes, Sir, a soldier was drownded in that hole.'

'And Dr Toole and Mr Nutter don't love him – both brisk fellows, and have fought.'

Blue-chin smiled on.

'Very clever dog – needs be sharp though, or he'll come to – ha!' and a grey trout came splashing and flickering along the top of the water upon the hook, and Irons placed the net in Dangerfield's outstretched hand, and the troutling was landed, to the distant music of 'God save the King', borne faintly on the air, by which the reader perceives that the band were now about to put up their instruments, and the gay folk to disperse. And at the same moment, Lord Castle-mallard was doing old General Chattesworth the honour to lean upon his arm, as they walked to and fro upon the parade-ground by the river's bank, and the general looked particularly grand and thoughtful, and my lord was more than usually gracious and impressive, and was saying: ''Tis a good match every way: he has good blood in his veins, Sir, the Dangerfields of Redminster; and you may suppose he's rich, when he was ready to advance Sir Sedley Hicks thirty-five thousand pounds on mortgage, and to my certain knowledge has nearly as much more out on good securities; and he's the most principled man I think I ever met with, and the cleverest dog, I believe, in these kingdoms; and I wish you joy, General Chattesworth.'

And he gave the general snuff out of his box, and shook hands, and said something very good, as he got into his carriage, for he laughed a good deal, and touched the general's ribs with the point of his gloved finger; and the general laughed too, moderately, and was instantaneously grave again, when the carriage whirled away.

Chapter Twenty-nine

Showing how poor Mrs Macnamara was troubled and haunted too, and opening a budget of gossip

Some score pages back, when we were all assembled at the King's House, my reader, perhaps, may not have missed our fat and consequential, but on the whole good-natured acquaintance, Mrs Macnamara; though, now I remember, he *did* overhear the gentle Magnolia, in that little colloquy in which she and Aunt Becky exchanged compliments, say, in substance, that she hoped that amiable parent might be better next day. She was not there, she was not well. Of late Mrs Macnamara had lost all her pluck, and half her colour, and some even of her fat. She was like one of those portly dowagers in Numbernip's select society of metamorphosed turnips, who suddenly exhibited sympathetic symptoms of failure, grew yellow, flabby, and wrinkled, as the parent bulb withered and went out of season. You would not have known her for the same woman.

A tall, pale female, dressed in black satin and a black velvet riding hood, had made her two visits in a hackney-coach; but whether these had any connection with the melancholy change referred to, I don't, at this moment, say. I know that they had a very serious bearing upon after events affecting persons who figure in this true history. Whatever her grief was she could not bring herself to tell it. And so her damask cheek, and portly form, and rollicking animal spirits continued to suffer.

The major found that her mind wandered at piquet. Toole also caught her thinking of something else in the midst of his best bits of local scandal; and Magnolia several times popped in upon her large mother in tears. Once or twice Toole thought, and he was right, that she was on the point of making a disclosure. But her heart failed her, and it came to nothing. The little fellow's curiosity was on fire. In his philosophy there was more in everything than met the eye, and he would not believe Magnolia, who laughed at him, that she did not know all about it.

On this present morning poor Mrs Macnamara had received a note, at which she grew pale as the large pat of butter before her, and she felt quite sick as she thrust the paper into her pocket, and tried to smile across the breakfast table at Magnolia, who was rattling away as usual, and the old major who was chuckling at her impudent mischief over his buttered toast and tea.

'Why, mother dear,' cried Mag suddenly, 'what the plague ails your pretty face? Did you ever see the like? It's for all the world like a bad batter pudding! I lay a crown, now, that was a bill. Was it a bill? Come now, Mullikins,' [a term of endearment for mother] 'show us the note. It is too bad, you poor dear, old, handsome, bothered angel, you should be fretted and tormented out of your looks and your health, by them dirty shopkeepers' bills, when a five-pound note, I'm certain sure, 'id pay every mothers skin o' them, and change to spare!' And the elegant Magnolia, whose soiclainet and Norwich crape petticoat were unpaid for, darted a glance of reproach full upon the major's powdered head, the top of which was cleverly presented to receive it, as he swallowed in haste his cup of tea, and rising suddenly, for his purse had lately suffered in the service of the ladies, and wanted rest –

'''Tis nothing at all but that confounded egg,' he said, raising that untasted delicacy a little towards his nose. 'Why the divil will you go on buying our eggs from that dirty old sinner, Poll Delany?' And he dropped it from its cup plump into the slop-basin.

'A then maybe it was,' said poor Mrs Mac, smiling as well as she could; 'but I'm better.'

'No you're not, Mullikins,' interposed Magnolia impatiently. 'There's Toole crossing the street, will I call him up?'

'Not for the world, Maggy darling. I'd have to pay him, and where's the money to come from?'

The major did not hear, and was coughing besides; and recollecting that he had a word for the adjutant's ear, took his sword off the peg where it hung, and his cocked hat, and vanished in a twinkling.

'Pay Toole, indeed! Nonsense, mother,' and up went the window.

'Good-morrow to your nightcap, doctor!'

'And the top of the morning to you, my pretty Miss chattering Mag, up on your perch there,' responded the physician.

'And what in the world brings you out this way at breakfast time, and where are you going? – Oh! Goosey, goosey gander, where do you wander?'

'Upstairs, if you let me,' said Toole, with a flourish of his hand, and a gallant grin, 'and to my lady's chamber.'

'And did you hear the news?' demanded Miss Mag.

The doctor glanced over his shoulder, and seeing the coast clear, he was by this time close under the little scarlet geranium pots that stood on the window-sill.

'Miss Chattesworth, eh?' he asked, in a sly, low tone.

'Oh, bother her, no. Do you remember Miss Anne Marjoribanks, that lodged in Doyle's house, down there, near the mills, last summer, with her mother, the fat woman with the poodle, and the – don't you know?'

'Ay, ay; she wore a flowered silk tabby sacque, on band days,' said Toole, who had an eye and a corner in his memory for female costume, 'a fine showy – I remember.'

'Well, middling: that's she.'

'And what of her?' asked Toole, screwing himself up as close as he could to the flower-pots.

'Come up and I'll tell you,' and she shut down the window and beckoned him slily, and up came Toole all alive.

Miss Magnolia told her story in her usual animated way, sometimes dropping her voice to a whisper, and taking Toole by the collar, sometimes rising to a rollicking roar of laughter, while the little doctor stood by, his hands in his breeches' pockets, making a pleasant jingle with his loose change there, with open mouth and staring eyes, and a sort of breathless grin all over his ruddy face. Then came another story, and more chuckling.

'And what about that lanky long maypole, Gertie Chattesworth, the witch? – Not that anyone cares tuppence if she rode on a broom to sweep the cobwebs off the moon, only a body may as well know, you know,' said Miss Mag, preparing to listen.

'Why, by Jupiter! They say – but d'ye mind, I don't know, and faith I don't believe it – but they do say she's going to be married to – who do you think now?' answered Toole.

'Old Colonel Bligh, of the Magazine, or Dr Walsingham, maybe,' cried Mag, with a burst of laughter; 'no young fellow would be plagued with her, I'm certain.'

'Well, ha, ha! You *are* a conjuror, Miss Mag, to be sure. He's *not* young – you're right there – but then, he's rich, he is, by Jove! There's no end of his – well, what do you say now to Mr Dangerfield?'

'Dangerfield! Well,' [after a little pause] 'he's ugly enough and old enough too, for the matter of that; but he's as rich as a pork-pie; and if he's worth half what they say, you may take my word for it, when he goes to church it won't be to marry the steeple.'

And she laughed again scornfully and added: ''Twas plain enough from the first, the whole family laid themselves out to catch the old quiz and his money. Let the Chattesworths alone for scheming, with all their grand airs. Much I mind them! Why, the old sinner was not an hour in the town when he was asked over the way to Belmont, and Miss dressed out there like a puppet, to simper and flatter the rich old land agent, and butter him up – my Lord Castlemallard's bailiff – if you please, ha, ha, ha! And the Duchess of Belmont, that ballyrags everyone round her, like a tipsy old soldier, as civil as six, my dear Sir, with her "Oh, Mr Dangerfield, this," and her "Dear Mr Dangerfield, that," and all to marry that long, sly hussy to a creature old enough to be her grandfather, though she's no chicken neither. Faugh! Filthy!' and Miss Magnolia went through an elegant pantomime of spitting over her shoulder into the grate.

Toole thought there was but one old fellow of his acquaintance who might be creditably married by a girl young enough to be his grand-daughter, and that was honest Arthur Slowe; and he was going to insinuate a joke of the sort; but perceiving that his sly preparatory glance was not pleasantly responded to, and that the stalworth nymph was quite in earnest, he went off to another topic.

The fact is that Toole knew something of Miss Mag's plans, as he did of most of the neighbours' beside. Old Slowe was, in certain preponderating respects, much to be preferred to the stalworth fireworker, Mr Lieutenant O'Flaherty. And the two gentlemen were upon her list. Two strings to a bow is a time-honoured provision. Cupid often goes so furnished. If the first snap at the critical moment, should we bow-string our precious throttles with the pieces? Far be it from us! Let us waste no time in looking foolish, but pick up the grey goose-shaft that lies so innocently at our feet among the daisies; and it's odds but the second plants it i' the clout. The lover, the hero of the piece, upon whose requited passion and splendid settlements the curtain goes down, is a role not always safely to be confided to the genius and discretion of a single performer. Take it that the captivating Frederick Belville, who is announced for the part, is, along with his other qualifications, his gallantry, his grace, his ringlets, his pathetic smile, his lustrous eyes, his plaintive tenor, and five-and-twenty years – a little bit of a rip – rather frail in the particular of brandy and water, and so, not quite reliable. Will not the prudent manager provide a substitute respectably to fill the part, in the sad event of one of those sudden indispositions to which Belville is but too liable? It may be somewhat 'fat and scant of breath', ay, and scant of hair and of teeth too. But though he has played Romeo thirty years ago, the perruquier, and the dentist, and the rouge-pot, and the friendly glare of the footlights will do wonders; and Podgers – steady fellow! – will be always at the right wing, at the right moment, know every line of his author, and contrive to give a very reasonable amount of satisfaction to all parties concerned. Following this precedent, then, that wise virgin, Miss Magnolia, and her sagacious mamma, had allotted the role in question to Arthur Slowe, who was the better furnished for the part, and, on the whole, the stronger 'cast'. But failing him, Lieutenant O'Flaherty was quietly, but unconsciously, as the phrase is, 'under-studying' that somewhat uncertain gentleman.

'And the general's off to Scarborough,' said Toole.

'Old Chattesworth! I thought it was to Bath.

'Oh, no, Scarborough; a touch of the old rheum, and stomach. I sent him there; and he's away in the Hillsborough packet for Holy-head this morning, and Colonel Stafford's left in command.'

'And my Lady Becky Belmont's superseded,' laughed Miss Magnolia, derisively.

'And who do you think's going to make the grand tour? From Paris to Naples, if you please, and from Naples to Rome, and up to Venice, and home through Germany, and deuce knows where beside; you'll not guess in a twel'month,' said Toole, watching her with a chuckle.

'Devereux, maybe,' guessed the young lady.

'No 'tisn't,' said Toole, delighted; 'try again!'

'Well, 'tis, let me see. Some wild young rogue, with a plenty of money, I warrant, if I could only think of him – come, don't keep me all day – who the plague is he, Toole?' urged the young lady, testily.

'Dan Loftus,' answered Toole, 'ha, ha, ha, ha!'

'Dan Loftus! – the grand tour – why, where's the world running to? Oh, ho, ho, ho, hoo! What a macaroni!' and they laughed heartily over it, and called him 'travelled monkey', and I know not what else.

'Why, I thought Dr Walsingham designed him for his curate; but what in the wide world brings Dan Loftus to foreign parts – "To dance and sing for the Spanish King, and to sing and dance for the Queen of France"?'

'Hey! Dan's got a good place, I can tell you – travelling tutor to the hopeful young lord that is to be – Devereux's cousin. By all the Graces, Ma'am, 'tis the blind leading the blind. I don't know which of the two is craziest. Hey, diddle-diddle – by Jupiter, such a pair – the dish ran away with the spoon; but Dan's a good creature, and we'll – we'll miss him. I like Dan, and he loves the rector – I like him for that; where there's gratitude and fidelity, Miss Mag, there's no lack of other virtues, I warrant you – and the good doctor has been a wonderful loving friend to poor Dan, and God bless him for it, say I, and amen.'

'And amen with all my heart,' said Miss Mag, gaily; ''tis an innocent creature – poor Dan; though he'd be none the worse of a little more lace to his hat, and a little less Latin in his head. But see here, doctor, here's my poor old goose of a mother (and she kissed her cheek) as sick as a cat in a tub.'

And she whispered something in Toole's wig, and they both laughed uproariously.

'I would not take five guineas and tell you what she says,' cried Toole.

'Don't mind the old blackguard, mother dear!' screamed Magnolia, dealing Aesculapius a lusty slap on the back; and the cook at that moment knocking at the door, called off the young lady to the larder, who cried over her shoulder as she lingered a moment at the door – 'Now, send her something, Toole, for my sake, to do her poor heart good. Do you mind – for faith and troth the dear old soul is sick and sad; and I won't let that brute, Sturk, though he does wear our uniform, next or near her.'

'Well, 'tisn't for me to say, eh? – and now she's gone – just let me try.' And he took her pulse.

Chapter Thirty

Concerning a certain woman in black

And Toole, holding her stout wrist, felt her pulse and said – 'Hem – I see – and – '

And so he ran on with half-a-dozen questions, and at the end of his catechism said, bluntly enough: 'I tell you what it is, Mrs Mack, you have something on your mind, my dear Madam, and till it's off, you'll never be better.'

Poor Mrs Mack opened her eyes, and made a gesture of amazed disclaimer, with her hands palm upwards. It was all affectation.

'Pish!' said Toole, who saw the secret almost in his grasp; 'don't tell me, my dear Madam – don't you think I know my business by this time o' day? I tell you again you'd better ease your mind – or take my word for it you'll be sorry too late. How would you like to go off like poor old Peggy Slowe – eh? There's more paralysis, apoplexy, heart-diseases, and lunacy, caused in one year by that sort of silly secrecy and moping, than by – hang it! my dear Madam,' urged Toole, breaking into a bold exhortation on seeing signs of confusion and yielding in his fat patient – 'you'd tell me all that concerns your health, and know that Tom Toole would put his hand in the fire before he'd let a living soul hear a symptom of your case; and here's some paltry little folly or trouble that I would not – as I'm a gentle-man – give a half-penny to hear, and you're afraid to tell me – though until you do, neither I, nor all the doctors in Europe, can do you a ha'porth o' good.'

'Sure I've nothing to tell, doctor dear,' whimpered poor Mrs Mack, dissolving into her handkerchief.

'Look ye – there's no use in trying to deceive a doctor that knows what he's about.' Toole was by this time half mad with curiosity. 'Don't tell me what's on your mind, though I'd be sorry you thought I wasn't ready and anxious to help you with my best and most secret services; but I confess, my dear Ma'am, I'd rather not hear – reserve it for some friend who has your confidence – but 'tis plain from the condition you're in' – and Toole closed his lips hard, and nodded twice or thrice – 'you have not told either the major or your daughter; and tell it you must to *someone*, or take the consequences.'

'Oh! Dr Toole, I *am* in trouble – and I'd like to tell you; but won't you – won't you promise me now, on your solemn honour, if I do, you won't tell a human being?' blubbered the poor matron.

'Conscience, honour, veracity, Ma'am – but why should I say any more – don't you know me, my dear Mrs Mack?' said Toole in a hot fidget, and with all the persuasion of which he was master.

'Indeed, I do – and I'm in great trouble – and sometimes think no-one can take me out of it,' pursued she.

'Come, come, my dear Madam, is it money?' demanded Toole.

'Oh! no – it's – 'tis a dreadful – that is, there *is* money in it – but oh! dear Doctor Toole, there's a frightful woman, and I don't know what to do: and I sometimes thought you might be able to help me – you're so clever – and I was going to tell you, but I was ashamed – there now, it's out,' and she blubbered aloud.

'*What's* out?' said Toole, irritated. 'I can't stop here all day, you know; and if you'd rather I'd go, say so.'

'Oh! no, but the major, nor Maggy does not know a word about it; and so, for your life, don't tell them; and – and – here it is.'

And from her pocket she produced a number of the *Freeman's Journal*, five or six weeks old and a great deal soiled.

'Read it, read it, doctor dear, and you'll see.'

'Read all this! Thank you, Ma'am; I read it a month ago,' said the doctor gruffly.

'Oh! no – this – only there – you see – *here*,' and she indicated a particular advertisement, which we here reprint for the reader's instruction; and thus it ran –

MARY MATCHWELL's most humble Respects attend the Nobility and Gentry. She has the Honour to acquaint them that she transacts all Business relative to Courtship and Marriage, with the utmost Dispatch and Punctuality. She has, at a considerable Expense, procured a complete List of all the unmarried Persons of both Sexes in this Kingdom, with an exact Account of their Characters, Fortunes, Ages, and Persons. Any Lady or Gentleman, by sending a Description of the Husband or Wife they would chuse, shall be informed where such a One is to be had, and put in a Method for obtaining him, or her, in the speediest Manner, and at the smallest Expense. Mrs Matchwell's Charges being always proportioned to the Fortunes of the Parties, and not to be paid till the Marriage takes place. She hopes the Honour and Secrecy she will observe in her Dealings, will encourage an unfortunate Woman, who hath experienced the greatest Vicissitudes of Life, as will be seen in her Memoirs, which are shortly to be published under the Title of *Fortune's Football*. All Letters directed to M. M., and sent Post paid to the Office where this Paper is published, shall be answered with Care.'

'Yes, yes, I remember that – a cheating gypsy – why, it's going on still – I saw it again yesterday, I think – a lying jade! – and this is the rogue that troubles you?' said Toole with his finger on the paragraph, as the paper lay on the table.

'Give it to me, doctor, dear. I would not have them see it for the world – and – and – oh! Doctor – sure you wouldn't tell.'

'Augh, bother! – didn't I swear my soul, Ma'am; and do you think I'm going to commit a perjury about "Mary Matchwell" – phiat!'

Well, with much ado, and a great circumbendibus, and floods of tears, and all sorts of deprecations and confusions, out came the murder at last.

Poor Mrs Mack had a duty to perform by her daughter. Her brother was the best man in the world; but what with 'them shockin' forfitures' in her father's time (a Jacobite grand-uncle had forfeited a couple of town-lands, value £37 per annum, in King William's time, and to that event, in general terms, she loved to refer the ruin of her family), and some youthful extravagances, his income, joined to hers, could not keep the dear child in that fashion and appearance her mother had enjoyed before her, and people without pedigree or solid pretension of any sort, looked down upon her, just because they had money (she meant the Chattesworths), and denied her the position which was hers of right, and so seeing no other way of doing the poor child justice, she applied to 'M. M.'

'To find a husband for Mag, eh?' said Toole.

'No, no. Oh, Dr Toole, 'twas – 'twas for *me*,' sobbed poor Mrs Mack. Toole stared for a moment, and had to turn quickly about, and admire some shell-work in a glass box over the chimney-piece very closely, and I think his stout short back was shaking tremulously as he did so; and, when he turned round again, though his face was extraordinarily grave, it was a good deal redder than usual.

'Well, my dear Madam, and where's the great harm in that, when all's done?' said Toole.

'Oh, doctor, I had the unpardonable *wake*ness, whatever come over me, to write her two letters on the subject, and she'll print them, and expose me, unless' – here she rolled herself about in an agony of tears, and buried her fat face in the back of the chair.

'Unless you give her money, I suppose,' said Toole. 'There's what invariably comes of confidential communications with female enchanters and gypsies! And what do you propose to do?'

'I don't know – what can I do? She got the £5 I borrowed from my brother, and he can't lend me more; and I can't tell him what I done with that; and she has £3 10s. I – I raised on my best fan, and the elegant soiclainet, you know – I bought it of Knox & Acheson, at the Indian Queen, in Dame-street;' and his poor patient turned up her small tearful blue eyes imploringly to his face, and her good-natured old features were quivering all over with tribulation.

'And Mag knows nothing of all this?' said Toole.

'Oh, not for the wide world,' whispered the matron, in great alarm. 'Whisht! Is that her coming?'

'No; there she is across the street talking to Mrs Nutter. Listen to me: I'll manage that lady, Mrs Mary – what's her name? – Matchwell. I'll take her in hands, and – whisper now.'

So Toole entered into details, and completed an officious little conspiracy; and the upshot of it was that Mrs Mack, whenever M. M. fixed a day for her next extortionate visit, was to apprise the doctor, who was to keep in the way; and, when she arrived, the good lady was just to send across to him for some 'peppermint drops', upon which hint Toole himself would come slily over, and place himself behind the arras in the bedroom, whither, for greater seclusion and secrecy, she was to conduct the redoubted Mary Matchwell, who was thus to be overheard, and taken by the clever doctor in the act; and then and there frightened not only into a surrender of the documents, but of the money she had already extracted, and compelled to sign such a confession of her guilt as would effectually turn the tables, and place her at the mercy of the once more happy Macnamara.

The doctor was so confident, and the scheme, to the sanguine Celtic imagination of the worthy matron, appeared so facile of execution and infallible of success, that I believe she would at that moment have embraced, and even kissed, little Toole, in the exuberance of her gratitude, had that learned physician cared for such fooleries.

The fact is, however, that neither the doctor nor his patient quite understood Mrs Matchwell or her powers, nor had the least inkling of the marvellous designs that were ripening in her brain, and involving the fate of more than one of the good easy people of Chapelizod, against whom nobody dreamed a thunderbolt was forging.

So the doctor, being a discreet man, only shook her cordially by the hand, at his departure, patting her encouragingly at the same time on her fat shoulder, and with a sly grin and a wink, and a wag of his head – offering to 'lay fifty', that between them 'they'd be too hard for the witch'.

Chapter Thirty-one

Being a short history of the great battle of Belmont that lasted for so many days, wherein the belligerents showed so much constancy and valour, and sometimes one side and sometimes t'other was victorious

So jolly old General Chattesworth was away to Scarborough, and matters went by no means pleasantly at Belmont; for there was strife between the ladies. Dangerfield – cunning fellow – went first to Aunt Becky with his proposal; and Aunt Becky liked it – determined it should prosper, and took up and conducted the case with all her intimidating energy and ferocity. But Gertrude's character had begun to show itself of late in new and marvellous lights, and she fought her aunt with cool, but invincible courage; and why should she marry, and above all, why marry that horrid, grim old gentleman, Mr Dangerfield? No, she had money enough of her own to walk through life in maiden meditation, fancy-free, without being beholden to anybody for a sixpence. Why, Aunt Rebecca herself had never married, and was she not all the happier of her freedom? Aunt Rebecca tried before the general went away, to inflame and stir him up upon the subject. But he had no capacity for coercion. She almost regretted she had made him so very docile. He would leave the matter altogether to his daughter. So Aunt Rebecca, as usual, took, as we have said, the carriage of the proceedings.

Since the grand *éclaircissement* had taken place between Mervyn and Gertrude Chattesworth, they met with as slight and formal a recognition as was possible, consistently with courtesy. Puddock had now little to trouble him upon a topic which had once cost him some uneasiness, and Mervyn acquiesced serenely in the existing state of things, and seemed disposed to be 'sweet upon' pretty Lilias Walsingham, if that young lady had allowed it; but her father had dropped hints about his history and belongings which surrounded him in her eyes with a sort of chill and dismal halo. There was something *funeste* and mysterious even in his beauty; and her spirits faltered and sank in his presence. Something of the same unpleasant influence, too, or was it fancy, she thought his approach seemed now to exercise upon Gertrude also, and that she, too, was unaccountably chilled and darkened by his handsome, but ill-omened presence.

Aunt Becky was not a woman to be soon tired, or even daunted. The young lady's resistance put her upon her mettle, and she was all the more determined, that she suspected her niece had some secret motive for rejecting a partner in some respects so desirable.

Sometimes, it is true, Gertrude's resistance flagged; but this was only the temporary acquiescence of fatigue, and the battle was renewed with the old spirit on the next occasion, and was all to be fought over again. At breakfast there was generally, as I may say, an affair of picquets, and through the day a dropping fire, sometimes rising to a skirmish; but the social meal of supper was generally the period when, for the most part, these desultory hostilities blazed up into a general action. The fortune of war as usual shifted. Sometimes Gertrude left the parlour and effected a retreat to her bedroom. Sometimes it was Aunt Rebecca's turn to slam the door, and leave the field to her adversary. Sometimes, indeed, Aunt Becky thought she had actually finished the exhausting campaign, when her artillery had flamed and thundered over the prostrate enemy for a full half-hour unanswered; but when, at the close of the cannonade she marched up, with drums beating and colours flying, to occupy the position and fortify her victory, she found, much to her mortification, that the foe had only, as it were, lain down to let her shrapnels and canister fly over, and the advance was arrested with the old volley and hurrah. And there they were – not an inch gained – peppering away at one another as briskly as ever, with the work to begin all over again.

'You think I have neither eyes nor understanding; but I can see, young lady, as well as another; ay, Madam, I've eyes, and some experience too, and 'tis my simple duty to my brother, and to the name I bear, not to mention *you*, niece, to prevent, if my influence or authority can do it, the commission of a folly which, I can't but suspect, may possibly be meditated, and which even you, niece, would live very quickly to repent.'

Gertrude did not answer; she only looked a little doubtfully at her aunt, with a gaze of deep, uneasy enquiry. That sort of insinuation seemed to disconcert her. But she did not challenge her aunt to define her meaning, and the attack was soon renewed at another point.

When Gertrude walked down to the town, to the King's House, or even to see Lily, at this side of the bridge, Dominick, the footman, was ordered to trudge after her – a sort of state she had never used in her little neighbourly rambles – and Gertrude knew that her aunt catechised that confidential retainer daily. Under this sort of management, the haughty girl winced and fretted, and finally sulked, grew taciturn and sarcastic, and shut herself up altogether within the precincts of Belmont.

Chapter Thirty-two

Narrating how Lieutenant Puddock and Captain Devereux brewed a bowl of punch, and how they sang and discoursed together

If people would only be content with that which is, let well alone, and allow today to resemble yesterday and tomorrow today, the human race would be much fatter at no greater cost, and sleep remarkably well. But so it is that the soul of man can no more rest here than the sea or the wind. We are always plotting against our own repose, and as no man can stir in a crowd without disturbing others, it happens that even the quietest fellows are forced to fight for their *status quo*, and sometimes, though they would not move a finger or sacrifice a button for the chance of 'getting on', are sulkily compelled to cut capers like the rest. Nature will have it so, and has no end of resources, and will not suffer even the sluggish to sit still, but if nothing else will do, pins a cracker to their skirts, in the shape of a tender passion, or some other whim, and so sets them bouncing in their own obese and clumsy way, to the trouble of others as well as their own discomfort. It is a hard thing, but so it is; the comfort of absolute stagnation is nowhere permitted us. And such, so multifarious and intricate our own mutual dependencies, that it is next to impossible to marry a wife, or to take a house for the summer at Brighton, or to accomplish any other entirely simple, good-humoured, and selfish act without affecting, not only the comforts, but the reciprocal relations of dozens of other respectable persons who appear to have nothing on earth to say to us or our concerns. In this respect, indeed, society resembles a pyramid of potatoes, in which you cannot stir one without setting others, in unexpected places, also in motion. Thus it was, upon very slight motives, the relations of people in the little world of Chapelizod began to shift and change considerably, and very few persons made a decided move of any sort without affecting or upsetting one or more of his neighbours.

Among other persons unexpectedly disturbed just now was our friend Captain Devereux. The letter reached him at night. Little

Puddock walked to his lodgings with him from the club, where he had just given a thplendid rethitation from Shakespeare, and was, as usual after such efforts, in a high state of excitement, and lectured his companion, for whom, by-the-bye, he cherished a boyish admiration, heightened very considerably by his not quite understanding him, upon the extraordinary dramatic capabilities and versatilities of Shakespeare's plays, which, he said, were not half comprehended.

'It was only on Tuesday – the night, you know, I fired the pistol at the robbers, near the dog-house, through the coach window, returning all alone from Smock-alley Theatre. I was thinking, upon my honour, if I had your parts, my dear Devereux, and could write, as I know you can, I'd make a variation upon every play of Shakespeare, that should be strictly moulded upon it, and yet in no respect recognisable.'

'Ay, like those Irish airs that will produce tears or laughter, as they are played slow or quick; or minced veal, my dear Puddock, which the cook can dress either savoury or sweet at pleasure; or Aunt Rebecca, that produces such different emotions in her different moods, and according to our different ways of handling her, is scarce recognisable in some of them, though still the same Aunt Becky,' answered Devereux, knocking at Irons's door.

'No, but seriously, by sometimes changing an old person to a young, sometimes a comical to a melancholy, or the reverse, sometimes a male for a female, or a female for a male – I assure you, you can so entirely disguise the piece, and yet produce situations so new and surprising –'

'I see, by all the gods at once, 'tis an immortal idea! Let's take *Othello* – I'll set about it tomorrow – tonight, by Jove! A gay young Venetian nobleman, of singular beauty, charmed by her tales of "anthropophagites and men whose heads do grow beneath their shoulders", is seduced from his father's house, and married by a middle-aged, somewhat hard-featured black woman, Juno, or Dido, who takes him away – not to Cyprus – we must be original, but we'll suppose to the island of Stromboli – and you can have an eruption firing away during the last act. There Dido grows jealous of our hero, though he's as innocent as Joseph; and while his valet is putting him to bed he'll talk to him and prattle some plaintive little tale how his father had a man called Barbarus. And then, all being prepared, and his bedroom candle put out, Dido enters, looking unusually grim, and smothers him with a pillow in spite of his cries and affecting entreaties, and – By Jupiter! Here's a letter from Bath, too.'

He had lighted the candles, and the letter with its great red eye of a seal, lying upon the table, transfixed his wandering glance, and smote somehow to his heart with an indefinite suspense and misgiving.

'With your permission, my dear Puddock?' said Devereux, before breaking the seal; for in those days they grew ceremonious the moment a point of etiquette turned up. Puddock gave him leave, and he read the letter.

'From my aunt,' he said, throwing it down with a discontented air; and then he read it once more, thought for a while, and put it into his pocket. 'The countess says I must go, Puddock. She has got my leave from the general; and hang it – there's no help for it – I can't vex her, you know. Indeed, Puddock, I *would* not vex her. Poor old aunt – she has been mighty kind to me – no-one knows how kind. So I leave tomorrow.'

'Not to stay away!' exclaimed Puddock, much concerned.

'I don't know, dear Puddock. I know no more than the man in the moon what her plans are. Lewis, you know, is ordered by the doctors to Malaga; and Loftus – honest dog – I managed that trifle for him – goes with him; and the poor old lady, I suppose, is in the vapours, and wants me – and that's all. And Puddock, we must drink a bowl of punch together – you and I – or something – anything – what you please.'

And so they sat some time longer, and grew very merry and friendly, and a little bit pathetic in their several ways. And Puddock divulged his secret but noble flame for Gertrude Chattesworth, and Devereux sang a song or two, defying fortune, in his sweet, sad tenor; and the nymph who skipt up and downstairs with the kettle grew sleepy at last; and Mrs Irons rebelled in her bed, and refused peremptorily to get up again, to furnish the musical topers with rum and lemons, and Puddock, having studied his watch – I'm bound to say with a slight hiccough and supernatural solemnity – for about five minutes, satisfied himself it was nearly one o'clock, and took an affecting, though soldier-like leave of his comrade, who, however, lent him his arm down the stairs, which were rather steep; and having with difficulty dissuaded him from walking into the clock, the door of which was ajar, thought it his duty to see the gallant little lieutenant home to his lodgings; and so in the morning good little Puddock's head ached. He had gone to bed with his waistcoat and leggings on – and his watch was missing and despaired of, till discovered, together with a lemon, in the pocket of his surtout, hanging against the wall; and a variety of other strange arrangements came to light, with not one of which could Puddock connect himself.

Indeed, he was 'dithguthted' at his condition; and if upon the occasion just described he had allowed himself to be somewhat 'intoxicated with liquor', I must aver that I do not recollect another instance in which this worthy little gentleman suffered himself to be similarly overtaken. Now and then a little 'flashy' he might be, but nothing more serious – and rely upon it, this was no common virtue in those days.

Chapter Thirty-three

*In which Captain Devereux's fiddle plays a prelude to
'Over the Hills and Far Away'*

There was some little undefinable coolness between old General
Chattesworth and Devereux. He admired the young fellow, and he
liked good blood in his corps, but somehow he was glad when he
thought he was likely to go. When old Bligh, of the Magazine,
commended the handsome young dog's good looks, the general
would grow grave all at once, and sniff once or twice, and say, 'Yes, a
good-looking fellow certainly, and might make a good officer, a
mighty good officer, but he's wild, a troublesome dog.' And, lowering his voice, 'I tell you what, colonel, as long as a young buck sticks
to his claret, it is all fair; but hang it, you see, I'm afraid he likes other
things, and he won't wait till after dinner – this between ourselves,
you know. 'Tis not a button to me, by Jupiter, what he does or
drinks, off duty; but hang it, I'm afraid some day he'll break out; and
once or twice in a friendly way, you know, I've had to speak with him,
and, to say truth, I'd rather he served under anyone else. He's a fine
fellow, 'tis a pity there should be anything wrong, and it would half
break my heart to have to take a public course with him; not, you
know, that it has ever come to anything like that – but – but I've
heard things – and – and he must pull up, or he'll not do for the
service.' So, though the thing did not amount to a scandal, there
was a formality between Devereux and his commanding officer, who
thought he saw bad habits growing apace, and apprehended that ere
long disagreeable relations might arise between them.

Lord Athenry had been no friend to Devereux in his nonage, and
the good-natured countess, to make amends, had always done her
utmost to spoil him, and given him a great deal more of his own way,
as well as of plum-cake, and Jamaica preserves, and afterwards a great
deal more money, than was altogether good for him. Like many a
worse person, she was a little bit capricious, and a good deal selfish;
but the young fellow was handsome. She was proud of his singularly

good looks, and his wickedness interested her, and she gave him more money than to all the best public charities to which she contributed put together. Devereux, indeed, being a fast man, with such acres as he inherited, which certainly did not reach a thousand, mortgaged pretty smartly, and with as much personal debt beside, of the fashionable and refined sort, as became a young buck of bright though doubtful expectations – and if the truth must be owned, sometimes pretty nearly pushed into a corner – was beholden, not only for his fun, but occasionally for his daily bread and even his liberty, to those benevolent doles.

He did not like her peremptory summons; but he could not afford to quarrel with his bread and butter, nor to kill by undutiful behaviour the fair, plump bird whose golden eggs were so very convenient. I don't know whether there may not have been some slight sign in the handwriting – in a phrase, perhaps, or in the structure of the composition, which a clever analysis might have detected, and which only reached him vaguely, with a foreboding that he was not to see Chapelizod again so soon as usual when this trip was made. And, in truth, his aunt had plans. She designed his retirement from the Royal Irish Artillery, and had negotiated an immediate berth for him on the Staff of the Commander of the Forces, and a prospective one in the household of Lord Townshend; she had another arrangement 'on the anvil' for a seat in Parliament, which she would accomplish, if that were possible; and finally a wife. In fact her ladyship had encountered old General Chattesworth at Scarborough only the autumn before, and they had had, in that gay resort, a good deal of serious talk (though serious talk with the good countess never lasted very long), between their cards and other recreations, the result of which was, that she began to think, with the good general, that Devereux would be better where one unlucky misadventure would not sully his reputation for life. Besides, she thought Chapelizod was not safe ground for a young fellow so eccentric, perverse, and impetuous, where pretty faces were plentier than good fortunes, and at every tinkling harpsichord there smiled a possible *mésalliance*. In the town of Chapelizod itself, indeed, the young gentleman did not stand quite so high in estimation as with his aunt, who thought nothing was good or high enough for her handsome nephew, with his good blood and his fine possibilities. The village folk, however, knew that he was confoundedly dipped; that he was sometimes alarmingly pestered by duns, and had got so accustomed to hear that his uncle, the earl, was in his last sickness, and his cousin, the next heir, dead, when another week disclosed that neither one nor the other was a bit worse than usual, that they began to think that Devereux's turn might very possibly never come at all. Besides, the towns-people had high notions of some of their belles, and not without reason. There was Miss Gertrude Chattesworth, for instance, with more than fourteen thousand pounds to her fortune, and Lilias Walsingham, who would inherit her mother's money, and the good rector's estate of twelve hundred a year beside, and both with good blood in their veins, and beautiful princesses too. However, in those days there was more parental despotism than now. The old people kept their worldly wisdom to themselves, and did not take the young into a scheming partnership; and youth and beauty, I think, were more romantic, and a great deal less venal.

Such being the old countess's programme – a plan, according to her lights, grand and generous – she might have dawdled over it for a good while, for she did not love trouble. It was not new; the airy castle had been some years built, and now, in an unwonted hurry, she wished to introduce the tenant to the well-aired edifice, and put him in actual possession. For a queer little attack in her head, which she called a fainting fit, and to which nobody dared afterwards to make allusion, and which she had bullied herself and everybody about her into forgetting, had, nevertheless, frightened her con-foundedly. And when her helpless panic and hysterics were over, she silently resolved, if the thing were done, then 'twere well 'twere done quickly.

Chapter Thirty-four

*In which Lilias hears a stave of an old song and there is a
leave-taking beside the river*

Devereux's move was very sudden, and the news did not reach the
Elms till his groom had gone on to Island-bridge with the horses,
and he himself, booted and spurred, knocked at the door. The doctor
was not at home; he had ridden into Dublin. Of course it was chiefly
to see him he had gone there.

'And Miss Walsingham?'

She was also out; no, not in the garden. John thought maybe at old
Miss Chattesworth's school; or, Sally said, maybe at Belmont; they
did not know.

Devereux looked into the large room at the right hand of the
hall, with the fair sad portrait of Lilias's young mother smiling, from
the wall. Like *her*, too – and the tall glasses of flowers – and the
harpsichord open, with the music she would play, just as usual, that
evening, he supposed; and he stood at the door, looking round the
room, booted and spurred, as I have said, with his cocked hat held to
his breast, in a reverie. It was not easy for old Sally to guess what was
passing in his mind, for whenever he was sad he smiled, but with the
somewhat of bitter in his smile, and when he suffered he used to joke.

Just at that moment Lilias Walsingham was walking along the high
street of the village to the King's House, and stopping to say a good-
natured little word to old Jenny Creswell, was overtaken by mild Mrs
Sturk, who was walking her little menagerie into the park.

'And oh! dear Miss Walsingham, did you hear the news?' she said;
'Captain Devereux is gone to England, and I believe we shan't see
him here again.'

Lilias felt that she grew pale, but she patted one of the children on
the head, and smiled, and asked him some foolish little question.

'But why don't you listen, dear Miss Lilias? You don't hear, I
think,' said Mrs Sturk.

'I do hear, indeed; when did he go?' she asked, coldly enough.

'About half an hour ago,' Mrs Sturk thought: and so, with a word or two more, and a kissing of hands, the good lady turned, with her brood, up the park lane, and Lily walked on to pay her visit to Mrs Colonel Stafford, feeling all the way a strange pang of anger and disappointment.

'To think of his going away without taking leave of my father!'

And when she reached the hall-door of the King's House for a moment she forgot what she had come for, and was relieved to find that good Mrs Strafford was in town.

There was then, I don't know whether there is not now, a little path leading by the river bank from Chapelizod to Island-bridge, just an angler's footpath, devious and broken, but withal very sweet and pretty. Leaving the King's House, she took this way home, and as she walked down to the river bank, the mortified girl looked down upon the grass close by her feet, and whispered to the daisies as she went along – 'No, there's no more kindness nor friendliness left in the world; the people are all cold creatures now, and hypocrites; and I'm glad he's gone.'

She paused at the stile which went over the hedge just beside an old fluted pier, with a grass-grown urn at top, and overgrown with a climbing rose-tree, just such a study as a young lady might put in her album; and then she recollected the long letter from old Miss Wardle that Aunt Becky had sent her to read, with a request, which from that quarter was a command, that she should return it by six o'clock, for Aunt Becky, even in matters indifferent, liked to name hours, and nail people sharp and hard to futile appointments and barren punctualities.

She paused at the stile; she liked the old pier; its partner next the river was in fragments, and the ruin and the survivor had both been clothed by good Mrs Strafford – who drew a little, and cultivated the picturesque – with the roses I have mentioned, besides woodbine and ivy. She had old Miss Wardle's letter in her hand, full, of course, of shocking anecdotes about lunatics, and the sufferings of Fleet prisoners, and all the statistics, and enquiries, and dry little commissions, with which that worthy lady's correspondence abounded. It was open in her hand, and rustled sharp and stiffly in the air, but it was not inviting just then. From that point it was always a pretty look down or up the river; and her eyes followed with the flow of its waters towards Inchicore. She loved the river; and in her thoughts she wondered why she loved it – so cold, so unimpressible – that went shining and rejoicing away into the sea. And just at that moment she heard a sweet tenor, with a gaiety somehow pathetic, sing not far away the words she remembered:

> And she smiled upon the stream,
> Like one that smiles at folly,
> A dreamer on a dream.

Devereux was coming – it was his playful salutation. Her large eyes dropped to the ground with the matchless blush of youth. She was strangely glad, but vexed at having changed colour; but when he came up with her, in the deep shadow thrown by the old pier, with its thick festooneries, he could not tell, he only knew she looked beautiful.

'My dreams take wing, but my follies will not leave me. And you have been ill, Miss Lilias?'

'Oh, nothing; only a little cold.'

'And I am going – I only knew last night – really going away.' He paused; but the young lady did not feel called upon to say anything, and only allowed him to go on. In fact, she was piqued, and did not choose to show the least concern about his movements. 'And I've a great mind now that I'm departing this little world,' and he glanced, it seemed to her, regretfully towards the village, 'to put you down, Miss Lily, if you will allow it, in my codicil for a legacy – '

She laughed a pleasant little careless laugh. How ill-natured! But, oh! wasn't it musical.

'Then I suppose, if you were not to see me for some time, or maybe for ever, the village folks won't break their hearts after Dick Devereux?'

And the gypsy captain smiled, and his eyes threw a soft violet shadow down upon her; and there was that in his tone which for a moment touched her with a strange reproach, like a bar of sweet music.

But little Lily was spirited; and if *he*, so early a friend, could go away without bidding goodbye, why he should not suppose *she* cared.

'Break our hearts? Not at all, perhaps; but of course I – the parson's daughter – I should, and old Moore, the barber, and Pat Moran, the hackney coachman, and Mrs Irons your fat landlady, you've been so very good to all of us, you know.'

'Well,' he interrupted, 'I've left my white surtout to Moran: a hat, let me see, and a pair of buckles to Moore; and my glass and china to dear Mrs Irons.'

'Hat – buckles – surtout – glass – china – gone! Then it seems to me your earthly possessions are pretty nearly disposed of, and your worldly cares at an end.'

'Yes; very nearly, but not quite,' he laughed. 'I have one treasure left – my poor monkey; he's a wonderful fellow – he has travelled half over the world, and is a perfect fine gentleman – and my true comrade until now. Do you think Dr Walsingham, of his charity, would give the poor fellow free quarters at the Elms?'

She was going to make answer with a jest, satirically; but her mood changed quickly. It was, she thought, saucy of Captain Devereux to fancy that she should care to have his pet; and she answered a little gravely: 'I can't say indeed; had you cared to see him, you might have asked him; but, indeed, Captain Devereux, I believe you're jesting.'

'Faith! Madam, I believe I am; or, it does not much matter – dreaming perhaps. There's our bugle!' And the sweet sounds quivered and soared through the pleasant air. 'How far away it sounds already; ours are sweet bugles – the sweetest bugles to my ear in the wide world. Yes, dreaming. I said I had but one treasure left,' he continued, with a fierce sort of tenderness that was peculiar to him: 'and I did not mean to tell you, but I will. Look at that, Miss Lily, 'tis the little rose you left on your harpsichord this morning. I stole it: 'tis mine; and Richard Devereux would die rather than lose it to another.'

So then, after all, he had been at the Elms; and she had wronged him.

'Yes, dreaming,' he continued, in his old manner; 'and 'tis time I were awake, awake and on the march.'

'You are then really going?' she said, so that no-one would have guessed how strangely she felt at that moment.

'Yes, really going,' he said, quite in his own way; 'Over the hills and far away; and so, I know, you'll first wish your old friend God speed.'

'I do, indeed.'

'And then you'll shake hands, Miss Lily, as in old times.'

And out came the frank little hand, and he looked on it, with a darkling smile, as it lay in his own sinewy but slender grasp; and she said with a smile – 'Goodbye.'

She was frightened lest he should possibly say more than she knew how to answer.

'And somehow it seems to me, I have a great deal to say.'

'And I've a great deal to read, you see;' and she just stirred old Miss Wardle's letter, that lay open in her hand, with a smile just the least in the world of comic distress.

'A great deal,' he said.

'And farewell, again,' said Lilias.

'Farewell! dear Miss Lily.'

And then, he just looked his old strange look upon her; and he went: and she dropped her eyes upon the letter. He had got into the far meadow, where the path makes a little turn round the clump of poplars, and hides itself. Just there he looked over his shoulder, a last look it might be, the handsome strange creature that had made so many of her hours pass so pleasantly; he that was so saucy with everyone else, and so gentle with her; of whom, she believed, she might make anything, a hero or a demigod! She knew a look would call him back – back, maybe, to her feet; but she could not give that little sign. There she stood, affecting to read that letter, one word of which she did not see. 'She does not care; but – but there's no-one like her. No – she does not care,' he thought; and she let him think it: but her heart swelled to her throat, and she felt as if she could have screamed, 'Come back – my only love – my darling – without you I must die!' But she did not raise her head. She only read on, steadily, old Miss Wardle's letter – over and over – the same half-dozen lines. And when, after five minutes more, she lifted up her eyes, the hoary poplars were ruffling their thick leaves in the breeze – and he gone; and the plaintive music came mellowed from the village, and the village and the world seemed all on a sudden empty for her.

Chapter Thirty-five

In which Aunt Becky and Dr Toole, in full blow, with Dominick the footman behind them, visit Miss Lily at the Elms

After such leave-takings, especially where something like a revelation takes place, there sometimes supervenes, I'm told, a sort of excitement before the chill and ache of separation sets in. So Lily, when she went home, found that her music failed her, all but the one strange little air, 'The river ran between them'; and then she left the harpsichord and went into the garden through the glass door, but the flowers had only half their interest, and the garden was solitary, and she felt restless, as if she were going to make a journey, or looking for strange news; and then she bethought her again of Mrs Colonel Stafford, that she might have by this time returned from Dublin, and there was some little interest about the good old lady, even in this, that she had just returned by the same road that he had gone away by, that she might have chanced to see him as he passed; that at least she might happen to speak of him, and to know something of the likelihood of his return, or even to speculate about him; for now any talk in which his name occurred was interesting, though she did not know it quite herself. So she went down to the King's House, and did find old Mrs Stafford at home: and after an entertaining gossip about some 'rich Nassau damask', at Haughton's in the Coombe, that had taken her fancy mightily, and how she had chosen a set of new Nankeen plates and fine oblong dishes at the Music Hall, and how Peter Raby, the watchman, was executed yesterday morning, in web worsted breeches, for the murder of Mr Thomas Fleming, of Thomas-street, she did come at last to mention Devereux: and she said that the colonel had received a letter from General Chattesworth, 'who by-the-bye', and then came a long parenthesis, very pleasant, you may be sure, for Lily to listen to; and the general, it appeared, thought it most likely that Devereux would not return to Chapelizod, and the Royal Irish Artillery; and then she went on to other subjects, and Lily staid a long time, thinking she might return to Devereux, but she did not mention him again. So home went little Lily more pensive than she came.

It was near eight o'clock, when who should arrive at the door, and flutter the crows in the old elms with an energetic double knock, but Aunt Rebecca, accompanied by no less a personage than Dr Toole in full costume, and attended by old Dominick, the footman.

The doctor was a little bit ruffled and testy, for having received a summons from Belmont, he had attended in full blow, expecting to prescribe for Aunt Rebecca or Miss Gertrude, and found, instead, that he was in for a barren and benevolent walk of half a mile on the Inchicore road, with the energetic Miss Rebecca, to visit one of her felonious pensioners who lay sick in his rascally crib. It was not the first time that the jolly little doctor had been entrapped by the good lady into a purely philanthropic excursion of this kind. But he could not afford to mutiny, and vented his disgust in blisters and otherwise drastic treatment of the malingering scoundrels whom he served out after his kind for the trouble and indignity they cost him.

'And here we are, Lily dear, on our way to see poor dear Pat Doolan, who, I fear, is not very long for this world. Dominick! – he's got a brain fever, my dear.'

The doctor said 'pish!' inaudibly, and Aunt Becky went on.

'You know the unhappy creature is only just out of prison, and if ever mortal suffered unjustly, he's the man. Poor Doolan's as innocent as you or I, my dear, or sweet little Spot, there,' pointing her fan like a pistol at that interesting quadruped's head. 'The disgrace has broken his heart, and that's at the bottom of his sickness. I wish you could hear him speak, poor dear wretch – Dominick!' and she had a word for that domestic in the hall.

'Hear him speak, indeed!' said Toole, taking advantage of her momentary absence. 'I wish you could, the drunken blackguard. King Solomon could not make sense of it. She gave that burglar, would you believe it, Ma'am? two guineas, by Jupiter: the first of this month – and whiskey only sixpence a pint – and he was drunk without intermission of course, day and night for a week after. Brain fever, indeed, 'tis just as sweet a little fit of delirium tremens, my dear Madam, as ever sent an innocent burglar slap into bliss;' and the word popped out with a venomous hiss and an angry chuckle.

'And so, my dear,' resumed Aunt Becky, marching in again; 'good Doctor Toole – our good Samaritan, here – has taken him up, just for love, and the poor man's fee – his blessing.'

The doctor muttered something about 'taking him up', but inarticulately, for it was only for the relief of his own feelings.

'And now, dear Lilias, we want your good father to come with us, just to pray by the poor fellow's bedside: he's in the study, is he?'

'No, he was not to be home until tomorrow morning.'

'Bless me!' cried Aunt Becky, with as much asperity as if she had said something different; 'and not a soul to be had to comfort a dying wretch in your father's parish – yes, he's dying; we want a minister to pray with him, and here we've a Flemish account of the rector. This tells prettily for Dr Walsingham!'

'Dr Walsingham's the best rector in the whole world, and the holiest man and the noblest,' cried brave little Lily, standing like a deer at bay, with her wild shy eyes looking full in Aunt Becky's, and a flush in her cheeks, and the beautiful light of truth beaming like a star from her forehead. And for a moment it looked like battle; but the old lady smiled a kind of droll little smile, and gave her a little pat on the cheek, saying with a shake of her head, 'saucy girl!'

'And you,' said Lily, throwing her arms about her neck, 'are my own Aunt Becky, the greatest darling in the world!' And so, as John Bunyan says, 'the water stood in their eyes', and they both laughed, and then they kissed, and loved one another the better. That was the way their little quarrels used always to end.

'Well, doctor, we must only do what we can,' said Aunt Becky, looking gravely on the physician: 'and I don't see why *you* should not read – you can lend us a prayer-book, darling – just a collect or two, and the Lord's Prayer – eh?'

'Why, my dear Ma'am, the fellow's howling about King Lewis and the American Indians, Dominick says, and ghosts and constables, and devils, and worse things, Madam, and – pooh – punch and laudanum's his only chance; don't mind the prayer-book, Miss Lily – there's no use in it, Mistress Chattesworth! I give you my honour, Ma'am, he could not make head or tale of it.'

In fact, the doctor was terrified lest Aunt Rebecca should compel him to officiate, and he was thinking how the fellows at the club, and the Aldermen of Skinner's-alley, would get hold of the story, and treat the subject less gravely than was desirable.

So Aunt Becky, with Lily's leave, called in Dominick, to examine him touching the soundness of Pat Doolan's mind, and the honest footman had no hesitation in pronouncing him wholly *non compos*.

'Pleasant praying with a chap like that, by Jove, as drunk as an owl, and as mad as a March hare, my dear Ma'am!' whispered Toole to Lilias.

'And, Lily dear, there's poor Gertrude all alone – 'twould be good-natured in you to go up and drink a dish of tea with her; but, then, you're cold – you're afraid?'

She was not afraid – she had been out today – and it had done her all the good in the world, and it was very good of Aunt Becky to think of it, for she was lonely too: and so off went the elder Miss Chattesworth, with her doctor and Dominick, in their various moods, on their mission of mercy; and Lily sent into the town for the two chairmen, Peter Brian and Larry Foy, the two-legged ponies, as Toole called them.

Chapter Thirty-six

Narrating how Miss Lilias visited Belmont, and saw a strange cocked hat in the shadow by the window

At that time, in every hall of gentility, there stood a sedan-chair, the property of the lady of the house; and by the time the chair-men had arrived and got the poles into their places, and trusty John Tracy had got himself into his brown surtout, trimmed with white lace, and his cane in his hand – (there was no need of a lantern, for the moon shone softly and pleasantly down) – Miss Lilias Walsingham drew her red riding hood about her pretty face, and stepped into the chair; and so the door shut, the roof closed in, and the young lady was fairly under weigh. She had so much to think of, so much to tell about her day's adventure, that before she thought she had come half the way, they were flitting under the shadows of the poplars that grew beside the avenue; and, through the window, she saw the hospitable house spreading out its white front as they drew near, and opening its wings to embrace her.

The hall-door stood half open, though it had been dark some time; and the dogs came down with a low growl, and plenty of sniffing, which forthwith turned into a solemn wagging of tails, for they were intimate with the chair-men, and with John Tracy, and loved Lilias too. So she got out in the hall, and went into the little room at the right, and opening the door of the inner and larger one – there was no candle there, and 'twas nearly dark – saw Gertrude standing by the window which looked out on the lawn toward the river. That side of the house was in shade, but she saw that the window was thrown up, and Gertrude, she thought, was looking toward her, though she did not move, until she drew nearer, wondering why she did not approach, and then, pausing in a kind of unpleasant doubt, she heard a murmured talking, and plainly saw the figure of a man, with a cloak, it seemed, wrapped about him, and leaning from outside, against the window-sill, and, as she believed, holding Gertrude's hand.

The thing that impressed her most was the sharp outline of the cocked hat, with the corners so peculiarly pinched in, and the feeling that she had never seen that particular hat before in the parish of Chapelizod.

Lily made a step backward, and Gertrude instantly turned round, and seeing her, uttered a little scream.

''Tis I, Gertrude, darling – Lily – Lily Walsingham,' she said, perhaps as much dismayed as Gertrude herself; 'I'll return in a moment.'

She saw the figure, outside, glide hurriedly away by the side of the wall.

'Lily – Lily, darling; no, don't go – I did not expect you;' and Gertrude stopped suddenly, and then as suddenly said: 'You are very welcome, Lily;' and she drew the window down, and there was another pause before she said – 'Had not we better go up to the drawing-room, and – and – Lily darling, you're very welcome. Are you better?'

And she took little Lily's hand, and kissed her.

Little Lilias all this time had said nothing, so entirely was she disconcerted. And her heart beat fast with a kind of fear: and she felt Gertrude's cold hand tremble she fancied in hers.

'Yes, darling, the drawing-room, certainly,' answered Lily. And the two young ladies went upstairs holding hands, and without exchanging another word.

'Aunt Becky has gone some distance to see a sick pensioner; I don't expect her return before an hour.'

'Yes – I know – and she came, dear Gertrude, to see me; and I should not have come, but that she asked me, and – and – '

She stopped, for she was speaking apologetically, like an intruder, and she was shocked to feel what a chasm on a sudden separated them, and oppressed with the consciousness that their old mutual girlish confidence was dead and gone; and the incident of the evening, and Gertrude's changed aspect, and their changed relations, seemed a dreadful dream.

Gertrude looked so pale and wretchedly, and Lily saw her eyes, wild and clouded, once or twice steal toward her with a glance of such dark alarm and enquiry, that she was totally unable to keep up the semblance of their old merry gossiping talk, and felt that Gertrude read in her face the amazement and fear which possessed her.

'Lily, darling, let us sit near the window, far away from the candles, and look out; I hate the light.'

'With all my heart,' said Lily. And two paler faces than theirs, that night, did not look out on the moonlight prospect.

'I hate the light, Lily,' repeated Gertrude, not looking at her companion, but directly out through the bow-window upon the dark outline of the lawn and river bank, and the high grounds on the other side. 'I hate the light – yes, I hate the light, because my thoughts are darkness – yes, my thoughts are darkness. No human being knows me; and I feel like a person who is *haunted*. Tell me what you saw when you came into the parlour just now.'

'Gertrude, dear, I ought not to have come in so suddenly.'

'Yes, 'twas but right – 'twas but kind in you, Lily – right and kind – to treat me like the open-hearted and intimate friend that, Heaven knows, I was to you, Lily, all my life. I think – at least, I think – till lately – but you were always franker than I – and truer. You've walked in the light, Lily, and that's the way to peace. I turned aside, and walked in mystery; and it seems to me I am treading now the valley of the shadow of death. Waking and talking, I am, nevertheless, in the solitude and darkness of the grave. And what did you see, Lily – I know you'll tell me truly – when you came into the parlour, as I stood by the window?'

'I saw, I think, the form of a man in a cloak and hat, as I believe, talking with you in whispers, Gertrude, from without.'

'The form of a man, Lily – you're right – not a man, but the form of a man,' she continued, bitterly; 'for it seems to me sometimes it can be no human fascination that has brought me under the tyranny in which I can scarce be said to breathe.'

After an interval she said: 'It will seem incredible. You've heard of Mr Dangerfield's proposal, and you've heard how I've received it. Well, listen.'

'Gertrude, dear!' said Lily, who was growing frightened.

'I'm going,' interrupted Miss Chattesworth, 'to tell you my strange, if you will, but not guilty – no, *not* guilty – secret. I'm no agent now, but simply passive in the matter. But you must first pledge me your sacred word that neither to my father nor to yours, nor to my aunt, nor to any living being, will you ever reveal what I am about to tell you, till I have released you from your promise.'

Did ever woman refuse a secret? Well, Lily wavered for a moment. But then suddenly stooping down, and kissing her, she said: 'No, Gertrude, darling – you'll not be vexed with me – but you must not tell me your secret. You have excuses such as I should not have – you've been drawn into this concealment, step by step, unwillingly;

but, Gertrude, darling, I must not hear it. I could not look Aunt
Becky in the face, nor the kind general, knowing that I was – '

She tried to find a word.

'*Deceiving* them, Lily,' said Gertrude, with a moan.

'Yes, Gertrude, darling.' And she kissed her again. 'And it might be
to your great hurt. But I thank you all the same from my heart for
your confidence and love; and I'm gladder than you'll ever know,
Gertie, that they are still the same.' And thus the two girls kissed
silently and fervently, and poor Gertrude Chattesworth wept uncom-
plainingly, looking out upon the dark prospect.

'And you'll tell me, darling, when you're happier, as you soon will
be?' said Lily.

'I will – I will indeed. I'm sometimes happier – sometimes quite
happy – but I'm very low tonight, Lily,' answered she.

Then Lily comforted and caressed her friend. And I must confess
she was very curious, too, and nothing but a terror of possessing a
secret under such terms, withheld her from hearing Gertrude's confession. But on her way home she thanked Heaven for her resolution,
and was quite sure that she was happier and better for it.

They were roused by Aunt Becky's knock at the hall-door, and her
voice and Dominick's under the window.

Chapter Thirty-seven

Showing how some of the feuds in Chapelizod waxed fiercer, and others were solemnly condoned

By this time little Dr Toole had stepped into the club, after his wont, as he passed the Phoenix. Sturk was playing draughts with old Arthur Slowe, and Dangerfield, erect and grim, was looking on the game, over his shoulder. Toole and Sturk were more distant and cold in their intercourse of late, though this formality partook of their respective characters. Toole used to throw up his nose, and raise his eyebrows, and make his brother mediciner a particularly stiff, and withal scornful reverence when they met. Sturk, on the other hand, made a short, surly nod – 'twas little more – and, without a word, turned on his heel, with a gruff pitch of his shoulder towards Toole.

The fact was, these two gentlemen had been very near exchanging pistol shots, or sword thrusts, only a week or two before; and all about the unconscious gentleman who was smiling in his usual pleasant fashion over the back of Sturk's chair. So Dangerfield's little dyspepsy had like to have cured one or other of the village leeches, for ever and a day, of the heart-ache and all other aches that flesh is heir to. For Dangerfield commenced with Toole: and that physician, on the third day of his instalment, found that Sturk had stept in and taken his patient bodily out of his hands.

I've seen one monkey force open the jaws of his brother, resolutely introduce his fingers, pluck from the sanctuary of his cheek the filbert he had just stowed there for his private nutrition and delight, and crunch and eat it with a stern ecstasy of selfishness, himself; and I fancy that the feelings of the quadrumanous victim, his jaws aching, his pouch outraged, and his bon-bouche in the miscreant's mouth, a little resembles those of the physician who has suffered so hideous a mortification as that of Toole.

Toole quite forgave Dangerfield. That gentleman gave him to understand that *his* ministrations were much more to his mind than those of his rival. But – and this was conveyed in strict confidence –

this change was put upon him by a – a – in fact a nobleman – Lord Castlemallard – with whom, just now, Dr Sturk can do a great deal; 'and you know I can't quarrel with my lord. It has pained me, I assure you, very much; and to say truth, whoever applied to him to interfere in the matter was, in my mind, guilty of an impertinence, though, as you see, I can't resent it.'

'*Whoever* applied? 'Tis pretty plain,' repeated Toole, with a vicious sneer. 'The whispering, undermining – and as stupid as the Hill of Howth. I wish you safe out of his hands, Sir.'

And positively, only for Aunt Becky, who was always spoiling this sort of sport, and who restrained the gallant Toole by a peremptory injunction, there would have been, in Nutter's unfortunate phrase, 'wigs on the green', next day.

So these gentlemen met on the terms I've described: and Nutter's antipathy also, had waxed stronger and fiercer. And indeed, since Dangerfield's arrival, and Sturk's undisguised endeavours to ingratiate himself with Lord Castlemallard, and push him from his stool, they had by consent ceased to speak to one another. When Sturk met Nutter, he, being of superior stature, looked over his head at distant objects: and when Nutter encountered Sturk, the little gentleman's dark face grew instantaneously darker – first a shade – then another shadow – then the blackness of thunder overspread it; and not only did he speak not a word to Sturk, but seldom opened his lips while that gentleman remained in the room.

On the other hand, if some feuds grew blacker and fiercer by time, there were others which were Christianly condoned; foremost among which was the mortal quarrel between Nutter and O'Flaherty. On the evening of their memorable meeting on the Fifteen Acres, Puddock dined out, and O'Flaherty was too much exhausted to take any steps toward a better understanding. But on the night following, when the club had their grand supper in King William's parlour, it was arranged with Nutter that a gentlemanlike reconciliation was to take place; and accordingly, about nine o'clock, at which time Nutter's arrival was expected, Puddock, with the pomp and gravity becoming such an occasion, accompanied by O'Flaherty, big with his speech, entered the spacious parlour.

When they came in there was a chorus of laughter ringing round, with a clapping of hands, and a Babel of hilarious applause; and Tom Toole was seen in the centre, sitting upon the floor, hugging his knees, with his drawn sword under his arm, his eyes turned up to the ceiling, and a contortion so unspeakably ludicrous upon his queer little face, as was very near causing little Puddock to explode in an unseemly burst of laughter.

Devereux, sitting near the door, luckily saw them as they entered, and announced them in a loud tone – 'Lieutenant Puddock, gentlemen, and Lieutenant Fireworker O'Flaherty.' For though Gypsy Devereux loved a bit of mischief, he did not relish it when quite so serious, as the Galwegian Fireworker was likely to make any sort of trifling on a point so tender as his recent hostilities on the Fifteen Acres.

Toole bounded to his feet in an instant, adjusting his wig and eyeing the newcomers with intense but uneasy solemnity, which produced some suppressed merriment among the company.

It was well for the serenity of the village that O'Flaherty was about to make a little speech – a situation which usually deprived him of half his wits. Still with the suspicion of conscious weakness, he read something affecting himself in the general buzz and countenance of the assembly; and said to Devereux, on purpose loud enough for Toole to hear – 'Ensign Puddock and myself would be proud to know what was the divarting tom-foolery going on about the floor, and for which we arrived unfortunately a little too leet?'

'Tom-foolery, Sir, is an unpleasant word!' cried the little doctor, firing up, for he was a gamecock.

'Tom Toolery he means,' interposed Devereux, 'the pleasantest word, on the contrary, in Chapelizod. Pray, allow me to say a word a degree more serious. I'm commissioned, Lieutenant Puddock and Lieutenant O'Flaherty,' [a bow to each] 'by Mr Mahony, who acted the part of second to Mr Nutter, on the recent occasion, to pray that you'll be so obliging as to accept his apology for not being present at this, as we all hope most agreeable meeting. Our reverend friend, Father Roach, whose guest he had the honour to be, can tell you more precisely the urgent nature of the business on which he departed.'

Father Roach tried to stop the captain with a reproachful glance, but that unfeeling officer fairly concluded his sentence notwithstanding, with a wave of his hand and a bow to the cleric; and sitting down at the same moment, left him in possession of the chair.

The fact was, that at an unseemly hour that morning three bailiffs – for the excursion was considered hazardous – introduced themselves by a stratagem into the reverend father's domicile, and nabbed the high-souled Patrick Mahony, as he slumbered peacefully in his bed, to the terror of the simple maid who let them in. Honest Father

Roach was for showing fight on behalf of his guest. On hearing the row and suspecting its cause – for Pat had fled from the kingdom of Kerry from perils of the same sort – his reverence jumped out of bed with a great pound on the floor, and not knowing where to look for his clothes in the dark, he seized his surplice, which always lay in the press at the head of his bed, and got into it with miraculous speed, whisking along the floor two pounds and a half of Mr Fogarty's best bacon, which the holy man had concealed in the folds of that sacred vestment, to elude the predatory instincts of the women, and from which he and Mr Mahony were wont to cut their jovial rashers.

The shutter of poor Mahony's window was by this time open, and the grey light disclosed the grimly form of Father Roach, in his surplice, floating threateningly into the chamber. But the bailiffs were picked men, broad-shouldered and athletic, and furnished with active-looking shillelaghs. *Veni, vidi, victus sum*! A glance showed him all was lost.

'My blessin' an you, Peg Finigan! And was it you let them in?' murmured his reverence, with intense feeling.

'At whose suit?' enquired the generous outlaw, sitting up among the blankets.

'Mrs Elizabeth Woolly, relict and administhrathrix of the late Mr Timotheus Woolly, of High-street, in the city of Dublin, tailor,' responded the choragus of the officers.

'Woolly – I was thinkin' so,' said the captive. 'I wisht I *had* her by the wool, bad luck to her!'

So away he went, to the good-natured ecclesiastic's grief, promising, nevertheless, with a disconsolate affectation of cheerfulness, that all should be settled, and he under the Priest's roof-tree again before night.

'I don't – exactly – know the nature of the business, gentlemen,' said Father Roach, with considerable hesitation.

'*Urgent*, however, it *was* – wasn't it?' said Devereux.

'Urgent – well; *certainly* – a – and – '

'And a summons there was no resisting – from a lady – eh? You said so, Father Roach,' persisted Devereux.

'A – from a leedy – a – yes – certainly,' replied he.

'A *widow* – is not she?' enquired Devereux.

'A widda, undoubtedly,' said the priest.

'Thay no more Thir,' said little Puddock, to the infinite relief of the reverend father, who flung another look of reproach at

Devereux, and muttered his indignation to himself. 'I'm perfectly satisfied; and so, I venture to thay, is Lieutenant O'Flaherty – '

'Is not he going to say something to Nutter?' enquired Devereux.

'Yes,' whispered Puddock, 'I hope he'll get through it. I – I wrote a few sentences myself; but he's by no means perfect – in fact, between ourselves, he's a somewhat slow study.'

'Suppose you purge his head again, Puddock?' Puddock did not choose to hear the suggestion: but Nutter, in reply to a complimentary speech from Puddock, declared, in two or three words, his readiness to meet Lieutenant O'Flaherty half-way; 'and curse me, Sir, if I know, at this moment, what I did or said to offend him.'

Then came a magnanimous, but nearly unintelligible speech from O'Flaherty, prompted by little Puddock, who, being responsible for the composition, was more nervous during the delivery of that remarkable oration, than the speaker himself; and 'thuffered indethcribably' at hearing his periods mangled; and had actually to hold O'Flaherty by the arm, and whisper in an agony – 'not yet – *curthe* it – not yet' – to prevent the incorrigible fireworker from stretching forth his bony red hand before he had arrived at that most effective passage which Puddock afterwards gave so well in private for Dick Devereux, beginning, 'and thus I greet – '

Thus was there a perfect reconciliation, and the gentlemen of the club, Toole included, were more than ever puzzled to understand the origin of the quarrel, for Puddock kept O'Flaherty's secret magnificently, and peace prevailed in O'Flaherty's breast until nearly ten months afterwards, when Cluffe, who was talking of the American war, asked O'Flaherty, who was full of volunteering, how he would like a 'clean shave with an Indian scalping knife,' whereupon O'Flaherty stood erect, and having glowered about him for a moment, strode in silence from the room, and consulted immediately with Puddock on the subject, who, after a moment's reflection found it no more than chance medley.

Chapter Thirty-eight

Dreams and troubles, and a dark lookout

So there was no feud in the club worth speaking of but those of which Dr Sturk was the centre; and Toole remarked this night that Sturk looked very ill – and so, in truth, he did; and it was plain, too, that his mind was not in the game, for old Slowe, who used not to have a chance with him, beat him three times running, which incensed Sturk, as small things will a man who is in the slow fever of a secret trouble. He threw down the three shillings he had lost with more force than was necessary, and muttering a curse, clapped on his hat and took up a newspaper at another table, with a rather flushed face. He happened to light upon a dolorous appeal to those 'whom Providence had blessed with riches', on behalf of a gentleman 'who had once held a commission under his Majesty, and was now on a sudden by some unexpected turns of fortune, reduced, with his unhappy wife and five small children, to want of bread, and implored of his prosperous fellow-citizens that charitable relief which, till a few months since, it was his custom and pleasure to dispense to others.' And this stung him with a secret pang of insecurity and horror. Trifles affected him a good deal now. So he pitched down the newspaper and walked across to his own house, with his hands in his pockets, and thought again of Dangerfield, and who the deuce he could be, or whether he had really ever, anywhere – in the body or in the spirit – encountered him, as he used to feel with a boding vagueness he had done. And then those accursed dreams: he was not relieved as he expected by disclosing them. The sense of an ominous meaning pointing at him in all their grotesque images and scenery, still haunted him.

'Parson Walsingham, with all his reading,' his mind muttered, as it were, to itself, 'is no better than an old woman; and that knave and buffoon, Mr Apothecary Toole, looked queer, the spiteful dog, just to disquiet me. I wonder at Dr Walsingham though. A sensible man would have laughed me into spirits. On my soul, I think he believes in dreams.' And Sturk laughed within himself scornfully. It was all affectation, and addressed strictly to himself, who saw through it all; but still he practised it. 'If these infernal losses had not come to spoil my stomach. I should not have remembered them, much less let them haunt me this way, like a cursed file of ghosts. I'll try gentian tomorrow.'

Everything and everyone was poking at the one point of his secret fears. Dr Walsingham preached a sermon upon the text, 'remember the days of darkness for they are many.' It went over the tremendous themes of death and judgment in the rector's own queer, solemn, measured way, and all the day after rang in Sturk's ear as the drums and fifes in the muffled peal of the Dead March used to do long ago, before his ear grew familiar with its thrilling roll. Sermons usually affected Sturk no more than they did other military gentlemen. But he was in a morbid state; and in this one or two terms or phrases, nothing in themselves, happened to touch upon a sensitive and secret centre of pain in the doctor's soul.

For instance, when he called death 'the great bankruptcy which would make the worldly man, in a moment, the only person in his house not worth a shilling,' the preacher glanced unconsciously at a secret fear in the caverns of Sturk's mind, that echoed back the sonorous tones and grisly theme of the rector with a hollow thunder.

There was a time when Sturk, like other shrewd, bustling fellows, had no objection to hear who had an execution in his house, who was bankrupt, and who laid by the heels; but now he shrunk from such phrases. He hated to think that a clever fellow was ever absolutely beggared in the world's great game. He turned his eye quickly from the *Gazette*, as it lay with other papers on the club table; for its grim pages seemed to look in his face with a sort of significance, as if they might some day or other have a small official duty to perform by him; and when an unexpected bankruptcy was announced by Cluffe or Toole in the club-room, it made his ear ring like a slap, and he felt sickish for half an hour after.

One of that ugly brood of dreams which haunted his nights, borrowed, perhaps, a hint from Dr Walsingham's sermon. Sturk thought he heard Toole's well-known, brisk voice, under his windows, exclaim, 'What is the dirty beggar doing there? Faugh! – he smells all over like carrion – ha, ha ha!' and looking out, in his dream, from his drawing-room window, he saw a squalid mendicant begging alms at his hall-door. 'Hollo, you, Sir; what do want there?' cried the surgeon, with a sort of unaccountable antipathy and fear. 'He lost his last shilling in the great bankruptcy, in October,' answered Dunstan's voice behind his ear; and in the earth-coloured face which the beggar turned up towards him, Sturk recognised his own features – ''Tis I' – he gasped out with an oath, and awoke in a horror, not knowing where he was. 'I – I'm dying.'

'October,' thought Sturk – 'bankruptcy. 'Tis just because I'm always thinking of that infernal bill, and old Dyle's renewal, and the rent.'

Indeed, the surgeon had a stormy look forward, and the navigation of October was so threatening, awful, and almost desperate, as he stood alone through the dreadful watches at the helm, with hot cheek and unsteady hand, trusting stoically to luck and hoping against hope, that rocks would melt, and the sea cease from drowning, that it was almost a wonder he did not leap overboard, only for the certainty of a cold head and a quiet heart, and one deep sleep.

And, then, he used to tot up his liabilities for that accursed month, near whose yawning verge he already stood; and then, think of every penny coming to him, and what might be rescued and wrung from runaways and bankrupts whose bills he held, and whom he used to curse in his bed, with his fists and his teeth clenched, when poor little Mrs Sturk, knowing naught of this danger, and having said her prayers, lay sound asleep by his side. Then he used to think, if he could only get the agency in time it would set him up – he could borrow £200 the day after his appointment; and he must make a push and extend his practice. It was ridiculous, that blackguard little Toole carrying off the best families in the neighbourhood, and standing in the way of a man like him; and Nutter, too – why, Lord Castlemallard knew as well as he did, that Nutter was not fit to manage the property, and that *he was* – and Nutter without a child or anyone, and *he* with seven! And he counted them over mentally with a groan. 'What was to become of them?' Then Nutter would be down upon him, without mercy, for the rent; and Dangerfield, if, indeed, he cared to do it [curse it, he trusted nobody], could not control him; and Lord Castlemallard, the selfish profligate, was away in Paris, leaving his business in the hands of that bitter old botch, who'd go any length to be the ruin of him.

Then he turned over the chances of borrowing a hundred pounds from the general – as he did fifty times every day and night, but always with the same result – 'No; curse him, he's as weak as water – petticoat government – he'll do nothing without his sister's leave, and she hates me like poison;' and then he thought – 'it would not be much to ask Lord Castlemallard – there's still time – to give me a month or two for the rent, but if the old sneak thought I owed twopence, I might whistle for the agency, and besides, faith! – I don't think he'd interfere.'

Then the clock downstairs would strike 'three', and he felt thankful, with a great sigh, that so much of the night was over, and yet dreaded the morning.

And then he would con over his chances again, and think which was most likely to give him a month or two. Old Dyle – 'Bah! He's a stone, he would not give me an hour. Or Carny, curse him, unless Lucas would move him. And, no, Lucas is a rogue, selfish beast: he owes me his place; and I don't think he'd stir his finger to snatch me from perdition. Or Nutter – Nutter, indeed! – why that fiend has been waiting half the year round to put in his distress the first hour he can.'

And then Sturk writhed round on his back, as we may suppose might St Anthony on his gridiron, and rolled his eyeballs up toward the dark bed; and uttered a dismal groan, and thought of the three inexorable fates, Carny, Nutter, and Dyle, who at that moment held among them the measure, and the thread, and the shears of his destiny: and standing desperately in the dark at the verge of the abyss, he mentally hurled the three ugly spirits together into his bag, and flung them whirling through the mirk into the lake that burns with fire and brimstone.

Chapter Thirty-nine

*Telling how Lilias Walsingham found two ladies awaiting
her arrival at the Elms*

When Lilias Walsingham, being set down in the hall at the Elms,
got out and threw back her hood, she saw two females sitting
there, who rose as she emerged, and bobbed a courtesy each. The
elder was a slight thin woman of fifty or upwards, dark of feature,
but with large eyes, the relics of early beauty. The other a youthful figure, an inch or two taller, slim and round, and showing only
a pair of eyes, large and dark as the others, looking from under
her red hood, earnestly and sadly as it seemed, upon Miss Walsingham.

'Good-evening, good neighbours,' said Miss Lily in her friendly
way; 'the master is in town, and won't return till tomorrow; but
maybe you wish to speak to me?'

' 'Tis no place for the like of yous,' said old John Tracy, gruffly, for
he knew them, with the privilege of an old servant. 'If you want to see
his raverence, you must come in the morning.'

'But it may be something, John, that can't wait, and that I can do,'
said Lily.

'And, true for you, so it is, my lady,' said the elder woman, with
another bob; 'an' I won't delay you, Ma'am, five minutes, if you
plaze, an' it's the likes of you,' she said, in a shrewish aside, with a
flash of her large eyes upon John Tracy, 'that stands betune them
that's willin' to be good and the poor – so yez do, saucepans and
bone-polishers, bad luck to yez.'

The younger woman plucked the elder by the skirt; but Lily did
not hear. She was already in the parlour.

'Ay, there it is,' grinned old John, with a wag of his head.

And so old Sally came forth and asked the women to step in, and
set chairs for them, while Lily was taking off her gloves and hood by
the table.

'You'll tell me first who you are,' said Lily, 'my good woman –

for I don't think we've met before – and then you will say what I can do for you.'

'I'm the Widdy Glynn, Ma'am, at your sarvice, that lives beyant Palmerstown, down by the ferry, af its playsin' to you; and this is my little girl, Ma'am, av you plaze. Nan, look up at the lady, you slut.'

She did not need the exhortation, for she was, indeed, looking at the lady, with a curious and most melancholy gaze.

'An' what I'm goin' to say, my lady, if you plase, id best be said alone;' and the matron glanced at old Sally, and bobbed another courtesy.

'Very well,' said Miss Walsingham. 'Sally, dear, the good woman wants to speak with me alone: so you may as well go and wait for me in my room.'

And so the young lady stood alone in presence of her two visitors, whereupon, with a good many courtesies, and with great volubility, the elder dame commenced: ''Tis what we heerd, Ma'am, that Captain Devereux, of the Artillery here in Chapelizod, Ma'am, that's gone to England, was coortin' you my lady; and I came here with this little girl, Ma'am, if you plaze, to tell you, if so be it's thrue, Ma'am, that there isn't this minute a bigger villian out iv gaol – who brought my poor little girl there to disgrace and ruin, Ma'am.'

Here Nan Glynn began to sob into her apron.

''Twas you, Richard Devereux, that promised her marriage – with his hand on the Bible, on his bended knee. 'Twas you, Richard Devereux, you hardened villian – yes, Ma'am, that parjured scoundrel – (don't be cryin', you fool) – put that ring there, you see, on her finger, Miss, an' a priest in the room, an' if ever man was woman's husband in the sight of God, Richard Devereux is married to Nan Glynn, poor an' simple as she stands there.'

'Stop, mother,' sobbed Nan, drawing her back by the arm; 'don't you see the lady's sick.'

'No – no – not anything; only – only shocked,' said poor Lilias, as white as marble, and speaking almost in a whisper; 'but I can't say Captain Devereux ever spoke to me in the way you suppose, that's all. I've no more to say.'

Nan Glynn, sobbing and with her apron still to her eyes, was gliding to the door, but her mother looked, with a coarse sort of cunning in her eye, steadily at the poor young lady, in some sort her victim, and added more sternly: 'Well, my lady, 'tis proud I am to hear it, an' there's no harm done, at any rate; an' I thought 'twas only right I should tell you the thruth, and give you this warnin', my lady;

an' here's the atturney's writin', Ma'am – if you'll plaze to read it – Mr Bagshot, iv Thomas Street – sayin', if you'll be plazed to look at it – that 'tis a good marriage, an' that if he marries any other woman, gentle or simple, he'll take the law iv him in my daughter's cause, the black, parjured villian, an' transport him, with a burnt hand, for bigamany; an' 'twas only right, my lady, as the townspeople was talking, as if it was as how he was thryin' to invagle you, Miss, the desaver, for he'd charrum the birds off the trees, the parjurer; and I'll tell his raverence all about it when I see him, in the morning – for 'tis only right he should know. Wish the lady good-night, Nan, you slut – an the same from myself, Ma'am.'

And, with another courtesy, the Glynns of Palmerstown withdrew.

Chapter Forty

*Of a messenger from Chapelizod vault who waited in the
Tiled House for Mr Mervyn*

Mervyn was just about this time walking up the steep Ballyfermot Road. It was then a lonely track, with great bushes and hedgerows overhanging it; and as other emotions subsided, something of the chill and excitement of solitude stole over him. The moon was wading through flecked masses of cloud. The breath of night rustled lightly through the bushes, and seemed to follow her steps with a strange sort of sigh and a titter. He stopped and looked back under the branches of an old thorn, and traced against the dark horizon the still darker outline of the ivied church tower of Chapelizod, and thought of the dead that lay there, and of all that those sealed lips might tell, and old tales of strange meetings on moors and desolate places with departed spirits, flitted across his brain; and the melancholy rush of the night air swept close about his ears, and he turned and walked more briskly toward his own gloomy quarters, passing the churchyard of Ballyfermot on his right. There were plenty of headstones among the docks and nettles: some short and some tall, some straight and some slanting back, and some with a shoulder up, and a lonely old ash-tree still and dewy in the midst, glimmering cold among the moveless shadows; and then at last he sighted the heavy masses of old elm, and the pale, peeping front of the 'Tyled House'; through the close and dismal avenue of elm, he reached the front of the mansion. There was no glimmer of light from the lower windows, not even the noiseless flitting of a bat over the dark little courtyard. His key let him in. He knew that his servants were in bed. There was something cynical in his ree-raw independence. It was unlike what he had been used to, and its savagery suited with his bitter and unsociable mood of late.

But his step sounding through the hall, and the stories about the place of which he was conscious? He battled with his disturbed foolish sensations, however, and though he knew there was a candle burning in his bedroom, he turned aside at the foot of the great stair, and stumbled and groped his way into the old wainscoted back-parlour, that looked out, through its great bow window, upon the haunted orchard, and sat down in its dismal solitude.

He ruminated upon his own hard fate – the meanness of mankind – the burning wrongs, as he felt confident, of other times, Fortune's inexorable persecution of his family, and the stygian gulf that deepened between him and the object of his love; and his soul darkened with a fierce despair, and with unshaped but evil thoughts that invited the tempter.

The darkness and associations of the place were unwholesome, and he was about to leave it for the companionship of his candle, but that, on a sudden, he thought he heard a sound nearer than the breeze among the old orchard trees.

This was the measured breathing of someone in the room. He held his own breath while he listened – 'One of the dogs,' he thought, and he called them quietly; but no dog came. 'The wind, then, in the chimney;' and he got up resolutely, designing to open the half-closed shutter. He fancied as he did so that he heard the respiration near him, and passed close to someone in the dark.

With an unpleasant expectation he threw back the shutters, and unquestionably he did see, very unmistakably, a dark figure in a chair; so dark, indeed, that he could not discern more of it than the rude but undoubted outline of a human shape; and he stood for some seconds, holding the open shutter in his hand, and looking at it with more of the reality of fear than he had, perhaps, ever experienced before. Pale Hecate now, in the conspiracy, as it seemed, withdrew on a sudden the pall from before her face, and threw her beams full upon the figure. A slim, tall shape, in dark clothing, and, as it seemed, a countenance he had never beheld before – black hair, pale features, with a sinister-smiling character, and a very blue chin, and closed eyes.

Fixed with a strange horror, and almost expecting to see it undergo some frightful metamorphosis, Mervyn stood gazing on the cadaverous intruder.

'Hollo! Who's that?' cried Mervyn sternly.

The figure opened his eyes, with a wild stare, as if he had not opened them for a hundred years before, and rose up with an uncertain motion, returning Mervyn's gaze, as if he did not know where he was.

'Who are you?' repeated Mervyn.

The phantom seemed to recover himself slowly, and only said: 'Mr Mervyn?'

'Who are you, Sir?' cried Mervyn, again.

'Zekiel Irons,' he answered.

'Irons? What *are* you, and what business have you here, Sir?' demanded Mervyn.

'The Clerk of Chapelizod,' he continued, quietly and remarkably sternly, but a little thickly, like a man who had been drinking.

Mervyn now grew angry.

'The Clerk of Chapelizod – here – sleeping in my parlour! What the devil, Sir, do you mean?'

'Sleep – Sir – sleep! There's them that sleeps with their eyes open, Sir – you know who they may be; there's some sleeps sound enough, like me and you; and some that's sleep-walkers,' answered Irons; and his enigmatical talk somehow subdued Mervyn, for he said more quietly: 'Well, what of all this, Sirrah?'

'A message,' answered Irons. The man's manner, though quiet, was dogged, and somewhat savage.

'Give it me, then,' said Mervyn, expecting a note, and extending his hand.

'I've nothing for your hand, Sir, 'tis for your ear,' said he.

'From whom, then, and what?' said Mervyn, growing impatient again.

'I ask your pardon, Mr Mervyn; I have a good deal to do, back and forward, sometimes early, sometimes late, in the church – Chapelizod Church – all alone, Sir; and I often think of you, when I walk over the south-side vault.'

'What's your message, I say, Sir, and who sends it,' insisted Mervyn.

'Your father,' answered Irons.

Mervyn looked with a black and wild sort of enquiry on the clerk – was he insane or what? – and seemed to swallow down a sort of horror, before his anger rose again.

'You're mistaken – my father's dead,' he said, in a fierce but agitated undertone.

'He's dead, Sir – yes,' said his saturnine visitor, with the same faint smile and cynical quietude.

'Speak out, Sirrah; whom do you come from?'

'The late Right Honourable the Lord Viscount Dunoran.' He spoke, as I have said, a little thickly, like a man who had drunk his modicum of liquor.

'You've been drinking, and you dare to mix my – my father's name with your drunken dreams and babble – you wretched sot!'

A cloud passed over the moon just then, and Irons darkened, as if about to vanish, like an offended apparition. But it was only for a minute, and he emerged in the returning light, and spoke: 'A naggin of whiskey, at the Salmon House, to raise my heart before I came here. I'm not drunk – that's sure,' he answered, quite unmoved, like one speaking to himself.

'And – why – what can you mean by speaking of him?' repeated Mervyn, unaccountably agitated.

'I speak *for* him, Sir, by your leave. Suppose he greets you with a message – and you don't care to hear it?'

'You're mad,' said Mervyn, with an icy stare, to whom the whole colloquy began to shape itself into a dream.

'Belike *you're* mad, Sir,' answered Irons, in a grim, ugly tone, but with face unmoved. ''Twas not a light matter brought me here – a message – there – well! – your right honourable father, that lies in lead and oak, without a name on his coffin-lid, would have you to know that what he said was – as it should be – and I can prove it – '

'What? – he said *what*? – what is it? – what can you prove? Speak out, Sirrah!' and his eyes shone white in the moonlight, and his hand was advanced towards Irons's throat, and he looked half beside himself, and trembling all over.

'Put down your hand or you hear no more from me,' said Irons, also a little transformed.

Mervyn silently lowered his hand clenched by his side, and, with compressed lips, nodded an impatient sign to him.

'Yes, Sir, he'd have you to understand he never did it, and I can prove it – *but I won't!*'

That moment, something glittered in Mervyn's hand, and he strode towards Irons, overturning a chair with a crash.

'I have you – come on and you're a dead man,' said the clerk, in a hoarse voice, drawing into the deep darkness toward the door, with the dull gleam of a pistol-barrel just discernible in his extended hand.

'Stay – don't go,' cried Mervyn, in a piercing voice; 'I conjure – I implore – whatever you are, come back – see, I'm unarmed,' and he flung his sword back toward the window.

'You young gentlemen are always for drawing upon poor bodies – how would it have gone if I had not looked to myself, Sir, and come furnished?' said Irons, in his own level tone.

'I don't know – I don't *care* – I don't care if I were dead. Yes, yes, 'tis true, I almost wish he had shot me.'

'Mind, Sir, you're on honour,' said the clerk, in his old tone, as he glided slowly back, his right hand in his coat pocket, and his eye with a quiet suspicion fixed upon Mervyn, and watching his movements.

'I don't know what or who you are, but if ever you knew what human feeling is – I say, if you are anything at all capable of compassion, you will kill me at a blow rather than trifle any longer with the terrible hope that has been my torture – I believe my insanity, all my life.'

'Well, Sir,' said Irons, mildly, and with that serene suspicion of a smile on his face, 'if you wish to talk to me you must take me different; for, to say truth, I was nearer killing you that time than you were aware, and all the time I mean you no harm! And yet, if I thought you were going to say to anybody living, Zekiel Irons, the clerk, was here on Tuesday night, I believe I'd shoot you now.'

'You wish your visit secret? Well, you have my honour, no-one living shall hear of it,' said Mervyn. 'Go on.'

'I've little to say, your honour; but, first, do you think your servants heard the noise just now?'

'The old woman's deaf, and her daughter dare not stir after nightfall. You need fear no interruption.'

'Ay, I know; the house is haunted, they say, but dead men tell no tales. 'Tis the living I fear, I thought it would be darker – the clouds broke up strangely; 'tis as much as my life's worth to me to be seen near this Tyled House; and never you speak to me nor seem to know me when you chance to meet me, do you mind, Sir? I'm bad enough myself, but there's some that's worse.'

''Tis agreed, there shall be no recognition,' answered Mervyn.

'There's them watching me that can see in the clouds, or the running waters, what you're thinking of a mile away, that can move as soft as ghosts, and can gripe as hard as hell, when need is. So be patient for a bit – I gave you the message – I tell you 'tis true; and as to my proving it at present, I can, you see, and I can't; but the hour is coming, only be patient, and swear, Sir, upon your soul and honour, that you won't let me come to perdition by reason of speaking the truth.'

'On my soul and honour, I mean it,' answered Mervyn. 'Go on.'

'Nor ever tell, high or low, rich or poor, man, woman, or child, that I came here; because – no matter.'

'That I promise, too; for Heaven's sake go on.'

'If you please, Sir, no, not a word more till the time comes,' answered Irons; 'I'll go as I came.' And he shoved up the window-sash and got out lightly upon the grass, and glided away among the gigantic old fruit-trees, and was lost before a minute.

Perhaps he came intending more. He had seemed for a while to have made up his mind, Mervyn thought, to a full disclosure, and then he hesitated, and, on second thoughts, drew back. Barren and tantalising, however, as was this strange conference, it was yet worth worlds, as indicating the quarter from which information might ultimately be hoped for.

Chapter Forty-one

In which the rector comes home, and Lily speaks her mind, and time glides on, and Aunt Rebecca calls at the Elms

Next morning, punctual at the early breakfast-hour of those days, the cheery voice of the old rector was heard at the garden rails that fronted the house, and out ran Tom Clinton, from the stable-yard, and bid his 'raverence', with homely phrase and with a pleasant grin, 'welcome home', and held his bridle and stirrup, while the parson, with a kind smile, and half a dozen enquiries, and the air of a man who, having made a long journey and a distant sojourn, expands on beholding old faces and the sights of home again; he had been away, to be sure, only one night and a part of a day, but his heart clave to his home and his darling; and Lilias ran to the garden gate to meet him, with her old smile and greeting, it seemed fonder and more tender than ever, and then they kissed and hugged and kissed again, and he patted her cheek and thought she looked a little pale, but would not say anything just then that was not altogether cheerful; and so they stepped up the two or three yards of gravel walk – she at his right side, with her right hand in his and her left clinging by his arm, and nestling close by his side, and leading him up to the house like a beloved captive.

And so at breakfast he narrated all his adventures, and told who were at the dinner party, and described two fine ladies' dresses – for the doctor had skill in millinery, though it was as little known as Don Quixote's talent for making bird-cages and toothpicks, confided, as we remember, in one of his conversations with honest Sancho, under the cork trees. He told her his whole innocent little budget of gossip, in his own simple, pleasant way; and his little Lily sat looking on her beloved old man, and smiling, but saying little, and her eyes often filling with tears; and he looked, when he chanced to see it – wistfully and sadly for an instant, but he made no remark.

And some time after, as she happened to pass the study-door, he called her – 'Little Lily, come here.' And in she came; and there was the doctor, all alone and erect before his bookshelves, plucking down a volume here, and putting up one there, and: 'Shut the door, little Lily,' said he gently and cheerily, going on with his work. 'I had a letter yesterday evening, my darling, from Captain Devereux, and he tells me that he's very much attached to you; and I don't wonder at his being in love with little Lily – he could not help it.' And he laughed fondly, and was taking down a volume that rather stuck in its place, so he could not turn to look at her; for, the truth was, he supposed she was blushing, and could not bear to add to her confusion; and he, though he continued his homely work, and clapped the sides of his books together, and blew on their tops, and went so simply and plainly to the point, was flushed and very nervous himself; for, though he thought of her marriage at some time or another as a thing that was to be, still it had seemed a long way off. And now, now it was come, and little Lily was actually going to be married – going away – and her place would know her no more; and her greeting and her music would be missed in the evening, and the garden lonely, and the Elms dark, without Lily.

'And he wants to marry my little Lily, if she'll have him. And what does my darling wish me to say to him?' and he spoke very cheerily.

'My darling, *you're* my darling; and your little Lily will never, never leave you. She'll stay.' And here the little speech stopped, for she was crying, with her arms about his neck; and the old man cried, too, and smiled over her, and patted her gracious head, with a little trembling laugh, and said, 'God bless you, my treasure.'

'Well, little Lily, will you have him?' he said, after a little pause.

'No, my darling, no!' she answered, still crying.

'You *won't* have him?'

'No – no – never!'

'Well, little Lily, I won't answer his letter today; there's no hurry, you know. And, if you are of the same mind tomorrow, you can just say you wish me to write.'

'Change, I can't; my answer will always be the same – always the same.'

And she kissed him again, and went toward the door; but she turned back, drying her eyes, with a smile, and said – 'No, your little Lily will stay with her darling old man, and be a pleasant old maid, like Aunt Becky: and I'll play and sing your favourite airs, and Sally and I will keep the house; and we'll be happier in the Elms, I'm determined, than ever we were – and won't you call me, darling, when you're going out?'

So little Lily ran away, and upstairs; and as she left the study and its beloved tenant, at every step the air seemed to darken round her, and her heart to sink. And she turned the key in her door, and threw herself on the bed; and, with her face to the pillow, cried as if her heart would break.

So the summer had mellowed into autumn, and the fall of the leaf, and Devereux did not return; and it was alleged in the club, on good authority, that he was appointed on the staff of the Commander of the Forces; and Puddock had a letter from him, dated in England, with little or no news in it; and Dr Walsingham had a long epistle from Malaga, from honest Dan Loftus, full of Spanish matter for Irish history, and stating, with many regrets, that his honourable pupil had taken ill of a fever. And this bit of news speedily took wind, and was discussed with a good deal of interest, and some fun, at the club; and the odds were freely given and taken upon the event.

The politics of Belmont were still pretty much in the old position. The general had not yet returned, and Aunt Rebecca and Gertrude fought pitched battles, as heretofore, on the subject of Dangerfield. That gentleman had carried so many points in his life by simply waiting, that he was nothing daunted by the obstacles which the caprice of the young lady presented to the immediate accomplishment of his plans. And those which he once deliberately formed, were never abandoned for trifles.

So when Aunt Becky and Miss Gertrude at length agreed on an armistice – the conditions being that the question of Mr Dangerfield's bliss or misery was to stand over for judgment until the general's return, which could not now be deferred more than two or three weeks – the amorous swain, on being apprised of the terms by Aunt Rebecca, acquiesced with alacrity, in a handsome, neat, and gallant little speech, and kissed Aunt Rebecca's slender and jewelled hand, with a low bow and a grim smile, all which she received very graciously.

Of course, Dangerfield knew pretty well how matters stood; he was not a man to live in a dream; facts were his daily bread. He knew to a month how old he was, and pretty exactly how time had dealt with his personal charms. He had a very exact and cynical appreciation of the terms on which Miss Chattesworth would – if at all – become and continue to be his wife. But he wanted her – she suited him exactly, and all he needed to make his kingdom sure, when he had obtained her, was his legal rights. He was no Petruchio; neither was it his theory to rule by love. He had a different way.

Without bluster, and without wheedling, he had the art of making those who were under his rule perfectly submissive; sooner or later they all came to fear him as a child does a spectre. He had no misgivings about the peace of his household.

In the meantime Gertrude grew happier and more like herself, and Aunt Rebecca had her own theories about the real state of that young lady's affections, and her generally unsuspected relations with others.

Aunt Rebecca called at the Elms to see Lilias Walsingham, and sat down beside her on the sofa.

'Lily, child, you're not looking yourself. I'll send you some drops. You must positively nurse yourself. I'm almost sorry I did not bring Dr Toole.'

'Indeed I'm glad you did not, Aunt Becky; I take excellent care of myself. I have not been out for three whole days.'

'And you must not budge, darling, while this east wind continues. D'ye mind? And what do you think, my dear, I do believe I've discovered the secret reason of Gertrude's repugnance to Mr Dangerfield's most advantageous offer.'

'Oh, indeed!' said Lily, becoming interested.

'Well, I suppose you suspected she *had* a secret?' said Aunt Rebecca.

'I can only say, dear Aunt Becky, she has not told it to *me*.'

'Now, listen to me, my dear,' said Aunt Becky, laying her fan upon Lily's arm. 'So sure as you sit there, Gertrude likes somebody, and I think I shall soon know who he is. Can you conjecture, my dear?' And Aunt Rebecca paused, looking, Lilias thought, rather pale, and with a kind of smile too.

'No,' said Lilias; 'no, I really can't.'

'Well, maybe when I tell you I've reason to think he's one of our officers here. Eh? Can you guess?' said Aunt Becky, holding her fan to her mouth, and looking straight before her.

It was now Lily's turn to look pale for a moment, and then to blush so much that her ears tingled, and her eyes dropped to the carpet. She had time to recover, though, for Aunt Becky, as I've said, was looking straight before her, a little pale, awaiting the result of Lily's presumed ruminations. A moment satisfied her it could not be Devereux, and she was soon quite herself again.

'An officer! No, Aunt Becky – there certainly is Captain Cluffe, who always joins your party when you and Gertrude go down to hear the band, and Lieutenant Puddock, too, who does the same – but you know – '

'Well, my dear, all in good time. Gertrude's very secret, and proud too; but I shall know very soon. I've ascertained, my dear, that an officer came under the window the other evening, and sang a verse of a French chanson, from the meadow, in a cloak, if you please, with a guitar. I could name his name, my dear – '

'Do pray tell me,' said Lily, whose curiosity was all alive.

'Why – a – not yet, my dear,' answered Aunt Becky, looking down; 'there are – there's a reason – but the affair, I may tell you, began, in earnest, on the very day on which she refused Mr Mervyn. But I forgot you did not know *that* either – however, you'll never mention it.' And she kissed her cheek, calling her 'my wise little Lily'.

'And my dear, it has been going on so regularly ever since, with, till very lately, so little disguise, that I only wonder everybody doesn't see it as plain as I do myself; and Lily, my dear,' continued Aunt Rebecca, energetically, rising from the sofa as some object caught her eye through the glass-door in the garden, 'your beautiful roses are all trailing in the mud. What on earth is Hogan about? And there, see, just at the door, a boxful of nails! – I'd nail his ear to the wall if he were mine,' and Aunt Rebecca glanced sharply through the glass, this way and that, for the offending gardener, who, happily, did not appear. Then off went Aunt Becky to something else; and in a little time remembered the famous academy in Martin's-row, and looking at her watch, took her leave in a prodigious hurry, and followed by Dominick, in full livery, and two dogs, left Lilias again to the society of her own sad thoughts.

Chapter Forty-two

*In which Dr Sturk tries this way and that for a reprieve
on the eve of execution*

So time crept on, and the day arrived when Sturk must pay his rent, or take the ugly consequences. The day before he spent in Dublin financiering. It was galling and barren work. He had to ask favours of fellows whom he hated, and to stand their refusals, and pretend to believe their lying excuses, and appear to make quite light of it, though every failure stunned him like a blow of a bludgeon, and as he strutted jauntily off with a bilious smirk, he was well nigh at his wits' end. It was dark as he rode out by the low road to Chapelizod – crestfallen, beaten – scowling in the darkness through his horse's ears along the straight black line of road, and wishing, as he passed the famous Dog-house, that he might be stopped and plundered, and thus furnished with a decent excuse for his penniless condition, and a plea in which all the world would sympathise for a short indulgence – and, faith! he did not much care if they sent a bullet through his harassed brain. But the highwaymen, like the bankers, seemed to know, by instinct, that he had not a guinea, and declined to give him even the miserable help he coveted.

When he got home he sent down for Cluffe to the Phoenix, and got him to take Nutter, who was there also, aside, and ask him for a little time, or to take part of the rent. Though the latter would not have helped him much; for he could not make out ten pounds just then, were it to save his life. But Nutter only said: 'The rent's not mine; I can't give it or lose it; and Sturk's not safe. Will *you* lend it? *I* can't.'

This brought Cluffe to reason. He had opened the business, like a jolly companion, in a generous, full-blooded way.

'Well, by Jove, Nutter, I can't blame you; for you see, between ourselves, I'm afraid 'tis as you say. We of the Royal Irish have done, under the rose, you know, all we can; and I'm sorry the poor devil has run himself into a scrape; but hang it, we must have a conscience; and if you think there's a risk of losing it, why I don't see that I can press you.

The reader must not suppose when Cluffe said, 'we of the Royal Irish', in connection with some pecuniary kindness shown to Sturk, that that sensible captain had given away any of his money to the surgeon; but Sturk, in their confidential conference, had hinted something about a 'helping hand', which Cluffe coughed off, and mentioned that Puddock had lent him fifteen pounds the week before.

And so he had, though little Puddock was one of the poorest officers in the corps. But he had no vices, and husbanded his little means carefully, and was very kindly and offhand in assisting to the extent of his little purse a brother in distress, and never added advice when so doing – for he had high notions of politeness – or, in all his life, divulged any of these little money transactions.

Sturk stood at his drawing-room window, with his hat on, looking towards the Phoenix, and waiting for Cluffe's return. When he could stand the suspense no longer, he went down and waited at his doorsteps. And the longer Cluffe stayed the more did Sturk establish himself in the conviction that the interview had prospered, and that his ambassador was coming to terms with Nutter. He did not know that the entire question had been settled in a minute-and-a-half, and that Cluffe was at that moment rattling away at backgammon with his arch-enemy, Toole, in a corner of the club parlour.

It was not till Cluffe, as he emerged from the Phoenix, saw Sturk's figure stalking in the glimpses of the moon, under the village elm, that he suddenly recollected and marched up to him. Sturk stood, with his face and figure mottled over with the shadows of the moving leaves and the withered ones dropping about him, his hands in his pockets, and a crown-piece – I believe it was his last available coin just then – shut up fast and tight in his cold fingers, with his heart in his mouth, and whistling a little to show his unconcern.

'Well,' said Sturk, 'he won't, of course?'

Cluffe shook his head.

'Very good – I'll manage it another way,' said Sturk, confidently. 'Good-night'; and Sturk walked off briskly towards the turnpike.

'He might have said "thank you", I think,' Cluffe said, looking after him with a haughty leer – 'mixing myself up in his plaguy affairs, and asking favours of fellows like Nutter.' But just then, having reached the corner next the Phoenix, Sturk hesitated, and Cluffe, thinking he might possibly turn back and ask him for money, turned on his heel, and, like a prudent fellow, trudged rapidly off to his lodgings.

Toole and O'Flaherty were standing in the doorway of the Phoenix, observing the brief and secret meeting under the elm.

'That's Sturk,' said Toole.

O'Flaherty grunted acquiescence.

Toole watched attentively till the gentlemen separated, and then glancing on O'Flaherty from the corner of his eye, with a knowing smile, 'tipped him the wink', as the phrase went in those days.

'An affair of honour?' said O'Flaherty, squaring himself. He smelt powder in everything.

'More like an affair of *dishonour*,' said Toole, buttoning his coat. 'He's been "kiting" all over the town. Nutter can distrain for his rent tomorrow, and Cluffe called him outside the bar to speak with him; put that and that together, Sir.' And home went Toole.

Sturk, indeed, had no plan, and was just then incapable of forming any. He changed his route, not knowing why, and posted over the bridge, and a good way along the Inchicore road, and then turned about and strode back again and over the bridge, without stopping, and on towards Dublin; and suddenly the moon shone out, and he recollected how late it was growing, and so turned about and walked homeward.

As he passed by the row of houses looking across the road towards the river, from Mr Irons's hall-door step a well-known voice accosted him. 'A thweet night, doctor – the moon tho thilver bright – the air tho thoft!'

It was little Puddock, whose hand and face were raised toward the sweet regent of the sky.

'Mighty fine night,' said Sturk, and he paused for a second. It was Puddock's way to be more than commonly friendly and polite with any man who owed him money; and Sturk, who thought, perhaps rightly, that the world of late had been looking cold and black upon him, felt, in a sort of way, thankful for the greeting and its cordial tone.

'A night like this,' pursued the little lieutenant, 'my dear Sir, brings us under the marble balconies of the palace of the Capulets, and sets us repeating "On such a night sat Dido on the wild seabanks" – you remember – "and with a willow wand, waved her love back to Carthage," – or places us upon the haunted platform, where buried Denmark revisits the glimpses of the moon. My dear doctor, 'tis wonderful – isn't it – how much of our enjoyment of Nature we owe to Shakespeare – 'twould be a changed world with us, doctor, if Shakespeare had not written – '

Then there was a little pause, Sturk standing still.

'God be wi' ye, lieutenant,' said he, suddenly taking his hand. 'If there were more men like you there would be fewer broken hearts in the world.' And away went Sturk.

Chapter Forty-three

*Showing how Charles Nutter's blow descended, and what part
the silver spectacles bore in the crisis*

In the morning the distress and keepers were in Sturk's house.

We must not be too hard upon Nutter. 'Tis a fearful affair, and
no child's play, this battle of life. Sturk had assailed him like a beast
of prey; not Nutter, to be sure, only Lord Castlemallard's agent.
Of that functionary his wolfish instinct craved the flesh, bones, and
blood. Sturk had no other way to live and grow fat. Nutter or he
must go down. The little fellow saw his great red maw and rabid
fangs at his throat. If he let him off, he would devour him, and lie in
his bed, with his cap on, and his caudles and cordials all round, as the
wolf did by Little Red Riding Hood's grandmamma; and with the
weapon which had come to hand – a heavy one too – he was going,
with Heaven's help, to deal him a brainblow.

When Sturk heard in the morning that the blow was actually struck,
he jumped out of bed, and was taken with a great shivering fit, sitting
on the side of it. Little Mrs Sturk, as white as her nightcap with terror,
was yet decisive in emergency, and bethought her of the brandy
bottle, two glasses from which the doctor swallowed before his teeth
gave over chattering, and a more natural tint returned to his blue face.

'Oh! Barney, dear, are we ruined?' faltered poor little Mrs Sturk.

'Ruined, indeed!' cried Sturk, with an oath, 'Come in here.' He
thought his study was on the same floor with his bedroom, as it had
been in old times in their house in Limerick, ten or twelve years
before.

'That's the nursery, Barney, dear,' she said, thinking, in the midst
of the horror, like a true mother, of the children's sleep.

Then he remembered and ran down to the study, and pulled out a
sheaf of bills and promissory notes, and renewals thereof, making a
very respectable show.

'Ruined, indeed!' he cried, hoarsely, talking to his poor little wife
in the tones and with the ferocity which the image of Nutter, with

which his brain was filled, called up. 'Look, I say, here's one fellow owes me that – and that – and that – and there – there's a dozen in that by another – there's two more sets there pinned together – and here's an account of them all – two thousand two hundred – and you may say three hundred – two thousand three hundred – owed me here; and that miscreant won't give me a day.'

'Is it the rent, Barney?'

'The rent? To be sure; what else should it be?' shouted the doctor, with a stamp.

And so pale little Mrs Sturk stole out of the room, as her lord with bitter mutterings pitched his treasure of bad bills back again into the *escritoire*: and she heard him slam the study door and run downstairs to browbeat and curse the men in the hall, for he had lost his head somewhat, between panic and fury. He was in his stockings and slippers, with an old flowered silk dressing-gown, and nothing more but his shirt, and looked, they said, like a madman. One of the fellows was smoking, and Sturk snatched the pipe from his mouth, and stamped it to atoms on the floor, roaring at them to know what the — brought them there; and without a pause for an answer, thundered, 'And I suppose you'll not let me take my box of instruments out of the house – mind, it's worth fifty pounds; and curse me, if one of our men dies for want of them in hospital, I'll indict you both, and your employer along with you, *for murder!*' And so he railed on, till his voice failed him with a sort of choking, and there was a humming in his ears, and a sort of numbness in his head, and he thought he was going to have a fit; and then up the stairs he went again, and into his study, and resolved to have Nutter out – and it flashed upon him that he'd say, 'Pay the rent first'; and then – what next? Why he'd post him all over Dublin, and Chapelizod, and Leixlip, where the Lord Lieutenant and Court were.

And down he sat to a sheet of paper, with his left hand clenched on the table, and his teeth grinding together, as he ransacked his vocabulary for befitting terms; but alas, his right hand shook so that his penmanship would not do, in fact, it half frightened him. 'By my soul! I believe something bad has happened me,' he muttered, and popped up his window, and looked out, half dreaming, over the churchyard on the park beyond, and the dewy overhanging hill, all pleasantly lighted up in the morning sun.

While this was going on, little Mrs Sturk, who on critical occasions took strong resolutions promptly, made a wonderfully rapid toilet, and let herself quietly out of the street door. She had thought of Dr

Walsingham; but Sturk had lately, in one of his imperious freaks of temper, withdrawn his children from the good doctor's catechetical class, and sent him besides, one of his sturdy, impertinent notes – and the poor little woman concluded there was no chance there. She knew little of the rector – of the profound humility and entire placability of that noble soul.

Well, she took the opposite direction, and turning her back on the town, walked at her quickest pace toward the Brass Castle. It was not eight o'clock yet, but the devil had been up betimes and got through a good deal of his day's work, as we have seen. The poor little woman had made up her mind to apply to Dangerfield. She had liked his talk at Belmont, where she had met him; and he enquired about the poor, and listened to some of her woeful tales with a great deal of sympathy; and she knew he was very rich, and that he appreciated her Barney, and so she trudged on, full of hope, though I don't think many people who knew the world better would have given a great deal for her chance.

Dangerfield received the lady very affably, in his little parlour, where having already despatched his early meal, he was writing letters. He looked hard at her when she came in, and again when she sat down; and when she had made an end of her long and dismal tale, he opened a sort of strongbox, and took out a thin quarto and read, turning the leaves rapidly over.

'Ay, here we have him – Chapelizod – Sturk, Barnabas – Surgeon, R.I.A., assignee of John Lowe – hey! one gale day, as you call it, only! – September. How came that? Rent, £40. Why, then, he owes a whole year's rent, £40, Ma'am. September, and his days of grace have expired. He ought to have paid it.'

Here there came a dreadful pause, during which nothing was heard but the sharp ticking of his watch on the table.

'Well, Ma'am,' he said, 'when a thing comes before me, I say yes or no promptly. I like your husband, and I'll lend him the amount of his rent.'

Poor little Mrs Sturk jumped up in an ecstasy, and then felt quite sick, and sat down almost fainting, with a deathlike smile.

'There's but one condition I attach, that you tell me truly, my dear Ma'am, whether you came to me directly or indirectly at his suggestion.'

No, indeed, she had not; it was all her own thought; she had not dared to mention it to him, lest he should forbid her, and now she should be almost afraid to tell him where she had been.

'He'll not be very angry, depend on't, my good Madam; you did wisely in coming to me. I respect your sense and energy; and should you hereafter stand in need of a friendly office, I beg you'll remember one who is disposed to help you.'

Then he sat down and wrote with a flying pen

My Dear Sir – I have just learned from Mrs Sturk that you have an immediate concern for forty pounds, to which, I venture to surmise, will be added some fees, etc. I take leave, therefore, to send herewith fifty guineas, which I trust will suffice for this troublesome affair. We can talk hereafter about repayment. Mrs Sturk has handed me a memorandum of the advance.

Your very obedient, humble servant,

Giles Dangerfield

The Brass Castle, Chapelizod
2nd October, 1767

Then poor little Mrs Sturk was breaking out into a delirium of gratitude. But he put his hand upon her arm kindly, and with a little bow and an emphasis, he said: 'Pray, not a *word*, my dear Madam. Just write a line,' and he slid his desk before her with a sheet of paper on it; 'and say Mr Dangerfield has this day handed me a loan of fifty guineas for my husband, Doctor Barnabas Sturk. Now sign, if you please, and add the date. Very good!'

'I'm afraid you can hardly read it – my fingers tremble a little,' said Mrs Sturk, with a wild little deprecatory titter, and for the first time very near crying.

' 'Tis mighty well,' said Dangerfield, politely; and he accompanied the lady with the note and fifty guineas, made up in a little rouleau, fast in her hand, across his little garden, and with – 'A fine morning truly', and 'God bless you, Madam', and one of his peculiar smiles, he let her out through his little wicket on the high road. And so away went Mrs Sturk, scarce feeling the ground under her feet; and Giles Dangerfield, carrying his white head very erect, with an approving conscience, and his silver spectacles flashing through the leaves of his lilacs and laburnums, returned to his parlour.

Mrs Sturk, who could hardly keep from running, glided along at a wonderful rate, wondering now and then how quickly the whole affair – so awful as it seemed to her in magnitude – was managed. Dangerfield had neither hurried her nor himself, and yet he despatched the matter and got her away in less than five minutes.

In little more than a quarter of an hour after, Dr Sturk descended his door-steps in full costume, and marched down the street and passed the artillery barrack, from his violated fortress, as it were, with colours flying, drums beating, and ball in mouth. He paid the money down at Nutter's table, in the small room at the Phoenix, where he sat in the morning to receive his rents, eyeing the agent with a fixed smirk of hate and triumph, and telling down each piece on the table with a fierce clink that had the ring of a curse in it. Little Nutter met his stare of suppressed fury with an eye just as steady and malign and a countenance blackened by disappointment. Not a word was heard but Sturk's insolent tone counting the gold at every clang on the table.

Nutter shoved him a receipt across the table, and swept the gold into his drawer.

'Go over, Tom,' he said to the bailiff, in a stern low tone, 'and see the men don't leave the house till the fees are paid.'

And Sturk laughed a very pleasant laugh, you may be sure, over his shoulder at Nutter, as he went out at the door.

When he was gone Nutter stood up, and turned his face toward the empty grate. I have seen some plain faces once or twice look so purely spiritual, and others at times so infernal, as to acquire in their homeliness a sort of awful grandeur; and from every feature of Nutter's dark wooden face was projected at that moment a super-natural glare of baffled hatred that dilated to something almost sublime.

Chapter Forty-four

Relating how, in the watches of the night, a vision came to Sturk, and his eyes were opened

Sturk's triumph was only momentary. He was in ferocious spirits, indeed, over the breakfast-table, and bolted quantities of buttered toast and eggs, swallowed cups of tea, one after the other, almost at a single gulp, all the time gabbling with a truculent volubility, and every now and then a thump, which made his spoon jingle in his saucer, and poor little Mrs Sturk start, and whisper, 'Oh, my dear!' But after he had done defying and paying off the whole world, and showing his wife, and half convincing himself, that he was the cleverest and finest fellow alive, a letter was handed to him which reminded him, in a dry, short way, of those most formidable and imminent dangers that rose up, apparently insurmountable, before him; and he retired to his study to ruminate again, and chew the cud of bitter fancy, and to write letters and tear them to pieces, and, finally, as was his wont, after hospital hours, to ride into Dublin, to bore his attorney with barren inventions and hopeless schemes of extrication.

Sturk came home that night with a hangdog and jaded look, and taciturn and half desperate. But he called for whiskey, and drank a glass of that cordial, and brewed a jug of punch in silence, and swallowed glass after glass, and got up a little, and grew courageous and flushed, and prated away, rather loud and thickly with a hiccough now and then, and got to sleep earlier than usual.

Somewhere among the 'small hours' of the night he awoke suddenly, recollecting something.

'I have it,' cried Sturk, with an oath, and an involuntary kick at the foot-board, that made his slumbering helpmate bounce.

'What is it, Barney, dear?' squalled she, diving under the bed-clothes, with her heart in her mouth.

'It's like a revelation,' cried Sturk, with another oath; and that was all Mrs Sturk heard of it for some time. But the surgeon was wide awake, and all alive about it, whatever it was. He sat straight up in the bed, with his lips energetically compressed, and his eyebrows screwed together, and his shrewd, hard eyes rolling thoughtfully over the curtains, in the dark, and now and then an ejaculation of wonder, or a short oath, would slowly rise up, and burst from his lips, like a great bubble from the fermentation.

Sturk's brain was in a hubbub. He had fifty plans, all jostling and clamouring together, like a nursery of unruly imps – 'Take *me*' – 'No, take *me*' – 'No, *me*!' He had been dreaming like mad, and his sensorium was still all alive with the images of fifty phantasmagoria, filled up by imagination and conjecture, and a strange, painfully-sharp remembrance of things past – all whirling in a carnival of roystering but dismal riot – masks and dice, laughter, maledictions, and drumming, fair ladies, tipsy youths, mountebanks and assassins: tinkling serenades, the fatal clang and rattle of the dice-box, and long-drawn, distant screams.

There was no more use in Sturk's endeavours to reduce all this to order, than in reading the Riot Act to a Walpurgis gathering. So he sat muttering unconscious ejaculations, and looking down, as it were, from his balcony, waiting for the uproar to abate; and when the air did clear and cool a little, there was just one face that remained impassive, and serenely winked before his eyes.

When things arrived at this stage, and he had gathered his recollections about him, and found himself capable of thinking, being a man of action, up he bounced and struck a light, vaulted into his breeches, hauled on his stockings, hustled himself into his roquelaure, and, candle in hand, in slippered feet, glided, like a ghost, downstairs to the back drawing-room, which, as we know, was his study.

The night was serene and breathless. The sky had cleared, and the moonlight slept mistily on the soft slopes of the park. The landscape was a febrifuge, and cooled and quieted his brain as he stood before it at his open window in solitary meditation. It was not till his slowly wandering eye lighted on the churchyard, with a sort of slight shock, that he again bestirred himself.

There it lay, with its white tombstones and its shadows spread under him, seeming to say – 'Ay, here I am; the narrow goal of all your plans. Not one of the glimmering memorials you see that does not cover what once was a living world of long-headed schemes, chequered remembrances, and well-kept secrets. Here lie your brother plotters, all in bond, only some certain inches below; with their legs straight and their arms by their sides, as when grim Captain DEATH called the stern word "attention!" with their sightless faces and un-thinking foreheads turned up to the moon. Dr Sturk, there are lots of places for you to choose among – suit yourself – here – or here – or maybe here.'

And so Sturk closed the window and remembered his dream, and looked out stealthily but sternly from the door, which was ajar, and shut it sharply, and with his hands in his breeches' pockets, took a quick turn to the window; his soul had got into harness again, and he was busy thinking. Then he snuffed the candle, and then quickened his invention by another brisk turn; and then he opened his desk, and sat down to write a note.

'Yes,' said he to himself, pausing for a minute, with his pen in his fingers, ''tis as certain as that I sit here.'

Well, he wrote the note. There was a kind of smile on his face, which was paler than usual all the while; and he read it over, and threw himself back in his chair, and then read it over again, and did not like it, and tore it up.

Then he thought hard for a while, leaning upon his elbow; and took a couple of great pinches of snuff, and snuffed his candle again, and, as it were, snuffed his wits, and took up his pen with a little flourish, and dashed off another, and read it, and liked it, and gave it a little sidelong nod, as though he said, 'You'll do;' and, indeed, considering all the time and thought he spent upon it, the compos-ition was no great wonder, being, after all, no more than this:

DEAR SIR – Will you give me the honour of a meeting at my house this morning, as you pass through the town? I shall remain within till noon, and hope for some minutes' private discourse with you.

> Your most obedient, very humble servant,
>
> BARNABAS STURK

Then he sealed it with a great red seal, large enough for a patent almost, impressed with the Sturk arms – a boar's head for crest, and a flaunting scroll, with '*Dentem fulmineum cave*' upon it. Then he peeped again from the window to see if the grey of the morning had come, for he had left his watch under his bolster, and longed for the time of action.

Then upstairs went Sturk; and so, with the note, like a loaded pistol, over the chimney, he popped into bed, where he lay awake in agit-ating rumination, determined to believe that he had seen the last of those awful phantoms – those greasy bailiffs – that smooth, smirking, formidable attorney; and – curse him – that bilious marshal's deputy, with the purplish, pimply tinge about the end of his nose and the tops of his cheeks, that beset his bed in a moving ring – this one pushing out a writ, and that rumpling open a parchment deed, and the other fumbling with his keys, and extending his open palm for the garnish. Avaunt. He had found out a charm to rout them all, and they shan't now lay a finger on him – a short and sharp way to clear himself; and so I believe he had.

Chapter Forty-five

Concerning a little rehearsal in Captain Cluffe's lodging, and a certain confidence between Dr Sturk and Mr Dangerfield

Mrs Sturk, though very quiet, was an active little body, with a gentle, anxious face. She was up and about very early, and ran down to the King's House, to ask Mrs Colonel Stafford, who was very kind to her, and a patroness of Sturk's, to execute a little commission for her in Dublin, as she understood she was going into town that day, and the doctor's horse had gone lame, and was in the hands of the farrier. So the good lady undertook it, and offered a seat in her carriage to Dr Sturk, should his business call him to town. The carriage would be at the door at half-past eleven.

And as she trotted home – for her Barney's breakfast-hour was drawing nigh – whom should she encounter upon the road, just outside the town, but their grim spectacled benefactor, Dangerfield, accompanied by, and talking in his usual short way to Nutter, the arch-enemy, who, to say truth, looked confoundedly black and she heard the silver spectacles say, ''Tis, you understand, my own thoughts *only* I speak, Mr Nutter.'

The fright and the shock of seeing Nutter so near her, made her salutation a little awkward; and she had, besides, an instinctive consciousness that they were talking about the terrible affair of yesterday. Dangerfield, on meeting her, bid Nutter good-morning suddenly, and turned about with Mrs Sturk, who had to slacken her pace a little, for the potent agent chose to walk rather slowly.

'A fine morning after all the rain, Madam. How well the hills look,' and he pointed across the Liffey with his cane; 'and the view down the river,' and he turned about, pointing towards Inchicore.

I believe he wanted to see how far Nutter was behind them. He was walking in the opposite direction, looking down on the kerb-stones of the footpath, and touching them with his cane, as if counting them as he proceeded. Dangerfield nodded, and his spectacles in the morning sun seemed to flash two sudden gleams of lightning after him.

'I've been giving Nutter a bit of my mind, Madam, about that procedure of his. He's very angry with me, but a great deal more so with your husband, who has my sympathies with him; and I think I'm safe in saying he's likely soon to have an offer of employment under my Lord Castlemallard, if it suits him.

And he walked on, and talked of other things in short sentences, and parted with Mrs Sturk with a grim brief kindness at the door, and so walked with his wiry step away towards the Brass Castle, where his breakfast awaited him, and he disappeared round the corner of Martin's Row.

'And which way was he going when you met him and that – that *Nutter*?' demanded Sturk, who was talking in high excitement, and not being able to find an epithet worthy of Nutter, made it up by his emphasis and his scowl. She told him.

'H'm! Then he can't have got my note yet!'

She looked at him in a way that plainly said, 'what note?' but Sturk said no more, and he had trained her to govern her curiosity.

As Dangerfield passed Captain Cluffe's lodgings, he heard the gay tinkle of a guitar, and an amorous duet, not altogether untunefully sung to that accompaniment; and he beheld little Lieutenant Puddock's back, with a broad scarlet and gold ribbon across it, supporting the instrument on which he was industriously thrumming, at the window, while Cluffe, who was emitting a high note, with all the tenderness he could throw into his robust countenance, and one of those involuntary distortions which in amateurs will sometimes accompany a vocal effort, caught the eye of the cynical wayfarer, and stopped short with a disconcerted little cough and a shake of his chops, and a grim, rather red nod, and 'Good-morning, Mr Dangerfield.' Puddock also saluted, still thrumming a low chord or two as he did so, for he was not ashamed, like his stout playmate, and saw nothing incongruous in their early minstrelsy.

The fact is, these gallant officers were rehearsing a pretty little entertainment they designed for the ladies at Belmont. It was a serenade, in short, and they had been compelled to postpone it in consequence of the broken weather; and though both gentlemen were, of course, romantically devoted to their respective objects, yet there were no two officers in his Majesty's service more bent upon making love with a due regard to health and comfort than our friends Cluffe and Puddock. Puddock, indeed, was disposed to conduct it in the true masquerading spirit, leaving the ladies to guess at the authors of that concord of sweet sounds with which the amorous air of night was to quiver round the walls and groves of Belmont; and Cluffe, externally acquiescing, had yet made up his mind, if a decent opportunity presented, to be detected and made prisoner, and that the honest troubadours should sup on a hot broil, and sip some of the absent general's curious Madeira at the feet of their respective mistresses, with all the advantage which a situation so romantic and so private would offer.

So 'tinkle, tinkle, twang, twang, THRUM!' went the industrious and accomplished Puddock's guitar; and the voices of the enamoured swains kept tolerable tune and time; and Puddock would say, 'Don't you think, Captain Cluffe, 'twould perhapth go better if we weren't to try that shake upon A. Do let's try the last two barth without it;' and 'I'm thorry to trouble you, but jutht wonth more, if you pleathe:

> But hard ith the chathe my thad heart mutht purthue,
> While Daphne, thweet Daphne, thtill flieth from my view.'

Puddock, indeed, had strict notions about rehearsing, and on occasions like this assumed managerial airs, and in a very courteous way took the absolute command of Captain Cluffe, who sang till he was purple, and his belts and braces cracked again, not venturing to mutiny, though he grumbled a little aside.

So when Dangerfield passed Cluffe's lodging again, returning on his way into Chapelizod, the songsters were at it still. And he smiled his pleasant smile once more, and nodded at poor old Cluffe, who this time was very seriously put out, and flushed up quite fiercely, and said, almost in a mutiny: 'Hang it, Puddock, I believe you'd keep a fellow singing ballads over the street all day. Didn't you see that cursed fellow, Dangerfield, sneering at us – curse him – I suppose he never heard a gentleman sing before; and, by Jove, Puddock, you know you do make a fellow go over the same thing so often it's enough to make a dog laugh.'

A minute after, Dangerfield had mounted Sturk's door-steps, and asked to see the doctor. He was ushered upstairs and into that back drawing-room which we know so well. Sturk rose as he entered.

'Your most obedient, Mr Dangerfield,' said the doctor, with an anxious bow.

'Good-morning, Sir,' said Dangerfield. 'I've got your note, and am here in consequence; what can I do?'

Sturk glanced at the door, to see it was shut, and then said: 'Mr Dangerfield, I've recollected a – *something*.'

'You *have*? Ho! Well, my good Sir?'

'You, I know, were acquainted with – with *Charles Archer*?'

Sturk looked for a moment on the spectacles, and then dropped his eyes.

'Charles Archer,' answered Dangerfield promptly, 'yes, to be sure. But Charles, you know, got into trouble, and 'tis not an acquaintance you or I can boast of; and in fact, we must not mention him; and I have long ceased to know anything of him.'

'But I've just remembered his address; and there's something about his private history which I very well know, and which gives me a claim upon his kind feeling, and he's now in a position to do me a material service; and there's no man living, Mr Dangerfield, has so powerful an influence with him as yourself. Will you use it in my behalf, and attach me to you by lasting gratitude?'

Sturk looked straight at Dangerfield; and Dangerfield looked at him, quizzically, perhaps a little ashamed, in return; after a short pause: 'I *will*,' said Dangerfield, with a sprightly decision. '*But*, you know, Charles is not a fellow to be trifled with – hey? And we must not mention his name – you understand – or hint where he lives, or anything about him, in short.'

'That's plain,' answered Sturk.

'You're going into town, Mrs Sturk tells me, in Mrs Strafford's carriage. Well, when you return this evening, put down in writing what you think Charles can do for you, and I'll take care he considers it.'

'I thank you, Sir,' said Sturk, solemnly.

'And hark ye, you'd better go about your business in town – do you see – just as usual; 'twill excite enquiry if you don't; so you must in this and other things proceed exactly as I direct you,' said Dangerfield.

'Exactly, Sir, depend on't,' answered Sturk.

'Good-day,' said Dangerfield.

'Adieu,' said the doctor; and they shook hands, gravely.

On the lobby Dangerfield encountered Mrs Sturk, and had a few pleasant words with her, patting the bull-heads of the children, and went downstairs smiling and nodding; and Mrs Sturk popped quietly into the study, and found her husband leaning on the chimney piece, and swabbing his face with his handkerchief – strangely pale – and looking, as the good lady afterwards said, for all the world as if he had seen a ghost.

Chapter Forty-six
The Closet scene, with the part of Polonius omitted

When Magnolia and the major had gone out, each on their several devices, poor Mrs Macnamara called Biddy, their maid, and told her, in a vehement, wheezy, confidential whisper in her ear, though there was nobody by but themselves, and the door was shut.

'Biddy, now mind – d'ye see – the lady that came to me in the end of July – do you remember? – in the black satin – you know? – she'll be here today, and we're going down together in her coach to Mrs Nutter's; but that does not signify. As soon as she comes, bring her in here, into this room – d'ye mind? – and go across that instant minute – d'ye see now? – straight to Dr Toole, and ask him to send me the peppermint drops he promised me.'

Then she cross-questioned Biddy, to ascertain that she perfectly understood and clearly remembered; and, finally, she promised her half-a-crown if she peformed this very simple commission to her mistress's satisfaction and held her tongue religiously on the subject. She had apprised Toole the evening before, and now poor Mrs Mack's sufferings, she hoped, were about to be brought to a happy termination by the doctor's ingenuity. She was, however, very nervous indeed, as the crisis approached; for such a beast as Mary Matchwell at bay was a spectacle to excite a little tremor even in a person of more nerve than fat Mrs Macnamara.

And what could Mary Matchwell want of a conjuring conference, of all persons in the world, with poor little Mrs Nutter? Mrs Mack had done in this respect simply as she was bid. She had indeed no difficulty to persuade Mrs Nutter to grant the interview. That harmless little giggling creature could not resist the mere mention of a fortune-teller. Only for Nutter, who set his face against this sort of sham witchcraft, she would certainly have asked him to treat her with a glimpse into futurity at that famous-sibyl's house; and now that she had an opportunity of having the enchantress *tête-à-tête* in her own snug parlour at the Mills, she was in a delightful fuss of mystery and delight.

Mrs Mack, indeed, from her own sad experience, felt a misgiving and a pang in introducing the formidable prophetess. But what could she do? She dared not refuse; all she could risk was an anxious hint to poor little Mrs Nutter, 'not to be telling her *anything*, good, bad, or indifferent, but just to ask her what questions she liked, and no more.' Indeed, poor Mrs Mack was low and feverish about this assignation, and would have been more so but for the hope that her Polonius, behind the arras, would bring the woman of Endor to her knees.

All on a sudden she heard the rumble and jingle of a hackney coach, and the clang of the horses' hoofs pulled up close under her window; her heart bounded and fluttered up to her mouth, and then dropped down like a lump of lead, and she heard a well-known voice talk a few sentences to the coachman, and then in the hall, as she supposed, to Biddy; and so she came into the room, dressed as usual in black, tall, thin, and erect, with a black hood shading her pale face, and the mist and chill of night seemed to enter along with her.

It was a great relief to poor Mrs Mack, that she actually saw Biddy at that moment run across the street toward Toole's hall-door, and she quickly averted her conscious glance from the light-heeled handmaid.

'Pray take a chair, Ma'am,' said Mrs Mack, with a pallid face and a low courtesy.

Mistress Matchwell made a faint courtesy in return, and, without saying anything, sat down, and peered sharply round the room.

'I'm glad, Ma'am, you had no dust today; the rain, Ma'am, laid it beautiful.'

The grim woman in black threw back her hood a little, and showed her pale face and thin lips, and prominent black eyes, altogether a grisly and intimidating countenance, with something wild and suspicious in it, suiting by no means ill with her supernatural and malign pretensions.

Mrs Mack's ear was strained to catch the sound of Toole's approach, and a pause ensued, during which she got up and poured out a glass of port for the lady, and she presented it to her deferentially. She took it with a nod, and sipped it, thinking, as it seemed, uneasily. There was plainly something more than usual upon her mind. Mrs Mack thought – indeed, she was quite sure – she heard a little fussing about the bedroom door, and concluded that the doctor was getting under cover.

When Mrs Matchwell had set her empty glass upon the table, she glided to the window, and Mrs Mack's guilty conscience smote her, as she saw her look towards Toole's house. It was only, however, for the coach; and having satisfied herself it was at hand, she said: 'We'll have some minutes quite private, if you please – 'tisn't my affair, you know, but yours,' said the weird woman.

There had been ample time for the arrangement of Toole's ambuscade. Now was the moment. The crisis was upon her. But poor Mrs Mack, just as she was about to say her little say about the front windows and opposite neighbours, and the privacy of the back bedroom, and to propose their retiring thither, felt a sinking of the heart – a deadly faintness, and an instinctive conviction that she was altogether overmatched, and that she could not hope to play successfully any sort of devil's game with that all-seeing sorceress. She had always thought she was a plucky woman till she met Mistress Mary. Before *her* her spirit died within her – her blood flowed hurriedly back to her heart, leaving her body cold, pale, and damp, and her soul quailing under her gaze.

She cleared her voice twice, and faltered an enquiry, but broke down in panic; and at that moment Biddy popped in her head – 'The doctor, Ma'am, was sent for to Lucan, an' he won't be back till six o'clock, an' he left no peppermint drops for you, Ma'am, an' do you want me, if you plase, Ma'am?'

'Go down, Biddy, that'll do,' said Mrs Mack, growing first pale, and then very red.

Mary Matchwell scented death afar off; for her the air was always tainted with ominous perfumes. Every unusual look or dubious word thrilled her with a sense of danger. Suspicion is the baleful instinct of self-preservation with which the devil gifts his children; and hers never slept.

'*What* doctor?' said Mrs Matchwell, turning her large, dismal, wicked gaze full on Mrs Mack.

'Doctor Toole, Ma'am.' She dared not tell a literal lie to that piercing, prominent pair of black eyes.

'And why did you send for Doctor O'Toole, Ma'am?'

'I did not send for the doctor,' answered the fat lady, looking down, for she could not stand that glance that seemed to light up all the caverns of her poor soul, and make her lies stand forth self-confessed. 'I did not send for him, Ma'am, only for some drops he promised me. I've been very sick – I – I – I'm so miserable.'

And poor Mrs Mack's nether lip quivered, and she burst into tears.

'You're enough to provoke a saint, Mrs Macnamara,' said the woman in black, rather savagely, though coldly enough. 'Why, you're on the point of fortune, as it seems to me.' Here poor Mrs Mack's inarticulate lamentations waxed more vehement. 'You don't believe it – very well – but where's the use of crying over your little difficulties, Ma'am, like a great baby, instead of exerting yourself and thanking your best friend?'

And the two ladies sat down to a murmuring *tête-à-tête* at the far end of the room; you could have heard little more than an inarticulate cooing, and poor Mrs Mack's sobs, and the stern – 'And is that all? I've had more trouble with you than with fifty reasonable clients – you can hardly be serious – I tell you plainly, you must manage matters better, my good Madam; for, frankly, Ma'am, *this* won't do.'

With which that part of the conference closed, and Mary Matchwell looked out of the window. The coach stood at the door, the horses dozing patiently with their heads together, and the coachman, with a black eye mellowing into the yellow stage, and a cut across his nose – both doing well – was marching across from the public-house over the way, wiping his mouth in the cuff of his coat.

'Put on your riding-hood, if you please, Madam, and come down with me in the coach to introduce me to Mrs Nutter,' said Mrs Matchwell, at the same time tapping with her long bony fingers to the driver.

'There's no need of that, Madam. I said what you desired, and I sent a note to her last night, and she expects you just now; and, indeed, I'd rather not go, Madam, if you please.'

''Tis past that now – just do as I tell you, for come you must,' answered Mrs Matchwell.

As the old woman of Berkley obeyed, and got up and went quietly away with her visitor, though her dead flesh quivered with fear, so poor Mrs Mack, though loath enough, submitted in silence.

'Now, you look like a body going to be hanged – you do; what's the matter with you, Madam? I tell you, you mustn't look that way. Here, take a sup o' this;' and she presented the muzzle of a small bottle like a pistol at her mouth as she spoke.

'There's a glass on the table, if you let me, Ma'am,' said Mrs Mack.

'Glass be — ; here, take a mouthful.'

And she popped it between her lips; and Mrs Mack was refreshed and her spirit revived within her.

Chapter Forty-seven

In which pale Hecate visits the Mills, and Charles Nutter, Esq., orders tea

Poor Mrs Nutter, I have an honest regard for her memory. If she was scant of brains, she was also devoid of guile – giggle and raspberry-jam were the leading traits of her character. And though she was slow to believe ill-natured stories, and made, in general, a horrid jumble when she essayed to relate news, except of the most elementary sort; and used to forget genealogies, and to confuse lawsuits and other family feuds, and would have made a most unsatisfactory witness upon any topic on earth, yet she was a ready sympathiser, and a restless but purblind matchmaker – always suggesting or suspecting little romances, and always amazed when the *éclaircissement* came off. Excellent for condoling – better still for rejoicing – she would, on hearing of a surprising good match, or an unexpected son and heir, or a pleasantly-timed legacy, go off like a mild little peal of joy-bells, and keep ringing up and down and zig-zag, and to and again, in all sorts of irregular roulades, without stopping, the whole day long, with 'Well, to be sure.' 'Upon my conscience, now, I scarce can believe it.' 'An' isn't it pleasant, though.' 'Oh! the creatures – but it was badly wanted!' 'Dear knows – but I'm glad – ha, ha, ha,' and so on. A train of reflection and rejoicing not easily exhausted, and readily, by simple transposition, maintainable for an indefinite period. And people, when good news came, used to say, 'Sally Nutter will be glad to hear that'; and though she had not a great deal of sense, and her conversation was made up principally of interjections, assisted by little gestures, and wonderful expressions of face; and though, when analysed, it was not much, yet she made a cheerful noise, and her company was liked; and her friendly little gesticulation, and her turning up of the eyes, and her smiles and sighs, and her 'whisht a bit', and her 'faith and troth now', and 'whisper', and all the rest of her little budget of idiomatic expletives, made the people somehow, along with her sterling qualities, fonder of her than perhaps, having her always at hand, they were quite aware.

So they both entered the vehicle, which jingled and rattled so incessantly and so loud that connected talk was quite out of the question, and Mrs Macnamara was glad 'twas so; and she could not help observing there was something more than the ordinary pale cast of devilment in Mary Matchwell's face – something, she thought, almost frightful, and which tempted her to believe in her necromantic faculty.

So they reached Nutter's house, at the Mills, a sober, grey-fronted mansion, darkened with tall trees, and in went Mrs Mack. Little Mrs Nutter received her in a sort of transport of eagerness, giggle, and curiosity.

'And is she really in the coach now? And, my dear, does she really tell the wonders they say? Mrs Molly told me – well, now, the most surprising things; and do you actually believe she's a conjuror? But mind you, Nutter must not know I had her here. He can't abide a fortune-teller. And what shall I ask her? I think about the pearl cross – don't you? For I *would* like to know, and then whether Nutter or his enemies – you know who I mean – will carry the day – don't you know? Doctor Sturk, my dear, and – and – but that's the chief question.'

Poor Mrs Mack glanced over her shoulder to see she wasn't watched, and whispered her in haste – 'For mercy's sake, my dear, take my advice, and that is, listen to all she tells you, but tell her nothing.'

'To be sure, my dear, that's only common sense,' said Mrs Nutter.

And Mary Matchwell, who thought they had been quite long enough together, descended from the carriage, and was in the hall before Mrs Nutter was aware; and the silent apparition overawed the poor little lady, who faltered a 'Good-evening, Madam – you're very welcome – pray step in.' So in they all trooped to Nutter's parlour.

So soon as little Mrs Nutter got fairly under the chill and shadow of this inauspicious presence, her giggle subsided, and she began to think of the dreadful story she had heard of her having showed Mrs Flemming through a glass of fair water, the apparition of her husband with his face half masked with blood, the day before his murder by the watchmen in John's-lane. When, therefore, this woman of Endor called for water and glasses, and told Mrs Mack that she must leave them alone together, poor little empty Mrs Nutter lost heart, and began to feel very queer, and to wish herself well out of the affair; and, indeed, was almost ready to take to her heels and leave the two ladies in possession of the house, but she had not decision for this.

'And mayn't Mrs Mack stay in the room with us?' she asked, following that good lady's retreating figure with an imploring look.

'By no means.'

This was addressed sternly to Mrs Mack herself, who, followed by poor Mrs Nutter's eyes, moved fatly and meekly out of the room.

She was not without her fair share of curiosity, but on the whole, was relieved, and very willing to go. She had only seen Mary Matchwell take from her pocket and uncase a small, oval-shaped steel mirror, which seemed to have the property of magnifying objects; for she saw her cadaverous fingers reflected in it to fully double their natural size, and she had half-filled a glass with water, and peered through it askew, holding it toward the light.

Well, the door was shut, and an interval of five minutes elapsed; and all of a sudden two horrible screams in quick succession rang through the house.

Betty, the maid, and Mrs Mack were in the small room on the other side of the hall, and stared in terror on one another. The old lady, holding Betty by the wrist, whispered a benediction; and Betty crying – 'Oh! my dear, what's happened the poor misthress?' crossed the hall in a second, followed by Mrs Mack, and they heard the door unlocked on the inside as they reached it.

In they came, scarce knowing how, and found poor little Mrs Nutter flat upon the floor, in a swoon, her white face and the front of her dress drenched with water.

'You've a scent bottle, Mrs Macnamara – let her smell to it,' said the grim woman in black, coldly, but with a scarcely perceptible gleam of triumph, as she glanced on the horrified faces of the women.

Well, it was a long fainting-fit; but she did come out of it. And when her bewildered gaze at last settled upon Mrs Matchwell, who was standing darkly and motionless between the windows, she uttered another loud and horrible cry, and clung with her arms round Mrs Mack's neck, and screamed: 'Oh! Mrs Mack, *there* she is – *there* she is – *there* she is.'

And she screamed so fearfully and seemed in such an extremity of terror, that Mary Matchwell, in her sables, glided, with a strange sneer on her pale face, out of the room across the hall, and into the little parlour on the other side, like an evil spirit whose mission was half accomplished, and who departed from her for a season.

'She's here – she's here!' screamed poor little Mrs Nutter.

'No, dear, no – she's not – she's gone, my dear, indeed she's gone,' replied Mrs Mack, herself very much appalled.

'Oh! is she gone – is she – *is* she gone?' cried Mrs Nutter, staring all round the room, like a child after a frightful dream.

'She's gone, Ma'am, dear – she isn't here – by this crass, she's gone!' said Betty, assisting Mrs Mack, and equally frightened and incensed.

'Oh! Oh! Betty, where is he gone? Oh! Mrs Mack – oh! no – no – never! It can't be – it couldn't. It *is* not he – he never did it.'

'I declare to you, Ma'am, she's not right in her head!' cried poor Betty, at her wits' ends.

'There – *there* now, Sally, darling – *there*,' said frightened Mrs Mack, patting her on the back.

'There – there – there – I see him,' she cried again. 'Oh! Charley – Charley, sure – sure I didn't see it aright – it was not real.'

'There now, don't be frettin' yourself, Ma'am dear,' said Betty.

But Mrs Mack glanced over her shoulder in the direction in which Mrs Nutter was looking, and with a sort of shock, not knowing whether it was a bodily presence or a simulacrum raised by the incantations of Mary Matchwell, she beheld the dark features and white eyeballs of Nutter himself looking full on them from the open door.

'Sally – what ails you, sweetheart?' said he, coming close up to her with two swift steps.

'Oh! Charley – 'twas a dream – nothing else – a bad dream, Charley. Oh! say it's a dream,' cried the poor terrified little woman. 'Oh! she's coming – she's coming!' she cried again, with an appalling scream.

'*Who* – what's the matter?' cried Nutter, looking in the direction of his poor wife's gaze in black wrath and bewilderment, and beholding the weird woman who had followed him into the room. As he gazed on that pale, wicked face and sable shape, the same sort of spell which she exercised upon Mrs Mack, and poor Mrs Nutter, seemed in a few seconds to steal over Nutter himself, and fix him in the place where he stood. His mahogany face bleached to sickly boxwood, and his eyes looked like pale balls of stone about to leap from their sockets.

After a few seconds, however, with a sort of gasp, like a man awaking from a frightful sleep, he said: 'Betty, take the mistress to her room;' and to his wife, 'go, sweetheart. Mrs Macnamara, this must be explained,' he added; and taking her by the hand, he led her in silence to the hall-door, and signed to the driver.

'Oh! thank you, Mr Nutter,' she stammered; 'but the coach is not mine; it came with that lady who's with Mrs Nutter.'

He had up to this moved with her like a somnambulist.

'Ay, that lady; and who the devil is she?' and he seized her arm with a sudden grasp that made her wince.

'Oh! that lady!' faltered Mrs Mack – 'she's, I believe – she's Mrs Matchwell – the – the lady that advertises her abilities.'

'Hey! I know – the fortune-teller, and go-between – her!'

She was glad he asked her no more questions, but let her go, and stood in a livid meditation, forgetting to bid her good-evening. She did not wait, however, for his courteous dismissal, but hurried away towards Chapelizod. The only thing connected with the last half-hour's events that seemed quite clear and real to the scared lady was the danger of being overtaken by that terrible woman, and a dreadful sense of her own share as an accessory in the untold mischief that had befallen poor Mrs Nutter.

In the midst of her horrors and agitation Mrs Mack's curiosity was not altogether stunned. She wondered vaguely, as she pattered along, with what dreadful exhibition of her infernal skill Mary Matchwell had disordered the senses of poor little Mrs Nutter – had she called up a red-eyed, sooty-raven to her shoulder – as old Miss Alice Lee (when she last had a dish of tea with her) told her she had once done before – and made the ominous bird speak the doom of poor Mrs Nutter from that perch? Or had she raised the foul fiend in bodily shape, or showed her Nutter's dead face through the water?

With these images flitting before her brain, she hurried on at her best pace, fancying every moment that she heard the rumble of the accursed coach behind her, and longing to see the friendly uniform of the Royal Irish Artillery, and the familiar house-fronts of the cheery little street, and above all, to hide herself securely among her own household gods.

When Nutter returned to the parlour his wife had not yet left it.

'I'll attend here, go you upstairs,' said Nutter. He spoke strangely, and looked odd, and altogether seemed strung up to a high pitch.

Out went Betty, seeing it was no good dawdling; for her master was resolute and formidable. The room, like others in old-fashioned houses with thick walls, had a double door. He shut the one with a stern slam, and then the other; and though the honest maid loitered in the hall, and, indeed, placed her ear very near the door, she was not much the wiser.

There was some imperfectly heard talk in the parlour, and cries, and sobs, and more talking. Then before Betty was aware, the door suddenly opened, and out came Mary Matchwell, with gleaming eyes, and a pale laugh of spite and victory and threw a look, as she passed, upon the maid that frightened her, and so vanished into her coach.

Nutter disengaged himself from poor Mrs Nutter's arms, in which he was nearly throttled, while she sobbed and shrieked: 'Oh! Charley, dear – dearest Charley – Charley, darling – isn't it frightful?' and so on.

'Betty, take care of her,' was all he said, and that sternly, like a man quietly desperate, but with a dismal fury in his face.

He went into the little room on the other side of the now darkening hall, and shut the door, and locked it inside. It was partly because he did not choose to talk just now any more with his blubbering and shrieking wife. He was a very kind husband, in his way, but a most incapable nurse, especially in a case of hysterics.

He came out with a desk in his hands.

'Moggy,' he said, in a low tone, seeing his other servant-woman in the dusk crossing at the foot of the stairs, 'here, take this desk, leave it in our bedroom – 'tis for the mistress; tell her so by-and-by.'

The wench carried it up; but poor Mrs Nutter was in no condition to comprehend anything, and was talking quite wildly, and seemed to be growing worse rather than better.

Nutter stood alone in the hall, with his back to the door from which he had just emerged, his hands in his pockets, and the same dreary and wicked shadow over his face.

'So that — Sturk will carry his point after all,' he muttered.

On the hall wainscot just opposite hung his horse-pistols; and when he saw them, and that wasn't for a while – for though he was looking straight at them, he was staring, really, quite through the dingy wooden panel at quite other objects three hundred miles away – when he *did* see them, I say, he growled in the same tone – 'I wish one of those bullets was through my head, so t'other was through his.'

And he cursed him with laconic intensity. Then Nutter slapped his pockets, like a man feeling if his keys and other portable chattels are all right before he leaves his home. But his countenance was that of one whose mind is absent and wandering. And he looked down on the ground, as it seemed in profound and troubled abstraction; and, after a while, he looked up again, and again glared on the cold pistols that hung before him – ready for anything. And he took down one with a snatch and weighed it in his hand, and fell to thinking again; and, as he did, kept opening and shutting the pan with a snap, and so for a long time, and thinking deeply to the tune of that castanet, and at last he roused himself, who knows from what dreams, and hung up the weapon again by its fellow, and looked about him.

The hall-door lay open, as Mary Matchwell had left it. Nutter stood on the door-step, where he could hear faintly, from above stairs, the cries and wails of poor, hysterical Mrs Nutter. He remained there a good while, during which, unperceived by him, Dr Toole's pestle-and-mortar-boy, who had entered by the back way, had taken a seat in the hall. He was waiting for an empty draught-bottle, in exchange for a replenished flask of the same agreeable beverage, which he had just delivered; for physic was one of poor Mrs Nutter's weaknesses, though, happily, she did not swallow half what came home for her.

When Nutter turned round, the boy – a sharp, tattling vagabond, he knew him well – was reading a printed card he had picked up from the floor, with the impress of Nutter's hob-nailed tread upon it. It was endorsed upon the back, 'For Mrs Macnamara, with the humble duty of her obedient servant, M. M.'

'What's that, Sirrah?' shouted Nutter.

'For Mrs Nutter, I think, Sir,' said the urchin, jumping up with a start.

'Mrs Nutter,' repeated he – 'No – Mrs Mac – Macnamara,' and he thrust it into his surtout pocket. 'And what brings you here, Sirrah?' he added savagely; for he thought everybody was spying after him now, and, as I said, he knew him for a tattling young dog – he had taken the infection from his master, who had trained him.

'Here, woman,' he cried to Moggy, who was passing again, 'give that pimping rascal his — answer; and see, Sirrah, if I find you sneaking about the place again, I'll lay that whip across your back.'

Nutter went into the small room again.

'An' how are ye, Jemmie – how's every inch iv you?' enquired Moggy of the boy, when his agitation was a little blown over.

'I'm elegant, thank ye,' he answered; 'an' what's the matther wid ye all? I cum through the kitchen, and seen no-one.'

'Och! Didn't you hear? The poor mistress – she's as bad as bad can be.' And then began a whispered confidence, broken short by Nutter's again emerging, with the leather belt he wore at night on, and a short back-sword, called a *couteau de chasse*, therein, and a heavy walking-cane in his hand.

'Get tea for me, wench, in half an hour,' said he, this time quite quietly, though still sternly, and without seeming to observe the quaking boy, who, at first sight, referred these martial preparations to a resolution to do execution upon him forthwith; 'you'll find me in the garden when it's ready.'

And he strode out, and pushing open the wicket door in the thick garden hedge, and, with his cane shouldered, walked with a quick, resolute step down towards the pretty walk by the river, with the thick privet hedge and the row of old pear trees by it. And that was the last that was heard or seen of Mr Nutter for some time.

Chapter Forty-eight

Swans on the water

At about half-past six that evening, Puddock arrived at Captain Cluffe's lodgings, and for the last time the minstrels rehearsed their lovelorn and passionate ditties. They were drest 'all in their best', under that outer covering which, partly for mystery and partly for bodily comfort – the wind, after the heavy rains of the last week, having come round to the east – these prudent troubadours wore.

Though they hardly glanced at the topic to one another, each had his delightful anticipations of the chances of the meeting. Puddock did not value Dangerfield a rush, and Cluffe's mind was pretty easy upon that point from the moment his proposal for Gertrude Chattesworth had taken wind.

Only for that cursed shower the other night, that made it incumbent on Cluffe, who had had two or three sharp little visits of his patrimonial gout, and no notion of dying for love, to get to his quarters as quickly as might be – he had no doubt that the last stave of their first duet rising from the meadow of Belmont, with that charming roulade – devised by Puddock, and the pathetic twang-twang of his romantic instrument, would have been answered by the opening of the drawing-room window, and Aunt Becky's imperious summons to the serenaders to declare themselves, and come in and partake of supper!

The only thing that at all puzzled him, unpleasantly connected with that unsuccessful little freak of musical love-making, was the fellow they saw getting away from under the open window – the very same at which Lilias Walsingham had unintentionally surprised her friend Gertrude. He had a surtout on, with the cape cut exactly after the fashion of Dangerfield, and a three-cocked hat with very pinched corners, in the French style, which identical hat Cluffe was ready to swear he saw upon Dangerfield's head very early one morning, as he accidentally espied him viewing his peas and tulips in the little garden of the Brass Castle by the river side. 'Twas fixed, in fact, in

Cluffe's mind that Dangerfield was the man; and what the plague need had a declared lover of any such clandestine manoeuvres? Was it possible that the old scoundrel was, after all, directing his night visits differently, and keeping the aunt in play, as a reserve, in the event of the failure of his suit to the niece? Plans as gross, he knew, had succeeded; old women were so devilish easily won, and loved money too, so well sometimes.

These sly fellows agreed that they must not go to Belmont by Chapelizod-bridge, which would lead them through the town, in front of the barrack, and under the very sign-board of the Phoenix. No, they would go by the Knockmaroon-road, cross the river by the ferry, and unperceived and unsuspected, enter the grounds of Belmont on the further side.

So away went the amorous musicians, favoured by the darkness, and talking in an undertone, and thinking more than they talked, while little Puddock, from under his cloak, scratched a faint little arpeggio and a chord, ever and anon, upon 'the inthrument'.

When they reached the ferry, the boat was tied at the near side, but deuce a ferryman could they see. So they began to shout and hallo, singly and together, until Cluffe, in much ire and disgust, exclaimed: 'Curse the sot – drunk in some whiskey-shop – the blackguard! That is the way such scoundrels throw away their chances, and help to fill the high roads with beggars and thieves; curse him, I shan't have a note left if we go on bawling this way. I suppose we must go home again.'

'Fiddle-thtick!' exclaimed the magnanimous Puddock. 'I pulled myself across little more than a year ago, and 'twas as easy as – as – anything. Get in, an' loose her when I tell you.'

This boat was managed by means of a rope stretched across the stream from bank to bank; seizing which, in both hands, the boatman, as he stood in his skiff, hauled it, as it seemed, with very moderate exertion across the river.

Cluffe chuckled as he thought how sold the rascally boatman would be, on returning, to find his bark gone over to the other side.

'Don't be uneathy about the poor fellow,' said Puddock; 'we'll come down in the morning and make him a present, and explain how it occurred.'

'Explain *yourself* – poor fellow, be hanged!' muttered Cluffe, as he took his seat, for he did not part with his silver lightly. 'I say, Puddock, tell me when I'm to slip the rope.'

The signal given, Cluffe let go, entertaining himself with a little jingle of Puddock's guitar, of which he had charge, and a verse or two of their last song, while the plump little lieutenant, standing upright, midships in the boat, hauled away, though not quite so deftly as was desirable. Some two or three minutes had passed before they reached the middle of the stream, which was, as Puddock afterwards remarked, 'gigantically thwollen'; and at this point they came to something very like a standstill.

'I say, Puddock, keep her head a little more up the stream, will you?' said Cluffe, thinking no evil, and only to show his nautical knowledge.

'It's easy to say keep her head up the stream,' gasped Puddock who was now labouring fearfully, and quite crimson in the face, tugging his words up with a desperate lisp, and too much out of breath to say more.

The shades of the night and the roar of the waters prevented Cluffe observing these omens aright.

'What the plague are you doing *now*?' cried Cluffe, arresting a decorative passage in the middle, and for the first time seriously uncomfortable, as the boat slowly spun round, bringing what Cluffe called her head – though head and tail were pretty much alike – toward the bank they had quitted.

'Curse you, Puddock, why – what are you going back for? You can't do it.'

'Lend a hand,' bawled Puddock, in extremity. 'I say, help, seize the rope; I say, Cluffe, quick, Sir, my arms are breaking.'

There was no exaggeration in this – there seldom was in anything Puddock said; and the turn of the boat had twisted his arms like the strands of a rope.

'Hold on, Puddock, curse you, I'm comin',' roared Cluffe, quite alive to the situation. 'If you let go, I'm *diddled* but I'll shoot you.'

'Catch the rope, I thay, Thir, or 'tith all over!'

Cluffe, who had only known that he was slowly spinning round, and that Puddock was going to commit him to the waves, made a vehement exertion to catch the rope, but it was out of reach, and the boat rocked so suddenly from his rising, that he sat down by mistake again, with a violent plump that made his teeth gnash, in his own place; and the shock and his alarm stimulated his anger.

'Hold on, Sir; hold on, you little devil, I say, one minute, here – hold – hollo!'

While Cluffe was shouting these words, and scrambling forward, Puddock was cryin, 'Curth it, Cluffe, quick – oh! hang it, I can't thtand it – bleth my *thoul*!

And Puddock let go, and the boat and its precious freightage, with a horrid whisk and a sweep, commenced its seaward career in the dark.

'Take the oars, Sir, hang you!' cried Cluffe.

'There are no oarth,' replied Puddock, solemnly.

'Or the helm.'

'There'th no helm.'

'And what the devil, Sir?' and a splash of cold water soused the silken calves of Cluffe at this moment.

'Heugh! Heugh! – and what the devil *will* you do, Sir? You don't want to drown me, I suppose?' roared Cluffe, holding hard by the gunwale.

'*You* can thwim, Cluffe; jump in, and don't mind me,' said little Puddock, sublimely.

Cluffe, who was a bit of a boaster, had bragged, one evening at mess, of his swimming, which he said was famous in his school days; 'twas a lie, but Puddock believed it implicitly.

'Thank you!' roared Cluffe. 'Swim, indeed! – buttoned up this way – and – and the gout too.'

'I say, Cluffe, save the guitar, if you can,' said Puddock.

In reply, Cluffe cursed that instrument through his teeth, with positive fury, and its owner; and, indeed, he was so incensed at this unfeeling request, that if he had known where it was, I think he would have gone nigh to smash it on Puddock's head, or at least, like the 'Minstrel Boy', to tear its chords asunder; for Cluffe was hot, especially when he was frightened. But he forgot – though it was hanging at that moment by a pretty scarlet and gold ribbon about his neck.

'Guitar be *diddled*!' cried he; ''tis gone – where *we're* going – to the bottom. What devil possessed you, Sir, to drown us this way?'

Puddock sighed. They were passing at this moment the quiet banks of the pleasant meadow of Belmont, and the lights twinkled from the bow-window in the drawing-room. I don't know whether Puddock saw them – Cluffe certainly did not.

'Hallo! hallo! – a rope!' cried Cluffe, who had hit upon this desperate expedient for raising the neighbourhood. 'A rope – a rope! Hallo! hallo! – a ro-o-o-ope!'

And Aunt Becky, who heard the wild whooping, mistook it for drunken fellows at their diversions, and delivered her sentiments in the drawing-room accordingly.

Chapter Forty-nine

Swans in the water

'We're coming to something – what's that?' said Puddock, as a long row of black stakes presented themselves at some distance ahead, in the dusky moonlight, slanting across the stream.

''Tis the salmon-weir!' roared Cluffe with an oath that subsided into something like a sickening prayer.

It was only a fortnight before that a tipsy fellow had been found drowned in the net. Cluffe had lost his head much more than Puddock, though Cluffe had fought duels. But then, he really could not swim a bit, and he was so confoundedly buckled up.

'Sit to the right. Trim the boat, Sir!' said little Puddock.

'Trim the devil!' bawled Cluffe, to whom this order of Puddock's, it must be owned a useless piece of marinetism in their situation, was especially disgusting; and he added, looking furiously ahead – ''Tisn't the boat I'd trim, I promise you: you – you ridiculous murderer!'

Just then Puddock's end of the boat touched a stone, or a post, or something in the current, and that in which Cluffe sat came wheeling swiftly round across the stream, and brought the gallant captain so near the bank that, with a sudden jerk, he caught the end of a branch that stretched far over the water, and, spite of the confounded tightness of his toilet, with the energy of sheer terror, climbed a good way; but, reaching a point where the branch forked, he could get no further, though he tugged like a brick. But what was a fat fellow of fifty, laced, and buckled, and buttoned up, like poor Cluffe – with his legs higher up among the foliage than his head and body – to do, and with his right calf caught in the fork of a branch, so as to arrest all progress, and especially as the captain was plainly too much for the branch, which was drooping toward the water, and emitting sounds premonitory of a smash.

With a long, screaking crash the branch stooped down to the water, and, so soon as the old element made itself acquainted with those parts that reached it first, the gallant captain, with a sort of sob, redoubled his efforts, and down came the faithless bough, more and more perpendicularly, until his nicely got-up cue and bag, then his powdered head, and finally Captain Cluffe's handsome features, went under the surface. When this occurred, he instantaneously disengaged his legs with a vague feeling that his last struggle above water was over.

His feet immediately touched the bottom; he stood erect, little above his middle, and quite out of the main current, within half-a-dozen steps of the bank, and he found himself – he scarcely knew how – on terra firma, impounded in a little flower-garden, with lilacs and laburnums, and sweet-briars, and, through a window close at hand, whom should he see but Dangerfield, who was drying his hands in a towel; and, as Cluffe stood for a moment, letting the water pour down through his sleeves, he further saw him make some queer little arrangements, and eventually pour out and swallow a glass of brandy, and was tempted to invoke his aid on the spot; but some small incivilities which he had bestowed upon Dangerfield, when he thought he cherished designs upon Aunt Rebecca, forbade; and at that moment he spied the little wicket that opened upon the road, and Dangerfield stept close up to the window, and cried sternly, 'Who's there?' with his grim spectacles close to the window.

The boyish instinct of 'hide and seek' took possession of Cluffe, and he glided forth from the precincts of the Brass Castle upon the high road, just as the little hall-door was pushed open, and he heard the harsh tones of Dangerfield challenging the gooseberry bushes and hollyhocks, and thrashing the evergreens with his cane.

Cluffe hied straight to his lodgings, and ordered a sack posset. Worthy Mrs Mason eyed him in silent consternation, drenched and dishevelled, wild, and discharging water from every part of his clothing and decorations, as he presented himself without a hat, before her dim dipt candle in the hall.

'I'll take that – that vessel, if you please, Sir, that's hanging about your neck,' said the mild and affrighted lady, meaning Puddock's guitar, through the circular orifice of which, under the chords, the water with which it was filled occasionally splashed.

'Oh – eh? – the instrument? – confound it!' and rather sheepishly he got the grey, red and gold ribbon over his dripping head, and placing it in her hand without explanation, he said – 'A warming-pan as quickly as may be, I beg, Mrs Mason – and the posset, I do earnestly request. You see – I – I've been nearly drowned – and – and I can't answer for consequences if there be one minute's delay.'

And up he went streaming, with Mrs Mason's candle, to his bed-room, and dragged off his clinging garments, and dried his fat body, like a man coming out of a bath, and roared for hot water for his feet, and bellowed for the posset and warming-pan, and rolled into his bed, and kept the whole house in motion.

And so soon as he had swallowed his cordial, and toasted his sheets, and with the aid of his man rolled himself in a great blanket, and clapped his feet in a tub of hot water, and tumbled back again into his bed, he bethought him of Puddock, and ordered his man to take his compliments to Captain Burgh and Lieutenant Lillyman, the tenants of the nearest lodging-house, and to request either to come to him forthwith on a matter of life or death.

Lillyman was at home, and came.

'Puddock's drowned, my dear Lillyman, and I'm little better. The ferry boat broke away with us. Do go down to the adjutant – they ought to raise the salmon nets – I'm very ill myself – very ill, indeed – else I'd have assisted; but you know *me*, Lillyman. Poor Puddock – 'tis a sad business – but lose no time.'

'And can't he swim?' asked Lillyman, aghast.

'Swim? – ay, like a stone, poor fellow! If he had only thrown himself out, and held by me, hang it, I'd have brought him to shore; but poor Puddock, he lost his head. And I – you see me here – don't forget to tell them the condition you found me in, and – and – now don't lose a moment.'

So off went Lillyman to give the alarm at the barrack.

Chapter Fifty

Treating of some confusion, in consequence, in the club-room of the
Phoenix and elsewhere, and of a hat that was picked up

When Cluffe sprang out of the boat, he was very near capsizing it
and finishing Puddock off-hand, but she righted and shot away
swiftly towards the very centre of the weir, over which, in a sheet of
white foam, she swept, and continued her route toward Dublin –
bottom upward, leaving little Puddock, however, safe and sound,
clinging to a post, at top, and standing upon a rough sort of plank,
which afforded a very unpleasant footing, by which the nets were
visited from time to time.

'Hallo! Are you safe, Cluffe?' cried the little lieutenant, quite firm,
though a little dizzy, on his narrow stand, with the sheets of foam
whizzing under his feet; what had become of his musical companion
he had not the faintest notion, and when he saw the boat hurled over
near the sluice, and drive along the stream upside down, he nearly
despaired.

But when the captain's military cloak, which he took for Cluffe
himself, followed in the track of the boat, whisking, sprawling, and
tumbling, in what Puddock supposed to be the agonies of drowning,
and went over the weir and disappeared from view, returning no
answer to his screams of 'Strike out, Cluffe! To your right, Cluffe.
Hollo! To your right,' he quite gave the captain over.

'Surrendhur, you thievin' villain, or I'll put the contints iv this gun
into yir carcass,' shouted an awful voice from the right bank, and
Puddock saw the outline of a gigantic marksman, preparing to fire
into his corresponding flank.

'What do you mean, Sir?' shouted Puddock, in extreme wrath and
discomfort.

'Robbin' the nets, you spalpeen; if you throw them salmon you're
hidin' undher your coat into the wather, be the tare-o-war – '

'What salmon, Sir?' interrupted the lieutenant. 'Why, salmon's
not in season, Sir.'

'None iv yer flummery, you schamin' scoundrel; but jest come here and give yourself up, for so sure as you don't, or dar to stir an inch from that spot, I'll blow you to smithereens!'

'Captain Cluffe is drowned, Sir; and I'm Lieutenant Puddock,' rejoined the officer.

'Tare-an-ouns, an' is it yerself, Captain Puddock, that's in it?' cried the man. 'I ax yer pardon; but I tuk you for one of thim vagabonds that's always plundherin' the fish. And who in the wide world, captain jewel, id expeck to see you there, meditatin' in the middle of the river, this time o' night; an' I dunna how in the world you got there, at all, at all, for the planking is carried away behind you since yistherday.'

'Give an alarm, if you please, Sir, this moment,' urged Puddock. 'Captain Cluffe has gone over this horrid weir, not a minute since, and is I fear drowned.'

'Dhrownded! Och! bloody wars.'

'Yes, Sir, send someone this moment down the stream with a rope –'

'Hollo, Jemmy?' cried the man, and whistled through his crooked finger.

'Jemmy,' said he to the boy who presented himself, 'run down to Tom Garret, at the Millbridge, and tell him Captain Cluffe's dhrownded over the weir, and to take the boat-hook and rope – he's past the bridge by this time – ay is he at the King's House – an' if he brings home the corpse alive or dead, before an hour, Captain Puddock here will give him twenty guineas reward.' So away went the boy.

''Tis an unaisy way you're situated yourself, I'm afeard,' observed the man.

'Have the goodness to say, Sir, by what meanth, if any, I can reach either bank of the river,' lisped Puddock, with dignity.

''Tis thrue for you, captain, *that's* the chat – how the divil to get you alive out o' the position you're in. Can you swim?'

'No, Thir.'

'An' how the dickens did you get there?'

'I'd rather hear, Sir, how I'm to get away, if you please,' replied Puddock, loftily.

'Are you bare-legged?' shouted the man.

'No, Sir,' answered the little officer, rather shocked.

'An' you're there wid shoes on your feet.

'Of course, Sir,' answered Puddock.

'Chuck them into the water this instant minute,' roared the man.

'Why, there are valuable buckles, Sir,' remonstrated Puddock.

'Do you mane to say you'd rather be dhrownded in yer buckles than alive in yer stockin' feet?' he replied.

There were some cross expostulations, but eventually the fellow came out to Puddock. Perhaps the feat was not quite so perilous as he represented; but it certainly was not a pleasant one. Puddock had a rude and crazy sort of banister to cling to, and a rugged and slippery footing; but slowly and painfully, from one post to another, he made his way, and at last jumped on the solid, though not dry, land, his life and his buckles safe.

'I'll give you a guinea in the morning, if you come to my quarterth, Mr — Thir,' and, without waiting a second, away he ran by the footpath, and across the bridge, right into the Phoenix, and burst into the club-room. There were assembled old Arthur Slowe, Tom Trimmer, from Lucan, old Trumble, Jack Collop, Colonel Stafford, and half-a-dozen more members, including some of the officers – O'Flaherty among the number, a little 'flashy with liquor' as the phrase then was.

Puddock stood in the wide opened door, with the handle in his hand. He was dishevelled, soused with water, bespattered with mud, his round face very pale, and he fixed a wild stare on the company. The clatter of old Trimmer's backgammon, Slowe's disputations over the draftboard with Colonel Stafford, Collop's dissertation on the points of that screw of a horse he wanted to sell, and the general buzz of talk, were all almost instantaneously suspended on the appearance of this phantom, and Puddock exclaimed: 'Gentlemen, I'm thorry to tell you, Captain Cluffe ith, I fear, drowned!'

'Cluffe?' 'Drowned?' 'By Jupiter!' 'You don't say so?' And a round of such ejaculations followed this announcement.

Allow me here to mention that I permit my people to swear by all the persons of the Roman mythology. There was a horrible profanity in the matter of oaths in those days, and I found that without changing the form of sentences, and sacrificing idioms, at times, I could not manage the matter satisfactorily otherwise.

'He went over the salmon weir – I saw him – Coyle's – weir – headlong, poor fellow! I shouted after him, but he could not anthwer, so pray let's be off, and – '

Here he recognised the colonel with a low bow and paused. The commanding officer instantaneously despatched Lieutenant Brady, who was there, to order out Sergeant Blakeney and his guard, and any six good swimmers in the regiment who might volunteer, with a reward of twenty guineas for whoever should bring in Cluffe alive, or ten guineas for his body; and the fat fellow all the time in his bed sipping sack posset!

So away ran Brady and a couple more of the young fellows at their best pace – no-one spared himself on this errand – and little Puddock and another down to the bridge. It was preposterous.

By this time Lillyman was running like mad from Cluffe's lodgings along Martin's Row to the rescue of Puddock, who, at that moment with his friends and the aid of a long pole, was poking into a little floating tanglement of withered leaves, turf, and rubbish, under the near arch of the bridge, in the belief that he was dealing with the mortal remains of Cluffe.

Lillyman overtook Toole at the corner of the street just in time to hear the scamper of the men, at double-quick, running down the sweep of the road to the bridge, and to hear the shouting that arose from the parade-ground by the river bank, from the men within the barrack precincts.

Toole joined Lillyman running.

'What the plague's this hubbub and hullo?' he cried.

'Puddock's drowned,' panted Lillyman.

'Puddock! Bless us! where?' puffed Toole.

'Hollo! You, Sir – have they heard it – is he *drowned*?' cried Lillyman to the sentry outside the gate.

'Dhrownded? Yes, Sir,' replied the man saluting.

'Is help gone?'

'Yes, Sir, Lieutenant Brady, and Sergeant Blakeney, and nine men.'

'Come along,' cried Lillyman to Toole, and they started afresh. They heard the shouting by the river bank, and followed it by the path round the King's House, passing the Phoenix; and old Colonel Stafford, who was gouty, and no runner, standing with a stern and anxious visage at the door, along with old Trumble, Slowe, and Trimmer, and some of the maids and drawers in the rear, all in consternation.

'Bring me the news,' screamed the colonel, as they passed.

Lillyman was the better runner. Toole a good deal blown, but full of pluck, was labouring in the rear; Lillyman jumped over the stile, at the river path; and Toole saw an officer who resembled 'poor Puddock', he thought, a good deal, cross the road, and follow in Lillyman's wake. The doctor crossed the stile next, and made his best gallop in rear of the plump officer, excited by the distant shouting, and full of horrible curiosity and good nature.

Nearly opposite Inchicore they fished up an immense dead pig; and Toole said, to his amazement, he found Puddock crying over it, and calling it 'my brother!' And this little scene added another very popular novelty to the doctor's stock of convivial monologues.

Toole, who loved Puddock, hugged him heartily, and when he could get breath, shouted triumphantly after the more advanced party, 'He's found, he's found!'

'Oh, thank Heaven!' cried little Puddock, with upturned eyes; 'but is he really found?'

The doctor almost thought that his perils had affected his intellect.

'Is he found – are *you* found?' cried the doctor, resuming that great shake by both hands, which in his momentary puzzle he had suspended.

'I – a – oh, dear! – I don't quite understand – is he lost? For mercy's sake, is Cluffe lost?' implored Puddock.

'Lost in his bedclothes, maybe,' cried Lillyman, who had joined them.

'But he's not – he's *not* drowned?'

'Pish! drowned, indeed! Unless he's drowned in the crock of hot water he's clapt his legs into.'

'Where is he – where's Cluffe?'

'Hang it! – he's in bed, in his lodging, drinking hot punch this half-hour.'

'But are you certain?'

'Why, I saw him there myself,' answered Lillyman, with an oath.

Poor little Puddock actually clasped his hands, looked up, and poured forth a hearty, almost hysterical, thanksgiving; for he had charged Cluffe's death altogether upon his own soul, and his relief was beyond expression.

In the meantime, the old gentlemen of the club were in a thrilling suspense, and that not altogether disagreeable state of horror in which men chew the cud of bitter fancy over other men's catastrophes. After about ten minutes in came young Spaight.

'Well,' said the colonel, 'is Cluffe safe or – eh?'

'Cluffe's safe – only half drowned; but poor Puddock's lost.'

'What!'

'Drowned, I'm afraid.'

'Drowned! Who says so?' repeated the colonel.

'Cluffe – everybody.'

'Why, there it is!' replied the colonel, with a great oath, breaking through all his customary reserve and stiffness, and flinging his cocked hat on the middle of the table, piteously, 'A fellow that can't swim a yard *will* go by way of saving a great – a large gentleman, like Captain Cluffe, from drowning, and he's pulled in himself; and so – bless my soul! what's to be done?'

So the colonel broke into a lamentation, and a fury, and a wonder. 'Cluffe and Puddock, the two steadiest officers in the corps! He had a devilish good mind to put Cluffe under arrest – the idiots – Puddock – he was devilish sorry. There wasn't a more honourable' – *et cetera*. In fact, a very angry and pathetic funeral oration, during which, accompanied by Doctor Toole, Lieutenant Puddock in person entered; and the colonel stopped short with his eyes and mouth very wide open, and said the colonel very sternly.

'I – I'm glad to see, Sir, you're safe: and – and – I suppose, I shall hear now that *Cluffe's* drowned?' and he stamped the emphasis on the floor.

While all this was going on, some of the soldiers had actually got into Dublin. The tide was in, and the water very high at 'Bloody Bridge'. A hat, near the corner, was whisking round and round, always trying to get under the arch, and always, when on the point, twirled round again into the corner – an image of the 'Flying Dutchman' and hope deferred. A watchman's crozier hooked the giddy thing. It was not a military hat; but they brought it back, and the captive was laid in the guard-room – mentioned by me because we've seen that identical hat before.

Chapter Fifty-one

How Charles Nutter's tea, pipe, and tobacco-box were all set out
for him in the small parlour at the Mills; and how that night
was passed in the House by the Churchyard

Mrs Nutter and Mrs Sturk, the wives of the two men who most hated one another within the vicinage of Chapelizod – natural enemies, holding aloof one from another, and each regarding the other in a puzzled way, with a sort of apprehension and horror, as the familiar of that worst and most formidable of men – her husband – were this night stricken with a common fear and sorrow.

Darkness descended on the Mills and the river – a darkness deepened by the umbrageous trees that grouped about the old grey house in which poor Mrs Nutter lay so ill at ease. Moggy carried the jingling tray of tea-things into Nutter's little study, and lighted his candles, and set the silver snuffers in the dish, and thought she heard him coming, and ran back again, and returned with the singing 'tea-kitchen', and then away again, for the thin buttered toast under its china cover, which our ancestors loved.

Then she listened – but 'twas a mistake – it was the Widow Macan's step, who carried the ten pailfuls of water up from the river to fill the butt in the backyard every Tuesday and Friday, for a shilling a week, and 'a cup o' tay with the girls in the kitchen'.

Then Moggy lighted the fire with the stump of a candle, for the night was a little chill, and she set the small round table beside it, and laid her master's pipe and tobacco-box on it, and listened, and began to wonder what detained him.

So she went out into the sharp still air, and stood on the hall-door step, and listened again. Presently she heard the Widow Macan walking up from the garden with the last pail on her head, who stopped when she saw her, and set down the vessel upon the corner of the clumsy little balustrade by the door-step. So Moggy declared her uneasiness, which waxed greater when Mrs Macan told her that 'the masther, God bless him, wasn't in the garden.'

She had seen him standing at the river's edge, while she passed and repassed. He did not move a finger, or seem to notice her, and was looking down into the water. When she came back the third or fourth time, he was gone.

At Moggy's command she went back into the garden, though she assured her, solemnly – ''twas nansince lookin' there' – and called Mr Nutter, at first in a deferential and hesitating way; but, emboldened and excited by the silence, for she began to feel unaccountably queer, in louder and louder a key, till she was certain that he was neither in the garden nor in the orchard, nor anywhere near the house. And when she stopped, the silence seemed awful, and the darkness under the trees closed round her with a supernatural darkness, and the river at the foot of the walk seemed snorting some inarticulate story of horror. So she locked the garden door quickly, looking over her shoulder for she knew not what, and ran faster than she often did along the sombre walk up to the hall-door, and told her tale to Moggy, and begged to carry the pail in by the hall-door.

In they came, and Moggy shut the hall-door, and turned the key in it. Perhaps 'twas the state in which the poor lady lay upstairs that helped to make them excited and frightened. Betty was sitting by her bedside, and Toole had been there, and given her some opiate, I suppose, for she had dropped into a flushed snoring sleep, a horrid counterfeit of repose. But she had first had two or three frightful fits, and all sorts of wild, screaming talk between. Perhaps it was the apparition of Mary Matchwell, whose evil influence was so horribly attested by the dismal spectacle she had left behind her, that predisposed them to panic; but assuredly each anticipated no good from the master's absence, and had a foreboding of something bad, of which they did not speak; but only disclosed it by looks, and listening, and long silences. The lights burning in Nutter's study invited them, and there the ladies seated themselves, and made their tea in the kitchen tea-pot, and clapped it on the hob, and listened for sounds from Mrs Nutter's chamber, and for the step of her husband crossing the little courtyard; and they grew only more nervous from listening, and there came every now and then a little tapping on the window-pane. It was only, I think, a little sprig of the climbing-rose that was nailed by the wall, nodding at every breath, and rapping like unseen finger-tops, on the glass. But, as small things will, with such folk, under such circumstances, it frightened them confoundedly.

Then, on a sudden, there came a great yell from poor Mrs Nutter's chamber, and they both stood up very pale. The Widow Macan, with the cup in her hand that she was 'tossing' at the moment, and Moggy, all aghast, invoked a blessing under her breath, and they heard loud cries and sudden volleys of talk, and Biddy's voice, soothing the patient.

Poor Mrs Nutter had started up, all on a sudden, from her narcotic doze, with a hideous scream that had frightened the women downstairs. Then she cried 'Where am I?' and 'Oh, the witch – the witch!'

'Oh! no, Ma'am, dear,' replied Betty; 'now, aisy, Ma'am, darling.'

'I'm going mad.'

'No, Ma'am, dear? – there now – sure 'tis poor Betty that's in it – don't be afear'd, Ma'am.'

'Oh, Betty, hold me – don't go – I'm mad – am I mad?'

Then in the midst of Betty's consolations, she broke into a flood of tears, and seemed in some sort relieved; and Betty gave her her drops again, and she began to mumble to herself, and so to doze.

At the end of another ten minutes, with a scream, she started up again.

'That's her step – where are you, Betty?' she shrieked, and when Betty ran to the bedside, she held her so hard that the maid was ready to cry out, leering all the time over her shoulder – 'Where's Charles Nutter? – I saw him speaking to you.'

Then the poor little woman grew quieter, and by her looks and moans, and the clasping of her hands, and her upturned eyes, seemed to be praying; and when Betty stealthily opened the press to take out another candle, her poor mistress uttered another terrible scream, crying 'You wretch! her head won't fit – you can't hide her;' and the poor woman jumped out of her bed, shrieking 'Charles, Charles, Charles!'

Betty grew so nervous and frightened, that she fairly bawled to her colleague, Moggy, and told her she would not stay in the room unless she sat up all night with her. So, together they kept watch and ward, and as the night wore on, Mrs Nutter's slumbers grew more natural and less brief, and her paroxysms of waking terror less maniacal. Still she would waken, with a cry that thrilled them, from some frightful vision, and seem to hear or see nothing aright for a good while after, and muttering to the frightened maids: 'Listen to the knocking – oh! – breathing outside the door – bolt it, Betty – girls, say your prayers – 'tis he,' or sometimes, ''tis she.'

And thus this heavy night wore over; and the wind, which began to rise as the hours passed, made sounds full of sad untranslatable meaning in the ears of the watchers.

Poor Mrs Sturk meanwhile, in the House by the Churchyard, sat listening and wondering, and plying her knitting-needles in the drawing-room. When the hour of her Barney's expected return had passed some time, she sent down to the barrack, and then to the club, and then on to the King's House, with her service to Mrs Stafford, to enquire after her spouse. But her first and her second round of enquiries, despatched at the latest minute at which she was likely to find any body out of bed to answer them, were altogether fruitless. And the lights went out in one house after another, and the Phoenix shut its doors, and her own servants were for hours gone to bed; and the little town of Chapelizod was buried in the silence of universal slumber. And poor Mrs Sturk still sat in her drawing-room, more and more agitated and frightened.

But her missing soldier did not turn up, and Leonora sat and listened hour after hour. No sound of return, not even the solemn clank and fiery snort of the fiend-horse under her window, or the 'ho-lo, ho-la – my life, my love!' of the phantom rider, cheated her with a momentary hope.

Poor Mrs Sturk! She raised the window a few inches, that she might the better hear the first distant ring of his coming on the road. She forgot he had not his horse that night, and was but a pedestrian. But somehow the night-breeze through the aperture made a wolfish howling and sobbing, that sounded faint and far away, and had a hateful character of mingled despair and banter in it.

She said every now and then aloud, to reassure herself – 'What a noise the wind makes to be sure!' and after a while she opened the window wider. But her candle flared, and the flame tossed wildly about, and the perplexed lady feared it might go out absolutely. So she shut down the window altogether, for she could not bear the ill-omened baying any longer.

So it grew to be past two o'clock, and she was afraid that Barney would be very angry with her for sitting up, should he return.

She went to bed, therefore, where she lay only more feverish – conjecturing, and painting frightful pictures, till she heard the crow of the early village cock, and the caw of the jackdaw wheeling close to the eaves as he took wing in the grey of the morning to show her that the business of a new day had commenced; and yet Barney had not returned.

Not long after seven o'clock, Dr Toole, with Juno, Cæsar, Dido, and Sneak at his heels, paid his half-friendly, half-professional visit at the Mills.

Poor little Mrs Nutter was much better – quiet for her was every-thing, packed up, of course, with a little physic; and having comforted her, as well as he was able, he had a talk with Moggy in the hall, and all about Nutter's disappearance, and how Mrs Macan saw him standing by the river's brink, and that was the last anyone near the house had seen of him; and a thought flashed upon Toole, and he was very near coming out with it, but checked himself, and only said: 'What hat had he on?'

So she told him.

'And was his name writ in it, or how was it marked?'

'Two big letters – a C and an N.'

'I see; and do you remember any other mark you'd know it by?'

'Well, yes; I stitched the lining only last month, with red silk, and that's how I remember the letters.'

'I know; and are you sure it was that hat he had on?'

'Certain sure – why, there's all the rest;' and she conned them over, as they hung on their pegs on the rack before them.

'Now, don't let the mistress be downhearted – keep her up, Moggy, do you mind. I told her the master was with Lord Castlemallard since yesterday evening, on business, and don't you say anything else; keep her quiet, do ye mind, and humour her.'

And away went Toole, at a swift pace, to the town again, and entered the barrack, and asked to see the adjutant, and then to look at the hat the corporal had fished up by 'Bloody Bridge'; and, by Jupiter! his heart gave a couple of great bounces, and he felt himself grow pale – they were the identical capitals, C N, and the clumsy red silk stitching in the lining.

Toole was off forthwith, and had a fellow dragging the river before three-quarters of an hour.

Dr Walsingham, returning from an early ride to Island Bridge, saw this artist at work, with his ropes and great hooks, at the other side of the river; and being a man of enquiring mind, and never having wit-nessed the process before, he cried out to him, after some moments lost in conjecture: 'My good man, what are you fishing for?'

'A land-agent,' answered Isaac Walton.

'A land-agent?' repeated the rector, misdoubting his ears.

The saturnine angler made no answer.

'And has a gentleman been drowned here?' he persisted.

The man only looked at him across the stream, and nodded.

'Eh! and his name, pray?'

'Old Nutter, of the Mills,' he replied.

The rector made a woeful ejaculation, and stared at the careless operator, who had a pipe in his mouth the while, which made him averse from conversation. He would have liked to ask him more questions, but he was near the village, and refrained himself; and he met Toole at the corner of the bridge who, leaning on the shoulder of the rector's horse, gave him the sad story in full.

Chapter Fifty-two

Concerning a rouleau of guineas and the crack of a pistol

Dangerfield went up the river that morning with his rod and net, and his piscatory *fidus Achates*, Irons, at his elbow. It was a nice grey sky, but the clerk was unusually silent even for him; and the sardonic piscator appeared inscrutably amused as he looked steadily upon the running waters. Once or twice the spectacles turned full upon the clerk, over Dangerfield's shoulder, with a cynical light, as if he were on the point of making one of his ironical jokes; but he turned back again with a little whisk, the jest untold, whatever it was, to the ripple and the fly, and the coy grey troutlings.

At last, Dangerfield said over his shoulder, with the same amused look, 'Do you remember Charles Archer?'

Irons turned pale, and looked down embarrassed as it seemed, and began plucking at a tangled piece of tackle, without making any answer.

'Hey? Irons,' persisted Dangerfield, who was not going to let him off.

'Yes, I do,' answered the man surlily; 'I remember him right well; but I'd rather not, *and* I won't speak of him, that's all.'

'Well, Charles Archer's *here*, we've seen him, haven't we? And just the devil he always was,' said Dangerfield with a deliberate chuckle of infinite relish, and evidently enjoying the clerk's embarrassment as he eyed him through his spectacles obliquely.

'He has seen *you*, too, he says; and thinks *you* have seen *him*, hey?' and Dangerfield chuckled more and more knowingly, and watched his shiftings and sulkings with a pleasant grin, as he teased and quizzed him in his own enigmatical way.

'Well, supposing I *did* see him,' said Irons, looking up, returning Dangerfield's comic glance with a bold and lowering stare; 'and supposing *he* saw *me*, so long as we've no business one of another, and never talks like, nor seems to remember – I think 'tisnt, no ways, no-one's business – that's what I say.'

'True, Irons, very true; you, I, and Sturk – the doctor I mean – are cool fellows, and don't want for nerve; but I think, don't you? we're afraid of Charles Archer, for all that.'

'Fear or no fear, I don't want to talk *to* him nor *of* him, no ways,' replied the clerk, grimly, and looking as black as a thunder-cloud.

'Nor I neither, but you know he's here, and what a devil he is; and we can't help it,' replied Dangerfield, very much tickled.

The clerk only looked through his nearly closed eyes, and with the same pale and surly aspect toward the point to which Dangerfield's casting line had floated, and observed: 'You'll lose them flies, Sir.'

'Hey?' said Dangerfield, and made another cast further into the stream.

'Whatever he may seem, and I think I know him pretty well,' he continued in the same sprightly way, 'Charles Archer would dispose of each of us – you understand – without a scruple, precisely when and how best suited his convenience. Now Doctor Sturk has sent him a message which I know will provoke him, for it sounds like a threat. If he reads it so, rely on't, he'll lay Sturk on his back, one way or another, and I'm sorry for him, for I wished him well; but if he will play at brag with the *devil*, I can't help him.'

'I'm a man that holds his tongue; I never talks none, even in my liquor. I'm a peaceable man, and no bully, and only wants to live quiet,' said Irons in a hurry.

'A disciple of *my* school, you're right, Irons, that's my way; *I* never *name* Charles except to the two or three who meet him, and then only when I can't help it, just as you do; fellows of that kidney I always take quietly, and I've prospered. Sturk would do well to reconsider his message. Were *I* in his shoes, I would not eat an egg or a gooseberry, or drink a glass of fair water from that stream, while he was in the country, for fear of *poison*! curse him! And to think of Sturk expecting to meet him, and walk with him, after such a message, together, as you and I do here. Do you see that tree?'

It was a stout poplar, just a yard away from Irons's shoulder; and as Dangerfield pronounced the word 'tree', his hand rose, and the sharp report of a pocket-pistol half-deafened Irons's ear.

'I say,' said Dangerfield, with a startling laugh, observing Irons wince, and speaking as the puff of smoke crossed his face, 'he'd lodge a bullet in the cur's heart, as suddenly as I've shot that tree;' the bullet had hit the stem right in the centre, 'and swear he was going to rob him.'

Irons eyed him with a livid squint, but answered nothing. I think he acquiesced in Dangerfield's dreadful estimate of Charles Archer's character.

'But we must give the devil his due; Charles can do a handsome thing sometimes. You shall judge. It seems he saw you, and you him – here, in this town, some months ago, and each knew the other, and you've seen him since, and done likewise; but you said nothing, and he liked your philosophy, and hopes you'll accept of this, which from its weight I take to be a little rouleau of guineas.'

During this speech Irons seemed both angry and frightened, and looked darkly enough before him on the water; and his lips were moving, as if in a running commentary upon it all the while.

When Dangerfield put the little roll in his hand, Irons looked suspicious and frightened, and balanced it in his palm, as if he had thoughts of chucking it from him, as though it were literally a satanic douceur. But it is hard to part with money, and Irons, though he still looked cowed and unhappy, put the money into his breeches' pocket, and he made a queer bow, and he said: 'You know, Sir, I never asked a farthing.'

'Ay, so he says,' answered Dangerfield.

'And,' with an imprecation, Irons added, 'I never expected to be a shilling the better of him.'

'He knows it; and now you have the reason why I mentioned Charles Archer; and having placed that gold in your hand, I've done with him, and we shan't have occasion, I hope, to name his name for a good while to come,' said Dangerfield.

Then came a long refreshing silence, while Dangerfield whipt the stream with his flies. He was not successful; but he did not change his flies. It did not seem to trouble him; indeed, mayhap he did not perceive it. And after fully twenty minutes thus unprofitably employed, he suddenly said, as if in continuation of his last sentence: 'And respecting that money, you'll use caution; a hundred guineas is not always so honestly come by. Your wife drinks – suppose a relative in England had left you that gold, by will, 'twould be best not to let *her* know; but give it to Dr Walsingham, secretly, to keep for you, telling him the reason. He'll undertake the trust and tell no-one – *that's* your plan – mind ye.'

Then came another long silence, and Dangerfield applied himself in earnest to catch some trout, and when he had accomplished half-a-dozen, he tired altogether of the sport, and followed by Irons, he sauntered homewards, where astounding news awaited him.

Chapter Fifty-three

Relating after what fashion Dr Sturk came home

As Dangerfield, having parted company with Irons at the corner of the bridge, was walking through the town, with his rod over his shoulder and his basket of troutlings by his side, his attention was arrested by a little knot of persons in close and earnest talk at the barrack-gate, nearly opposite Sturk's house.

He distinguished at a glance the tall grim figure of Oliver Lowe, of Lucan, the sternest and shrewdest magistrate who held the commission for the county of Dublin in those days, mounted on his iron-grey hunter, and holding the crupper with his right hand, as he leaned toward a ragged, shaggy little urchin, with naked shins, whom he was questioning, as it seemed closely. Half-a-dozen gaping villagers stood round.

There was an indescribable something about the group which indicated horror and excitement. Dangerfield quickened his pace, and arrived just as the adjutant rode out.

Saluting both as he advanced, Dangerfield asked – 'Nothing amiss, I hope, gentlemen?'

'The surgeon here's been found murdered in the park!' answered Lowe.

'Hey – *Sturk*?' said Dangerfield.

'Yes,' said the adjutant: 'this boy here says he's found him in the Butcher's Wood.'

'The Butcher's Wood! – why, what the plague brought him *there*?' exclaimed Dangerfield.

''Tis his straight road from Dublin across the park,' observed the magistrate.

'Oh! – I thought 'twas the wood by Lord Mountjoy's,' said Dangerfield; 'and when did it happen?'

'Pooh! – some time between yesterday afternoon and half an hour ago,' answered Mr Lowe.

'Nothing known?' said Dangerfield. ''Twill be a sad hearing over the way;' and he glared grimly with a little side-nod at the doctor's house.

Then he fell, like the others, to questioning the boy. He could tell them but little – only the same story over and over. Coming out of town, with tea and tobacco, a pair of shoes, and a bottle of whisky, for old Mrs Tresham – in the thick of the wood, among brambles, all at once he lighted on the body. He could not mistake Dr Sturk; he wore his regimentals; there was blood about him; he did not touch him, nor go nearer than a musket's length to him, and being frightened at the sight in that lonely place he ran away and right down to the barrack, where he made his report.

Just then out came Sergeant Bligh, with his men – two of them carrying a bier with a mattress and cloaks thereupon. They formed, and accompanied by the adjutant, at quick step marched through the town for the park. Mr Lowe accompanied them, and in the park-lane they picked up the ubiquitous Doctor Toole, who joined the party.

Dangerfield walked a while beside the adjutant's horse; and, said he: 'I've had as much walking as I can well manage this morning, and you don't want for hands, so I'll turn back when I've said just a word in your ear. You know, Sir, funerals are expensive, and I happen to know that poor Sturk was rather pressed for money – in fact, 'twas only the day before yesterday I myself lent him a trifle. So will you, through whatever channel you think best, let poor Mrs Sturk know that she may draw upon me for a hundred pounds, if she requires it?'

'Thank you, Mr Dangerfield; I certainly shall.'

And so Dangerfield lifted his hat to the party and fell behind, and came to a standstill, watching them till they disappeared over the brow of the hill.

When he reached his little parlour in the Brass Castle, luncheon was upon the table. But he had not much of an appetite, and stood at the window, looking upon the river with his hands in his pockets, and a strange pallid smile over his face, mingling with the light of the silver spectacles.

'When Irons hears of this,' he said, 'he'll come to my estimate of Charles Archer, and conclude he has had a finger in that pretty pie; 'twill frighten him.'

And somehow Dangerfield looked a little bit queer himself, and he drank off two small glasses, such as folks then used in Ireland – of Nantz; and setting down the glass, he mused: 'A queer battle life is; ha, ha! Sturk laid low – the wretched fool! Widow – yes; children – ay. Charles! Charles! If there be a reckoning after death, your score's an ugly one. I'm tired of playing my part in this weary game of defence. Irons and I remain with the secret between us. Glasscock had his fourth of it, and tasted death. Then we three had it; and Sturk goes next; and now I and Irons – Irons and I – which goes first?' And he fell to whistling slowly and dismally, with his hands in his breeches' pockets, looking vacantly through his spectacles on the ever-running water, an emblem of the eternal change and monotony of life.

In the meantime the party, with Tim Brian, the bare-shanked urchin, still in a pale perspiration, for guide, marched on, all looking ahead, in suspense, and talking little.

On they marched, till they got into the bosky shadow of the close old whitethorn and brambles, and there, in a lonely nook, the small birds hopping on the twigs above, sure enough, on his back, in his regimentals, lay the clay-coloured image of Sturk, some blood, nearly black now, at the corners of his mouth, and under his stern brows a streak of white eyeball turned up to the sky.

There was a pool of blood under his pomatumed, powdered, and curled head, more under his right arm, which was slightly extended, with the open hand thrown palm upwards, as if appealing to heaven.

Toole examined him.

'No pulse, by Jove! Quiet there! Don't stir!' Then he clapped his ear on Sturk's white Marseilles vest.

'Hush!' and a long pause. Then Toole rose erect, but still on his knees, '*Will* you be quiet there? I think there's some little action still; only don't talk, or shift your feet; and just – just, do be quiet!'

Then Toole rose to his knees again, with a side glance fixed on the face of Sturk, with a puzzled and alarmed look. He evidently did not well know what to make of it. Then he slipped his hand within his vest, and between his shirt and his skin.

'If he's dead, he's not long so. There's warmth here. And see, get me a pinch or two of that thistle-down, d'ye see?'

And with the help of this improvised test he proceeded to try whether he was still breathing. But there was a little air stirring, and they could not manage it.

'Well!' said Toole, standing this time quite erect, 'I – I think there's life there. And now, boys, d'ye see? Lift him very carefully, d'ye mind? Gently, very gently, for I tell you, if this haemorrhage begins again, he'll not last twenty seconds.'

So on a cloak they lifted him softly and deftly to the bier, and laid covering over him; and having received Toole's last injunctions, and especially a direction to Mrs Sturk to place him in a well-warmed bed, and introduce a few spoonfuls of warm port wine negus into his mouth, and if he swallowed, to continue to administer it from time to time, Sergeant Bligh and his men commenced their funereal march toward Sturk's house.

'And now, Mr Adjutant,' said Lowe, 'had not we best examine the ground, and make a search for anything that may lead to a conviction?'

Well, a ticket was found trod into the bloody mud, scarcely legible, and Sturk's cocked hat, the leaf and crown cut through with a blow of some blunt instrument. His sword they had found by his side not drawn.

'See! Here's a footprint, too,' said Lowe; 'don't move!'

It was remarkable. They pinned together the backs of two letters, and Toole, with his surgical scissors, cut the pattern to fit exactly into the impression; and he and Lowe, with great care, pencilled in the well-defined marks of the great hob-nails, and a sort of seam or scar across the heel.

'Twas pretty much after this fashion. It was in a slight dip in the ground where the soil continued soft. They found it in two other places coming up to the fatal spot, from the direction of the Magazine. And it was traceable on for some twenty yards more faintly; then, again, very distinctly, where – a sort of ditch interposing – a jump had been made, and here it turned down towards the park wall and the Chapelizod road, still, however, slanting in the Dublin direction.

In the hollow by the park wall it appeared again, distinctly; and here it was plain the transit of the wall had been made, for the traces of the mud were evident enough upon its surface, and the mortar at top was displaced, and a little tuft of grass in the mud, left by the clodded shoe-sole. Here the fellow had got over.

They followed, and, despairing of finding it upon the road, they diverged into the narrow slip of ground by the river bank, and just within the park-gate, in a slight hollow, the clay of which was still impressible, they found the track again. It led close up to the river bank, and there the villain seemed to have come to a standstill; for the sod just for so much as a good sized sheet of letter-paper might cover, was trod and broken, as if at the water's edge he had stood for a while, and turned about and shifted his feet, like a fellow that is uneasy while he is stationary.

From this standpoint they failed to discover any receding footprint; but close by it came a little horse track, covered with shingle, by which, in those days, the troops used to ride their horses to water. He might have stepped upon this, and following it, taken to the streets; or he might – and this was Lowe's theory – have swam the river at this point, and got into some of those ruffian haunts in the rear of Watling and St James's streets. So Lowe, who, with a thief or a murderer in the wind, had the soul of a Nimrod, rode round to the opposite bank, first telling Toole, who did not care to press his services at Sturk's house uninvited, that he would send out the great Doctor Pell to examine the patient, or the body, as the case might turn out.

By this time they were carrying Doctor Sturk – that gaudy and dismal image – up his own staircase – his pale wife sobbing and shivering on the landing, among whispered ejaculations from the maids, and the speechless wonder of the awe-stricken children, staring through the banisters – to lay him in the bed where at last he is to lie without dreaming.

Chapter Fifty-four

*In which Miss Magnolia Macnamara and Dr Toole, in different scenes,
prove themselves Good Samaritans; and the great Dr Pell mounts the
stairs of the House by the Churchyard*

So pulse or no pulse, dead or alive, they got Sturk into his bed.

Poor, cowed, quiet little Mrs Sturk, went quite wild at the bedside.

'Oh! My Barney – my Barney – my noble Barney,' she kept crying.
'He's gone – he'll never speak again. Do you think he hears? Oh,
Barney, my darling – Barney, it's your own poor little Letty – oh –
Barney, darling, don't you hear. It's your own poor, foolish Letty.'

But it was the same stern face, and ears of stone. There was no
answer and no sign.

And she sent a pitiful entreaty to Doctor Toole, who came very
good-naturedly – and indeed he was prowling about the doorway of
his domicile in expectation of the summons. And he shook her very
cordially by the hand, and quite 'filled-up', at her woebegone appeal,
and told her she must not despair yet.

And this time he pronounced most positively that Sturk was still
living.

'Yes, my dear Madam, so sure as you and I are. There's no mistaking.'

And as the warmth of the bed began to tell, the signs of life showed
themselves more and more unequivocally. But Toole knew that his
patient was in a state of coma, from which he had no hope of his
emerging.

So poor little Mrs Sturk – as white as the plaster on the wall – who
kept her imploring eyes fixed on the doctor's ruddy countenance,
during his moments of deliberation, burst out into a flood of tears,
and thanksgivings, and benedictions.

'He'll recover – something tells me he'll recover. Oh! my Barney –
darling – you will – you will.'

'While there's life – you know – my dear Ma'am,', said Toole,
doing his best. 'But then – you see – he's been very badly abused

about the head; and the brain you know – is the great centre – the – the – but, as I said, while there's life, there's hope.'

'And he's so strong – he shakes off an illness so easily; he has such courage.'

'So much the better, Ma'am.'

'And I can't but think, as he did not die outright, and has shown such wonderful endurance. Oh! my darling, he'll get on.'

'Well, well, Ma'am, there certainly have been wonderful recoveries.'

'And he's so much better already, you see, and I know so well how he gets through an illness, 'tis wonderful, and he certainly is mightily improved since we got him to bed. Why, I can *see* him breathe now, and you know it *must* be a good sign; and then there's a merciful God over us – and all the poor little children – what would become of us?' And then she wiped her eyes quickly. 'The promise, you know, of length of days – it often comforted me before – to those that honour father and mother; and I believe there never was so good a son. Oh! my noble Barney, never; 'tis my want of reliance and trust in the Almighty's goodness.'

And so, holding Toole by the cuff of his coat, and looking piteously into his face as they stood together in the doorway, the poor little woman argued thus with inexorable death.

Fools, and blind; when amidst our agonies of supplication the blow descends, our faith in prayer is staggered, as if it reached not the ear of the Allwise, and moved not His sublime compassion. Are we quite sure that we comprehend the awful and far-sighted game that is being played for us and others so well that we can sit by and safely dictate its moves?

How will Messrs. Morphy or Staunton, on whose calculations, I will suppose, you have staked £100, brook your insane solicitations to spare this pawn or withdraw that knight from prise, on the board which is but the toy type of that dread field where all the powers of eternal intellect, the wisdom from above and the wisdom from beneath – the stupendous intelligence that made, and the stupendous sagacity that would undo us, are pitted one against the other in a death-combat which admits of no reconciliation and no compromise?

About poor Mrs Nutter's illness, and the causes of it, various stories were current in Chapelizod. Some had heard it was a Blackamoor witch who had evoked the foul fiend in bodily shape from the parlour cupboard, and that he had with his cloven foot kicked her

and Sally Nutter round the apartment until their screams brought
in Charles Nutter, who was smoking in the garden; and that on
entering, he would have fared as badly as the rest, had he not had
presence of mind to pounce at once upon the great family Bible
that lay on the window-sill, with which he belaboured the infernal
intruder to a purpose. Others reported 'twas the ghost of old Philip
Nutter, who rose through the floor, and talked I know not what
awful rhodomontade. These were the confabulations of the tap-
room and the kitchen; but the speculations and rumours current
over the card-table and claret glasses were hardly more congruous
or intelligible. In fact, nobody knew well what to make of it. Nutter
certainly had disappeared, and there was an uneasy feeling about
him. The sinister terms on which he and Sturk had stood were
quite well known, and though nobody spoke out, everyone knew
pretty well what his neighbour was thinking of.

Our blooming friend, the handsome and stalworth Magnolia,
having got a confidential hint from agitated Mrs Mack, trudged up
to the Mills, in a fine frenzy, vowing vengeance on Mary Matchwell,
for she liked poor Sally Nutter well. And when, with all her roses in
her cheeks, and her saucy black eyes flashing vain lightnings across
the room in pursuit of the vanished woman in sable, the Amazon
with black hair and slender waist comforted and pitied poor Sally,
and anathematised her cowardly foe, it must be confessed she looked
plaguy handsome, wicked, and good-natured.

'Mary Matchwell, indeed! *I'll* match her well, wait a while, you'll
see if I don't. I'll pay her off yet, never mind, Sally, darling. Arrah!
Don't be crying, child, do you hear me. *What's* that? *Charles?* Why,
then, is it about Charles you're crying? Charles Nutter? Phiat!
woman dear! Don't you think he's come to an age to take care of
himself? I'll hold you a crown he's in Dublin with the sheriff, going
to cart that jade to Bridewell. And why in the world didn't you send
for *me*, when you wanted to discourse with Mary Matchwell? Where
was the good of my poor dear mother? Why, she's as soft as butter.
'Twas a devil like me you wanted, you poor little darling. Do you
think I'd a let her frighten you this way – the vixen – I'd a knocked
her through the window as soon as look at her. She saw with half an
eye she could frighten you both, you poor things. Oh! ho! How I
wish I was here. I'd a put her across my knee and – *no* – do you say?
Pooh! You don't know me, you poor innocent little creature; and, do
ye mind now, you must not be moping here. Sally Nutter, all alone,
you'll just come down to us, and drink a cup of tea and play a round

game and hear the news; and look up now and give me a kiss, for I like you, Sally, you kind old girl.'

And she gave her a hug, and a shake, and half-a-dozen kisses on each cheek, and laughed merrily, and scolded and kissed her again.

Little more than an hour after, up comes a little *billet* from the good-natured Magnolia, just to help poor little Sally Nutter out of the vapours, and vowing that no excuse should stand good, and that come she must to tea and cards. 'And, oh! what do you think?' it went on. 'Such a bit a newse, I'm going to tell you, so prepare for a chock;' at this part poor Sally felt quite sick, but went on. 'Doctor Sturk, that droav into town Yesterday, as grand as you Please, in Mrs Strafford's coach, all smiles and Polightness – whood a bleeved! Well He's just come back, with two great Fractions of his skull, riding on a Bear, insensible into The town – there's for you. Only Think of poor Mrs Sturk, and the Chock she's got on sight of Him: and how thankful and Pleasant you should be that Charles Nutter is not a Corpes in the Buchar's wood, and jiggin Home to you like Sturk did. But well in health, what I'm certain shure he is, taken the law of Mary Matchwell – bless the Mark – to get her emprisind and Publickly wiped by the commin hangman.' All which rhapsody conjured up a confused and dyspeptic dream, full of absurd and terrific images, which she could not well comprehend, except in so far as it seemed clear that some signal disaster had befallen Sturk.

That night, at nine o'clock, the great Doctor Pell arrived in his coach, with steaming horses, at Sturk's hall-door, where the footman thundered a tattoo that might have roused the dead; for it was the family's business, if they did not want a noise, to muffle the knocker. And the doctor strode up, directed by the whispering awestruck maid, to Sturk's bed-chamber, with his hands in his muff, after the manner of doctors in his day, without asking questions, or hesitating on lobbies, for the sands of his minutes ran out in gold-dust. So, with a sort of awe and suppressed bustle preceding and following him, he glided upstairs and straight to the patient's bed-side, serene, saturnine, and rapid.

In a twinkling the maid was running down the street for Toole, who had kept at home, in state costume, expecting the consultation with the great man, which he liked. And up came Toole, with his brows knit, and his chin high, marching over the pavement in a mighty fuss, for he knew that the oracle's time and temper were not to be trifled with.

In the club, Larry the drawer, as he set a pint of mulled claret by old Arthur Slowe's elbow, whispered something in his ear, with a solemn wink.

'Ho! – by Jove, gentlemen, the doctor's come – Doctor Pell. His coach stands at Sturk's door, Larry says, and we'll soon hear how he fares.' And up got Major O'Neill with a 'hey! ho-ho!' and out he went, followed by old Slowe, with his little tankard in his fist, to the inn-door, where the major looked on the carriage, lighted up by the footman's flambeau, beneath the old village elm – up the street – smoking his pipe still to keep it burning, and communicating with Slowe, two words at a time. And Slowe stood gazing at the same object with his little faded blue eyes, his disengaged hand in his breeches' pocket, and ever and anon wetting his lips with his hot cordial, and assenting agreeably to the major's conclusions.

'Seize ace! curse it!' cried Cluffe, who, I'm happy to say, had taken no harm by his last night's wetting; 'another gammon, I'll lay you fifty.'

'Toole, I dare thay, will look in and tell us how poor Sturk goes on,' said Puddock, playing his throw.

'Hang it, Puddock, mind your game – to be sure, he will. Cinque ace! Well, *curse* it! The same throw over again! 'Tis too bad. I missed taking you last time, with that stupid blot you've covered – and now, by Jove, it ruins me. There's no playing when fellows are getting up every minute to gape after doctors' coaches, and leaving the door open – hang it, I've lost the game by it – gammoned twice already. 'Tis very pleasant. I only wish when gentlemen interrupt play, they'd be good enough to pay the bets.'

It was not much, about five shillings altogether, and little Puddock had not often a run of luck.

'If you'd like to win it back, Captain Cluffe, I'll give you a chance,' said O'Flaherty, who was tolerably sober. 'I'll lay you an even guinea Sturk's dead before nine tomorrow morning; and two to one he's dead before this time tomorrow night.'

'I thank you – no, Sir – two doctors over him, and his head in two pieces – you're very obliging, lieutenant, but I'll choose a likelier wager,' said Cluffe.

Dangerfield, who was overlooking the party, with his back to the fire, appeared displeased at their levity – shook his head, and was on the point of speaking one of those polite but cynical reproofs, whose irony, cold and intangible, intimidated the less potent spirits of the club-room. But he dismissed it with a little shrug. And a minute after, Major O'Neill and Arthur Slowe became aware that Danger-field had glided behind them, and was looking serenely, like themselves, at the Dublin doctor's carriage and smoking team. The light from Sturk's bedroom window, and the red glare of the footman's torch, made two little trembling reflections in the silver spectacles as he stood in the shade, peering movelessly over their shoulders.

''Tis a sorry business, gentlemen,' he said in a stern, subdued tone. 'Seven children and a widow. He's not dead yet, though: whatever Toole might do, the Dublin doctor would not stay with a dead man; time's precious. I can't describe how I pity that poor soul, his wife – what's to become of her and her helpless brood I know not.'

Slowe grunted a dismal assent, and the major, with a dolorous gaze, blew a thin stream of tobacco-smoke into the night air, which floated off like the ghost of a sigh towards the glimmering window of Sturk's bedroom. So they all grew silent. It seemed they had no more to say, and that, in their minds, the dark curtain had come down upon the drama of which the 'noble Barney', as poor Mrs Sturk called him, was hero.

Chapter Fifty-five

In which Dr Toole, in full costume, stands upon the hearth-stone of the club, and illuminates the company with his back to the fire

Two or three minutes later, the hall-door of Sturk's mansion opened wide, and the figure of the renowned doctor from Dublin, lighted up with a candle from behind, and with the link from before, glided swiftly down the steps, and disappeared into the coach with a sharp clang of the door. Up jumps the footman, and gives his link a great whirl about his head. The maid stands on the step with her hand before the flaring candle. 'The Turk's Head, in Werburgh Street,' shouts the footman, and smack goes the coachman's whip, and the clang and rattle begin.

'That's Alderman Blunkett – he's dying,' said the major, by way of gloss on the footman's text; and away went the carriage with thundering wheels, and trailing sparks behind it, as if the wild huntsman had furnished its fleet and shadowy team.

'He has ten guineas in his pocket for that – a guinea a minute, by Jove, coining, no less,' said the major, whose pipe was out, and he thinking of going in to replenish it. 'We'll have Toole here presently, depend upon it.'

He had hardly spoken when Toole, in a halo of candle-light, emerged from Sturk's hall-door. With one foot on the steps, the doctor paused to give a parting direction about chicken-broth and white-wine whey.

These last injunctions on the door-steps had begun, perhaps in a willingness to let folk see and even hear that the visit was professional; and along with the lowering and awfully serious countenance with which they were delivered, had grown into a habit, so that, as now, he practised them even in solitude and darkness.

Then Toole was seen to approach the Phoenix, in full blow, his cane under his arm. With his full-dressed wig on, he was always grand and Aesculapian, and reserved withal, and walked with a measured tread, and a sad and important countenance, which somehow made him look more chubby; and he was a good deal more formal with his friends at the inn-door, and took snuff before he answered them. But this only lasted some eight or ten minutes after a consultation or momentous visit, and would melt away insensibly in the glow of the club-parlour, sometimes reviving for a minute, when the little mirror that sloped forward from the wall, showed him a passing portrait of his grand wig and toggery. And it was pleasant to observe how the old fellows unconsciously deferred to this temporary self-assertion, and would call him, not Tom, nor Toole, but 'doctor', or 'Doctor Toole', when the fit was upon him.

And Devereux, in his day, won two or three wagers by naming the doctor with whom Toole had been closeted, reading the secret in the countenance and by-play of their crony. When it had been with tall, cold, stately Dr Pell, Toole was ceremonious and deliberate, and oppressively polite. On the other hand, when he had been shut up with brusque, half-savage, energetic Doctor Rogerson, Tom was laconic, decisive, and insupportably ill-bred, till, as we have said, the mirage melted away, and he gradually acquiesced in his identity. Then, little by little, the irrepressible gossip, jocularity, and ballad minstrelsy were heard again, his little eyes danced, and his waggish smiles glowed once more, ruddy as a setting sun, through the nectarian vapours of the punch-bowl. The ghosts of Pell and Rogerson fled to their cold dismal shades, and little Tom Toole was his old self again for a month to come.

'Your most obedient, gentlemen – your most obedient,' said Toole, bowing and taking their hands graciously in the hall – 'a darkish evening, gentlemen.'

'And how does your patient, doctor?' enquired Major O'Neill.

The doctor closed his eyes, and shook his head slowly, with a gentle shrug.

'He's in a bad case, major. There's little to be said, and that little, Sir, not told in a moment,' answered Toole, and took snuff.

'How's Sturk, Sir?' repeated the silver spectacles, a little sternly.

'Well, Sir, he's not *dead*; but, by your leave, had we not better go into the parlour, eh? – 'tis a little chill, and, as I said, 'tis not all told in a moment – he's not dead, though, that's the sum of it – *you* first, pray proceed, gentlemen.'

Dangerfield grimly took him at his word; but the polite major got up a little ceremonious tussle with Toole in the hall. However, it was no more than a matter of half-a-dozen bows and waves of the hand, and 'after you, Sir'; and Toole entered, and after a general salutation in the style of Doctor Pell, he established himself upon the hearth-stone, with his back to the fire, as a legitimate oracle.

Toole was learned, as he loved to be among the laity on such occasions, and was in no undue haste to bring his narrative to a close. But the gist of the matter was this – Sturk was labouring under concussion of the brain, and two terrific fractures of the skull – so long, and lying so near together, that he and Doctor Pell instantly saw 'twould be impracticable to apply the trepan, in fact that 'twould be certain and instantaneous death. He was absolutely insensible, but his throat was not yet palsied, and he could swallow a spoonful of broth or sack whey from time to time. But he was a dead man to all intents and purposes. Inflammation might set in at any moment; at best he would soon begin to sink, and neither he nor Doctor Pell thought he had the smallest chance of awaking from his lethargy for one moment. He might last two or three days, or even a week – what did it signify? – what was he better than a corpse already? He could never hear, see, speak, or think again; and for any difference it could possibly make to poor Sturk, they might clap him in his grave and cover him up tonight.

Then the talk turned upon Nutter. Every man had his theory or his conjecture but Dangerfield, who maintained a discreet reserve, much to the chagrin of the others, who thought, not without reason, that he knew more about the state of his affairs, and especially of his relations with Lord Castlemallard, than perhaps all the world beside.

'Possibly, poor fellow, he was not in a condition to have his accounts overhauled, and on changing an agency things sometimes come out that otherwise might have kept quiet. He was the sort of fellow who would go through with a thing; and if he thought the best way on going out of the agency was to go out of the world also, out he'd go. They were always a resolute family – Nutter's great-uncle, you know, drowned himself in that little lake – what do you call it? – in the county of Cavan, and 'twas mighty coolly and resolutely done too.'

But there was a haunting undivulged suspicion in the minds of each. Every man knew what his neighbour was thinking of, though he did not care to ask about his ugly dreams, or to relate his own. They all knew what sort of terms Sturk and Nutter had been on. They tried to put the thought away, for though Nutter was not a joker, nor a songster, nor a storyteller, yet they liked him. Besides, Nutter might possibly turn up in a day or two, and in that case 'twould go best with those who had not risked an atrocious conjecture about him in public. So every man waited, and held his tongue upon that point till his neighbour should begin.

Chapter Fifty-six

Dr Walsingham and the Chapelizod Christians meet to the sound of the holy bell, and a vampire sits in the church

The next day the Sabbath bell from the ivied tower of Chapelizod Church called all good church-folk round to their pews and seats. Sturk's place was empty – already it knew him no more – and Mrs Sturk was absent; but the little file of children, on whom the neighbours looked with an awful and a tender curiosity, was there. Lord Townshend, too, was in the viceregal seat, with gentlemen of his household behind, splendid in star and peruke, and eyed over their prayer-books by many inquisitive Christians. Nutter's little pew, under the gallery, was void like Sturk's. These sudden blanks were eloquent, and many, as from time to time the dismal gap opened silent before their eyes, felt their thoughts wander and lead them away in a strange and dismal dance, among the nodding hawthorns in the Butcher's Wood, amidst the damps of night, where Sturk lay in his leggings and powder and blood, and the beetle droned by unheeding, and no-one saw him save the guilty eyes that gleamed back as the shadowy shape stole swiftly away among the trees.

Dr Walsingham's sermon had reference to the two-fold tragedy of the week, Nutter's supposed death by drowning, and the murder of Sturk. In his discourses he sometimes came out with a queer bit of erudition. Such as, while it edified one portion of his congregation, filled the other with unfeigned amazement.

'We may pray for rain,' said he on one occasion, when the collect had been read; 'and for other elemental influence with humble confidence. For if it be true, as the Roman annalists relate, that their augurs could, by certain rites and imprecations, produce thunderstorms – if it be certain that thunder and lightning were successfully invoked by King Porsenna, and as Lucius Piso, whom Pliny calls a very respectable author, avers that the same thing had frequently been done before his time by King Numa Pompilius, surely it is not presumption in a Christian congregation,' and so forth.

On this occasion he warned his parishioners against assuming that sudden death is a judgment. 'On the contrary, the ancients held it a blessing; and Pliny declares it to be the greatest happiness of life – how much more should we? Many of the Roman worthies, as you are aware, perished thus suddenly: Quintius Aemilius Lepidus, going out of his house, struck his great toe against the threshold and expired; Cneius Babius Pamphilus, a man of praetorian rank, died while asking a boy what o'clock it was; Aulus Manlius Torquatus, a gentleman of consular rank, died in the act of taking a cheese-cake at dinner; Lucius Tuscius Valla, the physician, deceased while taking a draught of mulsum; Appius Saufeius, while swallowing an egg: and Cornelius Gallus, the praetor, and Titus Haterius, a knight, each died while kissing the hand of his wife. And I might add many more names with which, no doubt, you are equally familiar.'

The gentlemen of the household opened their eyes; the officers of the Royal Irish Artillery, who understood their man, winked pleasantly behind their cocked hats at one another; and his excellency coughed, with his perfumed pocket-handkerchief to his nose, a good deal; and Master Dicky Sturk, a grave boy, who had a side view of his excellency, told his nurse that the lord lieutenant laughed in church! And was rebuked for that *scandalum magnatum* with proper horror.

Then the good doctor told them that the blood of the murdered man cried to heaven. That they might comfort themselves with the assurance that the man of blood would come to judgment. He reminded them of St Augustan's awful words, 'God hath woollen feet, but iron hands;' and he told them an edifying story of Mempricius, the son of Madan, the fourth king of England, then called Britaine, after Brute, who murdered his brother Manlius, and mark ye this, after twenty years he was devoured by wild beasts; and another of one Bessus – 'tis related by Plutarch – who having killed his father, was brought to punishment by means of swallows, which birds, his guilty conscience persuaded him, in their chattering language did say to one another, that Bessus had killed his father, whereupon he bewrayed his horrible crime, and was worthily put to death. 'The great Martin Luther,' he continued, 'reports such another story of a certain Almaigne, who, when thieves were in the act of murdering him, espying a flight of crows, cried aloud, "Oh crows, I take you for witnesses and revengers of my death." And so it fell out, some days afterwards, as these same thieves were drinking in an inn, a flight of crows came and lighted on the top of the house; whereupon the thieves, jesting, said to one another, "See, yonder are those who are to avenge the death of him we despatched t'other day," which the tapster overhearing, told forthwith to the magistrate, who arrested them presently, and thereupon they confessed, and were put to death.' And so he went on, sustaining his position with strange narratives culled here and there from the wilderness of his reading.

Among the congregation that heard this sermon, at the eccentricities of which I have hinted, but which had, beside, much that was striking, simply pathetic, and even awful in it, there glided – shall I say – a phantom, with the light of death, and the shadows of hell, and the taint of the grave upon him, and sat among these respectable persons of flesh and blood – impenetrable – secure – for he knew there were but two in the church for whom clever disguises were idle and transparent as the air. The blue-chinned sly clerk, who read the responses, and quavered the Psalms so demurely, and the white-headed, silver-spectacled, upright man, in my Lord Castlemallard's pew, who turned over the leaves of his prayer-book so diligently, saw him as he was, and knew him to be Charles Archer, and one of these at least, as this dreadful spirit walked, with his light burning in the noon-day, dogged by inexorable shadows through a desolate world, in search of peace, he knew to be the slave of his lamp.

Chapter Fifty-seven

In which Dr Toole and Mr Lowe make a visit at the Mills,
and recognise something remarkable while there

After church, Dr Toole walking up to the Mills, to pay an afternoon
visit to poor little Mrs Nutter, was overtaken by Mr Lowe, the
magistrate, who brought his tall, iron-grey hunter to a walk as he
reached him.

'Any tidings of Nutter?' asked he, after they had, in the old world
phrase, given one another the time of day.

'Not a word,' said the doctor; 'I don't know what to make of it; but
you know what's thought. The last place he was seen in was his own
garden. The river was plaguy swollen Friday night, and just where he
stood it's deep enough, I can tell you; often I bathed there when I was
a boy. He was consumedly in the dumps, poor fellow; and between
ourselves, he was a resolute dog, and atrabilious, and just the fellow to
make the jump into kingdom-come if the maggot bit: and you know
his hat was fished out of the river a long way down. They dragged next
morning, but – pish! – 'twas all nonsense and moonshine; why, there
was water enough to carry him to Ringsend in an hour. He was a good
deal out of sorts, as I said, latterly – a shabby design, Sir, to thrust him
out of my Lord Castlemallard's agency; but that's past and gone; and,
besides, I have reason to know there was some kind of an excitement –
a quarrel it could not be – poor Sally Nutter's too mild and quiet for
that; but a – a – *something* – a – an – agitation – or a bad news – or
something – just before he went out; and so, poor Nutter, you see, it
looks very like as if he had done something rash.'

Talking thus, they reached the Mills by the river side, not far from
Knockmaroon.

On learning that Toole was about making a call there, Lowe gave
his bridle to a little Chapelizod ragamuffin, and, dismounting, accompanied the doctor. Mrs Nutter was in her bed.

'Make my service to your mistress,' said Toole, 'and say I'll look
in on her in five minutes, if she'll admit me.' And Lowe and the

doctor walked on to the garden, and so side by side down to the river's bank.

'Hey! – look at that,' said Toole, with a start, in a hard whisper; and he squeezed Lowe's arm very hard, and looked as if he saw a snake.

It was the impression in the mud of the same peculiar footprint they had tracked so far in the park. There was a considerable pause, during which Lowe stooped down to examine the details of the footmark.

'Hang it – you know – poor Mrs Nutter – eh?' said Toole, and hesitated.

'We must make a note of that – the thing's important,' said Mr Lowe, sternly fixing his grey eye upon Toole.

'Certainly, Sir,' said the doctor, bridling; 'I should not like to be the man to hit him – you know; but it *is* remarkable – and, curse it, Sir, if called on, I'll speak the truth as straight as *you*, Sir – every bit, Sir.'

And he added an oath, and looked very red and heated.

The magistrate opened his pocket-book, took forth the pattern sole, carefully superimposed it, called Toole's attention, and said: '*You see.*'

Toole nodded hurriedly; and just then the maid came out to ask him to see her mistress.

'I say, my good woman,' said Lowe; 'just look here. Whose footprint is that – do you know it?'

'Oh, why, to be sure I do. Isn't it the master's brogues?' she replied, frightened, she knew not why, after the custom of her kind.

'You observe that?' and he pointed specially to the transverse line across the heel. 'Do you know that?'

The woman assented.

'Who made or mended these shoes?'

'Bill Heaney, the shoemaker, down in Martin's-row, there – 'twas he made them, and mended them, too, Sir.'

So he came to a perfect identification, and then an authentication of his paper pattern; then she could say they were certainly the shoes he wore on Friday night – in fact, every other pair he had were then on the shoe-stand on the lobby. So Lowe entered the house, and got pen and ink, and continued to question the maid and make little notes; and the other maid knocked at the parlour door with a message to Toole.

Lowe urged his going; and somehow Toole thought the magistrate suspected him of making signs to his witness, and he departed ill at ease; and at the foot of the stairs he said to the woman: 'You had better go in there – that stupid Lynn is doing her best to hang your master, by Jove!'

And the woman cried: 'Oh, dear, bless us!'

Toole was stunned and agitated, and so with his hand on the clumsy banister he strode up the dark staircase, and round the little corner in the lobby, to Mrs Nutter's door.

'Oh, Madam, 'twill all come right, be sure,' said Toole, uncomfortably, responding to a vehement and rambling appeal of poor Mrs Nutter's.

'And do you *really* think it will? Oh, doctor, doctor, *do* you think it will? The last two or three nights and days – how many is it? – Oh, my poor head – it seems like a month since he went away.'

'And where do you think he is? Do you think it's business?'

'Of course 'tis business, Ma'am.'

'And – and – oh, doctor! – you really think he's safe?'

'Of *course*, Madam, he's safe – what's to ail him?'

And Toole rummaged amongst the old medicine phials on the chimneypiece, turning their labels round and round, but neither seeing them nor thinking about them, and only muttering to himself with, I'm sorry to say, a curse here and there.

'You see, my dear Ma'am, you must keep yourself as quiet as you can, or physic's thrown away upon you; you really must,' said Toole.

'But doctor,' pleaded the poor lady, 'you don't know – I – I'm terrified – I – I – I'll never be the same again,' and she burst into hysterical crying.

'Now, really, Madam – confound it – my dear, good lady – you see – this will never do' – he was uncorking and smelling at the bottles in search of 'the drops' – 'and – and – here they are – and isn't it better, Ma'am, you should be well and hearty – here drink this – when – when he comes back – don't you see – than – a – a –'

'But – oh, I wish I could tell you. She said – she said – the – the – oh, you don't know –'

'*She* – who? *Who* said *what*?' cried Toole, lending his ear, for he never refused a story.

'Oh! Doctor, he's gone – I'll never – never – I know I'll never see him again. Tell me he's not gone – tell me I'll see him again.'

'Hang it, can't she stick to one thing at a time – the poor woman's half out of her wits,' said Toole, provoked; 'I'll wager a dozen of claret there's more on her mind than she's told to anyone.'

Before he could bring her round to the subject again, the doctor was called down to Lowe; so he took his leave for the present; and after his talk with the magistrate, he did not care to go up again to poor little Mrs Nutter; and Moggy was as white as ashes standing by, for Mr Lowe had just made her swear to her little story about the shoes; and Toole walked home to the village with a heavy heart, and a good deal out of humour.

Toole knew that a warrant would be issued next day against Nutter. The case against him was black enough. Still, even supposing he had struck those trenchant blows over Sturk's head, it did not follow that it was without provocation or in cold blood. It looked, however, altogether so unpromising, that he would have been almost relieved to hear that Nutter's body had been found drowned in the river.

Still there was a chance that he made good his retreat. If he had not paid his fare in Charon's packet-boat, he might, at least, have crossed the channel in the *Trevor* or *Hillsborough* to Holyhead. Then, deuce was in it, if he did not make a fair run for it, and earth himself snugly somewhere. 'Twas lighter work then than now. 'The old saying at London, among servants,' writes that good-natured theatrical wag, Tate Wilkinson, 'was, "I wish you were at York!" which the wronged cook has now changed for, "I wish you were at Jamaica." Scotland was then imagined by the cockney as a dreary place, distant almost as the West Indies; *now*' (reader, pray note the marvel) 'an agreeable party may, with the utmost ease, dine early in the week in Grosvenor Square, and without discomposure set down at table on Saturday or Sunday in the new town of Edinburgh!' From which we learn that miracles of celerity were already accomplishing themselves, and that the existing generation contemplated their triumphs complacently. But even upon these we have improved, and nowadays, our whole social organisation is subservient to detection. Cut your telegraph wires, substitute sail-boats for steam, and your old fair and easy forty-miles-a-day stage-coaches for the train and the rail, disband your City police and detective organisation, and make the transit of a letter between London and Dublin a matter of from five days to nearly as many weeks, and compute how much easier it was then than now for an adventurous highwayman, an absconding debtor, or a pair of fugitive lovers, to make good their retreat. Slow, undoubtedly, was the flight – they did not run, they walked away; but so was pursuit, and altogether, without authentic lights and official helps – a matter of post-chaises and perplexity, cross-roads and rumour, foundering in a wild waste of conjecture, or swallowed in the quag of some country inn-yard, where nothing was to be heard, and out of which there would be no relay of posters to pull you until nine o'clock next morning.

As Toole debouched from Martin's-row, on his return, into the comparative amplitude of the main street of Chapelizod, he glanced curiously up to Sturk's bedroom windows. There were none of the white signals of death there. So he ascended the door-step, and paid a visit – of curiosity, I must say – and looked on the snorting image of his old foe, and the bandaged head, spell-bound and dreamless, that had machinated so much busy mischief against his own medical sovereignty and the rural administration of Nutter.

As Toole touched his pulse, and saw him swallow a spoonful of chicken broth, and parried poor Mrs Sturk's eager quivering pleadings for his life with kind though cautious evasions, he rightly judged that the figure that lay there was more than half in the land of ghosts already – that the enchanter who met him in the Butcher's Wood, and whose wand had traced those parallel indentures in his skull, had not only exorcised for ever the unquiet spirit of intrigue, but wound up the tale of his days. It was true that he was never more to step from that bed, and that his little children would, ere many days, be brought there by kindly, horror-loving maids, to look their last on 'the poor master', and kiss awfully his cold stern mouth before the coffin lid was screwed down, and the white-robed image of their father hidden away for ever from their sight.

Chapter Fifty-eight

In which one of Little Bo-Peep's sheep comes home again, and various theories are entertained respecting Charles Nutter and Lieutenant Puddock

And just on Monday morning, in the midst of this hurly-burly of conjecture, who should arrive, of all the people in the world, and re-establish himself in his old quarters, but Dick Devereux. The gallant captain was more splendid and handsome than ever. But both his spirits and his habits had suffered. He had quarrelled with his aunt, and she was his bread and butter – ay, buttered on both sides. How lightly these young fellows quarrel with the foolish old worshippers who lay their gold, frankincense, and myrrh, at the feet of the handsome thankless idols. They think it all independence and high spirit, whereas we know it is nothing but a little egotistical tyranny, that unconsciously calculates even in the heyday of its indulgence upon the punctual return of the penitent old worshipper, with his or her votive offerings.

Perhaps the gypsy had thought better of it, and was already sorry he had not kept the peace. At all events, though his toilet and wardrobe were splendid – for fine fellows in his plight deny themselves nothing – yet morally he was seedy, and in temper soured. His duns had found him out, and pursued him in wrath and alarm to England, and pestered him very seriously indeed. He owed money beside to several of his brother officers, and it was not pleasant to face them without a guinea. An evil propensity, at which, as you remember, General Chattesworth hinted, had grown amid his distresses, and the sting of self-reproach exasperated him. Then there was his old love for Lilias Walsingham, and the pang of rejection, and the hope of a strong passion sometimes leaping high and bright, and sometimes nickering into ghastly shadows and darkness.

Indeed, he was by no means so companionable just now as in happier times, and was sometimes confoundedly morose and snappish;

for, as you perceive, things had not gone well with him latterly. Still he was now and then tolerably like his old self.

Toole, passing by, saw him in the window. Devereux smiled and nodded, and the doctor stopped short at the railings, and grinned up in return, and threw out his arms to express surprise, and then snapped his fingers, and cut a little caper, as though he would say – 'Now, you're come back – we'll have fun and fiddling again.' And forthwith he began to bawl his enquiries and salutations. But Devereux called him up peremptorily, for he wanted to hear the news – especially all about the Walsinghams. And up came Toole, and they had a great shaking of hands, and the doctor opened his budget and rattled away.

Of Sturk's tragedy and Nutter's disappearance he had already heard. And he now heard some of the club gossip, and all about Dangerfield's proposal for Gertrude Chattesworth, and how the old people were favourable, and the young lady averse – and how Dangerfield was content to leave the question in abeyance, and did not seem to care a jackstraw what the townspeople said or thought – and then he came to the Walsinghams, and Devereux for the first time really listened. The doctor was very well – just as usual; and wondering what had become of his old crony, Dan Loftus, from whom he had not heard for several months; and Miss Lily was not very well – a delicacy here (and he tapped his capacious chest), like her poor mother. 'Pell and I consulted about her, and agreed she was to keep within doors.' And then he went on, for he had a suspicion of the real state of relations between him and Lily, and narrated the occurrence rather with a view to collect evidence from his looks and manner, than from any simpler motive; and, said he, 'Only think, that confounded wench, Nan – you know – Nan Glynn.' And he related her and her mother's visit to Miss Lily, and a subsequent call made upon the rector himself – all, it must be confessed, very much as it really happened. And Devereux first grew so pale as almost to frighten Toole, and then broke into a savage fury – and did not spare hard words, oaths, or maledictions. Then off went Toole, when things grew quieter, upon some other theme, giggling and punning, spouting scandal and all sorts of news – and Devereux was looking full at him with large stern eyes, not hearing a word more. His soul was cursing old Mrs Glynn, of Palmerstown – that mother of lies and what not – and remonstrating with old Dr Walsingham – and protesting wildly against everything.

General Chattesworth, who returned two or three weeks after, was not half pleased to see Devereux. He had heard a good deal about him and his doings over the water, and did not like them. He had always had a misgiving that if Devereux remained in the corps, sooner or later he would be obliged to come to a hard reckoning with him. And the handsome captain had not been three weeks in Chapelizod, when more than the general suspected that he was in nowise improved. So General Chattesworth did not often see or talk with him; and when he did, was rather reserved and lofty with him. His appointment on the staff was in abeyance – in fact, the vacancy on which it was expectant had not definitely occurred – and all things were at sixes and sevens with poor Dick Devereux.

That evening, strange to say, Sturk was still living; and Toole reported him exactly in the same condition. But what did that signify? 'Twas all one. The man was dead – as dead to all intents and purposes that moment as he would be that day twelvemonth, or that day hundred years.

Dr Walsingham, who had just been to see poor Mrs Sturk – now grown into the habit of hoping, and sustained by the intense quiet fuss of the sick room – stopped for a moment at the door of the Phoenix, to answer the cronies there assembled, who had seen him emerge from the murdered man's house.

'He is in a profound lethargy,' said the worthy divine. ''Tis a subsidence – his life, Sir, stealing away like the fluid from the clepsydra – less and less left every hour – a little time will measure all out.'

'What the plague's a clepsydra?' asked Cluffe of Toole, as they walked side by side into the club-room.

'Ho! Pooh! One of those fabulous tumours of the epidermis mentioned by Pliny, you know, exploded ten centuries ago – ha, ha, ha!' and he winked and laughed derisively, and said, 'Sure you know Doctor Walsingham.'

And the gentlemen began spouting their theories about the murder and Nutter, in a desultory way; for they all knew the warrant was out against him.

'My opinion,' said Toole, knocking out the ashes of his pipe upon the hob; for he held his tongue while smoking, and very little at any other time; 'and I'll lay a guinea 'twill turn out as I say – the poor fellow's drowned himself. Few knew Nutter – I doubt if *anyone* knew him as I did. Why, he did not seem to feel anything, and you'd ha' swore nothing affected him, more than that hob, Sir; and all the time, there wasn't a more thin-skinned, atrabilious poor dog in all

Ireland – but honest, Sir – thorough steel, Sir. All I say is, if he had a finger in that ugly pie, you know, as some will insist, I'll stake my head to a china orange, 'twas a fair front-to-front fight. By Jupiter, Sir, there wasn't one drop of cur's blood in poor Nutter. No, poor fellow; neither sneak nor assassin *there* – '

'They thought he drowned himself from his own garden – poor Nutter,' said Major O'Neill.

'Well, that he did *not*,' said Toole. 'That unlucky shoe, you know, tells a tale; but for all that, I'm clear of the opinion that drowned he is. We tracked the step, Lowe and I, to the bank, near the horse-track, in Barrack Street, just where the water deepens – there's usually five feet of water there, and that night there was little short of ten. Now, take it that Nutter and Sturk had a tussle – and the thing happened, you know – and Sturk got the worst of it, and was, in fact, despatched, why, you know the kind of panic – and – and – the panic – you know – a poor dog, finding himself so situated, would be in – with the bitter, old quarrel between them – d'ye see? And this at the back of his vapours and blue-devils, for he was dumpish enough before, and would send a man like Nutter into a resolution of making away with himself; and that's how it happened, you may safely swear.'

'And what do *you* think, Mr Dangerfield?' asked the major.

'Upon my life,' said Dangerfield, briskly, lowering his newspaper to his knee, with a sharp rustle, 'these are questions I don't like to meddle in. Certainly, he had considerable provocation, as I happen to know; and there was no love lost – that I know too. But I quite agree with Doctor Toole – if he was the man, I venture to say 'twas a fair fight. Suppose, first, an altercation, then a hasty blow – Sturk had his cane, and a deuced heavy one – he wasn't a fellow to go down without knowing the reason why; and if they find Nutter, dead or alive, I venture to say he'll show some marks of it about him.'

Cluffe wished the whole company, except himself, at the bottom of the Red Sea; for he was taking his revenge of Puddock, and had already lost a gammon and two hits. Little Puddock won by the force of the dice. He was not much of a player; and the sight of Dangerfield – that repulsive, impenetrable, moneyed man, who had 'overcome him like a summer cloud', when the sky of his fortunes looked clearest and sunniest, always led him to Belmont, and the side of his lady-love.

If Cluffe's mind wandered in that direction, his reveries were rather comfortable. He had his own opinion about his progress with Aunt Rebecca, who had come to like his conversation, and talked with him a great deal about Puddock, and always with acerbity; Cluffe, who was a sort of patron of Puddock's, always, to do him justice, defended him respectfully. And Aunt Rebecca would listen very attentively, and then shake her head, and say, 'You're a great deal too good-natured, captain; and he'll never thank you for your pains, *never – I* can tell you.'

Well, Cluffe knew that the higher powers favoured Dangerfield; and that, beside his absurd sentiment, not to say passion, which could not but be provoking, Puddock's complicity in the abortive hostilities of poor Nutter and the gallant O'Flaherty rankled in Aunt Becky's heart. She was, indeed, usually appeasable and forgiving enough; but in this case her dislike seemed inveterate and vindictive; and she would say – 'Well, let's talk no more of him; 'tis easy finding a more agreeable subject: but you can't deny, captain, that 'twas an unworthy hypocrisy his pretending to sentiments against duelling to me, and then engaging as second in one on the very first opportunity that presented.'

Then Cluffe would argue his case, and plead his excuses, and fumbled over it a good while; not that he'd have cried a great deal if Puddock had been hanged; but, I'm afraid, chiefly because, being a fellow of more gaiety and accomplishment than quickness of invention, it was rather convenient, than otherwise, to have a topic, no matter what, supplied to him, and one that put him in an amiable point of view, and in a kind of graceful, intercessorial relation to the object of his highly prudent passion. And Cluffe thought how patiently she heard him, though he was conscious 'twas rather tedious, and one time very like another. But then, 'twasn't the talk, but the talker; and he was glad, at all risks, to help poor Puddock out of his disgrace, like a generous soul, as he was.

Chapter Fifty-nine

Telling how a coach drew up at the Elms, and two fine ladies, dressed for the ball, stepped in

It was now more than a fortnight since Sturk's mishap in the Butcher's Wood, and he was still alive, but still under the spell of coma. He was sinking, but very slowly; yet it was enough to indicate the finality of that 'life in death'.

Dangerfield once or twice attacked Toole rather tartly about Sturk's case.

'Can nothing be done to make him speak? Five minutes' consciousness would unravel the mystery.'

Then Toole would shrug, and say, 'Pooh – pooh! My dear Sir, you know nothing.'

'Why, there's *life*!'

'Ay, the mechanical functions of life, but the brain's over-powered,' replied Toole, with a wise frown.

'Well, relieve it.'

'By Jupiter, Sir, you make me laugh,' cried Toole with a grin, throwing up his eyebrows. 'I take it, you think we doctors can work miracles.'

'Quite the reverse, Sir,' retorted Dangerfield, with a cold scoff. 'But you say he may possibly live six weeks more; and all that time the wick is smouldering, though the candle's short – can't you blow it in, and give us even one minute's light?'

'Ay, a smouldering wick and a candle if you please; but enclosed in a glass bottle, how the deuce *are* you to blow it?'

'Pish!' said the silver spectacles, with an icy flash from his glasses.

'Why, Sir, you'll excuse me – but you don't understand,' said Toole, a little loftily. 'There are two contused wounds along the scalp as long as that pencil – the whole line of each partially depressed, the depression all along being deep enough to lay your finger in. You can ask Irons, who dresses them when I'm out of the way.'

'I'd rather ask you, Sir,' replied Dangerfield, in turn a little high.

'Well, you can't apply the trepan, the surface is too extended, and all unsound, and won't bear it – 'twould be simply killing him on the spot – don't you see? And there's no way else to relieve him.'

General Chattesworth had not yet returned. On his way home he had wandered aside, and visited the fashionable wells of Buxton, intending a three days' sojourn, to complete his bracing up for the winter. But the Pool of Siloam did not work pleasantly in the case of the robust general, who was attacked after his second dip with a smart fit of the gout in his left great-toe, where it went on charmingly, without any flickering upward, quite stationary and natural for three weeks.

About the end of which time the period of the annual ball given by the officers of the Royal Irish Artillery arrived. It was a great event in the town. To poor Mrs Sturk, watching by her noble Barney, it seemed, of course, a marvellous insensibility and an outrage. But the world must follow its instinct and vocation, and attend to its business and amuse itself too, though noble Barneys lie a-dying here and there.

Aunt Becky and Gertrude drew up at the Elms, the rector's house, with everything very handsome about them, and two laced footmen with flambeaux, and went in to see little Lily, on their way to the ball, and to show their dresses, which were very fine indeed, and to promise to come next day and tell her all the news; for Lily, as I mentioned, was an invalid, and balls and flicflacs were not for her.

Little Lily smiled her bright girlish smile, and threw both her arms round grand Aunt Becky's neck.

'You good dear Aunt Becky, 'twas so kind and like you to come – you and Gertie. And oh, Geminie! What a grand pair of ladies!' and she made a little rustic courtesy, like Nell in the farce. 'And I never saw this before (a near peep at Gertrude's necklace), and Aunt Becky, what beautiful lace. And does not she look handsome, Gertie? I *never* saw her look *so* handsome. She'll be the finest figure there. There's no such delicate waist anywhere.' And she set her two slender little forefingers and thumbs together, as if spanning it. 'You've no chance beside her, Gertie; she'll set all the young fellows a-sighing and simpering.'

'You wicked little rogue! I'll beat you black and blue, for making fun of old Aunt Becky,' cried Miss Rebecca, and ran a little race at her, about two inches to a step; her fan raised in her finger and thumb, and a jolly smile twinkling in her face, for she knew it was true about her waist, and she liked to be quizzed by the daring little girl. Her diamonds were on too, and her last look in her mirror had given her a satisfactory assurance, and she always played with little Lily, when they met; everyone grew gay and girlish with her.

So they stayed a full quarter of an hour, and the footman coughing laboriously outside the window reminded Aunt Rebecca at last how time flew; and Lily was for sitting down and playing a minuet and a country dance, and making them rehearse their steps, and calling in old Sally to witness the spectacle before they went; and so she and Aunt Becky had another little sportive battle – they never met, and seldom parted, without one. How was it that when gay little Lily provoked these little mimic skirmishes Aunt Becky would look for a second or two an inexpressibly soft and loving look upon her, and become quite girlish and tender? I think there is a way to every heart, and some few have the gift to reach it unconsciously and always.

So away rustled the great ladies, leaving Lily excited, and she stood at the window, with flushed cheek, and her fingers on the sash, looking after them, and she came back with a little smile and tears in her eyes. She sat down, with a bright colour in her cheeks, and did play a country dance, and then a merry old Irish air, full of frolic and spirit, on the harpsichord; and gentle old Sally's face peeped in with a wistful smile, at the unwonted sounds.

'Come, sober old Sally, my sweetheart! I've taken a whim in my head, and you shall dress me, for to the ball I'll go.'

'Tut, tut, Miss Lily, darling,' said old Sally, with a smile and a shake of the head. 'What would the doctors say?'

'What they please, my darling.'

And up stood little Lily, with her bright colour and lustrous eyes.

'Angel bright!' said the old woman, looking in that beloved and lovely young face, and quite 'filling up', as the saying is, 'there is not your peer on earth – no – not one among them all to compare with our Miss Lilias,' and she paused, smiling, and then she said – 'But, my darling, sure you know you weren't outside the door this five weeks.'

'And is not that long enough, and too long, to shut me up, you cruel old woman? Come, come, Sally, girl, I'm resolved, and to the ball I'll go; don't be frightened. I'll cover my head, and send in for Aunt Becky, and only just peep in, muffled up, for ten minutes; and I'll go and come in the chair, and what harm can I take by it?'

Was it spirit? Did she want to show the folk that she did not shrink from meeting somebody; or that, though really ill, she ventured to peep in, through sheer liking for the scrape of the fiddle, and the fun, to show them that at least she was not heart-sick? Or was it the mysterious attraction, the wish to see him once more, just through her hood, far away, with an unseen side glance, and to build endless speculations, and weave the filmy web of hope, for who knows how long, out of these airy tints, a strange, sad smile, or deep, wild glance, just seen and fixed for ever in memory? She had given him up in words, but her heart had not given him up. Poor little Lily! She hoped all that was so bad in him would one day mend. He was a hero still – and, oh! she hoped, would be true to her. So Lily's love, she scarce knew how, lived on this hope – the wildest of all wild hopes – waiting on the reformation of a rake.

'But, darling Miss Lily, don't you know the poor master would break his heart if he thought you could do such a wild thing as to go out against 'the doctor's orders, at this time o' night, and into that hot place, and out again among the cold draughts.'

Little Lily paused.

''Tis only a step, Sally; do you honestly think it would vex him?'

'Vex him, darling? No, but break his heart. Why, he's never done asking about you, and – oh! it's only joking you are, my darling, that's all.'

'No, Sally, dear love, I meant it,' said little Lily, sadly; 'but I suppose it was a wild thought, and I'm better at home.'

And she played a march that had somehow a dash of the pathetic in it, in a sort of reverie, and she said: 'Sally, do you know that?'

And Sally's gentle face grew reflective, and she said: 'Sure, Miss Lily, that's the tune – isn't it – the Artillery plays when they march out to the park?'

Lily nodded and smiled, and the tune moved on, conjuring up its pictured reverie. Those review days were grand things when little Lily was a child – magnanimous expenditure of hair and gunpowder was there. There sat General Chattesworth, behind his guns, which were now blazing away like fun, wearing his full uniform, point cravat and ruffles, and that dignified and somewhat stern aspect which he put on with the rest of his review-day costume, bestriding his cream-coloured charger, Bombardier, and his plume and powdered *ails de pigeon*, hardly distinguishable from the smoke which enveloped him, as a cloud does a demigod in an allegorical picture.

Chord after chord brought up all this moving pageant, unseen by Sally's dim old eyes, before the saddened gaze of little Lily, whose life was growing to a retrospect. She stood in the sunny street, again a little child, holding old Sally by the hand, on a soft summer day. The sentries presented arms, and the corps marched out resplendent. Old General Chattesworth, as proud as Lucifer, on Bombardier, who nods and champs, prancing and curvetting, to the admiration of the women; but at heart the mildest of quadrupeds, though passing, like an impostor as he was, for a devil incarnate; the band thundering melodiously that dashing plaintive march, and exhilarating and firing the souls of all Chapelizod. Up went the windows all along the street, the rabble-rout of boys yelled and huzzaed like mad. The maids popped their mob-caps out of the attics, and giggled, and hung out at the risk of their necks. The serving men ran out on the hall-door steps. The village roués emerged in haste from their public houses. The whole scene round and along from top to bottom, was grinning and agape. Nature seemed to brighten up at sight of them; and the sun himself came out all in his best, with an unparalleled effulgence.

Yes, the town was proud of its corps, and well it might. As gun after gun, with its complement of men and its lieutenant fireworkers, with a 'right wheel', rolled out of the gate upon the broad street, not a soul could look upon the lengthening pageant of blue and scarlet, with its symmetrical diagonals of snowy belt and long-flapped white cartouche boxes, moving together with measured swing; its laced cocked hats, leggings, and courtly white shorts and vests, and ruffles, and all its buttons and brasses flashing up to the sun, without allowing it was a fine spirited sight.

And Lily, beholding the phantom regiment, with mournful eyes, played their grand sad march proudly as they passed.

They looked so dashing and so grand; they were the tallest, shapeliest fellows. Faith, I can tell you, it was no such trifle, pulling along all those six and four pounders; and they needed to be athletic lads; and the officers were, with hardly an exception, martial, high-bred gentlemen, with aristocratic bearing, and some of them, without question, confoundedly handsome.

And always there was one light, tall shape; one dark handsome face, with darker, stranger eyes, and a nameless grace and interest, moving with the march of the gay pageant, before her mind's eye, to this harmonious and regretful music, which, as she played on, and her reverie deepened, grew slower and more sad, till old Sally's voice awoke the dreamer. The chords ceased, the vision melted, and poor little Lily smiled sadly and kindly on old Sally, and took her candle, and went up with her to her bed.

Chapter Sixty

Being a chapter of hoops, feathers, and brilliants, and bucks and fiddlers

It was a mighty grand affair, this ball of the Royal Irish Artillery. General Chattesworth had arrived that morning, just in time to preside over the hospitalities – he could not contribute much to the dancing – and his advent, still a little lame, but looking, as his friends told him, ten years younger for his snug little fit of the gout at Buxton, reinstated Aunt Becky in her place of power, to the secret disappointment of Madame Strafford, who had set her heart on doing the honours, and rehearsed for weeks, over her toilet, and even in bed, her little speeches, airs, and graces.

Lord Castlemallard was there, of course – and the gay and splendid Lady Moira – whom I mention because General Chattesworth opened the ball in a minuet with her ladyship – hobbling with wonderful grace, and beaming with great ceremonious smiles through his honourable martyrdom. But there were more than a score of peers there beside, with their peeresses in tall feathers, diamonds, and monstrous hoops. And the lord lieutenant was very near coming – and a lord lieutenant in those days, with a parliament to open, and all the regalia of his office about him, was a far greater personage than, in our democratic age, the sovereign in person.

Captain Cluffe had gone down in a chair to Puddock's lodgings, to borrow a pair of magnificent knee-buckles. Puddock had a second pair, and Cluffe's own had not, he thought, quite recovered their good looks since that confounded ducking on the night of the serenade. The gallant captain, learning that Puddock and Devereux intended walking – it was only a step across to the barrack-yard – and finding that Puddock could not at the moment lay his hand upon the buckles, and not wishing to keep the chair longer – for he knew delay would inflame the fare, and did not like dispensing his shillings, 'Hey! walk? I like the fancy,' cried the gay captain, sending half-a-crown downstairs to his 'two-legged ponies', as people pleasantly called them. 'I'd rather walk with you than jog along in a chair by myself, my gay fellows, any day.'

Most young fellows of spirit, at the eve of a ball, have their heads pretty full. There is always some one bright particular star to whom, even as they look on their own handsome features in the mirror, their adoration is paid.

Puddock's shoe-buckles flashed for Gertrude Chattesworth, as he turned out his toes. For her his cravat received its last careless touch – his ruffles shook themselves, and fell in rich elegance about his plump little hands. For her his diamond ring gleamed like a burning star from his white little finger; and for her the last fragrance was thrown over his pocket-handkerchief, and the last ogle thrown upon his looking-glass. All the interest of his elaborate toilet – the whole solemn process and detail – was but a worship of his divinity, at which he officiated. Much in the same way was Cluffe affected over his bedizenment in relation to his own lady-love; but in a calmer and more long-headed fashion. Devereux's toilet most of the young fellows held to be perfection; yet it seemed to trouble him less than all the rest. I believe it was the elegant and slender shape that would have set off anything, and that gave to his handsome costume and 'properties' an undefinable grace not their own. Indeed, as he leaned his elbow upon the window sash, looking carelessly across the river, he did not seem much to care what became of the labours of his toilet.

'I have not seen her since I came; and now I'm going to this stupid ball on the chance of meeting her there. And she'll not come – she avoids me – the chance of meeting her – and she'll not come. Well! If she be not kind to me, what care I for whom she be? And what great matter, after all, if she were there. She'd be, I suppose, on her high horse – and – and 'tis not a feather to me. Let her take her own way. What care I? If she's happy, why shouldn't I – why shouldn't I?'

Five minutes after: 'Who the plague are these fellows in the Phoenix? How the brutes howl over their liquor!' said Devereux, as he and Puddock, at the door-steps, awaited Cluffe, who was fixing his buckles in the drawing-room.

'The Corporation of Tailors,' answered Puddock, a little loftily, for he was not inwardly pleased that the precincts of the Phoenix should be profaned by their mechanical orgies.

Through the open bow-window of the great oak parlour of the inn was heard the mighty voice of the president, who was now in the thick of his political toasts.

'Odds bud!' lisped little Puddock, 'what a stentorian voice!'

'Considering it issues from a tailor!' acquiesced Devereux, who thought he recognised the accents, and hated tailors, who plagued him with long bills and dangerous menaces.

'May the friends of the Marquis of Kildare be ever blessed with the tailor's thimble,' declaimed the portentous toast master. 'May the needle of distress be ever pointed at all mock patriots; and a hot needle and a burning thread to all sewers of sedition!' and then came an applauding roar.

'And may you ride into town on your own goose, with a hot needle behind you, you roaring pigmy!' added Devereux.

'The Irish cooks that can't relish French sauce!' enunciated the same grand voice, that floated, mellowed, over the field.

'Sauce, indeed!' said Puddock, with an indignant lisp, as Cluffe, having joined them, they set forward together; 'I saw some of them going in, Sir, and to look at their vulgar, unthinking countenances, you'd say they had not capacity to distinguish between the taste of a quail and a goose; but, by Jove! Sir, they have a dinner. *You're* a politician, Cluffe, and read the papers. You remember the bill of fare – don't you? – at the Lord Mayor's entertainment in London.'

Cluffe, whose mind was full of other matters, nodded his head with a grunt.

'Well, I'll take my oath,' pursued Puddock, 'you couldn't have made a better dinner at the Prince of Travendahl's table. Spanish olea, if you please – ragou royal, cardoons, tendrons, shellfish in marinade, ruffs and rees, wheat-ears, green morels, fat livers, combs and notts. 'Tis rather odd, Sir, to us who employ them, to learn that our tailors, while we're eating the dinners we do – our *tailors*, Sir, are absolutely gorging themselves with such things – with *our* money, by Jove!'

'*Yours*, Puddock, not mine,' said Devereux. 'I haven't paid a tailor these six years. But, hang it, let's get on.'

So, in they walked by the barrack-yard, lighted up now with a splendid red blaze of torches, and with different emotions, entered the already crowded ball-room.

Devereux looked round the room, among nodding plumes and flashing brilliants, and smirking old bucks, and simpering young ones, amidst the buzz of two or three hundred voices, and the thunder and braying of the band. There were scores of pretty faces there – blondes and brunettes – blue eyes and brown – and more spirit and animation, and, I think, more grace too, in dance and talk, than the phlegmatic affectation of modern days allows; and there were some bright eyes that, not seeming to look, yet recognised, with a little thrill at the heart, and a brighter flush, the brilliant, proud Devereux – so handsome, so impulsive, so unfathomable – with his gypsy tint, and great enthusiastic eyes, and strange melancholy, sub-acid smile. But to him the room was lifeless, and the hour was dull, and the music but a noise and a jingle.

'I knew quite well she wasn't here, and she never cared for me, and I – why should I trouble my head about her? She makes her cold an excuse. Well, maybe yet she'll wish to see Dick Devereux, and I far away. No matter. They've heard slanders of me, and believe them. Amen, say I. If they're so light of faith, and false in friendship to cast me off for a foul word or an idle story – curse it – I'm well rid of that false and foolish friendship, and can repay their coldness and aversion with a light heart, a bow, and a smile. One slander I'll refute – yes – and that done, I'll close this idle episode in *my* cursed epic, and never, *never* think of her again.'

But fancy will not be controlled by resolutions, though ne'er so wise and strong, and precisely as the captain vowed 'never' – away glided that wild, sad sprite across the moonlit river, and among the old black elms, and stood unbidden beside Lilias. Little Lily, as they used to call her five years ago; and Devereux, who seemed to look so intently and so strangely on the flash and whirl of the dancers, saw but an old-fashioned drawing-room, with roses clustering by the windows, and heard the sweet rich voice, to him the music of Ariel, like a far-off dirge – a farewell – sometimes a forgiveness – and sometimes the old pleasant talk and merry little laugh, all old remembrances or vain dreams now.

But Devereux had business on his hands that night, and about eleven o'clock he had disappeared. 'Twas easy to go and come in such a crowd, and no-one perceive it.

But Puddock was very happy and excited. Mervyn, whom he had once feared, was there, a mere spectator, however, to witness that night's signal triumph. He had never danced so much with Miss Gertrude before, that is to say, at a great ball like this at which there was a plenty of bucks with good blood and lots of money; and indeed, it seemed to favour the idea of his success that Aunt Rebecca acknowledged him only with a silent and by no means gracious courtesy.

She was talking to Toole about Lilias, and saying how much better she had looked that evening.

'She's not better, Ma'am; I'd rather she hadn't the bright flush you speak of, there's something, you see, not quite right in that left lung, and that bright tint, Madam, is hectic – she's not better, Madam, not that we don't hope to see her so – Heaven forbid – but 'tis an anxious case;' and Toole shook his head gravely.

When Aunt Becky was getting on her hood and mantle, she invariably fell into talk with some crony who had a story to tell, or a point to discuss. So as she stood listening to old Colonel Bligh's hard, reedy gabble, and popping in her decisive word now and then, Gertrude, equipped for the night air, and with little Puddock for her escort, glided out and took her place in the great state coach of the Chattesworths, and the door being shut, she made a little nod and a faint smile to her true knight, and said with the slightest possible shrug, 'How cold it is tonight; my aunt, I think, will be obliged for your assistance, Lieutenant Puddock; as for me, I must shut up my window and wish you good-night.'

And with another smile she accordingly shut up the window, and when his best bow was accomplished, she leaned back with a pale and stricken countenance, and a great sigh – such a one as caused Lady Macbeth's physician, long ago, to whisper, 'What a sigh is there! The heart is sorely charged.' The footmen were standing by the open door, through which Aunt Becky was to come, and there were half a dozen carriages crowded side by side, the lackeys being congregated, with links lighted, about the same place of exit; and things being so, there came a small sharp tapping at the far window of the carriage, and with a start Gertrude saw the identical mantle, and the three-cocked hat with the peculiar corners, which had caused certain observers so much speculation on another night, and drawing close to the window, whereat this apparition presented itself, she let it down.

'I know, beloved Gertrude, what you would say,' he softly said; 'but be it frenzy or no, I cannot forbear; I am unalterable – be you the same.'

A white, slender hand glided in and seized hers, not resisting.

'Yes, Mordaunt, the same; but, oh! how miserable!' said Gertrude, and with just the slightest movement in the fingers of her small hand, hardly perceptible, and yet how fond a caress!

'I'm like a man who has lost his way among the catacombs – among the dead,' whispered this muffled figure, close to the window, still fervently holding her hand, 'and sees at last the distant gleam that shows him that his wanderings are to end. Yes, Gertrude, my beloved – yes, Gertrude, idol of my solitary love – the mystery is about to end – I'll end it. Be I what I may you know the worst, and have given me your love and troth – you are my affianced bride; rather than lose you, I would die; and I think, or I am walking in a dream, I've but to point my finger against two men, and all will be peace and light – light and peace – to me long strangers!'

At this moment Aunt Becky's voice was heard at the door, and the flash of the flambeaux glared on the window. He kissed the hand of the pale girl hurriedly, and the French cocked hat and mantle vanished.

In came Aunt Rebecca in a fuss, and it must be said in no very gracious mood, and rather taciturn and sarcastic; and so away they rumbled over the old bridge towards Belmont.

Chapter Sixty-one

In which the ghosts of a bygone sin keep tryst

Devereux, wrapped in his cloak, strode into the park, through Parson's-gate, up the steep hill, and turned towards Castleknock and the furze and hawthorn wood that interposes. The wide plain spread before him in solitude, with the thin vapours of night lying over it like a film in the moonlight.

Two or three thorn trees stood out from the rest, a pale and solitary group, stooping eastward with the prevailing sweep of a hundred years or more of westerly winds. To this the gypsy captain glided, in a straight military line, his eye searching the distance; and, after a while, from the skirts of the wood, there moved to meet him a lonely female figure, with her light clothing fluttering in the cold air. At first she came hurriedly, but as they drew near, she came more slowly.

Devereux was angry, and, like an angry man, he broke out first with: 'So, your servant, Mistress Nan! Pretty lies you've been telling of me – you and your shrew of a mother. You thought you might go to the rector and say what you pleased, and I hear nothing.'

Nan Glynn was undefinably aware that he was very angry, and had hesitated and stood still before he began, and now she said imploringly: 'Sure, Masther Richard, it wasn't me.'

'Come, my lady, don't tell me. You and your mother – curse her! – went to the Elms in my absence – *you* and she – and said I had promised to *marry* you! There – yes or no. Didn't you? And could you or could she have uttered a more utterly damnable lie?'

''Twas *she*, Master Richard – troth an' faith. I never knew she was going to say the like – no more I didn't.'

'A likely story, truly, Miss Nan!' said the young rake, bitterly.

'Oh! Masther Richard! By this cross! – you won't believe me – 'tis as true as you're standin' there – until she said it to Miss Lily – '

'Hold your tongue!' cried Devereux, so fiercely, that she thought him half wild; 'do you think 'tis a pin's point to me which of you first coined or uttered the lie? Listen to me; I'm a desperate man, and I'll take a course with you both you'll not like, unless you go tomorrow and see Dr Walsingham yourself, and tell him the whole truth – yes, the truth – what the devil do I care? – speak that, and make the most of it. But tell him plainly that your story about my having promised to marry you – do you hear – was a lie, from first to last – a lie – a lie – without so much as a grain of truth mixed up in it. All a cursed – devil's – woman's invention. Now, mind ye, Miss Nan, if you don't, I'll bring you and your mother into court, or I'll have the truth out of you.'

'But there's no need to threaten, sure, you know, Masther Richard, I'd do anything for you – I would. I'd beg, or I'd rob, or I'd die for you, Masther Richard; and whatever you bid me, your poor wild Nan 'ill do.'

Devereux was touched, the tears were streaming down her pale cheeks, and she was shivering.

'You're cold, Nan; where's your cloak and riding hood?' he said, gently.

'I had to part them, Masther Richard.'

'You want money, Nan,' he said, and his heart smote him.

'I'm not cold when I'm near you, Masther Richard. I'd wait the whole night long for a chance of seeing you; but oh! ho – ' [she was crying as if her heart would break, looking in his face, and with her hands just a little stretched towards him] 'Oh, Masther Richard, I'm nothing to you now – your poor wild Nan!'

Poor thing! Her mother had not given her the best education. I believe she was a bit of a thief, and she could tell fibs with fluency and precision. The woman was a sinner; but her wild, strong affections were true, and her heart was not in pelf.

'Now, don't cry – where's the good of crying – listen to me,' said Devereux.

'Sure I heerd you were sick, last week, Masther Richard,' she went on, not heeding, and with her cold fingers just touching his arm timidly – and the moon glittered on the tears that streamed down her poor imploring cheeks – 'an' I'd like to be caring you; an' I think you look bad, Masther Richard.'

'No, Nan – I tell you, no – I'm very well, only poor, just now, Nan, or *you* should not want.'

'Sure I know, Masther Richard: it is not that. I know you'd be good to me if you had it: and it does not trouble me.'

'But see, Nan, you must speak to your friends, and say – '

'Sorra a friend I have – sorra a friend, Masther Richard; and I did not spake to the priest this year or more, and I darn't go near him,' said the poor Palmerstown lass that was once so merry.

'Why won't you listen to me, child? I won't have you this way. You must have your cloak and hood. 'Tis very cold; and, by Heavens, Nan, you shall never want while I have a guinea. But you see I'm poor now, curse it – I'm poor – I'm sorry, Nan, and I have only this one about me.'

'Oh, no, Masther Richard, keep it – maybe you'd want it yourself.'

'No, child, don't vex me – there – I'll have money in a week or two, and I'll send you some more, Nan – I'll not forget you.' He said this in a sadder tone; 'and, Nan, I'm a changed man. All's over, you know, and we'll see one another no more. You'll be happier, Nan, for the parting, so here, and now, Nan, we'll say goodbye.'

'Oh! no – no – no – not goodbye; you couldn't – couldn't – couldn't – your poor wild Nan.'

And she clung to his cloak, sobbing in wild supplication.

'Yes, Nan, goodbye, it must be – no other word.'

'An' oh, Masther Richard, is it in airnest? You wouldn't, oh! sure you wouldn't.'

'Now, Nan, there's a good girl; I must go. Remember your promise, and I'll not forget you, Nan – on my soul, I won't.'

'Well, well, mayn't I chance to see you, maybe? Mayn't I look at you marching, Masther Richard, at a distance only? I wouldn't care so much, I think, if I could see you sometimes.'

'Now, there, Nan, you must not cry; you know 'tis all past and gone more than a year ago. 'Twas all d—d folly – all my fault; I'm sorry, Nan – I'm sorry; and I'm a changed man, and I'll lead a better life, and so do you, my poor girl.'

'But mayn't I see you? Not to spake to you, Masther Richard. Only sometimes to see you, far off, maybe.' Poor Nan was crying all the time she spoke. – 'Well, well, I'll go, I will, indeed, Masther Richard; only let me kiss your hand – an' oh! no, no, don't say goodbye, an' I'll go – I'm gone now, an' maybe – just maybe, you might some time chance to wish to see your poor, wild Nan again – only to see her, an' I'll be thinking o' that.'

The old feeling – if anything so coarse deserved the name – was gone; but he pitied her with all his heart; and that heart, such as it was – though she did not know it – was bleeding for her.

He saw her, poor creature, hurrying away in her light clothing, through the sharp, moonlight chill, which, even in the wrapping of his thick cloak, he felt keenly enough. She looked over her shoulder – then stopped; perhaps, poor thing, she thought he was relenting, and then she began to hurry back again. They cling so desperately to the last chance. But that, you know, would never do. Another pleading – another parting – So he turned sharply and strode into the thickets of the close brushwood, among which the white mists of night were hanging. He thought, as he stepped resolutely and quickly on, with a stern face and heavy heart, that he heard a wild sobbing cry in the distance, and that was poor Nan's farewell.

So Devereux glided on like a ghost, through the noiseless thicket, and scarcely knowing or caring where he went, emerged upon the broad open plateau, and skirting the Fifteen Acres, came, at last, to a halt upon the high ground overlooking the river – which ran, partly in long trains of silver sparkles, and partly in deep shadow beneath him. Here he stopped, and looked towards the village where he had passed many a pleasant hour – with a profound and remorseful foreboding that there were no more such pleasant hours for him; and his eye wandered among the scattered lights that still twinkled from the distant windows; and he fancied he knew, among them all, that which gleamed pale and dim through the distant elms – the star of his destiny; and he looked at it across the water – a greater gulf severed them – so near, and yet a star in distance – with a strange mixture of sadness and defiance, tenderness and fury.

Chapter Sixty-two

*Of a solemn resolution which Captain Devereux registered
among his household gods, with a libation*

When Devereux entered his drawing-room, and lighted his candles,
he was in a black and bitter mood. He stood at the window for a
while, and drummed on the pane, looking in the direction of the
barrack, where all the fun was going on, but thinking, in a chaotic
way, of things very different, and all toned with that strange sense of
self-reproach and foreboding which, of late, had grown habitual with
him – and not without just cause.

'This shall be the last. 'Twas dreadful, seeing that poor Nan; and
I want it – I can swear, I really and honestly want it – only one glass
to stay my heart. Everyone may drink in moderation – especially if
he's heart-sick, and has no other comfort – one glass and no more –
curse it.'

So one glass of brandy – I'm sorry to say, unmixed with water –
the handsome misanthropist sipped and sipped, to the last drop;
and then sat down before his fire, and struck, and poked, and
stabbed at it in a bitter, personal sort of way, until here and there
some blazes leaped up, and gave his eyes a dreamy sort of occupation; and he sat back, with his hands in his pockets, and his feet on
the fender, gazing among the Plutonic peaks and caverns between
the bars.

'I've had my allowance for tonight; tomorrow night, none at all.
'Tis an accursed habit: and I'll not allow it to creep upon me. No,
I've never fought it fairly, as I mean to do now – 'tis quite easy, if one
has but the will to do it.'

So he sat before his fire, chewing the cud of bitter fancy only; and
he recollected he had not quite filled his glass, and up he got with a
swagger, and says he: 'We'll drink fair, if you please – one glass – one
only – but that, hang it – a bumper.'

So he made a rough calculation.

'We'll say so much – here or there, 'tis no great matter. A thimble full won't drown me. Pshaw! That's too much. What am I to do with it? – hang it. Well, we can't help it – 'tis the last.'

So whatever the quantity may have been, he drank it too, and grew more moody; and was suddenly called up from the black abyss by the entrance of little Puddock, rosy and triumphant, from the ball.

'Ha! Puddock! Then the fun's over. I'm glad to see you. I've been *tête-à-tête* with my shadow – cursed bad company, Puddock. Where's Cluffe?'

'Gone home, I believe.'

'So much the better. You know Cluffe better than I, and there's a secret about him I never could find out. *You* have, maybe?'

'What's that?' lisped Puddock.

'What the deuce Cluffe's good for.'

'Oh! tut! We all know Cluffe's a very good fellow.'

Devereux looked from under his finely pencilled brows with a sad sort of smile at good little Puddock.

'Puddock,' says he, 'I'd like to have you write my epitaph.'

Puddock looked at him with his round eyes a little puzzled, and then he said: 'You think, maybe, I've a turn for making verses; and you think also I like you, and there you're quite right.'

Devereux laughed, but kindly, and shook the fat little hand he proffered.

'I wish I were like you, Puddock. We've the knowledge of good and evil between us. The knowledge of good is all yours: you see nothing but the good that men have; you see it – and, I dare say, truly – where I can't. The darker knowledge is mine.'

Puddock, who thought he thoroughly understood King John, Shylock, and Richard III, was a good deal taken aback by Devereux's estimate of his penetration.

'Well, I don't think you know me, Devereux,' resumed he with a thoughtful lisp. 'I'm much mistaken, or I could sound the depths of a villain's soul as well as most men.'

'And if you did you'd find it full of noble qualities,' said Dick Devereux. 'What book is that?'

'*The tragical history of Doctor Faustus*,' answered Puddock. 'I left it here more than a week ago. Have you read it?'

'Faith, Puddock, I forgot it! Let's see what 'tis like,' said Devereux. 'Hey day!' And he read:

> Now, Faustus, let thine eyes with horror stare
> Into that vast perpetual torture-house;

There are the furies tossing damned souls
On burning forks; their bodies boil in lead;
There are live quarters broiling on the coals
That ne'er can die; this ever-burning chair
Is for o'er-tortured souls to rest them in;
These that are fed with sops of flaming fire
Were gluttons, and loved only delicates,
And laughed to see the poor starve at their gates.

'Tailors! By Jupiter! Serve'em right, the rogues. Tailors dining upon ragou royal, Spanish olea, Puddock – fat livers, and green morels in the Phoenix, the scoundrels, and laughing to see poor gentlemen of the Royal Irish Artillery starving at their gates – hang 'em.'

'Well! Well! Listen to the *Good Angel*,' said Puddock, taking up the book and declaiming his best –

O thou hast lost celestial happiness,
Pleasures unspeakable, bliss without end.
Hadst thou affected sweet divinity,
Hell or the devil had no power on thee –
Hadst thou kept on that way. Faustus, behold
In what resplendent glory thou hadst sat,
On yonder throne, like those bright shining spirits,
And triumphed over hell! That hast thou lost;
And now, poor soul, must thy good angel leave thee;
The jaws of hell are open to receive thee.'

'Stop that; 'tis all cursed rant,' said Devereux. 'That is, the thing itself; you make the most it.'

'Why, truly,' said Puddock, 'there are better speeches in it. But 'tis very late; and parade, you know – I shall go to bed. And you – '

'No. I shall stay where I am.'

'Well, I wish you good-night, dear Devereux.'

'Good-night, Puddock'

And the plump little fellow was heard skipping downstairs, and the hall-door shut behind him. Devereux took the play that Puddock had just laid down, and read for a while with a dreary kind of interest. Then he got up, and, I'm sorry to say, drank another glass of the same strong waters.

'Tomorrow I turn over a new leaf;' and he caught himself repeating Puddock's snatch of Macbeth, 'Tomorrow, and tomorrow, and tomorrow'.

Devereux looked out, leaning on the window-sash. All was quiet now, as if the rattle of a carriage had never disturbed the serene cold night. The town had gone to bed, and you could hear the sigh of the river across the field. A sadder face the moon did not shine upon.

'That's a fine play, *Faustus* – Marlowe,' he said. Some of the lines he had read were booming funereally in his ear like a far-off bell. 'I wonder whether Marlowe had run a wild course, like some of us here – myself – and could not retrieve. That honest little mounte-bank, Puddock, does not understand a word of it. I wish I were like Puddock. Poor little fellow!'

So, after a while, Devereux returned to his chair before the fire, and on his way again drank of the waters of Lethe, and sat down, not forgetting, but remorseful, over the fire.

'I'll drink no more tonight – there – curse me if I do.'

The fire was waxing low in the grate. 'Tomorrow's a new day. Why, I never made a resolution about it before. I can keep it. 'Tis easily kept. Tomorrow I begin.'

And with fists clenched in his pockets, he vowed his vow, with an oath into the fire; and ten minutes were not past and over when his eye wandered thirstily again to the flask on the middle of the table, and with a sardonic, flushed smile, he quoted the 'Good Angel's' words:

O, Faustus, lay that damned book aside,
And gaze not on it lest it tempt thy soul.'

And then pouring out a dram, he looked on it, and said, with the 'Evil Angel':

Go forward, Faustus, in that famous art,
Wherein all Nature's treasure is contained:
Be thou on earth as Jove is in the sky,
Lord and commander of the elements.

And then, with a solitary sneer, he sipped it. And after a while he drank one glass more – they were the small glasses then in vogue – and shoved it back, with: 'There; that's the last.'

And then, perhaps, there was one other 'last'; and after that 'the *very* last'. 'Hang it! it *must* be the last', and so on, I suppose. And Devereux was pale, and looked wild and sulky, on parade next morning.

Chapter Sixty-three

*In which a liberty is taken with Mr Nutter's name, and
Mr Dangerfield stands at the altar*

Poor Mrs Nutter continued in a state of distracted and flighty tribulation, not knowing what to make of it, nor, indeed, knowing the
worst; for the neighbours did not tell her half they might, nor drop a
hint of the dreadful suspicion that dogged her absent helpmate.

She was sometimes up rummaging among the drawers, and fidget-
ing about the house, without any clear purpose, but oftener lying on
her bed, with her clothes on, crying. When she got hold of a friend,
she disburthened her soul, and called on him or her for endless
consolations and assurances, which, for the most part, she herself
prescribed. There were, of course, fits of despair as well as starts of
hope; and bright ideas, accounting for everything, and then clouds of
blackness, and tornadoes of lamentation.

Father Roach, a good-natured apostle whose digestion suffered
when anyone he liked was in trouble, paid her a visit; and being
somehow confounded with Dr Toole, was shown up to her bedroom, where the poor little woman lay crying under the coverlet.
On discovering where he was, the good father was disposed to
flinch, and get downstairs, in tenderness to his 'character', and
thinking what a story 'them villians o' the world 'id make iv it down
at the club there.' But on second thoughts, poor little Sally being
neither young nor comely, he ventured, and sat down by the bed,
veiled behind a strip of curtain, and poured his mellifluous consolations into her open ears.

And poor Sally became eloquent in return. And Father Roach
dried his eyes, although she could not see him behind the curtain,
and called her 'my daughter', and 'dear lady', and tendered such
comforts as his housekeeping afforded. 'Had she bacon in the house?'
or 'maybe she'd like a fat fowl?' 'She could not eat?' 'Why then she
could make elegant broth of it, and dhrink it, an' he'd keep another
fattenin' until Nutter himself come back.'

'And then, my honey, you an' himself'll come down and dine wid ould Father Austin; an' we'll have a grand evenin' of it entirely, laughin' over the remimbrance iv these blackguard troubles, acuishla! Or maybe you'd accept iv a couple o' bottles of claret or canaries? I see – you don't want for wine.'

So there was just one more offer the honest fellow had to make, and he opened with assurances 'twas only between himself an' her – an' not a sowl on airth 'id ever hear a word about it – and he asked her pardon, but he thought she might chance to want a guinea or two, just till Nutter came back, and he brought a couple in his waistcoat pocket.

Poor Father Roach was hard-up just then. Indeed, the being hard-up was a chronic affection with him. Two horses were not to be kept for nothing. Nor for the same moderate figure was it possible to maintain an asylum for unfortunates and outlaws – pleasant fellows enough, but endowed with great appetites and an unquenchable taste for consolation in fluid forms.

A clerical provision in Father Roach's day, and church, was not by any means what we have seen it since. At all events he was not often troubled with the possession of money, and when half-a-dozen good weddings brought him in fifty or a hundred pounds, the holy man was constrained forthwith to make distribution of his assets among a score of sour, and sometimes dangerous tradespeople. I mention this in no disparagement of Father Roach, quite the contrary. In making the tender of his two guineas – which, however, Sally declined – the worthy cleric was offering the widow's mite; not like some lucky dogs who might throw away a thousand or two and be nothing the worse; and you may be sure the poor fellow was very glad to find she did not want it.

'Rather hard measure, it strikes me,' said Dangerfield, in the club, 'to put him in the *Hue-and-Cry*.'

But there he was, sure enough, 'Charles Nutter, Esq., formerly of the Mills, near Knockmaroon, in the county of Dublin;' and a full description of the dress he wore, as well as of his height, complexion, features – and all this time his poor little wife still inhabiting the Mills, and quite unconscious that any man, woman, or child, who could prosecute him to conviction, for a murderous assault on Dr Sturk, should have £50 reward.

'News in today, by Jove,' said Toole, bustling solemnly into the club; 'by the packet that arrived at one o'clock: a man taken, answering Nutter's description exactly, just going aboard of a Jamaica brig at Gravesend, and giving no account of himself. He's to be sent over to Dublin for identification.'

And when that was thoroughly discussed two or three times over, they fell to talking of other subjects, and among the rest of Devereux, and wondered what his plans were; and, there being no brother officers by, whether he meant to keep his commission, and various speculations as to the exact cause of the coldness shown him by General Chattesworth. Dick Spaight thought it might be that he had not asked Miss Gertrude in marriage.

But this was pooh-poohed. 'Besides, they knew at Belmont,' said Toole, who was an authority upon the domestic politics of that family, and rather proud of being so, 'just as well as I did that Gypsy Dick was in love with Miss Lilias; and I lay you fifty he'd marry her tomorrow if she'd have him.'

Toole was always a little bit more intimate with people behind their backs, so he called Devereux 'Gypsy Dick'.

'She's ailing, I hear,' said old Slowe.

'She is, indeed, Sir,' answered the doctor, with a grave shake of the head.

'Nothing of moment, I hope?' he asked.

'Why, you see it may be; she had a bad cough last winter, and this year she took it earlier, and it has fallen very much on her lungs; and you see, we can't say, Sir, what turn it may take, and I'm very sorry she should be so sick and ailing – she's the prettiest creature, and the best little soul; and I don't know, on my conscience, what the poor old parson would do if anything happened her, you know. But I trust, Sir, with care, you know, 'twill turn out well.'

The season for trout-fishing was long past and gone, and there were no more pleasant rambles for Dangerfield and Irons along the flowery banks of the devious Liffey. Their rods and nets hung up, awaiting the return of genial spring; and the churlish stream, abandoned to its wintry mood, darkled and roared savagely under the windows of the Brass Castle.

One dismal morning, as Dangerfield's energetic step carried him briskly through the town, the iron gate of the churchyard, and the door of the church itself standing open, he turned in, glancing upward as he passed at Sturk's bedroom windows, as all the neighbours did, to see whether General Death's white banners were floating there, and his tedious siege ended – as end it must – and the garrison borne silently away in his custody to the prison house.

Up the aisle marched Dangerfield, not abating his pace, but with a swift and bracing clatter, like a man taking a frosty constitutional walk.

Irons was moping softly about in the neighbourhood of the reading-desk, and about to mark the places of psalms and chapters in the great church Bible and Prayer-book, and sidelong he beheld his crony of the angle marching, with a grim confidence and swiftness, up the aisle.

'I say, where's Martin?' said Dangerfield, cheerfully.

'He's gone away, Sir.'

'Hey! then you've no-one with you?'

'No, Sir.'

Dangerfield walked straight on, up the step of the communion-table, and shoving open the little balustraded door, he made a gay stride or two across the holy precinct, and with a quick right-about face, came to a halt; the white, scoffing face, for exercise never flushed it, and the cold, broad sheen of the spectacles, looked odd in the clerk's eyes, facing the church-door from beside the table of the sacrament, displayed, as it were, in the very frame – foreground, background, and all – in which he was wont to behold the thought-ful, simple, holy face of the rector.

'Alone among the dead; and not afraid?' croaked the white face pleasantly.

The clerk seemed always to writhe and sweat silently under the banter of his comrade of the landing-net, and he answered, without lifting his head, in a constrained and dogged sort of way, like a man who expects something unpleasant: 'Alone? Yes, Sir, there's none here but ourselves.'

And his face flushed, and the veins on his forehead stood out, as will happen with a man who tugs at a weight that is too much for him.

'I saw you steal a glance at Charles when he came into the church here, and it strikes me I was at the moment thinking of the same thing as you, to wit, will he require any special service at our hands? Well, he does! And you or I must do it. He'll give a thousand pounds, mind ye; and that's something in the way of fellows like you and me; and whatever else he may have done, Charles has never broke his word in a money matter. And, hark'ee, can't you thumb over that Bible and Prayer-book on the table here as well as *there*? Do so. Well –'

And he went on in a lower key, still looking full front at the church-door, and a quick glance now and then upon Irons, across the communion-table.

' 'Tis nothing at all – don't you see – what are you afraid of? It can't change events – 'tis only a question of today or tomorrow – a whim – a maggot – hey? You can manage it this way, mark ye.'

He had his pocket-handkerchief by the two corners before him, like an apron, and he folded it neatly and quickly into four.

'Don't you see – and a little water. You're a neat hand, you know; and if you're interrupted, 'tis only to blow your nose in't – ha, ha, ha! – and clap it in your pocket; and *you* may as well have the money – hey? Good-morning.'

And when he had got half-way down the aisle, he called back to Irons, in a loud, frank voice: 'And Martin's not here – could you say where he is?'

But he did not await the answer, and glided with quick steps from the porch, with a side leer over the wavy green mounds and tomb-stones. He had not been three minutes in the church, and across the street he went, to the shop over the way, and asked briskly where Martin, the sexton, was. Well, they did not know.

'Ho! Martin,' he cried across the street, seeing that functionary just about to turn the corner by Sturk's hall-door steps; 'a word with you. I've been looking for you. See, you must take a foot-rule, and make all the measurements of that pew, you know; don't mistake a hair's breadth, d'ye mind, for you must be ready to swear to it; and bring a note of it to me, at home, today, at one o'clock, and you shall have a crown-piece.'

From which the reader will perceive – as all the world might, if they had happened to see him enter the church just now – that his object in the visit was to see and speak with Martin; and that the little bit of banter with Irons, the clerk, was all by-play, and parenthesis, and beside the main business, and, of course, of no sort of consequence.

Mr Irons, like most men of his rank in life, was not much in the habit of exact thinking. His ruminations, therefore, were rather confused, but, perhaps, they might be translated in substance, into something like this: 'Why the —— can't he let them alone that's willing to let him alone? I wish he was in his own fiery home, and better people at rest. I *can't* mark them places – I don't know whether I'm on my head or heels.'

And he smacked the quarto Prayer-book down upon the folio Bible with a sonorous bang, and glided out, furious, frightened, and taciturn, to the Salmon House.

He came upon Dangerfield again only half-a-dozen steps from the turn into the street. He had just dismissed Martin, and was looking into a note in his pocket-book, and either did not see, or pretended not to see, the clerk. But someone else saw and recognised Mr Irons; and, as he passed, directed upon him a quick, searching glance. It was Mr Mervyn, who happened to pass that way. Irons and Dangerfield, and the churchyard – there was a flash of association in the group and the background which accorded with an old suspicion. Dangerfield, indeed, was innocently reading a leaf in his red and gilt leather pocket-book, as I have said. But Irons's eyes met the glance of Mervyn, and contracted oddly, and altogether there gleamed out something indefinable in his look. It was only for a second – a glance and an intuition; and from that moment it was one of Mervyn's immovable convictions, that Mr Dangerfield knew something of Irons's secret. It was a sort of intermittent suspicion before – now it was a monstrous, but fixed belief.

So Mr Irons glided swiftly on to the Salmon House, where, in a dark corner, he drank something comfortable, and stalked back again to the holy pile with his head aching, and the world round him like a wild and evil dream.

Chapter Sixty-four

*Being a night scene, in which Miss Gertrude Chattesworth,
being adjured by Aunt Becky, makes answer*

In Aunt Becky's mind, the time could not be far off when the odd sort of relations existing between the Belmont family and Mr Dangerfield must be defined. The Croesus himself, indeed, was very indulgent. He was assiduous and respectful, but he wisely abstained from pressing for an immediate decision, and trusted to reflection and to Aunt Becky's good offices; and knew that his gold would operate by its own slow, but sure, gravitation.

At one time he had made up his mind to be peremptory – and politely to demand an unequivocal 'yes' or 'no'. But a letter reached him from London; it was from a great physician there. Whatever was in it, the effect was to relieve his mind of an anxiety. He never, indeed, looked anxious, or moped like an ordinary man in blue-devils. But his servants knew when anything weighed upon his spirits, by his fierce, short, maniacal temper. But with the seal of that letter the spell broke, the evil spirit departed for a while, and the old jocose, laconic irony came back, and glittered whitely in the tall chair by the fire, and sipped its claret after dinner, and sometimes smoked its long pipe and grinned into the embers of the grate. At Belmont, there had been a skirmish over the broiled drumsticks at supper, and the ladies had withdrawn in towering passions to their nightly devotions and repose.

Gertrude had of late grown more like herself, but was quite resolute against the Dangerfield alliance, which Aunt Becky fought for, the more desperately that in their private confidences under the poplar trees she had given the rich cynic of the silver spectacles good assurance of success.

Puddock drank tea at Belmont – nectar in Olympus – that evening. Was ever lieutenant so devoutly romantic? He had grown more fanatical and abject in his worship. He spoke less, and lisped in very low tones. He sighed often, and sometimes mightily; and ogled unhappily, and smiled lackadaisically. The beautiful damsel was, in her high, cold way, kind to the guest, and employed him about the room on little commissions, and listened to his speeches without hearing them, and rewarded them now and then with the gleam of a smile, which made his gallant little heart flutter up to his solitaire, and his honest powdered head giddy.

'I marvel, brother,' ejaculated Aunt Becky, suddenly appearing in the parlour, where the general had made himself comfortable over his novel, and opening her address with a smart stamp on the floor. The veteran's heart made a little jump, and he looked up over his gold spectacles.

'I marvel, brother, what you can mean, desire, or intend, by all this ogling, sighing, and love-making; 'tis surely a strange way of forwarding Mr Dangerfield's affair.'

He might have blustered a little, as he sometimes did, for she had startled him, and her manner was irritating; but she had caught him in a sentimental passage between Lovelace and Miss Harlowe, which always moved him – and he showed no fight at all; but his innocent little light blue eyes looked up wonderingly and quite gently at her.

'Who – I? *What* ogling, Sister Becky?'

'You! Tut! That foolish, ungrateful person, Lieutenant Puddock; what can you propose to yourself, brother, in bringing Lieutenant Puddock here? I hate him.'

'Why, what about Puddock – what has he done?' asked the general, with round eyes still, and closing his book on his finger.

'What has he done! Why, he's at your daughter's feet,' cried Aunt Becky, with scarlet cheeks, and flashing eyes; 'and she – artful gypsy, has brought him there by positively making love to him.'

'Sweet upon Toodie (the general's old pet name for Gertrude); why, half the young fellows are – you know – pooh, pooh,' and the general stood up with his back to the fire – looking uneasy; for, like many other men, he thought a woman's eyes saw further in such a case than his.

'Do you wish the young hussy – do you – to marry Lieutenant Puddock? I should not wonder! Why, of course, her fortune you and she may give away to whom you like; but remember, she's young, and has been much admired, brother; and may make a great match; and in our day, young ladies were under direction, and did not marry without apprising their parents or natural guardians. Here's Mr Dangerfield, who proposes great settlements. Why won't she have him? For my part, I think we're little better than cheats; and I mean to write tomorrow morning and tell the poor gentleman that you and

I have been bamboozling him to a purpose, and meant all along to marry the vixen to a poor lieutenant in your corps. Speak truth, and shame the devil, brother; for my part, I'm sick of the affair; I'm sick of deception, ingratitude, and odious fools.

Aunt Becky had vanished in a little whirlwind, leaving the general with his back to the fire, looking blank and uncomfortable. And from his little silver tankard he poured out a glassful of his mulled claret, not thinking, and smelled to it deliberately, as he used to do when he was tasting a new wine, and looked through it, and set the glass down, forgetting he was to drink it, for his thoughts were elsewhere.

On reaching her bedroom, which she did with impetuous haste, Aunt Becky shut the door with a passionate slam, and said, with a sort of choke and a sob, 'There's nought but ingratitude on earth – the odious, odious, *odious* person!'

And when, ten minutes after, her maid came in, she found Aunt Rebecca but little advanced in her preparations for bed; and her summons at the door was answered by a fierce and shrilly nose-trumpeting, and a stern 'Come in, hussy – are you deaf, child?' And when she came in, Aunt Becky was grim, and fussy, and her eyes red.

Miss Gertrude was that night arrived just on that dim and delicious plateau – that debatable land upon which the last waking reverie and the first dream of slumber mingle together in airy dance and shifting colours – when, on a sudden, she was recalled to a consciousness of her grave bed-posts, and damask curtains, by the voice of her aunt.

Sitting up, she gazed on the redoubted Aunt Becky through the lace of her *bonnet de nuit*, for some seconds, in a mystified and incredulous way.

Mistress Rebecca Chattesworth, on the other hand, had drawn the curtains, and stood, candle in hand, arrayed in her night-dress like a ghost, only she had on a pink and green quilted dressing-gown loosely over it.

She was tall and erect, of course; but she looked softened and strange; and when she spoke, it was in quite a gentle, humble sort of way, which was perfectly strange to her niece.

'Don't be frightened, sweetheart,' said she, and she leaned over and with her arm round her neck, kissed her. 'I came to say a word, and just to ask you a question. I wish, indeed I do – Heaven knows, to do my duty; and, my dear child, will you tell me the whole truth – will you tell me truly? – You will, when I ask it as a kindness.'

There was a little pause, and Gertrude looked with a pale gaze upon her aunt.

'Are you,' said Aunt Becky – 'do you, Gertrude – do you like Lieutenant Puddock?'

'Lieutenant Puddock!' repeated the girl, with the look and gesture of a person in whose ear something strange has buzzed.

'Because, if you really are in love with him, Gertie; and that he likes you; and that, in short – ' Aunt Becky was speaking very rapidly, but stopped suddenly.

'In love with Lieutenant Puddock!' was all that Miss Gertrude said.

'Now, do tell me, Gertrude, if it be so – tell *me*, dear love. I know 'tis a hard thing to say,' and Aunt Becky considerately began to fiddle with the ribbon at the back of her niece's nightcap, so that she need not look in her face; 'but, Gertie, tell me truly, do you like him; and – and – why, if it be so, I will mention Mr Dangerfield's suit no more. There now – there's all I want to say.'

'Lieutenant Puddock!' repeated young Madam in the nightcap; and by this time the film of slumber was gone; and the suspicion struck her somehow in altogether so comical a way that she could not help laughing in her aunt's sad, earnest face.

'Fat, funny little Lieutenant Puddock! – was ever so diverting a disgrace? Oh! dear aunt, what have I done to deserve so prodigious a suspicion?'

It was plain, from her heightened colour, that her aunt did not choose to be laughed at.

'What have you done?' said she, quite briskly; 'why – what have you done?' and Aunt Becky had to consider just for a second or two, staring straight at the young lady through the crimson damask curtains. 'You have – you – you – why, what have you *done*?' And she covered her confusion by stooping down to adjust the heel of her slipper.

'Oh! It's delightful – plump little Lieutenant Puddock!' and the graver her aunt looked the more irrepressibly she laughed; till that lady, evidently much offended, took the young gentlewoman pretty roundly to task.

'Well! I'll tell you what you have done,' said she, almost fiercely. 'As absurd as he is, you have been twice as sweet upon him as he upon you; and you have done your endeavour to fill his brain with the notion that you are in love with him, young lady; and if you're not, you have acted, I promise you, a most unscrupulous and unpardonable part by a most honourable and well-bred gentleman – for that character I believe he bears. Yes – you may laugh, Madam, how you please; but he's allowed, I say, to be as honest, as true, as fine a gentleman as – as – '

'As ever surprised a weaver,' said the young lady, laughing till she almost cried. In fact, she was showing in a new light, and becoming quite a funny character upon this theme. And, indeed, this sort of convulsion of laughing seemed so unaccountable on natural grounds to Aunt Rebecca, that her irritation subsided into perplexity, and she began to suspect that her extravagant merriment might mean possibly something which she did not quite understand.

'Well, niece, when you have quite done laughing at nothing, you will, perhaps, be so good as to hear me. I put it to you now, young lady, as your relation and your friend, once for all, upon your sacred honour – remember you're a Chattesworth – upon the honour of a Chattesworth' (a favourite family form of adjuration on serious occasions with Aunt Rebecca), 'do you like Lieutenant Puddock?'

It was now Miss Gertrude's turn to be nettled, and to remind her visitor, by a sudden flush in her cheek and a flash from her eyes, that she was, indeed, a Chattesworth; and with more disdain than, perhaps, was quite called for, she repelled the soft suspicion.

'I protest, Madam,' said Miss Gertrude, ''tis *too* bad. Truly, Madam, it *is vastly* vexatious to have to answer so strange and affronting a question. If you ever took the trouble, aunt, to listen to, or look at, Lieutenant Puddock, you might – '

'Well, niece,' quoth Aunt Becky, interrupting, with a little toss of her head, 'young ladies weren't quite so hard to please in my time, and I can't see or hear that he's so much worse than others.'

'I'd sooner die than have him,' said Miss Gertie, peremptorily.

'Then, I suppose, if ever, and whenever he asks you the question himself, you'll have no hesitation in telling him so?' said Aunt Becky, with becoming solemnity.

'Laughable, ridiculous, comical and absurd as I always thought and believed Lieutenant Puddock to be, I yet believe the asking such a question of me to be a stretch of absurdity, from which his breeding, for he is a gentleman, will restrain him. Besides, Madam, you can't possibly be aware of the subjects on which he has invariably discoursed whenever he happened to sit by me – plays and players, and candied fruit. Really, Madam, it is too absurd to have to enter upon one's defence against so incredible an imagination.'

Aunt Rebecca looked steadily for a few seconds in her niece's face, then drew a long breath, and leaning over, kissed her again on the forehead, and with a grave little nod, and looking on her again for a short space, without saying a word more, she turned suddenly and left the room.

Miss Gertrude's vexation again gave way to merriment; and her aunt, as she walked sad and stately upstairs, heard one peal of merry laughter after another ring through her niece's bedroom. She had not laughed so much for three years before; and this short visit cost her, I am sure, two hours' good sleep at least.

Chapter Sixty-five

Relating some awful news that reached the village, and how Dr
Walsingham visited Captain Richard Devereux at his lodgings

And now there was news all over the town, to keep all the tongues
there in motion.

News – news – great news! – terrible news! Peter Fogarty, Mr
Tresham's boy, had it that morning from his cousin, Jim Redmond,
whose aunt lived at Ringsend, and kept the little shop over against
the 'Plume of Feathers,' where you might have your pick and choice
of all sorts of nice and useful things – bacon, brass snuff-boxes, penny
ballads, eggs, candles, cheese, tobacco-pipes, pinchbeck buckles for
knee and instep, soap, sausages, and who knows what beside.

No-one quite believed it – it was a tradition at third hand, and
Peter Fogarty's cousin, Jim Redmond's aunt, was easy of faith – Jim,
it was presumed, not very accurate in narration, and Peter, not much
better. Though, however, it was not actually 'intelligence', it was a
startling thesis. And though some raised their brows and smiled
darkly, and shook their heads, the whole town certainly pricked their
ears at it. And not a man met another without 'Well! Anything more?
You've heard the report, Sir – eh?'

It was not till Doctor Toole came out of town, early that day, that
the sensation began in earnest.

'There could be no doubt about it – 'twas a wonderful strange
thing certainly. After so long a time – and so well preserved too.'

'*What* was it – what *is* it?'

'Why, Charles Nutter's corpse is found, Sir!'

'Corpse – hey!'

'So Toole says. Hollo! Toole – Doctor Toole – I say. Here's Mr
Slowe hasn't heard about poor Nutter.'

'Ho! Neighbour Slowe – give you good-day, Sir – not heard it? By
Jove, Sir – poor Nutter! – 'tis true – his body's found – picked up this
morning, just at sunrise, by two Dunleary fishermen, off Bullock.
Justice Lowe has seen it – and Spaight saw it too. I've just been

speaking with him, not an hour ago, in Thomas Street. It lies at Ringsend – and an inquest in the morning.'

And so on in Doctor Toole's manner, until he saw Dr Walsingham, the good rector, pausing in his leisurely walk just outside the row of houses that fronted the turnpike, in one of which were the lodgings of Dick Devereux.

The good Doctor Toole wondered what brought his reverence there, for he had an inkling of something going on. So he bustled off to him, and told his story with the stern solemnity befitting such a theme, and that pallid, half-suppressed smile with which an exciting horror is sometimes related. And the good rector had many ejaculations of consternation and sympathy, and not a few enquiries to utter. And at last, when the theme was quite exhausted, he told Toole, who still lingered on, that he was going to pay his respects to Captain Devereux.

'Oh!' said cunning little Toole, 'you need not, for I told him the whole matter.'

'Very like, Sir,' answered the doctor; 'but 'tis on another matter I wish to see him.'

'Oh! – ho! – certainly – very good, Sir. I beg pardon – and – and – he's just done his breakfast – a late dog, Sir – ha! ha! Your servant, Doctor Walsingham.'

Devereux puzzled his comrade Puddock more than ever. Sometimes he would descend with his blue devils into the abyss, and sit there all the evening in a dismal sulk. Sometimes he was gayer even than his old gay self; and sometimes in a bitter vein, talking enigmatical ironies, with his strange smile; and sometimes he was dangerous and furious, just as the weather changes without rhyme or reason. Maybe he was angry with himself, and thought it was with others; and was proud, sorry, and defiant, and let his moods, one after another, possess him as they came.

They were his young days – beautiful and wicked – days of clear, rich tints, and sanguine throbbings, and *gloria mundi* – when we fancy the spirit perfect, and the body needs no redemption – when, fresh from the fountains of life, death is but a dream, and we walk the earth like heathen gods and goddesses, in celestial egotism and beauty. Oh, fair youth! – gone for ever. The parting from thee was a sadness and a violence – sadder, I think, than death itself. We look behind us, and sigh after thee, as on the pensive glories of a sunset, and our march is toward the darkness. It is twilight with us now, and will soon be starlight, and the hour and place of slumber, till the reveille sounds, and the day of wonder opens. Oh, grant us a good hour, and take us to Thy mercy! But to the last those young days will be remembered and worth remembering; for be we what else we may, young mortals we shall never be again.

Of course Dick Devereux was now no visitor at the Elms. All *that* for the present was over. Neither did he see Lilias; for little Lily was now a close prisoner with doctors, in full uniform, with shouldered canes, mounting guard at the doors. 'Twas a hard winter, and she needed care and nursing. And Devereux chafed and fretted; and, in truth, 'twas hard to bear this spite of fortune – to be so near, and yet so far – quite out of sight and hearing.

A word or two from General Chattesworth in Doctor Walsingham's ear, as they walked to and fro before the white front of Belmont, had decided the rector on making this little call; for he had now mounted the stair of Devereux's lodging, and standing on the carpet outside, knocked, with a grave, sad face on his door panel, glancing absently through the lobby window, and whistling inaudibly the while.

The doctor was gentle and modest, and entirely kindly. He held good Master Feltham's doctrine about reproofs. 'A man,' says he, 'had better be convinced in private than be made guilty by a proclamation. Open rebukes are for Magistrates and Courts of Justice! for Stelled Chambers and for Scarlets, in the thronged Hall. Private are for friends; where all the witnesses of the offender's blushes are blinde and deaf and dumb. We should do by them as Joseph thought to have done by Mary, seeke to cover blemishes with secrecy. Public reproofe is like striking of a Deere in the Herd; it not only wounds him to the loss of enabling blood, but betrays him to the Hound, his Enemy, and makes him by his fellows be pusht out of company.'

So on due invitation from within, the good parson entered, and the handsome captain in all his splendours – when you saw him after a little absence 'twas always with a sort of admiring surprise – you had forgot how *very* handsome he was – this handsome slender fellow, with his dark face and large, unfathomable violet eyes, so wild and wicked, and yet so soft, stood up surprised, with a look of welcome quickly clouded and crossed by a gleam of defiance.

They bowed, and shook hands, however, and bowed again, and each was the other's 'servant'; and being seated, they talked *de generalibus*; for the good parson would not come like an executioner and take his prisoner by the throat, but altogether in the spirit of the shepherd, content to walk a long way about, and wait till he came up with the truant, and entreating him kindly, not dragging or beating him back to the flock, but leading and carrying by turns, and so awaiting his opportunity. But Devereux was in one of his moods. He thought the doctor no friend to his suit, and was bitter, and formal, and violent.

Chapter Sixty-six

*Of a certain tempest that arose and shook the captain's spoons
and tea-cups; and how the wind suddenly went down*

'I'm very glad, Sir, to have a few quiet minutes with you,' said
the doctor, making then a little pause; and Devereux thought he
was going to re-open the matter of his suit. 'For I've had no answer to my last letter, and I want to know all you can tell me of that
most promising young man, Daniel Loftus, and his most curious
works.'

'Dan Loftus is dead and – ' (I'm sorry to say he added something
else); 'and his works have followed him, Sir,' said the strange captain,
savagely; for he could not conceive what business the doctor had to
think about *him*, when Captain Devereux's concerns were properly
to be discussed. So though he had reason to believe he was quite well,
and in Malaga with his 'honourable' and sickly cousin, he killed him
off-hand, and disposed summarily of his works.

There was an absolute silence of some seconds after this scandalous explosion; and Devereux said – 'In truth, Sir, I don't know. They
hold him capable of taking charge of my wise cousin – hang him! – so
I dare say he can take care of himself; and I don't see what the plague
ill's to happen him.'

The doctor's honest eyes opened, and his face flushed a little. But
reading makes a full man, not a quick one; and so while he was
fashioning his answer, the iron cooled. Indeed he never spoke in
anger. When on sudden provocation he carried his head higher and
flushed a little, they supposed he was angry; but if he was, this was all
he showed of the old Adam, and he held his peace.

So now the doctor looked down upon the table-cloth, for Devereux's breakfast china and silver were still upon the table, and he
marshalled some crumbs he found there, sadly, with his finger, in a
row first, and then in a circle, and then, goodness knows how; and he
sighed profoundly over his work.

Devereux was in his mood. He was proud – he had no notion of apologising. But looking another way, and with his head rather high, he hoped Miss Lilias was better.

Well, well, the spring was coming; and Parson Walsingham knew the spring restored little Lily. 'She's like a bird – she's like a flower, and the winter is nearly past,' and the beautiful words of the 'Song of Songs', which little Lily so loved to read, mingled like a reverie in his discourse, and he said, 'the flowers will soon appear in the earth, the time of the singing birds will come, and the voice of the turtle be heard in our land.'

'Sir,' said Dick Devereux, in a voice that sounded strangely, 'I have a request; may I make it? – a favour to beg. 'Tisn't, all things remembered, very much. If I write a letter, and place it open in your hand – a letter, Sir, to Miss Lily – will you read it to her, or else let her read it? Or even a message – a spoken message – will you give it?'

'Captain Devereux,' said the doctor, in a reserved but very sad sort of way, 'I must tell you that my dear child is by no means well. She has had a cold, and it has not gone away so soon as usual – something I think of her dear mother's delicacy – and so she requires care, my little Lily, a great deal of care. But, thank God, the spring is before us. Yes, yes; the soft air and sunshine, and then she'll be out again. You know the garden, and her visits, and her little walks. So I don't fret or despair. Oh, no.' He spoke very gently, in a reverie, after his wont, and he sighed heavily. 'You know 'tis growing late in life with me, Captain Devereux,' he resumed, 'and I would fain see her united to a kind and tender partner, for I think she's a fragile little flower. Poor little Lily! Something, I often think, of her dear mother's delicacy, and I have always nursed her, you know. She has been a great pet;' and he stopped suddenly, and walked to the window. 'A great pet. Indeed, if she could have been spoiled, I should have spoiled her long ago, but she could not. Ah, no! Sweet little Lily!'

Then quite firmly but gently Parson Walsingham went on: 'Now, the doctors say she mustn't be agitated, and I can't allow it, Captain Devereux. I gave her your message – let me see – why 'tis four, ay, five months ago. I gave it with a good will, for I thought well of you.'

'And you don't any longer – there, 'tis all out,' broke in Devereux, fiercely.

'Well, you know her answer; it was not lightly given, nor in haste, and first and last 'twas quite decided, and I sent it to you under my own hand.'

'I thought you were a friend to me, Dr Walsingham, and now I'm sure you're none,' said the young fellow, in the same bitter tone.

'Ah, Captain Devereux, he can be no friend to you who is a friend to your faults; and you no friend to yourself if you be an enemy to him that would tell you of them. Will you like him the worse that would have you better?'

'We've *all* faults, Sir; mine are not the worst, and I'll have neither shrift nor absolution. There's some reason here you won't disclose.'

He was proud, fierce, pale, and looked damnably handsome and wicked.

'She gave *no* reason, Sir;' answered Dr Walsingham. No, she gave none; but, as I understood, she did not love you, and she prayed me to mention it no more.'

'She gave no reason; but you *know* the reason,' glared out Devereux.

'Indeed, Sir, I do *not* know the reason,' answered the rector.

'But you know – you *must* – you *meant* – *you*, at least had heard some ill of me, and you no longer wish my suit to prosper.'

'I have, indeed, of late, heard *much* ill of you, Captain Devereux,' answered Dr Walsingham, in a very deliberate but melancholy way, 'enough to make me hold you no meet husband for any wife who cared for a faithful partner, or an honourable and a quiet home.'

'You mean – I know you do – that Palmerstown girl, who has belied me?' cried Devereux.

'That unhappy young woman, Captain Devereux, her name is Glynn, whom you have betrayed under a promise of marriage.'

That moment Devereux was on his feet. It was the apparition of Devereux; a blue fire gleaming in his eyes, not a word from his white lips, while three seconds might have ticked from Mrs Irons's prosy old clock on the stair-head; his slender hand was outstretched in appeal and defiance, and something half-celestial, half-infernal – the fallen angelic – in his whole face and bearing.

'May my merciful Creator strike me dead, here at your feet, Doctor Walsingham, but 'tis a lie,' cried he. 'I never promised – she'll tell you. I thought she told you long ago. 'Twas that devil incarnate, her mother, who forged the lie, why or wherefore, except for her fiendish love of mischief, I know not.'

'I cannot tell, Sir, about your promise,' said the doctor gravely; 'with or without it, the crime is heinous, the cruelty immeasurable.'

'Dr Walsingham,' cried Dick Devereux, a strange scorn ringing in his accents, 'with all your learning you don't know the world; you don't know human nature; you don't see what's passing in this very village before your eyes every day you live. I'm not worse than others; I'm not half so bad as fifty older fellows who ought to know better; but I'm *sorry*, and 'tisn't easy to say that, for I'm as proud, proud as the devil, proud as you; and if it were to my Maker, what more can I say? I'm sorry, and if Heaven forgives us when we repent, I think our wretched fellow-mortals may.'

'Captain Devereux, I've nothing to forgive,' said the parson, kindly.

'But I tell you, Sir, this cruel, unmeaning separation will be my eternal ruin,' cried Devereux. 'Listen to me – by Heaven, you shall. I've fought a hard battle, Sir! I've tried to forget her – to *hate* her – it won't do. I tell you, Dr Walsingham, 'tis not in your nature to comprehend the intensity of my love – you can't. I don't blame you. But I think, Sir – I think I *might* make her like me, Sir. They come at last, sometimes, to like those that love them so – so *desperately*: *that* may not be for me, 'tis true. I only ask to plead my own sad cause. I only want to see her – gracious Heaven – but to see her – to show her how I was wronged – to tell her she can make me what she will – an honourable, pure, self-denying, devoted man, or leave me in the dark, alone, with nothing for it but to wrap my cloak about my head, and leap over the precipice.'

'Captain Devereux, why will you doubt me? I've spoken the truth. I have already said I must not give your message; and you are not to suppose I dislike you, because I would fain have your faults mended.'

'Faults! have I? To be sure I have. So have *you*, *more*, Sir, and *worse* than I, maybe,' cried Devereux, wild again; 'and you come here in your spiritual pride to admonish and to lecture, and to *insult* a miserable man, who's better, perhaps, than yourself. You've heard ill of me? You hear I sometimes drink maybe a glass too much – who does not? You can drink a glass yourself, Sir; drink more, and show it less than I maybe; and you listen to every damned slander that any villain, to whose vices and idleness you pander with what you call your alms, may be pleased to invent, and you deem yourself charitable; save us from such charity! *Charitable*, and you refuse to deliver my miserable message: hard-hearted Pharisee!'

It is plain poor Captain Devereux was not quite himself – bitter, fierce, half-mad, and by no means so polite as he ought to have been. Alas! as Job says, 'ye imagine to reprove words; and the speeches of one that is desperate, which are as wind.'

'Yes, hard-hearted, unrelenting Pharisee.' The torrent roared on, and the wind was up; it was night and storm with poor Devereux. 'You who pray every day – oh – damnable hypocrisy – lead us not into temptation – you neither care nor ask to what courses your pride and obstinacy are driving me – your fellow-creature.'

'Ah, Captain Devereux, you are angry with me, and yet it's not my doing; the man that is at variance with himself will hardly be at one with others. You have said much to me that is unjust, and, perhaps, unseemly; but I won't reproach you; your anger and trouble make wild work with your words. When one of my people falls into sin, I ever find it is so through lack of prayer. Ah! Captain Devereux, have you not of late been remiss in the duty of private prayer?'

The captain laughed, not pleasantly, into the ashes in the grate. But the doctor did not mind, and only said, looking upward – 'Lord, if thou hadst been here, my brother had not died.'

There was kindness, and even tenderness, in the tone in which simple Dr Walsingham spoke the appellative, brother; and it smote Devereux now, as sometimes happens with wayward fellows, and his better nature was suddenly moved.

'I'm *sorry*, Sir – I am. You're too patient – I'm *very* sorry; 'tis like an angel – you're noble, Sir, and I such an outcast. I – I wish you'd strike me, Sir – you're too kind and patient, Sir, and so pure – and how have I spoken to you? A *trial*, Sir, if you *can* forgive me – one trial – my vice – you shall see me changed, a new man. Oh, Sir, let me swear it. I *am*, Sir – I'm reformed; don't believe me till you see it. Oh! Good Samaritan – don't forsake me – I'm all one wound.'

Well! they talked some time longer, and parted kindly.

Chapter Sixty-seven

In which a certain troubled spirit walks

Mr Dangerfield was at the club that night, and was rather in spirits than otherwise, except, indeed, when poor Charles Nutter was talked of. Then he looked grave, and shrugged, and shook his head, and said: 'A bad business, Sir; and where's his poor wife?'

'Spending the night with us, poor soul,' said Major O'Neill, mildly, 'and hasn't an idaya, poor thing; and indeed, I hope, she mayn't hear it.'

'Pooh! Sir, she must hear it; but you know she might have heard worse, Sir, eh?' rejoined Dangerfield.

'True for you, Sir,' said the major, suspending the filling of his pipe to direct a quiet glance of significance at Dangerfield, and then closing his eyes with a nod.

And just at this point in came Spaight.

'Well, Spaight!'

'Well, Sir.'

'You saw the body, eh?' and a dozen other interrogatories followed, as, cold and wet with melting snow, dishevelled and storm-beaten – for it was a plaguy rough night – the young fellow, with a general greeting to the company, made his way to the fire.

' 'Tis a tremendous night, gentlemen, so by your leave I'll stir the fire – and, yes, I seen him, poor Nutter – and, paugh, an ugly sight he is, I can tell you; here Larry, bring me a rummer-glass of punch – his right ear's gone, and a'most all his right hand – and screeching hot, do you mind – an', phiew – altogether 'tis sickening – them fishes, you know – I'm a'most sorry I went in – you remember Dogherty's whiskey shop in Ringsend – he lies in the back parlour, and wondherful little changed in appearance.'

And so Mr Spaight, with a little round table at his elbow, and his heels over the fender, sipped his steaming punch, and thawed inwardly and outwardly, as he answered their questions and mixed in their speculations.

Up at the Mills, which had heard the awful news, first from the Widow Macan, and afterwards from Pat Moran, the maids sat over their tea in the kitchen in high excitement and thrilling chat – 'The poor master!' 'Oh, the poor man!' 'Oh, la, what's that?' with a start and a peep over the shoulders. 'And oh dear, and how in the world will the poor little misthress ever live over the news?' and so forth, made a principal part of their talk. There was a good accompaniment of wind outside, and a soft pelting of snow on the window panes, 'and oh, my dear life, but wasn't it dark!'

Up went Moggy, with her thick-wicked kitchen candle, to seek repose; and Betty, resolving not to be long behind, waited only 'to wash up her plates' and slack down the fire, having made up her mind, for she grew more nervous in solitude, to share Moggy's bed for that night.

Moggy had not been twenty minutes gone, and her task was nearly ended, when – 'Oh, blessed saints!' murmured Betty, with staring eyes, and dropping the sweeping-brush on the flags, she heard, or thought she heard, her master's step, which was peculiar, crossing the floor overhead.

She listened, herself as pale as a corpse, and nearly as breathless; but there was nothing now but the muffled gusts of the storm, and the close soft beat of the snow, so she listened and listened, but nothing came of it.

''Tis only the vapours,' said Betty, drawing a long breath, and doing her best to be cheerful; and so she finished her labours, stopping every now and then to listen, and humming tunes very loud, in fits and starts. Then it came to her turn to take her candle and go upstairs; she was a good half-hour later than Moggy – all was quiet within the house – only the sound of the storm – the creak and rattle of its strain, and the hurly-burly of the gusts over the roof and chimneys.

Over her shoulder she peered jealously this way and that, as with flaring candle she climbed the stairs. How black the window looked on the lobby, with its white patterns of snow-flakes in perpetual succession sliding down the panes. Who could tell what horrid face might be looking in close to her as she passed, secure in the darkness and that drifting white lace veil of snow? So nimbly and lightly up the stairs climbed Betty, the cook.

If listeners seldom hear good of themselves, it is also true that peepers sometimes see more than they like; and Betty, the cook, as she reached the landing, glancing askance with ominous curiosity, beheld a spectacle, the sight of which nearly bereft her of her senses.

Crouching in the deep doorway on the right of the lobby, the cook, I say, saw something – a figure – or a deep shadow – only a deep shadow – or maybe a dog. She lifted the candle – she peeped under the candlestick: 'twas no shadow, as I live, 'twas a well-defined figure!

He was draped in black, cowering low, with the face turned up. It was Charles Nutter's face, fixed and stealthy. It was only while the fascination lasted – while you might count one, two, three, deliberately – that the horrid gaze met mutually. But there was no mistake there. She saw the stern dark picture as plainly as ever she did. The light glimmered on his white eyeballs.

Starting up, he struck at the candle with his hat. She uttered a loud scream, and flinging stick and all at the figure, with a great clang against the door behind, all was swallowed in instantaneous darkness; she whirled into the opposite bedroom she knew not how, and locked the door within, and plunged head-foremost under the bedclothes, half-mad with terror.

The squall was heard of course. Moggy heard it, but she heeded not; for Betty was known to scream at mice, and even moths. And as her door was heard to slam, as was usual in panics of the sort, and as she returned no answer, Moggy was quite sure there was nothing in it.

But Moggy's turn was to come. When spirits 'walk', I've heard they make the most of their time, and sometimes pay a little round of visits on the same evening.

This is certain; Moggy was by no means so great a fool as Betty in respect of hobgoblins, witches, banshees, pookas, and the world of spirits in general. She eat heartily, and slept soundly, and as yet had never seen the devil. Therefore such terrors as she that night experienced were new to her, and I can't reasonably doubt the truth of her narrative. Awaking suddenly in the night, she saw a light in the room, and heard a quiet rustling going on in the corner, where the old white-painted press showed its front from the wall. So Moggy popped her head through her thin curtains at the side, and – blessed hour! – there she saw the shape of a man looking into the press, the doors being wide open, and the appearance of a key in the lock.

The shape was very like her master. The saints between us and harm! The glow was reflected back from the interior of the press, and showed the front part of the figure in profile with a sharp line of light. She said he had some sort of thick slippers over his boots, a dark coat, with the cape buttoned, and a hat flapping over his face; coat and hat and all, sprinkled over with snow.

As if he heard the rustle of the curtain, he turned toward the bed, and with an awful ejaculation she cried, ''Tis you, Sir!'

'Don't stir, and you'll meet no harm,' he said, and over he posts to the bedside, and he laid his cold hand on her wrist, and told her again to be quiet, and for her life to tell no-one what she had seen, and with that she supposed she swooned away; for the next thing she remembered was listening in mortal fear, the room being all dark, and she heard a sound at the press again, and then steps crossing the floor, and she gave herself up for lost; but he did not come to the bedside any more, and the tread passed out at the door, and so, as she thought, went downstairs.

In the morning the press was locked and the door shut, and the hall-door and back-door locked, and the keys on the hall-table, where they had left them the night before.

You may be sure these two ladies were thankful to behold the grey light, and hear the cheerful sounds of returning day; and it would be no easy matter to describe which of the two looked most pallid, scared, and jaded that morning, as they drank a hysterical dish of tea together in the kitchen, close up to the window, and with the door shut, discoursing, and crying, and praying over their tea-pot in miserable companionship.

Chapter Sixty-eight

How an evening passes at the Elms, and Dr Toole makes a little excursion; and two choice spirits discourse, and Hebe trips in with the nectar

Up at the Elms, little Lily that night was sitting in the snug, old-fashioned room, with the good old rector. She was no better; still in doctors' hands and weak, but always happy with him, and he more than ever gentle and tender with her; for though he never would give place to despondency, and was naturally of a trusting, cheery spirit, he could not but remember his young wife, lost so early; and once or twice there was a look – an outline – a light – something, in little Lily's fair, girlish face, that, with a strange momentary agony, brought back the remembrance of her mother's stricken beauty, and plaintive smile. But then his darling's gay talk and pleasant ways would reassure him, and she smiled away the momentary shadow.

And he would tell her all sorts of wonders, old-world gaieties, long before she was born; and how finely the great Mr Handel played upon the harpsichord in the Music Hall, and how his talk was in German, Latin, French, English, Italian, and half-a-dozen languages besides, sentence about; and how he remembered his own dear mother's dress when she went to Lord Wharton's great ball at the castle – dear, oh! dear, how long ago that was! And then he would relate stories of banshees, and robberies, and ghosts, and hair-breadth escapes, and 'rapparees', and adventures in the wars of King James, which he heard told in his nonage by the old folk, long vanished, who remembered those troubles.

'And now, darling,' said little Lily, nestling close to him, with a smile, 'you *must* tell me all about that strange, handsome Mr Mervyn; who he is, and what his story.'

'Tut, tut! Little rogue – '

'Yes, indeed, you must, and you will; you've kept your little Lily waiting long enough for it, and she'll promise to tell nobody.'

'Handsome he is, and strange, no doubt – it was a strange fancy that funeral. Strange, indeed,' said the rector.

'What funeral, darling?'

'Why, yes, a funeral – the bringing his father's body to be laid here in the vault, in my church; it is their family vault. 'Twas a folly; but what folly will not young men do?'

And the good parson poked the fire a little impatiently.

'Mr Mervyn – *not* Mervyn – that was his mother's name; but – see, you must not mention it, Lily, if I tell you – *not* Mr Mervyn, I say, but my Lord Dunoran, the only son of that disgraced and blood-stained nobleman, who, lying in gaol, under sentence of death for a foul and cowardly murder, swallowed poison, and so closed his guilty life with a tremendous crime, in its nature inexpiable. There, that's all, and too much, darling.'

'And was it very long ago?'

'Why, 'twas before little Lily was born; and long before *that* I knew him – only just a little. He used the Tiled House for a hunting-lodge, and kept his dogs and horses there – a fine gentleman, but vicious, always, I fear, and a gamester; an overbearing man, with a dangerous cast of pride in his eye. You don't remember Lady Dunoran? – pooh, pooh, what am I thinking of? No, to be sure! You could not. 'Tis from her, chiefly, poor lady, he has his good looks. Her eyes were large, and very peculiar, like *his* – his, you know, are very fine. She, poor lady, did not live long after the public ruin of the family.'

'And has he been recognised here? The townspeople are so curious.'

'Why, dear child, not one of them ever saw him before. He's been lost sight of by all but a few, a very few friends. My Lord Castle-mallard, who was his guardian, of course, knows; and to me he disclosed himself by letter; and we keep his secret, though it matters little who knows it, for it seems to me he's as unhappy as aught could ever make him. The townspeople take him for his cousin, who squandered his fortune in Paris; and how is he the better of their mistake, and how were he the worse if they knew him for who he is? 'Tis an unhappy family – a curse haunts it. Young in years, old in vice, the wretched nobleman who lies in the vault, by the coffin of that old aunt, scarcely better than himself, whose guineas supplied his early profligacy – alas! he ruined his ill-fated, beautiful cousin, and she died heart-broken, and her little child, both there – in that melancholy and contaminated house.'

So he rambled on, and from one tale to another, till little Lily's early bed-hour came.

I don't know whether it was Doctor Walsingham's visit in the morning, and the chance of hearing something about it, that prompted the unquiet Tom Toole to roll his cloak about him, and buffet his way through storm and snow, to Devereux's lodgings. It was only a stone's-throw; but even that, on such a night, was no trifle.

However, up he went to Devereux's drawing-room, and found its handsome proprietor altogether in the dumps. The little doctor threw off his sleety cloak and hat in the lobby, and stood before the officer fresh and puffing, and a little flustered and dazzled after his romp with the wind.

Devereux got up and received him with a slight bow and no smile, and a 'Pray take a chair, Doctor Toole.'

'Well, this *is* a bright fit of the dismals,' said little Toole, nothing overawed. 'May I sit near the fire?'

'Upon it,' said Devereux, sadly.

'Thank'ee,' said Toole, clapping his feet on the fender, with a grin, and making himself comfortable. 'May I poke it?'

'Eat it – do as you please – anything – everything; play that fiddle,' [pointing to the ruin of Puddock's guitar, which the lieutenant had left on the table] 'or undress and go to bed, or get up and dance a minuet, or take that pistol, with all my heart, and shoot me through the head.'

'Thank'ee, again. A fine choice of amusements, I vow,' cried the jolly doctor.

'There, don't mind me, nor all I say, Toole. I'm, I suppose, in the vapours; but, truly, I'm glad to see you, and I thank you, indeed I do, heartily, for your obliging visit; 'tis very neighbourly. But, hang it, I'm weary of the time – the world is a dull place. I'm tired of this planet, and should not mind cutting my throat and trying a new star. Suppose we make the journey together, Toole; there is a brace of pistols over the chimney, and a fair wind for some of them.'

'Rather too much of a gale for my taste, thanking you again,' answered Toole with a cosy chuckle; 'but, if *you're* bent on the trip, and can't wait, why, at least let's have a glass together before parting.'

'With all my heart, what you will. Shall it be punch?'

'Punch be it. Come, hang saving; get us up a ha'porth of whiskey,' said little Toole, gaily.

'Hallo, Mrs Irons, Madam, will you do us the favour to make a bowl of punch as soon as may be?' cried Devereux, over the banister.

'Come, Toole,' said Devereux, 'I'm very dismal. Losses and crosses, and deuce knows what. Whistle or talk, what you please, I'll listen;

tell me anything: stories of horses, dogs, dice, snuff, women, cocks, parsons, wine – what you will. Come, how's Sturk? He's beaten poor Nutter, and won the race; though the stakes, after all, were scarce worth taking – and what's life without a guinea? – He's grown, I'm told, so confoundedly poor, "*quis pauper? Avarus.*" A worthy man was Sturk, and, in some respects, resembled the prophet, Shylock; but you know nothing of him – why the plague don't you read your Bible, Toole?'

'Well,' said Toole, candidly, 'I don't know the Old Testament as well as the New; but certainly, whoever he's like, he's held out wonderfully. 'Tis nine weeks since he met that accident, and there he's still, above ground; but that's all – just above ground, you see.'

'And how's Cluffe?'

'Pooh, Cluffe indeed! Nothing ever wrong with him but occasional over-eating. Sir, you'd a laughed today had you seen him. I gave him a bolus, twice the size of a gooseberry. "What's this?" said he. "A bolus," says I. "The devil," says he; "dia-bolus, then," says I – "hey?" said I, "well?" Ha! ha! And by Jove, Sir, it actually half stuck in his oesophagus, and I shoved it down like a bullet, with a probang; you'd a died a-laughing, yet 'twasn't a bit too big. Why, I tell you, upon my honour, Mrs Rebecca Chattesworth's black boy, only t'other day, swallowed a musket bullet twice the size, ha! ha! – he did – and I set him to rights in no time with a little powder.'

'Gunpowder?' said Devereux. 'And what of O'Flaherty? I'm told he was going to shoot poor Miles O'More.'

'Ha, ha! Hey? Well, I don't think either remembered in the morning what they quarrelled about,' replied Toole; 'so it went off in smoke, Sir.'

'Well, and how is Miles?'

'Why, ha, ha! He's back again, with a bill, as usual, and a horse to sell – a good one – the black one, don't you remember? He wants five and thirty guineas; 'tisn't worth two pounds ten. "Do you know anyone who wants him? I would not mind taking a bill, with a couple of good names upon it," says he. Upon my credit I believe he thought I'd buy him myself. "Well," says I, "I think I do know a fellow that would give you his value, and pay you cash besides," says I. 'Twas as good as a play to see his face. "Who is he?" says he, taking me close by the arm. "The knacker," says I. 'Twas a bite for Miles; hey? Ha, ha, ha!'

'And is it true old Tresham's going to join our club at last?'

'He! Hang him! He's like a brute beast, and never drinks but when he's dry, and then small beer. But, I forgot to tell you, by all that's lovely, they do say the charming Magnolia – a fine bouncing girl that – is all but betrothed to Lieutenant O'Flaherty.'

Devereux laughed, and thus encouraged, Toole went on, with a wink and a whisper.

'Why, the night of the ball, you know, he saw her home, and they say he kissed her – by Bacchus, on both sides of the face – at the door there, under the porch; and you know, if he had not a right, she'd a-knocked him down.'

'Psha! The girl's a Christian, and when she's smacked on one cheek she turns the other. And what says the major to it?'

'Why, as it happened, he opened the door precisely as the thing occurred; and he wished Lieutenant O'Flaherty good-night, and paid him a visit in the morning. And they say 'tis all satisfactory; and – by Jove! 'tis good punch.' And Mrs Irons entered with a china bowl on a tray.

Chapter Sixty-nine

Concerning a second hurricane that raged in Captain Devereux's drawing-room, and relating how Mrs Irons was attacked with a sort of choking in her bed

And the china bowl, with its silver ladle, and fine fragrance of lemon and old malt whiskey, and a social pair of glasses, were placed on the table by fair Mistress Irons; and Devereux filled his glass, and Toole did likewise; and the little doctor rattled on; and Devereux threw in his word, and finally sang a song. 'Twas a ballad, with little in the words; but the air was sweet and plaintive, and so was the singer's voice:

> A star so High,
> In my sad sky,
> I've early loved and late:
> A clear lone star,
> Serene and far,
> Doth rule my wayward fate.
>
> Tho' dark and chill
> The night be still,
> A light comes up for me:
> In eastern skies
> My star doth rise,
> And fortune dawns for me.
>
> And proud and bold,
> My way I hold;
> For o'er me high I see,
> In night's deep blue,
> My star shine true,
> And fortune beams on me.
>
> Now onward still,
> Thro' dark and chill,
> My lonely way must be;

In vain regret,
My star will set,
And fortune's dark for me.

And whether glad,
Or proud, or sad,
Or howsoe'er I be;
In dawn or noon,
Or setting soon,
My star, I'll follow thee.

And so there was a pause and a silence. In the silvery notes of the singer there was the ring of a prophecy; and Toole half read its meaning. And himself loving a song, and being soft over his music, he remained fixed for a few seconds, and then sighed, smiling, and dried his light blue eyes covertly; and he praised the song and singer briskly; and sighed again, with his fingers on the stem of his glass. And by this time Devereux had drawn the window-curtain, and was looking across the river, through the darkness, towards the Elms, perhaps for that solitary distant light – his star – now blurred and lost in the storm. Whatever his contemplations, it was plain, when he turned about, that the dark spirit was upon him again.

'Curse that punch,' said he, in language still more emphatic. 'You're like Mephistopheles in the play – you come in upon my quiet to draw me to my ruin. 'Twas the devil sent you here, to kill my soul, I believe; but you shan't. *Drink*, will you? – Ay – I'll give you a draught – a draught of *air* will cool you. Drink to your heart's content.'

And to Toole's consternation up went the window, and a hideous rush of eddying storm and snow whirled into the room. Out went the candles – the curtains flapped high in air, and lashed the ceiling – the door banged with a hideous crash – papers, and who knows what beside, went spinning, hurry-scurry round the room; and Toole's wig was very near taking wing from his head.

'Hey – hey – hey! Holloo!' cried the doctor, out of breath, and with his artificial ringlets frisking about his chops and eyes.

'Out, sorcerer – temptation, begone – avaunt, Mephistopheles – cauldron, away!' thundered the captain; and sure enough, from the open window, through the icy sleet, whirled the jovial bowl; and the jingle of the china was heard faint through the tempest.

Toole was swearing, in the whirlwind and darkness, like a trooper.

'Thank Heaven! 'tis gone,' continued Devereux; 'I'm safe – no thanks to you, though; and, hark ye, doctor, I'm best alone; leave me – leave me, pray – and pray forgive me.'

The doctor groped and stumbled out of the room, growling all the while, and the door slammed behind him with a crash like a cannon.

'The fellow's brain's disordered – *delirium tremens*, and jump out of that cursed window, I wouldn't wonder,' muttered the doctor, adjusting his wig on the lobby, and then calling rather mildly over the banisters, he brought up Mrs Irons with a candle, and found his cloak, hat, and cane; and with a mysterious look beckoned that matron to follow him, and in the hall, winking up towards the ceiling at the spot where Devereux might at the moment be presumed to be standing: 'I say, has he been feverish or queer, or – eh? – any way humoursome or out of the way?' And then – 'See now, you may as well have an eye after him, and if you remark anything strange, don't fail to let me know – d'ye see? And for the present you had better get him to shut his window and light his candles.'

And so the doctor, wrapped in his mantle, plunged into the hurricane and darkness; and was sensible, with a throb of angry regret, of a whiff of punch rising from the footpath, as he turned the corner of the steps.

An hour later, Devereux being alone, called to Mrs Irons, and receiving her with a courteous gravity, he said: 'Madam, will you be so good as to lend me your Bible?'

Devereux was prosecuting his reformation, which, as the reader sees, had set in rather tempestuously, but was now settling in serenity and calm.

Mrs Irons only said – 'My – ?' and then paused, doubting her ears.

'Your *Bible*, if you please, Madam.'

'Oh? – oh! my Bible? I – to be sure, captain, jewel,' and she peeped at his face, and loitered for a while at the door, for she had unpleasant misgivings about him, and did not know what to make of his request, so utterly without parallel. She'd have fiddled at the door some time longer, speculating about his sanity, but that Devereux turned full upon her with a proud stare, and rising, he made her a slight bow, and said: 'I *thank* you, Madam,' with a sharp courtesy, that said: 'avaunt, and quit my sight!' so sternly, though politely, that she vanished on the instant; and downstairs she marvelled with Juggy Byrne, 'what the puck the captain could want of a Bible! Upon my conscience it sounds well. It's what he's not right in his head, I'm afeared. A Bible!' – and an aërial voice seemed to say, 'a pistol', and another, 'a coffin' – 'An' I'm sure I wish that quare little Lieutenant Puddock id come up and keep him company. I dunno' what's come over him.'

And they tumbled about the rattletraps under the cupboard, and rummaged the drawers in search of the sacred volume. For though Juggy said there was no such thing, and never had been in her time, Mrs Irons put her down with asperity. It was not to be found, however, and the matron thought she remembered that old Mrs Legge's cook had borrowed it some time ago for a charm. So she explained the accident to Captain Devereux, who said, 'I thank you, Madam; 'tis no matter. I wish you a good-night, Madam;' and the door closed.

'No Bible!' said Devereux, 'the old witch!'

Mrs Irons, as you remember, never spared her rhetoric, which was fierce, shrill, and fluent, when the exercise of that gift was called for. The parish clerk bore it with a cynical and taciturn patience, not, perhaps, so common as it should be in his sex; and this night, when she awoke, and her eyes rested on the form of her husband at her bedside, with a candle lighted, and buckling on his shoes, with his foot on the chair, she sat up straight in her bed, wide awake in an instant, for it was wonderful how the sight of that meek man roused the wife in her bosom, especially after an absence, and she had not seen him since four o'clock that evening; so you may suppose his reception was warm, and her expressions every way worthy of her feelings.

Meek Irons finished buckling that shoe, and then lifted the other to the edge of the chair, and proceeded to do the like for it, serenely, after his wont, and seeming to hear nothing. So Mrs Irons proceeded, as was her custom when that patient person refused to be roused – she grasped his collar near his cheek, meaning to shake him into attention.

But instantly, as the operation commenced, the clerk griped her with his long, horny fingers by the throat, with a snap so sure and energetic that not a cry, not a gasp even, or a wheeze, could escape through 'the trachea', as medical men have it; and her face and forehead purpled up, and her eyes goggled and glared in her head; and her husband looked so insanely wicked, that, as the pale picture darkened before her, and she heard curse after curse, and one foul name after another hiss off his tongue, like water off a hot iron, in her singing ears, she gave herself up for lost. He closed this exercise by chucking her head viciously against the board of the bed half-a-dozen times, and leaving her thereafter a good deal more confused even than on the eventful evening when he had first declared his love.

So soon as she came a little to herself, and saw him coolly button-ing his leggings at the bedside, his buckles being adjusted by this time, her fear subsided, or rather her just indignation rose above it, and drowned it; and she was on the point of breaking out afresh, only in a way commensurate with her wrongs, and proportionately more formidable; when, on the first symptom of attack, he clutched her, if possible, tighter, the gaping, goggling, purpling, the darkening of vision and humming in ears, all recommenced; likewise the knocking of her head with improved good-will, and, spite of her struggles and scratching, the bewildered lady, unused to even a show of insurrec-tion, underwent the same horrid series of sensations at the hands of her rebellious lord.

When they had both had enough of it, Mr Irons went on with his buttoning, and his lady gradually came to. This time, however, she was effectually frightened – too much so even to resort to hysterics, for she was not quite sure that when he had buttoned the last button of his left legging he might not resume operations, and terminate their conjugal relations.

Therefore, being all of a tremble, with her hands clasped, and too much terrified to cry, she besought Irons, whose bodily strength surprised her, for her life, and his pale, malign glance, askew over his shoulder, held her with a sort of a spell that was quite new to her – in fact, she had never respected Irons so before.

When he had adjusted his leggings, he stood lithe and erect at the bedside, and with his fist at her face, delivered a short charge, the point of which was, that unless she lay like a mouse till morning he'd have her life, though he hanged for it. And with that he drew the curtain, and was hidden from her sight for some time.

Chapter Seventy

*In which an unexpected visitor is seen, in the cedar-parlour of
the Tiled House, and the story of Mr Beauclerc and the
Flower de Luce begins to be unfolded*

It was an awful night, indeed, on which all this occurred, and that
apparition had shown itself up at the Mills. And truly it would seem
the devil had business on his hands, for in the cedar-parlour of the
Tiled House another unexpected manifestation occurred just about
the same hour.

What gentleman is there of broken fortunes, undefined rights, and
in search of evidence, without a legal adviser of some sort? Mr
Mervyn, of course, had his, and paid for the luxury according to
custom. And every now and then off went a despatch from the Tiled
House to the oracular London attorney; sometimes it was a budget
of evidence, and sometimes only a string of queries. Tonight, to the
awful diapason of the storm – he was penning one of these – the fruit
of a tedious study of many papers and letters, tied up in bundles by
his desk, all of them redolent of ominous or fearful associations.

I don't know why it is the hours fly with such a strange celerity in
the monotony and solitude of such nightwork. But Mervyn was
surprised, as many a one similarly occupied has been, on looking at
his watch, to find that it was now long past midnight; so he threw
himself back in his chair with a sigh, and thought how vainly his life
was speeding away, and heard, with a sort of wonder, how mad was
the roar of the storm without, while he had quietly penned his long
rescript undisturbed.

The wild bursts of supernatural fury and agony which swell and
mingle in a hurricane, I dare say, led his imagination a strange aërial
journey through the dark. Now it was the baying of hell-hounds, and
the long shriek of the spirit that flies before them. Anon it was the
bellowing thunder of an ocean, and the myriad voices of shipwreck.
And the old house quivering from base to cornice under the strain;
and then there would come a pause, like a gasp, and the tempest once

more rolled up, and the same mad hubbub shook and clamoured at the windows.

So he let his Pegasus spread his pinions on the blast, and mingled with the wild rout that peopled the darkness; or, in plainer words, he abandoned his fancy to the haunted associations of the hour, the storm, and the house, with a not unpleasant horror. In one of these momentary lulls of the wind, there came a sharp, distinct knocking on the window-pane. He remembered with a thrill the old story of the supernatural hand which had troubled that house, and began its pranks at this very window.

Ay, ay, 'twas the impatient rapping of a knuckle on the glass quite indisputably.

It is all very well weaving the sort of dream or poem with which Mervyn was half amusing and half awing himself, but the sensation is quite different when a questionable sound or sight comes uninvited to take the matter out of the province of our fancy and the control of our will. Mervyn found himself on his legs, and listening in a less comfortable sort of horror, with his gaze fixed in the direction of that small sharp knocking. But the storm was up again, and drowning every other sound in its fury.

If Mr Mervyn had been sufficiently frightened, he would have forthwith made good his retreat to his bedroom, or, if he had not been frightened at all, he would have kept his seat, and allowed his fancies to return to their old channel. But, in fact, he took a light in his hand, and opened a bit of the window-shutter. The snow, however, was spread over the panes in a white, sliding curtain, that returned the light of his candle, and hid all without. 'Twas idle trying to peer through it, but as he did, the palm of a hand was suddenly applied to the glass on the outside, and began briskly to rub off the snow, as if to open a peep-hole for distinct inspection.

It was to be more this time than the apparition of a hand – a human face was immediately presented close to the glass – not that of Nutter either – no – it was the face of Irons – pale, with glittering eyes and blue chin, and wet hair quivering against the glass in the storm.

He nodded wildly to Mervyn, brushing away the snow, beckoning towards the back-door, as he supported himself on one knee on the window-stone, and, with his lips close to the glass, cried, 'let me in'; but, in the uproar of the storm, it was by his gestures, imperfectly as they were seen, rather than by his words, that Mervyn comprehended his meaning.

Down went Mr Mervyn, without a moment's hesitation, leaving the candle standing on the passage table, drew the bolts, opened the door, and in rushed Irons, in a furious gust, his cloak whirling about his head amidst a bitter eddying of snow, and a distant clapping of doors throughout the house.

The door secured again, Mr Irons stood in his beflaked and dripping mantle, storm-tossed, dishevelled, and alone once again in the shelter of the Tiled House, to explain the motive of his visit.

'Irons! I could hardly believe it,' and Mervyn made a pause, and then, filled with the one idea, he vehemently demanded, 'In Heaven's name, have you come to tell me all you know?'

'Well, maybe – no,' answered the clerk: 'I don't know; I'll tell you something. I'm going, you see, and I came here on my way; and I'll tell you more than last time, but not all – not all yet.'

'Going? And where? – what are your plans?'

'Plans? – I've *no* plans. Where am I going? – Nowhere – anywhere. I'm going away, that's all.'

'You're leaving this place – eh, to return no more?'

'I'm leaving it tonight; I've the doctor's leave, Parson Walsingham. What d'ye look at, Sir? D'ye think it's what I murdered anyone? Not but if I stayed here I might though,' and Mr Irons laughed a frightened, half-maniacal sort of laugh. 'I'm going for a bit, a fortnight or so, maybe, till things get quiet' – [lead us not into temptation!] – 'to Mullingar, or anywhere; only I won't stay longer at hell's door, within stretch of that devil's long arm.'

'Come to the parlour,' said Mervyn, perceiving that Irons was chilled and shivering.

There, with the door and window-shutters closed, a pair of candles on the table, and a couple of faggots of that pleasant bog-wood, which blazes so readily and fragrantly on the hearth, Irons shook off his cloak, and stood, lank and grim, and, as it seemed to Mervyn, horribly scared, but well in view, and trying, sullenly, to collect his thoughts.

'I'm going away, I tell you, for a little while; but I'm come to see you, Sir, to think what I may tell you now, and above all, to warn you again' saying to any living soul one word of what passed between us when I last was here; you've kept your word honourable as yet; if you break it I'll not return,' and he clenched it with an oath, 'I *daren't* return.'

'I'll tell you the way it happened,' he resumed. ''Tis a good while now, ay twenty-two years; your noble father's dead these twenty-two years and upwards. 'Twas a bad murdher, Sir: they wor both bad murdhers. I look on it, *he's* a murdhered man.'

'He – who?' demanded the young man.

'Your father, Sir.'

'My father murdered?' said Mervyn.

'Well, I see no great differ; I see none at all. I'll tell you how it was.'

And he looked over his shoulder again, and into the corners of the room, and then Mr Irons began: 'I believe, Sir, there's no devil like a vicious young man, with a hard heart and cool courage, in want of money. Of all the men I ever met with, or heard tell of, Charles Archer was the most dreadful. I used sometimes to think he *was* the devil. It wasn't long-headed or cunning he was, but he knew your thoughts before you half knew them yourself. He knew what *everyone* was thinking of. He made up his mind at a glance, and struck like a thunderbolt. As for pity or fear, he did not know what they were, and his cunning was so deep and sure there was no catching him.

'He came down to the Pied Horse Inn, where I was a drawer, at Newmarket, twice.'

Mervyn looked in his face, quickly, with a ghastly kind of a start.

'Ay, Sir, av coorse you know it; you read the trial; av coorse you did. Well, he came down there twice. 'Twas a good old house, Sir, lots of room, and a well-accustomed inn. An' I think there was but two bad men among all the servants of the house – myself and Glascock. He was an under-hostler, and a bad boy. He chose us two out of the whole lot, with a look. He never made a mistake. He knew us some way like a crow knows carrion, and he used us cleverly.'

And Irons cursed him.

'He's a hard master, like his own,' said Irons; 'his wages come to nothing, and his services is hell itself. He could sing, and talk, and drink, and keep things stirring, and the gentlemen liked him; and he was, 'twas said, a wonderful fine player at whist, and piquet, and ombre, and all sorts of card-playing. So you see he could afford to play fair. The first time he came down, he fought three duels about a tipsy quarrel over a pool of Pope Joan. There was no slur on his credit, though; 'twas just a bit of temper. He wounded all three; two but trifling; but one of them – Chapley, or Capley, I think, was his name – through the lungs, and he died, I heard, abroad. I saw him killed – 'twasn't the last; it was done while you'd count ten. Mr Archer came up with a sort of a sneer, pale and angry, and 'twas a clash of the small swords – one, two, three, and a spring like a tiger – and all over. He was frightful strong; ten times as strong as he looked – all a deception.'

'Well, Sir, there was a Jew came down, offering wagers, not, you see, to gentlemen, Sir, but to poor fellows. And Mr Archer put me and Glascock up to bite him, as he said; and he told us to back Strawberry, and we did. We had that opinion of his judgment and his knowledge – you see, we thought he had ways of finding out these things – that we had no doubt of winning, so we made a wager of twelve pounds. But we had no money – not a crown between us – and we must stake gold with the host of the Plume of Feathers; and the long and the short of it was, I never could tell how he put it into our heads, to pledge some of the silver spoons and a gold chain of the master's, intending to take them out when we won the money. Well, Strawberry lost, and we were left in the lurch. So we told Mr Archer how it was; for he was an off-handed man when he had anything in view, and he told us, as we thought, he'd help us if we lost. "Help you," says he, with a sort of laugh he had, "I want help myself; I haven't a guinea, and I'm afraid you'll be hanged: and then," says he, "stay a bit, and I'll find a way."

'I think he *was* in a bad plight just then himself; he was awful expensive with horses and – and – other things; and I think there was a writ, or maybe more, out against him, from other places, and he wanted a lump of money in his hand to levant with, and go abroad. Well, listen, and don't be starting, or making a row, Sir,' and a sulky, lowering, hang-dog shadow, came over Irons. 'Your father, Lord Dunoran, played cards; his partner was Mr Charles Archer. Whist it was – with a gentleman of the name of Beauclerc, and I forget the other – he wore a chocolate suit, and a black wig. 'Twas I carried them their wine. Well, Mr Beauclerc won, and Mr Archer stopped playing, for he had lost enough; and the gentleman in the chocolate – what was his name? – Edwards, I think – ay, 'twas – *yes*, Edwards, it was – was tired, and turned himself about to the fire, and took a pipe of tobacco; and my lord, your father, played piquet with Mr Beauclerc; and he lost a power of money to him, Sir; and, by bad luck, he paid a great part of it, as they played, in rouleaus of gold, for he had won at the dice downstairs. Well, Mr Beauclerc was a little hearty, and he grew tired, and was for going to bed. But my lord was angry, and being disguised with liquor too, he would not let him go till they played more; and play they did, and the luck still went the same way; and my lord grew fierce over it, and cursed and drank, and that did not mend his luck you may be sure; and at last Mr

Beauclerc swears he'd play no more; and both kept talking together, and neither heard well what t'other said; but there was some talk about settling the dispute in the morning.

'Well, Sir, in goes Mr Beauclerc, staggering – his room was the Flower de Luce – and down he throws himself, clothes an' all, on his bed; and then my lord turned on Mr *Edwards*, I'm sure that was his name, and persuades him to play at piquet; and to it they went.

'As I was coming in with more wine, I meets Mr Archer coming out, "Give them their wine," says he, in a whisper, "and follow me." An' so I did. "You know something of Glascock, and have a fast hold of him," says he, "and tell him quietly to bring up Mr Beauclerc's boots, and come back along with him; and bring me a small glass of rum." And back he goes into the room where the two were stuck in their cards, and talking and thinking of nothing else.'

Chapter Seventy-one

In which Mr Irons's narrative reaches Merton Moor

'Well, I did as he bid me, and set the glass of rum before him, and in place of drinking it, he follows me out. "I told you," says he, "I'd find a way, and I'm going to give you fifty guineas apiece. Stand you at the stair-head," says he to Glascock, "and listen; and if you hear anyone coming, step into Mr Beauclerc's room with his boots, do you see, for I'm going to rob him." I thought I'd a fainted, and Glascock, that was a tougher lad than me, was staggered; but Mr Archer had a way of taking you by surprise, and getting you into a business before you knew where you were going. "I see, Sir," says Glascock. "And come you in, and I'll do it," says Mr Archer, and in we went, and Mr Beauclerc was fast asleep.

'I don't like talking about it,' said Irons, suddenly and savagely, and he got up and walked, with a sort of a shrug of the shoulders, to and fro half-a-dozen times, like a man who has a chill, and tries to make his blood circulate.

Mervyn commanded himself, for he knew the man would return to his tale, and probably all the sooner for being left to work off his transient horror how he might.

'Well, he did rob him, and I often thought how cunningly, for he took no more than about half his gold, well knowing, I'm now sure, neither he nor my lord, your father, kept any count; and there was a bundle of notes in his pocket-book, which Mr Archer was thinning swiftly, when all of a sudden, like a ghost rising, up sits Mr Beauclerc, an unlucky rising it was for him, and taking him by the collar – he was a powerful strong man – "You've robbed me, Archer," says he. I was behind Mr Archer, and I could not see what happened, but Mr Beauclerc made a sort of a start and a kick out with his foot, and seemed taken with a tremble all over, for while you count three, and he fell back in the bed with his eyes open, and Mr Archer drew a thin long dagger out of the dead man's breast, for dead he was.

'"What are you afraid of, you — fool?" says he, shaking me up; "I know what I'm about; I'll carry you through; your life's in my hands, mine in yours, only be cool." He was that himself, if ever man was, and quick as light he closed the dead man's eyes, saying, "in for a penny in for a pound," and he threw a bit of the coverlet over his breast, and his mouth and chin, just as a man might draw it rolling round in the bed, for I suppose he thought it best to hide the mouth that was open, and told its tale too plainly, and out he was on the lobby the next instant. "Don't tell Glascock what's happened, 'twill make him look queer; let him put in the boots, and if he's asked, say Mr Beauclerc made a turn in the bed, and a grumbling, like a man turning over in his sleep, while he was doing so, d'ye see, and divide this, 'twill settle your little trouble, you know." 'Twas a little paper roll of a hundred guineas. An' that's the way Mr Beauclerc came by his death.'

This to Mervyn was the sort of shock that might have killed an older man. The dreadful calamity that had stigmatised and beggared his family – the horror and shame of which he well remembered, when first revealed to him, had held him trembling and tongue-tied for more than an hour before tears came to his relief, and which had ever since blackened his sky, with a monotony of storm and thunder, was in a moment shown to be a chimera. No wonder that he was for a while silent, stunned, and bewildered. At last he was able – pale and cold – to lift up his clasped hands, his eyes, and his heart, in awful gratitude, to the Author of Mercy, the Revealer of Secrets, the Lord of Life and Truth.

'And where is this Charles Archer – is he dead or living?' urged Mervyn with an awful adjuration.

'Ay, where to catch him, and how – Dead? Well, he's dead to some, you see, and living to others; and living or dead, I'll put you on his track some fine day, if you're true to me; but not yet awhile, and if you turn a stag, or name my name to living soul (and here Mr Irons swore an oath such as I hope parish clerks don't often swear, and which would have opened good Dr Walsingham's eyes with wonder and horror), you'll never hear word more from me, and I think, Sir, you'll lose your life beside.'

'Your threats of violence are lost on me, I can take care of myself,' said Mervyn, haughtily.

The clerk smiled a strange sort of smile.

'But I've already pledged my sacred honour not to mention your name or betray your secret.'

'Well, just have patience, and maybe I'll not keep you long; but 'tis no trifle for a man to make up his mind to what's before *me*, maybe.'

After a pause, Irons resumed – 'Well, Sir, you see, Mr Archer sat down by the fire and smoked a pipe, and was as easy and pleased, you'd say, to look on him, as a man need be; and he called for cards when my lord wanted them, and whatever else he needed, making himself busy and bustling – as I afterwards thought to make them both remember well that he was in the room with them.

'In and out of the chamber I went with one thing or another, and every time I passed Mr Beauclerc's room I grew more and more frightened; and, truth to say, I was a scared man, and I don't know how I got through my business; every minute expecting to hear the outcry from the dead man's room.

'Mr Edwards had an appointment, he said – nothing good, you may be sure – they were a rake-helly set – saving your presence. Neither he nor my lord had lost, I believe, anything to signify to one another; and my lord, your father, made no difficulty about his going away, but began to call again for Mr Beauclerc, and to curse him – as a half-drunk man will, making a power of noise; and, "Where's he gone to?" and, "Where's his room?" and, " — him, he shall play, or fight me." You see, Sir, he had lost right and left that time, and was an angry man, and the liquor made him half-mad; and I don't think he knew rightly what he was doing. And out on the lobby with him swearing he should give him his revenge, or he'd know the reason why.

'"Where's Mr Beauclerc's room?" he shouts to me, as if he'd strike me; I did not care a rush about that, but I was afraid to say – it stuck in my throat like – and I stared at Mr Archer; and he calls to the chamber-maid, that was going upstairs, "Where does Mr Beauclerc lie?" and she, knowing him, says at once, "The Flower de Luce", and pointed to the room; and with that, my lord staggered up to the door, with his drawn sword in hand, bawling on him to come out, and fumbling with the pin; he could not open it; so he knocked it open with a kick, and in with him, and Mr Archer at his elbow, soothing him like; and I, I don't know how – behind him.

'By this time he had worked himself into a mad passion, and says he, "Curse your foxing – if you won't play like a man, you may die like a dog." I think 'twas them words ruined him; the chamber-maid heard them outside; and he struck Mr Beauclerc half-a-dozen blows with the side of the small-sword across the body, here and there, quite unsteady; and "Hold, my lord, you've hurt him," cries Mr

Archer, as loud as he could cry. "Put up your sword for Heaven's sake," and he makes a sort of scuffle with my lord, in a friendly way, to disarm him, and push him away, and "Throw down the coverlet and see where he's wounded," says he to me; and so I did, and there was a great pool of blood – we knew all about that – and my lord looked shocked when he seen it. "I did not mean that," says my lord; "but," says he, with a sulky curse, "he's well served."

'I don't know whether Glascock was in the room or not all this while, maybe he was; at any rate, he swore to it afterwards; but you've read the trial, I warrant. The room was soon full of people. The dead man was still warm – 'twas well for us. So they raised him up; and one was for trying one thing, and another; and my lord was sitting stupid-like all this time by the wall; and up he gets, and says he, "I hope he's not dead, but if he be, upon my honour, 'tis an accident – no more. I call Heaven to witness, and the persons who are now present; and pledge my sacred honour, as a peer, I meant no more than a blow or two."

"You hear, gentlemen, what my lord says, he meant only a blow or two, and not to take his life," cries Mr Archer.

'So my lord repeats it again, cursing and swearing, like St Peter in the judgment hall.

'So, as nobody was meddling with my lord, out he goes, intending, I suppose, to get away altogether, if he could. But Mr Underwood missed him, and he says, "Gentlemen, where's my Lord Dunoran? We must not suffer him to depart;" and he followed him – two or three others going along with him, and they met him with his hat and cloak on, in the lobby, and he says, stepping between him and the stairs, "My lord, you must not go, until we see how this matter ends."

''Twill end well enough," says he, and without more ado he walks back again.

'So you know the rest – how that business ended, at least for him.'

'And you are that very Zekiel Irons who was a witness on the trial?' said Mervyn, with a peculiar look of fear and loathing fixed on him.

'The same,' said Irons, doggedly; and after a pause, 'but I swore to very little; and all I said was true – though it wasn't the whole truth. Look to the trial, Sir, and you'll see 'twas Mr Archer and Glascock that swore home against my lord – not I. And I don't think myself, Glascock was in the room at all when it happened – so I don't.'

'And where is that wretch, Glascock, and that double murderer Archer; where is he?'

'Well, Glascock's making clay.'

'What do you mean?'

'Under ground, this many a day. Listen: Mr Archer went up to London, and he was staying at the Hummums, and Glascock agreed with me to leave the Pied Horse. We were both uneasy, and planned to go up to London together; and what does he do – nothing less would serve him – but he writes a sort of letter, asking money of Mr Archer under a threat. This, you know, was after the trial. Well, there came no answer; but after a while – all on a sudden – Mr Archer arrives himself at the Pied Horse; I did not know then that Glascock had writ to him – for he meant to keep whatever he might get to himself. "So," says Mr Archer to me, meeting me by the pump in the stable-yard, "that was a clever letter you and Glascock wrote to me in town."

'So I told him 'twas the first I heard of it.

'"Why," says he, "do you mean to tell me you don't want money?"

'I don't know why it was, but a sort of a turn came over me and I said "No".

'"Well," says he, "I'm going to sell a horse, and I expect to be paid tomorrow; you and Glascock must wait for me outside" – I think the name of the village was Merton – I'm not sure, for I never seen it before or since – "and I'll give you some money then."

'"I'll have none," says I.

'"What, no money?" says he. "Come, come."

'"I tell you, Sir, I'll have none," says I. Something, you see, came over me, and I was more determined than ever. I was always afeard of him, but I feared him like Beelzebub now. "I've had enough of your money, Sir; and I tell you what, Mr Archer, I think 'tis best to end our dealings, and I'd rather, if you please, Sir, never trouble you more."

'"You're a queer dog," says he, with his eye fast on me, and musing for a while – as if he could see into my brain, and was diverted by what he found there; – "you're a queer dog, Irons. Glascock knows the world better, you see; and as you and he are going up to London together, and I must give the poor devil a lift, I'll meet you at the other side of Merton, beyond the quarry – you know the moor – on Friday evening, after dark – say seven o'clock – we must be quiet, you know, or people will be talking."

'Well, Sir, we met him, sure enough, at the time and place.'

Chapter Seventy-two
In which the apparition of Mr Irons is swallowed in darkness

''Twas a darkish night – very little moon – and he made us turn off the road, into the moor – black and ugly it looked, stretching away four or five miles, all heath and black peat, stretches of little broken hillocks, and a pool or tarn every now and again. An' he kept looking back towards the road, and not a word out of him. Well, I did not like meeting him at all if I could help it, but I was in dread of him; and I thought he might suppose I was plotting mischief if I refused. So I made up my mind to do as he bid me for the nonce, and then have done with him.

'By this time we were in or about a mile from the road, and we got over a low rising ground, and back nor forward, nor no way could we see anything but the moor; and I stopped all of a sudden, and says I, "We're far enough, I'll go no further."

'"Good," says Mr Archer; "but let's go yonder, where the stones are – we can sit as we talk – for I'm tired."

'There was half-a-dozen white stones there by the side of one of these black tarns. We none of us talked much on that walk over the moor. We had enough to think of, each of us, I dare say.

'"This will do," says Mr Archer, stopping beside the pool; but he did not sit, though the stones were there. "Now, Glascock, here I am, with the price of my horse in my pocket; what do you want?"

'Well, when it came to the point so sudden, Glascock looked a bit shy, and hung his head, and rowled his shoulders, and shuffled his feet a bit, thinking what he'd say.

'"Hang it, man; what are you afraid of? We're friends," says Mr Archer, cheerfully.

'"Surely, Sir," says Glascock, "I did not mean aught else."

'And with that Mr Archer laughed, and says he "Come – you beat about the bush – let's hear your mind."

'"Well, Sir, 'tis in my letter," says he.

' "Ah, Glascock," says he, "that's a threatening letter. I did not think you'd serve me so. Well, needs must when the devil drives." And he laughed again, and shrugs up his shoulders, and says he, putting his hand in his pocket, "there's sixty pounds left; 'tis all I have; come, be modest – what do you say?"

' "You got a lot of gold off Mr Beauclerc," says Glascock.

' "Not a doit more than I wanted," says he, laughing again. "And who, pray, had a better right – did not I murder him?"

'His talk and his laughing frightened me more and more.

' "Well, I stood to you then, Sir; didn't I?" says Glascock.

' "Heart of oak, Sir – true as steel; and now, how much do you want? Remember, 'tis all I have – and I out at elbows; and here's my friend Irons, too – eh?"

' "I want nothing, and I'll take nothing," says I; "not a shilling – not a halfpenny." You see there was something told me no good would come of it, and I was frightened besides.

' "What! You won't go in for a share, Irons?" says he.

' "No; 'tis your money, Sir – I've no right to a sixpence – and I won't have it," says I; "and there's an end."

' "Well, Glascock, what say you? – you hear Irons."

' "Let Irons speak for himself – he's nothing to me. You should have considered me when all that money was took from Mr Beauclerc – one done as much as another – and if 'twas no more than holding my tongue, still 'tis worth a deal to you."

' "I don't deny – a deal – everything. Come – there's sixty pounds here – but, mark, 'tis all I have – how much?"

' "I'll have thirty, and I'll take no less," says Glascock, surly enough.

' "Thirty! 'Tis a good deal – but all considered – perhaps not too much," says Mr Archer.

'And with that he took his right hand from his breeches' pocket, and shot him through the heart with a pistol.

'Neither word, nor stir, nor groan, did Glascock make; but with a sort of a jerk, flat on his back he fell, with his head on the verge of the tarn.

'I believe I said something – I don't know – I was almost as dead as himself – for I did not think anything *that* bad was near at all.

' "Come, Irons – what ails you – steady, Sir – lend me a hand, and you'll take no harm."

'He had the pistol he discharged in his left hand by this time, and a loaded one in his right.

' " 'Tis his own act, Irons. *I* did not want it; but I'll protect myself, and won't hold my life on ransom, at the hands of a Jew or a Judas," said he, smiling through his black hair, as white as a tombstone.

'"I am neither," says I.

'"I know it," says he; "and so you're *here*, and he *there*."

'"Well, 'tis over now, I suppose," says I. I was thinking of making off.

'"Don't go yet," says he, like a man asking a favour; but he lifted the pistol an inch or two, with a jerk of his wrist, "you must help me to hide away this dead fool."

'Well, Sir, we had three or four hours cold work of it – we tied stones in his clothes, and sunk him close under the bank, and walled him over with more. 'Twas no light job, I can tell you the water was near four feet deep, though 'twas a dry season; and then we slipped out a handsome slice of the bank over him; and, making him all smooth, we left him to take his chance; and I never heard any talk of a body being found there; and I suppose he's now where we left him.'

And Irons groaned.

'So we returned silent and tired enough, and I in mortal fear of him. But he designed me no hurt. There's luckily some risk in making away with a fellow, and 'tisn't done by any but a fool without good cause; and when we got on the road again, I took the London road, and he turned his back on me, and I don't know where he went; but no doubt his plans were well shaped.

''Twas an ugly walk for me, all alone, over that heath, I can tell you. 'Twas mortal dark; and there was places on the road where my footsteps echoed back, and I could not tell but 'twas Mr Archer following me, having changed his mind, maybe, or something as bad, if that could be; and many's the time I turned short round, expecting to see him, or may be that other lad, behind, for you see I got a start like when he shot Glascock; and there was a trembling over me for a long time after.

'Now, you see, Glascock's dead, and can't tell tales no more nor Mr Beauclerc, and Dr Sturk's a dead man too, you may say; and I think he knew – that is – brought to mind somewhat. He lay, you see, on the night Mr Beauclerc lost his life, in a sort of a dressing-room, off his chamber, and the door was open; but he was bad with a fall he had, and his arm in splints, and he under laudanum – in a trance like – and on the inquest he could tell nothing; but I think he remembered something more or less concerning it after.' And Mr Irons took a turn, and came back very close to Mervyn, and said very gently, 'and I think Charles Archer murdered him.'

'Then Charles Archer *has* been in Dublin, perhaps in Chapelizod, within the last few months,' exclaimed Mervyn, in a sort of agony.

'I didn't say so,' answered Irons. 'I've told you the truth – 'tis the truth – but there's no catching a ghost – and who'd believe my story? And them things is so long ago. And suppose I make a clean breast of it, and that I could bring you face to face with him, the world would not believe my tale, and I'd then be a lost man, one way or another – no-one, mayhap, could tell how – I'd lose my life before a year, and all the world could not save me.'

'Perhaps – perhaps Charles Nutter's the man; and Mr Dangerfield knows something of him,' cried Mervyn.

Irons made no answer, but sat quite silent for some seconds, by the fire, the living image of apathy.

'If you name me, or blab one word I told you, I hold my peace for ever,' said he, slowly, with a quiet oath, but very pale, and how blue his chin looked – how grim his smile, with his face so shiny, and his eyelids closed. You're to suppose, Sir, 'tis possible Mr Dangerfield has a guess at him. Well, he's a clever man, and knows how to put this and that together; and has been kind to Dr Sturk and his family. He's a good man, you know; and he's a long-headed gentleman, they say; and if he takes a thing in hand, he'll be as like as another to bring it about. But sink or swim my mind's made up. Charles Archer, wherever he is, will not like my going – he'll sniff danger in the wind, Sir. I could not stay – he'd have had me – you see, body and soul. 'Twas time for me to go – and go or stay, I see nothing but bad before me. 'Twas an evil day I ever saw his face; and 'twould be better for me to have a cast for my life at any rate, and that I'm nigh-hand resolved on; only you see my heart misgives me – and that's how it is. I can't quite make up my mind.'

For a little while Mervyn stood in an agony of irresolution. I'm sure I cannot understand all he felt, having never been, thank Heaven! in a like situation. I only know how much depended on it, and I don't wonder that for some seconds he thought of arresting that lank, pale, sinister figure by the fire, and denouncing him as, by his own confession, an accessory to the murder of Beauclerc. The thought that he would slip through his fingers, and the clue to vindication, fortune, and happiness, be for ever lost, was altogether so dreadful that we must excuse his forgetting for a moment his promise, and dismissing patience, and even policy, from his thoughts.

But 'twas a transitory temptation only, and common sense seconded honour. For he was persuaded that whatever likelihood there was of leading Irons to the critical point, there was none of driving him thither; and that Irons, once restive and impracticable, all his hopes would fall to the ground.

'I am going,' said Irons, with quiet abruptness; 'and right glad the storm's up still,' he added, in a haggard rumination, and with a strange smile of suffering. 'In dark an' storm – curse him! – I see his face everywhere. I don't know how he's got this hold over me,' and he cursed him again and groaned dismally. 'A night like this is my chance – and so here goes.'

'Remember, for Heaven's sake, remember,' said Mervyn, with agonised urgency, as he followed him with a light along the passage to the back-door.

Irons made no answer; and walking straight on, without turning his head, only lifted his hand with a movement backward, like a man who silently warns another from danger.

So Irons went forth into the night and the roaring storm, dark and alone, like an evil spirit into desert places; and Mervyn barred the door after him, and returned to the cedar parlour, and remained there alone and long in profound and not unnatural agitation.

Chapter Seventy-three

Concerning a certain gentleman, with a black patch over his eye, who made some visits with a lady, in Chapelizod and its neighbourhood

In the morning, though the wind had somewhat gone down, 'twas still dismal and wild enough; and to the consternation of poor Mrs Macnamara, as she sat alone in her window after breakfast, Miss Mag and the major being both abroad, a hackney coach drew up at the door, which stood open. The maid was on the step, cheapening fish with a virulent lady who had a sieve-full to dispose of.

A gentleman, with a large, unwholesome face, and a patch over one eye, popped his unpleasant countenance, black wig, and three-cocked hat, out of the window, and called to the coachman to let him out.

Forth he came, somewhat slovenly, his coat not over-well brushed, having in his hand a small trunk, covered with gilt crimson leather, very dingy, and somewhat ceremoniously assisted a lady to alight. This dame, as she stepped with a long leg, in a black silk stocking, to the ground, swept the front windows of the house from under her velvet hood with a sharp and evil glance; and in fact she was Mistress Mary Matchwell.

As she beheld her, poor Mrs Mack's heart fluttered up to her mouth, and then dropped with a dreadful plump, into the pit of her stomach. The dingy, dismal gentleman, swinging the red trunk in his hand, swaggered lazily back and forward, to stretch his legs over the pavement, and air his large cadaverous countenance, and sniff the village breezes.

Mistress Matchwell in the meantime, exchanging a passing word with the servant, who darkened and drew back as if a ghost had crossed her, gathered her rustling silks about her, and with a few long steps noiselessly mounted the narrow stairs, and stood, sallow and terrible in her sables, before the poor gentlewoman.

With two efforts Mrs Mack got up and made a little, and then a great courtesy, and then a little one again, and tried to speak, and felt very near fainting.

'See,' says Mary Matchwell, 'I must have twenty pounds – but don't take on. You must make an effort, my dear – 'tis the last. Come, don't be cast down. I'll pay you when I come to my property, in three weeks' time; but law expenses must be paid, and the money I must have.'

Hereupon Mrs Mack clasped her hands together in an agony, and 'set up the pipes'.

M. M. was like to lose patience, and when she did she looked most feloniously, and in a way that made poor soft Mrs Mack quiver.

' 'Tis but twenty pounds, woman,' she said, sternly. 'Hub-bub-bub-boo-hoo-hoo,' blubbered the fat and miserable Mrs Macnamara. 'It will be all about – I may as well tell it myself. I'm ruined! My Venetian lace – my watch – the brocade not made up. It won't do. I must tell my brother; I'd rather go out for a charwoman and starve myself to a skeleton, than try to borrow more money.'

Mrs Matchwell advanced her face towards the widow's tearful countenance, and held her in the spell of her dreadful gaze as a cat does a bird.

'Why, curse you, woman, do you think 'tis to rob you I mean? – 'tisn't a present even – only a loan. Stop that blubbering, you great old mouth! Or I'll have you posted all over the town in five minutes. A *loan*, Madam; and you need not pay it for three months – three whole months – *there*!'

Well, this time it ended as heretofore – poor Mrs Mack gave way. She had not a crown-piece, indeed, that she could call her own; but M. M. was obliging, and let her off for a bill of exchange, the nature of which, to her dying day, the unhappy widow could never comprehend, although it caused her considerable affliction some short time subsequently.

Away went Mary Matchwell with her prize, leaving an odour of brandy behind her. Her dingy and sinister squire performed his clumsy courtesies, and without looking to the right or left, climbed into the coach after her, with his red trunk in his hand; and the vehicle was again in motion, and jingling on at a fair pace in the direction of Nutter's house, The Mills, where her last visit had ended so tragically.

Now, it so happened that just as this coach, with its sombre occupants, drew up at The Mills, Doctor Toole was standing on the steps, giving Moggy a parting injunction, after his wont; for poor little Mrs Nutter had been thrown into a new paroxysm by the dreadful tidings of her Charlie's death, and was now lying on her bed, and bathing the pillow in her tears.

'Is this the tenement called the Mills, formerly in the occupation of the late Charles Nutter – eh?' demanded the gentleman, thrusting his face from the window, before the coachman had got to the door.

'It is, Sir,' replied Toole, putting Moggy aside, and suspecting, he could not tell what amiss, and determined to show front, and not averse from hearing what the visit was about. 'But Mrs Nutter is very far from well, Sir; in fact, in her bed-chamber, Sir, and laid upon her bed.'

'Mrs Nutter's *here*, Sir,' said the man phlegmatically. He had just got out on the ground before the door, and extended his hand toward Mary Matchwell, whom he assisted to alight.

'*This* is Mrs Nutter, relict of the late Charles Nutter, of The Mills, Knockmaroon, in the parish of Chapelizod.'

'At your service, Sir,' said Mary Matchwell, dropping a demure courtesy, and preparing to sail by him.

'Not so fast, Ma'am, if you please,' said Toole, astonished, but still sternly and promptly enough. 'In with you, Moggy, and bar the kitchen door.'

And shoving the maid back, he swung the door to, with a slam. He was barely in time, and Mary Matchwell, baffled and pale, confronted the doctor, with the devil gleaming from her face.

'Who are you, man, that dare shut my own door in my face?' said the beldame.

'Toole's my name, Madam,' said the little doctor, with a lofty look and a bow. 'I have the honour to attend here in a professional capacity.'

'Ho! a village attorney,' cried the fortune-teller, plainly without having consulted the cards or the planets. 'Well, Sir, you'd better stand aside, for I am the Widow Nutter, and this is my house; and burn me, but one way or another, in I'll get.'

'You'd do well to avoid a trespass, Ma'am, and better to abstain from house-breaking; and you may hammer at the knocker till you're tired, but they'll not let you in,' rejoined Toole. 'And as to you being the Widow Nutter, Ma'am, that is widow of poor Charles Nutter, lately found drowned, I'll be glad to know, Ma'am, how you make *that* out.'

'Stay, Madam, by your leave,' said the cadaverous, large-faced man, interposing. 'We are here, Sir, to claim possession of this tenement and the appurtenances, as also of all the money, furniture, and other chattels whatsoever of the late Charles Nutter; and being denied admission, we shall then serve certain cautionary and other notices, in such a manner as the court will, under the circumstances, and in your presence, being, by your admission, the attorney of Sarah Hearty, calling herself Nutter – '

'I did not say I was,' said Toole, with a little toss of his chin.

The gentleman's large face here assumed a cunning leer.

'Well, we have our thoughts about that, Sir,' he said. 'But by your leave, we'll knock at the hall-door.'

'I tell you what, Sir,' said Toole, who had no reliance upon the wisdom of the female garrison, and had serious misgivings lest at the first stout summons the maids should open the door, and the ill-favoured pair establish themselves in occupation of poor Mrs Nutter's domicile, 'I'll not object to the notices being received. There's the servant up at the window there – but you must not make a noise; Mrs Nutter, poor woman, is sick and hypochondriac, and can't bear a noise; but I'll permit the service of the notices, because, you see, we can afford to snap our fingers at you. I say, Moggy, open a bit of that window, and take in the papers that this gentleman will hand you. *There*, Sir, on the end of your cane, if you please – very good.'

' 'Twill do, she has them. Thank you, Miss,' said the legal practitioner, with a grin. 'Now, Ma'am, we'd best go to the Prerogative Court.'

Mary Matchwell laughed one of her pale malevolent laughs up at the maid in the window, who stood there, with the papers in her hand, in a sort of horror.

'Never mind,' said Mary Matchwell, to herself, and, getting swiftly into the coach, she gleamed another ugly smile up at the window of The Mills, as she adjusted her black attire.

'To the Prerogative Court,' said the attorney to the coachman.

'In that house I'll lie tonight,' said Mary Matchwell, with a terrible mildness, as they drove away, still glancing back upon it, with her peculiar smile; and then she leaned back, with a sneer of superiority on her pallid features, and the dismal fatigue of the spirit that rests not, looked savagely out from the deep, haggard windows of her eyes.

When Toole saw the vehicle fairly off, you may be sure he did not lose time in getting into the house, and there conning over the papers, which puzzled him unspeakably.

Chapter Seventy-four

In which Dr Toole, in his boots, visits Mr Gamble, and sees an ugly client of that gentleman's, and something crosses an empty room

'Here's a conspiracy with a vengeance!' muttered Toole, 'if a body could only make head or tail of it. Widow! – eh! – we'll see: why, she's like no woman ever *I* saw. Mrs Nutter, forsooth!' and he could not forbear laughing at the conceit. 'Poor Charles! 'Tis ridiculous – though upon my life, I don't like it. It's just possible it may be all as true as gospel – they're the most devilish-looking pair I've seen out of the dock – curse them – for many a day. I would not wonder if they were robbers. The *widow* looks consumedly like a man in petticoats – hey! – devilish like. I think I'll send Moran and Brien up to sleep tonight in the house. But, hang it! if they were, they would not come out in the daytime to give an alarm. Hollo! Moggy, throw me out one of them papers till I see what it's about.'

So he conned over the notice which provoked him, for he could not half understand it, and he was very curious.

'Well, keep it safe, Moggy,' said he. 'H'm – it *does* look like law business, after all, and I believe it *is*. No – they're not housebreakers, but robbers of another stamp – and a worse, I'll take my davy.'

'See,' said he, as a thought struck him, 'throw me down both of them papers again – there's a good girl. They ought to be looked after, I dare say, and I'll see the poor master's attorney today, d'ye mind? And we'll put our heads together – and, that's right – *relict* indeed!'

And, with a solemn injunction to keep doors locked and windows fast, and a nod and a wave of his hand to Mistress Moggy, and muttering half a sentence or an oath to himself, and wearying his imagination in search of a clue to this new perplexity, he buttoned his pocket over the legal documents, and strutted down to the village, where his nag awaited him saddled, and Jimmey walking him up and down before the doctor's hall-door.

Toole was bound upon a melancholy mission that morning. But though properly a minister of life, a doctor is also conversant with death, and inured to the sight of familiar faces in that remarkable disguise. So he spurred away with more coolness, though not less regret than another man, to throw what light he could upon the subject of the inquest which was to sit upon the body of poor Charles Nutter.

The little doctor, on his way to Ringsend, without the necessity of diverging to the right or left, drew bridle at the door of Mr Luke Gamble, on the Blind Quay, attorney to the late Charles Nutter, and jumping to the ground, delivered a rattling summons thereupon.

It was a dusty, dreary, wainscoted old house – indeed, two old houses intermarried – with doors broken through the partition walls – the floors not all of a level – joined by steps up and down – and having three great staircases, that made it confusing. Through the windows it was not easy to see, such a fantastic mapping of thick dust and dirt coated the glass.

Luke Gamble, like the house, had seen better days. It was not his fault, but an absconding partner had well nigh been his ruin: and, though he paid their liabilities, it was with a strain, and left him a poor man, shattered his connection, and made the house too large by a great deal for his business.

Doctor Toole came into the clerk's room, and was ushered by one of these gentlemen through an empty chamber into the attorney's sanctum. Up two steps stumbled the physician, cursing the house for a place where a gentleman was so much more likely to break his neck than his fast, and found old Gamble in his velvet cap and dressing-gown, in conference with a hard-faced, pale, and pock-marked elderly man, squinting unpleasantly under a black wig, who was narrating something slowly, and with effort, like a man whose memory is labouring to give up its dead, while the attorney, with his spectacles on his nose, was making notes. The speaker ceased abruptly, and turned his pallid visage and jealous, oblique eyes on the intruder.

Luke Gamble looked embarrassed, and shot one devilish angry glance at his clerk, and then made Doctor Toole very welcome.

When Toole had ended his narrative, and the attorney read the notices through, Mr Gamble's countenance brightened, and darkened and brightened again, and with a very significant look, he said to the pale, unpleasant face, pitted with small-pox: 'M. M.', and nodded.

His companion extended his hand toward the papers.

'Never mind,' said the attorney; 'there's that here will fix M. M. in a mighty tight vice.'

'And who's M. M., pray?' enquired Toole.

'When were these notices served, doctor?' asked Mr Gamble.

'Not an hour ago; but, I say, who the plague's M. M.?' answered Toole.

'M. M.,' repeated the attorney, smiling grimly on the backs of the notices which lay on the table; 'why there's many queer things to be heard of M. M.; and the town, and the country, too, for that matter, is like to know a good deal more of her before long; and who served them – a process-server, or who?'

'Why, a fat, broad, bull-necked rascal, with a double chin, and a great round face, the colour of a bad suet-dumplin', and a black patch over his eye,' answered Toole.

'Very like – was he alone?' said Gamble.

'No – a long, sly she-devil in black, that looked as if she'd cut your windpipe, like a cat in the dark, as pale as paper, and mighty large, black, hollow eyes.'

'Ay – that's it,' said Gamble, who, during this dialogue, had thrown his morning-gown over the back of the chair, and got on his coat, and opened a little press in the wall, from which he took his wig, and so completed his toilet.

'That's it?' repeated Toole. 'What's it? – What's *what*?'

'Why, 'tis David O'Regan – Dirty Davy, as we call him. I never knew him yet in an honest case; and the woman's M. M.'

'Hey! To be sure – a woman – I know – I remember – ' and he was on the point of breaking out with poor Mrs Macnamara's secret, but recovered in time. 'That's the she fortune-teller, the witch, M. M., Mary Matchwell; 'twas one of her printed cards, you know, was found lying in Sturk's blood. Dr Sturk, you remember, that they issued a warrant for, against our poor friend, you know.'

'Ay, ay – poor Charles – poor Nutter. Are you going to the inquest?' said Gamble; and, on a sudden, stopped short, with a look of great fear, and a little beckon of his hand forward, as if he had seen something.

There was that in Gamble's change of countenance which startled Toole, who, seeing that his glance was directed through an open door at the other end of the room, skipped from his chair and peeped through it. There was nothing, however, visible but a tenebrose and empty passage.

'What did you see – eh? What frightens you?' said Toole. 'One would think you saw Nutter – like – like.'

Gamble looked horribly perturbed at these words.

'Shut it,' said he, nearing the door, on which Toole's hand rested. Toole took another peep, and did so.

'Why, there's nothing there – like – like the women down at the Mills there,' continued the doctor.

'What about the women?' enquired Gamble, not seeming to know very well what he was saying, agitated still – perhaps intending to keep Toole talking.

'Why, the women – the maids, you know – poor Nutter's servants, down at the Mills. They swear he walks the house, and they'll have it they saw him last night.'

'Pish! Sir – 'tis all conceit and vapours – women's fancies – a plague o' them all. And where's poor Mrs Nutter?' said Gamble, clapping on his cocked hat, and taking his cane, and stuffing two or three bundles of law papers into his coat pockets.

'At home – at the Mills. She slept at the village and so missed the ghost. The Macnamaras have been mighty kind. But when the news was told her this morning, poor thing, she would not stay, and went home; and there she is, poor little soul, breaking her heart.'

Mr Gamble was not ceremonious; so he just threw a cursory and anxious glance round the room, clapped his hands on his coat pockets, making a bunch of keys ring somewhere deep in their caverns. And all being right, 'Come along, gentlemen,' says he, 'I'm going to lock the door;' and without looking behind him, he bolted forth abstractedly into his dusty ante-room.

'Get your cloak about you, Sir – remember your *cough*, you know – the air of the streets is sharp,' said he with a sly wink, to his ugly client, who hastily took the hint.

'Is that *coach* at the door?' bawled Gamble to his clerks in the next room, while he locked the door of his own snuggery behind him; and being satisfied it was so, he conducted the party out by a side door, avoiding the clerks' room, and so downstairs.

'Drive to the courts,' said the attorney to the coachman; and that was all Toole learned about it that day. So he mounted his nag, and resumed his journey to Ringsend at a brisk trot.

I suppose, when he turned the key in his door, and dropped it into his breeches' pocket, the gentleman attorney assumed that he had made everything perfectly safe in his private chamber, though Toole thought he had not looked quite the same again after that sudden change of countenance he had remarked.

Now, it was a darksome day, and the windows of Mr Gamble's room were so obscured with cobwebs, dust, and dirt, that even on a sunny day they boasted no more than a dim religious light. But on this day a cheerful man would have asked for a pair of candles, to dissipate the twilight and sustain his spirits.

He had not been gone, and the room empty ten minutes, when the door through which he had seemed to look on that unknown something that dismayed him, opened softly – at first a little – then a little more – then came a knock at it – then it opened more, and the dark shape of Charles Nutter, with rigid features and white eye-balls, glided stealthily and crouching into the chamber, and halted at the table, and seemed to read the endorsements of the notices that lay there.

Chapter Seventy-five
*How a gentleman paid a visit at the Brass Castle, and there
read a paragraph in an old newspaper*

Dangerfield was, after his wont, seated at his desk, writing letters,
after his early breakfast, with his neatly-labelled accounts at his
elbow. There was a pleasant frosty sun glittering through the twigs
of the leafless shrubs, and flashing on the ripples and undulations of
the Liffey, and the redbreasts and sparrows were picking up the
crumbs which the housekeeper had thrown for them outside. He had
just sealed the last of half-a-dozen letters, when the maid opened his
parlour-door, and told him that a gentleman was at the hall-step,
who wished to see him.

Dangerfield looked up with a quick glance. 'Eh? – to be sure. Show
him in.'

And in a few seconds more, Mr Mervyn, his countenance more
than usually pale and sad, entered the room. He bowed low and
gravely, as the servant announced him.

Dangerfield rose with a prompt smile, bowing also, and advanced
with his hand extended, which, as a matter of form rather than of
cordiality, his visitor took, coldly enough, in his.

'Happy to see you here, Mr Mervyn – pray, take a chair – a
charming morning for a turn by the river, Sir.'

'I have taken the liberty of visiting you, Mr Dangerfield – '

'Your visit, Sir, I esteem an honour,' interposed the lord of the
Brass Castle.

A slight and ceremonious bow from Mervyn, who continued – 'for
the purpose of asking you directly and plainly for some light upon a
matter in which it is in the highest degree important I should be
informed.'

'You may command me, Mr Mervyn,' said Dangerfield, crossing
his legs, throwing himself back, and adjusting himself to attention.

Mervyn fixed his dark eyes full and sternly upon that white and
enigmatical face, with its round glass eyes and silver setting, and

those delicate lines of scorn he had never observed before, traced about the mouth and nostril.

'Then, Sir, I venture to ask you for all you can disclose or relate about one Charles Archer.'

Dangerfield cocked his head on one side, quizzically, and smiled the faintest imaginable cynical smile.

'I can't *disclose* anything, for the gentleman never told me his secrets; but all I can relate is heartily at your service.'

'Can you point him out, Sir?' asked Mervyn, a little less sternly, for he saw no traces of a guilty knowledge in the severe countenance and prompt, unembarrassed manner of the gentleman who leaned back in his chair, with the clear bright light full on him, and his leg crossed so carelessly.

Dangerfield smiled, shook his head gently, and shrugged his shoulders the least thing in the world.

'Don't you know him, Sir?' demanded Mervyn.

'Why,' said Dangerfield, with his chin a little elevated, and the tips of his fingers all brought together, and his elbows resting easily upon the arms of his chair, and altogether an involuntary air of hauteur, 'Charles Archer, perhaps you're not aware, was not exactly the most reputable acquaintance in the world; and my knowledge of him was very slight indeed – wholly accidental – and of very short duration.'

'May I ask you, if, without leaving this town, you can lay your finger on him, Sir?'

'Why, not conveniently,' answered Dangerfield, with the same air of cynical amusement. ''Twould reach in that case all the way to Florence, and even then we should gain little by the discovery.'

'But you do know him?' pursued Mervyn.

'*I did*, Sir, though very slightly,' answered Dangerfield.

'And I'm given to understand, Sir, he's to be found occasionally in this town?' continued his visitor.

'There's just one man who sees him, and that's the parish clerk – what's his name? – Zekiel Irons – he sees him. Suppose we send down to his house, and fetch him here, and learn all about it?' said Dangerfield, who seemed mightily tickled by the whole thing.

'He left the town, Sir, last night; and I've reason to suspect, with a resolution of returning no more. And I must speak plainly, Mr Dangerfield, 'tis no subject for trifling – the fame and fortune of a noble family depend on searching out the truth; and I'll lose my life, Sir, or I'll discover it.'

Still the old cynical, quizzical smile on Dangerfield's white face, who said encouragingly, 'Nobly resolved, Sir, upon my honour!'

'And Mr Dangerfield, if you'll only lay yourself out to help me, with your great knowledge and subtlety – disclosing everything you know or conjecture, and putting me in train to discover the rest – so that I may fully clear this dreadful mystery up – there is no sacrifice of fortune I will not cheerfully make to recompense such immense services, and you may name with confidence your own terms, and think nothing exorbitant.'

For the first time Dangerfield's countenance actually darkened and grew stern, but Mervyn could not discern whether it was with anger or deep thought, and the round spectacles returned his intense gaze with a white reflected sheen, sightless as death.

But the stern mouth opened, and Dangerfield, in his harsh, brief tones, said: 'You speak without reflection, Sir, and had nigh made me lose my temper; but I pardon you; you're young, Sir, and besides, know probably little or nothing of me. Who are you, Sir, who thus think fit to address me, who am by blood and education as good a gentleman as any alive? The inducements you are pleased to offer – you may address elsewhere – they are not for me. I shall forget your imprudence, and answer frankly any questions, within my knowledge, you please to ask.'

Mervyn bowed apologetically, and a silence ensued; after which he thus availed himself of his host's permission to question him: 'You mentioned Irons, the clerk, Mr Dangerfield, and said that he sees Charles Archer. Do you mean it?'

'Why, thus I mean it. He *thinks* he sees him; but, if he does, upon my honour, he sees a ghost,' and Dangerfield chuckled merrily.

'Pray, Mr Dangerfield, consider me, and be serious, and in Heaven's name explain,' said Mervyn, speaking evidently in suppressed anguish.

'Why, you know – don't you? The poor fellow's not quite right here,' and he tapped the centre of his own towering forehead with the delicate tip of his white middle finger. 'I've seen a little of him; he's an angler, so am I; and he showed me the fishing of the river, here, last summer, and often amused me prodigiously. He's got some such very odd maggots! I don't say, mind ye, he's *mad*, there are many degrees, and he's quite a competent parish clerk. He's only wrong on a point or two, and one of them is Charles Archer. I believe for a while he thought *you* were he; and Dangerfield laughed his dry, hard chuckle.

'Where, Sir, do you suppose Charles Archer is now to be found?' urged Mervyn.

'Why, what remains of him, in Florence,' answered Dangerfield.

'You speak, Sir, as if you thought him dead.'

'Think? I know he's dead. I knew him but three weeks, and visited him in his sickness – was in his room half an hour before he died, and attended his funeral,' said Dangerfield.

'I implore of you, Sir, as you hope for mercy, don't trifle in this matter,' cried Mervyn, whose face was white, like that of a man about to swoon under an operation.

'Trifle! What d'ye mean, Sir?' barked out Dangerfield, rabidly.

'I mean, Sir, *this* – I've information he's positively living, and can relieve my father's memory from the horrible imputation that rests upon it. You know who I am!'

'Ay, Sir, Lord Castlemallard told me.'

'And my life I cheerfully devote to the task of seizing and tracing out the bloody clue of the labyrinth in which I'm lost.'

'Good – 'tis a pious as well as a prudent resolve,' said Dangerfield, with a quiet sneer. 'And now, Sir, give me leave to say a word. Your information that Charles Archer is living, is not worth the breath of the madman that spoke it, as I'll presently show you. By an odd chance, Sir, I required this file of newspapers, last week, to help me in ascertaining the date of Sir Harry Wyatt's marriage. Well, only last night, what should I hit on but this. Will you please to read?'

He had turned over the pages rapidly, and then he stopped at this little piece of news packed up in a small paragraph at the bottom of a column, and, pointing his finger to it, he slid the volume of newspapers over to Mervyn, who read:

Died on the 4th of August, of a lingering disease, at his lodgings in Florence, whither he had gone for the improvement of his health, Charles Archer, Esq., a gentleman who some three years since gave an exceeding clear evidence against Lord Dunoran, for the murder of Mr Beauclerc, and was well-known at New-market. His funeral, which was private, was attended by several English gentlemen, who were then at Florence.'

Mervyn, deadly pale, with gleaming eyes, and hand laid along his forehead, as if to screen off an insupportable light and concentrate his gaze upon the words, read and re-read these sentences with an agony of scrutiny such as no critic ever yet directed upon a disputed passage in his favourite classic. But there was no possibility of fastening any consolatory interpretation upon the paragraph. It was all too plain and outspoken.

''Tis possible this may be true – *thus* much. *A* Charles Archer is dead, and yet another Charles Archer, the object of my search, still living,' said Mervyn.

'Hey! that didn't strike me,' said Dangerfield, as much amused as was consistent with moderately good breeding. 'But I can quite account, Mr Mervyn,' he continued, with a sudden change of tone and manner, to something almost of kindness, 'for your readiness to entertain any theory not quite destructive of hopes, which, notwithstanding, I fear, rest simply on the visions of that poor hypochondriac, Irons. But, for all that, 'tis just possible that something may strike either you or me in the matter not quite so romantic – hey? But still something. – You've not told me how the plague Charles Archer could possibly have served you. But on that point, perhaps, we can talk another time. I simply desire to say, that any experience or ability I may possess are heartily at your service whenever you please to task them, as my good wishes are already.'

So, stunned, and like a man walking in a dream – all his hopes shivered about his feet – Mervyn walked through the door of the little parlour in the Brass Castle, and Dangerfield, accompanying him to the little gate which gave admission from the high-road to that tenement, dismissed him there, with a bow and a pleasant smile; and, standing, for a while, wiry and erect, with his hands in his pockets, he followed him, as he paced dejectedly away, with the same peculiar smile.

When he was out of sight, Dangerfield returned to his parlour, smiling all the way, and stood on the hearthrug, with his back to the fire. When he was alone, a shadow came over his face, and he looked down on the fringe with a thoughtful scowl – his hands behind his back – and began adjusting and smoothing it with the toe of his shoe.

'Sot, fool, and poltroon – triple qualification for mischief – I don't know why he still lives. Irons – a new vista opens, and this d—d young man!' All this was not, as we sometimes read, 'mentally ejaculated', but quite literally muttered, as I believe everyone at times mutters to himself. 'Charles Archer living – Charles Archer dead – or, as I sometimes think, neither one nor t'other quite – half-man, half-corpse – a vampire – there is no rest for thee: no sabbath in the days of thy week. Blood, blood – blood, 'tis tiresome. Why should I be a slave to these d—d secrets. I don't think 'tis my judgment, so much as the devil, holds me here. Irons has more brains than I – instinct – calculation – which is oftener right? Miss Gertrude Chattesworth, a mere whim, I think understood her game too. I'll deal with that tomorrow. I'll send Daxon the account, vouchers, and cheque for Lord Castlemallard – tell Smith to sell my horses, and, by the next packet – hey?' and he kissed his hand, with an odd smirk, like a gentleman making his adieus, 'and so leave those who court the acquaintance of Charles Archer, to find him out, and catch their Tartar how they may.'

Chapter Seventy-six

Relating how the castle was taken, and how Mistress Moggy took heart of grace

That evening there came to the door of the Mills, a damsel, with a wide basket on her arm, the covering of which being removed, a goodly show of laces, caps, fans, wash-balls, buckles, and other attractions, came out like a parterre of flowers, with such a glow as dazzled the eyes of Moggy, at the study window.

'Would you plaze to want any, my lady?' enquired the pedlar.

Moggy thought they were, perhaps, a little bit too fine for her purse, but she could not forbear longing and looking, and asking the prices of this bit of finery and that, at the window; and she called Betty, and the two maids conned over the whole contents of the basket.

At last she made an offer for an irresistible stay-hook of pinchbeck, set with half-a-dozen resplendent jewels of cut glass, and after considerable chaffering, and a keen encounter of their wits, they came at last to terms, and Moggy ran out to the kitchen for her money, which lay in a brass snuff-box, in a pewter goblet, on the dresser.

As she was counting her coin, and putting back what she did not want, the latch of the kitchen door was lifted from without, and the door itself pushed and shaken. Though the last red gleam of a stormy sunset was glittering among the ivy leaves round the kitchen window, the terrors of last night's apparition were revived in a moment, and, with a blanched face, she gazed on the door, expecting, breathlessly, what would come.

The door was bolted and locked on the inside, in accordance with Doctor Toole's solemn injunction; and there was no attempt to use violence. But a brisk knocking began thereat and Moggy, encouraged by hearing the voices of Betty and the vender of splendours at the little parlour window, and also by the amber sunlight on the rustling ivy leaves, and the loud evening gossip of the sparrows, took heart of grace, and demanded shrilly 'Who's there?'

A whining beggar's voice asked admission.

'But you can't come in, for the house is shut up for the night,' replied the cook.

''Tis a quare hour you lock your doors at,' said the besieger.

'Mighty quare, but so it is,' she answered.

'But 'tis a message for the misthress I have,' answered the applicant.

'Who from?' demanded the porteress.

''Tis a present o' some wine, acushla.'

'Who from?' repeated she, growing more uneasy.

'Auch! woman, are you going to take it in, or no?'

'Come in the morning, my good man,' said she, 'for sorrow a foot you'll put inside the house tonight.'

'An' that's what I'm to tell them that sent me.'

'Neither more nor less,' replied she.

And so she heard a heavy foot clank along the pavement, and she tried to catch a glimpse of the returning figure, but she could not, though she laid her cheek against the window-pane. However, she heard him whistling as he went, which gave her a better opinion of him, and she thought she heard the road gate shut after him.

So feeling relieved, and with a great sigh, she counted her money over; and answering Betty's shrill summons to the study, as the woman was in haste, with a 'Coming, coming this minute,' she replaced her treasure, and got swiftly into poor Charles Nutter's little chamber. There was his pipe over the chimney, and his green and gold-laced Sunday waistcoat folded on the little walnut table by the fire, and his small folio, *Maison Rustique, the Country Farme*, with his old green worsted purse set for a marker in it where he had left off reading the night before all their troubles began; and his silk dressing-gown was hanging by the window-frame, and his velvet morning-cap on the same peg – the dust had settled on them now. And after her fright in the kitchen, all these mementoes smote her with a grim sort of reproach and menace, and she wished the window barred, and the door of the ominous little chamber locked for the night.

''Tis growing late,' said the dealer from without, 'and I daren't be on the road after dark. Gi' me my money, good girl; and here, take your stay-hook.'

And so saying, she looked a little puzzled up and down, as not well knowing how they were to make their exchange.

'Here,' says Moggy, 'give it in here.' And removing the fastening, she shoved the window up a little bit. 'Hould it, Betty; hould it up,' said she. And in came the woman's hard, brown hand, palm open, for her money, and the other containing the jewel, after which the vain soul of Moggy lusted.

'That'll do,' said she; and crying shrilly, 'Give us a lift, sweetheart,' in a twinkling she shoved the window up, at the same time kneeling, with a spring, upon the sill, and getting her long leg into the room, with her shoulder under the window-sash, her foot firmly planted on the floor, and her face and head in the apartment. Almost at the same instant she was followed by an ill-looking fellow, buttoned up in a surtout, whose stature seemed enormous, and at sight of whom the two women shrieked as if soul and body were parting.

The lady was now quite in the room, and standing upright showed the tall shape and stern lineaments of Mary Matchwell. And as she stood she laughed a sort of shuddering laugh, like a person who had just had a plunge in cold water.

'Stop that noise,' said she, recognising Betty, who saw her with unspeakable terror. 'I'm the lady that came here, you know, some months ago, with Mrs Macnamara; and I'm Mrs Nutter, which the woman upstairs *is not*. I'm Mrs Nutter, and *you're my* servants, do ye mind? And I'll act a fair mistress by you, if you do me honest service. Open the hall-door,' she said to the man, who was by this time also in the room. And forth he went to do her bidding, and a gentleman, who turned out to be that respectable pillar of the law whom Mr Gamble in the morning had referred to as 'Dirty Davy', entered. He was followed by Mrs Mary Matchwell's maid, a giggling, cat-like gypsy, with a lot of gaudy finery about her, and a withered devilment leering in her face; and a hackney-coach drove up to the door, which had conveyed the party from town; and the driver railing in loud tones, after the manner of his kind in old times, at all things, reeking of whiskey and stale tobacco, and cursing freely, pitched in several trunks, one after the other; and, in fact, it became perfectly clear that M. M. was taking possession. And Betty and Moggy, at their wits' end between terror and bewilderment, were altogether powerless to resist, and could only whimper a protest against the monstrous invasion, while poor little Sally Nutter upstairs, roused by the wild chorus of strange voices from the lethargy of her grief, and even spurred into active alarm, locked her door, and then hammered with a chair upon the floor, under a maniacal hallucination that she was calling I know not what or whom to the rescue.

Then Dirty Davy read aloud, with due emphasis, to the maids, copies, as he stated, of the affidavits sworn to that day by Mistress

Mary Matchwell, or as he called her, Mrs Nutter, relict of the late Charles Nutter, gentleman, of the Mills, in the parish of Chapel-izod, barony of Castleknock, and county of Dublin, deposing to her marriage with the said Charles Nutter having been celebrated in the Church of St Clement Danes, in London, on the 7th of April, 1750. And then came a copy of the marriage certificate, and then a statement how, believing that deceased had left no 'will' making any disposition of his property, or naming an executor, she applied to the Court of Prerogative for letters of administration to the deceased, which letters would be granted in a few days; and in the meantime the bereaved lady would remain in possession of the house and chattels of her late husband.

All this, of course, was so much 'Hebrew-Greek', as honest Father Roach was wont to phrase it, to the scared women. But M. M. – [Greek: nykti eoikos] – fixing them both with her cold and terrible gaze, said quite intelligibly, 'What's your name?'

'Moggy Sullivan, if you please, Ma'am.'

'And what's yours?'

'Lizabet – Betty they call me – Madam; Lizabet Burke, if you please, Madam.'

'Well, then, Moggy Sullivan and Elizabeth Burke, harkee both, while I tell you a thing. I'm mistress here by law, as you've just heard, and you're my servants; and if you so much as wind the jack or move a tea-cup, except as I tell you, I'll find a way to punish you; and if I miss to the value of a pin's head, I'll indict you for a felony, and have you whipped and burnt in the hand – you know what that means. And now, where's Mistress Sarah Harty? For she must pack and away.'

'Oh! Ma'am, jewel, the poor misthress.'

'*I'm* the mistress, slut.'

'Ma'am, dear, she's very bad.'

'*Where* is she?'

'In her room, Ma'am,' answered Betty, with blubbered cheeks.

'Where are you going, minx?' cried M. M., with a terrible voice and look, and striding toward the door, from which Moggy was about to escape.

Now, Moggy was a sort of heroine, not in the vain matter of beauty, for she had high cheek bones, a snub nose, and her figure had no more waist, or other feminine undulations, than the clock in the hall; but like that useful piece of furniture, presented an oblong parallelogram, unassisted by art; for, except on gala days, these homely maidens never sported hoops. But she was, nevertheless, a heroine of the Amazonian species. She tripped up Pat Morgan, and laid that athlete suddenly on his back, upon the grass plot before the hall door, to his eternal disgrace, when he 'offered' to kiss her, while the fiddler and tambourine-man were playing. She used to wring big boys by the ears; overawe fishwives with her voluble invective; put dangerous dogs to rout with sticks and stones, and evince, in all emergencies, an adventurous spirit and an alacrity for battle.

For her, indeed, as for others, the spell of 'M. M.'s' evil eye and witchlike presence was at first too much; but Moggy rallied, and, thus challenged, she turned about at the door and stoutly confronted the intruder.

'Minx, yourself, you black baste; I'm goin' just wherever it plases me best, and I'd like to know who'll stop me; and first, Ma'am, be your lave, I'll tell the mistress to lock her door, and keep you and your rake-helly squad at the wrong side of it, and then, Ma'am, wherever the fancy takes me next – and that's how it is, and my sarvice to your ladyship.'

Off went Moggy, with a leer of defiance and a snap of her fingers, cutting a clumsy caper, and rushed like a mad cow up the stairs, shouting all the way, 'Lock your door, Ma'am – lock your door.'

Growing two or three degrees whiter, M. M., so soon as she recovered herself, glided in pursuit, like the embodiment of an evil spirit, as perhaps she was, and with a gleam of insanity, or murder, in her eye, which always supervened when her wrath was moved.

The sullen face of the bailiff half lighted up with a cynical grin of expectation, for he saw that both ladies were game, and looked for a spirited encounter. But Dirty Davy spoiled all by interposing his person, and arresting the pursuit of his client, and delivering a wheezy expostulation close in her ear.

''Tis a strange thing if I can't do what I will with my own – fine laws, i'faith!'

'I only tell you, Madam, and if you do, it may embarrass us mightily by-and-by.'

'I'd wring her neck across the banister,' murmured M. M.

'An' now, plase your ladyship, will I bring your sarvice to the ladies and gentlemen down in the town, for 'tis there I'm going next,' said Moggy, popping in at the door, with a mock courtesy, and a pugnacious cock in her eye, and a look altogether so provoking and warlike as almost tempted the bailiff at the door to clap her on the back, and cry, had he spoken Latin, *macte virtute puer*!

'Catch the slut. You shan't budge – not a foot – hold her,' cried M. M. to the bailiff.

'Baugh!' was his answer.

'See, now,' said Davy, 'Madam Nutter's not serious – you're *not*, Ma'am? We don't detain you, mind. The door's open. There's no false imprisonment or duress, mind ye, thanking you all the same, Miss, for your offer. We won't detain you, ah, ah. No, I thank you. Chalk the road for the young lady, Mr Redmond.'

And Davy fell to whisper energetically again in M. M.'s ear.

And Moggy disappeared. Straight down to the town she went, and to the friendly Dr Toole's house, but he was not expected home from Dublin till morning. Then she had thoughts of going to the barrack, and applying for a company of soldiers, with a cannon, if necessary, to retake the Mills. Then she bethought her o' good Dr Walsingham, but he was too simple to cope with such seasoned rogues. General Chattesworth was too far away, and not quite the man either, no more than Colonel Stafford; and the young beaux, 'them captains, and the like, 'id only be funnin' me, and knows nothing of law business.' So she pitched upon Father Roach.

Chapter Seventy-seven
In which Irish melody prevails

Now, Father Roach's domicile was the first house in the Chapel-lane, which consisted altogether of two, not being very long. It showed a hall-door, painted green – the national hue – which enclosed, I'm happy to say, not a few of the national virtues, chief among which reigned hospitality. As Moggy turned the corner, and got out of the cold wind under its friendly shelter, she heard a stentorian voice, accompanied by the mellifluous drone of a bagpipe, concluding in a highly decorative style the last verse of the 'Colleen Rue'.

Respect for this celestial melody, and a desire to hear a little more of what might follow, held Moggy on the steps, with the knocker between her finger and thumb, unwilling to disturb by an unseasonable summons the harmonies from which she was, in fact, separated only by the thickness of the window and its shutter. And when the vocal and instrumental music came to an end together with a prolonged and indescribable groan and a grunt from the songster and the instrument, there broke forth a shrilly chorus of female cackle, some in admiration and some in laughter; and the voice of Father Roach was heard lustily and melodiously ejaculating 'More power to you, Pat Mahony!'

As this pleasant party all talked together, and Moggy could not clearly unravel a single sentence, she made up her mind to wait no longer, and knocked with good emphasis, under cover of the uproar.

The maid, who had evidently been in the hall, almost instantaneously opened the door; and with a hasty welcome full of giggle and excitement, pulled in Moggy by the arm, shutting the door after her; and each damsel asked the other, 'An' how are you, and are you elegant?' and shaking her neighbour by both hands. The clerical handmaid, in a galloping whisper in Moggy's ear, told her, ''Twas a weddin' party, and such tarin' fun she never see – sich dancin' and singin', and laughin' and funnin'; and she must wait a bit, and see the quality,' a portion of whom, indeed, were visible as well as overpoweringly audible, through the half-open door of the front parlour; 'and there was to be a thunderin' fine supper – a round of beef and two geese, and a tubful of oysters,' &c, &c.

Now I must mention that this feast was, in fact, in its own way, more romantically wonderful than that of the celebrated wedding of Camacho the Rich, and one of the many hundred proofs I've met with in the course of my long pilgrimage that the honest prose of everyday life is often ten times more surprising than the unsubstantial fictions of even the best epic poets.

The valiant Sir Jaufry, it is true, was ordered to a dungeon by the fair Brunissende, who so soon as she beheld him, nevertheless became enamoured of the knight, and gave him finally her hand in wedlock. But if the fair Brunissende had been five and forty, or by'r lady, fifty, the widow of a tailor, herself wondrous keen after money, and stung very nigh to madness by the preposterous balance due (as per ledger), and the inexhaustible and ingenious dodges executed by the insolvent Sir Jaufry, the composer of that chivalric romance might have shrunk from the happy winding-up as bordering too nearly upon the incredible.

Yet good Father Roach understood human nature better. Man and woman have a tendency to fuse. And given a good-looking fellow and a woman, no matter of what age, who but deserves the name, and bring them together, and let the hero but have proper opportunities, and deuce is in it if nothing comes of the matter. Animosity is no impediment. On the contrary 'tis a more advantageous opening than indifference. The Cid began his courtship by shooting his lady-love's pigeons, and putting her into a pet and a frenzy. The Cid knew what he was about. Stir no matter *what* passions, provided they *be* passions, and get your image well into your lady's head, and you may repeat, with like success, the wooing (which superficial people pronounce so unnatural) of crook-backed Richard and the Lady Anne. Of course, there are limits. I would not advise, for instance, a fat elderly gentleman, bald, carbuncled, dull of wit, and slow of speech, to hazard that particular method, lest he should find himself the worse of his experiment. My counsel is for the young, the tolerably good-looking, for murmuring orators of the silver-tongue family, and romantic athletes with coaxing ways.

Worthy Father Roach constituted himself internuncio between Mahony, whom we remember first in his pride of place doing the honours of that feast of Mars in which his 'friend' Nutter was to have carved up the great O'Flaherty on the Fifteen Acres, and next, *quantum mutatus ab illo*! a helpless but manly captive in the hands of the Dublin bailiffs, and that very Mrs Elizabeth Woolly, relict and sole executrix of the late Timotheus Woolly, of High-street, tailor, &c., &c., who was the cruel cause of his incarceration.

Good Father Roach, though a paragon of celibacy, was of a gallant temperament, and a wheedling tongue, and unfolded before the offended eye of the insulted and vindictive executrix so interesting a picture of 'his noble young friend, the victim of circumstance, breaking his manly heart over his follies and misfortunes'; and looking upon her, Mrs Woolly, afar off, with an eye full of melancholy and awe, tempered with, mayhap, somewhat of romantic gallantry, like Sir Walter Raleigh from the Tower window on Queen Elizabeth, that he at length persuaded the tremendous 'relict' to visit her captive in his dungeon. This she did, in a severe mood, with her attorney, and good Father Roach; and though Mahony's statement was declamatory rather than precise, and dealt more with his feelings than his resources, and was carried on more in the way of an appeal to the 'leedy' than as an exposition to the man of law, leaving matters at the end in certainly no clearer state than before he began, yet the executrix consented to see the imprisoned youth once more, this time dispensing with her attorney's attendance, and content with the protection of the priest, and even upon that, on some subsequent visits, she did not insist.

And so the affair, like one of those medleys of our Irish melodies arranged by poor M. Jullien, starting with a martial air, breathing turf and thunder, fire and sword, went off imperceptibly into a pathetic and amorous strain. Father Roach, still officiating as internuncio, found the dowager less and less impracticable, and at length a treaty was happily concluded. The captive came forth to wear thenceforward those lighter chains only, which are forged by Hymen and wreathed with roses; and the lady applied to his old promissory notes the torch of love, which in a moment reduced them to ashes. And here, at the hermitage of our jolly Chapelizod priest – for bride and bridegroom were alike of the 'ancient faith' – the treaty was ratified, and the bagpipe and the bridegroom, in tremendous unison, splitting the rafters with 'Hymen, Hymen, O Hymenæe!'

In the midst of this festive celebration, his reverence was summoned to the hall, already perfumed with the incense of the geese, the onions, the bacon browned at the kitchen-fire, and various other delicacies, toned and enriched by the vapours that exhaled from the little bottle of punch which, in consideration of his fatigues, stood by the elbow of the piper.

When the holy man had heard Moggy's tale, he scratched his tonsure and looked, I must say, confoundedly bored.

'Now, Moggy, my child, don't you see, acushla, 'tisn't to me you should ha' come; I'm here, my dear, engaged,' and he dried his moist and rubicund countenance, 'in one of the sacred offices iv the Church, the sacrament, my dear, iv' – here Mahony and the piper struck up again in so loud a key in the parlour, that as Moggy afterwards observed, 'they could not hear their own ears', and the conclusion of the sentence was overwhelmed in 'Many's the bottle I cracked in my time'. So his reverence impatiently beckoned to the hall-door, which he opened, and on the steps, where he was able to make himself audible, he explained the nature of his present engagement, and referred her to Doctor Toole. Assured, however, that he was in Dublin, he scratched his tonsure once more.

'The divil burn the lot o' them, my dear, an' purty evenin' they chose for their vagaries – an' law papers too, you say, an' an attorney into the bargain – there's no influence you can bring to bear on them fellows. If 'twas another man, an' a couple more at his back, myself an' Pat Moran 'id wallop them out of the house, an' into the river, be gannies; as aisy as say an *ave*.'

The illustration, it occurred to him, might possibly strike Moggy as irreverent, and the worthy father paused, and, with upturned eyes, murmured a Latin ejaculation, crossing himself; and having thus reasserted his clerical character, he proceeded to demonstrate the uselessness of his going.

But Father Roach, though sometimes a little bit testy, and, on the whole, not without faults, was as good-natured an anchorite as ever said mass or brewed a contemplative bowl of punch. If he refused to go down to the Mills, he would not have been comfortable again that night, nor indeed for a week to come. So, with a sigh, he made up his mind, got quietly into his surtout and mufflers which hung on the peg behind the hall-door, clapped on his hat, grasped his stout oak stick, and telling his housekeeper to let them know, in case his guests should miss him, that he was obliged to go out for ten minutes or so on parish business, forth sallied the stout priest, with no great appetite for knight-errantry, but still anxious to rescue, if so it might be, the distressed princess, begirt with giants and enchanters, at the Mills.

At the Salmon House he enlisted the stalworth Paddy Moran, with the information conveyed to that surprised reveller, that he was to sleep at 'Mrs Nutter's house' that night; and so, at a brisk pace, the clerical knight, his squire, and demoiselle-errant, proceeded to the Mills.

Chapter Seventy-eight

In which, while the harmony continues in Father Roach's front parlour, a few discords are introduced elsewhere; and Dr Toole arrives in the morning with a marvellous budget of news

The good people who had established themselves in poor Nutter's domicile did not appear at all disconcerted by the priest's summons. His knock at the hall-door was attended to with the most consummate assurance by M. M.'s maid, just as if the premises had belonged to her mistress all her days.

Between this hussy and his reverence, who was in no mood to be trifled with, there occurred in the hall some very pretty sparring, which ended by his being ushered into the parlour, where sat Mistress Matchwell and Dirty Davy, the 'tea-things' on the table, and an odour more potent than that of the Chinese aroma circulating agreeably through the chamber.

I need not report the dialogue of the parties, showing how the honest priest maintained, under sore trial, his character for politeness while addressing a lady, and how he indemnified himself in the style in which he 'discoorsed' the attorney; how his language fluctuated between the persuasively religious and the horribly profane; and how, at one crisis in the conversation, although he had self-command enough to bow to the matron, he was on the point of cracking the lawyer's crown with the fine specimen of Irish oak which he carried in his hand, and, in fact, nothing but his prudent respect for that gentleman's cloth prevented his doing so.

'But supposin', Ma'am,' said his reverence, referring to the astounding allegation of her marriage with Nutter; 'for the sake of argumint, it should turn out to be so, in coorse you would not like to turn the poor woman out iv doors, without a penny in her pocket, to beg her bread?'

'Your friend upstairs, Sir, intended playing the lady for the rest of her days,' answered M. M., with a cat-like demureness, sly and cruel, 'at my cost and to my sorrow. For twenty long years, or nigh hand it, she has lived with my husband, consuming my substance, and keeping me in penury. What did she allow me all that time? – Not so much as that crust – ha! ha! – no, not even allowed my husband to write me a line, or send me a shilling. I suppose she owes me for her maintenance here – in my house, out of my property – fully two thousand pounds. Make money of that, Sir; – and my lawyer advises me to make her pay it.'

'Or rather to make her account, Ma'am; or you will, if she's disposed to act fairly, take anything you may be advised to be reasonable and equitable, Ma'am,' interposed Dirty Davy.

'That's it,' resumed Madam Mary. 'I don't want her four bones. Let her make up one thousand pounds – that's reason, Sir – and I'll forgive her the remainder. But if she won't, then to gaol I'll send her, and there she may rot for me.'

'You persave, Sir,' continued the attorney; 'your client – I mane your friend – has fixed herself in the character of an agent – all the late gintleman's money, you see, went through her hands – an agent or a steward to Charles Nutther, desased – an' a coort iv equity'll hould her liable to account, ye see; an' we know well enough what money's past through her hands annually – an' whatever she can prove to have been honestly applied, we'll be quite willin' to allow; but, you see, we must have the balance!'

'Balance!' said the priest, incensed beyond endurance; 'if you stay balancin' here, my joker, much longer, you'll run a raysonable risk of balancin' by the neck out iv one of them trees before the doore.'

'So you're threatenin' my life, Sir!' said the attorney, with a sly defiance.

'You lie like the divil, Sir – savin' your presence, Ma'am. Don't you know the differ, Sir, between a threat an' a warnin', you bosthoon?' thundered his reverence.

'You're sthrivin' to provoke me to a brache iv the pace, as the company can testify,' said Dirty Davy.

'Ye lie again, you – you fat crature – 'tis thryin' to provoke you to *keep* the pace I am. Listen to me, the both o' yez – the leedy upstairs, the misthress iv this house, and widow of poor Charles Nutter – Mrs Sally Nutther, I say – is well liked in the parish; an' if they get the wind o' the word, all I say 's this – so sure as you're found here houldin' wrongful possession of her house an' goods, the boys iv Palmerstown, Castleknock, and Chapelizod will pay yez a visit you won't like, and duck yez in the river, or hang yez together, like a pair of common robbers, as you unquestionably *are – not*,' he added, with a sudden sense of legal liability.

'Who's that?' demanded the lynx-eyed lady, who saw Pat Moran cross the door in the shadow of the lobby.

'That's Mr Moran, a most respectable and muscular man, come here to keep possession, Madam, for Mrs Sally Nutther, our good friend and neighbour, Ma'am,' replied the priest.

'As you plase, Sir,' replied the attorney; 'you're tumblin' yourself and your friend into a nice predicament – as good a consthructive ousther, *vi et armis*, as my client could possibly desire. Av coorse, Sir, we'll seek compensation in the regular way for this violent threspass; and we have you criminally, you'll obsarve, no less than civilly.'

'Now, look – onderstand me – don't affect to misteek, av you plase,' said the priest, not very clear or comfortable, for he had before had one or two brushes with the law, and the recollection was disagreeable: 'I – Mr Moran – we're here, Sir – the both iv us, as you see – pacibly – and – and – all to that – and at the request of Mrs Sally Nutther – mind that, too – at her special desire – an' I tell you what's more – if you make any row here – do you mind – I'll come down with the magisthrate an' the soldiers, an' lave it to them to dale with you accordin' – mind ye – to law an' equity, civil, human, criminal, an' divine – an' make money o' that, ye – ye – mountain in labour – savin' your presence, Ma'am.'

'I thank you – that'll do, Sir,' said the lawyer, with a lazy chuckle.

'I'll now do myself the honour to make my compliments to Mrs Sally Nutther,' said Father Roach, making a solemn bow to Mrs Matchwell, who, with a shrill sneer, pursued him as he disappeared with 'The lady in the bedroom, your reverence?'

Whereat Dirty Davy renewed his wheezy chuckle.

Nothing daunted, the indignant divine stumped resolutely upstairs, and found poor Sally Nutter, to whose room he was joyfully admitted by honest Betty, who knew his soft honest brogue in a panic, the violence of which had almost superseded her grief. So he consoled and fortified the poor lady as well as he could, and when she urged him to remain in the house all night, 'My dear Ma'am,' says he, lifting his hand and shaking his head, with closed eyes, 'you forget my ca*rac*ter. Why, the house is full iv faymales. My darlin' Mrs Nutter, I – I couldn't enthertain sich an idaya; and, besides,' said he, with sudden energy, recollecting that the goose might be overdone, 'there's a religious duty, my dear Ma'am – the holy sacrament waitin' – a pair to be married; but Pat Moran will keep them quiet till mornin,' and I'll be down myself to see you then. So my sarvice to you, Mrs Nutther, and God bless you, my dear Ma'am.'

And with this valediction the priest departed, and from the road he looked back at the familiar outline of the Mills, and its thick clumps of chimneys, and two twinkling lights, and thought of the horrible and sudden change that had passed over the place and the inmates, and how a dreadful curse had scathed them: making it, till lately the scene of comfort and tranquillity, to become the hold of every foul spirit, and the cage of every unclean and hateful bird.

Doctor Toole arrived at ten o'clock next morning, with news that shook the village. The inquest was postponed to the evening, to secure the attendance of some witnesses, who could throw a light, it was thought, on the enquiry. Then Doctor Toole was examined, and identified the body at first, confidently.

'But,' said he, in the great parlour of the Phoenix, where he held forth, 'though the features were as like as two eggs, it struck me the forehead was a thought broader. So, said I, I can set the matter at rest in five minutes. Charles Nutter's left upper arm was broken midway, and I set it; there would be the usual deposit where the bone knit, and he had a sword thrust through his right shoulder, cicatrised, and very well defined; and he had lost two under-teeth. Well, the teeth *were* gone, but three instead of two, and on laying the arm-bone bare, 'twas plain it had never been broken, and, in like manner, nothing wrong with the right shoulder, and there was nothing like so much deltoid and biceps as Nutter had. So says I, at once, be that body whose it may, 'tis none of Charles Nutter's, and to that I swear, gentlemen; and I had hardly made an end when 'twas identified for the corpse of the French hairdresser, newly arrived from Paris, who was crossing the Liffey, on Tuesday night, you remember, at the old ferry-boat slip, and fell in and was drowned. So that part of the story's ended.

'But, gentlemen,' continued Toole, with the important and resolute bearing of a man who has a startling announcement to make, 'I am sorry to have to tell you that poor Charles Nutter's in gaol.'

In gaol! was echoed in all sorts of tones from his auditory, with an abundance of profane ejaculations of wonderment, concern, and horror.

'Ay, gentlemen, in the body of the gaol.'

Then it came out that Nutter had been arrested that very morning, in a sedan-chair, at the end of Cook Street, and was now in the county prison awaiting his trial; and that, no doubt, bail would be refused, which, indeed, turned out truly.

So, when all these amazing events had been thoroughly discussed, the little gathering dispersed to blaze them abroad, and Toole wrote to Mr Gamble, to tell him 'that the person, Mary Matchwell, claiming to be the wife of Charles Nutter, has established herself at the Mills, and is disposed to be troublesome, and terrifies poor Mrs Sally Nutter, who is ill; it would be a charity to come out, and direct measures. I know not what ought to be done, though confident her claim is a bag of moonshine and lies, and, if not stopped, she'll make away with the goods and furniture, which is mighty hard upon this unfortunate lady,' etc., etc.

'That Mary Matchwell, as I think, ought to be in gaol for the assault on Sturk; her card, you know, was found in the mud beside him, and she's fit for any devil's work.'

This was addressed by Toole to his good wife.

'That *card*?' said Jimmey, who happened to be triturating a powder in the corner for little Master Barney Sturk, and who suspended operations, and spoke with the pestle in his fingers, and a very cunning leer on his sharp features: 'I know all about that card.'

'You do – do you? And why didn't you spake out long ago, you vagabond?' said Toole. 'Well, then! Come now! – what's in your knowledge-box? – out with it.'

'Why, I had that card in my hand the night Mr Nutter went off.'

'Well? – Go on.'

''Twas in the hall at the Mills, Sir; I knew it again at the Barracks the minute I seen it.'

'Why, 'tis a printed card – there's hundreds of them – how d'ye know one from t'other, wisehead?'

'Why, Sir, 'twas how this one was walked on, and the letter M. in Mary was tore across, an' on the back was writ, in red ink, for Mrs Macnamara, and they could not read it down at the Barracks, because the wet had got at it, and the end was mostly washed away, and they thought it was MacNally, or MacIntire; but I knew it the minute I seen it.'

'Well, my tight little fellow, and what the dickens has all that to do with the matter?' asked Toole, growing uneasy.

'The dickens a much, I believe, Sir; only as Mr Nutter was goin' out he snatched it out o' my hand – in the hall there – and stuffed it into his pocket.'

'You did not tell that lying story, did you, about the town, you mischievous young spalpeen?' demanded the doctor, shaking his disciple rather roughly by the arm.

'No – I – I didn't – I did not tell, Sir – what is it to me?' answered the boy, frightened.

'You didn't tell – not you, truly. I lay you a tenpenny-bit there isn't a tattler in the town but has the story by rote – a pretty kettle o' fish you'll make of it, with your meddling and lying. If 'twas true, 'twould be another matter, but – hold your tongue; – how the plague are you to know one card from another when they're all alike, and Mrs Macnamara, Mrs Macfiddle. I suppose *you* can read better than the *adjutant*, ha, ha! Well, mind my words, you've got yourself into a pretty predicament; I'd walk twice from this to the county court-house and back again, only to look at it; a pleasant cross-hackling the counsellors will give you, and if you prevaricate – you know what that is, my boy – the judge will make short work with you, and you may cool your heels in gaol as long as he pleases, for me.'

'And, look'ee,' said Toole, returning, for he was going out, as he generally did, whenever he was profoundly ruffled, 'you remember the affidavit-man that was whipped and pilloried this time two years for perjury, eh? Look to it, my fine fellow. There's more than me knows how Mr Nutter threatened to cane you that night – and a good turn 'twould have been – and 'twouldn't take much to persuade an honest jury that you wanted to pay him off for that by putting a nail in his coffin, you young miscreant! Go on – do – and I promise you'll get an airing yet you'll not like – you will.'

And so Toole, with a wag of his head, and a grin over his shoulder, strutted out into the village street, where he was seen, with a pursed mouth, and a flushed visage, to make a vicious cut or two with his cane in the air as he walked along. And it must be allowed that Master Jimmey's reflections were a little confused and uncomfortable, as he pondered over the past and the future with the pestle in his fingers and the doctor's awful words ringing in his ears.

Chapter Seventy-nine

Showing how little Lily's life began to change into a retrospect; and how on a sudden she began to feel better

As time wore on, little Lilias was not better. When she had read her Bible, and closed it, she would sit long silent, with a sad look, thinking; and often she would ask old Sally questions about her mother, and listen to her, looking all the time with a strange and earnest gaze through the glass door upon the evergreens and the early snowdrops. And old Sally was troubled somehow, and saddened at her dwelling so much upon this theme.

And one evening, as they sat together in the drawing-room – she and the good old rector – she asked him, too, gently, about her; for he never shrank from talking of the beloved dead, but used to speak of her often, with a simple tenderness, as if she were still living.

In this he was right. Why should we be afraid to *speak* of those of whom we think so continually? She is not dead, but sleepeth! I have met a few, and they very good men, who spoke of their beloved dead with this cheery affection, and mingled their pleasant and loving remembrances of them in their common talk; and often I wished that, when I am laid up in the bosom of our common mother earth, those who loved me would keep my memory thus socially alive, and allow my name, when I shall answer to it no more, to mingle still in their affectionate and merry intercourse.

'Some conflicts my darling had the day before her departure,' he said; 'but such as through God's goodness lasted not long, and ended in the comfort that continued to her end, which was so quiet and so peaceable, we who were nearest about her, knew not the moment of her departure. And little Lily was then but an infant – a tiny little thing. Ah! if my darling had been spared to see her grown-up, such a beauty, and so like her!'

And so he rambled on; and when he looked at her, little Lily was weeping; and as he looked she said, trying to smile – 'Indeed, I don't know why I'm crying, darling. There's nothing the matter with your little Lily – only I can't help crying: and I'm your foolish little Lily, you know.'

And this often happened, that he found she was weeping when he looked on her suddenly, and she used to try to smile, and both, then, to cry together, and neither say what they feared, only each unspeakably more tender and loving. Ah, yes! in their love was mingling now something of the yearning of a farewell, which neither would acknowledge.

Now, while they lay here [says sweet John Bunyan, in his *Pilgrim's Progress*] and waited for the good hour, there was a noise in the town that there was a post come from the celestial city, with matter of great importance to one Christiana. So enquiry was made for her, and the house was found out where she was; so the post presented her with a letter, the contents whereof were, 'Hail, thou good one! I bring thee tidings that the Master calleth for thee, and expecteth that thou shouldst stand in his presence, in clothes of immortality, within these ten days.'

When he had read this letter to her, he gave her therewith a sure token that he was a true messenger, and was come to bid her make haste to be gone. The token was an arrow with a point sharpened with love, let easily into her heart, which by degrees wrought so effectually with her, that at the time appointed she must be gone.

When Christiana saw that her time was come, and that she was the first of this company that was to go over, she called for Mr Greatheart, her guide, and told him how matters were.

And so little Lily talked with Mr Greatheart in her own way; and hearing of her mother, gave ear to the story as to a sweet and solemn parable, that lighted her dark steps. And the old man went on:

It is St John who says, 'And the sea arose by reason of a great wind that blew. So when they had rowed about five-and-twenty, or thirty furlongs, they see the Lord walking on the sea, and drawing nigh unto the ship: and they were afraid. But he saith unto them, It is I, be not afraid.' So is it with the frail bark of mortality and the trembling spirit it carries. When 'it is now dark', and the sea arises, and the 'great wind' blows, the vessel is tost, and the poor heart fails within it; and when they see the dim form which they take to be the angel of death walking the foaming waters, they cry out in terror, but the voice of the sweet Redeemer, the Lord of Life is heard, 'It is I; be not afraid', and so the faithful ones 'willingly receive him into the ship', and immediately it is at the land whither they go: yes, at the land whither they go. But, oh! the lonely ones, left behind on the other shore.

One morning, old Sally, who in her quiet way used to tell all the little village news she heard, thinking to make her young mistress smile, or at least listen, said: 'And that wild young gentleman, Captain Devereux, is growing godly, they say; Mrs Irons tells me how he calls for his Bible o' nights, and how he does not play cards, nor eat suppers at the Phoenix, nor keep bad company, nor go into Dublin, but goes to church; and she says she does not know what to make of him.'

Little Lily did not speak or raise her head; she went on stirring the little locket, that lay on the table, with the tip of her finger, looking on it silently. She did not seem to mind old Sally's talk, almost to hear it, but when it ended, she waited, still silent, as a child, when the music is over, listens for more.

When she came down she placed her chair near the window, that she might see the snowdrops and the crocuses.

'The spring, at last, Sally, my darling, and I feel so much better;' and Lily smiled on the flowers through the windows, and I fancy the flowers opened in that beautiful light.

And she said, every now and then, that she felt 'so much better – so much stronger', and made old Sally sit by her, and talk to her, and smiled so happily, and there again were all her droll engaging little ways. And when the good rector came in, that evening, she welcomed him in the old pleasant way: though she could not run out, as in other times, when she heard his foot on the steps, to meet him at the door, and there was such a beautiful colour in her clear, thin cheeks, and she sang his favourite little song for him, just one verse, with the clear, rich voice he loved so well, and then tired. The voice remained in his ears long after, and often came again, and that little song, in lonely reveries, while he sat listening, in long silence, and twilight, a swan's song.

'You see, your little Lily is growing quite well again. I feel so much better.'

There was such a childish sunshine in her smile, his trembling heart believed it.

'Oh! little Lily, my darling!' he stopped – he was crying, and yet delighted. Smiling all the time, and crying, and through it a little laugh, as if he had waked from a dream of having lost her, and found her there – his treasure – safe. 'If anything happened to little Lily, I think the poor old man' – and the sentence was not finished; and, after a little pause, he said, quite cheerily – 'But I knew the spring would bring her back. I knew it, and here she is; the light of the house; little Lily, my treasure.'

And so he blessed and kissed her, and blessed her again, with all his fervent soul, laying his old hand lightly on her fair young head; and when she went up for the night, with gentle old Sally, and he heard her room door shut, he closed his own, and kneeling down, with clasped hands and streaming eyes, in a rapture of gratitude, he poured forth his thanksgivings before the Throne of all Mercies.

These outpourings of gratitude, all premature, for blessings not real but imagined, are not vain. They are not thrown away upon that glorious and marvellous God who draws near to all who will draw near to Him, reciprocates every emotion of our love with a tenderness literally parental, and is delighted with his creatures' appreciation of his affection and his trustworthiness; who knows whereof we are made, and remembers that we are but dust, and is our faithful Creator. Therefore, friend, though thou fearest a shadow, thy prayer is not wasted; though thou rejoicest in an illusion, thy thanksgiving is not in vain. They are the expressions of thy faith recorded in Heaven, and counted – oh! marvellous love and compassion! – to thee for righteousness.

Chapter Eighty

In which two acquaintances become, on a sudden, marvellously friendly in the churchyard; and Mr Dangerfield smokes a pipe in the Brass Castle, and resolves that the dumb shall speak

On Sunday, Mervyn, after the good doctor's sermon and benediction, wishing to make enquiry of the rector touching the movements of his clerk, whose place was provisionally supplied by a corpulent and unctuous mercenary from Dublin, whose fat presence and panting delivery were in signal contrast with the lank figure and deep cavernous tones of the absent official, loitered in the churchyard to allow time for the congregation to disperse, and the parson to disrobe and emerge.

He was reading an epitaph on an expansive black flagstone, in the far corner of the churchyard – it is still there – upon several ancestral members of the family of Lowe, who slept beneath 'in hope', as the stone-cutter informed the upper world; and musing, as sad men will, upon the dates and vanities of the record, when a thin white hand was lightly laid upon his sleeve from behind; and looking round, in expectation of seeing the rector's grave, simple, kindly countenance, he beheld, instead, with a sort of odd thrill, the white glittering face of Mr Paul Dangerfield.

'Hamlet in the churchyard!' said the white gentleman, with an ambiguous playfulness, very like a sneer. 'I'm too old to play Horatio; but standing at his elbow, if the Prince permits, I have a friendly word or two to say, in my own dry way.'

There was in Mervyn's nature something that revolted instinctively from the singular person who stood at his shoulder. Their organisations and appetites were different, I suppose, and repellent. Cold and glittering was the *'gelidus anguis in herba'* – the churchyard grass – who had lifted his baleful crest close to his ear.

There was a slight flush on 'Hamlet's' forehead, and a glimmer of something dangerous in his eye, as he glanced on his stark acquaintance. But the feeling was transitory and unreasonable, and he greeted him with a cold and sad civility.

'I was thinking, Mr Mervyn,' said Mr Dangerfield, politely, 'of walking up to the Tiled House, after church, to pay my respects, and ask the favour of five minutes' discourse with you; and seeing you here, I ventured to present myself.'

'If I can do anything to serve Mr Dangerfield,' began Mervyn.

Dangerfield smiled and bowed. He was very courteous; but in his smile there was a character of superiority which Mervyn felt almost like an insult.

'You mistake me, Sir. I'm all gratitude; but I don't mean to trouble you further than to ask your attention for two or three minutes. I've a thing to tell you, Sir. *I'm* really anxious to serve *you*. I wish I could. And 'tis only that I've recollected since I saw you, a circumstance of which possibly you may make some use.'

'I'm deeply obliged, Sir – deeply,' said Mervyn, eagerly.

'I'm only, Sir, too happy. It relates to Charles Archer. I've recollected, since I saw you, a document concerning his death. It had a legal bearing of some sort, and was signed by at least three gentlemen. One was Sir Philip Drayton, of Drayton Hall, who was with him at Florence in his last illness. I may have signed it myself, but I don't recollect. It was by his express desire, to quiet, as I remember, some proceedings which might have made a noise, and compromised his family.'

'Can you bring to mind the nature of the document?'

'Why, thus much. I'm quite sure it began with a certificate of his death; and then, I think, was added a statement, at his last request, which surprised, or perhaps, shocked us. I only say I *think* – for though I remember that such a statement was solemnly made, I can't bring to mind whether it was set out in the writing of which I speak. Only I am confident it referred to some crime – a confession of something; but for the life o' me I can't recollect what. If you could let me know the subject of your suspicion it might help me. I should never have remembered this occurrence, for instance, had it not been for our meeting t'other day. I can't exactly – in fact, *at all* – bring to mind what the crime was: forgery, or perjury – eh?'

'Why, Sir, 'twas this,' said Mervyn, and stopped short, not knowing how far even this innocent confidence might compromise Irons. Dangerfield, his head slightly inclined, was disconcertingly silent and attentive.

'I – I suspect,' resumed Mervyn, 'I suspect, Sir, 'twas *perjury*,' said Mervyn.

'Oh! perjury? I see – in the matter of his testimony in that distressing prosecution. My Lord Dunoran – hey?'

Mervyn bowed, and Dangerfield remained silent and thoughtful for a minute or two, and then said: 'I see, Sir – I *think* I see; but, who then was the guilty man, who killed Mr — pooh, what's-his-name – the deceased man, – you know?'

'Why, upon that point, Sir, I should have some hesitation in speaking. I can only now say thus much, that I'm satisfied he, Charles Archer, in swearing as he did, committed wilful perjury.'

'You are? – oho! – oh! This is satisfactory. You don't, of course, mean mere conjecture – eh?'

'I know not, Sir, how you would call it, but 'tis certainly a feeling fixed in my mind.'

'Well, Sir, I trust it may prove well founded. I wish I had myself a copy of that paper; but, though I have it not, I think I can put you in a way to get it. It was addressed, I perfectly recollect, to the Messrs. Elrington, gentlemen attorneys, in Chancery-lane, London. I remember it, because my Lord Castlemallard employed them eight or nine years afterwards in some law business, which recalled the whole matter to my mind before it had quite faded. No doubt they have it there. 'Twas about a week after his death. The date of that you can have from newspapers. You'll not mention my name when writing, because they mayn't like the trouble of searching, and my Lord Castlemallard would not approve my meddling in other persons' affairs – even in yours.'

'I shan't forget. But what if they refuse to seek the paper out?'

'Make it worth their while in money, Sir; and, though they may grumble over it, I warrant they'll find it.'

'Sir,' said Mervyn, suddenly, 'I cannot thank you half enough. This statement, should it appear attached, as you suppose, to the certificate, may possibly place me on the track of that lost witness, who yet may restore my ruined name and fortunes. I thank you, Sir. From my heart I *do* thank you.'

And he grasped Dangerfield's white thin hand in his, with a fervour how unlike his cold greeting of only a few minutes before, and shook it with an eager cordiality.

Thus across the grave of these old Lowes did the two shake hands, as they had never done before; and Dangerfield, white and glittering, and like a frolicsome man entering into a joke, wrung his with an exaggerated demonstration, and then flung it downward with a sudden jerk, as if throwing down a glove. The gesture, the smile, and the suspicion of a scowl, had a strange mixture of cordiality, banter and defiance, and he was laughing a quiet 'ha, ha, ha'; and, wagging his head, he said – 'Well, I thought 'twould please you to hear this; and anything more I can do or think of is equally at your service.'

So, side by side they returned, picking their steps among the graves and headstones, to the old church porch.

For a day or two after the storm, the temper of our cynical friend of the silver spectacles had suffered. Perhaps he did not like the news which had reached him since, and would have preferred that Charles Nutter had made good his escape from the gripe of justice.

The management of Lord Castlemallard's Irish estates had devolved provisionally upon Mr Dangerfield during the absence of Nutter and the coma of his rival; and the erect white gentleman, before his desk in his elbow-chair, when, after his breakfast, about to open the letters and the books relating to this part of his charge, used sometimes to grin over his work, and jabber to himself his hard scoffs and gibes over the sins and follies of man, and the chops and changes of this mortal life.

But from and after the night of the snow-storm he had contracted a disgust for this part of his labours, and he used to curse Nutter with remarkable intensity, and with an iteration which, to a listener who thought that even the best thing may be said too often, would have been tiresome.

Perhaps a little occurrence, which Mr Dangerfield himself utterly despised, may have had something to do with his bitter temper, and gave an unsatisfactory turn to his thoughts. It took place on the eventful night of the tempest.

If some people saw visions that night, others dreamed dreams. In a midnight storm like this, time was when the solemn peal and defiant clang of the holy bells would have rung out confusion through the winged hosts of 'the prince of the powers of the air', from the heights of the abbey tower. Everybody has a right to his own opinion on the matter. Perhaps the prince and his army are no more upon the air on such a night than on any other; or that being so, they no more hastened their departure by reason of the bells than the eclipse does by reason of the beating of the Emperor of China's gongs. But this I aver, whatever the cause, upon such nights of storm, the sensoria of some men are crossed by such wild variety and succession of images, as amounts very nearly to the Walpurgis of a fever. It is not the mere noise – other noises won't do it. The air, to be sure, is thin, and blood-vessels expand, and perhaps the brain is pressed upon unduly. Well, I don't know. Material laws may possibly account for it. I can only speak with certainty of the phenomenon. I've experienced it; and some among those of my friends who have reached that serene period of life in which we con over our ailments, register our sensations, and place ourselves upon regimens, tell me the same story of themselves. And this, too, I know, that upon the night in question, Mr Paul Dangerfield, who was not troubled either with vapours or superstitions, as he lay in his green-curtained bed in the Brass Castle, had as many dreams flitting over his brain and voices humming and buzzing in his ears, as if he had been a poet or a pythoness.

He had not become, like poor Sturk before his catastrophe, a dreamer of dreams habitually. I suppose he did dream. The beasts do. But his visions never troubled him; and I don't think there was one morning in a year on which he could have remembered his last night's dream at the breakfast-table.

On this particular night, however, he did dream. *Vidit somnium.* He thought that Sturk was dead, and laid out in a sort of state in an open coffin, with a great bouquet on his breast, something in the continental fashion, as he remembered it in the case of a great, stern, burly ecclesiastic in Florence. The coffin stood on tressels in the aisle of Chapelizod church; and, of all persons in the world, he and Charles Nutter stood side by side as chief mourners, each with a great waxen taper burning in one hand, and a white pocket-handkerchief in the other.

Now in dreams it sometimes happens that men undergo sensations of awe, and even horror, such as waking they never know, and which the scenery and situation of the dream itself appear wholly inadequate to produce. Mr Paul Dangerfield, had he been called on to do it, would have kept solitary watch in a dead man's chamber, and smoked his pipe as serenely as he would in the club-room of the Phoenix. But here it was different. The company were all hooded and silent, sitting in rows: and there was a dismal sound of distant waters, and an indefinable darkness and horror in the air; and, on a sudden, up sat the corpse of Sturk, and thundered, with a shriek, a dreadful denunciation, and Dangerfield started up in his bed aghast, and cried – 'Charles Archer!'

The storm was bellowing and shrieking outside, and for some time that grim, white gentleman, bolt upright in his shirt, did not know distinctly in what part of the world, or, indeed, in what world he was.

'So,' said Mr Dangerfield, soliloquising, 'Charles Nutter's alive, and in prison, and what comes next? 'Tis enough to make one believe in a devil almost! Why wasn't he drowned, d—n him? How did he get himself taken, d—n him again? From the time I came into this unlucky village I've smelt danger. That accursed beast, a corpse, and a ghost, and a prisoner at last – well, he has been my evil genius. *If* he were drowned or hanged; born to be hanged, I hope: all I want is quiet – just *quiet*; but I've a feeling the play's not played out yet. He'll give the hangman the slip, will he? Not if I can help it, though; but caution, Sir, caution; life's at stake – my life's on the cast. The clerk's a wise dog to get out of the way. Death's walking. What a cursed fool I was when I came here and saw those beasts, and knew them, not to turn back again, and leave them to possess their paradise! I think I've lost my caution and common sense under some cursed infatuation. That handsome, insolent wench, Miss Gertrude, 'twould be something to have her, and to humble her, too; but – but 'tis not worth a week in such a neighbourhood.'

Now this soliloquy, which broke into an actual mutter every here and there, occurred at about eleven o'clock a.m., in the little low parlour of the Brass Castle, that looked out on the wintry river.

Mr Dangerfield knew the virtues of tobacco, so he charged his pipe, and sat grim, white, and erect by the fire. It is not everyone that is 'happy thinking', and the knight of the silver spectacles followed out his solitary discourse, with his pipe between his lips, and saw all sorts of things through the white narcotic smoke.

'It would not do to go off and leave affairs thus; a message might follow me, eh? No; I'll stay and see it out, quite out. Sturk – Barnabas Sturk. If he came to his speech for five minutes – hum – we'll see. I'll speak with Mrs Sturk about it – we must help him to his speech – a prating fellow; 'tis hard he should hold his tongue; yes, we'll help him to his speech; 'tis in the interest of justice – eternal justice – ha, ha, the truth, the whole truth, and nothing but the truth. Let Dr Sturk be sworn – ha, ha – *magna est veritas* – there is nothing hidden that shall not be revealed; ha, ha. Let Dr Sturk be called.'

So the white, thin phantom of the spectacles and tobacco pipe, sitting upright by the fire, amused himself with a solitary banter. Then he knocked the white ashes out upon the hob, stood up with his back to the fire, in grim rumination, for about a minute, at the end of which he unlocked his desk, and took forth a letter with a large red seal. If was more than two months old by this time, and was, in fact, that letter from the London doctor which he had expected with some impatience.

It was not very long, and standing he read it through, and his white face contracted, and darkened, and grew strangely intense and stern as he did so.

' 'Tis devilish strong – ha, ha, ha – conclusive, indeed.' He was amused again. 'I've kept it long enough – *igni reservata*.'

And holding it in the tongs, he lighted a corner, and as the last black fragment of it, covered with creeping sparks, flew up the chimney, he heard the voice of a gentleman hallooing in the courtyard.

Chapter Eighty-one
In which Mr Dangerfield receives a visitor, and makes a call

Dangerfield walked out and blandly greeted the visitor, who turned out to be Mr Justice Lowe.

'I give you good-morning, Sir; pray, alight and step in. Hallo, Doolan, take Mr Justice Lowe's horse.'

So Mr Lowe thanked him, in his cold way, and bowing, strode into the Brass Castle; and after the customary civilities, sat himself down, and says he, 'I've been at the Crown Office, Sir, about this *murder*, we may call it, upon Sturk, and I told them you could throw a light, as I thought, on the matter.'

'As how, Sir?'

'Why, regarding the kind of feeling that subsisted between the prisoner, Nutter, and Doctor Sturk.'

''Tis unpleasant, Sir, but I can't object.'

'There was an angry feeling about the agency, I believe? Lord Castlemallard's agency, eh?' continued Lowe.

'Well, I suppose it *was* that; there certainly was an unpleasant feeling – *very* unpleasant.'

'You've heard him express it?'

'Yes; I think most gentlemen who know him have. Why, he made no disguise of it; he was no great talker, but we've heard him on that subject.'

'But you specially know how it stood between them in respect of the agency?'

'Yes.'

'Very good, Sir,' said Lowe.

'And I've a notion that something decisive should be done toward effecting a full discovery, and I'll consider of a method,' replied Dangerfield.

'How do you mean?' said Lowe, looking up with a glance like a hawk.

'How! Why I'll talk it over with Mrs Sturk this evening.'

'Why, what has she got to tell?'

'Nothing, as I suppose; I'll see her today; there's nothing to tell; but something, I think, to be done; it hasn't been set about rightly; 'tis a botched business hitherto – that's in *my* judgment.'

'Yet 'tis rather a strong case,' answered Mr Lowe, superciliously.

'Rather a strong case, so it is, but I'll clench it, Sir; it ought to be certain.'

'Well, Sir?' said Lowe, who expected to hear more.

'Yes,' said Dangerfield, briskly, ''twill depend on *her*; *I'll* suggest, *she'll* decide.'

'And why *she*, Sir?' said Lowe sharply.

'Because 'tis her business and her right, and no-one else can,' answered Dangerfield just as tartly, with his hands in his breeches' pockets, and his head the least thing o' one side, and then with a bow, 'won't you drink a glass of wine, Sir?' which was as much as to say, you'll get no more from me.

'I thank you, Sir, no; 'tis a little too early for me.' And so with the usual ceremonies, Mr Lowe departed, the governor of the Brass Castle walking beside his horse, as far as the iron gate, to do him honour; and as he rode away towards Lucan, Mr Dangerfield followed him with a snowy smirk.

Then briskly, after his wont, the knight of the shining spectacles made his natty toilet; and in a few minutes his cocked hat was seen gliding along the hedge toward Chapelizod.

He glanced up at Sturk's window – it was a habit now – so soon as he came in sight, but all looked as usual. So he mounted the steps, and asked to see Mrs Sturk.

'My dear Madam,' said he, after due courtesies interchanged, 'I've but a few minutes; my horse waits yonder at the Phoenix, and I'm away to town. How does your patient today?'

'Oh, mighty well – wonderful – that is considering how cold the weather is. The doctor says he's lower, indeed, but I don't mind that, for he must be lower while the cold continues; I always say that; and I judge very much by the eye; don't you, Mr Dangerfield? By his looks, you know; they can't deceive me, and I assure you – '

'Your house is quiet; are the children out, Ma'am?'

'Oh, yes, with Mag in the park.'

'Perhaps, Ma'am, you'd let me see him?'

'See him?'

'Yes, look on him, Ma'am, only for a moment you know.'

She looked very much surprised, and perhaps a little curious and frightened.

'I hope you haven't heard he's worse, Mr Dangerfield. Oh, Sir, sure you haven't?'

'No, Madam, on my honour, except from yourself, I've heard nothing of him today; but I'd like to see him, and speak a word to you, with your permission.'

So Mrs Sturk led the way upstairs, whispering as she ascended; for she had always the fancy in her head that her Barney was in a sweet light sleep, from which he was on no account to be awakened, forgetting, or not clearly knowing, that all the ordnance in the barrack-yard over the way had not voice enough to call him up from that dread slumber.

'You may go down, my dear,' said Mr Dangerfield to the little girl, who rose silently from the chair as they entered; 'with your permission, Mistress Sturk – I say, child, you may run down,' and he smiled a playful, sinister smile, with a little wave of his finger toward the door. So she courtesied and vanished obediently.

Then he drew the curtain, and looked on Doctor Sturk. There lay the hero of the tragedy, his smashed head strapped together with sticking-plaster, and a great white fold of fine linen, like a fantastic turban, surmounting his grim yellow features.

Then he slipped his fingers under the coverlet, and took his hand; a strange greeting that! But it was his pulse he wanted, and when he had felt it for a while, 'Psha!' said he in a whisper – for the semblance of sleep affected everyone alike – 'his pulse is just gone. Now, Madam, listen to me. There's not a soul in Chapelizod but yourself who does not know his wounds are mortal – he's *dying*, Ma'am.'

'Oh – oh – o – o – oh, Mr Dangerfield, you don't – you don't think so,' wildly cried the poor little lady, growing quite white with terror and agony.

'Now, pray, my dear Mistress Sturk, compose yourself, and hear me out: 'Tis my belief he has a chance; but none, absolutely *no* chance, Madam, unless my advice be taken. There's not an evening, Ma'am, I meet Doctor Toole at the club, but I hear the same report – a little lower – always the same – lower – sinking – and *no hope*.'

Here Mrs Sturk broke out again.

'Now, Madam,' I protest you'll make me regret my visit, unless you please to command yourself. While the doctors who are about him have got him in hands, there's neither hope for his life, nor for his recovering, for one moment, the use of his speech. Pray, Madam, hear me. They state as much themselves. Now, Madam, I say, we must have a chance for his life, and if that fails, a chance for his speech. The latter, Madam, is of more consequence than, perhaps, you are aware.'

Poor little Mrs Sturk was looking very pale, and breathing very hard, with her hand pressed to her heart.

'I've done what I could, you know, to see my way through his affairs, and I've succeeded in keeping his creditors quiet.'

At this point poor Mrs Sturk broke out, 'Oh! may the Father of the fatherless, if such they are to be, bless and reward – oh-oh – ho-ho, Mr Dangerfield – oh – oh-oh – Sir.'

'Now, pray, Madam, oblige me and be tranquil. I say, Madam, his affairs, I suspect, are by no means in so bad a case as we at first supposed, and he has got, or I'm mistaken, large sums out, but where, neither I nor you can tell. Give him five minutes' speech, and it may be worth a thousand pounds to you – well, not to you, if you will, but to his children. And again, Madam, 'tis of the utmost importance that he should be able to state who was the villain who struck him – Charles – a – Charles – Mr Nutter – you know, Madam.'

'Oh! that dreadful – dreadful man – may Heaven forgive him. Oh, my Barney! Look at him there – he'd forgive him if he could speak. You would, my blessed Barney – you would.'

'To be sure he would. But see, Ma'am, the importance of having his evidence to settle the fact. Well, I know that he would not like to hang anybody. But suppose, Ma'am, Charles Nutter is innocent, don't you think he'd like to acquit him? Ay, you do. Well, Ma'am, 'tis due to the public, you see, and to his children that he should have a chance of recovering his speech, and to common humanity that he should have a chance for his *life* – eh? And *neither* will the doctors who have him in hands allow him. Now, Madam, there's a simple operation, called trepanning, you have heard of it, which would afford him such a chance, but fearing its failure they won't try it, although they allege that without it *he must die*, d'ye see? – ay, *die he must*, without a cast for his life if you won't try it.'

And so, by harping on the alternatives, and demonstrating the prudence, humanity, and duty of action, and the inevitably fatal consequences of the other course, he wrought upon her at last to write a note to Surgeon Dillon to come out on the evening following, and to perform the operation. The dreadful word 'today', the poor little woman could not abide. She pleaded for a respite, and so, half-distracted, fixed tomorrow.

'I hope, my dear Madam, you've some little confidence in me. I think I have shown an interest, and I've striven to be of use.'

'Oh, Sir, Mr Dangerfield, you've been too good, our guardian angel; but for you, Sir, we should not have had a roof over our heads, or a bed to lie on; oh! may – '

'Well, Ma'am, you please to speak too highly of my small services; but I would plead them, humble as they are, as a claim on your confidence, and having decided upon this wise and necessary course, pray do not say a word about it to anybody but myself. I will go to town, and arrange for the doctor's visit, and you'll soon, I hope, have real grounds for gratitude, not to me, Ma'am, but to Heaven.'

Chapter Eighty-two

*In which Mr Paul Dangerfield pays his respects and compliments
at Belmont; where other visitors also present themselves*

Before going to town, Mr Dangerfield, riding over the bridge and up
the Palmerstown-road, dismounted at Belmont door-steps, and asked
for the general. He was out. Then for Miss Rebecca Chattesworth.
Yes, she was in the withdrawing-room. And so, light, white, and wiry,
he ascended the stairs swiftly.

'Mr Dangerfield,' cried Dominick, throwing open the door; and
that elderly and ill-starred wooer glided in thereat.

'Madam, your most humble servant.'

'Oh! Mr Dangerfield? You're very welcome, Sir,' said Aunt Becky,
with a grand courtesy, and extending her thin jewelled hand, which
he took gallantly, with another bow, and a smile, and a flash from his
spectacles.

Aunt Becky laid down her volume of Richardson. She was quite
alone, except for her little monkey – Goblin – with a silver hoop about
his waist, and a chain thereto attached; two King Charles's dogs,
whose barking subsided after a while; and one grey parrot on a perch
in the bow-window, who happily was not in a very chatty mood just
then. So the human animals were able to edge in a sentence easily
enough. And Mr Dangerfield said: 'I'm happy in having found you,
Madam; for whatever be my disappointments else, to Miss Rebecca
Chattesworth at least I owe a debt of gratitude, which, despairing to
repay it, I can only acknowledge; and leaving unacknowledged, I
should have departed from Ireland most unhappily.'

'What a fop! What a fop,' said the parrot.

'You rate my poor wishes too highly, Mr Dangerfield. I over-
estimated, myself, my influence with the young lady; but why speak
of your departure, Sir, so soon? A little time may yet work a change.'

'You lie, you dog! You lie, you lie, you lie,' said the parrot.

'Madam,' said he with a shake of his head, ''tis hoping against hope.
Time will add to *my* wrinkles without softening *her* aversion. I utterly

despair. While there remained one spark of hope I should never have dreamed of leaving Chapelizod.'

Here there was a considerable pause, during which the parrot occasionally repeated, 'You lie, you lie – you dog – you lie.'

'Of course, Sir, if the chance be not worth waiting for, you do well to be gone wherever your business or your pleasures, Sir, invite you,' said Aunt Becky, a little loftily.

'What a fop!' said the parrot. 'You lie, you dog!'

'Neither business, Madam, nor pleasures invite me. My situation here has been most distressing. So long as hope cheered me, I little regarded what might be said or thought; but I tell you honestly that hope is extinguished; and it has grown to me intolerable longer to remain in sight of that treasure for which I cannot cease to wish, and which I never can possess. I've grown, Madam, to detest the place.'

Aunt Becky, with her head very high, adjusted in silence the two China mandarins on the mantelpiece – first, one very carefully, then the other. And there was a pause, during which one of the lapdogs screamed; and the monkey, who had boxed his ears, jumped, with a ringing of his chain, chattering, on the back of the armchair in which the grim suitor sat. Mr Dangerfield would have given the brute a slap in the face, but that he knew how that would affect Miss Rebecca Chattesworth.

'So, Madam,' said he, standing up abruptly, 'I am here to thank you most gratefully for the countenance given to my poor suit, which, here and now, at last and for ever, I forego. I shall leave for England so soon as my business will allow; and as I made no secret of my suit, so I shall make none of the reasons of my departure. I'm an out-spoken man, Madam; and as the world knew my hopes, I shall offer them no false excuses for my departure; but lift my hat, and bow to fortune – a defeated man.'

'*Avez-vous diné, mon petit coquin?*' said the parrot.

'Well, Sir, I will not altogether deny you have reason for what you design; and it may be, 'tis as well to bring the matter to a close, though your resolution has taken me by surprise. She hath shown herself so perverse in this respect, that I allow I see no present likelihood of a change; and indeed I do not quite understand my niece; and, very like, she does not comprehend herself.'

Mr Dangerfield almost smiled one of his grim disconcerting smiles, and a cynical light played over his face; and the black monkey behind him grinned and hugged himself like his familiar. The disappointed gentleman thought he understood Miss Gertrude pretty well.

'I thought,' said Aunt Becky; 'I suspected – did you – a certain young gentleman in this neighbourhood –'

'As having found his way to the young lady's good graces?' asked Dangerfield.

'Yes; and I conjecture you know whom I mean,' said Aunt Rebecca.

'Who – pray, Madam?' he demanded.

'Why, Lieutenant Puddock,' said Aunt Becky, again adjusting the china on the chimneypiece.

'Eh? – truly? – that did not strike me,' replied Dangerfield.

He had a disconcerting way of saying the most ordinary things, and there was a sort of latent meaning, like a half-heard echo, under-running the surface of his talk, which sometimes made people undefinably uncomfortable; and Aunt Becky looked a little stately and flushed; but in a minute more the conversation proceeded.

'I have many regrets, Miss Chattesworth, in leaving this place. The loss of your society – don't mistake me, I never flatter – is a chief one. Some of your views and plans interested me much. I shall see my Lord Castlemallard sooner than I should had my wishes prospered; and I will do all in my power to engage him to give the site for the building, and stones from the quarry free; and I hope, though no longer a resident here, you will permit me to contribute fifty pounds towards the undertaking.'

'Sir, I wish there were more gentlemen of your public spirit and Christian benevolence,' cried Aunt Becky, very cordially; 'and I have heard of all your goodness to that unhappy family of Doctor Sturk's – poor wretched man!'

'A bagatelle, Madam,' said Dangerfield, shaking his head and waving his hand slightly; 'but I hope to do them, or at least the public, a service of some importance, by bringing conviction home to the assassin who struck him down, and that in terms so clear and authentic, as will leave no room for doubt in the minds of any; and to this end I'm resolved to stick at no trifling sacrifice, and, rather than fail, I'll drain my purse.'

'*Mon petit coquin!*' prattled the parrot in the bow-window.

'And, Madam,' said he, after he had risen to take his leave, 'as I before said, I'm a plain man. I mean, so soon as I can wind my business up, to leave this place and country – I would *tonight*, if I could; but less, I fear, than some days – perhaps a week will not suffice. When I'm gone, Madam, I beg you'll exercise no reserve respecting the cause of my somewhat abrupt departure; I could easily make a pretext of something else; but the truth, Madam, is easiest as well as best to be told; I protracted my stay so long as hope continued. Now my suit is ended, I can no longer endure the place. The remembrance of your kindness only, sweetens the bitterness of my regret, and that I shall bear with me so long, Madam, as life remains.' And saying this, as Mr Richardson writes, 'he bowed upon her passive hand,' and Miss Rebecca made him a grand and gracious courtesy.

As he retreated, whom should Dominick announce but Captain Cluffe and Lieutenant Puddock. And there was an odd smile on Mr Dangerfield's visage, as he slightly acknowledged them in passing, which Aunt Rebecca somehow did not like.

So Aunt Becky's levee went on; and as Homer, in our schoolboy ear, sang the mournful truth, that 'as are the generations of the forest leaves so are the succession of men,' the Dangerfield efflorescence had no sooner disappeared, and that dry leaf whisked away down the stairs, than Cluffe and Puddock budded forth and bloomed in his place, in the sunshine of Aunt Rebecca's splendid presence.

Cluffe, in virtue of his rank and pretensions, marched in the van, and, as Aunt Becky received him, little Puddock's round eyes swept the room in search, perhaps, of some absent object.

'The general's not here,' said Aunt Becky loftily and severely, interpreting Puddock's wandering glance in that way. 'Your visit, perhaps, is for him – you'll find him in his study, with the orderly.'

'My visit, Madam,' said Puddock, with a slight blush, 'was intended for you, Madam – not for the general, whom I had the honour of seeing this morning on parade.'

'Oh! for me? I thank you,' said Aunt Rebecca, with a rather dry acknowledgment. And so she turned and chatted with Cluffe, who, not being at liberty to talk upon his usual theme – his poor, unhappy friend, Puddock, and his disgraces – was eloquent upon the monkey, and sweet upon the lapdogs, and laughed till he grew purple at the humours of the parrot, and swore, as gentlemen then swore, 'twas a conjuror, a wonder, and as good as a play. While this entertaining conversation was going on, there came a horrid screech and a long succession of yelps from the courtyard.

'Good gracious mercy,' cried Aunt Rebecca, sailing rapidly to the window, ''tis Flora's voice. Sweet creature, have they killed you – my angel; what is it? – where *are* you, sweetheart? – where *can* she be? Oh, dear – oh, dear!' – and she looked this way and that in her distraction.

But the squeak subsided, and Flora was not to be seen; and Aunt Becky's presence of mind returned, and she said: 'Captain Cluffe, 'tis a great liberty; but you're humane – and, besides, I know that *you* would readily do me a kindness.' That emphasis was shot at poor Puddock. 'And may I pray you to try on the steps if you can see the dear animal, anywhere – you know Flora?'

'Know her? – Oh dear, yes,' cried Cluffe with alacrity, who, however, did *not*, but relied on her answering to her name, which he bawled lustily from the door-steps and about the courtyard, with many terms of endearment, intended for Aunt Becky's ear, in the drawing-room.

Little Puddock, who was hurt at that lady's continued severity, was desirous of speaking; for he liked Aunt Becky, and his heart swelled within him at her injustice; but though he hemmed once or twice, somehow the exordium was not ready, and his feelings could not find a tongue.

Aunt Becky looked steadfastly from the window for a while, and then sailed majestically toward the door, which the little ensign, with an humble and somewhat frightened countenance, hastened to open.

'Pray, Sir, don't let me trouble you,' said Aunt Becky, in her high, cold way.

'Madam, 'tis no trouble – it would be a happiness to me, Madam, to serve you in any way you would permit; but *'tis* a trouble to me, Madam, indeed, that you leave the room, and a greater trouble,' said little Puddock, waxing fluent as he proceeded, 'that I have incurred your displeasure – indeed, Madam, I know not how – your goodness to me, Madam, in my sickness, I never can forget.'

'You *can* forget, Sir – you *have* forgot. Though, indeed, Sir, there was little to remember, I – I'm glad you thought me kind, Sir. I – I wish you well, Sir,' said Aunt Becky. She was looking down and a little pale, and in her accents something hurried and almost sad. 'And as for my displeasure, Sir, who said I was displeased? And if I were, what could my displeasure be to you? No, Sir,' she went on almost fiercely, and with a little stamp on the floor, 'you don't care; and why should you? – You've proved it – you don't, Lieutenant Puddock, and you *never* did.'

And, without waiting for an answer, Aunt Becky flashed out of the room, and upstairs to her chamber, the door of which she slammed fiercely; and Gertrude, who was writing a letter in her own chamber, heard her turn the key hastily in the lock.

When Cluffe, who for some time continued to exercise his lungs in persuasive invitations to Flora, at last gave over the pursuit, and returned to the drawing-room, to suggest that the goddess in question had probably retreated to the kitchen, he was a good deal chagrined to find the drawing-room 'untreasured of its mistress'.

Puddock looked a good deal put out, and his explanation was none of the clearest; and he could not at all say that the lady was coming back.

'I think, Lieutenant Puddock,' said Cluffe, who was much displeased, and had come to regard Aunt Rebecca very much as under his especial protection, 'it might have been better we hadn't called here. I – you see – you're not – you see it yourself – you've offended Miss Rebecca Chattesworth somehow, and I'm afraid you've not mended matters while I was downstairs bawling after that cursed – that – the – little dog, you know. And – and for my part, I'm devilish sorry I came, Sir.'

This was said after a wait of nearly ten minutes, which appeared at least twice as long.

'I'm sorry, Sir, I embarrassed you with the disadvantage of my company,' answered little Puddock, with dignity.

'Why, 'tisn't that, you know,' rejoined Cluffe, in a patronising 'my good-fellow' sort of way; 'you know I always liked your company devilish well. But where's the good of putting oneself in the way of being thought *de trop* – don't you see – by other people – and annoyed in this way – and – you – you don't know the *world*, Puddock – you'd much better leave yourself in any hands, d'ye see; and so, I suppose, we may as well be off now – 'tis no use waiting longer.'

And discontentedly and lingeringly the gallant captain, followed by Puddock, withdrew himself – pausing to caress the wolf-dog at the corner of the courtyard, and loitering as long as it was decent in the avenue.

All this time Miss Gertrude Chattesworth, like her more mature relative, was in the quiet precincts of her chamber. She, too, had locked her door, and, with throbbing temples and pale face, was writing a letter, from which I take the liberty of printing a few scarcely coherent passages.

I saw you on Sunday – for near two hours – may Heaven forgive me, thinking of little else than you. And, oh! what would I not have given to speak, were it but ten words to you? When is my miserable probation to end? Why is this perverse mystery persisted in? I sometimes lose all hope in my destiny, and well-nigh all trust in you. I feel that I am a deceiver, and cannot bear it. I assure you, on my sacred honour, I believe there is nothing gained by all this – oh! forgive the word – deception. How or when is it to terminate? – What do you purpose? – Why does the clerk's absence from the town cause you so much uneasiness? – Is there any danger you have not disclosed? A friend told me that you were making preparations to leave Chapelizod and return to England. I think I was on the point of fainting when I heard it. I almost regret I did not, as the secret would thus have been discovered, and my emancipation accomplished. How have you acquired this strange influence over me, to make me so deceive those in whom I should most naturally confide? I am persuaded they believe I really recoil from you. And what is this new business of Doctor Sturk? I am distracted with uncertainties and fears. I hear so little, and imperfectly from you, I cannot tell from your dark hints whether some new danger lurks in those unlooked-for quarters. I know not what magic binds me so to you, to endure the misery of this strange deceitful mystery – but you are all mystery; and yet be not – you cannot be – my evil genius. You will not condemn me longer to a wretchedness that must destroy me. I conjure you, declare yourself. What have we to fear? I will brave all – anything rather than darkness, suspense, and the consciousness of a continual dissimulation. Declare yourself, I implore of you, and be my angel of light and deliverance.

There is a vast deal more, but this sample is quite enough; and when the letter was finished, she signed it –

> Your most unhappy and too-faithful,
> GERTRUDE

And having sealed it, she leaned her anxious head upon her hand, and sighed heavily.

She knew very well by what means to send it; and the letter awaited at his house him for whom it was intended on his return that evening.

Chapter Eighty-three

In which the knight of the silver spectacles makes the acquaintance of the sage 'Black Dillon', and confers with him in his retreat

At that time there had appeared in Dublin an erratic genius in the medical craft, a young surgeon, 'Black Dillon', they called him, the glory and disgrace of his calling; such as are from time to time raised up to abase the pride of intellect, and terrify the dabblers in vice. A prodigious mind, illuminating darkness and shivering obstacles at a blow, with an electric force – possessing the power of a demigod, and the lusts of a swine. Without order, without industry; defying all usages and morality; lost for weeks together in the catacombs of vice; and emerging to reassert in an hour the supremacy of his intellect; without principles or shame; laden with debt; and shattered and poisoned with his vices; a branded and admired man.

In the presence of this outcast genius and prodigy of vice, stood Mr Dangerfield. There were two other gentlemen in the same small room, one of whom was doggedly smoking, with his hat on, over the fire; the other snoring in a crazy armchair, on the back of which hung his wig. The window was small and dirty; the air muddy with tobacco-smoke, and inflamed with whiskey. Singing and the clang of glasses was resounding from the next room, together with peals of coarse laughter; and from that on the other side, the high tones and hard swearing, and the emphatic slapping of a heavy hand upon the table, indicating a rising quarrel, were heard. From one door through another, across the narrow floor on which Mr Dangerfield stood, every now and then lounged some neglected, dirty, dissipated-looking inmate of these unwholesome precincts. In fact, Surgeon Dillon's present residence was in that *diversorium pecatorum*, the Four Courts Marshalsea in Molesworth-court. As these gentlemen shuffled or swaggered through, they generally nodded, winked, grunted, or otherwise saluted the medical gentleman, and stared at his visitor. For as the writer of the Harleian tract – I forget its name – pleasantly observes – 'In gaol they are no proud men, but will be quickly acquainted without ceremony.'

Mr Dangerfield stood erect; all his appointments were natty, and his dress, though quiet, rich in material; and there was that air of reserve, and decision, and command about him, which suggests money, an article held much in esteem in that retreat. He had a way of seeing everything in a moment without either staring or stealing glances, and nobody suspected him of making a scrutiny. In the young surgeon he saw an object in strong contrast with himself. He was lean and ungainly, shy and savage, dressed in a long greasy silk morning gown, blotched with wine and punch over the breast. He wore his own black hair gathered into a knot behind, and in a neglected dusty state, as if it had not been disturbed since he rolled out of his bed. This being placed his large, red, unclean hands, with fingers spread, like a gentleman playing the harpsichord, upon the table, as he stood at the side opposite to Mr Dangerfield, and he looked with a haggard, surly stare on his visitor, through his great dark, deep-set prominent eyes, streaming fire, the one feature that transfixed the attention of all who saw him. He had a great brutal mouth, and his nose was pimply and inflamed, for Bacchus has his fires as well as Cupid, only he applies them differently. How polished showed Mr Dangerfield's chin opposed to the three days' beard of Black Dillon! How delicate his features compared with the lurid proboscis, and huge, sensual, sarcastic mouth of the gentleman in the dirty morning-gown and shapeless slippers, who confronted him with his glare, an image of degradation and power!

'Tuppince, Docthor Dillon,' said a short, fat, dirty nymph, without stays or hoop, setting down a 'naggin o' whiskey' between the medical man and his visitor.

The doctor, to do him justice, for a second or two looked confoundedly put out, and his eyes blazed fiercer as his face flushed.

'Three halfpence outside, and twopence here, Sir,' said he with an awkward grin, throwing the money on the table; 'that's the way our shepherd *deglubat oves*, Sir; she's brought it too soon, but no matter.'

It was not one o'clock, in fact.

'They *will* make mistakes, Sir; but you will not suffer their blunders long, I warrant,' said Dangerfield, lightly. 'Pray, Sir, can we have a room for a moment to ourselves?'

'We can, Sir, 'tis a liberal house; we can have anything; liberty itself, Sir – for an adequate sum,' replied Mr Dillon.

Whatever the sum was, the room was had, and the surgeon, who had palpably left his 'naggin' uneasily in company with the gentleman in the hat, and him without a wig, eyed Dangerfield curiously, thinking that possibly his grand-aunt Molly had left him the fifty guineas she was rumoured to have sewed up in her stays.

'There's a great deal of diversion, Sir, in five hundred guineas,' said Mr Dangerfield, and the spectacles dashed pleasantly upon the doctor.

'Ye may say that,' answered the grinning surgeon, with a quiet oath of expectation.

''Tis a handsome fee, Sir, and you may have it.'

'Five hundred guineas!'

'Ah, you've heard, Sir, perhaps, of the attempted murder in the park, on Doctor Sturk, of the Artillery; for which Mr Nutter now lies in prison?' said Mr Dangerfield.

'That I have, Sir.'

'Well, you shall have the money, Sir, if you perform a simple operation.'

''Tis not to hang him you want me?' said the doctor, with a gloomy sneer.

'Hang him! – ha, ha – no, Sir, Doctor Sturk still lives, but insensible. He must be brought to consciousness, and speech. Now, the trepan is the only way to effect it; and I'll be frank with you: Doctor Pell has been with him half a dozen times, and he says the operation would be instantaneously fatal. I don't believe him. So also says Sir Hugh Skelton, to whom I wrote in London – I don't believe him, either. At all events, the man is dying, and can't last very many days longer, so there's nothing risked. His wife wishes the operation; here's her note; and I'll give you five hundred guineas and – what are you here for?'

'Only eighteen, unless some more has come in this morning,' answered the doctor.

'And your liberty, Sir, *that* on the spot, if you undertake the operation, and the fee so soon as you have done it.'

The doctor's face blazed with a grin of exultation; he squared his shoulders and shook himself a little; and after a little silence, he demanded: 'Can you describe the case, Sir, as you stated it to Sir Hugh Skelton?'

'Surely, Sir, but I rely for it and the terms, upon the description of a village doctor, named Toole; an ignoramus, I fear.'

And with this preface he concisely repeated the technical description which he had compiled from various club conversations of

Dr Toole's, to which no person imagined he had been listening so closely.

'If that's the case, Sir, 'twill kill him.'

'Kill or cure, Sir, 'tis the only chance,' rejoined Dangerfield.

'What sort is the wife, Sir?' asked Black Dillon, with a very odd look, while his eye still rested on the short note that poor Mrs Sturk had penned.

'A nervous little woman of some two or three and forty,' answered the spectacles.

The queer look subsided. He put the note in his pocket, and looked puzzled, and then he asked – 'Is he any way related to you, Sir?'

'None in life, Sir. But that does not affect, I take it, the medical question.'

'No, it does *not* affect the medical question – nothing *can*,' observed the surgeon, in a sulky, sardonic way.

'Of course not,' answered the oracle of the silver spectacles, and both remained silent for a while.

'You want to have him speak? Well, suppose there's a hundred chances to one the trepan kills him on the spot – what then?' demanded the surgeon, uncomfortably.

Dangerfield pondered, also uncomfortably for a minute, but answered nothing; on the contrary, he demanded – 'And what then, Sir?'

'But here, in this case,' said Black Dillon, 'there's no chance at all, do you see, there's *no* chance, good, bad or indifferent; none at all.'

'But *I* believe there *is*,' replied Dangerfield, decisively.

'You believe, but *I* know.'

'See, Sir,' said Dangerfield, darkening, and speaking with a strange snarl; 'I know what I'm about. I've a desire, Sir, that he should speak, if 'twere only two minutes of conscious articulate life, and then death – 'tis not a pin's point to me how soon. Left to himself he must die; therefore, to shrink from the operation on which depends the discovery both of his actual murderer and of his money, Sir, otherwise lost to his family, is – is a damned affectation! *I* think it – so do *you*, Sir; and I offer five hundred guineas as your fee, and Mrs Sturk's letter to bear you harmless.'

Then there was a pause. Dangerfield knew the man's character as well as his skill. There were things said about him darker than we have hinted at.

The surgeon looked very queer and gloomy down upon the table, and scratched his head, and he mumbled gruffly – 'You see – you know – 'tis a large fee, to be sure; but then – '

'Come, Sir,' said Dangerfield, looking as though he'd pull him by the ear; 'it *is* a large fee, and you'll get no more – you should not stick at trifles, when there's – a – a – justice and humanity – and, to be brief, Sir – yes or no?'

'*Yes*,' answered the doctor; 'but how's the fee secured?'

'Hey! I'd forgot. Right, Sir – you shall be satisfied.' And he took a pen, and wrote on the back of a letter –

SIR – Considering the hopeless condition in which Dr Sturk now lies, and the vast importance of restoring him, Dr Sturk, of the R.I.A., to the power of speech, even for a few minutes, I beg to second Mrs Sturk's request to you; and when you shall have performed the critical operation she desires, I hereby promise, whether it succeed or fail, to give you a fee of five hundred guineas.

PAUL DANGERFIELD
The Brass Castle, Chapelizod

And he dated it, and handed it to the surgeon, who read it through, and then looked with a gruff hesitation at the writer.

'Oh, you've only to enquire – anyone who knows Chapelizod will tell you who I am; and you'll want something – eh? – to take you out of this – how much?'

'Only seven guineas. There's a little score here, and some fees. Eighteen will cover everything, unless something has come in this morning.'

So they went to 'the Hatch', and made enquiries, and all being well, Mr Dangerfield dealt liberally with the surgeon, who promised to be in attendance at Dr Sturk's house in Chapelizod, at seven o'clock next evening.

'And pray, Dr Dillon, come in a coach,' said Dangerfield, 'and in costume – you understand. They've been accustomed, you know, to see Pell and other doctors who make a parade.'

And with these injunctions they parted; and the surgeon, whose luggage was trifling, jumped into a coach with it, and jingled home to his den and his liberty.

Chapter Eighty-four

In which Christina goes over; and Dan Loftus comes home

This evening Lily Walsingham was early tired and very weak, Sally thought, and more glad than usual to lie down in her bed; and there her old and loving nurse fancied that she looked a little strange, and that her thoughts sometimes wandered.

She lay very quietly for a good while, and suddenly, with a beautiful look, and in a clear, glad voice, she said 'Mother!'

And old Sally said: 'There's no-one, dear Miss Lily, but me.'

But she was looking earnestly, and, with a rapt smile, only said: 'Oh!'

She thought she saw her, I believe.

Are these always illusions? Or is it only that, as the twilight deepens, and the shapes of earth melt into night, the stars of heaven, changeless and serene, reveal themselves, and shine out to the darkened eyes of mortals?

As Aunt Becky sat that night in the drawing-room with her niece, a maid, with a whisper, placed a little note in Miss Gertrude's hand. There was a little pause.

'Oh! aunt – oh!' and she looked so terrified. 'Oh! aunt,' and she threw her arms round her aunt's neck, and began crying wildly. 'Poor Lily's gone – there's the note.'

Then arose the wild wailing of unavailing grief, and sobs, mixed with early recollections of childhood, and all poor Lily's sweet traits poured out.

Old Aunt Rebecca took the note. Her stoicism was the point on which she piqued herself most. She looked very pale, and she told her niece to be composed; for Aunt Becky had a theory that feelings ought to be commanded, and that it only needed effort and resolution. So she read the note, holding her head very high, but the muscles of her face were quivering.

'Oh! Gertrude, if ever there was an angel – and the poor desolate old man – '

The theory broke down, and old Aunt Rebecca cried and sat down, and cried heartily, and went and put her thin arms round her niece, and kissed her, and cried, and cried, and kissed her again.

'She was such – such a darling – oh! Gertrude dear, we must never quarrel any more.'

Death had come so near, and all things less than itself were rebuked in that sublime presence; and Lily Walsingham was gone; and she who was so lately their gay companion, all at once so awfully angelic in the unearthly light of death.

'Who'd ha' thought it was so near, Ma'am,' said the maid; 'the poor little thing! Though to be sure, Ma'am, a winding sheet came three times in the candle last night, and I turns it round and picks it off, that way, with my nail, unknownst to Mrs Heany, for fear she'd be frettin' about the little boy that's lyin' at home in the small-pox; and indeed I thought 'twas for him it was; but man proposes, and God disposes – and death forgets none, the Lord be praised – and everyone has their hour, old and young, Ma'am; and as I was sayin', they had no notion or expectation up at the Elms, Ma'am, she was so bad, the heavens be her bed this night. 'Twas all in an instant like, Miss, she made as if she'd sit up, bein' leanin' on pillows – and so she put out them purty little hands of hers, with a smile, and that was all – the purty crature – everyone's sorry afther her. The man was cryin' in the hall that brought the note.'

The poor came to the door, and made their rude and kindly lamentations – they were all quite sincere – 'His reverence was very good, but he couldn't have the thought, you know.' It was quite true – 'everyone was sorry'. The brave Magnolia's eyes were red, when she looked out of the window next morning, and jolly little Doctor Toole said at the club: 'Ah, Sir, she was a bright little thing – a born lady – such a beauty – and the best little creature. The town might well be proud of her, in every way, Sir.' And he fell a-blubbering; and old Major O'Neill, who was a quiet and silent officer, cried in a reserved way, looking into the fire, with his elbow on the mantelpiece. And Toole said, 'I don't know how I'll pass that house.'

And many felt the same. Little Lily was there no more – and the Elms were changed – the light and the grace were gone – and they were only dark old trees now.

And everyone felt a great desire to find some way – any way – to show their respect and affection for their good old rector. And I'm sure he understood it – for liking and reverence, one way or another, will tell their story. The hushed enquiries at the door, and little offers of useless services made by stealth through the servants, and such like foolish kindnesses at such a time – the evidence of a great but helpless sympathy – are sweet as angelic music.

And who should arrive at night, with all his trunks, or at least a considerable number of them, and his books and rattletraps, but honest, simple Dan Loftus. The news was true about his young charge. He had died of fever at Malaga, and Dick Devereux was at last a step, and a long one – nearer to the title. So Dan was back again in his old garret. Travel had not educated him in the world's ways. In them he was the same queer, helpless tyro. And his costume, though he had a few handsome articles – for, travelling with a sprig of nobility, he thought it but right and seemed to dress accordingly – was on that account, perhaps, only more grotesque than ever. But he had acquired mountains of that lore in which he and good Doctor Walsingham delighted. He had transcribed old epitaphs and translated interminable extracts from archives, and bought five Irish manuscripts, all highly illustrative of that history on which he and the doctor were so pleasantly engaged. It was too late that night to go up to the Elms; but he longed to unpack his trunkful of manuscripts, and to expound to his beloved doctor the treasures he had amassed.

And over his solitary tea-cup and his book the sorrowful news from the Elms reached him, and all his historical castles in the air were shivered. In the morning, before the town was stirring, he crossed the bridge, and knocked softly at the familiar hall-door. Honest old John Tracy opened it, and Dan shook hands with him, and both cried for a while quietly.

'How is the honoured master?' at last said Loftus.

'He's there in the study, Sir. Thank God, you're come, Sir. I'm sure he'd like to see you – I'll ask him.'

Dan went into the drawing-room. He looked out at the flowers, and then at the harpsichord, and on her little walnut table, where her work-basket lay, and her thimble, and the little coral necklace – a childish treasure that she used to wear when she was quite a little thing. It was like a dream; and everything seemed to say – 'Poor little Lily!'

So old John came in, and 'Sir,' said he, 'the master will be glad to see you.' And Dan Loftus found himself in the study; and the good doctor and he wrung one another's hands for a long time.

'Oh, Dan – Dan – she's gone – little Lily.'

'You'll see her again, Sir – oh, you'll see her again.'

'Oh, Dan! Dan! Till the heavens be no more they shall not awake, nor be raised out of their sleep. Oh, Dan, a day's so long – how am I to get over the time?'

'The loving Lord, Sir, will find a way.'

'But, oh! was there no pitying angel to stay the blow – to plead for a few years more of life? I deserved it – oh, Dan, yes! – I know it – I deserved it. But, oh! could not the avenger have pierced me, without smiting my innocent darling?'

'Oh! she was taken in love, not in judgment, Sir – my pastor – but in love. It was the voice of the Redeemer that called her.'

And honest Dan repeated, through his sobs, a verse of that 'Song of Songs' which little Lily had loved so well:

> My well-beloved spake, and said unto me:
> Arise, my love, my fair one, and come thy way.

The old man bowed his sorrowful head listening.

'You never saw anything so beautiful,' said he after a while. 'I think, Dan, I could look at her for ever. I don't think it was partiality, but it seems to me there never was – I never saw a creature like her.'

'Oh, noble! noble!' sobbed poor Dan.

The doctor took him by the arm, and so into the solemn room.

'I think you'd like to see her, Dan?'

'I would – I would indeed, Sir.'

And there was little Lily, never so like the lily before. Poor old Sally had laid early spring flowers on the white coverlet. A snowdrop lay by her pale little finger and thumb, just like a flower that has fallen from a child's hand it its sleep. He looked, at her – the white angelic apparition – a smile, or a light upon the face.

'Oh, my darling, my young darling, gone – "He is not a man as I am, that I should answer him."'

But poor Dan, loudly crying, repeated the noble words of Paul, that have spoken down to us through the sorrows of nigh two thousand years: 'For this we say unto you by the word of the Lord, that we which are alive, and remain unto the coming of the Lord, shall not prevent them which are asleep. For the Lord himself shall descend from heaven with a shout, with the voice of the archangel, and with the trump of God; and the dead in Christ shall rise first.'

And so there was a little pause, and the old man said: 'It was very good of you to come to me, my good young friend, in my helplessness and shipwreck, for the Lord hath hid himself from me; but he speaks to his desolate creature, my good Dan, through your gracious lips. My faith! – I thought I had faith till it was brought to the test, and then it failed! But my good friend Loftus was sent to help me – to strengthen the feeble knees.'

And Dan answered, crying bitterly, and clasping the rector's hand in both of his: 'Oh, my master, all that ever I knew of good, I learned from you, my pastor, my benefactor.'

So, with a long, last look, Dan followed the old man to the study, and they talked long there together, and then went out into the lonely garden, and paced its walks side by side, up and down.

Chapter Eighty-five

In which Captain Devereux hears the news; and Mr Dangerfield
meets an old friend after dinner

On the night when this great sorrow visited the Elms, Captain Richard Devereux, who had heard nothing of it, was strangely saddened and disturbed in mind. They say that a distant death is sometimes felt like the shadow and chill of a passing iceberg; and if this ominous feeling crosses a mind already saddened and embittered, it overcasts it with a feeling akin to despair.

Mrs Irons knocked at his door, and with the eagerness of a messenger of news, opened it without awaiting his answer.

'Oh, captain, jewel, do you know what? There's poor Miss Lily Walsingham; and what do you think but she's dead – the poor little thing; gone tonight, Sir – not half an hour ago.'

He staggered a little, and put his hand toward his sword, like a man struck by a robber, and looked at her with a blank stare. She thought he was out of his mind, and was frightened.

' 'Tis only me, Sir, Mrs Irons.'

'A – thank you;' and he walked towards the chimney, and then towards the door, like a man looking for something; and on a sudden clasping his forehead in his hands, he cried a wild and terrible appeal to the Maker and Judge of all things.

' 'Tis impossible – oh, no – oh, no – it's *not* true.'

He was in the open air, he could not tell how, and across the bridge, and before the Elms – a dream – the dark Elms – dark everything.

'Oh, no – it can't be – oh, no – oh, no;' and he went on saying as he stared on the old house, dark against the sky, 'Oh, no – oh, no.'

Two or three times he would have gone over to the hall-door to make enquiry, but he sickened at the thought. He clung to that hope, which was yet not a hope, and he turned and walked quickly down the river's side by the Inchicore-road. But the anguish of suspense soon drew him back again; and now his speech was changed, and he said: 'Yes, she's gone – she's gone – oh, she's gone – she's certainly gone.'

He found himself at the drawing-room window that looked into the little garden at the front of the house, and tapping at the window-pane. He remembered, all on a sudden – it was like waking – how strange was such a summons. A little after he saw a light crossing the hall, and he rang the door-bell. John Tracy opened the door. Yes, it was all true.

The captain was looking very pale, John thought, but otherwise much as usual. He stared at the old servant for some seconds after he told him all, but said nothing, not even good-night, and turned away. Old John was crying; but he called after the captain to take care of the step at the gate: and as he shut the hall-door his eye caught, by the light of his candle, a scribbling in red chalk, on the white door-post, and he stooped to read it, and muttered, 'Them mischievous young blackguards!' and began rubbing it with the cuff of his coat, his cheek still wet with tears. For even our grief is volatile; or, rather, it is two tunes that are in our ears together, the requiem of the organ, and, with it, the faint hurdy-gurdy jig of our vulgar daily life; and now and then this latter uppermost.

It was not till he had got nearly across the bridge that Captain Devereux, as it were, waked up. It was no good waking. He broke forth into sheer fury. It is not my business to note down the horrors of this impious frenzy. It was near five o'clock when he came back to his lodgings; and then, not to rest. To sit down, to rise again, to walk round the room and round, and stop on a sudden at the window, leaning his elbows on the sash, with hands clenched together, and teeth set; and so those demoniac hours of night and solitude wore slowly away, and the cold grey stole over the east, and Devereux drank a deep draught of his fiery Lethe, and cast himself down on his bed, and fell at once into a deep, exhausted lethargy.

When his servant came to his bedside at seven o'clock, he was lying motionless, with flushed cheeks, and he could not rouse him. Perhaps it was well, and saved him from brain-fever or madness.

But after such paroxysms comes often a reaction, a still, stony, awful despondency. It is only the oscillation between active and passive despair. Poor Leonora, after she had worked out her fit, tearing 'her raven hair', and reviling heaven, was visited in sadder and tenderer guise by the vision of the past; but with that phantom went down in fear and isolation to the grave.

This morning several of the neighbours went into Dublin, for the bills were to be presented against Charles Nutter for a murderous assault, with intent to kill, made upon the person of Barnabas Sturk,

Esq., Doctor of Medicine, and Surgeon to the Royal Irish Artillery. As the day wore on, the honest gossips of Chapelizod looked out anxiously for news. And everybody who met anyone else asked him – 'Any news about Nutter, eh?' – and then they would stop to speculate – and then one would wonder that Dr Walsingham's man, Clinton, had not yet returned – and the other would look at his watch, and say 'twas one o'clock – and then both agreed that Spaight, at all events, must soon come – for he has appointed two o'clock for looking at that brood mare of Fagan's.

At last, sure enough, Spaight appeared. Toole, who had been detained by business in another quarter, had ridden into the town from Leixlip, and was now dismounted and talking with Major O'Neill upon the absorbing topic. These cronies saw Spaight at the turnpike, and as he showed his ticket, he talked with the man. Of course, the news was come. The turnpike-man knew it by this time; and off scampered Toole, and the major followed close at his heels, at double-quick. He made a dismal shake or two of his head, and lifted his hand as they drew near. Toole's heart misgave him.

'Well, how is it? – What's the news?' he panted.

'A true bill,' answered Spaight, with a solemn stare; 'a true bill, Sir.'

Toole uttered an oath of consternation, and taking the words out of Spaight's mouth, told the news to the major.

'Do you tell me so?' exclaimed the major. 'Bedad, Sir, I'm un-common sorry.'

'A bad business, Sir,' observed Spaight.

'No worse,' said Toole. 'If they convict him on this, you know – in case Sturk dies, and die he will – they'll indict and convict him on the more *serious* charge,' and he winked gloomily, 'the evidence is all one.'

'That poor little Sally Nutter!' ejaculated the major. 'She's to be pitied, the crature!'

''Tis mighty slender evidence to take a man's life on,' said Toole, with some disgust. 'Be the law, Sir, the whole thing gives me a complete turn. Are you to dine with Colonel Strafford today?'

'I am, Sir,' said the major; 'an' it goes again' the colonel's grain to have a party at all just now, with the respect he has for the family up there,' and he nodded his head, pensively, toward the Elms. 'But he asked Lowe ten days ago, and Mr Dangerfield, and two or three more; and you know he could not put them off on that ground – there being no relationship, you see – and, 'pon my oath, Sir, I'd rather not go myself, just now.'

That evening, at five o'clock, Colonel Stafford's dinner party assembled at the King's House. The colonel was a serene man, and hospitality – even had he been in the dumps – demands her sacrifices. He, therefore, did the honours as beseemed a genial and courteous old officer of the Royal Irish Artillery, who, if his conversation was not very remarkable in quality, and certainly not exorbitant in quantity, made up by listening a great deal, and supplying no end of civility, and an affluence of very pretty claret. Mr Justice Lowe was there, and Mr Dangerfield, and old Colonel Bligh, of the Magazine, and honest Major O'Neill, notwithstanding his low spirits. Perhaps they required keeping up; and claret like Colonel Stafford's is consoling.

The talk turned, of course, a good deal on Charles Nutter; and Mr Dangerfield, who was in great force, and, indeed, in particularly pleasant spirits, except when unfortunate Nutter was actually under discussion – when he grew grave and properly saddened – told, in his clear, biting way, a curious rosary of Newgate stories – of highwaymen's disguises – of clever constables – of circumstantial evidence, marvellously elicited, and exquisitely put together – of monsters, long concealed, drawn from the deep by the finest tackle, into upper light, and dropped deftly into the landing-net of Justice. These curious anecdotes of Bow-street dexterity and Bagshot dodges – thrust and parry – mine and counter-mine – ending, for the most part, in the triumph of Bow-street, Justice crowned, and a Tyburn speech – tickled Lowe mightily, who quite enjoyed himself, and laughed more than his friend Colonel Stafford ever remembered to have heard him before, over some of the ingenious stratagems described so neatly by Dangerfield, and the gay irony with which he pointed his catastrophes. And Lowe actually, having obtained Colonel Stafford's leave, proposed that gallant officer's health in a bumper, and took occasion to mention their obligations to him for having afforded them the opportunity of enjoying Mr Dangerfield's sprightly and instructive sallies; and hoped, with all his heart, that the neighbourhood was long to enjoy the advantage and pleasure of his residence among them. And Mr Dangerfield replied gaily, that all that was needed to make such sweet scenery and charming company as the place commanded absolutely irresistible, was the sense of safety conferred by the presence of such a magistrate as Mr Lowe, and the convivial inspiration of such wine as their gallant host provided; and that, for his part, being somewhat of an old boy, and having had enough of rambling, nothing would better please him than to spend the residue of his days amidst the lively quietude of their virtuous and hilarious neighbourhood; and some more to the like purpose, which pleased the good company highly, who all agreed that the white gentleman – fluent, easy, and pointed in his delivery – was a mighty fine speaker, indeed. Though there was a lurking consciousness in each, which none cared to publish, that there was, at times, an indefinable flavour of burlesque and irony in Mr Dangerfield's compliments, which excited momentary suspicions and qualms, which the speaker waived off, however, easily with his jewelled fingers, and smiled mockingly away.

Lowe was mightily taken with him. There was little warmth or veneration in that hard justice's nature. But Mr Dangerfield had a way with him that few men with any sort of taste for the knowledge of evil could resist; and the cold-eyed justice of the peace hung on his words with an attentive rapture, and felt that he was drinking deep and pleasant draughts from the sparkling fountains of knowledge; and was really sorry, and shook him admiringly by the hand, when Dangerfield, who had special business at home, rose up in his brisk way, and flashed a farewell over the company from his spectacles.

'If Mr Dangerfield really means to stay here, he must apply for the commission of the peace,' said Mr Lowe, so soon as the door shut. 'We must put it upon him. I protest I never met a man so fitted by nature and acquirements to make a perfectly useful magistrate. He and I, Sir, between us, we'd give a good account of this part of the county; and there's plenty of work, Sir, if 'twere only between this and Dublin; and, by George, Sir, he's a wonderful diverting fellow, full of anecdote. Wonderful place London, to be sure.'

'And a good man, too, in a quiet way,' said Colonel Strafford, who could state a fact. ''Tisn't every rich man has the heart to part with his money as he does; he has done many charities here, and especially he has been most bountiful to poor Sturk's family.'

'I know that,' said Lowe.

'And he sent a fifty pound note by the major there to poor Sally Nutter o' Monday last; he'll tell you.'

And thus it is, as the foul fiend, when he vanishes, leaves a smell of brimstone after him, a good man leaves a fragrance; and the company in the parlour enjoyed the aroma of Mr Dangerfield's virtues, as he buttoned his white surtout over his breast, and dropped his vails into the palms of the carbuncled butler and fuddled footman in the hall.

It was a clear, frosty, starlit night. White and stern was the face which he turned upward for a moment to the sky. He paused for a second in the ray of candle-light that gleamed through Puddock's window-shutter, and glanced on the pale dial of his large gold watch. It was only half-past eight o'clock. He walked on, glancing back over his shoulder, along the Dublin road.

'The drunken beast. My mind misgives me he'll disappoint,' muttered the silver spectacles, gliding briskly onward.

When he reached the main street he peered curiously before him under the village tree, in quest of carriage lights.

'A lawless brute like that may be before his time as well as after.' So he walked briskly forward, and up Sturk's door-steps, and knocked.

'The Dublin doctor hasn't come, eh?' – he asked.

'No, Sir, he isn't come yet – 'twas nine o'clock, the mistress told me.'

'Very good. Tell Mrs Sturk, pray, that I, Mr Dangerfield, you know, will call, as I promised, at nine o'clock precisely.'

And he turned again and walked briskly over the bridge, and away along the Inchicore road overhanging the river. All was silent there. Not a step but his own was stirring, and the road in places so overhung with old trees that it was difficult to see a yard before one.

He slackened his pace, and listened, like a man who keeps an assignation, and listened again, and laughed under his breath; and sure enough, before long, the clink of a footstep was heard approaching swiftly from the Dublin direction.

Mr Dangerfield drew aside under the deep shadow of a high hawthorn hedge, overhung by trees; and watching intently, he saw a tall, lank figure, with a peculiar gait and stoop of its own, glide stealthily by. He smiled after it in the dark.

The tall figure was that of our old friend, Zekiel Irons, the clerk. A sable form, as beseemed his ecclesiastical calling – and now a white figure was gliding without noise swiftly after him.

Suddenly, as he reached an open part of the road, a thin hand was laid on his shoulder, and, with a start, and a 'hollo', he sprung round.

'Hey! Why, you're as frightened as if you had seen Charles – Charles *Nutter*. Hey? – Don't be uneasy. I heard from the parson yesterday morning you were to be with him tonight before nine o'clock, about that money you left in his hands, and I've chanced to meet you; and this I want you to understand, Charles Nutter is in gaol, and we must not let him get out – do you see? That business settled, we're at rest. So, Mr Irons, you must not show the white feather. Be bold – speak out what you know – now's the time to strike. I'll put your evidence, as you reported it to me, into shape, and you come to me tomorrow morning at eight o'clock; and mind you,

I'll reward you this time, and better than ever you've fared before. Go on. Or stay – I'll go before.'

And Mr Dangerfield laughed one of his chilly laughs – and, with a nod to Irons, repeated – 'eight o'clock' – and so walked on a little bit.

The clerk had not said a word. A perspiration broke forth on his forehead, and, wiping the drops away, he said: 'Lord have mercy upon us – Lord deliver us – Lord have mercy upon us,' like a man dying.

Mr Dangerfield's bold proposition seemed quite to overpower and unman him.

The white figure turned short, facing the clerk, and said he: 'See you, Mr Irons, I'm serious – there must be no shirking. If you undertake, you must go through; and, hark! in your ear – you shall have five hundred pounds. I put no constraint – say yes or no – if you don't like you needn't. Justice, I think, will be done even without your help. But till he's quiet – you understand – *nothing* sure. He has been dead and alive again – curse him; and till he's at rest, and on the surgeon's table – ha! ha! – we shan't feel quite comfortable.'

'Lord have mercy upon us!' muttered Irons, with a groan.

'Amen,' said Dangerfield, with a sneering imitation. '*There*, 'tis enough – if you have nerve to speak truth and do justice, you may have the money. We're men of business – you and I. If not, I shan't trouble you any more. If you like it, come to me at eight o'clock in the morning; if not, why, stay away, and no harm's done.'

And with these words, Mr Dangerfield turned on his heel once more, and started at a lively pace for Chapelizod.

Chapter Eighty-six

In which Mr Paul Dangerfield mounts the stairs of the House by the Churchyard, and makes some arrangements

The white figure glided duskily over the bridge. The river rushed beneath in Egyptian darkness. The air was still, and a thousand celestial eyes twinkled down brightly through the clear deep sky upon the actors in this true story. He kept the left side, so that the road lay between him and the Phoenix door, which gaped wide with a great hospitable grin, and crimsoned the night air with a glow of candle-light.

The white figure turned the corner, and glided onward in a straight, swift line – straight and swift as fate – to the door of Doctor Sturk.

He knocked softly at the hall-door, and swiftly stepped in and shut it.

'How's your master?'

'Jist the same way, plaze yer honour; jist sleepin' – still sleepin' – sleepin' always,' answered the maid.

'Has the Dublin doctor come?'

'No.'

'The mistress – where's she?'

'In the room, Sir, with the masther.'

'Present my service to her – Mr Dangerfield's compliments, you know – and say I await her permission to come upstairs.'

Presently the maid returned, with poor Mrs Sturk's invitation to Mr Dangerfield to walk up.

Up he went, leaving his white surtout and cocked hat in the hall, and entered the chamber where pale little Mrs Sturk, who had been crying a great deal, sat in a dingy old tabby saque, by the light of a solitary mould-candle at the bedside of the noble Barney.

The mutton-fat wanted snuffing; but its light danced and splintered brilliantly over Mr Dangerfield's resplendent shoe-buckles, and up and down his cut-steel buttons, and also glimmered in a more phosphoric way upon his silver spectacles, as he bowed at the door, arrayed in a puce cut velvet coat, lined with pink, long embroidered satin waistcoat, fine lace ruffles and cravat, his well-shaped leg gleaming glossily in silk, and altogether, in his glimmering jewellery, and purple and fine linen, resembling Dives making a complimentary visit to the garret of Lazarus.

Poor little Mrs Sturk felt her obligations mysteriously enlarged by so much magnificence, and wondered at the goodness of this white-headed angel in point, diamonds, and cut velvet, who had dropped from the upper regions upon the sad and homely floor of her Barney's sick chamber.

'Dr Dillon not yet arrived, Madam? Well, 'tis precisely his hour; we shall have him soon. How does the patient? Ha! just as usual. How? – why, there's a change, isn't there?'

'As how, Sir?' enquired Mrs Sturk, with a scared look.

'Why, don't you see? But you mustn't be frightened; there's one coming in whom I have every confidence.'

'I don't see, Sir. What is it, Mr Dangerfield? Oh, *pray*, Sir?'

'Why – a – nothing very particular, only he looks more languid than when I saw him last, and discoloured somewhat, and his face more sunk, I think – eh?'

'Oh, no, Sir – 'tis this bad light – nothing more, indeed, Sir. This evening, I assure you, Mr Dangerfield, at three o'clock, when the sun was shining, we were all remarking how well he looked. I never saw – you'd have said so – such a wonderful improvement.'

And she snuffed the candle, and held it up over Barney's grim features.

'Well, Madam, I hope we soon may find it. 'Twill be a blessed sight – eh? – when he sits up in that bed, Madam, as I trust he may this very night, and speak – eh?'

'Oh! My precious Barney!' and the poor little woman began to cry, and fell into a rhapsody of hopes, thanksgiving, anecdote and prayer.

In the meanwhile Dangerfield was feeling his pulse, with his watch in the hollow of his hand.

'And aren't they better – his pulse, Sir – they were stronger this morning by a great deal than last night – it was just at ten o'clock – don't you perceive, Sir?'

'H'm – well, I hope, Ma'am, we'll soon find *all* better. Now, have you got all things ready – you have, of course, a sheet well aired?'

'A sheet – I did not know 'twas wanted.'

'Hey, this will never do, my dear Madam – he'll be here and nothing ready; and you'll do well to send over to the mess-room for a lump of ice. 'Tis five minutes past nine. If you'll see to these things, I'll sit here, Madam, and take the best care of the patient – and, d'ye see, Mistress Sturk, 'twill be necessary that you take care that Toole hears nothing of Dr Dillon's coming.'

It struck me, when originally reading the correspondence which is digested in these pages, as hardly credible that Doctor Sturk should have continued to live for so long a space in a state of coma. Upon this point, therefore, I took occasion to ask the most eminent surgeon of my acquaintance, who at once quieted my doubts by detailing a very remarkable case cited by Sir A. Cooper in his lectures, vol. i., p. 172. It is that of a seaman, who was pressed on board one of his Majesty's ships, early in the revolutionary war; and while on board this vessel, fell from the yard-arm, and was taken up insensible, in which state he continued living for thirteen months and some days!

So with a little more talk, Mrs Sturk, calling one of her maids, and leaving the little girl in charge of the nursery, ran down with noiseless steps and careworn face to the kitchen, and Mr Danger-field was left alone in the chamber with the spellbound sleeper on the bed.

In about ten seconds he rose sharply from his chair and listened: then very noiselessly he stepped to the door and listened again, and gently shut it.

Then Mr Dangerfield moved to the window. There was a round hole in the shutter, and through it he glanced into the street, and was satisfied.

By this time he had his white pocket-handkerchief in his hands. He folded it deftly across and across into a small square, and then the spectacles flashed coldly on the image of Dr Sturk, and then on the door; and there was a pause.

'What's that?' he muttered sharply, and listened for a second or two.

It was only one of the children crying in the nursery. The sound subsided.

So with another long silent step, he stood by the capriole-legged old mahogany table, with the scallop shell containing a piece of soap and a washball, and the basin with its jug of water standing therein. Again he listened while you might count two, and dipped the hand-kerchief, so folded, into the water, and quietly squeezed it; and stood white and glittering by Sturk's bedside.

People moved very noiselessly about that house, and scarcely a minute had passed when the door opened softly, and the fair Magnolia Macnamara popped in her glowing face and brilliant glance, and whispered.

'Are you there, Mrs Sturk, dear?'

At the far side of the bed, Dangerfield, with his flashing spectacles and snowy aspect, and a sort of pant, rose up straight, and looked into her eyes, like a white bird of prey disturbed over its carrion.

She uttered a little scream – quite pale on a sudden – for she did not recognise the sinister phantom who glimmered at her over the prostrate Sturk.

But Dangerfield laughed his quiet hollow 'Ha! ha! ha!' and said promptly, 'A strange old nurse I make, Miss Macnamara. But what can I do? Mrs Sturk has left me in charge, and faith I believe our patient's looking mighty badly.'

He had observed Miss Mag glancing from him to the dumb figure in the bed with a puzzled kind of horror.

The fact is, Sturk's face had a leaden tint; he looked, evidently enough, even in that dim candle-light, a great deal worse than the curious Miss Mag was accustomed to see him.

'He's very low, tonight, and seems oppressed, and his pulse is failing; in fact, my dear young lady, he's plainly worse tonight than I like to tell poor Mrs Sturk, you understand.'

'And his face looks so shiny and damp-like,' said Miss Mag, with a horrible sort of scrutiny.

'Exactly so, Miss, 'tis *weakness*,' observed Dangerfield.

'And you were wiping it with your pocket-handkerchief when I looked in,' continued Miss Mag.

'Was I – ha, ha – 'tis wonderful how quick we learn a new business. I vow I begin to think I should make a very respectable nursetender.'

'And what the dickens brings *him* up here?' asked Miss Mag of herself; so soon as the first shock was over, the oddity of the situation struck her as she looked with perplexed and unpleasant sort of enquiry at Mr Dangerfield.

Just then up came the meek little Mrs Sturk, and the gentleman greeted her with a 'Well, Madam, I have not left his bedside since you went down; and I think he looks a little better – just a little – eh?'

'I trust and pray, Sir, that when the doctor – ' began Mrs Sturk, and stopped short, for Mr Dangerfield frowned quickly, and pointed towards Miss Mag, who was now, after her wont, looking round the room for matter of interest.

'And is Pell comin' out tonight?' asked Miss Mag quickly.

'No, truly. Madam,' answered the gentleman: 'Dr Pell's not comin' – is he, Mrs Sturk?'

'Dr Pell! – oh, la – no, Sir. No, my dear.' And, after a pause, 'Oh, ho. I wish it was over,' she groaned, with her hand pressed to her side, looking with a kind of agony on Sturk.

'*What over*?' asked Miss Mag.

Just then a double-knock came to the hall-door, and Mr Dangerfield signed sternly to Mrs Sturk, who first stood up, with her eyes and mouth wide open, and then sat down, like a woman going to faint.

But the maid came up and told Miss Mag that her mother and Lieutenant O'Flaherty were waiting on the steps for her; and so, though loath to go unsatisfied, away she went, with a courtesy to Mr Dangerfield and a kiss to Mrs Sturk, who revived on hearing it was only her fat kindly neighbour from over the way, instead of Black Doctor Dillon, with his murderous case of instruments.

The gentleman in the silver spectacles accompanied her to the lobby, and offered his hand; but she dispensed with his attendance, and jumped down the stairs with one hand to the wall and the other on the banisters, nearly a flight at a time; and the cackle of voices rose from the hall door, which quickly shut, and the fair vision had vanished.

Dangerfield's silver spectacles gleamed phosphorically after her from under his lurid forehead. It was not a pleasant look, and his mouth was very grim. In another instant he was in the room again, and glanced at his watch.

' 'Tis half-past nine,' he said, in a quiet tone, but with a gleam of intense fury over his face, 'and that – that – doctor named *nine*.'

Dangerfield waited, and talked a little to Mrs Sturk and the maid, who were now making preparations, in short sentences, by fits and starts of half-a-dozen words at a time. He had commenced his visit ceremoniously, but now he grew brusque, and took the command: and his tones were prompt and stern, and the women grew afraid of him.

Ten o'clock came. Dangerfield went downstairs, and looked from the drawing-room windows. He waxed more and more impatient. Down he went to the street. He did not care to walk towards the King's House, which lay on the road to Dublin; he did not choose to meet his boon companions again, but he stood for full ten minutes, with one of Dr Sturk's military cloaks about him, under the village tree, directing the double-fire of his spectacles down the street, with an incensed steadiness, unrewarded, unrelieved. Not a glimmer of a link; not a distant rumble of a coach-wheel. It was a clear, frosty night, and one might hear a long way.

If any of the honest townsfolk had accidentally lighted upon that muffled, glaring image under the dark old elm, I think he would have mistaken it for a ghost, or something worse. The countenance at that moment was not prepossessing.

Mr Dangerfield was not given to bluster, and never made a noise; but from his hollow jaws he sighed an icy curse towards Dublin, which had a keener edge than all the roaring blasphemies of Donnybrook together; and, with another shadow upon his white face, he re-entered the house.

'He'll not come tonight, Ma'am,' he said with a cold abruptness.

'Oh, thank Heaven! – that is – I'm so afraid – I mean about the operation.'

Dangerfield, with his hands in his pockets, said nothing. There was a sneer on his face, white and dark, somehow. That was all. Was he baffled, and was Dr Sturk, after all, never to regain his speech?

At half-past ten o'clock, Mr Dangerfield abandoned hope. Had it been Dr Pell, indeed, it would have been otherwise. But Black Dillon had not a patient; his fame was in the hospitals. There was nothing to detain him but his vices, and five hundred pounds to draw him to Chapelizod. He had not come. He must be either brained in a row, or drunk under a table. So Mr Dangerfield took leave of good Mrs Sturk, having told her in case the doctor should come, to make him wait for his arrival before taking any measures, and directing that he should be sent for immediately.

So Mr Dangerfield got into his white surtout silently in the hall, and shut the door quickly after him, and waited, a grim sentry, under the tree, with his face towards Dublin. Father Time had not blunted the white gentleman's perceptions, touched his ear with his numb fingers, or blown the smoke of his tobacco-pipe into his eyes. He was keen of eye, sharp of hearing; but neither sight nor sound rewarded him, and so he turned, after a few minutes, and glided away, like a white ghost, toward the Brass Castle.

In less than five minutes after, the thunder of a coach shook Dr Sturk's windows, followed by a rousing peal on the hall-door, and Dr Dillon, in dingy splendours, and a great draggled wig, with a gold-headed cane in his bony hand, stepped in; and, diffusing a reek of whiskey-punch, and with a case of instruments under his arm, pierced the maid who opened the door, through with his prominent black eyes, and frightened her with his fiery face, while he demanded to see Mrs Sturk, and lounged, without ceremony, into the parlour; where he threw himself on the sofa, with one of his bony legs extended on it, and his great ugly hand under his wig scratching his head.

Chapter Eighty-seven

In which two comrades are tête-à-tête in their old quarters, and Dr Sturk's cue is cut off, and a consultation commences

The buzz of a village, like the hum of a city, represents a very wonderful variety of human accent and feeling. It is marvellous how few families thrown together will suffice to furnish forth this *dubia coena* of sweets and bitters.

The roar of many waters – the *ululatus* of many-voiced humanity – marvellously monotonous, considering the infinite variety of its ingredients, booms on through the dark. The storyteller alone can take up the score of the mighty medley, and read at a glance what every fife and fiddle-stick is doing. That pompous thrum-thrum is the talk of the great white Marseilles paunch, *pietate gravis*; the whine comes from Lazarus, at the area rails; and the bass is old Dives, roaring at his butler; the piccolo is contributed by the studious schoolboy, whistling over his *Latin Grammar*; that wild, long note is poor Mrs Fondle's farewell of her dead boy; the ugly barytone, rising from the tap-room, is what Wandering Willie calls a sculduddery song – shut your ears, and pass on; and that clear soprano, in nursery, rings out a shower of innocent idiotisms over the half-stripped baby, and suspends the bawl upon its lips.

So, on this night, as usual, there rose up toward the stars a throbbing murmur from our village – a wild chaos of sound, which we must strive to analyse, extracting from the hurly-burly each separate tune it may concern us to hear.

Captain Devereux was in his lodging. He was comparatively tranquil now; but a savage and impious despair possessed him. Serene outwardly – he would not let the vulgar see his scars and sores, and was one of those proud spirits who build to themselves desolate places.

Little Puddock was the man with whom he had least reserve. Puddock was so kindly, and so true and secret, and cherished beside, so great an admiration for him, that he greeted him rather kindly at a moment when another visitor would have fared scurvily enough.

Puddock was painfully struck with his pallor, his wild and haggard eye, and something stern and brooding in his handsome face, which was altogether new and shocking to him.

'I've been *thinking*, Puddock,' he said; 'and thought with me has grown strangely like despair – and that's all. Why, man, *think* – what is there for me? – All my best stakes I've lost already; and I'm fast losing myself. How different, Sir, is my fate from others? Worse men than I – every way incomparably worse – and d— them, *they* prosper, while I go down the tide. 'Tisn't just!' And he swore a great oath. ''Tis enough to make a man blaspheme. I've done with life – I hate it. I'll volunteer. 'Tis my first thought in the morning, and my last at night, how well I'd like a bullet through my brain or heart. D— the world, d— feeling, d— memory. I'm not a man that can always be putting prudential restraints upon myself. I've none of those plodding ways. The cursed fools that spoiled me in my childhood, and forsake me now, have all to answer for – I charge them with my ruin.' And he launched a curse at them (meaning his aunt) which startled the plump soul of honest little Puddock.

'You must not talk that way, Devereux,' he said, still a good deal more dismayed by his looks than his words. 'Why are you so troubled with vapours and blue devils?'

'Nowhy!' said Devereux, with a grim smile.

'My dear Devereux, I say, you mustn't talk in that wild way. You – you talk like a ruined man!'

'And I so comfortable!'

'Why, to be sure, Dick, you have had some little rubs, and, maybe, your follies and your vexations; but, hang it, you are young; you can't get experience – at least, so I've found it – without paying for it. You mayn't like it just now; but it's well worth the cost. Your worries and miscarriages, dear Richard, will make you steady.'

'Steady!' echoed Devereux, like a man thinking of something far away.

'Ay, Dick – you've sown your wild oats.'

On a sudden, says the captain, 'My dear little Puddock,' and he took him by the hand, with a sort of sarcastic flicker of a smile, and looked in his face almost contemptuously; but his eyes and his voice softened before the unconscious bonhomie of the true little gentleman. 'Puddock, Puddock, did it never strike you, my boy, that Hamlet never strives to speak a word of comfort to the forlorn old Dane? He felt it would not do. Every man that's worth a button knows his own case best; and I know the secrets of my own prison-house. Sown my

wild oats! To be sure I have, Puddock, my boy; and the new leaf I've
turned over is just this; I've begun to reap them; and they'll grow, my
boy, and grow as long as grass grows; and – Macbeth has his dagger,
you know, and I've my sickle – the handle towards my hand, that you
can't see; and in the sweat of my brow, I must cut down and garner
my sheaves; and as I sowed, so must I reap, and grind, and bake, the
black and bitter grist of my curse. Don't talk nonsense, little Puddock.
Wasn't it Gay that wrote the *Beggar's Opera*? Ay! why don't you play
Macheath? Gay! – Ay – a pleasant fellow, and his poems too. He
writes – don't you remember – he writes,

> So comes a reckoning when the banquet's o'er –
> The dreadful reckoning, and men smile no more.

'Puddock, throw up that window, the room's too hot – or stay,
never mind; read a book, Puddock, you like it, and I'll stroll a little
along the path, and find you when I come back.'

'Why it's dark,' remonstrated his visitor.

'Dark? I dare say – yes, of course – very dark – but cool; the air
is cool.'

He talked like a man who was thinking of something else; and
Puddock thought how strangely handsome he looked, with that pale
dash of horror, like King Saul when the evil spirit was upon him; and
there was a terrible misgiving in his mind. The lines of the old ballad
that Devereux used to sing with a sort of pathetic comicality were
humming in his ear,

> He walked by the river, the river so clear –
> The river that runs through Kilkenny;
>> His name was Captain Wade,
>> And he died for that fair maid.

and so following. What could he mean by walking, at that hour,
alone, by the river's brink? Puddock, with a sinking and flutter at his
heart, unperceived, followed him downstairs, and was beside him in
the street.

'The path by the river?' said Puddock.

'The river – the path? Yes, Sir, the path by the river. I thought I
left you upstairs,' said Devereux, with an odd sort of sulky shrinking.

'Why, Devereux, I may as well walk with you, if you don't object,'
lisped Puddock.

'But I do object, Sir,' cried Devereux, suddenly, in a fierce high
key, turning upon his little comrade. 'What d'ye mean, Sir? You

think I mean to – to *drown* myself – ha, ha, ha! Or what the devil's running in your head? I'm not a madman, Sir, nor you a mad-doctor. Go home, Sir – or go to – to where you will, Sir; only go your own way, and leave me mine.'

'Ah, Devereux, you're very quick with me,' said Puddock, placing his plump little hand on Devereux's arm, and looking very gently and gravely in his face.

Devereux laid his hand upon Puddock's collar with an agitated sort of sneer. But he recollected himself, and that diabolical gloom faded from his face, and he looked more like himself, and slid his cold hand silently into little Puddock's; and so they stood for a while, by the door-step, to the admiration of Mrs Irons – whom Devereux's high tones had called to her window.

'Puddock, I don't think I'm well, and I don't know quite what I've been saying. I ask your pardon. You've always been very good to me, Puddock. I believe – I believe you're the only friend I have, and – Puddock, you won't leave me.'

So upstairs they went together; and Mrs Irons, from what she had overheard, considered herself justified in saying, that 'Captain Devereux was for drowning himself in the Liffey, and would have done so only for Lieutenant Puddock.' And so the report was set a-going round the garrulous town of Chapelizod.

As Mr Dangerfield glided rapidly along the silent road towards the Brass Castle, the little gate of his now leafless flower-garden being already in sight, he saw a dark figure awaiting him under the bushes which overhung it. It was Mr Irons, who came forward, without speaking, and lifted his hat respectfully, perhaps abjectly, and paused for recognition.

'Hey! Irons?' said Mr Dangerfield.

'At your service, Sir.'

'Well, and what says his worship?' asked the gentleman, playfully.

'I wanted to tell your honour that it won't make no odds, and I'll do it.'

'Of course. You're right. It does make no odds. He'll hang whatever you do; and I tell you 'tis well he should, and only right *you* should speak the truth, too – 'twill make assurance doubly sure.'

'At eight o'clock in the morning, Sir, I'll attend you,' said Irons, with a sort of shiver.

'Good! And I'll jot down your evidence, and we'll drive over to Mr Lowe's, to Lucan, and you shall swear before him. And, you understand – I don't forget what I promised – you'll be a happier man every way for having done your duty; and here's half-a-crown to spend in the Salmon House.'

Irons only moaned, and then said: 'That's all, Sir. But I couldn't feel easy till it was off my mind.'

'At eight o'clock I shall expect you. Good-night, Irons.'

And with his hands in his pockets he watched Irons off the ground. His visage darkened as for a while his steady gaze was turned toward Dublin. He was not quite so comfortable as he might have been.

Meanwhile Black Dillon, at Mrs Sturk's request, had stalked upstairs to the patient's bedside.

'Had not I best send at once for Mr Dangerfield?' she enquired.

'No occasion, Ma'am,' replied the eminent but slightly fuddled 'Saw-bones', spitting beside him on the floor 'until I see whether I'll operate tonight. What's in that jug, Ma'am? Chicken-broth? That'll do. Give him a spoonful. See – he swallows free enough;' and then Black Dillon plucked up his eyelids with a roughness that terrified the reverential and loving Mrs Sturk, and examined the distorted pupils.

'You see the cast in that eye, Ma'am; there's the pressure on the brain.'

Dillon was lecturing her upon the case as he proceeded, from habit, just as he did the students in the hospital.

'No convulsions, Ma'am?'

'Oh, no, Sir, thank Heaven; nothing in the least – only quiet sleep, Sir; just like that.'

'Sleep, indeed – that's no sleep, Ma'am. Boo-hooh! I couldn't bawl that way in his face, Ma'am, without disturbing him, Ma'am, if it was. Now we'll get him up a bit – there, that's right – aisy. He was lying, Ma'am, I understand, on his back, when they found him in the park, Ma'am – so Mr Dangerfield says – ay. Well, slip the cap off – backward – backward, you fool; that'll do. Who plastered his head, Ma'am?'

'Doctor Toole, Sir.'

'Toole – Toole – h'm – I see – hey – hi – tut! 'tis the devil's pair of fractures, Ma'am. See – nearer – d'ye see, there's two converging lines – d'ye see, Ma'am?' and he indicated their directions with the silver handle of an instrument he held in his hand, 'and serrated at the edges, I'll be bound.'

And he plucked off two or three strips of plaster with a quick whisk, which made poor little Mrs Sturk wince and cry, 'Oh, dear, Sir!'

'Threpan, indeed!' murmured Black Dillon, with a coarse sneer, 'did they run the scalpel anywhere over the occiput, Ma'am?'

'I – I – truly, Sir – I'm not sure,' answered Mrs Sturk, who did not perfectly understand a word he said.

The doctor's hair had not been cut behind. Poor Mrs Sturk, expecting his recovery every day, would not have permitted the sacrilege, and his dishevelled cue lay upon his shoulders. With his straight surgical scissors Black Dillon snipped off this sacred append-age before the good lady knew what he was about, and cropped the back of his head down to the closest stubble.

'Will you send, if you please, Ma'am, for Doctor – Doctor – Thingumee?'

'Doctor Toole?' enquired Mrs Sturk.

'Doctor Toole, Ma'am; yes,' answered the surgeon.

He himself went down to the coach at the hall-door, and in a few minutes returned with a case, and something in a cloth. From the cloth he took an apparatus, like the cushioned back of a chair, with straps and buckles attached to it, and a sort of socket, the back of which was open, being intended to receive the head in.

'Now, Ma'am, we'll prop him up comfortable with this, if you please.'

And having got it into place, and lowered by a screw, the cushions intended to receive his head, and got the lethargic trunk and skull of the Artillery doctor well-placed for his purpose, he took out a roll of sticking-plaster and a great piece of lint, and laid them on the table, and unlocked his box, which was a large one, and took out several instruments, silver-mounted, straight and crooked, with awful adaptations to unknown butcheries and tortures, and then out came another – the veritable trepan – resembling the homely bit-and-brace, but slender, sinister, and quaint, with a murderous sort of elegance.

'You may as well order in half-a-dozen clean towels, if you please, Ma'am.'

'Oh! Doctor, you're not going to have an operation tonight, gasped Mrs Sturk, her face quite white and damp, and her clasped hands trembling.

'Twenty to one, Ma'am,' he replied with a slight hiccup, 'we'll have nothing of the kind; but have them here, Ma'am, and some warm water for fear of accidents – though maybe 'tis only for a dhrop of punch we'll be wanting it,' and his huge, thirsty mouth grinned facetiously; and just then Dr Toole entered the room. He was confoundedly surprised when he found Black Dillon there. Though bent on meeting him with hauteur and proper reserve, on account of his damnable character, he was yet cowed by his superior knowledge, so that Tom Toole's address was strangely chequered with pomposity and alarm.

Dillon's credentials there was, indeed, no disputing, so they sent for Moore, the barber; and, while he was coming, they put the women out of the room, and sat in consultation.

Chapter Eighty-eight

*In which Mr Moore the barber arrives, and the medical
gentlemen lock the door*

The ladies were not much the wiser, though, I confess, they were not
far removed from the door. The great men inside talked indistinctly
and technically, and once Doctor Dillon was so unfeeling as to crack
a joke – they could not distinctly hear what – and hee-haw brutally
over it. And poor little Mrs Sturk was taken with a great palpitation,
and looked as white as a ghost, and was, indeed, so obviously at the
point of swooning that her women would have removed her to the
nursery, and placed her on the bed, but that such a procedure would
have obliged them to leave the door of their sick master's room, just
then a point of too lively interest to be deserted. So they consoled
their mistress, and supported her with such strong moral cordials as
compassionate persons in their rank and circumstances are prompt
to administer.

'Oh! Ma'am, jewel, don't be takin' it to heart that way – though,
dear knows, 'tis no way surprisin' you would; for may I never sin if
ever I seen such a murtherin' steel gimblet as the red-faced docthor –
I mane the Dublin man – has out on the table beside the poor
masther – 'tid frighten the hangman to look at it – an' six towels, too!
Why, Ma'am dear, if 'twas what they wor goin' to slaughter a bullock
they wouldn't ax more nor that.'

'Oh! don't. Oh! Katty, Katty – don't, oh don't'

'An' why wouldn't I, my darlin' misthress, tell you what's doin', the
way you would not be dhruv out o' your senses intirely if you had no
notion, Ma'am dear, iv what they're goin' to do to him?'

At this moment the door opened, and Doctor Dillon's carbuncled
visage and glowing eyes appeared.

'Is there a steady woman there – not a child, you know, Ma'am?
A – *you'll* do.' [to Katty] 'Come in here, if you please, and we'll tell
you what you're to do.'

So, being nothing loath, she made her courtesy and glided in.

'Oh! Doctor,' gasped poor Mrs Sturk, holding by the hem of his garment, 'do you think it will kill him?'

'No, Ma'am – not tonight, at any rate,' he answered, drawing back; but still she held him.

'Oh! Doctor, you think it *will* kill him?'

'No, Ma'am – there's always some danger.'

'Danger of what, Sir?'

'Fungus, Ma'am – if he gets over the chance of inflammation. But, on the other hand, Ma'am, we may do him a power of good; and see, Ma'am, 'twill be best for you to go down or into the nursery, and we'll call you, Ma'am, if need be – that is, if he's better, Ma'am, as we hope.'

'Oh! Mr Moore, it's you,' sobbed the poor woman, holding fast by the sleeve of the barber, who that moment, with many reverences and 'your servant, Ma'am', had mounted to the lobby with the look of awestruck curiosity in his long, honest face, which the solemn circumstance of his visit warranted.

'You're the man we sent for?' demanded Dillon, gruffly.

''Tis good Mr Moore,' cried trembling little Mrs Sturk, deprecating and wheedling him instinctively to make him of her side, and lead him to take part with her and resist all violence to her husband – flesh of her flesh, and bone of her bone.

'Why don't you spake, Sor-r-r? Are you the barber we sent for or no? What ails you, man?' demanded the savage Doctor Dillon, in a suppressed roar.

'At your sarvice, Ma'am – Sir,' replied Moore, with submissive alacrity.

'Come in here, then. Come in, will you?' cried the doctor, hauling him in with his great red hand.

'There now – there now – there – there,' he said gruffly, extending his palm to keep off poor Mrs Sturk.

So he shut the door, and poor Mrs Sturk heard him draw the bolt, and felt that her Barney had passed out of her hands, and that she could do nothing for him now but clasp her hands and gasp up her prayers for his deliverance; and so great indeed was her anguish and panic, that she had not room for the feminine reflection how great a brute Doctor Dillon was.

So she heard them walking this way and that, but could not distinguish what they said, only she heard them talking; and once or twice a word reached her, but not very intelligible, such as: ''Twas Surgeon Beauchamp's – see that.'

'Mighty curious.'

Then a lot of mumbling, and 'Cruciform, of course.'

This was said by Doctor Dillon, near the door, where he had come to take an additional candle from the table that stood there; as he receded it lost itself in mumble again, and then she heard quite plainly, 'Keep your hand there.'

And a few seconds after, 'Hold it there and don't let it drip.'

And then a little more mumbled dialogue, and she thought she heard, 'Begin now.'

And there was a dead silence of many seconds; and Mrs Sturk felt as if she must scream, and her heart beat at a gallop, and her dry, white lips silently called upon her Maker for help, and she felt quite wild, and very faint; and heard them speak brief, and low together, and then another long silence; and then a loud voice, in a sort of shriek, cry out that name – holy and awful – which we do not mix in tales like this. It was Sturk's voice; and he cried in the same horrid shriek, 'Murder – mercy – Mr Archer!'

And poor Mrs Sturk, with a loud hysterical cry, that quivered with her agony, answered from without, and wildly rattled at the door-handle, and pushed with all her feeble force to get in, in a kind of crescendo screaming – 'Oh, Barney – Barney – *Barney, sweetheart* – what are they *doing*?'

'Oh! blessed hour! – Ma'am – 'tis the master himself that is talking;' and with a very pale face the maid, who stood in the doorway beside her, uttered her amazed thanksgiving.

And the doctors' voices were now heard plainly enough soothing the patient, and he seemed to have grown more collected; and she heard him – she thought – repeat a snatch of a prayer, as a man might just rescued from a shipwreck; and he said in a tone more natural in one so sick and weak, 'I'm a dead man – he's done it – where is he? – he's murdered me.'

'Who?' demanded Toole's well-known voice.

'Archer – the villain – Charles Archer.'

'Give me the cup with the claret and water, and the spoon – there it is,' said Dillon's rough bass tones.

And she heard the maid's step crossing the floor, and then there was a groan from Sturk.

'Here, take another spoonful, and don't mind talking for a while. It's doing mighty well. There, don't let him slip over – that's enough.'

Just then Toole opened the door enough to put his head through, and gently restraining poor Mrs Sturk with his hand, he said with a vigorous whisper: ' 'Twill all go well, Ma'am, we hope, if he's not agitated; you must not go in, Ma'am, nor talk to him – by-and-by you may see him, but he must be quiet now; his pulse is very regular at present – but you see, Ma'am, we can't be too cautious.'

While Toole was thus discoursing her at the door, she heard Dr Dillon washing his hands, and Sturk's familiar voice, sounding so strange after the long silence, say very languidly and slowly: 'Take a pen, Sir – someone – take and write – write down what I say.'

'Now, Ma'am, you see he's bent on talking,' said Toole, whose quick ear caught the promise of a revelation. 'I must be at my post, Ma'am – the bed post – hey! we may joke now, Ma'am, that the patient's recovered his speech; and, you know, you mustn't come in – not till we tell you it's safe – there now – rely on me – I give you my word of honour he's doing as well as we could have hoped for.'

And Toole shook her trembling little hand very cordially, and there was a very good-natured twinkle in his eye.

And Toole closed the door again, and they heard Sturk murmur something more; and then the maid, who was within, was let out by Toole, and the door closed and bolted again, and a sort of cooing and murmuring recommenced.

After a while, Toole, absolutely pale, and looking very stern, opened the door, and, said he, in a quiet way, 'Ma'am, may I send Katty down to the King's House, with a note to Mr – a note to the King's House, Ma'am – I thank you – and see, Katty, good girl, ask to see the gentleman himself, and take his answer from his own lips.'

And he tore off the back of a letter, and pencilled on it these words:

MY DEAR SIR – Dr Sturk has been successfully operated upon by me and another gentleman; and being restored to speech and recollection, but very weak, desires earnestly to see you, and make an important disclosure to you as a justice of the peace.

I am, Sir, your very obedient, humble servant,

THOMAS TOOLE

Upon this note he clapt a large seal with the Toole arms, and when it was complete, placed it in the hands of Katty, who, with her riding-hood on and her head within it teeming with all sorts of wild conjectures and horrible images, and her whole soul in a whirl of curiosity, hurried along the dark street, now and then glinted on by a gleam through a shutter, or enlivened by the jingle of a harpsichord, or a snatch of talk and laughter heard faintly through the windows, and along the Dublin-road to the gate of the King's House. The hall-door of this hospitable mansion stood open, and a flood of red candle-light fell upon one side of the grey horse, saddle, and holster pipes, which waited the descent of Mr Lowe, who was shaking hands with the hospitable colonel at the threshold.

Katty was just in time, and the booted gentleman, in his surtout and cape, strode back again into the light of the hall-door, and breaking the seal, there read, with his clear cold eye, the lines which Toole had pencilled, and thrusting it into his coat pocket, and receiving again the fuddled butler's benedictions – he had given him half-a-crown – he mounted his grey steed, and at a brisk trot, followed by his servant, was, in little more than two minutes' time, at Dr Sturk's door.

Moore, the barber, *functus officio*, was now sitting in the hall, with his razors in his pocket, expecting his fee, and smelling pleasantly of the glass of whiskey which he had just drunk to the health and long life of the master – God bless him – and all the family.

Doctor Toole met Mr Lowe on the lobby; he was doing the honours of the ghastly *éclaircissement*, and bowed him up to the room, with many an intervening whisper, and a sort of apology for Dillon, whom he treated as quite unpresentable, and resolved to keep as much as practicable in the background.

But that gentleman, who exulted in a good stroke of surgery, and had no sort of professional delicacy, calling his absent fathers and brethren of the scalpel and forceps by confounded hard names when he detected a blunder or hit a blot of theirs, met Mr Lowe on the upper lobby.

'Your servant, Sir,' said he, rubbing his great red hands with a moist grin; 'you see what I've done. Pell's no surgeon, no more than that – ' ['Toole', he was going to say, but modified the comparison in time] – 'that candlestick! To think of him never looking at the occiput; and *he* found lying on his back – 'twas well Mr Dangerfield pitched on me – though I say it – why *shouldn't* I say it – a depression, the size of a shilling in the back of the head – a bit of depressed bone, you see, over the cerebellum – the trepan has relieved him.'

'And was it Mr Dangerfield?' enquired Lowe, who was growing to admire that prompt, cynical hero more and more every hour.

'By gannies, it just was. He promised me five hundred guineas to make him speak. What all them solemn asses could not compass, that's sweeping in their thousands every quarter, thanks to a discerning public. Baugh! He had heard of a rake-helly dog, with some stuff in his brain-pan, and he came to me – and I done it – Black Dillon done it – ha, ha! That's for the pack of them. Baugh!'

Doctor Dillon knew that the profession slighted him; and every man's hand against him, his was against every man.

Sturk was propped up and knew Lowe, and was, in a ghastly sort of way, glad to see him. He looked strangely pale and haggard, and spoke faintly.

'Take pen and ink,' said he.

There were both and paper ready.

'He would not speak till you came,' whispered Toole, who looked hotter than usual, and felt rather small, and was glad to edge in a word.

'An' don't let him talk too long; five minutes or so, and no more,' said Doctor Dillon; 'and give him another spoonful now – and where's Mr Dangerfield?'

'And do you really mean to say, Sir, he promised you a fee of *five* – eh?' said Toole, who could not restrain his somewhat angry curiosity.

'Five hundred guineas – ha, ha, ha! Be gannies, Sir, there's a power of divarsion in that.'

'''Tis a munificent fee, and prompted by a fine public spirit. We are all his debtors for it! And to you, Sir, too. He's an early man, Sir, I'm told. You'll not see him tonight. But, whatever he has promised is already performed; you may rely on his honour.'

'If you come out at nine in the morning, Dr Dillon, you'll find him over his letters and desk, in his breakfast parlour,' said Toole, who, apprehending that this night's work might possibly prove a hit for the disreputable and savage luminary, was treating him, though a good deal stung and confounded by the prodigious amount of the fee, with more ceremony than he did at first. 'Short accounts, you know,' said Dillon, locking the lid of his case down upon his instruments. 'But maybe, as you say, 'tis best to see him in the morning – them rich fellows is often testy – ha! ha! An' a word with you, Dr Toole,' and he beckoned his brother aside to the corner near the door – and whispered something in his ear, and laughed a little awkwardly, and Toole, very red and grave, lent him – with many misgivings, two guineas.

'An' see – don't let them give him too much of that – the chicken broth's too sthrong – put some wather to that, Miss, i' you plaze – and give him no more tonight – d'ye mind – than another half a wine-glass full of clar't unless the docthor here tells you.'

So Dr Dillon took leave, and his fiery steeds, whirling him onward, devoured, with their resounding hoofs, the road to Dublin, where he had mentally devoted Toole's two guineas to the pagan divinities whose worship was nightly celebrated at the old St Columbkill.

'We had best have it in the shape of a deposition, Sir, at once,' said Lowe, adjusting himself at the writing-table by the bedside, and taking the pen in his fingers, he looked on the stern and sunken features of the resuscitated doctor, recalled, as it were, from 'the caverns of the dead and the gates of darkness', to reveal an awful secret, and point his cold finger at the head of the undiscovered murderer.

'Tell it as shortly as you can, Sir, but without haste,' said Toole, with his finger on his pulse. Sturk looked dismal and frightened, like a man with the hangman at his elbow.

'It was that d—d villain – Charles Archer – write that down – 'twas a foul blow – Sir, I'm murdered, I suppose.'

And then came a pause.

'Give me a spoonful of wine – I was coming out of town at dusk – this evening – '

'No, Sir; you're here some time, stunned and unconscious.'

'Eh! How long?'

'No matter, Sir, now. Just say the date of the night it happened.'

Sturk uttered a deep groan.

'Am I dying?' said he.

'No, Sir, please goodness – far from it,' said Toole.

'Fracture?' asked Sturk, faintly.

'Why – yes – something of the sort – indeed – altogether a fracture; but going on mighty well, Sir.'

'Stabbed anywhere – or gunshot wound?' demanded Sturk.

'Nothing of the kind, Sir, upon my honour.'

'You think – I have a chance?' and Sturk's cadaverous face was moist with the dews of an awful suspense.

'Chance,' said Toole, in an encouraging tone, 'well, I suppose you have, Sir – ha, ha! But, you know, you must not tire yourself, and we hope to have you on your legs again, Sir, in a reasonable time.'

'I'm very bad – the sight's affected,' groaned Sturk.

'See, Sir, you tire yourself to no purpose. You're in good hands, Sir – and all will go well – as we expect – Pell has been with you twice – '

'H'm! Pell – that's good.'

'And you're going on mighty well, Sir, especially tonight.'

'Doctor, upon your honour, have I a chance?'

'You have, Sir – certainly – yes, upon my honour.'

'Thank God!' groaned Sturk, turning up the whites of his eyes, and lifting up two very shaky hands.

'But you must not spoil it – and fatigue will do that for you,' remarked Toole.

'But, Sir, Sir – I beg pardon, Doctor Toole – but this case is not quite a common one. What Doctor Sturk is about to say may acquire an additional legal value by his understanding precisely the degree of danger in which he lies. Now, Doctor Sturk, you must not be over much disturbed,' said Lowe.

'No, Sir – don't fear me – I'm not much disturbed,' said Sturk.

'Well, Doctor Toole,' continued Lowe, 'we must depart a little here from regular medical routine – tell Doctor Sturk plainly all you think.'

'Why – a' – and Doctor Toole cleared his voice, and hesitated.

'Tell him what you and Doctor Dillon think, Sir. Why, Doctor Dillon spoke very plainly to me.'

'I don't like his pulse, Sir. I think you had better not have agitated him,' muttered Toole with an impatient oath.

' 'Tis worse to keep his mind doubtful, and on the stretch,' said Lowe. 'Doctor Toole, Sir, has told you the bright side of the case. It is necessary, making the deposition you propose, that you should know t'other.'

'Yes, of course – quite right – go on,' said Sturk faintly.

'Why, you know,' said Toole, sniffing, and a little sulkily, 'you know, Doctor Sturk, we doctors like to put the best foot foremost; but you can't but be aware, that with the fractures – *two* fractures – along the summit of the skull, and the operation by the trepan, behind your head, just accomplished, there must be, of course, some danger.'

'I see. Sir,' said Sturk, very quietly, but looking awfully cadaverous; 'all I want to know is, how long you think I may live?'

'You may recover altogether, Sir – you may – but, of course – you may – there's a chance; and things might not go right,' said Toole, taking snuff.

'I see – Sir – 'tis enough' – and there was a pause. 'I'd like to have the sacrament, and pray with the clergyman a little – Lord help me! – and my will – only a few words – I don't suppose there's much left me; but there's a power of appointment – a reversion of £600, stock – I'm tired.'

'Here, take this,' said Toole, and put half-a-dozen spoonsful of claret and water into his lips, and he seemed to revive a little. 'There's no immediate hurry – upon my honour, Doctor Sturk, there isn't,' said Toole. 'Just rest aisy a bit; you're disturbed a good deal, Sir; your pulse shows it; and you need not, I assure you, upon my conscience and honour – 'tis quite on the cards you may recover.'

And as he spoke, Toole was dropping something from a phial into a wine-glass – sal volatile – ether – I can't say; but when Dr Sturk swallowed it there was a 'potter-carrier's' aroma about the room.

Then there was a pause for a while, and Toole kept his fingers on his pulse; and Sturk looked, for some time, as if he were on the point of fainting, which, in his case, might have proved very like dying.

'Have you the claret bottle in the room?' demanded Toole, a little flurried; for Sturk's pulses were playing odd pranks, and bounding and sinking in a dance of death.

'The what, Sir?' asked the maid.

'The *wine*, woman – this instant,' said the doctor, with a little stamp.

So, the moment he had the bottle, he poured out half a large glass, and began spooning it into Sturk's white parted lips.

Lowe looked on very uneasily; for he expected, as Toole did also, prodigious revelations; though each had a suspicion that he divined their nature tolerably clearly.

'Give him some more,' said Toole, with his fingers on the sick man's wrist, and watching his countenance. 'D— it, don't be afraid – more, some more – more!'

And so the Artillery doctor's spirit revived within him; though with flickerings and tremblings; and he heaved some great sighs, and moved his lips. Then he lay still for a while; and after that he spoke.

'The pen, Sir, – write,' he said. 'He met me in the Butcher's Wood; he said he was going to sleep in town,' and Sturk groaned dismally; 'and he began talking on business – and turned and walked a bit with me. I did not expect to see him there – he was frank – and spoke me fair. We were walking slowly. He looked up in the sky with his hands in his coat pockets and was a step, or so, in advance of me; and he turned short – I didn't know – I had no more fear than you – and struck me a blow with something he had in his hand. He rose to the blow on his toes – 'twas so swift, I had no time – I could not see what he struck with, 'twas like a short bit of rope.'

'Charles Archer? Do you know him, Dr Toole?' asked Lowe. Toole shook his head.

'Charles Archer!' he repeated, looking at Sturk; 'where does he live?' and he winked to Toole, who was about speaking, to hold his peace.

'Here – in this town – Chapelizod, up the river a bit, with – with a – changed name,' answered Sturk. And at the name he mentioned, Lowe and Toole, in silence and steadfastly, exchanged a pale, grim glance that was awful to see.

Chapter Eighty-nine

In which a certain songster treats the company to a dolorous ballad whereby Mr Irons is somewhat moved

It seemed that Mr Dangerfield had taken Zekiel Irons's measure pretty exactly. The clerk had quite made up his mind to take the bold step urged upon him by that gentleman. He was a slow man. When one idea had fairly got into his head there was no room there for another. Cowardly and plotting, but when his cowardice was wrought upon to a certain pitch, he would wax daring and fierce from desperation.

He walked down to the village from the little gate of the Brass Castle, where he had talked with Mr Dangerfield, appointing eight o'clock next morning for making the deposition; late now for all purposes; but to nail him to a line of *viva voce* evidence when he should come to be examined on Charles Nutter's approaching trial. The whole way along he walked with the piece of silver, which Mr Paul Dangerfield had given him, griped tight in his crooked fingers, in his breeches' pocket – no change in his grim and sinister face – no turn of the head – no side glance of the eye – all dark, rigid, and tense.

The mechanism of long habit brought him round the corner to the door of the Salmon House, the 'public' facing, but with the length of the street interposing, the Phoenix, whose lights were visible through and under the branches of the village tree. His mind wandered back to the Mills with a shock, and glided stealthily past the Brass Castle without dwelling there, and he looked down the street. Over the bridge at the Elms, lay death in its awful purity. At his left, in the grey stone house, was Doctor Sturk – the witness with sealed lips – the victim of Charles Archer's mysterious prowess; and behind lay the churchyard, and the quiet little church with that vault and nameless coffin. Altogether, the suggestions and associations about him were not cheerful or comfortable. He squeezed the silver – Dangerfield's little remembrance – with a furious strain, and ground his teeth.

'I'm like a man surrounded. I wish I was out of it all!' he muttered, with a careworn glance.

So he entered the public-house.

There was not much business doing. Three friends, Smithfield dealers or some such folk, talking loudly over their liquor of prices and prospects; and one fat fellow, by the fire, smoking a pipe, with a large glass of punch at his elbow.

'Ah, then, Mr Irons, an' is it yourself that's in it? And where in the world wor ye all this time?' said the landlady.

'Business, Ma'am, business, Mrs Molloy.'

'An' there's your chair waitin' for you beside the fire, Mr Irons, this month an' more – a cowld evening – and we all wondherin' what in the wide world was gone widg ye – this I do'no how long.'

'Thank ye, Ma'am – a pipe and a glass o' punch.'

Irons was always a man of few words, and his laconics did not strike Mistress Molloy as anything very strange. So she wiped the little table at his side, and with one foot on the fender, and his elbow on his knee, he smoked leisurely into the fireplace.

To look at his face you would have supposed he was thinking; but it was only that sort of foggy vacuity which goes by the name of 'a brown study'. He never thought very clearly or connectedly; and his apathetic reveries, when his mood was gloomy, were furnished forth in a barren and monotonous way, with only two or three frightful figures, and a dismal scenery that seldom shifted.

The three gentlemen at the table called for more liquor, and the stout personage sitting opposite to Irons, dropped into their talk, having smoked out his pipe, and their conversation became more general and hilarious; but Irons scarce heard it. Curiosity is an idle minx, and a soul laden like the clerk's has no entertainment for her. But when one of the three gentlemen who sat together – an honest but sad-looking person with a flaxen wig, and a fat, florid face – placing his hand in the breast of his red plush waistcoat, and throwing himself back in his chair, struck up a dismal tune, with a certain character of psalmody in it, the clerk's ear was charmed for a moment, and he glanced on the singer and sipped some punch; and the ballad, rude and almost rhymeless, which he chanted had an undefined and unpleasant fascination for Irons. It was thus:

A man there was near Ballymooney,
   Was guilty of a deed o' blood,
For thravellin' alongside iv ould Tim Rooney.
   He kilt him in a lonesome wood.

He took his purse, and his hat and cravat.
　And stole his buckles and his prayer-book, too;
And neck-and-heels, like a cruel savage,
　His corpus through the wood he drew.

He pult him over to a big bog-hole,
　And sunk him undher four-foot o' wather,
And built him down wid many a thumpin' stone.
　And slipt the bank out on the corpus afther.'

Here the singer made a little pause, and took a great pull at the beer-can, and Irons looked over his shoulder at the minstrel; but his uneasy and malignant glance encountered only the bottom of the vessel; and so he listened for more, which soon came thus:

An' says he, 'Tim Rooney, you're there, my boy,
　Kep' down in the bog-hole wid the force iv suction,
An 'tisn't myself you'll throuble or annoy,
　To the best o' my opinion, to the resurrection.

With that, on he walks to the town o' Drumgoole,
　And sot by the fire in an inn was there;
And sittin' beside him, says the ghost – 'You fool!
　'Tis myself's beside ye, Shamus, everywhere.'

At this point the clerk stood up, and looked once more at the songster, who was taking a short pull again, with a suspicious and somewhat angry glance. But the unconscious musician resumed:

'Up through the wather your secret rises;
　The stones won't keep it, and it lifts the mould,
An' it tracks your footsteps, and yoar fun surprises
　An' it sits at the fire beside you black and cowld.

'At prayers, at dances, or at wake or hurling;
　At fair, or funeral, or where you may;
At your going out, and at your returning,
　'Tis I'll be with you to your dying day.'

'Is there much more o' that?' demanded Irons, rather savagely.
The thirsty gentleman in the red plush waistcoat was once more, as he termed it, 'wetting his whistle'; but one of his comrades responded tartly enough: 'I'd like there was – an' if you mislike it, neighbour, there's the door.'

If he expected a quarrel, however, it did not come; and he saw by Irons's wandering eye, fierce as it looked, that his thoughts for the moment were elsewhere. And just then the songster, having wiped his mouth in his coat-sleeve, started afresh in these terms:

'You'll walk the world with a dreadful knowledge,
  And a heavy heart and a frowning brow;
And thinking deeper than a man in college,
  Your eye will deaden, and your back will bow.

'And when the pariod iv your life is over,
  The frightful hour of judgment then will be;
And, Shamus Hanlon, heavy on your shoulder,
  I'll lay my cowld hand, and you'll go wid me.'

This awful ditty died away in the prolonged drone which still finds favour in the ears of our Irish rustic musicians, and the company now began to talk of congenial themes, murders, ghosts, and retributions, and the horrid tune went dismally booming on in Mr Irons's ear.

Trifling, and apparently wholly accidental, as was this occurrence, the musical and moral treat had a very permanent effect upon the fortunes of Irons, and those of other persons who figure in our story. Mr Irons had another and another glass of punch. They made him only more malign and saturnine. He sat in his corner by the fire, silent and dismal; and no-one cared what was passing in the brain behind that black and scowling mask. He paid sternly and furiously, like a villain who has lost at play; and without a 'good-night', or any other leave taking, glided ominously from the room; and the gentlemen who carried on the discourse and convivialities of the Salmon House, followed him with a gibe or two, and felt the pleasanter for the removal of that ungracious presence.

A few minutes later, Mr Lowe stood on the hall-door step, and calling to his man, gave him a little note and some silver, and a message – very impressively repeated – and the groom touched his hat, and buttoned up his coat about his neck, the wind being from the east, and he started, at something very near a gallop, for Dublin.

There was a man at the door of the Salmon House, who, with a taciturn and saturnine excitement, watched the unusual bustle going on at the door-steps of Doctor Sturk's dwelling. This individual had been drinking there for a while; and having paid his shot, stood with his back to the wall, and his hands in his pockets, profoundly agitated, and with a chaos of violent and unshaped thoughts rising and rolling in his darkened brain.

After Lowe went into the house again, seeing the maid still upon the steps, talking with Mr Moore, the barber, who was making his lingering adieux there, this person drew near, and just as the tonsor made his final farewell, and strode down the street towards his own dwelling, he presented himself in time to arrest the retreat of the damsel.

'By your leave, Mistress Katty,' said he, laying his hand on the iron rail of the door-steps.

'Oh, good jewel! An' is that yourself, Mr Irons? And where in the world wor you this month an' more?'

'Business – nothin' – in Mullingar – an' how's the docthor tonight?'

The clerk spoke a little thickly, as he commonly did on leaving the Salmon House.

'He's elegant, my dear – beyant the beyants – why, he's sittin' up, dhrinking chicken-broth, and talking law-business with Mr Lowe.'

'He's talkin'!'

'Ay is he, and Mr Lowe just this minute writ down all about the way he come by the breakin' of his skull in the park, and we'll have great doings on the head of it; for the master swore to it, and Doctor Toole – '

'An'who done it?' demanded Irons, ascending a step, and grasping the iron rail.

'I couldn't hear – nor no-one, only themselves.'

'An' who's that rode down the Dublin road this minute?'

'That's Mr Lowe's man; 'tis what he's sent him to Dublin wid a note.'

'I see,' said Irons, with a great oath, which seemed to the maid wholly uncalled for; and he came up another step, and held the iron rail and shook it, like a man grasping a battle-axe, and stared straight at her, with a look so strange, and a visage so black, that she was half-frightened.

'A what's the matther wid you, Misther Irons?' she demanded.

But he stared on in silence, scowling through her face at vacancy, and swaying slightly as he griped the metal banister.

'I *will*,' he muttered, with another most unclerklike oath, and he took Katty by the hand, and shook it slowly in his own cold, damp grasp as he asked, with the same intense and forbidding look,

'Is Mr Lowe in the house still?'

'He is, himself and Doctor Toole, in the back parlour.'

'Whisper him, Katty, this minute, there's a man has a thing to tell him.'

'What about?' enquired Katty.

'About a great malefactor.'

Katty paused, with her mouth open, expecting more.

'Tell him now; at once, woman; you don't know what delay may cost.'

He spoke impetuously, and with a bitter sort of emphasis, like a man in a hurry to commit himself to a course, distrusting his own resolution.

She was frightened at his sudden fierceness, and drew back into the hall and he with her, and he shut the door with a clang behind him, and then looked before him, stunned and wild, like a man called up from his bed into danger.

'Thank God. I'm in for it,' muttered he, with a shudder and a sardonic grin, and he looked for a moment something like that fine image of the Wandering Jew, given us by Gustave Doré, the talisman of his curse dissolved, and he smiling cynically in the terrible light of the judgment day.

The woman knocked at the parlour door, and Lowe opened it.

'Who's here?' he asked, looking at Irons, whose face he remembered, though he forgot to whom it belonged.

'I'm Zekiel Irons, the parish-clerk, please your worship, and all I want is ten minutes alone with your honour.'

'For what purpose?' demanded the magistrate, eyeing him sharply.

'To tell you all about a damned murder.'

'Hey – why – who did it?'

'Charles Archer,' he answered; and screwed up his mouth with a convulsive grimace, glaring bloodlessly at the justice.

'Ha! Charles Archer! I think we know something already about that.'

'I don't think you do, though; and by your leave, you'll promise, if I bring it home to him, you'll see me safe through it. 'Tis what I'm the only witness living that knows all about it.'

'Well, what is it about?'

'The murder of Mr Beauclerc, that my Lord Dunoran was tried and found guilty for.'

'Why, all very good; but that did not happen in Ireland.'

'No. At Newmarket, the Pied Horse.'

'Ay, in England. I know, and that's out of our jurisdiction.'

'I don't care. I'll go to London if you like – to Bow-street –

anywhere – so as I make sure to hang him; for my life is worse than death while he's at this side of the grave – and I'd rather be in my coffin – I would – than live within five miles of him. Anyway, you'll hear what I have to say, and to *swear*, and send me safe across the water to Bow-street, or wherever else you think best; for, if he has his liberty, and gets sight o' me again, I'm a dead man.'

'Come in here, Mr Irons, and take a chair,' said the justice.

Doctor Toole was in the room, in a balloon-backed chair, regaling himself with a long pipe, and Mr Lowe shut the door.

'We have another deposition, doctor, to take; Mr Irons, here, is prepared to swear informations of very singular importance.'

'Irons, hollo! From what planet did you drop tonight?'

'Mullingar, Sir.'

'Nothing about the burning of the old woman at Tyrrell's Pass, eh?'

'No – 'tis an old story. I don't care what comes of it, I'm innocent, only you'll say I kept it too long to myself. But you can't touch my life. I'm more afeard of him than you, and with good cause; but I think he's in a corner now, and I'll speak out and take my chance, and you mustn't allow me to be murdered.'

By this time Lowe had procured writing materials, and all being ready, he and the curious and astonished doctor heard a story very like what we have already heard from the same lips.

Chapter Ninety

Mr Paul Dangerfield has something on his mind, and
Captain Devereux receives a message

Mr Dangerfield having parted with Irons, entered the little garden or shrubbery, which skirted on either side the short gravel walk, which expanded to a miniature courtyard before the door of the Brass Castle. He flung the little iron gate to with a bitter clang, so violent that the latch sprang from its hold, and the screaking iron swung quivering open again behind him.

Like other men who have little religion, Mr Paul Dangerfield had a sort of vague superstition. He was impressible by omens, though he scorned his own weakness, and sneered at, and quizzed it sometimes in the monologues of his ugly solitude. The swinging open of the outer gate of his castle sounded uncomfortably behind him, like an invitation to shapeless danger to step in after him. The further he left it behind him, the more in his spirit was the gaping void between his two little piers associated with the idea of exposure, defencelessness, and rashness. This feeling grew so strong, that he turned about before he reached his hall-door, and, with a sensation akin to fury, retraced the fifteen or twenty steps that intervened, and grasped the cold iron with the fiercest tension of his sinews, as if it had resented his first violence by a dogged defiance of his wishes, and spluttering a curse between his teeth, he dashed it to again – and again, as once more it sprang open from the shock.

'Who's master *now*?' snarled Mr Paul Dangerfield, through his clenched teeth, and smiting the senseless iron with a vindictive swoop of his cane. I fancy his face at this moment had some of the peculiar lines and corrugations which we observe in that of Retzsch's Mephistopheles, when he gripes the arm of Faust to drag him from Margaret's cell. So he stood behind his iron grating, glaring and grinning defiance into the darkness, with his fingers clenched hard upon his cane.

Black Dillon's failure was a blow to the progress of his plans. It incensed him. 'That d—d outcast! That *he* should presume so to treat a man who could master him so easily at any game, and buy and sell him body and soul, and had actually bargained to give him five hundred guineas – the needy, swinish miscreant! And paid him earnest beside – the stupid cheat! Drink – dice – women! Why, five hundred guineas made him free of his filthy paradise for a twelvemonth, and the leprous oaf could not quit his impurities for an hour, and keep the appointment that was to have made him master of his heart's desires.'

At his hall-door he paused, listening intently, with his spectacles glimmering toward Chapelizod, for the sound of a distant step; but there was no messenger afoot. He heard only the chill sigh of the air through the leafless branches.

Mr Dangerfield had not his key with him; and he beat an unnecessarily loud and long tattoo upon his door, and before it could possibly have been answered, he thundered a second through the passages.

Mrs Jukes knew the meaning of that harsh and rabid summons. 'There was something on the master's mind.' His anxieties never depressed him as they did other men, but strung up his energies to a point of mental tension and exasperation which made him terrible to his domestics. It was not his acts – his conduct was always under control, but chiefly his looks, and accents, and an influence that seemed to take possession of him at such times that rendered him undefinably formidable to his servants.

'Ha! – mighty obleeging,' [he so pronounced the word] ' – let in at last – cold outside, Ma'am. You've let out the fire, I suppose?'

His tones were like the bark of a wolf, and there was a devilish smirk in his white face, as he made her a mock salutation, and glided into his parlour. The fire was bright enough, however, as Mrs Jukes was much relieved to see; and dropping a courtesy she enquired whether he would like a dish of tea, or anything?

'No, Ma'am!' he snarled.

'Would he like his dressing-gown and slippers?'

'No, Ma'am,' again. So she dropped another courtesy, and sneaked away to the kitchen, with short, noiseless steps, and heard Mr Dangerfield shut the door sharply.

His servants were afraid of him. They could not quite comprehend him. They knew it was vain trying to deceive him, and had quite given up lying and prevaricating. Neither would he stand much talking. When they prattled he brought them to the point sternly; and whenever a real anxiety rested on his mind he became pretty nearly diabolical. On the whole, however, they had a strange sort of liking for him. They were proud of his wealth, and of his influence with great people. And though he would not allow them to rob, disobey, or deceive him, yet he used them handsomely, paid like a prince, was a considerate master, and made them comfortable.

Now Mr Dangerfield poked up his fire and lighted his candles. Somehow, the room looked smaller he thought than it had ever seemed before. He was not nervous – nothing could bring him to that; but his little altercation with the iron gate, and some uncomfortable thoughts had excited him. It was an illusion merely – but the walls seemed to have closed in a foot or two, and the ceiling to have dropped down proportionably, and he felt himself confined and oppressed.

'My head's a little bit heated – *ira furor brevis*,' and he sneered a solitary laugh, more like himself, and went out into his tiny hall, and opened the door, and stood on the step for air, enjoying the cold wind that played about his temples. Presently he heard the hollow clink of two pair of feet walking toward the village. The pedestrians were talking eagerly; and he thought, as they passed the little iron gate of his domain, he heard his own name mentioned, and then that of Mervyn. I dare say it was mere fancy; but, somehow, he did not like it, and he walked swiftly down to the little gate by the roadside – it was only some twenty yards – keeping upon the grass that bounded it, to muffle the sound of his steps. This white phantom noiselessly stood in the shadow of the road side. The interlocutors had got a good way on, and were talking loud and volubly. But he heard nothing that concerned him from either again, though he waited until their steps and voices were lost in the distance.

The cool air was pleasant about his bare temples, and Mr Paul Dangerfield waited a while longer, and listened, for any sound of footsteps approaching from the village, but none such was audible; and beginning to feel a little chilly, he entered his domicile again, shut the hall-door, and once more found himself in the little parlour of the Brass Castle.

His housekeeper heard his harsh voice barking down the passage at her, and rising with a start from her seat, cried, 'At your service, Sir.'

'At a quarter to twelve o'clock fetch me a sandwich, and a glass of absynthe, and meanwhile, don't disturb me.'

And she heard him enter his little parlour, and shut the door.

'There's something to vex, but nothing to threaten – nothing. It's all that comical dream – curse it! What tricks the brain plays us! 'Tis fair it should though. We work it while we please, and it plays when it may. The slave has his saturnalia, and flouts his tyrant. Ha, ha! 'tis time these follies were ended. I've something to do tonight.'

So Mr Dangerfield became himself again, and applied himself keenly to his business.

When I first thought of framing the materials which had accumulated in my hands into a narrative, dear little Lily Walsingham's death was a sore trouble to me. 'Little' Lily I call her, but though slight, she was not little – rather tall, indeed.

It was, however, the term I always heard connected with her pretty name in my boyhood, when the old people, who had remembered her very long ago, mentioned her, as they used, very kindly, a term of endearment that had belonged to her, and in virtue of the childlike charm that was about her, had grown up with her from childhood. I had plans for mending this part of the record, and marrying her to handsome Captain Devereux, and making him worthy of her; but somehow I could not. From very early times I had known the sad story. I had heard her beauty talked about in my childhood: the rich, clear tints, the delicate outlines, those tender and pleasant dimples, like the wimpling of a well; an image so pure, and merry, and melancholy withal, had grown before me, and in twilight shadows visited the now lonely haunts of her brief hours; even the old church, in my evening rambles along the uplands of the park, had in my eyes so saddened a grace in the knowledge that those slender bones lay beneath its shadows, and all about her was so linked in my mind with truth, and melancholy, and altogether so sacred, that I could not trifle with the story, and felt, even when I imagined it, a pang and a reproach, as if I had mocked the sadness of little Lily's fate; so, after some ponderings and trouble of mind I gave it up, and quite renounced the thought.

And, after all, what difference should it make? Is not the generation among whom her girlish lot was cast long passed away? A few years more or less of life. What of them now? When honest Dan Loftus cited those lines from the 'Song of Songs', did he not make her sweet epitaph? Had she married Captain Devereux, what would her lot have been? She was not one of those potent and stoical spirits who can survive the wreck of their best affections, and retort injury with scorn. In forming that simple spirit, Nature had forgotten arrogance and wrath. She would never have fought against the cruelty of changed affections if that or the treasons of an unprincipled husband had come.

His love would have been her light and life, and when that was turned away, like a northern flower that has lost its sun, she would have only hung her pretty head, and died, in her long winter. So viewing now the ways of wisdom from a distance, I think I can see they were the best, and how that fair young mortal, who seemed a sacrifice, was really a conqueror.

Puddock and Devereux on this eventful night, as we remember, having shaken hands at the door-steps, turned and went upstairs together, very amicably again, to the captain's drawing-room.

So Devereux, when they returned to his lodgings, had lost much of his reserve, and once on the theme of his grief, stormed on in gusts, and lulls, and thunder, and wild upbraidings, and sudden calms; and the good-natured soul of little Puddock was touched, and though he did not speak, he often dried his eyes quietly, for grief is conversant not with self, but with the dead, and whatever is generous moves us.

'There's no-one stirring now, Puddock – I'll put my cloak about me and walk over to the Elms, to ask how the rector is tonight,' said Devereux, muffling himself in his military mantle.

It was only the restlessness of grief. Like all other pain, grief is haunted with the illusion that change means relief; motion is the instinct of escape. Puddock walked beside him, and they went swiftly and silently together.

When they reached the other side of the bridge, and stood under the thorn-hedge fronting the leafless elms, Devereux was irresolute.

'Would you wish *me* to enquire?' asked Puddock. Devereux held him doubtfully by the arm for a moment or two, and then said gently – 'No, I thank you, Puddock – I'll go – yes – I'll go myself;' and so Captain Devereux went up to the door.

John Tracy, at the steps, told him that he thought his master wished to speak with him; but he was not quite sure. The tall muffled figure therefore waited at the door while John went in to tell his master, and soon returned to say that Doctor Walsingham would be much obliged to him to step into the study.

When the doctor saw Devereux, he stood up to meet him.

'I hope, Sir,' said Devereux, very humbly, 'you have forgiven me.'

The doctor took his hand and shook it very hard, and said, 'There's nothing – we're both in sorrow. Everyone – everyone is sorry, Sir, but you more.'

Devereux did not say anything, being moved, as I suppose. But he had drawn his cloak about his face, and was looking down.

'There was a little message – only a word or two,' said the doctor; 'but everything of hers is sacred.'

He turned over some papers in his desk, and chose one. It was in Lily's pretty handwriting.

'I am charged with this little message. Oh, my darling!' and the old man cried bitterly. 'Pray, read it – you will understand it – 'tis easily read. What a pretty hand it was!'

So Devereux took the little paper, and read just the words which follow:

> My beloved father will, I hope, if he thinks it right, tell Captain Richard Devereux that I was not so unkind and thankless as I may have seemed, but very grateful for his preference, of which I know, in many ways, how unworthy I was. But I do not think we could have been happy; and being all over, it is a great comfort to friends who are separated here, that there is a place where all may meet again, if God will; and as I did not see or speak with him since my dear father brought his message, I wished that so much should be said, and also to say a kind goodbye, and give him all good wishes.

LILIAS
Friday evening

Captain Richard Devereux read this simple little record through, and then he said: 'Oh, Sir, may I have it – isn't it mine?'

We who have heard those wondrous aërial echoes of Killarney, when the breath has left the bugle and its cadences are silent, take up the broken links of the lost melody with an answer far away, sad and celestial, real yet unreal, the fleeting yet lingering spirit of music that is past and over, have something in memory by which we can illustrate the effect of these true voices of the thoughts and affections that have perished, returning for a few charmed moments regretfully and sweetly from the sea of eternal silence.

And so that sad and clear farewell, never repeated, was long after, in many a lonely night, answered by the voice of Devereux.

'Did she – did she know how I loved her? Oh, never, never! I'll never love any but you. Darling, darling – you can't die. Oh, no, no, no! Your place knows you still; your place is here – here – here.'

And he smote his breast over that heart which, such as it was, cherished a pure affection for her.

Chapter Ninety-one

Concerning certain documents which reached Mr Mervyn,
and the witches' revels at the Mills

I would be ashamed to say how soon after Dangerfield had spoken to Mr Mervyn in the churchyard on the Sunday afternoon, when he surprised him among the tombstones, the large-eyed young gentleman with the long black hair was at his desk, and acting upon his suggestion. But the *Hillsborough* was to sail next day; and Mr Mervyn's letter, containing certain queries and an order for twenty guineas on a London house, glided in that packet with a favouring breeze from the Bay of Dublin, on its way to the London firm of Elrington Brothers.

On the morning of the day whose events I have been describing in the last half-dozen chapters, Mr Mervyn received his answer, which was to the following effect:

SIR – Having made search for the Paper which you enquire after, we have Found one answering your description in a General way; and pursuant to your request and Direction, beg leave to forward you a Copy thereof, together with a copy of a letter concerning it, received by the same post from Sir Philip Drayton, of Drayton Hall, Sometime our Client, and designed in Part to explain his share in the matter. Your order for twenty guineas, on Messrs. Trett and Penrose, hath come to hand, and been duly honoured, and we thankfully Accept the same, in payment for all trouble had in this matter. &c, &c, &c.'

The formal document which it enclosed said:

This is to certify that Charles Archer, Esq., aged, as shortly before his death he reported himself, thirty-five years, formerly of London, departed this life, on the 4th August, 1748, in his lodgings, in the city of Florence, next door to the Red Lion, and over against the great entrance of the Church of the Holy Cross, in the which, having conformed to the holy Roman faith, he is buried. – Signed this 12th day of August, 1748.

> PHILIP DRAYTON, Baronet
> GAETANO MELONI, M.D.
> ROBERT SMITH, Musician
> [we three having seen the said Charles Archer
> during his sickness, and after his decease]

Then followed the copy of the baronet's letter to his attorneys, which was neither very long nor very businesslike.

Why the plague don't you make the scoundrel, Jekyl, pay? His mother's dead only t'other day, and he must be full of money. I've scarce a marvedy in hand, now; so let him have a writ in his, drat him. About that certificate, I'm almost sorry I signed it. I've bin thinking 'tis like enough I may be troubled about it. So you may tell 'em I know no more only what is there avouched. No more I do. He played at a faro-table here, and made a very pretty figure. But I hear now from Lord Orland that there are many bad reports of him. He was the chief witness against that rogue, Lord Dunoran, who swallowed poison in Newgate, and, they say, leaned hard against him, although he won much money of him, and swore with a bloodthirsty intention. But that is neither here nor there; I mean ill reports of his rogueries at play, and other doings, which, had I sooner known, my name had not bin to the paper. So do not make a noise about it, and maybe none will ask for't. As for Jack Jekyl, why not take the shortest way with him. You're very pitiful fellows; but I wish o' my conscience you'd take some pity o' me, and not suffer me to be bubbled,' &c., &c.

There was only a sentence or two more, referring in the same strain to other matters of business, of which, in the way of litigation, he seemed to have no lack, and the letter ended.

I'll go direct to London and see these people, and thence to Florence. Gaetano Meloni – he may be living – who knows? He will remember the priest who confessed him. A present to a religious house may procure – in a matter of justice, and where none can be prejudiced, for the case is very special – a dispensation, if he be the very Charles Archer – and he may – why not? – have disclosed all on his deathbed. First, I shall see

Mr Dangerfield – then those attorneys; and next make search in Florence; and, with the aid of whatever I can glean there, and from Irons, commence in England the intensest scrutiny to which a case was ever yet subjected.

Had it not been so late when he found this letter on his return, he would have gone direct with it to the Brass Castle; but that being quite out of the question, he read it again and again. It is wonderful how often a man will spell over and over the same commonplace syllables, if they happen to touch a subject vitally concerning himself, and what theories and speculations he will build upon the accidental turn of a phrase, or the careless dash of a pen.

As we see those wild animals walk their cages in a menagerie, with the fierce instincts of suppressed action rolling in the vexed eye and vibrating in every sinew, even so we behold this hero of the flashing glance and sable locks treading, in high excitement, the floor of the cedar parlour. Every five minutes a new hope – a new conjecture, and another scrutiny of the baronet's letter, or of the certificate of Archer's death, and hour after hour speeding by in the wild chase of successive chimeras.

While Mr Justice Lowe's servant was spurring into town at a pace which made the hollow road resound, and struck red flashes from the stones, up the river, at the Mills, Mistress Mary Matchwell was celebrating a sort of orgie. Dirty Davy and she were good friends again. Such friendships are subject to violent vicissitudes, and theirs had been interrupted by a difference of opinion, of which the lady had made a note with a brass candlestick over his eye. Dirty Davy's expressive feature still showed the green and yellow tints of convalescence. But there are few philosophers who forgive so frankly as a thorough scoundrel, when it is his interest to kiss and be friends. The candlestick was not more innocent of all unpleasant feeling upon the subject than at that moment was Dirty Davy.

Dirty Davy had brought with him his chief clerk, who was a facetious personage, and boozy, and on the confidential footing of a common rascality with his master, who, after the fashion of Harry V in his nonage, condescended in his frolics and his cups to men of low estate; and Mary Matchwell, though fierce and deep enough, was not averse on occasion to partake of a bowl of punch in sardonic riot, with such agreeable company.

Charles Nutter's unexpected coming to life no more affected Mary Matchwell's claim than his supposed death did her spirits.

Widow or wife, she was resolved to make good her position, and the only thing she seriously dreaded was that an intelligent jury, an eminent judge, and an adroit hangman, might remove him prematurely from the sphere of his conjugal duties, and forfeit his worldly goods to the crown.

Next morning, however, a writ or a process of some sort, from which great things were expected, was to issue from the court in which her rights were being vindicated. Upon the granting of this, Mistress Matchwell and Dirty Davy – estranged for some time, as we have said – embraced. She forgot the attorney's disrespectful language, and he the lady's brass candlestick, and, over the punch-bowl of oblivion and vainglory, they celebrated their common victory.

Under advice, M. M. had acquiesced, pending her vigorous legal proceedings, in poor little Sally Nutter's occupying her bedroom in the house for a little while longer. The beleagured lady was comforted in her strait by the worthy priest, by honest Dr Toole, and not least, by that handsome and stalworth nymph, the daring Magnolia. That blooming Amazon was twice on the point of provoking the dismal sorceress, who kept her court in the parlour of the Mills, to single combat. But fortune willed it otherwise, and each time the duel had been interrupted in its formal inception, and had gone no further than that spirited prologue in which the female sex so faithfully preserve the tradition of those thundering dialogues which invariably precede the manual business of the Homeric fray.

This was the eve of a great triumph and a memorable gala. Next morning, Sally Nutter was to be scalped, roasted, and eaten up, and the night was spent in savage whoopings, songs and dances. They had got a reprobate blind fiddler into the parlour, where their punch-bowl steamed – a most agreeable and roistering sinner, who sang indescribable songs to the quaver of his violin, and entertained the company with Saturnalian vivacity, jokes, gibes, and wicked stories. Larry Cleary, thou man of sin and music! methinks I see thee now. Thy ugly, cunning, pitted face, twitching and grinning; thy small, sightless orbs rolling in thy devil's merriment, and thy shining forehead red with punch.

In the kitchen things were not more orderly; M.M.'s lean maid was making merry with the bailiff, and a fat and dreadful trollop with one eye – tipsy, noisy, and pugnacious.

Poor little Sally Nutter and her maids kept dismal vigil in her bedroom. But that her neighbours and her lawyer would in no sort permit it, the truth is, the frightened little soul would long ago have made herself wings, and flown anywhere for peace and safety.

It is remarkable how long one good topic, though all that may be said upon it has been said many scores of times, will serve the colloquial purposes of the good folk of the kitchen or the nursery. There was scarcely half-an-hour in the day during which the honest maids and their worthy little mistress did not discuss the dreadful Mary Matchwell. They were one and all, though in different degrees, indescribably afraid of her. Her necromantic pretensions gave an indistinctness and poignancy to their horror. She seemed to know, by a diabolical intuition, what everybody was about – she was so noiseless and stealthy, and always at your elbow when you least expected. Those large dismal eyes of hers, they said, glared green in the dark like a cat's; her voice was sometimes so coarse and deep, and her strength so unnatural, that they were often on the point of believing her to be a man in disguise. She was such a blasphemer, too; and could drink what would lay a trooper under the table, and yet show it in nothing but the superintensity of her Satanic propensities. She was so malignant, and seemed to bear to all God's creatures so general a malevolence, that her consistent and superlative wickedness cowed and paralysed them. The enigma grew more horrible every day and night, and they felt, or fancied, a sort of influence stealing over them which benumbed their faculty of resistance, and altogether unstrung their nerves.

The grand compotation going on in the parlour waxed louder and wilder as the night wore on. There were unseen guests there, elate and inspiring, who sat with the revellers – phantoms who attend such wassail, and keep the ladle of the punch-bowl clinking, the tongue of the songster glib and tuneful, and the general mirth alive and furious. A few honest folk, with the gift of a second sight in such matters, discover their uncanny presence – leprous impurity, insane blasphemy, and the stony grin of unearthly malice – and keep aloof.

To heighten their fun, this jovial company bellowed their abominable ballads in the hall, one of them about 'Sally M'Keogh', whose sweetheart was hanged, and who cut her throat with his silver-mounted razor, and they hooted their gibes up the stairs. And at last Mary Matchwell, provoked by the passive quietude of her victim, summoned the three revellers from the kitchen, and invaded the upper regions at their head – to the unspeakable terror of poor Sally Nutter – and set her demon fiddler a-scraping, and made them and

Dirty Davy's clerk dance a frantic reel on the lobby outside her bedroom door, locked and bolted inside, you may be sure.

In the midst of this monstrous festivity and uproar, there came, all on a sudden, a reverberating double-knock at the hall-door, so loud and long that every hollow, nook, and passage of the old house rang again. Loud and untimely as was the summons, it had a character, not of riot, but of alarm and authority. The uproar was swallowed instantly in silence. For a second only the light of the solitary candle shone upon the pale, scowling features of Mary Matchwell, and she quenched its wick against the wall. So the Walpurgis ended in darkness, and the company instinctively held their breaths.

There was a subdued hum of voices outside, and a tramping on the crisp gravel, and the champing and snorting of horses, too, were audible.

'Does none o' yez see who's in it?' said the blind fiddler.

'Hold your tongue,' hissed Mary Matchwell with a curse, and visiting the cunning pate of the musician with a smart knock of the candlestick.

'I wisht I had your thumb undher my grinder,' said the fiddler, through his teeth, 'whoever you are.'

But the rest was lost in another and a louder summons at the hall-door, and a voice of authority cried sternly,

'Why don't you open the door? – Hollo! there – I can't stay here all night.'

'Open to him, Madam, I recommend you,' said Dirty Davy, in a hard whisper; 'will I go?'

'Not a step; not a word;' and Mary Matchwell griped his wrist.

But a window in Mrs Nutter's room was opened, and Moggy's voice cried out: 'Don't go, Sir; for the love o' goodness, don't go. Is it Father Roach that's in it?'

' 'Tis I, woman – Mr Lowe – open the door, I've a word or two to say.'

Chapter Ninety-two
The Wher-wolf

About a quarter of an hour before this, Mr Paul Dangerfield was packing two trunks in his little parlour, and burning letters industriously in the fire, when his keen ear caught a sound at which a prophetic instinct within him vibrated alarm. A minute or two before he had heard a stealthy footstep outside. Then he heard the cook walk along the passage, muttering to herself, to the hall-door, where there arose a whispering. He glanced round his shoulder at the window. It was barred. Then lifting the table and its load lightly from before him, he stood erect, fronting the door, and listening intently. Two steps on tiptoe brought him to it, and he placed his fingers on the key. But he recollected a better way. There was one of those bolts that rise and fall perpendicularly in a series of rings, and bar or open the door by a touch to a rope connected with it by a wire and a crank or two.

He let the bolt softly drop into its place; the rope was within easy reach, and with his spectacles gleaming white on the door, he kept humming a desultory tune, like a man over some listless occupation.

Mr Paul Dangerfield was listening intently, and stepped as softly as a cat. Then, with a motion almost elegant, he dropt his right hand lightly into his coat-pocket, where it lay still in ambuscade.

There came a puffing night air along the passage, and rattled the door; then a quiet shutting of the hall-door, and a shuffling and breathing near the parlour.

Dangerfield, humming his idle tune with a white and sharpening face, and a gaze that never swerved, extended his delicately-shaped fingers to the rope, and held it in his left hand. At this moment the door-handle was suddenly turned outside, and the door sustained a violent jerk.

'Who's there?' demanded the harsh, prompt accents of Dangerfield, suspending his minstrelsy. 'I'm busy.'

'Open the door – we've a piece of intelligence to gi'e ye.'

'Certainly – but don't be tedious.' (He drew the string, and the bolt shot up.) 'Come in, Sir.'

The door flew open; several strange faces presented themselves on the threshold, and at the same instant, a stern voice exclaimed: 'Charles Archer, I arrest you in the king's name.'

The last word was lost in the stunning report of a pistol, and the foremost man fell with a groan. A second pistol already gleamed in Dangerfield's hand, and missed. With a spring like a tiger he struck the hesitating constable in the throat, laying his scalp open against the door-frame, and stamping on his face as he fell; and clutching the third by the cravat, he struck at his breast with a knife, already in his hand. But a pistol-shot from Lowe struck his right arm, scorching the cloth; the dagger and the limb dropped, and he staggered back, but recovered his equilibrium, and confronted them with a white skull-like grin, and a low 'ha, ha, ha!'

It was all over, and the silver spectacles lay shattered on the floor, like a broken talisman, and a pair of grey, strangely-set, wild eyes glared upon them.

The suddenness of his assault, his disproportioned physical strength and terrific pluck, for a second or two confounded his adversaries; but he was giddy – his right arm dead by his side. He sat down in a chair confronting them, his empty right hand depending near to the floor, and a thin stream of blood already trickling down his knuckles, his face smiling, and shining whitely with the damp of anguish, and the cold low 'ha, ha, ha!' mocking the reality of the scene.

'Heinous old villain!' said Lowe, advancing on him.

'Well, gentlemen, I've shown fight, eh? – and now I suppose you want my watch, and money, and keys – eh?'

'Read the warrant, Sir,' said Lowe, sternly.

'Warrant! Hey – warrant? – why, this is something new – will you be so good as to give me a glass of water – thank you – hold the paper a moment longer – I can't get this arm up.' With his left hand he set down the tumbler-glass, and then held up the warrant.

'Thank ye. Well, this warrant's for Charles Archer.'

'Alias Paul Dangerfield – if you read, Sir.'

'Thank you – yes – I see – that's news to me. Oh! Mr Lowe – I did not see *you* – I haven't hurt you, I hope? Why the plague do you come at these robbing hours? We'd have all fared better had you come by daylight.'

Lowe did not take the trouble to answer him.

'I believe you've *killed* that constable in the exercise of his duty, Sir; the man's dead,' said Lowe, sternly.

'Another gloss on my text; why invade me like housebreakers?' said Dangerfield with a grim scoff.

'No violence, Sirrah, on your peril – the prisoner's wounded,' said Lowe, catching the other fellow by the collar and thrusting him back: he had gathered himself up giddily, and swore he'd have the scoundrel's life.

'Well, gentlemen, you have made a *false* arrest, and shot me while defending my person – *you* – four to one! – and caused the death of your accomplice; what more do you want?'

'You must accompany us to the county gaol, Sir; where I'll hand in your committal.'

'Dr Toole, I presume, may dress my arm?'

'Certainly, Sir.'

'Good! What more?'

'There's a coach at the door, you'll please to step in, Sir.'

'Good, Sir, again; and now permit me to make a remark. I submit, Sir, to all this violence, and will go with you, under protest, and with a distinct warning to you, Mr Lowe, and to your respectable body-guard of prize-fighters and ruffians – how many? – two, four, five, six, upon my honour, counting the gentleman upon the floor, and yourself, Sir – seven, pitted against one old fellow, ha, ha, ha! – a distinct warning, Sir, that I hold you accountable for this outrage, and all its consequences.'

'See to that man; I'm afraid he has killed him,', said Lowe.

He was not dead, however, but, as it seemed, suffering intense pain, and unable to speak except in a whisper. They got him up with his back to the wall.

'You issue a warrant against another man whom I believe to be dead, and execute it upon *me* – rather an Irish proceeding, Sir; but, perhaps, if not considered impertinent, you will permit me to enquire what is the particular offence which that other person has committed, and for which you have been pleased to shoot me?'

'You may read it on the warrant, Sir; 'tis for a murderous assault on Doctor Sturk.'

'Hey? Better and better! Why, I'm ready to pay five hundred guineas to make him speak; and you'll soon find how expensive a blunder you've committed, Sir,' observed Dangerfield, with a glare of menace through his hollow smile.

'I'll stand that hazard, Sir,' rejoined Lowe, with a confident sneer.

The dreadful sounds of the brief scuffle had called up the scared and curious servants. The smell of the pistol-smoke, the sight of blood, the pale faces of the angry and agitated men, and the spectacle of their master, mangled, ghastly, and smiling, affrighted Mrs Jukes; and the shock and horror expressed themselves in tears and distracted lamentations.

'I must have your keys, Sir, if you please,' said Mr Lowe.

'A word first – here, Jukes,' he addressed his housekeeper; 'stop that, you fool!' [she was blubbering loudly] ''tis a mistake, I tell you; I shall be back in an hour. Meanwhile, here are my keys; let Mr Lowe, there, have them whenever he likes – all my papers, Sir.' [turning to Lowe] 'I've nothing, thank Heaven! to conceal. Pour some port wine into that large glass.'

And he drank it off, and looked better; he appeared before on the point of fainting.

'I beg pardon, gentlemen – will you drink some wine?'

'I thank you, no, Sir. You'll be good enough to give me those keys.' [to the housekeeper].

'Give them – certainly,' said Dangerfield.

'Which of them opens the chest of drawers in your master's bedchamber facing the window?' He glanced at Dangerfield, and thought that he was smiling wider, and his jaws looked hollower, as he repeated: 'If she does not know it, I'll be happy to show it you.'

With a surly nod, Mr Lowe requited the prisoner's urbanity, and followed Mrs Jukes into her master's bed-chamber; there was an old-fashioned oak chest of drawers facing the window.

'Where's Captain Cluffe?' enquired Lowe.

'He stopped at his lodgings, on the way,' answered the man; 'and said he'd be after us in five minutes.'

'Well, be good enough, Madam, to show me the key of these drawers.'

So he opened the drawers in succession, beginning at the top, and searching each carefully, running his fingers along the inner edges, and holding the candle very close, and grunting his disappointment as he closed and locked each in its order.

In the meantime, Doctor Toole was ushered into the little parlour, where sat the disabled master of the Brass Castle. The fussy little mediciner showed in his pale, stern countenance, a sense of the shocking reverse and transformation which the great man of the village had sustained.

'A rather odd situation you find me in, Doctor Toole,' said white Mr Dangerfield, in his usual harsh tones, but with a cold moisture shining on his face; 'under *duresse*, Sir, in my own parlour, charged with murdering a gentleman whom I have spent five hundred guineas to bring to speech and life, and myself half murdered by a justice of the peace and his discriminating followers, ha, ha, ha! I'm suffering a little pain, Sir; will you be so good as to lend me your assistance?'

Toole proceeded to his task much more silently than was his wont, and stealing, from time to time, a glance at his noticeable patient with the wild grey eyes, as people peep curiously at what is terrible and repulsive.

' 'Tis broken, of course,' said Dangerfield.

'Why, yes, Sir,' answered Toole; 'the upper arm – a bullet, Sir. H'm, ha – yes; it lies only under the skin, Sir.'

And with a touch of the sharp steel it dropped into the doctor's fingers, and lay on a bloody bit of lint on the table by the wineglasses. Toole applied his sticking-plaster, and extemporised a set of splints, and had the terrified cook at his elbow tearing up one of her master's shirts into strips for bandages; and so went on neatly and rapidly with his shifty task.

In the mean time, Cluffe had arrived. He was a little bit huffed and grand at being nailed as an evidence, upon a few words carelessly, or, if you will, confidentially dropped at his own mess-table, where Lowe chanced to be a guest; and certainly with no suspicion that his little story could in any way be made to elucidate the mystery of Sturk's murder. He would not have minded, perhaps, so much, had it not been that it brought to light and memory again the confounded ducking sustained by him and Puddock, and which, as an officer and a very fine fellow, he could not but be conscious was altogether an undignified reminiscence.

'Yes, the drawers were there, he supposed; those were the very ones; he stooped but little; it must have been the top one, or the next to it. The thing was about as long as a drumstick, like a piece of whip handle, with a spring in it; it bent this way and that, as he dried it in the towel, and at the butt it was ribbed round and round with metal rings – devilish heavy.'

So they examined the drawers again, took everything out of them, and Captain Cluffe, not thinking it a soldier-like occupation, tacitly declined being present at it, and, turning on his heel, stalked out of the room.

'What's become of it, Ma'am?' said Lowe, suddenly and sternly, turning upon Mrs Jukes, and fixing his eyes on hers. There was no guilty knowledge there.

'He never had any such thing that I know of,' she answered stoutly; 'and nothing could be hid from me in these drawers, Sir; for I had the key, except when it lay in the lock, and it must ha' been his horse-whip; it has some rings like of leather round it, and he used to lay it on these drawers.'

Cluffe was, perhaps, a little bit stupid, and Lowe knew it; but it was the weakness of that good magistrate to discover in a witness for the crown many mental and moral attributes which he would have failed to recognise in him had he appeared for the prisoner.

'And where's that whip, now?' demanded Lowe.

'By the hall-door, with his riding-coat, Sir,' answered the bewildered housekeeper.

'Go on, if you please, Ma'am, and let me see it.'

So to the hall they went, and there, lying across the pegs from which Mr Dangerfield's surtout and riding-coat depended, there certainly was a whip with the butt fashioned very much in the shape described by Captain Cluffe; but alas, no weapon — a mere toy — leather and cat-gut.

Lowe took it in his hand, and weighing it with a look of disgust and disappointment, asked rather impatiently, 'Where's Captain Cluffe?'

The captain had gone away.

'Very well, I see,' said Lowe, replacing the whip; 'that will do. The hound!'

Mr Lowe now re-entered the little parlour, where the incongruous crowd, lighted up with Mr Dangerfield's wax lights, and several kitchen candles flaring in greasy brass sticks, were assisting at the treatment of the master of the castle and the wounded constables.

'Well, Sir,' said Mr Dangerfield, standing erect, with his coat sleeve slit, and his arm braced up in splints, stiff and helpless in a sling, and a blot of blood in his shirt sleeve, contrasting with the white intense smirk of menace upon his face; 'if you have quite done with my linen and my housekeeper, Sir, I'm ready to accompany you under protest, as I've already said, wherever you design to convey my mangled person. I charge you, Sir, with the safety of my papers and my other property which you constrain me to abandon in this house; and I think you'll rue this night's work to the latest hour of your existence.'

'I've done, and will do, my duty, Sir,' replied Lowe, with dry decision.

'You've committed a d—d outrage; duty? Ha, ha, ha!'

'The coach is at the door, hey?' asked Lowe

'I say, Sir,' continued Dangerfield, with a wolfish glare, and speaking in something like a suppressed shriek, 'you *shall* hear my warning and my protest, although it should occupy the unreasonable period of two whole minutes of your precious time. You half murder, and then arrest me for the offence of another man, and under the name of a man who has been dead and buried full twenty years. I can prove it; the eminent London house of Elrington Brothers can prove it; the handwriting of the late Sir Philip Drayton, Baronet, of Drayton Hall, and of two other respectable witnesses to a formal document, can prove it; dead and rotten – *dust*, Sir. And in your stupid arrogance, you blundering Irishman, you dare to libel me – your superior in everything – with his villainous name, and the imputation of his crimes – to violate my house at the dead of night – to pistol me upon my own floor – and to carry me off by force, as you purpose, to a common gaol. Kill Dr Sturk, indeed! Are you mad, Sir? *I* who offered a fee of five hundred guineas even to bring him to speech! *I* who took the best medical advice in *London* on his behalf; *I* who have been his friend only too much with my Lord Castlemallard, and who, to stay his creditors, and enable his family to procure for him the best medical attendance, and to afford him, in short, the best chance of recovery and life, have, where *you* neither lent or bestowed a shilling – poured out my money as profusely as you, Sir, have poured out my blood, every drop of which, Sir, shall cost you a slice of your estate. But even without Sturk's speaking one word, I've evidence which escaped *you*, conceited blockhead, and which, though the witness is as mad almost as yourself, will yet be enough to direct the hand of justice to the right man. There *is* a Charles, Sir, whom all suspect, who awaits trial, judgment, and death in this case, the wretched Charles Nutter of the Mills, Sir, whose motive is patent, and on whose proceedings a light will, I believe, be thrown by the evidence of Zekiel Irons, whatever that evidence may be worth.'

'I don't care to tell you, Sir, that 'tis partly on the evidence of that same Zekiel Irons that I've arrested *you*,' said Mr Justice Lowe.

'Zekiel Irons, *me*! What! Zekiel Irons charge me with the crime which he was here, not two hours since, fastening on oath upon Charles Nutter! Why, Sir, he asked me to bring him to your residence in the morning, that he might swear to the information which he repeated in my presence, and of which there's a note in that desk. 'Pon my life, Sir, 'tis an agreeable society, this; bedlam broke loose –

the mad directing the mad, and both falling foul of the sane. One word from Doctor Sturk, Sir, will blast you, so soon as, please Heaven, he shall speak.'

'He *has* spoken, Sir,' replied Lowe, whose angry passions were roused by the insults of Dangerfield, and who had, for the moment, lost his customary caution.

'Ha!' cried Dangerfield, with a sort of gasp, and a violent smirk, the joyousness of which was, however, counteracted by a lurid scowl and a wonderful livid glare in his wild eyes. 'Ha! he has? Bravo, Sir, bravissimo!' and he smirked wider and wider, and beat his uninjured hand upon the table, like a man applauding the *dénouement* of a play. 'Well, Sir; and notwithstanding his declaration, you arrest me upon the monstrous assertion of a crazy clerk, you consummate blockhead!'

''Twon't do, Sir, you shan't sting me by insult into passion; nor frighten me by big words and big looks into hesitation. My duty's clear, and be the consequences what they may, I'll carry the matter through.'

'Frighten you! Ha, ha, ha!' and Dangerfield glared at his bloody shirt-sleeve, and laughed a chilly sneer; 'no, Sir, but I'll punish you, with Doctor Sturk's declaration against the babble of poor Zekiel Irons. I'll quickly close your mouth.'

'Sir, I never made it a practice yet to hide evidence from a prisoner. Why should I desire to put you out of the world, if you're innocent? Doctor Sturk, Sir, has denounced you distinctly upon oath: Charles Archer, going by the name of Paul Dangerfield, and residing in this house, called the Brass Castle, as the person who attempted to murder him in the Butcher's Wood.'

'*What*, Sir? Doctor Sturk denounce *me*! 'Fore heaven, Sir – it seems to me you've all lost your wits. Doctor Sturk! – Doctor Sturk charge *me* with having assaulted him! Why – curse it, Sir – it can't possibly be – you can't believe it; and, if he said it, the man's raving still.'

'He has said it, Sir.'

'Then, Sir, in the devil's name, didn't it strike you as going rather fast to shoot me on my own hearth-stone – *me*, knowing all you do about me – with no better warrant than the talk of a man with a shattered brain, awakening from a lethargy of months? Sir, though the laws afford no punishment exemplary enough for such atrocious precipitation, I promise you I'll exact the last penalty they provide; and now, Sir, take me where you will; I can't resist. Having shot me, do what you may to interrupt my business; to lose my papers and accounts; to prevent my recovery, and to blast my reputation – Sir, I shall have compensation for all.'

So saying, Dangerfield, with his left hand, clapt his cocked hat on, and with a ghastly smile nodded a farewell to Mrs Jukes, who, sobbing plentifully, had placed his white surtout cloakwise over his shoulders, buttoning it about his throat. The hall-door stood open; the candles flared in the night air, and with the jaunty, resolute step of a man marching to victory and revenge, he walked out, and lightly mounted to his place. She saw the constables get in, and one glimpse more of the white grim face she knew so well, the defiant smirk, the blood-stained shirt-sleeve, and the coach-door shut. At the crack of the whip and the driver's voice, the horses scrambled into motion, the wheels revolved, and the master of the Brass Castle and the equipage glided away like a magic lantern group, from before the eyes and the candle of the weeping Mrs Jukes.

Chapter Ninety-three

In which Dr Toole and Dirty Davy confer in the blue room

The coach rumbled along toward Dublin at a leisurely jog. Notwithstanding the firm front Mr Lowe had presented, Dangerfield's harangue had affected him unpleasantly. Cluffe's little bit of information respecting the instrument he had seen the prisoner lay up in his drawer on the night of the murder, and which corresponded in description with the wounds traced upon Sturk's skull, seemed to have failed. The handle of Dangerfield's harmless horsewhip, his mind misgave him, was all that would come of *that* piece of evidence; and it was impossible to say there might not be something in all that Dangerfield had uttered. Is it a magnetic force, or a high histrionic vein in some men, that makes them so persuasive and overpowering, and their passion so formidable? But with Dangerfield's presence, the effect of his plausibilities and his defiance passed away. The pointed and consistent evidence of Sturk, perfectly clear as he was upon every topic he mentioned, and the corroborative testimony of Irons, equally distinct and damning – the whole case blurred and disjointed, and for a moment grown unpleasantly hazy and uncertain in the presence of that white sorcerer, readjusted itself now that he was gone, and came out in iron and compact relief – impregnable.

'Run boys, one of you, and open the gate of the Mills,' said Lowe, whose benevolence, such as it was, expanded in his intense feeling of relief. ''Twill be good news for poor Mistress Nutter. She'll see her husband in the morning.'

So he rode up to the Mills, and knocked his alarm, as we have seen and heard, and there told his tidings to poor Sally Nutter, vastly to the relief of Mistress Matchwell, the Blind Fiddler, and even of the sage, Dirty Davy; for there are persons upon the earth to whom a sudden summons of any sort always sounds like a call to judgment, and who, in any such ambiguous case, fill up the moments of suspense with wild conjecture, and a ghastly summing-up against themselves; can it be this – or that, or the other – old, buried, distant villainy, that comes back to take me by the throat?

Having told his good news in a few dry words to Mrs Sally, Mr Lowe superadded a caution to the dark lady downstairs, in the face of which she, being quite reassured by this time, grinned and snapped her fingers, and in terms defied, and even cursed the tall magistrate without rising from the chair in which she had re-established herself in the parlour. He mounted his hunter again, and followed the coach at a pace which promised soon to bring him up with that lumbering conveyance; for Mr Lowe was one of those public officers who love their work, and the tenant of the Brass Castle was no common prisoner, and well worth seeing, though at some inconvenience, safely into his new lodging.

Next morning, you may be sure, the news was all over the town of Chapelizod. All sorts of cross-rumours and wild canards, of course, were on the wind, and every new fact or fib borne to the door-step with the fresh eggs, or the morning's milk and butter, was carried by the eager servant into the parlour, and swallowed down with their toast and tea by the staring company.

Upon one point all were agreed: Mr Paul Dangerfield lay in the county gaol, on a charge of having assaulted Dr Sturk with intent to kill him. The women blessed themselves, and turned pale. The men looked queer when they met one another. It was altogether so astounding – Mr Dangerfield was so rich – so eminent – so moral – so charitable – so above temptation. It had come out that he had committed, some said three, others as many as fifteen secret murders. All the time that the neighbours had looked on his white head in church as the very standard of probity, and all the prudential virtues rewarded, they were admiring and honouring a masked assassin. They had been bringing into their homes and families an undivulged and terrible monster. The wher-wolf had walked the homely streets of their village. The ghoul, unrecognised, had prowled among the graves of their churchyard. One of their fairest princesses, the lady of Belmont, had been on the point of being sacrificed to a vampire. Horror, curiosity and amazement were everywhere.

Charles Nutter, it was rumoured, was to be discharged on bail early, and it was mooted in the club that a deputation of the neighbours should ride out to meet him at the boundaries of Chapelizod, welcome him there with an address, and accompany him to the Mills as a guard of honour; but cooler heads remembered the threatening and unsettled state of things at that domicile, and thought that Nutter would, all things considered, like a quiet return best; which view of the affair was, ultimately, acquiesced in.

For Mary Matchwell, at the Mills, the tidings which had thrown the town into commotion had but a solitary and a selfish interest. She was glad that Nutter was exculpated. She had no desire that the king should take his worldly goods to which she intended helping herself: otherwise he might hang or drown for aught she cared. Dirty Davy, too, who had quaked about his costs, was greatly relieved by the turn which things had taken; and the plain truth was that, not-withstanding his escape from the halter, things looked very black and awful for Charles Nutter and his poor little wife, Sally.

Doctor Toole, at half-past nine, was entertaining two or three of the neighbours, chiefly in oracular whispers, by the fire in the great parlour of the Phoenix, when he was interrupted by Larry, the waiter, with 'Your horse is at the door, docther,' [Toole was going into town, but was first to keep an appointment at Doctor Sturk's with Mr Lowe] 'and,' continued Larry, 'there's a fat gentleman in the blue room wants to see you, if you plase.'

'Hey? – ho! Let's see then,' said little Toole, bustling forth with an important air. 'The blue room, hey?'

When he opened the door of that small apartment there stood a stout, corpulent, rather seedy and dusty personage, at the window, looking out and whistling with his hat on. He turned lazily about as Toole entered, and displayed the fat and forbidding face of Dirty Davy.

'Oh! I thought it might be professionally, Sir,' said Toole, a little grandly; for he had seen the gentleman before, and had, by this time, found out all about him, and perceived he had no chance of a fee.

'It *is* professionally, Sir,' quoth Dirty Davy, 'if you'll be so obleeging as to give me five minutes.'

With that amiable egotism which pervades human nature, it will be observed, each gentleman interpreted 'professionally' as referring to his own particular calling.

So Toole declared himself ready and prepared to do his office, and Dirty Davy commenced.

'You know me, I believe, Sir?'

'Mr David O'Reegan, as I believe,' answered Toole.

'The same, Sir,' replied Davy. 'I'm on my way, Sir, to the Mills, where my client, Mrs Nutter (here Toole uttered a disdainful grunt), resides; and I called at your house, doctor, and they sent me here;

and I am desirous to prove to you, Sir, as a friend of Miss Sarah Harty, styling herself Mrs Nutter, that my client's rights are clear and irresistible, in order that you may use any interest you may have with that ill-advised faymale – and I'm told she respects your advice and opinion highly – to induce her to submit without further annoyance; and I tell you, in confidence, she has run herself already into a very sarious predicament.'

'Well, Sir, I'll be happy to hear you,' answered Toole.

''Tis no more, Sir, than I expected from your well-known candour,' replied Dirty Davy, with the unctuous politeness with which he treated such gentlemen as he expected to make use of. 'Now, Sir, I'll open our case without any reserve or exaggeration to you, Sir, and that, Doctor Toole, is what I wouldn't do to many beside yourself. The facts is in a nutshell. We claim our conjugal rights. Why, Sir? Because, Sir, we married the oppugnant, Charles Nutter, gentleman, of the Mills, and so forth, on the 7th of April, Anno Domini, 1750, in the Church of St Clement Danes, in London, of which marriage this, Sir, is a verbatim copy of the certificate. Now, Sir, your client – I mane your friend – Misthress Mary Harty, who at present affects the state and usurps the rights of marriage against my client – the rightful Mrs Nutter, performed and celebrated a certain pretended marriage with the same Charles Nutter, in Chapelizod Church, on the 4th of June, 1758, seven years and ten months, wanting three days, subsequent to the marriage of my client. Well, Sir, I see exactly, Sir, what you'd ask: "Is the certificate genuine?" '

Toole grunted an assent.

'Well, Sir, upon that point I have to show you this,' and he handed him a copy of Mr Luke Gamble's notice served only two days before, to the effect that, having satisfied himself by enquiring on the spot of the authenticity of the certificate of the marriage of Charles Nutter of the Mills, and so forth, to Mary Duncan, his client did not mean to dispute it. 'And, Sir, further, as we were preparing evidence in support of my client's and her maid's affidavit, to prove her identity with the Mary Duncan in question, having served your client – I mane, Sir, asking your pardon again – your friend, with a notice that such corroboratory evidence being unnecessary, we would move the court, in case it were pressed for, to give us the costs of procuring it, Mr Luke Gamble forthwith struck, on behalf of his client, and admitted the sufficiency of the evidence. Now, Sir, I mention these things, not as expecting you to believe them upon my statement, you see, but simply to enquire of Mr Gamble whether they be true or no;

and if true, Sir, upon his admission, then, Sir, I submit we're entitled to your good offices, and the judicious inthurfarence of the Rev. Mr Roach, your respectable priest, Sir.'

'My friend, Sir, not my priest. I'm a Churchman, Sir, as everybody knows.'

'Of course, Sir – I ask your pardon again, Doctor Toole – Sir, your friend to induce your client – *friend* I mane again, Sir – Mistress Sarah Harty, formerly housekeeper of Mr Charless (so he pronounced it) Nutther, gentleman, of the Mills, and so forth, to surrendher quiet and peaceable possession of the premises and chattels, and withdraw from her tortuous occupation dacently, and without provoking the consequences, which must otherwise follow in the sevarest o' forms;' or, as he pronounced it, 'fawrums'.

'The sevarest o' grandmothers. Humbug and flummery! Sir,' cried Toole, most unexpectedly incensed, and quite scarlet.

'D'ye mane I'm a liar, Sir? Is that what you mane?' demanded Dirty Davy, suddenly, like the doctor, getting rid of his ceremonious politeness.

'I mane what I mane, and that's what I mane,' thundered Toole, diplomatically.

'Then, tell your *friend* to prepare for consequences,' retorted Dirty Davy, with a grin.

'And make my compliments to your client, or conjuror, or wife, or whatever she is, and tell her that whenever she wants her dirty work done, there's plenty of other Dublin blackguards to be got to do it, without coming to Docther Thomas Toole, or the Rev. Father Roach.'

Which sarcasm he delivered with killing significance, but Dirty Davy had survived worse thrusts than that.

'She's a conjuror, is she? I thank you, Sir.'

'You're easily obliged, Sir,' says Toole.

'We all know what that manes. And these documents *sworn* to by my client and myself, is a pack o' lies! Betther and betther! I thank ye again, Sir.'

'You're welcome, my honey,' rejoined Toole, affectionately.

'An' you live round the corner. I know your hall-door, Sir – a light brown, wid a brass knocker.'

'Which is a fine likeness iv your own handsome face, Sir,' retorted Toole.

'An' them two documents, Sir, is a fabrication and a forgery, backed up wid false affidavits?' continued Mr O'Reegan.

'Mind that, Larry,' says the doctor, with a sudden inspiration addressing the waiter, who had peeped in; 'he admits that them two documents you see there, is forgeries, backed up with false affidavits; you heard him say so, and I'll call you to prove it.'

'*You lie!*' said Dirty Davy, precipitately, for he was quite disconcerted at finding his own sophistical weapons so unexpectedly turned against him.

'You scum o' the airth!' cried Toole, hitting him, with his clenched fist, right upon the nose, so vigorous a thump, that his erudite head with a sonorous crash hopped off the wainscot behind it; 'you lying scullion!' roared the doctor, instantaneously repeating the blow, and down went Davy, and down went the table with dreadful din, and the incensed doctor bestrode his prostrate foe with clenched fists and flaming face, and his grand wig all awry, and he panting and scowling.

'Murdher, murdher, *murdher*!' screamed Dirty Davy, who was not much of a Spartan, and relished nothing of an assault and battery but the costs and damages.

'You – you – you – '

'Murdher – help – help – murdher – murdher!'

'Say it again, you cowardly, sneaking, spying viper; say it *again*, can't you?'

It was a fine tableau, and a noble study of countenance and attitude.

'Sich a bloody nose I never seen before,' grinned Larry rubbing his hands over the exquisite remembrance. 'If you only seed him, flat on his back, the great ould shnake, wid his knees and his hands up bawling murdher; an' his big white face and his bloody nose in the middle, like nothin' in nature, bedad, but the ace iv hearts in a dirty pack.'

How they were separated, and who the particular persons that interposed, what restoratives were resorted to, how the feature looked half an hour afterwards, and what was the subsequent demeanour of Doctor Toole, upon the field of battle, I am not instructed; my letters stop short at the catastrophe, and run off to other matters.

Doctor Toole's agitations upon such encounters did not last long. They blew off in a few thundering claps of bravado and defiance in the second parlour of the Phoenix, where he washed his hands and readjusted his wig and ruffles, and strutted forth, squaring his elbows, and nodding and winking at the sympathising waiters in the inn hall; and with a half grin at Larry, 'Well, Larry, I think I showed him Chapelizod, hey?' said the doctor, buoyantly, to that functionary, and marched diagonally across the broad street toward Sturk's house, with a gait and a countenance that might have overawed an army.

Chapter Ninety-four
What Dr Sturk brought to mind, and all that Dr Toole heard at Mr Luke Gamble's

Just as he reached Sturk's door, wagging his head and strutting grimly – and, palpably, still in debate with Dirty Davy – his thoughts received a sudden wrench in a different direction by the arrival of Mr Justice Lowe, who pulled up his famous grey hunter at the steps of the House by the Churchyard.

'You see, Doctor Toole, it won't do, waiting. The thing's too momentous.'

And so they walked upstairs and into the drawing-room, and sent their compliments to Mrs Sturk, who came down in *déshabille*, with her things pinned about her, and all over smiles. Poor little woman! Toole had not observed until now how very thin she had grown.

'He's going on delightfully, gentlemen; he drank a whole cup of tea, weak of course, Doctor Toole, as you bid me; and he eat a slice of toast, and liked it, and two Naples biscuits, Mr Lowe, and I know he'll be delighted to see you.'

'Very good, Madam, *very* good,' said Toole.

'And he's looking better already. He waked out of that sweet sleep not ten minutes after you left this morning.'

'Ay, he was sleeping very quietly,' said Toole to Lowe. 'May we go up, Ma'am?'

'Oh! he'll be overjoyed, gentlemen, to see you, and 'twill do him an infinity of good. I can scarce believe my eyes. We've been tidying the study, the maid and I, and airing the cushions of his chair;' and she laughed a delighted little giggle. 'And even the weather has taken up such beautiful sunshine; everything favourable.'

'Well, Doctor Sturk,' said Toole, cheerily, 'we have a good account of you – a vastly good account, doctor; and, by St George, Sir, we've been tidying – '

He was going to say the study, but little Mrs Sturk put her finger to her lip in a wonderful hurry, raising her eyebrows and drawing a breath through her rounded lips, in such sort as arrested the sentence; for she knew how Barney's wrath always broke out when he thought the women had been in his study, and how he charged every missing paper for a month after upon their cursed meddling. But Sturk was a good deal gentler now, and had a dull and awful sort of apathy upon him; and I think it was all one to him whether the women had been in the study or not. So Toole said instead: 'We've been thinking of getting you down in a little while, doctor, if all goes pleasantly; 'tis a lovely day, and a good omen – see how the sun shines in at the curtain.'

But there was no responsive sunshine upon Sturk's stern, haggard face, as he said very low – still looking on the foot-board – 'I thank you, doctor.'

So after a few more questions, and a little bit of talk with Mrs Sturk, they got that good lady out of the room, and said Lowe to the patient: 'I'm sorry to trouble you, Dr Sturk, but there's a weighty matter at which you last night hinted; and Dr Toole thought you then too weak; and in your present state, I would not now ask you to speak at any length, were the matter of less serious moment.'

'Yes, Sir,' said Sturk, but did not seem about to speak any more; and after a few seconds, Lowe continued.

'I mean, Dr Sturk, touching the murder of Mr Beauclerc, which you then said was committed by the same Charles Archer who assaulted you in the park.'

'Ay, Sir,' said Sturk.

'The same murder of which Lord Dunoran was adjudged guilty.'

Sturk moved his lips with a sort of nod.

'And, Doctor Sturk, you remember you then said you had yourself *seen* Charles Archer do that murder.'

Sturk lifted his hand feebly enough to his forehead, and his lips moved, and his eyes closed. They thought he was praying – possibly he was; so they did not interrupt him; and he said, all on a sudden, but in a low dejected way, and with many pauses: 'Charles Archer. I never saw another such face; 'tis always before me. He was a man that everybody knew was dangerous – a damnable profligate besides – and, as all believed, capable of anything, though nobody could actually bring anything clearly home to him but his bloody duels, which, however, were fairly fought. I saw him only thrice in my life before I saw him here. In a place, at Newmarket, where they played hazard, was once; and I saw him fight Beau Langton; and I saw him murder Mr Beauclerc. I saw it all!' And the doctor swore a shuddering oath.

'I lay in the small room or closet, off the chamber in which he slept. I was suffering under a bad fracture, and dosed with opium. 'Tis all very strange, Sir. I saw everything that happened. I saw him stab Beauclerc. Don't question me; it tires me. I think 'twas a dagger. It looked like a small bayonet. I'll tell you how – all, by-and-by.'

He sipped a little wine and water, and wiped his lips with a very tremulous handkerchief.

'I never spoke of it, for I could not. The whole of that five minutes' work slipped from my mind, and was gone quite and clean when I awoke. What I saw I could not interrupt. I was in a cataleptic state, I suppose. I could not speak; but I saw like a lynx, and heard every whisper. When I awakened in the morning I remembered nothing. I did not know I had a secret. The knowledge was sealed up until the time came. A sight of Charles Archer's face at any time would have had, as I suppose, the same effect. When I saw him here, the first time, it was at the general's at Belmont; though he was changed by time, and carefully disguised, all would not do. I felt the sight of him was fatal. I was quite helpless; but my mind never stopped working upon it till – till – '

Sturk groaned.

'See now,' said Toole, 'there's time enough, and don't fatigue yourself. There, now, rest quiet a minute.'

And he made him swallow some more wine; and felt his pulse and shook his head despondingly at Lowe, behind his back.

'How is it?' said Sturk, faintly.

'A little irritable – that's all,' said Toole.

'Till one night, I say' – Sturk resumed, after a minute or two, 'it came to me all at once, awake – I don't know – or in a dream; in a moment I had it all. 'Twas like a page cut out of a book – lost for so many years.' And Sturk moaned a despairing wish to Heaven that the secret had never returned to him again.

'Yes, Sir – like a page cut out of a book, and never missed till 'twas found again; and then sharp and clear, every letter from first to last. Then, Sir – then – thinking 'twas no use at that distance of time taking steps to punish him, I – I foolishly let him understand I knew him. My mind misgave me from the first. I think it was my good angel that warned me. But 'tis no use now. I'm not a man to be easily frightened. But it seemed to me he was something altogether worse than a man, and like – like Satan; and too much for me every way. If I was wise I'd have left him alone. But 'tis no good fretting now. It was to be. I was too outspoken – 'twas always my way – and I let him know; and – and you see, he meant to make away with me. He tried to take my life, Sir; and I think he has done it. I'll never rise from this bed, gentlemen. I'm done for.'

'Come, Doctor Sturk, you mustn't talk that way, Pell will be out this evening, and Dillon may be – though faith! I don't quite know that Pell will meet him – but we'll put our heads together, and deuce is in it or we'll set you on your legs again.'

Sturk was screwing his lips sternly together, and the lines of his gruff haggard face were quivering, and a sullen tear or two started down from his closed eye.

'I'm – I'm a little nervous, gentlemen – I'll be right just now. I'd like to see the – the children, if they're in the way, that's all – by-and-by, you know.'

'I've got Pell out, you see – not that there's any special need, you know; but he was here before, and it wouldn't do to offend him; and he'll see you this afternoon.'

'I thank you, Sir,' said Sturk, in the same dejected way.

'And, Sir,' said Lowe, 'if you please, I'll get this statement into the shape of a deposition or information, for you see 'tis of the vastest imaginable importance, and exactly tallies with evidence we've got elsewhere, and 'twouldn't do, Sir, to let it slip.'

And Toole thought he saw a little flush mount into Sturk's sunken face, and he hastened to say, 'What we desire, Dr Sturk, is to be able to act promptly in this case of my Lord Dunoran. Measures must be taken instantly, you see, for 'tis of old standing, and not a day to be lost, and there's why Mr Lowe is so urgent to get your statement in white and black.'

'And sworn to,' added Mr Lowe.

'I'll swear it,' said Sturk, in the same sad tones.

And Mrs Sturk came in, and Toole gave leave for chicken broth at twelve o'clock, about two tablespoonsful, and the same at half-past one, when he hoped to be back again. And on the lobby he gave her, with a cheery countenance, all the ambiguous comfort he could. And Lowe asked Mrs Sturk for more pens and paper, and himself went down to give his man a direction at the door, and on the way, in the hall, Toole looking this way and that, to see they weren't observed, beckoned him into the front parlour, and, said he, in a low key: 'The pulse is up a bit, not very much, but still I don't like it – and very hard, you see – and what we've to dread, you know's inflammation; and he's so shocking low, my dear Sir, we must let him have wine and other things, or we'll lose him that way; and you see it's a mighty unpleasant case.'

And coming into the hall, in a loud confident voice he cried: 'And I'll be here again by half-past one o'clock.'

And so he beckoned to the boy with his horse to come up, and chatted in the interim with Mr Lowe upon the steps, and told him how to manage him if he grew exhausted over his narrative; and then mounting his nag, and kissing his hand and waving his hat to Mrs Sturk, who was looking out upon him from Barney's window, he rode away for Dublin.

Toole, on reaching town, spurred on to the dingy residence of Mr Luke Gamble. It must be allowed that he had no clear intention of taking any step whatsoever in consequence of what he might hear. But the little fellow was deuced curious; and Dirty Davy's confidence gave him a sort of right to be satisfied.

So with his whip under his arm, and a good deal out of breath, for the stairs were steep, he bounced into the attorney's sanctum.

'Who's that? *Is* that? – Why, bless my soul and body! 'tis yourself,' cried Toole, after an astonished pause of a few seconds at the door, springing forward and grasping Nutter by both hands, and shaking them vehemently, and grinning very joyously and kindly the while.

Nutter received him cordially, but a little sheepishly. Indeed, his experiences of life, and the situations in which he had found himself since they had last met, were rather eccentric and instructive than quite pleasant to remember. And Nutter, in his way, was a proud fellow, and neither liked to be gaped at nor pitied.

But Toole was a thorough partisan of his, and had been urgent for permission to see him in gaol, and they knew how true he had been to poor Sally Nutter, and altogether felt very much at home with him.

So sitting in that twilight room, flanked with piles of expended briefs, and surrounded with neatly docketed packets of attested copies, notices, affidavits, and other engines of legal war – little Toole having expended his congratulations, and his private knowledge of Sturk's revelations, fell upon the immediate subject of his visit.

'That rogue, Davy O'Reegan, looked in on me not an hour ago, at the Phoenix,' [and he gave them a very spirited, but I'm afraid a somewhat fanciful description of the combat] 'and I'm afraid he'll give us a deal of trouble yet. He told me that the certificate – '

'Ay – here's a copy;' and Luke Gamble threw a paper on the table before him.

'That's it – Mary Duncan – 1750 – the very thing – the rascal! Well, he said, you know, but I knew better, that you had admitted the certificate formally.'

'So I have. Sir,' said. Mr Gamble, drily, stuffing his hands into his breeches' pockets, and staring straight at Toole with elevated eyebrows, and as the little doctor thought, with a very odd expression in his eyes.

'You *have*, Sir?'

'I have!' and then followed a little pause, and Mr Gamble said – 'I did so, Sir, because there's no disputing it – and – and I think, Doctor Toole, I know something of my business.'

There was another pause, during which Toole, flushed and shocked, turned his gaze from Gamble to Nutter.

''Tis a true bill, then?' said Toole, scarcely above his breath, and very dismally.

A swarthy flush covered Nutter's dark face. The man was ashamed.

''Tis nigh eighteen years ago, Sir,' said Nutter embarrassed, as he well might be. 'I was a younger man, then, and was bit, Sir, as many another has been, and that's all.'

Toole got up, stood before the fireplace, and hung his head, with compressed lips, and there was a silence, interrupted by the hard man of the law, who was now tumbling over his papers in search of a document, and humming a tune as he did so.

'It may be a good move for Charles Nutter, Sir, but it looks very like a checkmate for poor Sally,' muttered Toole angrily.

Mr Luke Gamble either did not hear him, or did not care a farthing what he said; and he hummed his tune very contentedly.

'And I had, moreover,' said he, 'to make another admission for the same reason, videlicet, that Mary Matchwell, who now occupies a portion of the Mills, the promovent in this suit, and Mary Duncan mentioned in that certificate, are one and the same person. Here's our answer to their notice, admitting the fact.'

'I thank you,' said Toole again, rather savagely, for a glance over his shoulder had shown him the attorney's face grinning with malicious amusement, as it seemed to him, while he readjusted the packet of papers from which he had just taken the notice; 'I saw it, Sir, your brother lawyer, Mr O'Reegan, Sir, showed it me this morning.'

And Toole thought of poor little Sally Nutter, and all the wreck and ruin coming upon her and the Mills, and began to con over his own liabilities, and to reflect seriously whether, in some of his brisk altercations on her behalf with Dirty Davy and his client, he might not have committed himself rather dangerously; and especially the consequences of his morning's collision with Davy grew in darkness and magnitude very seriously, as he reflected that his entire statement had turned out to be true, and that he and his client were on the winning side.

'It seems to me, Sir, you might have given some of poor Mrs Nutter's friends at Chapelizod a hint of the state of things. I, Sir, and Father Roach – we've meddled, Sir, more in the business – than – than – but no matter now – and all under a delusion, Sir. And poor Mistress Sally Nutter – *she* doesn't seem to trouble you much, Sir.'

He observed that the attorney was chuckling to himself still more and more undisguisedly, as he slipped the notice back again into its place.

'You gentlemen of the law think of nothing, Sir, but your clients. I suppose 'tis a good rule, but it may be pushed somewhat far. And what do you propose to do for poor Mistress Sally Nutter?' demanded Toole, very sternly, for his blood was up.

'She has heard from us this morning,' said Mr Gamble, grining on his watch, 'and she knows all by this time, and 'tisn't a button to her.'

And the attorney laughed in his face; and Nutter who had looked sulky and uncomfortable, could resist no longer, and broke into a queer responsive grin. It seemed to Toole like a horrid dream.

There was a tap at the door just at this moment.

'Come in,' cried Mr Gamble, still exploding in comfortable little bursts of half-suppressed laughter.

'Oh! 'tis you? Very good, Sir,' said Mr Gamble, sobering a little. He was the same lanky, vulgar, and slightly-squinting gentleman, pitted with the small-pox, whom Toole had seen on a former occasion. And the little doctor thought he looked even more cunning and meaner than before. Everything had grown to look repulsive, and every face was sinister now; and the world began to look like a horrible masquerade, full of half-detected murderers, traitors, and miscreants.

'There isn't a soul you can trust – 'tis enough to turn a man's head; 'tis sickening, by George!' grumbled the little doctor, fiercely.

'Here's a gentleman, Sir,' said Gamble, waving his pen towards Toole, with a chuckle, 'who believes that ladies like to recover their husbands.'

The fellow grew red, and grinned a sly uneasy grin, looking stealthily at Toole, who was rapidly growing angry.

'Yes, Sir, and one who believes, too, that gentlemen ought to protect their wives,' added the little doctor hotly.

'As soon as they know who they are,' muttered the attorney to his papers.

'I think, gentlemen, I'm rather in your way,' said Toole with a gloomy briskness; 'I think 'tis better I should go. I – I'm somewhat amazed, gentlemen, and I – I wish you a good-morning.'

And Toole made them a very stern bow, and walked out at the wrong door.

'This way, by your leave, doctor,' said Mr Gamble, opening the right one; and at the head of the stairs he took Toole by the cuff, and said he: 'After all, 'tis but just the wrong Mrs Nutter should give place to the right; and if you go down to the Mills tomorrow, you'll find she's by no means so bad as you think her.'

But Toole broke away from him sulkily, with: 'I wish you a good-morning, Sir.'

It was quite true that Sally Nutter was to hear from Charles and Mr Gamble that morning; for about the time at which Toole was in conference with those two gentlemen in Dublin, two coaches drew up at the Mills.

Mr Gamble's conducting gentleman was in one, and two mysterious personages sat in the other.

'I want to see Mrs Nutter,' said Mr Gamble's emissary.

'Mrs Nutter's in the parlour, at your service,' answered the lean maid who had opened the door, and who recognising in that gentleman an adherent of the enemy, had assumed her most impertinent leer and tone on the instant.

The ambassador looked in and drew back.

'Oh, then, 'tisn't the mistress you want, but the master's old housekeeper; ask *her*.'

And she pointed with her thumb towards Molly, whose head was over the banister.

So, as he followed that honest handmaiden upstairs, he drew from his coat-pocket a bundle of papers, and glanced at their endorsements, for he had a long exposition to make, and then some important measures to execute.

Toole had to make up for lost time; and as he rode at a smart canter into the village, he fancied he observed the signs of an unusual excitement there. There were some faces at the windows, some people on the door-steps; and a few groups in the street; they were all looking in the Dublin direction. He had a nod or two as he passed. Toole thought forthwith of Mr David O'Reegan – people generally refer phenomena to what most concerns themselves – and a dim horror of some unknown summary process dismayed him; but his hall-door shone peaceably in the sun, and his boy stood whistling on the steps, with his hands in his pockets. Nobody had been there since, and Pell had not yet called at Sturk's.

'And what's happened – what's the neighbours lookin' after?' said Toole, as his own glance followed the general direction, so soon as he had dismounted.

''Twas a coach that had driven through the town, at a thundering pace, with some men inside, from the Knockmaroon direction, and a lady that was screeching. She broke one of the coach windows in Martin's-row, and the other – *there*, just opposite the Phoenix.' The glass was glittering on the road. 'She had rings on her hand, and her knuckles were bleeding, and it was said 'twas poor Mrs Nutter going away with the keepers to a mad-house.'

Toole turned pale and ground his teeth, looking towards Dublin.

'I passed it myself near Island-bridge; I did hear screeching, but I thought 'twas from t'other side of the wall. There was a fellow in an old blue and silver coat with the driver – eh?'

'The same,' said the boy; and Toole, with difficulty swallowing down his rage, hurried into the house, resolved to take Lowe's advice on the matter, and ready to swear to poor Sally's perfect sanity – 'the crature! – the villains!'

But now he had only a moment to pull off his boots, to get into his grand costume, and seize his cane and his muff, too – for he sported one; and so transformed and splendid, he marched down the paved *trottoir* – Doctor Pell happily not yet arrived – to Sturk's house. There was a hackney coach near the steps.

Chapter Ninety-five

In which Dr Pell declines a fee, and Dr Sturk a prescription

In entering the front parlour from whence, in no small excitement, there issued the notes of a coarse diapason, which he fancied was known to him, he found Mr Justice Lowe in somewhat tempestuous conference with the visitor.

He was, in fact, no other than Black Dillon; black enough he looked just now. He had only a moment before returned from a barren visit to the Brass Castle, and was in no mood to be trifled with.

''Twasn't *I*, Sir, but Mr Dangerfield, who promised you five hundred guineas,' said Mr Lowe, with a dry nonchalance.

'Five hundred fiddles,' retorted Doctor Dillon – his phrase was coarser, and Toole at that moment entering the door, and divining the situation from the doctor's famished glare and wild gestures, exploded, I'm sorry to say, in a momentary burst of laughter, into his cocked hat. 'Twas instantly stifled, however; and when Dillon turned his flaming eyes upon him, the little doctor made him a bow of superlative gravity, which the furious hero of the trepan was too full of his wrongs to notice in any way.

'I was down at his house, bedad, the Brass Castle, if you plase, and not a brass farthin' for my pains, nothing there but an ould woman, as ould and as ugly as himself, or the divil – be gannies! An' he's levanted, or else tuck for debt. Brass Castle! Brass *forehead*, bedad. Brass, like Goliath, from head to heels; an' by the heels he's laid, I'll take my davy, considherin' at his laysure which is strongest – a brass castle or a stone jug. An' where, Sir, am I to get my five hundred guineas – where, Sir?' he thundered, staring first in Lowe's face, then in Toole's, and dealing the table a lusty blow at each interrogatory.

'I think, Sir,' said Lowe, anticipating Toole, 'you'd do well to consider the sick man, Sir.' The noise was certainly considerable.

'I don't know, Sir, that the sick man's considherin' me much,' retorted Doctor Dillon. 'Sick man – sick grandmother's aunt! If you can't speak like a man o' sense, *don't* spake, at any rate, like a justice o' the pace. Sick man, indeed! Why there's not a crature livin' barrin' a natural eediot, or an apothecary, that doesn't know the man's dead; he's *dead*, Sir; but 'tisn't so with me, an' I can't get on without vittles, and vittles isn't to be had without money; that's logic, Mr Justice; that's a medical fact Mr Docthor. An' how am I to get my five hundred guineas? I say, *you* and *you* – the both o' ye – that prevented me of going last night to his brass castle – brass snuff-box – there isn't room to stand in it, bedad – an' gettin' my money. I hold you both liable to me – one an' t'other – the both o' ye.'

'Why, Sir,' said Lowe, ' 'tis a honorarium.'

' 'Tis no such thing, Sir; 'tis a contract,' thundered Dillon, pulling Dangerfield's note of promise from his pocket, and dealing it a mighty slap with the back of his hand.

'Contract or no, Sir, there's nobody liable for it but himself.'

'We'll try that, Sir; and in the meantime, what the divil am I to do, I'd be glad to know; for strike me crooked if I have a crown piece to pay the coachman. Trepan, indeed; I'm nately trepanned myself.'

'If you'll only listen, Sir, I'll show you your case is well enough. Mr Dangerfield, as you call him, has not left the country; and though he's arrested, 'tisn't for debt. If he owes you the money, 'tis your own fault if you don't make him pay it, for I'm credibly informed he's worth more than a hundred thousand pounds.'

'And where is he, Sir?' demanded Black Dillon, much more cheerfully and amicably. 'I hope I see you well, Doctor Toole.'

That learned person acknowledged the somewhat tardy courtesy, and Lowe made answer: 'He lies in the county gaol, Sir, on a serious criminal charge; but a line from me, Sir, will, I think, gain you admission to him forthwith.'

'I'll be much obliged for it, Sir,' answered Dillon. 'What o'clock is it?' he asked of Toole; for though it is believed he owned a watch, it was sometimes not about him; and while Lowe scribbled a note, Toole asked in a dignified way: 'Have you seen our patient, Sir?'

'Not I. Didn't I see him last night? The man's dead. He's in the last stage of exhaustion with an inflammatory pulse. If you feed him up he'll die of inflammation; and if you don't he'll die of wakeness. So he lies on the fatal horns of a dilemma, you see; an' not all the men in Derry'll take him off them alive. He's gone, Sir. Pell's coming, I hear. I'd wait if I could; but I must look afther business; and there's no good to be done here. I thank you, Mr Lowe – Sir – your most obedient servant, Doctor Toole.' And with Lowe's note in his breeches' pocket, he strode out to the steps, and whistled for his coachman, who drove his respectable employer tipsily to his destination.

I dare say the interview was characteristic; but I can find no account of it. I am pretty sure, however, that he did not get a shilling. So at least he stated in his declaration, in the action against Lowe, in which he, or rather his attorney, was non-suited, with grievous loss of costs. And judging by the sort of esteem in which Mr Dangerfield held Black Dillon, I fancy that few things would have pleased him better in his unfortunate situation than hitting that able practitioner as hard as might be.

Just as he drove away, poor little Mrs Sturk looked in.

'Is there anything, Ma'am?' asked Toole, a little uneasily.

'Only – only, I think he's just a little frightened – he's so nervous you know – by that Dublin doctor's loud talking – and he's got a kind of trembling – a shivering.'

'Eh – a shivering, Ma'am?' said Toole. 'Like a man that's taken a cold, eh?'

'Oh, he hasn't got cold – I'm sure – there's no danger of that. It's only nervous; so I covered him up with another pair of blankets, and gave him a hot drink.'

'Very good, Ma'am; I'll follow you up in a minute.'

'And even if it was, you know he shakes off cold in no time, he has such a fine constitution.'

'Yes, Ma'am – that's true – very good, Ma'am. I'll be after you.'

So upstairs went Mrs Sturk in a fuss.

'That's it,' said Toole so soon as they were alone, nodding two or three times dejectedly, and looking very glum. 'It's set in – the inflammation – it's set in, Sir. He's gone. That's the rigor.'

'Poor gentleman,' said Lowe, after a short pause, 'I'm much concerned for him, and for his family.'

''Tis a bad business,' said Toole, gloomily, like a man that's frightened. And he followed Mrs Sturk, leaving Lowe adjusting his papers in the parlour.

Toole found his patient laden with blankets, and shivering like a man in an ague, with blue sunken face. And he slipped his hand under the clothes, and took his pulse, and said nothing but – 'Ay – ay – ay' – quietly to himself, from time to time, as he did so; and Sturk – signing, as well as he could, that he wanted a word in his ear – whispered, as well as his chattering teeth would let him, 'You know what *this* is.'

'Well – well – there now, there; drink some of this,' said Toole, a little flurried, and trying to seem cool.

'I think he's a little bit better, doctor,' whispered poor little Mrs Sturk, in Toole's ear.

' 'Twill pass away. Ma'am.'

Toole was standing by the bedside, looking rather woefully and frightened on Sturk's face, and patting and smoothing the coverlet with the palm of his stumpy red hand; and whispering to himself from time to time, 'Yes, yes,' although with rather a troubled and helpless air.

Just then came the roll of a coach to the door, and a long peal at the knocker; and little Toole ran down to meet the great Doctor Pell in the hall. He was in, in a moment, and turned aside with Toole into the drawing-room. And Toole's voice was heard pretty volubly. It was only a conference of about two minutes. And Dr Pell said in his usual *tall* way, as they came out – 'How long ago, Sir?'

'About ten – no, hardly so much – *eight* minutes ago,' answered Toole, as he followed that swift phantom up the stairs.

'Your most obedient, Ma'am,' said the slim and lofty doctor, parenthetically saluting the good lady; and he stood by the bedside, having laid his muff on the chair.

'Well, Sir, and how do you feel? There now, that will do, Sir; don't mind speaking; *I* see. And he put his hand under the clothes, and laid it on Sturk's arm, and slid it down to his hand, and felt his pulse.

'And he's been near ten minutes this way?' said the doctor.

'Oh, he was a great deal worse; 'tis a vast deal better now; isn't it, Doctor Toole?'

'The rigor is subsiding, then. Has he had a sweat, Ma'am?' said Pell.

'Oh, no – nothing like – quite nice and cool, doctor – and no fever; nice quiet sleep; and his appetite wonderful; tell him, Doctor Toole.'

'Oh, yes, Ma'am – Doctor Pell knows; I told him all, Ma'am,' said Toole, who was looking with a blank and dismal sort of contemplation upon Sturk's fallen countenance.

'Well, Ma'am,' said Pell, as he looked on his watch, 'this rigor, you see, will soon pass away, and you're doing everything we could wish, and (for he found he had time to scribble a prescription), we'll just order him a trifle. Good-day, Sir. Your most obedient, Ma'am.'

'Pen and ink in the drawing-room, Doctor Pell,' said Toole, reverentially.

'Oh! no, *no*, Madam, excuse me,' murmured Doctor Pell, gently pressing back Mrs Sturk's fee, the residuum of Dangerfield's bounty, with his open palm.

'Oh, but Doctor Pell,' urged she, in a persuasive aside, half behind him, in the shadow of the doorway.

'Pray, Madam, no more – pardon me,' and Doctor Pell, with a peremptory bow, repelled his fee.

Why do physicians take their honest earnings in this clandestine way – transacted like favours, secret, sweet, and precious; and pocketed in dark corners, and whispers, like the wages of sin? Cold Doctor Pell here refused a very considerable fee. He could on occasion behave handsomely; but I can't learn that blustering, hilarious Doctor Rogerson ever refused his.

And the doctor descended, not hastily, but very swiftly, and was in the drawing-room, and the door shut.

'Gone, poor gentleman!' said Toole, in an undertone – his phraseology became refined in Pell's presence; he'd have said 'poor devil', or 'poor dog', if he had been with Doctor Rogerson.

Pell held the pen in his thin lips, while he tore off half-a-sheet of paper, and only shook his head funereally.

So, taking the pen in his fingers, he said, 'We'll give him so and so, if you approve.'

'Very good, Sir,' said Toole, deferentially; and Pell, not seeming to hear, dashed off a few spattered lines, with necromantic circles and zigzags at the end of each.

When Sturk afterwards saw that paper in the fingers of the maid, being very weak, he did not care to speak; but he signed with a little motion of his head, and she leaned down to listen.

'Recipe?' whispered the doctor; 'put it – in – the fire;' and he shut his eyes – tired.

Pell, looking again at his watch, was Doctor Toole's very obedient servant, and was waylaid by poor little Mrs Sturk on the lobby.

'Well, Madam, we've put our heads together, and ordered a little matter, and that rigor – that shivering fit – will subside; and we trust he'll be easier then; and you've a very competent adviser in Doctor a – a –'

'Toole,' suggested the eager little woman.

'Doctor Toole, Madam, and he'll direct whatever may be necessary; and should he wish to consult again, you can send for me; but he's quite competent, Madam, and he'll tell you all we think.'

He had got to the end of the stairs while talking, and made his adieux, and glided down and out; and before poor little Mrs Sturk bethought her how little she had got from him, she heard the roll of his coach wheels whirling him back again to Dublin. I believe few doctors grow so accustomed to the ghastly *éclaircissement* as not very willingly to shirk it when they may.

Toole shrank from it, too, and dodged, and equivocated, and evaded all he could; but he did admit there was an unfavourable change; and when he had gone – promising to be back at four o'clock – poor little Mrs Sturk broke down – all alone in the drawing-room – and cried a passionate flood of tears; and thinking she was too long away, dried her eyes quickly, and ran up, and into Barney's room with a smile on; and she battled with the evil fear; and hope, that faithful angel that clings to the last, hovered near her with blessed illusions, until an hour came, next day, in the evening, about four o'clock, when from Barney's room there came a long, wild cry. It was 'his poor foolish little Letty' – the long farewell – and the 'noble Barney' was gone. The courtship and the married days – all a faded old story now; and a few days later, reversed arms, and muffled drums, and three volleys in the churchyard, and a little file of wondering children, dressed in black, whom the old general afterwards took up in his arms, one by one, very kindly, and kissed, and told them they were to come and play in Belmont whenever they liked, and to eat fruit in the garden, and a great deal more; for all which a poor little lady, in a widow's cap and a lonely room hard by, was very grateful.

Chapter Ninety-six

About the rightful Mrs Nutter of the Mills, and how Mr Mervyn received the news

Little Doctor Toole came out feeling rather queer and stunned from Sturk's house. It was past three o'clock by this time, and it had already, in his eyes, a changed and empty look, as his upturned eye for a moment rested upon its grey front, and the window-panes glittering in the reddening sun. He looked down the street towards the turnpike, and then up it, towards Martin's-row and the Mills. And he bethought him suddenly of poor Sally Nutter, and upbraided himself, smiting the point of his cane with a vehement stab upon the pavement, for having forgotten to speak to Lowe upon her case. Perhaps, however, it was as well he had not, inasmuch as there were a few not unimportant facts connected with that case about which he was himself in the dark.

Mr Gamble's conducting clerk had gone upstairs to Mrs Nutter's door, and being admitted, had very respectfully asked leave to open, for that lady's instruction, a little statement which he was charged to make.

This was in substance, that Archibald Duncan, Mary Matchwell's husband, was in Dublin, and had sworn informations against her for bigamy; and that a warrant having been issued for her arrest upon that charge, the constables had arrived at the Mills for the purpose of executing it, and removing the body of the delinquent, M. M., to the custody of the turnkey; that measures would be taken on the spot to expel the persons who had followed in her train; and that Mr Charles Nutter himself would arrive in little more than an hour, to congratulate his good wife, Sally, on the termination of their troubles, and to take quiet possession of his house.

You can imagine how Sally Nutter received all this, with clasped hands and streaming eyes, looking in the face of the man of notices and attested copies, unable to speak – unable quite to believe. But before he came to the end of his dry and delightful narrative, a loud yell and a scuffle in the parlour were heard; a shrilly clamour of warring voices; a dreadful crash of glass: a few curses and oaths in basses and barytones; and some laughter from the coachmen, who viewed the fray from outside through the window; and a brief, wild, and garrulous uproar, which made little Sally Nutter – though by this time used to commotion – draw back with her hands to her heart, and hold her breath. It was the critical convulsion; the evil spirit was being eliminated, and the tenement, stunned, bruised, and tattered, about to be at peace.

Of Charles Nutter's doings and adventures during the terrible interval between his departure on the night of Mary Matchwell's first visit to the Mills, and his return on this evening to the same abode, there is a brief outline, in the first person, partly in answer to questions, and obviously intended to constitute a memorandum for his attorney's use. I shall reprint it with your leave – as it is not very long – verbatim.

When that woman, Sir, came out to the Mills [says this document], I could scarce believe my eyes; I knew her temper; she was always damnably wicked; but I had found out all about her long ago, and I was amazed at her audacity. What she said was true – we *were* married; or rather, we went through the ceremony, at St Clement Danes, in London, in the year '50. I could not gainsay that; but I well knew what she thought was known but to herself and another. She had a husband living then. We lived together little more than three months. We were not a year parted when I found out all about him; and I never expected more trouble from her.

I knew all about him then. But seventeen years bring many changes; and I feared he might be dead. He was a saddler in Edinburgh, and his name was Duncan. I made up my mind to go thither straight. Next morning the *Lovely Betty*, packet, was to sail for Holyhead. I took money, and set out without a word to anybody. The wretch had told my poor wife, and showed her the certificate, and so left her half mad.

I swore to her 'twas false. I told her to wait a bit and she would see. That was everything passed between us. I don't think she half understood what I said, for she was at her wits' ends. I was scarce better myself first. 'Twas a good while before I resolved on this course, and saw my way, and worse thoughts were in my head; but so soon as I made up my mind to this I grew cool. I don't know how it happened that my footprints by the river puzzled them; 'twas all accident; I was thinking of no such matter; I did not go through the village, but through the Knockmaroon gate; 'twas dark by that time; I only met two men with a cart – they did not know me – Dublin men, I think. I crossed the park in a straight line for Dublin; I did not meet a living soul; 'twas dark, but not very dark. When I reached the Butcher's Wood, all on a sudden, I heard a horrid screech, and two blows quick, one after the other, to my right, not three score steps away – heavy blows – they sounded like the strokes of a man beating a carpet.

With the first alarm, I hollo'd, and ran in the direction shouting as I went; 'twas as I ran I heard the second blow; I saw no-one, and heard no other sound; the noise I made myself in running might prevent it. I can't say how many seconds it took to run the distance – not many; I ran fast; I was not long in finding the body; his white vest and small clothes showed under the shadow; he seemed quite dead. I thought when first I took his hand, there was a kind of a quiver in his fingers; but that was over immediately. His eyes and mouth were a bit open; the blood was coming very fast, and the wounds on his head looked very deep – frightful – as I conjectured they were done with a falchion (a name given to a heavy wooden sword resembling a New Zealand weapon); there was blood coming from one ear, and his mouth; there was no sign of life about him, and I thought him quite dead. I would have lifted him against a tree, but his head looked all in a smash, and I daren't move him. I knew him for Dr Sturk, of the Artillery; he wore his regimentals; I did not see his hat; his head was bare when I saw him.

When I saw 'twas Doctor Sturk, I was frightened; he had treated me mighty ill, and I resented it, which I did not conceal; and I thought 'twould look very much against me if I were any way mixed up in this dreadful occurrence – especially not knowing who did it – and being alone with the body so soon after 'twas done. I crossed the park wall therefore; but by the time I came near Barrack-street, I grew uneasy in my mind, lest Doctor Sturk should still have life in him, and perish for want of help. I went down to the river-side, and washed my hands, for there was blood upon 'em, and while so employed, by mischance I lost my hat in the water and could not recover it. I stood for a while by the river-bank; it was a lonely place; I was thinking of crossing there first, I was so frightened; I changed my mind, however, and went round by Bloody-bridge.

'The further I went the more fearful I grew, lest Sturk should die for want of help that I might send him; and although I thought him dead, I got such a dread of this over me as I can't describe. I saw two soldiers opposite the Royal Oak inn, and I told them I overheard a fellow speak of an officer that lay wounded in the Butcher's Wood, not far from the park-wall, and gave them half-a-crown to have search made, which they promised, and took the money.

I crossed Bloody-bridge, and got into a coach, and so to Luke Gamble's. I told him nothing of Sturk; I had talked foolishly to him, and did not know what even he might think. I told him all about M. M.'s, that is Mary Duncan's turning up; she went by that name in London, and kept a lodging-house. I took his advice on the matter, and sailed next morning. The man Archie Duncan had left Edinburgh, but I traced him to Carlisle and thence to York, where I found him. He was in a very poor way, and glad to hear that Demirep was in Dublin, and making money. When I came back I was in the *Hue-and-Cry* for the assault on Sturk.

I took no precaution, not knowing what had happened; but 'twas night when we arrived, Duncan and I, and we went straight to Gamble's and he concealed me. I kept close within his house, except on one night, when I took coach. I was under necessity, as you shall hear, to visit Chapelizod. I got out in the hollow of the road by the Knockmaroon pond, in the park; an awful night it was – the night of the snow-storm, when the brig was wrecked off the Black Rock, you remember. I wanted to get some papers necessary to my case against Mary Duncan. I had the key of the glass door; the inside fastening was broke, and there was no trouble in getting in. But the women had sat up beyond their hour, and saw me. I got the papers, however, and returned, having warned them not to speak. I ventured out of doors but once more, and was took on a warrant for assaulting Sturk. 'Twas the women talking as they did excited the officer's suspicions.

I have lain in prison since. The date of my committal and discharge are, I suppose, there.

And so ends this rough draft, with the initials, I think, in his own hand, C. N., at the foot.

At about half-past four o'clock Nutter came out to the Mills in a coach. He did not drive through Chapelizod; he was shy, and wished to feel his way a little. So he came home privily by the Knockmaroon Park-gate. Poor little Sally rose into a sort of heroine. With a wild cry, and 'Oh, Charlie!' she threw her arms about his neck; and the 'good little crayture', as Magnolia was wont to call her, had fainted. Nutter said nothing, but carried her in his arms to the sofa, and himself sobbed very violently for about a minute, supporting her tenderly. She came to herself very quickly, and hugged her Charlie with such a torrent of incoherent endearments, welcomes, and benedictions as I cannot at all undertake to describe. Nutter didn't speak. His arms were about her, and with wet eyes, and biting his netherlip, and smiling, he looked into her poor little wild, delighted face with an unspeakable world of emotion and affection beaming from the homely lines and knots of that old mahogany countenance; and the maids smiling, blessing, courtesying, and welcoming him home again, added to the pleasant uproar which amazed even the tipsy coachman from the hall.

'Oh! Charlie, I have you fast, my darling. Oh! But it's wonderful; you, yourself – my Charlie, your own self – never, never, oh! *never* to part again!' and so on.

And so for a rapturous hour, it seemed as if they had passed the dark valley, and were immortal; and no more pain, sorrow, or separation for them. And, perhaps, these blessed illusions are permitted now and again to mortals, like momentary gleams of paradise, and distant views of the delectable mountains, to cheer poor pilgrims with a foretaste of those meetings beyond the river, where the separated and beloved shall embrace.

It is not always that the person most interested in a rumour is first to hear it. It was reported in Chapelizod, early that day, that Irons, the clerk, had made some marvellous discovery respecting Lord Dunoran, and the murder of which an English jury had found that nobleman guilty. Had people known that Mervyn was the son of that dishonoured peer – as in that curious little town they would, no doubt, long since have at least suspected, had he called himself by his proper patronymic Mordaunt – he would not have wanted a visitor to enlighten him half-an-hour after the rumour had began to proclaim itself in the streets and public haunts of the village. No-one, however, thought of the haughty and secluded young gentleman who lived so ascetic a life at the Tiled House, and hardly ever showed in the town, except in church on Sundays; and who when he rode on his black hunter into Dublin, avoided the village, and took the high-road by Inchicore.

When the report did reach him, and he heard that Lowe, who knew all about it, was at the Phoenix, where he was holding a conference with a gentleman from the Crown Office, half-wild with excitement, he hurried thither. There, having declared himself to the magistrate and his companion, in that little chamber where Nutter was wont to transact his agency business, and where poor Sturk had told down his rent, guinea by guinea, with such a furious elation, on the morning but one before he received his death-blow, he heard, with such feelings as may be imagined, the magistrate read aloud, not only the full and clear information of Irons, but the equally distinct deposition of Doctor Sturk, and was made aware of the complete identification of the respectable and vivacious Paul Dangerfield with the dead and damned Charles Archer!

On hearing all this, the young man rode straight to Belmont, where he was closeted with the general for fully twenty minutes. They parted in a very friendly way, but he did not see the ladies. The general, however, no sooner bid him farewell at the door-steps than he made his way to the drawing-room, and, big with his amazing secret, first, in a very grave and almost agitated way, told little 'Toodie', as he called his daughter, to run away and leave him together with Aunt Rebecca, which being done, he anticipated that lady's imperious summons to explain himself by telling her, in his blunt, soldierly fashion, the wondrous story.

Aunt Becky was utterly confounded. She had seldom before in her life been so thoroughly taken in. What a marvellous turn of fortune! What a providential deliverance and vindication for that poor young Lord Dunoran! What an astounding exposure of that miscreant Mr Dangerfield!

'What a blessed escape the child has had!' interposed the general with a rather testy burst of gratitude.

'And how artfully she and my lord contrived to conceal their engagement!' pursued Aunt Rebecca, covering her somewhat confused retreat.

But, somehow, Aunt Rebecca was by no means angry. On the contrary, anyone who knew her well would have perceived that a great weight was taken off her mind.

The consequences of Dangerfield's incarceration upon these awful charges, were not confined altogether to the Tiled House and the inhabitants of Belmont.

No sooner was our friend Cluffe well assured that Dangerfield was in custody of the gaoler, and that his old theory of a certain double plot carried on by that intriguing personage, with the object of possessing the hand and thousands of Aunt Rebecca, was now and for ever untenable, than he wrote to London forthwith to countermand the pelican. The answer, which in those days was rather long about coming, was not pleasant, being simply a refusal to rescind the contract.

Cluffe, in a frenzy, carried this piece of mercantile insolence off to his lawyer. The stout captain was, however, undoubtedly liable, and, with a heavy heart, he wrote to beg they would, with all despatch, sell the bird in London on his account, and charge him with the difference. 'The scoundrels! – they'll buy him themselves at half-price, and charge me a percentage besides; but what the plague better can I do?

In due course, however, came an answer, informing Captain Cluffe that his letter had arrived too late, as the bird, pursuant to the tenor of his order, had been shipped for him to Dublin by the *Fair Venus*, with a proper person in charge, on the Thursday morning previous. Good Mrs Mason, his landlady, had no idea what was causing the awful commotion in the captain's room; the fitful and violent soliloquies; the stamping of the captain up and down the floor; and the contusions, palpably, suffered by her furniture. The captain's temper was not very pleasant that evening, and he was fidgety and feverish besides, expecting every moment a note from town to apprise him of its arrival.

However, he walked up to Belmont a week or two after, and had a very consolatory reception from Aunt Becky. He talked upon his old themes, and upon the subject of Puddock, was, as usual, very friendly and intercessorial; in fact, she showed at last signs of yielding.

'Well, Captain Cluffe, tell him if he cares to come, he *may* come, and be on the old friendly footing; but be sure you tell him he owes it all to *you*.'

And positively, as she said so, Aunt Rebecca looked down upon her fan; and Cluffe thought looked a little flushed, and confused too; whereat the gallant fellow was so elated that he told her all about the pelican, discarding as unworthy of consideration, under circumstances so imminently promising, a little plan he had formed of keeping the bird privately in Dublin, and looking out for a buyer.

Poor little Puddock, on the other hand, had heard, more than a week before this message of peace arrived, the whole story of

Gertrude's engagement to Lord Dunoran, as we may now call Mr Mervyn, with such sensations as may be conjectured. His heart, of course, was torn; but having sustained some score of similar injuries in that region upon other equally harrowing occasions, he recovered upon this with all favourable symptoms, and his wounds healed with the first intention. He wore his chains very lightly, indeed. The iron did not enter into his soul; and although, of course, 'he could never cease but with his life to dwell upon the image of his fleeting dream – the beautiful nymph of Belmont,' I have never heard that his waist grew at all slimmer, or that his sleep or his appetite suffered during the period of his despair.

The good little fellow was very glad to hear from Cluffe, who patronised him most handsomely, that Aunt Rebecca had consented to receive him once more into her good graces.

'And the fact is, Puddock, I think I may undertake to promise you'll never again be misunderstood in that quarter,' said Cluffe, with a mysterious sort of smile.

'I'm sure, dear Cluffe, I'm grateful as I ought, for your generous pleading on my poor behalf, and I do prize the good will of that most excellent lady as highly as any, and owe her, beside, a debt of gratitude for care and kindness such as many a mother would have failed to bestow.'

'Mother, indeed! Why, Puddock, my boy, you forget you're no chicken,' said Cluffe, a little high.

'And tomorrow I will certainly pay her my respects,' said the lieutenant, not answering Cluffe's remark.

So Gertrude Chattesworth, after her long agitation – often despair – was tranquil at last, and blessed in the full assurance of the love which was henceforth to be her chief earthly happiness.

'Madam was very sly,' said Aunt Becky, with a little shake of her head, and a quizzical smile; and holding up her folded fan between her finger and thumb, in mimic menace as she glanced at Gertrude. 'Why, Mr Mordaunt, on the very day – the day we had the pleasant luncheon on the grass – when, as I thought, she had given you your quietus – 'twas quite the reverse, and you had made a little betrothal, and duped the old people so cleverly ever after.'

'You have forgiven me, dear aunt,' said the young lady, kissing her very affectionately, 'but I will never quite forgive myself. In a moment of great agitation I made a hasty promise of secrecy, which, from the moment 'twas made, was to me a never-resting disquietude, misery, and reproach. If you, my dearest aunt, knew, as *he* knows, all the anxieties, or rather the terrors, I suffered during that agitating period of concealment – '

'Indeed, dear Madam,' said Mordaunt – or as we may now call him, Lord Dunoran – coming to the rescue, ''twas all my doing; on me alone rests all the blame. Selfish it hardly was. I could not risk the loss of my beloved; and until my fortunes had improved, to declare our situation would have been too surely to lose her. Henceforward I have done with mystery. *I* will never have a secret from her, nor she from you.'

He took Aunt Becky's hand. 'Am I, too, forgiven?'

He held it for a second, and then kissed it.

Aunt Becky smiled, with one of her pleasant little blushes, and looked down on the carpet, and was silent for a moment; and then, as they afterwards thought a little oddly, she said, 'That censor must be more severe than I, who would say that concealment in matters of the heart is never justifiable; and, indeed, my dear,' she added, quite in a humble way, 'I almost think you were right.'

Aunt Becky's looks and spirits had both improved from the moment of this *éclaircissement*. A load was plainly removed from her mind. Let us hope that her comfort and elation were perfectly unselfish. At all events, her heart sang with a quiet joy, and her good humour was unbounded. So she stood up, holding Lord Dunoran's hand in hers, and putting her white arm round her niece's neck, she kissed her again and again, very tenderly, and she said: 'How very happy, Gertrude, you must be!' and then she went quickly from the room, drying her eyes.

Happy indeed she was, and not least in the termination of that secrecy which was so full of self-reproach and sometimes of distrust. From the evening of that dinner at the King's House, when in an agony of jealousy she had almost disclosed to poor little Lily the secret of their engagement, down to the latest moment of its concealment, her hours had been darkened by care, and troubled with ceaseless agitations.

Everything was now going prosperously for Mervyn – or let us call him henceforward Lord Dunoran. Against the united evidence of Sturk and Irons, two independent witnesses, the crown were of opinion that no defence was maintainable by the wretch, Archer. The two murders were unambiguously sworn to by both witnesses. A correspondence, afterwards read in the Irish House of Lords, was carried on between the Irish and the English law officers of the crown – for the case, for many reasons, was admitted to be momentous – as to which crime he should be first tried for – the murder of Sturk, or that of Beauclerc. The latter was, in this respect, the most momentous – that the cancelling of the forfeiture which had ruined the Dunoran family depended upon it.

'But are you not forgetting, Sir,' said Mr Attorney in consultation, 'that there's the finding of *felo de se* against him by the coroner's jury?'

'No, Sir,' answered the crown solicitor, well pleased to set Mr Attorney right. 'The jury being sworn, found only that he came by his death, but whether by gout in his stomach, or by other disease, or by poison, they had no certain knowledge; there was therefore no such coroner's verdict, and no forfeiture therefore.'

'And I'm glad to hear it, with all my heart. I've seen the young gentleman, and a very pretty young nobleman he is,' said Mr Attorney. Perhaps he would not have cared if this expression of his good will had got round to my lord.

The result was, however, that their prisoner was to be first tried in Ireland for the murder of Doctor Barnabas Sturk.

A few pieces of evidence, slight, but sinister, also turned up. Captain Cluffe was quite clear he had seen an instrument in the prisoner's hand on the night of the murder, as he looked into the little bed-chamber of the Brass Castle, so unexpectedly. When he put down the towel, he raised it from the toilet, where it lay. It resembled the butt of a whip – was an inch or so longer than a drumstick, and six or seven inches of the thick end stood out in a series of circular bands or rings. He washed the thick end of it in the basin; it seemed to have a spring in it, and Cluffe thought it was a sort of loaded baton. In those days robbery and assault were as common as they are like to become again, and there was nothing remarkable in the possession of such defensive weapons. Dangerfield had only run it once or twice hastily through the water, rolled it in a red handkerchief, and threw it into his drawer, which he locked. When Cluffe was shown the whip, which bore a rude resemblance to this instrument, and which Lowe had assumed to be all that Cluffe had really seen, the gallant captain peremptorily pooh-poohed it. 'Twas no such thing. The whip-handle was light in comparison, and it was too long to fit in the drawer.

Now, the awful fractures which had almost severed Sturk's skull corresponded exactly with the wounds which such an instrument would inflict, and a tubular piece of broken iron, about two inches long, exactly corresponding with the shape of the loading described by Cluffe, was actually discovered in the sewer of the Brass Castle. It had been in the fire, and the wood or whalebone was burnt completely away. It was conjectured that Dangerfield had believed it to be lead, and having burnt the handle, had broken the metal which he could not melt, and made away with it in the best way he could. So preparations were pushed forward, and Sturk's dying declaration, sworn to late in the evening before his dissolution, in a full consciousness of his approaching death, was, of course, relied on, and a very symmetrical and logical bill lay, neatly penned, in the Crown Office, awaiting the next commission for the county.

Chapter Ninety-seven

In which Obediah arrives

In the meantime our worthy little Lieutenant Puddock – by this time quite reconciled to the new state of things, walked up to Belmont, with his head a great deal fuller – such and so great are human vagaries – of the interview pending between him and Aunt Becky than of the little romance which had exploded so unexpectedly about a fortnight ago.

He actually saw Miss Gertrude and my Lord Dunoran walking side by side, on the mulberry walk by the river; and though he looked and felt a little queer, perhaps a little absurd, he did not sigh, or murmur a stanza, or suffer a palpitation; but walked up to the hall-door, and asked for Miss Rebecca Chattesworth.

Aunt Becky received him in the drawing-room. She was looking very pale, and spoke very little, and very gently for her. In a reconciliation between two persons of the opposite sexes – though the ages be wide apart – there is almost always some little ingredient of sentiment.

The door was shut, and Puddock's voice was heard in an indistinct murmur, upon the lobby. Then there was a silence, or possibly, some speaking in a still lower key. Then Aunt Becky was crying, and the lieutenant's voice cooing through it. Then Aunt Becky, still crying, said: 'A longer time than *you* think for, lieutenant; two years, and more – *always*! And the lieutenant's voice rose again; and she said – 'What a fool I've been!' which was again lost in Puddock's accents; and the drawing-room door opened, and Aunt Rebecca ran upstairs, with her handkerchief to her red nose and eyes, and slammed her bedroom door after her like a boarding-school miss.

And the general's voice was heard shouting 'luncheon' in the hall; and Dominick repeated the announcement to Puddock, who stood, unusually pale and very much stunned, with the handle of the open drawing-room door in his hand, looking up toward the bedroom in an undecided sort of way, as if he was not clear whether it was not his duty to follow Aunt Becky. On being told a second time, however, that the general awaited him at luncheon, he apprehended the meaning of the message, and went down to the parlour forthwith.

The general, and my lord Dunoran, and Miss Gertrude, and honest Father Roach, were there; and Aunt Becky being otherwise engaged, could not come.

Puddock, at luncheon, was abstracted – frightened – silent, for the most part; talking only two or three sentences during that sociable meal, by fits and starts; and he laughed once abruptly at a joke he did not hear. He also drank three glasses of port.

Aunt Rebecca met him with her hood on in the hall. She asked him, with a faltering sort of carelessness, looking very hard at the clock, and nearly with her back to him: 'Lieutenant, will you take a turn in the garden with me?'

To which Puddock, with almost a start – for he had not seen her till she spoke – and, upon my word, 'tis a fact, with a blush, too – made a sudden smile, and a bow, and a suitable reply in low tones; and forth they sallied together, and into the garden, and up and down the same walk, for a good while – a long while – people sometimes don't count the minutes – with none but Peter Brian, the gardener, whom they did not see, to observe them.

When they came to the white wicket-door of the garden, Aunt Rebecca hastily dropped his arm, on which she had leaned; and together they returned to the house very affably; and there Aunt Becky bid him goodbye in a whisper, a little hastily; and Puddock, so soon as he found Dominick, asked for the general.

He had gone down to the river; and Puddock followed. As he walked along the court, he looked up; there was a kind of face at the window. He smiled a great deal and raised his hat, and placed it to his heart, and felt quite bewildered, like a man in a dream; and in this state he marched down to the river's bank.

They had not been together for a full minute when the stout general threw back his head, looking straight in his face; and then he stepped first one, then another, fat little pace backward, and poked his cane right at the ribs of the plump little lieutenant, then closing with him, he shook both Puddock's hands in both his, with a hearty peal of laughter.

Then he took Puddock under his arm. Puddock had to stoop to pick up his hat which the general had dislodged. And so the general walks him slowly towards the house; sometimes jogging his elbow a little under his ribs; sometimes calling a halt and taking his collar in his finger and thumb, thrusting him out a little, and eyeing him over with a sort of swagger, and laughing and coughing, and whooping, and laughing again, almost to strangulation; and altogether extraordinarily boisterous, and hilarious, and familiar, as Cluffe thought, who viewed this spectacle from the avenue.

Mr Sterling would not have been quite so amused at a similar freak of Mrs Hidleberg's – but our honest general was no especial worshipper of money – he was rich, too, and his daughter, well dowered, was about to marry a peer, and beside all this, though he loved 'Sister Becky', her yoke galled him; and I think he was not altogether sorry at the notion of a little more liberty.

At the same moment honest Peter Brien, having set his basket of winter greens down upon the kitchen-table, electrified his auditory by telling them, with a broad grin and an oath, that he had seen Lieutenant Puddock and Aunt Rebecca kiss in the garden, with a good smart smack, 'by the powers, within three yards of his elbow, when he was stooping down cutting them greens!' At which profanity, old Mistress Dorothy, Aunt Rebecca's maid, was so incensed that she rose and left the kitchen without a word. The sensation there, however, was immense; and Mistress Dorothy heard the gabble and laughter fast and furious behind her until she reached the hall.

Captain Cluffe was asking for Aunt Rebecca when Puddock and the general reached the hall-door, and was surprised to learn that she was not to be seen. 'If she knew 'twas I,' he thought, 'but no matter.'

'Oh, *we* could have told you that; eh, Puddock?' cried the general; ''tisn't everybody can see my sister today, captain; a very peculiar engagement, eh, Puddock?' And a sly wink and a chuckle.

Cluffe smiled a little, and looked rather conscious and queer, but pleased with himself; and his eyes wandered over the front windows hastily, to see if Aunt Becky was looking out, for he fancied there was something in the general's quizzing, and that the lady might have said more than she quite intended to poor little Puddock on the subject of the gallant mediator; and that, in fact, he was somehow the theme of some little sentimental disclosure of the lady's. What the plague else could they both mean by quizzing Cluffe about her?

Puddock and he had not gone half-way down the short avenue, when Cluffe said, with a sheepish smile: 'Miss Rebecca Chattesworth dropped something in her talk with you, Puddock, I see that plain enough, my dear fellow, which the general has no objection I should hear, and, hang it, I don't see any myself. I say, I may as well hear it, eh? I venture to say there's no great harm in it.'

At first Puddock was reserved, but recollecting that he had been left quite free to tell whom he pleased, he made up his mind to unbosom; and suggested, for the sake of quiet and a longer conversation, that they should go round by the ferry.

'No, I thank you, I've had enough of that; we can walk along as quietly as you like, and turn a little back again if need be.'

So slowly, side by side, the brother-officers paced toward the bridge; and little Puddock, with a serious countenance and blushing cheeks, and looking straight before him, made his astounding disclosure.

Puddock told things in a very simple and intelligible way, and Cluffe heard him in total silence; and just as he related the crowning fact, that he, the lieutenant, was about to marry Miss Rebecca Chattesworth, having reached the milestone by the footpath, Captain Cluffe raised his foot thereupon, without a word to Puddock, and began tugging at the strap of his legging, with a dismal red grin, and a few spluttering curses at the artificer of the article.

'And the lady has had the condescension to say that she has liked me for at least *two years*.'

'And she hating you like poison, to my certain knowledge,' laughed Captain Cluffe, very angrily, and swallowing down his feelings. So they walked on a little way in silence, and Cluffe, who, with his face very red, and his mouth a good deal expanded, and down in the corners, was looking steadfastly forward, exclaimed suddenly – '*Well*!'

'I see, Cluffe,' said Puddock; 'you don't think it prudent – you think we mayn't be happy?'

'*Prudent*,' laughed Cluffe, with a variety of unpleasant meanings; and after a while – 'And the general knows of it?'

'And approves it most kindly,' said Puddock.

'What else can he do?' sneered Cluffe; ''tis a precious fancy – they *are* such cheats! Why you might be almost her *grand*-son, my dear Puddock, ha, ha, ha. 'Tis preposterous; you're sixteen years younger than I.'

'If you can't congratulate me, 'twould be kinder not to say anything, Captain Cluffe; and nobody must speak in my presence of that lady but with proper respect; and I – I thought, Cluffe, you'd have wished me well, and shaken hands and said something – something – '

'Oh, as for that,' said Cluffe, swallowing down his emotions again, and shaking hands with Puddock rather clumsily, and trying to smile, 'I wish you well, Heaven knows – everything good; why shouldn't I, by George? You know, Puddock, 'twas I who brought you together. And – and – am I at liberty to mention it?'

Puddock thought it better the news should be proclaimed from Belmont.

'Well, so I think myself,' said Cluffe, and relapsed into silence till they parted, at the corner of the broad street of Chapelizod, and Cluffe walked at an astounding pace on to his lodgings.

'Here's Captain Cluffe,' said Mrs Mason, to a plump youth, who had just made the journey from London, and was standing with the driver of a low-backed car, and saluted the captain, who was stalking in without taking any notice.

'Little bill, if you please, captain.'

'What is it?' demanded the captain, grimly.

'Obediar's come, Sir.'

'Obediar!' said the captain. 'What the plague do you mean, Sir?'

'Obediar, Sir, is the name we give him. The pelican, Sir, from Messrs. Hamburgh and Slighe.'

And the young man threw back a piece of green baize, and disclosed Obediar, who blinked with a tranquil countenance upon the captain through the wires of a strong wooden cage. I doubt if the captain ever looked so angry before or since. He glared at the pelican, and ground his teeth, and actually shook his cane in his fist; and if he had been one bit less prudent than he was, I think Obediar would then and there have slept with his fathers.

Cluffe whisked himself about, and plucked open the paper.

'And what the devil is all this for, Sir? Ten – twelve pounds ten shillings freightage and care on the way – and twenty-five, by George, Sir – not far from forty pounds, Sir,' roared Cluffe.

'Where'll I bring him to, Sir?' asked the driver.

The captain bellowed an address we shan't print here.

'Curse him – curse the brute! Forty pounds!' and the captain swore hugely, 'you scoundrel! Drive the whole concern out of that, Sir. Drive him away, Sir, or by Jove, I'll break every bone in your body, Sir.'

And the captain scaled the stairs, and sat down panting, and outside the window he heard the driver advising something about putting the captain's bird to livery, 'till sich time as he'd come to his sinses'; and himself undertaking to wait opposite the door of his lodgings until his fare from Dublin was paid.

Though Cluffe was occasionally swayed by the angry passions, he was, on the whole, in his own small way, a long-headed fellow. He hated law, especially when he had a bad case; and accordingly he went down again, rumpling the confounded bill in his hand, and told the man that he did not blame *him* for it – though the whole thing was an imposition; but that rather than have any words about it, he'd pay the account, and have done with it; and he stared again in the face of the pelican with an expression of rooted abhorrence and disgust, and the mild bird clapped its bill, perhaps expecting some refreshment, and looking upon the captain with a serene complacency very provoking under the circumstances.

'How the devil people can like such misshapen, idiotic-looking, selfish, useless brutes; and, by George, it smells like a polecat – curse it! But some people have deuced queer fancies in more matters than one. The brute! On my soul, I'd like to shoot it.'

However, with plenty of disputation over the items, and many oaths and vows, the gallant captain, with a heavy and wrathful heart, paid the bill; and although he had sworn in his drawing-room that he'd eat the pelican before Aunt Rebecca should have it, he thought better also upon this point too, and it arrived that evening at Belmont, with his respectful compliments.

Cluffe was soon of opinion that he was in absolute possession of his own secret, and resolved to keep it effectually. He hinted that very evening at mess, and afterwards at the club, that he had been managing a very nice and delicate bit of diplomacy which not a soul of them suspected, at Belmont; and that by George, he thought they'd stare when they heard it. He had worked like a lord chancellor to bring it about; and he thought all was pretty well settled, now. And the Chapelizod folk, in general, and Puddock, as implicitly as any, and Aunt Rebecca, for that matter, also believed to their dying day that Cluffe had managed that match, and been a true friend to little Puddock.

Cluffe never married, but grew confoundedly corpulent by degrees, and suffered plaguily from gout; but was always well dressed, and courageously buckled in, and, I dare say, two inches less in girth, thanks to the application of mechanics, than nature would have presented him.

Chapter Ninety-eight
In which Charles Archer puts himself upon the country

The excitement was high in Chapelizod when the news reached that a true bill was found against Charles Archer for the murder of Barnabas Sturk. Everywhere, indeed, the case was watched with uncommon interest; and when the decisive day arrived, and the old judge, furrowed, yellow, and cross, mounted the bench, and the jury were called over, and the challenges began, and the grim, gentle-manlike person with the white hair, and his right arm in a black silk sling, whispering to his attorney and now and again pencilling, with his left hand, a line to his counsel with that indescribable air of confidence and almost defiance, pleaded to the indictment 'not guilty', and the dreadful business of the day began, the court was crowded as it seldom had been before.

A short, clear, horrible statement unfolded the case for the crown. Then the dying deposition of Sturk was put in evidence; then Irons the clerk was put up, and told his tale doggedly and distinctly, and was not to be shaken. 'No, it was not true that he had ever been confined in a mad-house.' 'He had never had delirium tremens.' 'He had never heard that his wife thought him mad.' 'Yes, it was true he had pledged silver of his master's at the Pied Horse at Newmarket.' 'He knew it was a felony, but it was the prisoner who put it into his head and encouraged him to do it.' 'Yes, he would swear to that.' 'He had several times spoken to Lord Dunoran, when passing under the name of Mervyn, on the subject of his father being wronged.' 'He never had any promise from my lord, in case he should fix the guilt of that murder on some other than his father.' Our friend, Captain Cluffe, was called, and delivered his evidence in a somewhat bluff and peremptory, but on the whole effective way.

Charles Nutter, after some whispered consultation, was also called, and related what we have heard. 'Yes, he had been arrested for the murder of Dr Sturk, and now stood out on bail to answer that charge.' Then followed some circumstances, one of which, the discovery of a piece of what was presumed to be the weapon with which the murder was perpetrated, I have already mentioned. Then came some evidence, curious but quite clear, to show that the Charles Archer who had died at Florence was *not* the Charles Archer who had murdered Beauclerc, but a gentleman who had served in the army, and had afterwards been for two years in Italy, in the employment of a London firm who dealt in works of art, and was actually resident in *Italy* at the time when the Newmarket murder occurred, and that the attempt to represent him as the person who had given evidence against the late Lord Dunoran was an elaborate and cunning contrivance of the prisoner at the bar. Then came the medical evidence.

Pell was examined, and delivered only half a dozen learned sentences; Toole, more at length, made a damaging comparison of the fragment of iron already mentioned, and the outline of the fractures in the deceased man's head; and Dillon was questioned generally, and was not cross-examined. Then came the defence.

The points were, that Sturk was restored to speech by the determined interposition of the prisoner at the bar, an unlikely thing if he was ruining himself thereby! That Sturk's brain had been shattered, and not cleared from hallucinations before he died; that having uttered the monstrous dream, in all its parts incredible, which was the sole foundation of the indictment against that every way respectable and eminent gentleman who stood there, the clerk, Irons, having heard something of it, had conceived the plan of swearing to the same story, for the manifest purpose of securing thereby the favour of the young Lord Dunoran, with whom he had been in conference upon this very subject without ever once having hinted a syllable against Mr Paul Dangerfield until after Doctor Sturk's dream had been divulged; and the idea of fixing the guilt of Beauclerc's murder upon that gentleman of wealth, family, and station, occurred to his intriguing and unscrupulous mind.

Mr Dangerfield, in the dock, nodded sometimes, or sneered or smirked with hollow cheeks, or shook his head in unison with the passing sentiment of the speaker, directing, through that hot atmosphere, now darkening into twilight, a quick glance from time to time upon the aspect of the jury, the weather-gauge of his fate, but altogether with a manly, sarcastic, and at times a somewhat offended air, as though he should say, ''Tis somewhat too good a jest that I, Paul Dangerfield, Esq., a man of fashion, with my known character, and worth nigh two hundred thousand pounds sterling, should stand here, charged with murdering a miserable Chapelizod doctor!' The minutes had stolen away; the judge read his notes by candle-light, and charged, with dry and cranky emphasis, dead against that man of integrity, fashion, and guineas; and did not appear a bit disturbed at the idea of hanging him.

When the jury went in he had some soup upon the bench, and sipped it with great noise. Mr Dangerfield shook hands with his counsel, and smirked and whispered. Many people there felt queer, and grew pale in the suspense, and the general gaze was fixed upon the prisoner with a coarse curiosity, of which he seemed resolutely unconscious; and five minutes passed by and a minute or two more – it seemed a very long time – the minute-hands of the watches hardly got on at all – and then the door of the jury-room opened, and the gentlemen came stumbling in, taking off their hats, and silence was called. There was no need; and the foreman, with a very pale and frightened face, handed down the paper.

And the simple message sounded through the court: 'Guilty!'

And Mr Dangerfield bowed, and lifted up a white, smiling countenance, all over shining now with a slight moisture.

Then there was some whispering among the conductors of the prosecution; and the leader stood up to say, that, in consequence of a communication from the law officers in England, where the prisoner was to be arraigned on a capital indictment, involving serious consequences to others – for the murder, he meant, of Mr Beauclerc – the crown wished that he should stand over for judgment until certain steps in that case had been taken at the other side. Then the court enquired whether they had considered so and so; and the leader explained and satisfied his lordship, who made an order accordingly. And Mr Dangerfield made a low bow, with a smirk, to his lordship, and a nod, with the same, to his counsel; and he turned, and the turnkey and darkness received him.

Mr Dangerfield, or shall we say the villain, Charles Archer, with characteristic promptitude and coolness, availed himself of the interval to try every influence he could once have set in motion, and as it were to gather his strength for a mighty tussle with the king of terrors, when his pale fingers should tap at his cell door. I have seen two of his letters, written with consummate plausibility and adroitness, and which have given me altogether a very high idea of his powers. But they were all received with a terrifying coldness or with absolute silence. There was no reasoning against an intuition. Every human being felt that the verdict was true, and that the judgment, when it came, would be right: and recoiled from the smiling gentleman, over whose white head the hempen circle hung like a diabolical glory. Dangerfield, who had something of the Napoleonic faculty of never 'making pictures' to himself, saw this fact in its literality, and acquiesced in it.

He was a great favourite with the gaoler, whom, so long as he had the command of his money, he had treated with a frank and convivial magnificence, and who often sat up to one o'clock with him, and enjoyed his stories prodigiously, for the sarcastic man of the world lost none of his amusing qualities: and – the fatigues of his barren correspondence ended – slept, and eat, and drank, pretty much as usual.

This Giant Despair, who carried the keys at his girdle, did not often get so swell a pilgrim into his castle, and was secretly flattered by his familiarity, and cheered by his devilish gaiety, and was quite willing to make rules bend a little, and the place as pleasant as possible to his distinguished guest, and give him in fact, all his heart could desire, except a chance of escape.

'I've one move left – nothing very excellent – but sometimes, you know, a scurvy card enough will win the trick. Between you and me, my good friend, I have a thing to tell that 'twill oblige my Lord Dunoran very much to hear. My Lord Townshend will want his vote. He means to prove his peerage immediately and he may give a poor devil a lift, you see – hey?'

So next day there came my Lord Dunoran and a magistrate, not Mr Lowe – Mr Dangerfield professed a contempt for him, and preferred any other. So it was Mr Armstrong this time, and that is all I know of him.

Lord Dunoran was more pale than usual; indeed he felt like to faint on coming into the presence of the man who had made his life so indescribably miserable, and throughout the interview he scarcely spoke six sentences, and not one word of reproach. The villain was down. It was enough.

Mr Dangerfield was, perhaps, a little excited. He talked more volubly than usual, and once or twice there came a little flush over his pallid forehead and temples. But, on the whole, he was very much the same brisk, sardonic talker and polite gentleman whom Mr Mervyn had so often discoursed with in Chapelizod. On this occasion, his narrative ran on uninterruptedly and easily, but full of horrors, like a satanic reverie.

'Upon my honour, Sir,' said Paul Dangerfield, with his head erect, 'I bear Mr Lowe no ill-will. He is, you'll excuse me, a thief-catcher by nature. He can't help it. He thinks he works from duty, public spirit, and other fine influences; I know it is simply from an irrepressible instinct. I do assure you, I never yet bore any man the least ill-will. I've had to remove two or three, not because I hated them – I did not care a button for any – but because their existence was incompatible with my safety, which, Sir, is the first thing to me, as yours is to you. Human laws we respect – ha, ha! – you and I, because they subserve our convenience, and just so long. When they tend to our destruction, 'tis, of course, another thing.'

This, it must be allowed, was frank enough; there was no bargain here; and whatever Mr Dangerfield's plan might have been, it certainly did not involve making terms with Lord Dunoran beforehand, or palliating or disguising what he had done. So on he went.

'I believe in luck, Sir, and there's the sum of my creed. I was wrong in taking that money from Beauclerc *when* I did, 'twas in the midst of a dismal run of ill-fortune. There was nothing unfair in taking it, though. The man was a cheat. It was not really his, and no-one could tell to whom it belonged; 'twas no more his because I had found it in his pocket than if I had found it in a barrel on the high seas. I killed him to prevent his killing me. Precisely the same motive, though in your case neither so reasonable nor so justifiable, as that on which, in the name of justice, which means only the collective selfishness of my fellow-creatures, you design in cool blood to put me publicly to death. 'Tis only that you, gentlemen, think it contributes to your safety. That's the spirit of human laws. I applaud and I adopt it in my own case. Pray, Sir,' [to Mr Armstrong] 'do me the honour to try this snuff, 'tis real French rappee.

'But, Sir, though I have had to do these things, which you or any other man of nerve would do with a sufficient motive, I never hurt any man without a necessity for it. My money I've made fairly, though in great measure by play, and no man can say I ever promised that which I did not perform. 'Tis quite true I killed Beauclerc in the manner described by Irons. That was put upon me, and I could not help it. I did right. 'Tis also true, I killed that scoundrel Glascock, as Irons related. Shortly after, being in trouble about money and in danger of arrest, I went abroad, and changed my name and disguised my person.

'At Florence I was surprised to find a letter directed to Charles Archer. You may suppose it was not agreeable. But, of course, I would not claim it; and it went after all to him for whom it was intended. There was actually there a Mr Charles Archer, dying of a decline.

Three respectable English residents had made his acquaintance, knowing nothing of him but that he was a sick countryman. When I learned all about it, I, too, got an introduction to him; and when he died, I prevailed with one of them to send a note signed by himself and two more to the London lawyer who was pursuing me, simply stating that Charles Archer had died in Florence, to their knowledge, they having seen him during his last illness, and attended his funeral.

'I told them that he had begged me to see this done, as family affairs made it necessary; 'twas as well to use the event – and they did it without difficulty. I do not know how the obituary announcement got into the newspapers – it was not my doing – and naming him as the evidence in the prosecution of my Lord Dunoran was a great risk, and challenged contradiction, but none came. Sir Philip Drayton was one of the signatures, and it satisfied the attorney.

'When I came to Chapelizod, though, I soon found that the devil had not done with me, and that I was like to have some more unpleasant work on my hands. I did not know that Irons was above ground, nor he either that I was living. We had wandered far enough asunder in the interval to make the chances very many we should never meet again. Yet here we met, and I knew him, and he me. But he's a nervous man, and whimsical.

'He was afraid of me, and never used his secret to force money from me. Still it was not pleasant. I did not know but that if I went away he might tell it. I weighed the matter; 'tis true I thought there might have come a necessity to deal with him; but I would not engage in anything of the sort, without an absolute necessity. But Doctor Sturk was different – a bull-headed, conceited fool. I thought I remembered his face at Newmarket, and changed as it was, I was right, and learned all about him from Irons. I saw his mind was at work on me, though he could not find me out, and I could not well know what course a man like that might take, or how much he might have seen or remembered. That was not pleasant either.

'I had taken a whim to marry; there's no need to mention names; but I supposed I should have met no difficulty with the lady – relying on my wealth. Had I married, I should have left the country.

'However, it was not to be. It might have been well for all had I never thought of it. For I'm a man who, when he once places an object before him, will not give it up without trying. I can wait as well as strike, and know what's to be got by one and t'other. Well, what I've once proposed to myself I don't forego, and that helped to hold me where I was.

'The nature of the beast, Sturk, and his circumstances were danger-ous. 'Twas necessary for my safety to make away with him. I tried it by several ways. I made a quarrel between him and Toole, but somehow it never came to a duel; and a worse one between him and Nutter, but that too failed to come to a fight. It was to be, Sir, and my time had come. What I long suspected arrived, and he told me in his own study he knew me, and wanted money. The money didn't matter; of that I could spare abundance, though 'tis the nature of such a tax to swell to confiscation. But the man who gets a sixpence from you on such terms is a tyrant and your master, and I can't brook slavery.

'I owed the fellow no ill-will; upon my honour as a gentleman, I forgive him, as I hope he has forgiven me. It was all fair he should try. We can't help our instincts. There's something wolfish in us all. I was vexed at his d—d folly, though, and sorry to have to put him out of the way. However, I saw I must be rid of him.

'There was no immediate hurry. I could afford to wait a little. I thought he would walk home on the night I met him. He had gone into town in Colonel Strafford's carriage. It returned early in the afternoon without him. I knew his habits; he dined at Keating's ordinary at four o'clock; and Mercer, whom he had to speak with, would not see him, on his bill of exchange business, in his counting-house. Sturk told me so; and he must wait till half-past five at his lodgings. What he had to say was satisfactory, and I allowed five minutes for that.

'Then he might come home in a coach. But he was a close-fisted fellow and loved a shilling; so it was probable he would walk. His usual path was by the Star Fort, and through the thorn woods between that and the Magazine. So I met him. I said I was for town, and asked him how he had fared in his business; and turned with him, walking slowly as though to hear. I had that loaded whalebone in my pocket, and my sword, but no pistol. It was not the place for firearms; the noise would have made an alarm. So I turned sharp upon him and felled him. He knew by an intuition what was about to happen, for as the blow fell he yelled "murder". That d—d fellow Nutter, in the wood at our right, scarce a hundred yards away, halloed in answer. I had but time to strike him two blows on the top of his head that might have killed an ox. I felt the metal sink at the second in his skull, and would have pinked him through with my sword, but the fellow was close on me, and I thought I knew the voice for Nutter's. I stole through the bushes swiftly, and got along into the hollow under the Magazine, and thence on.

'There was a slight fog upon the park, and I met no-one. I got across the park-wall, over the quarry, and so down by the stream at Coyles, and on to the road near my house. No-one was in sight, so I walked down to Chapelizod to show myself. Near the village tree I met Dr Toole. I asked him if Nutter was in the club, and he said no – nor at home, he believed, for his boy had seen him more than half-an-hour ago leave his hall door, dressed for the road.

'So I made as if disappointed, and turned back again, assured that Nutter was the man. I was not easy, for I could not be sure that Sturk was dead. Had I been allowed a second or two more, I'd have made sure work of it. Still I was *nearly* sure. I could not go back now and finish the business. I could not say whether he lay there any longer, and if he did, how many men Nutter might have about him by this time. So, Sir, the cast was made, I could not mend it, and must abide my fortune be it good or ill.

'Not a servant saw me go out or return. I came in quietly, and went into my bedroom and lighted a candle. 'Twas a blunder, a blot, but a thousand to one it was not hit. I washed my hands. There was some blood on the whalebone, and on my fingers. I rolled the loaded whalebone up in a red handkerchief, and locked it into my chest of drawers, designing to destroy it, which I did, so soon as the servants were in bed; and then I felt a chill and a slight shiver – 'twas only that I was an older man. I was cool enough, but a strain on the mind was more to me then than twenty years before. So I drank a dram, and I heard a noise outside my window. 'Twas then that stupid dog, Cluffe, saw me, as he swears.

'Well, next day Sturk was brought home; Nutter was gone, and the suspicion attached to him. That was well. But, though Pell pronounced that he must die without recovering consciousness, and that the trepan would kill him instantaneously, I had a profound misgiving that he might recover speech and recollection. I wrote as exact a statement of the case to my London physician – a very great man – as I could collect, and had his answer, which agreed exactly with Doctor Pell's. 'Twas agreed on all hands the trepan would be certain death. Days, weeks, or months – it mattered not what the interval – no returning glimmer of memory could light his death-bed. Still, Sir, I presaged evil. He was so long about dying.

'I'm telling you everything, you see. I offered Irons what would have been a fortune to him – he was attending occasionally in Sturk's sick-room, and assisting in dressing his wounds – to watch his opportunity and smother him with a wet handkerchief. I would have done it myself afterwards, on the sole opportunity that offered, had I not been interrupted.

'I engaged, with Mrs Sturk's approval, Doctor Dillon. I promised him five hundred guineas to trepan him. That young villain, I could prove, bled Alderman Sherlock to death to please the alderman's young wife. Who'd have thought the needy profligate would have hesitated to plunge his trepan into the brain of a dying man – a corpse, you may say, already – for five hundred guineas? I was growing feverish under the protracted suspense. I was haunted by the apprehension of Sturk's recovering his consciousness and speech, in which case I should have been reduced to my present rueful situation; and I was resolved to end that cursed uncertainty.

'When I thought Dillon had forgot his appointment in his swinish vices, I turned my mind another way. I resolved to leave Sturk to *nature*, and clench the case against Nutter, by evidence I would have compelled Irons to swear. As it turned out, *that* would have been the better way. Had Sturk died without speaking, and Nutter hanged for his death, the question could have opened no more, and Irons would have been nailed to my interest.

'I viewed the problem every way. I saw the danger from the first, and provided many expedients, which, one after the other, fortune frustrated. I can't confidently say even now that it would have been wiser to leave Sturk to die, as the doctors said he must. I had a foreboding, in spite of all they could say, he would wake up before he died and denounce me. If 'twas a mistake, 'twas a fated one, and I could not help it.

'So, Sir, you see I've nothing to blame myself for – though all has broken down.

'I guessed when I heard the sound at the hall-door of my house that Sturk or Irons had spoken, and that they were come to take me. Had I broken through them, I might have made my escape. It was long odds against me, but still I had a chance – that's all. And the matter affecting my Lord Dunoran's innocence, I'm ready to swear, if it can serve his son – having been the undesigned cause of some misfortunes to you, my lord, in my lifetime.'

Lord Dunoran said nothing, he only bowed his head.

So Dangerfield, when his statement respecting the murder of Beauclerc had been placed clearly in writing, made oath of its truth, and immediately when this was over (he had, while they were preparing the statement, been walking up and down his flagged chamber), he grew all on a sudden weak, and then very flushed, and they thought he was about to take a fit; but speedily he recovered himself, and in five minutes' time was much as he had been at the commencement.

After my lord and Mr Armstrong went away, he had the gaoler with him, and seemed very sanguine about getting his pardon, and was very brisk and chatty, and said he'd prepare his petition in the morning, and got in large paper for drafting it on, and said, 'I suppose at the close of this commission they will bring me up for judgment; that will be the day after tomorrow, and I must have my petition ready.' And he talked away like a man who had got a care off his mind, and is in high spirits; and when grinning, beetle-browed Giant Despair shook his hand, and wished him luck at parting, he stopped him, laying his white hand upon his herculean arm, and, said he, 'I've a point to urge they don't suspect. I'm sure of my liberty; what do you think of that – hey?' and he laughed. 'And when I get away what do you say to leaving this place and coming after me? Upon my life, you must, Sir. I like you, and if you don't, rot me, but I'll come and take you away myself.'

So they parted in a sprightly, genial way; and in the morning the turnkey called the gaoler up at an unseasonable hour, and told him that Mr Dangerfield was dead.

The gaoler lay in the passage outside the prisoner's cell, with his bed across the door, which was locked, and visited him at certain intervals. The first time he went in there was nothing remarkable. It was but half-an-hour after the gaoler had left. Mr Dangerfield, for so he chose to be called, was dozing very quietly in his bed, and just opened his eyes, and nodded on awaking, as though he would say, 'Here I am,' but did not speak.

When, three hours later, the officer entered, having lighted his candle at the lamp, he instantly recoiled. 'The room felt so queer,' said he, 'I thought I'd a fainted, and I drew back. I tried it again a bit further in, and 'twas worse, and the candle almost went out –'twas as if the devil was there. I drew back quick, and I called the prisoner, but no word was there. Then I locks the door, and called Michael; and when he came we called the prisoner again, but to no purpose. Then we opened the door, and I made a rush, and smashed the glass of the window to let in air. We had to wait outside a good while before we could venture in; and when we did, there he was lying like a man asleep in his bed, with his nightcap on, and his hand under his cheek, and he smiling down on the flags, very sly, like a man who has won something cleverly. He was dead, and his limbs cold by this time.'

There was an inquest. Mr Dangerfield 'looked very composed in death', says an old letter, and he lay 'very like sleep' in his bed, 'his fingers under his cheek and temple', with the countenance turned 'a little downward, as if looking upon something on the floor', with an 'ironical smile'; so that the ineffaceable lines of sarcasm, I suppose, were traceable upon that jaundiced mask.

Some said it was a heart disease, and others an exhalation from the prison floor. He was dead, that was all the jury could say for certain, and they found 'twas 'by a visitation of God'. The gaoler, being a superstitious fellow, was plaguily nervous about Mr Dangerfield's valediction, and took clerical advice upon it, and for several months after became a very serious and ascetic character; and I do believe that the words were spoken in reality with that sinister jocularity in which his wit sported like churchyard meteors, when crimes and horrors were most in his mind.

The niece of this gaoler said she well remembered her uncle, when a very old man, three years before the rebellion, relating that Mr Dangerfield came by his death in consequence of some charcoal in a warming pan he had prevailed on him to allow him for his bed, he having complained of cold. He got it with a design to make away with himself, and it was forgotten in the room. He placed it under the bed, and waited until the first call of the turnkey was over, and then he stuffed his surtout into the flue of the small fire-place, which afforded the only ventilation of his cell, and so was smothered. It was not till the winter following that the gaoler discovered, on lighting a fire there, that the chimney was stopped. He had a misgiving about the charcoal before, and now he was certain. Of course, he said nothing about his suspicions at first, nor of his discovery afterwards.

So, sometimes in my musings, when I hear of clever young fellows taking to wild courses, and audaciously rushing – where good Christians pray they may not be led – into temptation, there rises before me, with towering forehead and scoffing face, a white image smoking his pipe grimly by a plutonic fire; and I remember the words of the son of Sirach – 'The knowledge of wickedness is not wisdom, neither at any time the counsel of sinners prudence.'

Mr Irons, of course, left Chapelizod. He took with him the hundred guineas which Mr Dangerfield had given him, as also, it was said, a handsome addition made to that fund by open-handed Dr Walsingham; but somehow, being much pressed for time, he forgot good Mistress Irons, who remained behind and let lodgings pretty much as usual, and never heard from that time forth anything very distinct about him; and latterly it was thought was, on the whole, afraid rather than desirous of his turning up again.

Doctor Toole, indeed, related in his own fashion, at the Phoenix, some years later, a rumour which, however, may have turned out to be no better than smoke.

'News of Zekiel, by Jove! The prophet was found, Sir, with a friend in the neighbourhood of Hounslow, with a brace of pistols, a mask, a handful of slugs, and a powder-horn in his pocket, which he first gave to a constable, and then made his compliments to a justice o' the peace, who gave him and his friend a note of commendation to my Lord Chief Justice, and his lordship took such a fancy to both that, by George, he sent them in a procession in his best one-horse coach, with a guard of honour and a chaplain, the high-sheriff dutifully attending, through the City, where, by the king's commands, they were invested with the grand collar of the order of the hempen cravat, Sir, and with such an attention to their comfort they were not required to descend from their carriage, by George, and when it drove away they remained in an easy, genteel posture, with their hands behind their backs, in a sort of an ecstasy, and showed their good humour by dancing a reel together with singular lightness and agility, and keeping it up till they were both out of breath, when they remained quiet for about half an hour to cool, and then went off to pay their respects to the President of the College of Surgeons,' and so forth; but I don't think Irons had pluck for a highwayman, and I can't, therefore, altogether, believe the story.

We all know Aunt Rebecca pretty well by this time. And looking back upon her rigorous treatment of Puddock, recorded in past chapters of this tale, I think I can now refer it all to its true source.

She was queer, quarrelsome, and sometimes nearly intolerable; but she was generous and off-handed, and made a settlement, reserving only a life interest, and nearly all afterwards to Puddock.

'But in a marriage settlement,' said the attorney (so they called themselves in those days), 'it is usual – ' and here his tone became so gentle that I can't say positively what he uttered.

'Oh – a – that,' she said, 'a – well, you can speak to Lieutenant Puddock, if you wish. I only say for myself a life estate; Lieutenant Puddock can deal with the remainder as he pleases.' And Aunt Rebecca actually blushed a pretty little pink blush. I believe she did not think there was much practical utility in the attorney's suggestion, and if an angel in her hearing had said of her what he once said of Sarah, she would not have laughed indeed, but I think she would have shaken her head.

She was twenty years and upwards his senior; but I don't know which survived the other, for in this life the battle is not always to the strong.

Their wedding was a very quiet affair, and the talk of the village was soon directed from it to the approaching splendours of the union of Miss Gertrude and my Lord Dunoran.

Chapter Ninety-nine
The story ends

The old minutes of the Irish House of Lords can better explain than I the parliamentary process by which all the consequences of the judgment against the late Lord Dunoran were abrogated, as respected his son. An ancient name rescued from the shadow of dishonour, and still greater estates, made my lord and lady as happy as things can. So for the recluse Mervyn, and the fair Gertrude Chattesworth, our story ends like a fairy tale.

A wedding in those days was a celebration and a feast; and it was deemed fitting that the union of Gertrude Chattesworth and the youthful Lord Dunoran should await the public vindication of his family, and the authentic restoration of all their rights and possessions. On the eve of this happy day, leaning on the youthful arm of kindly Dan Loftus, there came a figure not seen there for many months before, very much changed, grown, oh, how old! It was the good rector, who asked to see Miss Gertrude.

And so when he entered the room, she ran to meet him with a little cry; and she threw her arms about his neck and sobbed a good deal on that old, cassocked shoulder, and longed to ask him to let her be as a daughter to him. But he understood her and, after a while, he wished her joy, very kindly. And my Lord Dunoran came in, and was very glad to see him, and very tender and reverent too; and the good doctor, as he could not be at the wedding, wished to say a word 'on the eve of the great change which my dear young friend – little Gertie, we used to call her – is about to make.' And so he talked to them both. It was an affectionate little homily, and went on something in this sort.

'But I need not say how honourable an estate it is, only, my lord, you will always remember your wooing is not over with your wedding. As you did first choose your love, you must hereafter love your choice. In Solomon's Song, the Redeemer the bridegroom, and the Church His spouse, one calls the other "love", to show that though both did not honour alike, yet both should love alike.

'And always be kind, and the kinder the more her weakness needs it. Elkanah says to his wife, "Am not I better unto thee than ten sons?" As though he favoured her more for that which she thought herself despised. So a good husband will not love his wife less, but comfort her more for her infirmities, as this man did, that she may bear with his infirmities too. And if she be jealous – ay, they will be jealous – '

He spoke in a reverie, with a sad fond look, not a smile, but something like a smile, and a little pensive shake of the head; he was thinking, perhaps, of very old times. And 'my lord' glanced with a sly smile at Gertrude, who was looking on the carpet with, I think, a blush, and I'm sure saw my lord's glance seeking hers, but made as though she did not.

'If she be jealous, her jealousy, you know, is still the measure of her love. Bless God that he hath made thee to her so dear a treasure that she cannot hide her fears and trouble lest she should lose even a portion of thy love; and let thy heart thank *her* too.

'And if the husband would reprove her, it must be in such a mood as if he did chide with himself, and his words like Jonathan's arrows, which were not shot to hurt but to give warning. She must have no words but loving words from thee. She is come to thee as to a sanctuary to defend her from hurt, and canst thou hurt her thyself? Does the king trample his crown? Solomon calls the wife the crown of her husband; therefore, he who despiseth her woundeth his own honour. I am resolved to honour virtue in what sex soever I find it.'

The doctor was speaking this like a soliloquy, slowly, and looking on the floor.

'And I think in general I shall find it more in women than in men.'

Here the young people exchanged another smile, and the doctor looked up and went on. 'Ay – though weaker and more infirmly guarded, I believe they are better; for everyone is so much the better, by how much he comes nearer to God; and man in nothing is more like him than in being merciful. Yet woman is far more merciful than man. God is said to be love; and I am sure in that quality woman everywhere transcends.'

The doctor's serious discourses were a mosaic of old divines and essayists, and Greek and Latin authors, as the writings of the Apostolic Fathers are, in a great measure, a tesselation of holy writ. He assumed that everybody knew where to find them. His business was only to repeat the truth wherever gleaned. So I can't tell how much was the doctor's and how much theirs.

And when he had done upon this theme, and had risen to take leave, he said in his gentle and simple way And I brought you a little present – a necklace and earrings – old-fashioned, I'm afraid – they were my dear mother's diamonds, and were to have been – '

Here there was a little pause – they knew what was in his mind – and he dried his eyes quickly.

'And won't you take them, Gertie, for poor little Lily's keepsake? And so – well, well – little Gertie – I taught you your catechism – dear, dear! Little Gertie going to be married! And may God Almighty bless her to you, and you to her, with length of days, and all goodness; and with children, the inheritors of your fair forms, and all your graces, to gladden your home with love and duty, and to close your eyes at last with tender reverence; and to walk after you, when your time is over, in the same happy and honourable paths.'

Miss Gertrude was crying, and with two quick little steps she took his knotted old hand, and kissed it fervently and said: 'I thank you, Sir, you've always been so good to me; I wish I could tell you – and won't you come to us, Sir, and see us very often – when we are settled – and bring good Mr Loftus, and dear old Sally; and thank you, Sir, with all my heart, for your beautiful presents, and for your noble advice, Sir, which I will never forget, and for your blessing, and I wish I could show you how very much I love and reverence you.'

And my Lord Dunoran, though he was smiling, looked as if he had been crying too. But men, you know, don't like to be detected in that weakness, though everybody knows there are moments when *bonus Homerus dormitat*.

Good Doctor Walsingham made Dan Loftus his curate. But when in the course of time a day came when the old rector was to meet his parishioners no more, and the parish was vacant, I do not hear that honest Dan succeeded to it. Indeed I'm afraid that it needs sometimes a spice of the devil, or at least of the world, to get on in the Church. But Lord Dunoran took him with him on the embassage to Lisbon, and afterwards he remained in his household as his domestic chaplain, much beloved and respected. And there he had entire command of his lordship's fine library, and compiled and composed, and did everything but publish and marry.

In due time the fair Magnolia made the amorous and formidable O'Flaherty happy. Single blessedness was not for her, and it is due to her to say, she turned out one of the best housewives in Chapelizod, and made the fireworker account for every shilling of his pay and other revenues, and managed the commissariat and all other departments to admiration. She cured her lord very nearly of boozing, and altogether of duelling. One combat only he fought after his marriage, and it was rumoured that the blooming Magnolia actually chastised the gigantic delinquent with her own fair hand. That, however, I don't believe. But unquestionably she did, in other ways, lead the contumacious warrior so miserable a life for some months after that, as he averred to the major, with tears in his eyes, it would have been 'more to his teeste to have been shot on the occasion'. At first, of course, the fireworker showed fight, and sometimes broke loose altogether; but in the end 'his mouth was made', his paces formed, and he became a very serviceable and willing animal. But if she was strong she was also generous, and very popular for her good nature and fearlessness. And they made a very happy, as well as a comely couple. And many handsome children were nursed at her fair breast, and drew many a Celtic virtue from that kindly fountain, and one of the finest grenadiers who lay in his red coat and sash within the French lines on the field of Waterloo, in that great bivouac which knows no *reveille* save the last trumpet, was a scion of that fine military stock.

At length came the day of the nuptials – a grand day for Belmont – a grand day for the town. Half-a-dozen flags were up and floating in the autumnal sun. The band of the Royal Irish Artillery played noble and cheering strains upon the lawns of Belmont. There were pipers and fiddlers beside for rustic merrymakers under the poplars. Barrels of strong ale and sparkling cider were broached on the grass; and plenty of substantial fare kept the knives and forks clattering under the marquees by the hedgerow. The rude and hospitable feudalism of old times had not died out yet; marriage being an honourable estate, the bride and bridegroom did not steal away in a travelling carriage, trying to pass for something else, to unknown regions, but remained courageously upon the premises, the central figures of a genial gala.

Need I describe the wedding? It always seems to me that I saw it, and see it still, I've heard the old folk talk it over so often. The reader's fancy will take that business off my hands. 'What's a play without a marriage? And what is a marriage if one sees nothing of it?' says Sir Roger in Gay's tragi-comic pastoral. 'Let him have his humour, but set the doors wide open, that we may see how all goes on.'

[*Sir Roger at the door, pointing*]
'So natural! D'ye see now, neighbours? The ring, i'faith. To have and to hold! Right again; well play'd, doctor; well play'd, son *Thomas*. Come, come, I'm satisfied. Now for the fiddles and dances.'

And so are we – now, then, for the fiddles and dances! And let those who love to foot it keep it up – after sack-posset and stocking thrown – till two o'clock i' the morning; and the elder folk, and such as are 'happy thinking', get home betimes; and smiling still, get to their beds; and with hearty laughter – as it were mellowed by distance – still in their ears, and the cheery scrape of the fiddle, all-pervading, still humming on; and the pleasant scuffle of light feet, and with kindly ancient faces, and blushing young ones all round in airy portraiture; grinning, roguish, faithful, fuddled old servants, beflowered and liveried, pronouncing benedictions at the foot of the stairs, and pocketing their vails; and buxom maids in their best Sunday finery, giggling and staring, with eyes starting out of their heads, at the capering 'quality', through the half-open doors; let us try to remember the 'sentiment' delivered by that ridiculous dog, Tom Toole, after supper, at which we all laughed so heartily. And, ah! there were some pretty faces that ought to have been there – faces that were pleasant to see, but that won't smile or blush any more; and I missed them, though I said nothing. And so, altogether, it went down among my pleasant recollections, and I think will always remain so, for it was all kindly, and had its root in the heart; and the affections were up and stirring, and mixed in the dance with the graces, and shook hands kindly with old father Bacchus; and so I pull my nightcap about my ears, drop the extinguisher on the candle, and wish you all pleasant dreams.

THE END